"KHAR, WHAT ARE WE MISSING?"

Doyce still had the nagging conviction that the Seeker General had not told her everything she knew about their mission, about Oriel's death. *Is the truth so fearsome that the Seeker General is apprehensive I'll refuse if I know it? What Doyce had heard and surmised so far already gave her nightmares.*

Khar's tail twitched, the tip flickering back and forth in an angry tattoo. **"They don't expect us to succeed,"'** the ghatti mindspoke. **"They think that someone, that we, have to try but they don't believe we can do it. They're convinced something worse will happen, something terrible, but they don't know what. They want to warn us, but they don't even know where to begin."**

"Wonderful," Doyce mindspoke back. *"Two more sacrificial lambs. Why not stake us out somewhere and be done with it?"*

The Ghatti's Tale

Book One: Finders-Seekers

Gayle Greeno

DAW BOOKS, INC.
DONALD A. WOLLHEIM, FOUNDER
375 Hudson Street, New York, NY 10014
ELIZABETH R. WOLLHEIM
SHEILA E. GILBERT
PUBLISHERS

DAW TRADEMARK REGISTERED
U.S. PAT. OFF. AND FOREIGN COUNTRIES
—MARCA REGISTRADA
HECHO EN U.S.A.

PRINTED IN THE U.S.A.

This book is dedicated to two people and one cat—to my parents, Doris L. and G. Alfred Greeno, for raising me with wit, wisdom, and a sense of wonder at the world around me, and to Tulip, for nineteen years, beloved feline, literary "mews."

"Ask, and it shall be given to you; seek, and ye shall find; knock, and it shall be opened unto you. Every one that asketh receiveth; and he that seeketh findeth"
—St. Matthew, 7: 7-8

❖

PART
ONE

❖

The silver medallion with its eight faintly curved sides swayed from the chain around Vesey's neck, swung closer and closer to the baby's face as the boy leaned over Briony's cradle, his long, quick-bitten fingers trapping each side, halting the cradle's rocking. It glinted and glittered, sharded by sunlight, then seemed to grow larger, engulfing the space, round and glowing as a cataracted eye, and Doyce sensed that she lay in the cradle looking up and out, instead of her daughter Briony.

It unnerved Doyce, the medallion with its rhythmic back and forth swaying, but why should she be frightened of a Lady's Medal . . . or of the stepson who wore it? She started upright, throwing the rumpled blanket off her shoulders, eyes half-open to the summer-starred sky above. Barely awake, conscious enough to know that she dreamed, yet unable or unwilling to pull herself out of the dream. She collapsed, head tossing against the worn black saddle that served as her pillow, and reluctantly fell into the dream again. It was distasteful, though not entirely unpleasant. The dream people looked achingly familiar, said familiar things, did familiar things, as did she. A habitual dream, yet subtly different. Surely she was no babe in the cradle to be watched over by Vesey? The octagonal medallion swung before her face again, blindly eyeing her, and she burrowed deep in the blanket, hiding.

Khar, all silvery shadowed with dark stripes and swirls, slipped beside Doyce, touched the flickering eyelid with her pink nose and felt the lid flutter, then subside. The ghatta sat motionless, staring down at her sleeping Bondmate. She'd had to touch, to remold Doyce's dreams more and more often lately to allow her to sleep. She knew her intrusiveness had been gentle, a careful redirection, a reemphasis of thought, but it had occurred oftener than she liked. Why, she wondered? Perhaps it was simply because they were both tired from the circuit.

But the ghatta suspected she knew the true reason: the closer they came to the capital of Gaernett, the sooner Doyce would have to reach a decision about Oriel Faltran. Would she agree to marry him or not? And the more she thought on that, the more Doyce fled backward in her dreams to her previous marriage, relived her times with Varon, their baby Briony, and her stepson Vesey, all dead now.

Doyce craved the known rather than the unknown, Khar decided. Still, it puzzled the ghatta. She knew the old dreams inside and out, had experienced them time and again. These alterations were minutely different, yet there all the same. It made no sense: a dream relived, retold past history, but could not reinvent the past or change it. How could a dream form an untruth, something that had never happened like that? Every ghatt and ghatta, down to the littlest ghatten, knew better. Humans had such a strange way of mixing truth with desires, with wishes, should haves and could haves. How could they stumble forth whole from their pretending each morning? How much easier to know that a dream was truth. She sniffed again at Doyce's forehead, rubbed her chin against the woman's ear, and felt her shift away from the tickling whiskers. Khar moved to the end of the blanket and settled, curled her shoulders tight against the back of Doyce's knees and slumped her chin on her chest, slitted her golden eyes. Other voices, other dreams drifted on the air as well tonight; she brushed by some, tasted at others; picked up the thread of mindspeech that Mem'now unwound toward her so invitingly and shared

'speech with the yellow, tiger-striped ghatt back at
Seeker Veritas Headquarters in Gaernett.

Although Mem'now sensed her presence, neither rushed
their conversation, and Khar's thoughts hovered, sharing
his sensations as he paused outside the kitchens, listened,
and found the quality of silence to his satisfaction. It
would be rude to interrupt until he was ready. Mem'now
was set in his ways, but to her thinking it gave the big
yellow tom a sense of solidity, the knowledge that he
could be trusted with anything. Why else would he have
been chosen to lead the Tale-Telling as a way of training
the ghatten in mindspeech, that unique gift that enhanced
and expanded the scope of their native falanese tongue?

Pushing against the swinging door with his shoulder,
he slipped his head and shoulders through the opening
and stopped, rubbed against the door casing and surveyed the darkened kitchen quarters. His right hip radiated a dull ache and he grimaced as he flexed that leg.
He gave a little snort, a sound of fond disgust that Khar
recognized, and still without formally acknowledging her
presence, Mem'now mindwalked with her. His Bond,
Twylla, *would* insist on staying out too long to gather
her medicinal herbs that morning—yesterday morning,
he corrected himself pedantically—and with the sun
barely risen the dew dapples weighted the plant stems,
the grass blades, and shrubs as heavily as wet laundry
bows a clothesline on a breezeless day. That and the
coolness, plus Twylla's insistence on scrambling up and
around and down amongst the boulders and loose soil by
the riverbank, slipping on damp, moss-greened rocks,
had caused her old injury to flare up, muscles and im-
properly mended bones protesting at the ill use. Still, she'd
been pleased with what she'd gathered, her marigold-
haired head, fuzzy and furzy with exertion, bent as she
cradled the cane-woven basket of dripping water parsley
and bulbous typha roots close to her chest and hauled
herself up the bank, her right leg dragging behind, useful
only as a support or prop.

Khar knew it was Twylla's pain that Mem'now felt, a
pain that had become an old and familiar presence to
him, just as it had to Twylla. It would always be a part
of him, and Khar felt him detach himself momentarily

from their sharing as he reached to caress Twylla's dreams, felt the feather of contentment that emanated from him as he entered his Bondmate's sleep memories of their gathering expedition earlier that day. Khar envied him the safe prosaicality of Twylla's dreams.

"Greetings," Mem'now's mindvoice boomed in her ear and Khar started despite herself. The ghatt had incredible resonance and reach to his mindspeech; she knew it but had forgotten how near he could seem, almost as if he curled on the blanket beside her. **"I hoped you'd be within range to join us tonight. Twylla and I have missed you both, though not as much as Oriel and Saam undoubtedly have missed you. Has Doyce decided anything yet?"**

Khar fought a vague reluctance to share her thoughts and was shamed by her denial of Mem'now's concern. Still, she convinced herself, they were Doyce's thoughts, and her Bondmate had the right to privacy. It was just that Doyce's sense of privacy sometimes seemed to exclude Khar, and the ghatta writhed with private embarrassment at the thought.

"Greetings. Will she, won't she? Won't she, will she? I don't know yet, Mem'now." She sniffed in exasperation.

The ghatt chuckled as he made his way through the darkened, still kitchen, navigating the carefully swept flagstones with their still-moist puddles from the final nightly scrubbing. **"Ah, Bondmates . . ."** he shook his broad head from side to side, not bothering to finish the thought. **"What is it that humans do with flowers? He loves me, he loves me not?"**

"Mem'now!"

He bowed his head in mock supplication, let his ears furl dejectedly, and searched for inspiration. **"Saam may mindwalk with us later as well. Would you like me to link you?"** The Seeker's circuit that Saam and his Bondmate Oriel rode ranged too far from Khar and Doyce's circuit for the ghatti to mindlink with each other, but with Mem'now positioned between them as an intermediary link, it was possible.

She mentally shook her head. **"No, just give him my Greetings. We'll see each other soon enough. Ghatti don't plot, you know that."**

"Not even in a good cause, such as romance?" Mem'-now shot back and then winced at the emphatic negation Khar 'spoke at him. He licked at his ruff, considering. "There's a surprise for tonight, you know. Something special for the ghatten—and us as well. Might make it worth your staying awake." He courteously neglected to add that he sensed she'd be awake all night, monitoring Doyce's dreams.

"You already 'speak the best ghatti Tales that could ever be told. Your guidance in the mindwalk is a treasure. Isn't that enough for the lucky younglings?"

He was pleased with her commendation, she could sense it, but didn't allow it to go to his head. "And your Tales, my lovely ghatta, have delighted many as well. But be that as it may regarding both our skills, I've some-one special for tonight."

Pointing her nose toward the stars, Khar sensed and sought the essence of Doyce's dream, then settled back, satisfied, and gave Mem'now her attention once more. "Who?"

"You hardly do credit to the curiosity of the ghatti race if all you can manage is a simple 'who.' " He wound his way around the legs of the work-scarred trestle tables, past stools high and low, and brushed his tail against the long, fire-blackened ladle that swung, along with toasting forks and other implements, from a row of hooks and hangers. There was the slightest jangle, and that amused him, because it was precisely the amount of sound he meant to set off. He sat at last, compact and sturdy, back to the banked fire, gold earhoop reflecting a circlet of light, and waited, sniffing with contentment at the yeasty smell of fresh bread rising beneath tucked linen towels.

She considered saying nothing, outwaiting him, falling back on ghatti politesse to override the insatiable inquisitiveness, the need to know. But she liked Mem'now far too much not to let him have his satisfaction, especially when she could sense him fractionally shifting from fore-leg to foreleg, eagerness barely suppressed.

"Mem'now, who is it? Don't keep me in suspense. Is it Ghra'm? I'd heard that he and Selwa Alun were com-ing to visit. We haven't seen him since they retired and moved so far south. Selwa was always lonely when she

lived here, too far distant from the sea. But it's too far
for Ghra'm to mindspeak—there aren't enough others to
join with him. Is it Ghra'm?"

"Ghra'm would be deeply welcome, but it's someone
who visits even more infrequently than Ghra'm," Mem'-
now allowed. His claws flexed in and out of their sheaths,
the faintest of scraping sounds against the flagged floor.

She thought, thought hard, and a distant sensation rif-
fled the delicate hairs within her ears, a brief memory of
mindspeech from another, someone so far removed and
so seldom heard from that she could scarcely credit it.
She shook her head to clear it and nearly pounced on
Mem'now with the answer, then halted, remembering decorum, refusing to spoil his pleasure. And were she
wrong, he'd think her half daft. **"Who, beloved ghatt-
friend, who?"**

Mem'now looked down shyly, green eyes squinted
shut. **"One of the Eldest."**

Exhaling a breathy little pleasure purr, Khar pulled
herself into a more upright position, claws heedlessly
kneading the blanket with excitement. Doyce winced in
her sleep as a claw struck home through the blanket,
and Khar apologized, soothed. **"Which one, Mem? Who?
W'han? Or Reux? She hasn't mindspoken us in the longest time. Some thought she might have finally passed
on."**

"Even Elder than W'han and Reux," Mem'now hinted.
"It's Mr'rhah."

"Mr'rhah . . ." she sighed her pleasure, turning the
name in her mind. Mem'now told the truth, no doubt of
that . . . but Mr'rhah! The thought stunned her, and still
threatened to overwhelm Mem'now as he contemplated
the enormity of the honor of such a visit.

Doyce stirred again, thrashed a bare arm free of the
covers, and whimpered, a tear streaking down her cheek.
With scant farewell Khar exited from her mindwalk with
Mem'now and spirited herself into Doyce's dream, stalking stealthy and silent, waiting to surprise and entrap any
tiny bit of untruth that had slipped into Doyce's sleep
tales. She prowled back and forth within the unguarded
thoughts of her beloved Bondmate, tested each tendril
of memory for the traitor. Each piece rang true and

whole, simply another vision of Doyce's past life before Khar had 'Printed with her. It was not a happy dream, Khar had replayed it too often, for the memory visitors lived only in the dream now, but it accurately depicted her past life. She whispered reassurance of her presence, of her love, and pressing tight against Doyce's legs, hummed lullaby purrs.

Still, Khar stayed on guard, alert for the slightest change. She'd slip back and rejoin Mem'now later when the other ghatti had arrived, if Doyce stayed fast asleep. To miss the opportunity to hear Mr'rhah Tale-Tell was almost more than she could bear; it might even be enough to raise Khar into the next spiral of cognizance, to formally mindwalk the path of a Major Tale told by an Elder of Mr'rhah's standing—if Mr'rhah would permit the ultimate sharing, allow Khar the flawless imprinting of the Tale in her memory. It was an Elder's duty to guide younglings through the spirals of knowledge-lore, the sharing of level upon level of enlightenment, each as different as commencing a new life.

But then Khar had to face the harsh and unpalatable truth: with or without Mr'rhah's Elder pattern of the Tale etched in her mindspeech, she was unlikely to ascend higher on the spiral until she and Doyce merged as a totality in the sharing of thoughts. Was she to blame? Was Doyce? Their Bonding linked sound and true, a match of minds, and yet somehow a very intimate part of Doyce always eluded her. **"Please,"** Khar mindwalked, mindspoke as hard as she could to any who might hear, any who might care, and prayed the Elders of the Race listened tonight. Listened and felt inclined to do something about it, not simply record her as a ghatta Bondmate not quite capable of reaching the core of her beloved's being, doomed constantly to repeat the same spiral, learning and relearning the same lesson yet never achieving perfection. **"Perhaps attaining another spiral will mean I have the capacity to reach her."** She closed her amber, slanted eyes in humility. **"You know I ask it for both of us, to use the wisdom to make us both more perceptive."**

But no answer whispered on the tentative summer breeze, just the sound of a nightjar's wings swishing, feathered mouth gaping wide to entrap a moth. She waited, every iota of her being alert, warding Doyce's dream, waiting for an answer. That there was no answer was an answer in itself; Khar acknowledged the bitter truth of that. She must strive with what she had, with all she had.

Near dawn soon, the moons had traversed the sky, fading to ghost-white cauls insubstantial as a worn nightshift. Had she missed the Tale-Telling, missed passing a greeting to Saam? She spun a delicate guard into Doyce's dreams and soared outward with the rest of her being, mindwalking, her thoughts sliding without effort down the mindpath Mem'now had so considerately left open for her. She entered the kitchen quietly, not wishing to disturb the tale or the listeners. Two tiny ghatten, almost ready to 'Print, sat spellbound at Mr'rhah's feet where once, long ago, Khar had sat, so young, so tiger-striped bold and promising. Might they rise more swiftly and surely through the turnings than she had. Another ghatten, barely an oct old, eyes not even open, ears still pinned tight to its head, nursed with innocent greed, drinking in the Tale with his mother's milk. Murmurous greetings echoed from the other adults although not a slitted eye shifted from Mr'rhah's spellbinding. Khar felt the Tale-patterns meshing, mindwalking the past in the middle of one of her favorite Tales, *Newcomers to Methuen.* . . .

"We quivered with vibrations of delight as we directed our mindthoughts at these strange visitors from the skyways, so like and yet so unlike the Erakwa. We could read these beings' thoughts, even though we could not fully comprehend them. We trilled with curiosity—asked question after question—and oh, the disappointment so strong that our tails drooped as we accepted at last that they could not seem to hear us though we could hear them so clearly. So many more tantalizing potentialities than the Erakwa, prickle-burred tight that we could never force open to seed, impervious to our questing and our questioning, shielding themselves from our search for truth. . . ."

The Tale wound on and on, rising and falling in the rich inflections, the power of Mr'rhah's mindvoice. Khar listened intently to the old, beloved Tale, the words buoying her spirits.

". . .And some erected shelters, while others sought for food, and still others pounded and thumped at the strange sleek silver forms that had brought them, plunging down like a plummeting osprey striking the surface of the lake for a fish. Some trekked all across the land carrying heavy burdens. We stalked these walkers, sampled their thoughts, and wished for understanding that not even our Elders could provide. We hid and watched, eyes glowing bright and inquisitive from behind rocky crags; we stretched long and still on branches over their heads, our eyes reflecting green and gold with leaf-light, and slipped silent and supple as dawn mist from place to place to follow them. Every so often we encouraged one of them to see us, and they invariably responded by making strange little lip-smacking noises, finger-snappings, and word-soundings of 'Here, kitty, kitty.' We were touched that they had already named us, though it was not our own name.

"And as they wandered over the land, they bored holes into the earth, sank small bundles into those holes, and lovingly packed dirt over them. They talked at their wrists, and listened, too, and we wondered why—if they could listen to their wrists—they could not hear us. We yearned to know what they were burying, and claw-carefully pried loose a few of the shell-like cylinders to see, but we could not make heads nor tails of them. They did not smell of food, though at first we suspected they cached these things as the squirrels bury nuts and the woodmice store seeds against winter."

Khar trembled with anticipation. This was the part of the tale that set the hairs along her spine atingle, that never failed to inject a tiny frisson of fear. She formed the human word and concept in her mind, reveling in the sheer sound of it: Plumb—Periodic Linear Ultra-Mensuration Beamer. Neither falanese, the ghatti common tongue, nor their original mindspeech contained a comparable word for the object or the idea.

Indeed, her early ghatti ancestors had no conception of anything that could explode like that; that was one of the things the human visitors inadvertently had taught not only the ghatti but themselves as well. They had brought with them an unintentional devastation that nothing native to Methuen could envision. Khar knew the history of Doyce's people as well as her own: how the patient survey teams had set the bores in place, drilling some by hand to avoid disturbing delicate geological layerings, inserting the ultrasensitive probes to listen, see, and feel the land around them, to touch and taste the earth and to report back to the monitors, the glowing green screens, and the men and women who collated and interpreted the raw data flowing in from hundreds of isolated sites.

The Plumbs could report on any sort of danger, from sudden, random earth shifts to the mass gatherings of potentially dangerous indigenous life-forms, though the Erakwa shrank from the offworlders as though their very touch defiled the earth. But most important of all to the Newcomers, the Plumbs assayed what the earth held close to her bosom, her jewels and treasures: raw ores, precious metals, gems, and the less valuable but still highly coveted geological formations of marble, slate, limestone, granite, and more. The veritable building blocks of a people with the yearning to literally carve themselves a place in history, people with a severe lack of natural resources on their home planet. Hence the Newcomers' expedition to Methuen. But then the Plumbs began to explode. . . .

The ghatten would learn the delicate interlinking of the tales as they grew older, the interweaving of ghatti and human history, and would begin to understand the story as a whole. For now the tales gave the younglings the first taste of the answers, the truths that helped assuage ghatti curiosity. And for Khar, the complete comprehension of the intricacies of a Major Tale would mean she had risen a turn higher on the spiral toward Elderdom. Ah, if only she could succeed. . . . Khar listened again with her whole concentration, putting her own thoughts aside.

". . . **We despaired for these Newcomers, for with each fresh turmoil of the earth they became less and less a society. After three of the six original silver ospreys suddenly sprang into the air, the Newcomers who re-**

mained seemed to lose all hope, fledglings crying pite-
ously, abandoned in their nest. Their fear left a bitter
metallic bite to the air that we could smell and taste.
They became fainthearted, looked shabby as if they had
not groomed themselves or each other properly in a long
time. And they turned on each other in their fear, fighting for food, for shelter, killing each other as a rabid
animal runs wild, biting and snapping at anything within
reach.

"We wanted so badly to aid them, to share our
thoughts, but still we could not, our season had not yet
come, and their minds were unripe. We watched their
society crumbling and feared that these creatures would
destroy themselves before we could make contact. Some
counseled we should desist, that the fightings and killings
proved they were not worthy of sharing our thoughts,
but others countered that we must show them the truth,
make them see the errors of their ways. But how? They
would not, could not listen."

Yes, how? Khar asked herself. How could she show
Doyce the truth if she wouldn't completely share with
Khar? Shamed, Khar concentrated anew as Mr'rhah
lifted her listeners to the Tale's climax, her mindvoice
soaring as she sang of the Bonding of a Newcomer's
youngling with a tiny female ghatten and the sudden on-
rush of shared mindspeech, comprehension, communion
at last. The story of Matthias Vandersma and the ghatten
Kharm was worthy of a Tale of its own, and, indeed,
formed the next Major Tale on the spiral.

With a calculated pause, Mr'rhah leaned to sniff one
of the younglings, her old, leathery nose with its v-
notched scar touching against the fresh, unmarred gray
of the ghatten's. She lifted her head, then held it poised
in an attitude of listening; Khar strove to hear as well, a
foreboding anticipation coursing through her.

"And so, my loves, it happened one day that. . . ."
Mr'rhah hesitated as if she'd lost her place, shook her
head. An impossibility; no Elder ever dropped the thread
of a Tale; they could recite it endless times, commence
and stop anywhere, wind it backward and forward without losing a word, truth flowing as steadily alive as heart-
throbs. ". . .It happened one. . . ." Her head began an

involuntary palsied swaying and shaking and then her whole body snapped rigid in a silent mindscream. Her body stretched and stretched, a tensile elongation as her grizzled muzzle pointed toward the ceiling, her mouth gaping, lips peeled back in pain to reveal the worn teeth. Khar could feel the pain, knew that each and every ghatt and ghatta in the room and any others mindlinked with the Tale could feel it as well. But they were all locked in it with Mr'rhah, feeling the pain bore through them, mindspeech fraying as surely as an old hempen rope frays and snaps.

"**Break them free, snap the younglings out of the mindsharing,**" Mr'rhah screamed, rolling on the flagstones, head arched backward, flecks of foam whitening her muzzle. "**Mem'now, break them free now! I haven't the strength! Break them free or we'll lose them, and they'll mindwalk alone forever!**"

Mem'now's broad yellow head jerked back and forth as Mr'rhah's scream buffeted him. At last he reacted, a stinging slap at the ghatten nearest him, raking across the sensitive little charcoal gray nose with his claws until the ghatten howled, then looked at him clear-eyed, questioning him in frightened falanese. Others reacted as well, tearing the two other younglings out of the mindlink with cuffs and blows, and that was the last Khar recalled of the scene, for her fears and Mr'rhah's pain shivered in tandem as the links snapped one by one, the joining destroyed, sundered, leaving each participating ghatt and ghatta to pull themselves back toward sanity as best they could.

Mad fear clawing at her, Khar exploded, leaping over Doyce's sleeping form and landing near the dwindling campfire. The next mindscream came fainter but equally potent. "**Saam!**" The ghatta wailed. "**Saam, what is it, what?**" The mindlink snapped and crumbled even further, broke into a thousand fragmenting cries as the Elder One severed her last linkage, withdrew to escape, wheeling free to elude the terror she could not control. Khar tumbled back on her haunches at the suddenness of the final release. No reason, no reason at all, she argued with herself, to believe the horror involved Saam, but in her heart of hearts she sensed it did. Proof! Where was the truth? With so many snapping out of the link in disorder, truth was not lost but immured so deeply in subconscious memory that it was practically impossible to resurrect.

She spun a frail thread of mindspeech through the night, felt it wither and recede at the lack of contact. Alone, ah, so alone! She screamed again, this time aloud, and a part of her saw Doyce come thrashing out of her bedroll, sword scraping from her scabbard as she stumbled erect, a slight figure in small clothes with a lethal weapon in her hand. The woman spun in a terse, controlled circle, one bare heel planted for stability, sword flickering from half-extension to guard as she patrolled, searching for danger. After a few moments, she risked bending and tossing branches into the fire, the flames flickering, then crackling, soaring high. Doyce continued checking outward, searching the aspened copse behind her and watching the clear stretch of meadow with a cautious, assessing gaze.

Khar screamed again and yet again, could not help herself, her eyes widening in the sudden spurt of flame, yet seeing nothing, envisioning something beyond the normally acute ghatti-sight. Each hair of her silky coat stood erect, and she could not control the sound issuing from her throat, mourning the dark and danger of the unknown and unknowable. She heard her own voice rise and fall—challenge, plaint, yearning, fury—and at last strain to reach a crescendo and die. But no one heard; there was no one to hear. Nothing, nothing she could do; it was done.

Dully, not caring, she watched Doyce ease her way alongside the little mare, trying to snag Lokka's halter as the horse's hooves churned the soft earth, sending up the smell of bruised, torn grass, her eyes rolled to whites as she strained against the lead-line, ready to bolt as soon as the leather parted. Escape, to run as far away as she could, Khar desired it as well, to escape the nightmare sounds that had flooded her brain. But she could not escape, would not go; she had Bonded, she had Chosen.

Now Doyce knelt beside her, stroking the prickling hair along her spine, trying to 'speak her, babbling senseless sounds at her, words she couldn't bear to listen to

16   *Gayle Greeno*

or answer. Doyce sighed, rose to her feet and surveyed the woods and slope around her again. "Khar?" she asked tentatively, not wishing to intrude.

Khar's response was brusque and to the point. **"You are safe. I will watch."**

And so they both sat until morning, Doyce half-dressed, body quivering with waves of cold and tension, her sword bared to greet the unknown, Khar a short distance away, beyond reach, back turned to her beloved Bondmate. Neither spoke.

♣

"Com-ing!"

The only indication that the shout had penetrated was that horse and rider both leaned their weight to the right, in the direction of the sound, but made no other move. From their position atop the small rise they contemplated a sparkling blue pond fringed with reeds that formed a gold-brown and deep green frieze interwoven at one point with the figure of a bittern, its elongated shape synchronous with the vertical pattern. The rest of nature appeared unalarmed and unaware of the shout; a bronze-speckled starling tilted its head from side to side searching for seeds and bugs among the meadow grass, and a black squirrel sat upright and scrubbed at its face with busy paws, briefly curious about horse and rider, then it began to scamper about its business. Indeed, no one but the horse and rider had heard the shout.

The hemlock growth to the right of the two exploded with motion and a large cat hurtled across the rise, launching itself squarely at the target the woman and the trim little sorrel mare presented. The cat, bull's-eye striped in gray-brown and black, sprang upward, hind legs bunching as the muscles contracted, and leaped on the saddle platform in front of the woman. It made a half-turn, wrapped its tail around white feet and sat facing forward, gazing out over the horse's head. A gold hoop glinted in its left ear near the base, and a gold ball dotted the tip of its right ear. The cat was nearly as big as a three-year-old child.

"Well?" Doyce asked, scratching the ghatta between

her ears. "Anything, nothing, something?" The ghatta craned its neck as if loosening tense muscles but refused to look back at the woman. It took immense interest in a nonexistent speck of dust on one white forepaw and began to lick assiduously. "Well?" Doyce repeated.

"Nothing," the ghatta allowed and licked some more. **"Nothing that you could see or hear or taste or feel. But something . . . I don't know what . . . so very faint, like the barest remnant of a nightmare. I can feel it, but I can't form it."**

The mare whickered consolingly, for she, too, understood the words mind-directed as they were so that only the three were privy to the conversation. The small creatures of the meadow, frozen or frantic from the ghatta's sudden rush, began at last to resume their normal activities in the absence of further sound or movement, but they continued to keep a wary eye on the large feline.

"Maybe you're being too sensitive, still too keyed up after last night," Doyce consoled as her fingers continued their patter behind the ghatta's ears. Khar'pern shook her head in disgust and Doyce stopped. It was going to take more to pacify the ghatta than she'd anticipated. The eldritch scream last night had spooked Khar, no two ways about it. And understandably so—the merest hint of it had coiled through her sleep, tightening a noose around her own less-than-restful dreams.

And that was all she could make of it, for this morning Khar still refused to discuss the night's alarum. She mindspoke, but whenever Doyce questioned her, the ghatta broke the mindlink. Her slanted amber eyes welled with deep loss and disillusionment, the look of a child discovering that all the seeming verities of love and trust, home and safety were false, seductive dancing shadows cloaking the final misstep into the dreary pit of nothingness. If it hadn't been for that, and for the fact that Lokka had strained her lead nearly to the breaking, Doyce would have accounted it a terror of the night, formless but frightening, that sometimes overtook weary travelers. That, and the knowledge that the back of her own neck still prickled.

Doyce sighed and gave the ghatta a final gentle pat. For a moment Khar pressed back against the comforting touch, then she sat up straight, claws extended to grip the shearling on the pommel platform. "If we ride straight through, we can make Myllard's Ale House tonight. We can take the cut above Tavistock. It's a harder climb but quicker, and I didn't promise anyone that we'd stop at Tavistock, only that we might." Somehow she wanted to be back at the capital tonight, and she sensed the ghatta would prefer it, too. And there was always the chance that Oriel would have the same idea, that he and Saam would have pushed to finish the final days of their circuit and ridden straight back as well. If anyone knew her mind, he did, and that bothered her because she could never see into his the same way. Instead, all she saw were reflections of her own doubts as to how durable their relationship would prove to be. *"Ask Lokka if she minds the climb?"* she asked with her mind.

"Fine . . . with us both." Doyce shook out the reins, and the little sorrel mare turned away from the down-slope and trotted toward the rolling foothills that led to the Hightmont, where the trail would wind up and around its high, sheltering flank and finally down to Gaernett, the capital. She looked longingly over her shoulder at the pond and wiped her sweaty face with a forearm, shoving red-brown curls off her forehead. Individual silver strands almost lost in the red highlights glinted in the sunlight.

Lady take the shearling tabard when it was hot! A quick swim would have been nice. The ghatta half-turned and the faintest, fleetingest of grins appeared. **"Leeches,"** she murmured. **"And hungry."** Leave it to a ghatta to take the pleasure out of a daydream by providing the truth!

The trail snaking through the low ridges at the Hight-mont's base showed minimal upkeep, and Doyce clucked in disapproval as she kept a firm seat while Lokka picked her way around potholes and rough washouts, rocks and rubble that had cut loose and sluiced downslope onto the trail after the summer storms. Brush untrimmed since spring cleanup reached out toward her, spears of leathery-tough, sharp-bladed leaves and wiry branches exuding a rich, spicy scent in the full heat of the sun. Still too low for a finger of breeze to ease down her collar, but she could hear it rustling and beckoning not far above. She'd have to report the condition of the pass-through when she got back. Doyce made a face at the thought: bureaucracy, another report to fill out and file with someone.

The sudden, sharp noise of a rock ricocheting and tumbling downslope, sand and loose earth slithering after it, jarred her out of her daydreams.

"Plumb!" she shouted and bent low over the mare, jamming her heels into Lokka's sides and urging her toward a jutting overhang about one hundred meters ahead. Shaken and sweaty, she pulled up and looked back along the path, trembling as the final cascade and the random pattering of loose stones and freshly fractured earth hit and bounced along the trail just about where she'd been caught woolgathering.

Chagrined, she looked down at the ghatta, unperturbed by their unexpected dash, her only reaction having been to dig her claws deeper into her shearling pad. "Avalanche," Doyce emended. "Just a small one, not a Plumb. Sorry."

"Better to react and then decide what it is," the ghatta commented. "Rock slides hurt just as much as Plumbs if you're under them."

"True enough." She took a deep breath and exhaled with relief, spreading her fingers to form the eight-pointed Lady's sign and be damned if anyone called her superstitious. Then a reassuring pat at her pocket to make sure that the misshapen, melted remains of Vesey's Lady's Medal were there. It hadn't brought him luck, but it was all she had for remembrance. "And there hasn't been a Plumb exploding in years, they're all inoperative by now."

"One hundred and . . . eighty-seven years."

"Now who's 'scribing the records?" Doyce's hazel eyes slid away from the ghatta's cool amber expression, her tone cross from the exactitude of the ghatta's correction. She was the one who usually pulled facts and figures from her capacious memory and her years as a transcriber and record-keeper. "Well, onward and upward?

I suppose we might as well continue. And hope that we won't have to dodge again."

Plumb. Funny how the word reverberated in her mind, an unexperienced terror that had been drummed into her throughout her childhood, as it had through the childhoods of countless generations of children. To frighten a recalcitrant child into obedience all an adult had to do was utter the word "Plumb," followed by an explosive sound or sharp handclap.

Of course, to children the word translated as "plum," as if the succulent summer fruit with its purple-black skin and golden-moist flesh had some mysterious, destructive powers capable of leveling a house, a hamlet, a town, a mountain. And there was always one child somewhere, more curious, braver than the rest, who would cautiously gather some of the fallen fruit and bury it, then crouch behind a sheltering rock and wait all day to see if the plums would detonate. Or worse yet, threaten to throw the dark, soft fruits grenadelike at childish enemies.

One hundred and eighty-seven years. Doyce shook her head at the passage of time. They must all be dead, deactivated, or harmless by now, delicate contact points corroded by years of rain and snow, leaching minerals from the earth, or destroyed by their own tiny circuit-breaker sensor chips. But for nearly fifty years before that they had exploded wherever they'd been planted—in fields, beneath towns and villages, throughout the mountain ranges, along river beds—wherever man had felt the need for a monitoring system that plumbed the depths of the earth.

Plumbs. Why were they so vividly in her mind this morning? *"Did I dream about them last night, Khar?"* The ghatta's shoulders rose, then her spine snapped rigid in surprise. Doyce took the movement as a negative and rode on, lost in past history, while the large striped ghatta sat erect, ears twitching for the slightest sound of a grain of sand, a pebble, a stone's abrupt shift or fall. Nothing moved that shouldn't have, and the ghatta relaxed but wondered, truly wondered, if the woman had inadvertently shared in the Tale-Telling the previous night. It had never happened that way before.

Jenret Wycherley swung sideways to slip his back into the right angle where bench back met bench arm and shoved a cushion behind him to stop the slatlike armrest from digging into his ribs. The cushion wasn't *too* dirty, he judged, just worn. Had Myllard, the proprietor of this Ale House, or his wife, Fala, heard Jenret's pronouncement on the cleanliness of the cushion, the young man would have been unceremoniously tossed out the door. He swung a foot up on the bench and balanced his wineglass on his cocked knee.

As it was, Rawn heard Jenret's internal comment about the freshness of the cushion. **"It's perfectly clean, as well you know. Though how it stays clean when louts like you put their booted feet on the seat cushions, I'll never fathom."** The midnight black ghatt half-raised himself under the table, and his eyes glowed, caught in the beam of late afternoon sun streaming through the mullioned windows. **"And is the wine satisfactory?"**

Jenret paused, flourished his glass toward the light to show wine as golden as the sunbeams, and took a considering, judicious sip. *"Obviously must be, it's my second glass."* But he took his booted foot off the cushion. *"Why so grumpy today, my favorite Bondmate, my best friend?"*

"The *only* Bondmate you'll ever have, and sometimes, I think, your *only* friend." Rawn subsided back under the table, flopped on his side, his tail drubbing the floor in warning. His head still buzzed from the strange panics and alarums of the previous night. The mindwalking crumbling, disintegrating . . . the shrieks and wails. . . . He had not been mindwalking the Tale, had not been a part of the linkage, but the fallout of pain had exploded within him anyway. Ghatti all over the capital and who knew how far distant were still reeling from the inexplicable horror. But he would not tell this to Jenret, at least not yet. Jenret and the others, be they Seekers or not, knew only the tragic end of last night's turmoil. There was more to be learned and ghatti everywhere planned on finding out, himself amongst them.

A serving maid—and they were always maids at Myllard's Ale House, never wenches—swung by, pretty and

pert, to check whether Jenret's glass needed refilling. It
didn't, but he debated the idea if it would mean she'd
linger to chat. She was trim, with a saucy look to her
warm brown eyes, and a lace fichu discreetly veiled other
notable attributes. Still, if he wanted that kind of companionship, there were other ale houses, other inns. A
thought for later that night.

Part of the reason he came to Myllard's was the reverse
side of the coin: Jenret Wycherley knew himself to be a
handsome man, his jet black hair set against almost ala-
baster skin that showed the need for a shave practically
as soon as he'd finished with one. But his real downfall—
or rather, the ladies' downfall—were his gentian-blue
eyes, hedged with the longest, darkest, curled lashes that
made them the envy of half the women, young and old,
in Gaernett. At Myllard's the proprietor would brook no
nonsense about outrageous flirtations or worse. Myllard's
serving maids might sigh about the handsome Seeker
once they reached the kitchens, but while they served
him they would be nothing but polite and professional.
He could manage the same.

"Need the looking glass, or is memory enough to
serve?" Rawn growled.

Stung, Jenret set the glass down hard, harder than he'd
intended, and watched the wine slop over onto his cuff.
The ghatt was certainly bad-tempered today. He daubed
with his handkerchief, folding it to find a dry spot, glad
all the same that he planned on changing for dinner—no
Seeker's garb this evening. His aunt was certain to prof-
fer an astringent comment about his drinking habits if his
clothing reeked of wine. Still, his voice came patiently as
he continued to blot at his sleeve. *"Rawn, peace, old
friend. I know you're upset about the day's events, we all
are. A sad loss for the Seekers Veritas."* He reached under
the table and rumpled the big ghatt's ears, tugged at the
earhoop. *"But, thank the Lady, we've still each other."*

Rawn rubbed his chin against the seeking hand,
gnawed at the thumb. "Sorry," he apologized and rubbed
harder. "Don't want to have to hear about it all over
again at dinner tonight with your Aunt Mahafny. She
doesn't really approve of me anyway."

"Of course she does. Just because she's a eumedico

doesn't mean she's like so many who think it beneath human dignity to share a mindlink with an animal. I'm not related to Mahafny by blood, but she is *bloodlinked to Swan Maclough, her cousin. If being related to the Seeker General isn't good enough for you—and I know being related to me is no recommendation—I don't know what is."*

"When do we have to leave?"

"Not for a while yet." Jenret considered the angle of the sun. Later than he'd thought, close to dusk. *"Mahafny prefers to eat early, but not that early. Time for another glass of wine before I go change. Besides, I want to hear her views on the day's events. Mahafny's wise beyond her eumedico training, and I'm anxious to hear what she makes of this. You'll go, won't you? She won't throw plates at you as long as you stay on my side of the table."*

"Who's paying for dinner?" Rawn responded. Jenret laughed and waved the serving maid over to order another glass of wine and instructed himself to keep his eyes on her face, not her fichu.

♣

Late, ripe dusk of a lazy day balanced between the growth and the harvest seasons, and the lights of Gaernett began winking on, one by one, as the three descended the final switchback and merged into the main thoroughfare leading toward the capital. After the solitary ride through the cut, the jostle of humanity—full-laden carts and wagons wheeling toward the city dammed the outward exodus of clustered walkers, riders on horseback, and passenger rigs—filled the air with good-natured cursing and comments as everyone jockeyed for position. Lokka sliced through the throngs, sidestepped capering children and work-weary adults, moving Doyce and Khar with slow assurance along the broad road.

Even after all these years the wonder of the small, secure city with its pink and gray granites, its white and green and gold-veined marbles, its slates of mauve and gray, rose and blue, still enchanted her, the way it all fit together as if the city were an extension of the mountains

it nestled against. And in a way it was, for all the building
stones of the city were quarried in the heart of the low,
hummocky ranges scattered throughout the continent of
Princept, although none were ever mined from the heart
of the Hightmont itself. Doyce had ventured to Gaernett
late in life, not born of the city but discovering it with
the rapturous interest that an adolescent brings to everything that is new and exciting and different. She'd been
sixteen, done with her Tierce and pledged to the eumedicos, deserting her family, as her weaver mother had so
baldly stated it. But she had dreamed so of being a eumedico, had earned the scholarship for it, though she
knew her leaving would make her mother's life more
difficult, fearful that without Doyce to partner her in the
weaving the income would be too scanty to support her
and Doyce's older, crippled sister.

She relinquished the old memories and concentrated
on the distant mosaic of colored stones that tiled the city,
certain landmarks catching her eye just as the features
of an old and familiar friend stand out from the sea of
faces in a crowd. Ensconced on the highest hill within
the city-center stood the Monitor's Hall with its plain,
pale green marble with the barest relief of a darker
green, decorated tracery above its fluted pillars, a tracery
that charted the history of their new world. The seat of
their government and the dwelling place of the Monitor,
duly elected by the populace after nominations from the
Wards.

Ticking them off against her fingers, Doyce squinted
to spot the dancing colors of each Ward House flag: Merchanters, Growers, Artisans, Builders, the Delvers or
miners, and the Transitors, all those involved in road-
work, the canals, shipping, and transport. Her former
Ward, the Eumedicos, would come into sight soon
enough. And, of course, the largest, most disparate
Ward—the Commonality, made up of any citizen who
came of age and did not hold membership in one of the
other seven Wards.

Nearest to the Monitor's Hall yet surpassing it in grandeur, in its yearning for the heavens, stood the dove gray
stonework of the Bethel of Our Lady, its eight outer
walls forming the points of an octagon with gently flared

sides. From its topmost level eight flying buttresses supported the penultimate spire, its complex, curved masonry delicate as antique lacery from this distance. The Bethel served as mankind's symbol of the perfect moon that never waxed nor waned over Methuen, encircled by her eight companion satellites that showed the changing phases of each Octant.

Doyce strained to locate the next emblem, though the edifice itself stood starkly visible, located halfway between the Monitor's Hall and the western side of the outer Ring Wall. Her eyes sought the Ward banner, a deep cerulean blue with three four-pointed white stars arrayed in a triangle: the sign of the Eumedico Hospice. Three hanging lanterns would soon announce its presence by night. The Hospice pained the eye with its uncompromising lines and austere rise of pure white marble, built not for aesthetics but for total utility: the healing of the sick, the final hope of a populace against the ravages of illness, injury, and age; and for the training of novice eumedicos, as she had once been. Uncompromising— that was the word for it, and the brief smile that flickered across her face honored the positive attributes of the word, but the bleakness in her eyes acknowledged other possibilities.

Good at last to let her sight drift to the final major building situated nearest the outer wall, the youngest in construction, a scant hundred years old. A pale rose-tinted cupola capped the front of a spacious four-story building of mottled gray-rose granite, while two darker gray wings of later vintage jutted to form a gentle V-shape sheltering the parkland's green slope. The training ground and the burial ground, the starting point and the end point of all Seekers were encompassed within that gentle embrace.

Seeker Veritas headquarters. The place where she began and ended each octant-long circuit, the repository of her hopes and dreams, her life as she now lived it, and the storage place of the few artifacts of her other lives, harbored inside its gray-rose walls. The closest thing she could claim as a permanent home for the past ten years. She waved a sketchy but heartfelt salute of welcome, a homecoming of sorts, though she was still distant from it. Not tonight, she'd promised herself that, a night at Myllard's first, and then, the next day, home.

"Khar, love, you've been awfully silent. How are you?"

"Fine." The ghatta twitched an ear. **"Watching people is more fun than watching buildings."**

Doyce laughed. *"Are you insinuating that I haven't been watching where I'm going?"*

"You've been watching where you're going, not where you are. But Lokka and I have taken care of that for you."

"Then let's see if I can't get Lokka and the two of us to the gate a little more quickly." She patted Lokka's neck, gave a chirrup and slapped the reins, and they were off, weaving their way through the knots of traffic.

❖

The Ring Wall's smooth outer facade of black basalt—still stoutly maintained despite the fact there had been no direct assault since Marchmont's only foray about one hundred years ago—loomed over Doyce as she reached a small, patient assembly of people awaiting formal recognition to enter. They parted to let her reach the head of the line; the deference wasn't necessary, but it was pleasing. She pulled Lokka ahead as the four Guardians on duty snapped to attention, their leather and bronze half-armor brightly polished. Two she recognized by sight and nodded to in greeting; they'd stood her an ale one night at Myllard's. They gave the faintest acknowledgment, a slight bob of the head, and stared straight ahead, true to their duty and their training.

The closest Canderis could claim to a standing army, there was little need for the Guardians in the military sense. Trained and constantly tested to the highest degree of readiness in mock combat and group battle strategy, the Guardians seldom found themselves engaged in traditional battles in these long years of peace. Instead, they served wherever the sight of them reassured the populace of their safety, and turned their hands to whatever emergency tasks might prove useful, as well as serving as a constabulary in cities and towns. Surprisingly enough, the life suited them well, for the Guardians recruited no brawlers, nor men with naught on their minds but mayhem and aggression, the love of killing. Instead they took pains to enlist men with good hearts, who cared about the land and the people and the protection of them, but who yearned for a touch of adventure as well.

Flanked by the four Guardians, Doyce waited until the gatekeeper emerged, rubbing the remains of his evening meal off his face, jostling past the Guardians. Doyce straightened herself in the saddle and intoned, "Seeker Veritas Doyce Marbon and the ghatta Bondmate Khar'pern. Enter we may?" Pure ritual, for a Seeker-Bondmate pair would never be denied access anywhere.

"Ah. Aye, enter ye may," the gatekeeper rasped, then tossed a sneer back over his shoulder at the soldiers. " 'Nother of those damn Stealthers and her cat. Ye get rid of one, 'nother appears." The youngest Guardian, cheeks and chin sunburned scarlet where a beard had recently been barbered clean, and flushing redder at the insult he'd heard, narrowed his lips and his armor gave a warning jangle as he started forward, then restrained himself under the watchful eye of his Sergeant. Khar's ears pricked forward as she stared through the gatekeeper. The one word transmitted to Doyce's mind described offal that had begun to rot and that any self-respecting ghatt would scratch dirt over to bury.

"Apt, but hardly original," she whispered back.

"Why waste originality?"

Lokka's hooves echoed on the cobble streets as they wound their way off the broad entry avenue and into the twists and turns of the old quarter where Myllard's Ale House was located. Shopkeepers dragged forth the clumsy night-shutters and chatted back and forth with each other about the day's business while children noisily played tag in the shadows, shrieking and chasing each other, darting away minnowlike when "it" drew too near. A few early drunks already saluted the power of the five nearly full Lady's moons creeping up into the sky and serenaded them in a cacophony of sound. "The Guardians will have their hands full tonight." She plugged fingers in her ears. The tune was long past having any identity she'd care to know.

"And for the next few nights," Khar murmured, ears twitching.

Tired, Doyce looked to see who watched them as they rode down the street. Fascinating to see how many gazed after a Seeker and Bondmate, either overtly or covertly. Some with a faint look of disgust on their faces, the ones who referred to them as Stealthers; while many others called greetings, smiled at the trio. A few children jogged companionably alongside, some stretching up gingerly to pat Khar, saying "Hey, ghatty, hey, kitty," and then dropping back to rejoin the tag game. Khar licked her rumpled fur into place, swiveled her head to check if more grubby hands waggled fingers toward her. Still other watchers made their ignoring obvious, backs stiff-turned, as if not seeing meant the three did not exist.

Once she had been one of those who had ignored, during her training as a eumedico. She had truly believed that the need for a ghatt as an intermediary, a mindlink from human to human, affronted any intelligent, educated mind, and the Lady's as well, if one believed in the panacea of religion. Almost a sin to let a four-legged lesser being slink into one's mind. Now that she wore the tabard of a Seeker Veritas she could imagine no other way, *would* feel that way even if she did not know the truth about the eumedicos and their vaunted link from human mind to human mind, from eumedico to patient.

That sharing, a personal mindlink with Khar, was wondrous. So wondrous that she never dared let herself delve as profoundly as she might. For when Khar was gone, dead, the link would be sundered, and the thought of another loss, another desertion, hurt more than she could bear. No more losses, she thought, and touched at the familiar lump of the medallion in her pocket.

To be Chosen as a Seeker Veritas meant a gift beyond riches or power, that singular sharing with Khar. True, it required embarking on a tireless search for the truth, not randomly, but in a rigorously supervised and sanctioned role as a Seeker Veritas, a Truth Seeker charged with hearing disputes to determine the veracity of the matter. The gift did not allow one to sit in judgment on one's fellow beings, although some outsiders interpreted it that way. Why else look so dubiously at a Seeker-

Bondmate pair except for the feeling of violation that their presence triggered in some, the sensation that their every thought, every feeling, whether consciously acknowledged or not, could be read, assayed, analyzed. An unfair assessment of their roles, but it happened. She'd tried to argue people out of it before. "If it's not a formal Seeking, why should a ghatt want to busybody himself through your mind every particle of the day, or *any* particle of the day?" A ghatt Sought only where instructed to, as part of the ceremony.

For others, the look of the ghatti engendered fear: so close to a common house or barn cat—and yet not. Three to four times the size of an average cat, proportionately longer of limb, more solid of body, the ghatt face broadened more than a cat's, with ears that sat a shade lower on the head, and the ear tips a little less pointed. In their coloration and their general habits they were practically identical. Too easy to make the assumption of sameness when they were anything but—with their thieving minds sucking the thoughts right out of your brain. Just as cats were sometimes accused of sucking the breath from a sleeping baby's lips, so did the ghatti with human thoughts—or so the common thinking went. And if they did that, what was a human left with?

Yet in nearly two hundred years of formal Seeker-Bondmate service across the whole of Canderis, with thousands of individual circuits to their credit, never had there been a major rebellion against them. The true dissidents were those who refused to admit that what the ghatti read in their minds during a Seeking was what was actually there, no matter how they might try to delude themselves. And what was read there was left intact.

Well, no sense in worrying about how many cast disapproving stares their way. Never *that* many, and so be it, they wouldn't change. Lady bright, it felt good to be coming off an octant-long Truth-Seeking circuit! Did the forty days seem longer now simply because she was older or because she was eager to be back with Oriel for a few brief days? Lokka picked up her feet more sharply, forgetting her tiredness, showing off for the many who greeted the trio as they rode along. Mintor the shoemaker whooped hello as he lowered the shutters of his shop into place with a crash and slammed the bolts home.

"Some supple green leather just waiting to be boots for you, Doyce-dear," he cried. For Mintor, pleasure came from finding the right materials to create the perfect boots and shoes for his favorites. If Mintor swore he had the right leather, she should consider it. His boots were minor works of genius—flawlessly molded to the wearer, supple, strong—and expensive.

She jingled the pouch at her side in his direction to let him hear the high-pitched chink that indicated more copper and silver than gold. Seekers drew pay, though not extravagantly. Unless she dipped into her account at Headquarters, she doubted she'd have enough. Worth it or not? "We'll see, Mintor, and thank you for the thought," she shouted over her shoulder.

"Almost forgot!" He ran panting for a few steps in her wake. "Rault asked that you stop by, too. Something he owes you." He halted in consternation as if he'd said too much and hurried back to his bars and locks.

What could Rault possibly owe her, she speculated, eyebrows climbing at the idea, but nothing came to mind. Not that it would be such a bad thing to have a jeweler in one's debt; would that she did!

Puzzling over the thought, she thumped the ghatta on her rump. The ghatta's mood still balanced between two worlds, here-and-now alternating with abstracted worry. Blast the ghatta for her silences sometimes. Why wouldn't Khar share her problems with her? *"Rolapin stew,"* Doyce began, wondering if Khar were even listening. *"Myllard makes the best rolapin stew—to hear the oldsters tell it, nearly as good as the original lapin."*

"Rolapin stew. . . ." The ghatta wrenched herself away from private thoughts, tried to participate. **"Not that those oldsters ever tasted the real thing either . . . long before their time."**

"No doubt it becomes tastier through generations of memory," Doyce agreed. *"But Myllard's is still in a class of its own. How many appalling imitations have we consumed on other circuits? Nobody remembers what real lapin tasted like—they were too tame, not used to the wild when they were brought here—but the scientist who gener-*

*ated rolapin didn't do us a disservice, especially when
Myllard's wife Fala is the chef."*

At those words Lokka swung into the courtyard that
marked Myllard's Ale House, a large building grown
higgledy-piggledy over its plot of land. Doyce tilted her
head to admire its lavish, crazy-quilt architecture, and bit
her lip to suppress a laugh. It couldn't be missed, all
three stories of it, the first of natural oak, then the next
level painted peach, and the final story a sky blue,
topped by a green slate roof. Fala's favorite color, sea
foam green, Myllard had confided to her once. Wings
and porches and gables jutted in every direction, each
touched with fanciful gilded wood carvings. She shook
her head at the whimsicality of it all. No granite or marble for Myllard; it didn't answer his inner soul the way
wood did.

Forest green apron flapping around his paunch, Myllard himself came rushing out the front door, hurtling
down the beam of light cast through the opening. "I *told*
them you'd be in, said you'd be early if you possibly
could," he roared as he reached up to stroke Khar, one
of the few adult non-Seekers who dared the familiarity
without reaping a sheaf of scratches. He swatted Lokka's
withers and then pounded Doyce on the thigh. She
winced; being friendly with Myllard was a tactile business, his sense of touch reassuring himself and his friends
that they really were so.

"Edert! Edert! Take Lokka round back. No skimping,
now. There's other work to do, but not while our favorite
little mare is waiting."

Khar leaped earthward light as thistledown and rubbed
once in greeting against Myllard's stout, gaitered calf.
Doyce dismounted more slowly, wondering if her leg
muscles really wanted to stretch. A knee popped, loud
as an exploding chestnut by the fire. She looked around
disingenuously, pretending the sound came from somewhere else in the yard. The muscles and joints would
limber up, she knew, but it wasn't as easy as it had been
at the beginning. But then thirty-seven was old by the
ways of Seekers, the age at which most went into semiretirement or returned to the lives they'd left before
they'd been Chosen. And Lady willing, she and Khar

had at least another seven or eight years left before retirement. After all, what other life did she have to return
to?

Myllard capered around her, patting one shoulder,
then the other as they started across the yard. "Parcellus
and Per'la are in, and Rolf and Chak. Can't say they
waited dinner for you, inconsiderate devils, though I
swore to them you'd be here."

Out of the corner of her eye she saw Jenret Wycherley
saunter out the door and swing left, heading toward the
stables. No mistaking the black garb. Rawn followed,
then onyx-statue froze as he looked back over his shoulder at her and Khar. Should she shout a hello? She decided not. In all honesty, she didn't care that much for
the man. He'd trained two years ahead of her, and while
they maintained a cordial work relationship, that more
than sufficed. A totally vain, self-indulgent man. She
wrinkled her nose at the thought, then turned her attention back to Myllard.

"Did Oriel come in early?" she asked.

Myllard stopped short, his mouth a little, round "o"
as he seemed to consider the question. One hand tugged
at the tuft of faded sandy hair over his left ear, and the
lines around his eyes grew deeper, more pronounced.
The pause stretched painfully long, enough to make her
consider why, but then he rushed ahead as if to make up
for lost time. "No, no, not that I've seen. Did ye think
he'd be in by now?"

She touched his shoulder to reassure him that he
wasn't at fault. "No, just a chance." So Oriel hadn't read
her mind this time. Khar stiffened and pressed herself
against Doyce's leg. She reached down and stroked her
head in sympathy; she wasn't sure she wanted any other
company than Oriel's tonight. Just food and ale and bed.
Still, Parcellus and Per'la and Rolf and Chak were
friends, more than fellow-Seekers. It could have been
far, far worse company. It could have been Jenret
Wycherley if he'd seen her. Doyce made a face at the
thought. She just wasn't in the mood for his superciliou-
ness tonight, even for the space of one casual drink,
though with Jenret it was far more likely to be more than
one.

"And I suppose you'll want rolapin stew—two helpings, at least—I can tell you look hungry." The innkeeper
winked at Doyce, not his usual twinkle of shared complicity, but almost a physical tic of nervousness. What
ailed the man? She looked at him more closely in the
harsh light spilling out of the door, but the light and
shadows made it hard to judge anything. "And while
we're at it, perhaps those two helpings on two separate
plates in case it should overflow . . . or someone wants
to share the meal with you."

She nodded agreeably and let Myllard shepherd her
into the Ale House, Khar by her side.

The carillon in the tower of the Lady's Bethel peeled
a two-note hesitation, then a cascade of seven descending
chimes, and Mahafny Annendahl slammed the heavy,
leather-bound book shut, keeping one finger in her place.
Should she mark it, she wondered, then shook her head,
pulling her hand free. She hadn't absorbed a jot of what
she'd been reading—genotypes, phenotypes, damn that
little monk puttering in his pea patch so many centuries
ago on another world. It had been pretense, something
to keep her occupied until dinner with her nephew Jenret. She'd considered canceling dinner after her meeting
late that afternoon with Swan Maclough; the summons
had been unexpected and unnerving. True, they were
cousins, but cousins who had journeyed their very separate ways since childhood, one rising to Seeker General
of the Seekers Veritas, the other becoming a respected
eumedico, one of the Senior Staff. Friendship remained,
but their respective roles emphasized the disparity of
their different worlds.

The last thing she'd expected today was to hear from
Swan, not with the capital buzzing with the news. Swan
should have been far too busy, and she was—except that
she had needed her cousin's knowledge, both professional and personal. But now Swan's suppositions and
half-knowledge were hers, the chorus to a lament, a melody of despair she had inked in through years of re-

search. How much of a facade could she marshal to hide
it from Jenret tonight?

She rose, slid a lucifer from the emerald enameled box
and struck a light, touching the wick of the candle in its
silver holder, curved like a fanciful smiling fish. The box
and the candlestick, she realized, were both gifts from
Jenret. The presents followed no pattern that she could
trace, not birth days, not naming days, nor halidays, no
regular schedule. Simply whenever the spirit moved him.
The giftings always a tad too extravagant for her taste
and sense of propriety; they were not blood kin, just kin
by marriage. Strange, to have two meetings in one day
with kin and near-kin, she who had so few close relatives
or friends left.

Dragging the candlestick to one side of the cherry-
framed mirror, she began to work her fingers through
her hair, twisting and turning the long silvered locks into
a chignon. Her fingers reflected in the looking glass, darting about, long and slender and white as fish bones, skel-
etal fish swimming through a sea of silver hair. She
reached down for the silver fastener in the jumble on top
of her bureau, then tossed it back, reached into her
pocket for her old leather and wood fastener, and clipped
it into place, shook her head to make sure it was secure.

Well, what *was* she going to tell Jenret tonight? Thrusting her hands in the pockets of her white laboratory coat,
she wheeled away from the mirror and walked toward
the window. Or what might he tell her? Affected he
might be at times, but he was no young fool; and every
underling knew more about some things, certain things,
than his superiors did. Best to draw him out first and
see.

She leaned elbows against windowsill, rested her head
on clasped hands. She'd never mentioned Doyce Marbon
to him before, nor had he ever mentioned Doyce to her.
No reason that he should; Doyce Marbon was one of a
hundred and fifty Seeker pairs that he knew. More, if
you counted those retired. But she'd mention Doyce tonight; how, she wasn't sure, but she'd find a way, had
to find one. Jenret might prove no help at all, but if he
could, even inadvertently . . . well, she'd cling to whatever fragile straws she could find. But shifting some of

the burden on him was unfair, not unless she armed him
with all she knew, or worse, suspected, and she wasn't
ready for that yet. Still so much more research to do, so
many more questions to ask. Damn all that she hadn't
been able to concentrate more on her reading!

Footsteps crackled along the cindered path, and she
peered down, waving at the dark-haired young man
nearly swallowed by the wall's dark shadow. No question
it was he, Rawn silhouetted near his leg. She'd hoped
the ghatt might stay away, that she might not have to
meet those questioning eyes. Jenret swore on his honor
that Rawn would never 'speak her unless she requested
it, but tonight she feared things might slip past her conscious control. She waved again, palm down to forestall
him coming up to her private chambers, then turned from
the window and stripped off her white coat, tossed it
over the chair. Somehow she didn't want any physical
reminder of being a eumedico tonight; her secret knowledge more than sufficed.

Doyce and Myllard paused in the entryway, then the
innkeep absently rubbed her back before heading behind
the crowded counter while Doyce and Khar pushed their
way between the trestles to the corner where the Seekers
traditionally sat. Rolf looked up and waved, nudged Parcellus, deep in thought over a puzzle-toy. The ghatta sitting next to Parcellus and the ghatt at Rolf's side were
already aware of the newcomers. Chak rose to his feet
and stretched, head and shoulders dipping down and up
in an elegant, fluid motion that belied his solidity, a staid
and proper gentleman ghatt, gray coat, dapper white feet
and a hint of white at the ruff, a discreet jabot. He
stretched up, whiskers coarse against Doyce's hand, and
then turned with a delicate greet-sniff to Khar.

If Seeker and Bond truly did assume each other's mental signature after years of companionship, Doyce counted
Rolf and Chak as living examples. Rolf Cardamon, elegantly neat, trim—too trim? she asked herself—and gray-
goateed, touched her hand in brief affection and shifted
so she could sit. Although in his late forties, Rolf looked

at least ten years older, and she worried, not for the first time, about his health. Skin and muscle blanched vellum-thin over his bones. Chak at twenty-six could best be described as venerable, although his age sat more lightly on him than it did on his Bondmate. Rolf and Chak, she realized with a pang, could probably manage no more than a season or two of circuits before retirement became necessity rather than choice. They'd tried retiring once before, applied for half-duty as trainers, but it hadn't worked, and they'd petitioned to ride the circuits again.

"Myllard's just opened a cask of New Golden," Rolf greeted her. "It's not at all bad. Shall I get you some?" She gave him a grateful smile and turned to extricate herself from Per'la's frenzy of affection.

Rolf and Chak might be subdued, self-contained, but Per'la was anything but—a fluffy, long-haired ghatta the color and sweetness of a buttercream bonbon. Simply stated, Per'la loved the world and everything in it, her round peridot eyes wide with pleasure at every new happening. And at this moment, Doyce and Khar were the newest event. But that didn't make her a distracted simpleton on the job, far from it. She'd reviewed Parse and Per'la at several Seekings near the completion of their training; the ghatta held a place as one of the most discerning, sensitive ghatti on circuit, capable of delicate transmittings without losing the human nuances. Sometimes Doyce teased the ghatta that Per'la's first tongue had been human speech, not falanese, not mindspeech.

Without meaning to, Doyce found herself staring at Per'la's Bondmate, Parcellus, his carroty hair wisping in all directions, in need of a trim as usual. The Lady only knew what had drawn Per'la to Choose Parse as her Bondmate. Parcellus Rudyard seemed an ill match for the ghatta, a young man of sudden intensities and equally sudden lapses, impetuous one moment, foot-dragging the next as if the two sides of himself warred over who had the upper hand. If Parcellus were truly engrossed in his puzzle, she doubted he'd have much to say for the evening, but in one of his sudden turns, he became voluble, thin, aesthete's hands orchestrating the air, words of welcome spilling forth.

"Good to see you well, Parse," she managed as she strove to untangle herself from Per'la's affections, "but Per'la's demanded first greetings." The ghatta wreathed herself round and round Doyce's body, ducking under one arm, bouncing across her lap, head butting under her chin. Khar looked on, momentarily diverted, edging along the bench so that Per'la's long, plumed tail didn't swat her in the face.

Rolf, competently balancing three steins of New Golden from the bar, made the traditional greeting first, cutting through Parse's chatter. "Mindwalk if ye will." It was that greeting which threw open all levels of their conversation so that each ghatt might mindspeak with the other Seekers, not just with its Bondmate. Without invitation the ghatti were too reticent to break into another Bondmate's thoughts unless it proved absolutely crucial. The Bond was sacred, and to trespass into the mind of another ghatt's Bondmate and share converse displayed an unspeakable rudeness and ill-breeding.

"Have you heard, did you feel it . . . ?" Parcellus stifled a sneeze as he waved exclamations across the table-top, nearly toppling his ale. Rolf moved to steady it, starting to speak at the same time, but Per'la beat him to it.

"**Hush!**" Her plumed tail gave one snap, the same hint of exasperation in her voice. "**Tired, give them a chance, a few sips. Let them go wash and eat.**" Strangely enough, Per'la had not administered the reprimand on the intimate or personal mode. Doyce ignored her momentary uneasiness; Parcellus and Per'la always relished an audience, or managed to create one, whether they craved it or not.

Expression serious, Parcellus literally sat on his hands, as if by controlling them he could curb his tongue. "But, but, it's important that they. . . ."

"**And so they shall, but a few moments more or less won't change it,**" Chak's deep mindvoice rumbled.

"Mmph. He's right, Parse. Ease off. Now," Rolf commanded, letting go of Parcellus's stein. "How was the last circuit, Doyce? The usual, more or less? Lucky you for the mountains this time of year. I had the coast trip that swings down through that ooze of a marshland that

the S.G.'s office and the Transitors swear is solid land—
maybe it was the last time they bothered to go out and
ride it. Well, talk about unseasonably hot and rainy, plus
a trick tide that forced a shoal of skipperfish in and
stranded them on the mud flats. Chak didn't uncrinkle
his nose from the smell of dead fish for three days, did
you, old gent?" Chak's nose wrinkled in agreement, and
Doyce smiled in sympathy as she scratched the gray ears.

Myllard brought a bowl of fresh water for Khar, and
the ghatta drank, beads of water springing up and clinging to her white whiskers. "Thanks for bringing over the
ale, Rolf. Couldn't get here before. Not that it's that
busy, but there were some stories needed to be quashed.
It's getting out of hand." A glance of shared concern
bordering on fear passed between them, then Myllard
grabbed Rolf's shoulder, massaged it ruminatively, and
bustled back toward the bar where two traders from the
outlands and a drover huddled deep in conversation,
heads together, with an occasional sidelong glance at the
Seekers in the far corner. No need to pay attention to
that; covert looks in a crowded ale house were a part of
life. Someone was always curious.

She drank down half her ale in greedy gulps, then slid
off the bench. "Let me go get some of the dust and grime
rearranged," she apologized. "Khar, want to come? A
quick brush and polish, anyway, or do you want to stay?"

Khar examined her white paws, impeccable as always.
"Do my ears?" The ghatta had an inordinate liking for
having her ears tickled with a hairbrush. **"And your hair
looks like last year's bird's nest."** The final comment was
transmitted on the intimate mode so that the others
wouldn't hear. Doyce ran a hand over the tangles and
pulled a face in agreement.

Back a little later, the worst of the day's dust slapped
from clothes, hands and face glowing from soap and
water, and her unruly curls dampened, forced to wave in
nearly the same direction, Doyce reentered the taproom.
From across the way she saw Rolf let go of Parcellus's
shoulder, while Per'la jumped into his lap. Parse shook
his head emphatically and sneezed three times, face reddening as he strove to contain them. "I finished your ale,
Doyce, so this one's on me," he called, voice strained

and nervous, wiping his nose with the clean, capacious white handkerchief Rolf tossed at him. "Except you'll have to bring it over yourself."

Rolf made a disgusted face, jutting his goatee in Parse's direction and pushed himself up, braced against the table. "Never mind, love, I'm closer than you. No sense you threading your way through to us and then beyond to the counter. I'll get them. Now behave!" He directed the last comment toward his table-mate.

As if seeking inspiration anywhere he could, Parcellus rolled watering, pink-rimmed eyes at the ceiling, at the bird's-eye mapled wall behind her shoulder, everywhere except at Doyce as she sat down. "Twins'll be in later this evening." His voice reverberated so brittlely-bright she thought it might crack. She also had the distinct impression that he relaxed after that statement, as if Per'la had withdrawn her claws from his thigh. But Per'la, too, seemed intent on letting her peridot eyes wander, and Doyce suppressed her mindthought to the ghatta. What had gotten into Parse tonight? He tended to be as volatile as his allergies, but something was bursting to escape him. Perhaps it had something to do with the Ambwasali twins: Parse adored a good gossip and the twins made up some of his favorite material.

"Didn't think I'd see the twins this time around. Aren't they already on another circuit, or just about due to head out?" Parse raised the nearly empty stein, her stein, come to think of it, to his face and muttered something unintelligible into its depths.

She knew the twins, knew them fairly well, as far as that went, which meant she didn't really know them at all. She'd spent time with them when Oriel was present, and a bit when he wasn't, but she could never fathom their differentness. Their looks unconventional by Canderisian standards, Bard and Byrta would have stood out in any crowd without their twinship—that was an added fillip to their foreignness. Oriel had told her the tale of how their grandparents had come from the Sunderlies, so far distant and fragilely joined to Princept by a narrow chain of islands that most knew nothing of it other than that it was broiling hot and its people dark-skinned and wild. Dark-skinned was true enough, but the wildness had no doubt grown out of travelers' embroidering, the embellishing and redecorating of a tale told so often that something new had to be tacked on each time for freshness.

She half-turned away from Parse, leaned against the table, and heard Oriel's voice in her head, telling the tale. Not the best of tale-tellers, what with his interruptions and asides, but he more than made up for it with his eagerness. "Now you see, Bard's and Byrta's grandfather and his three wives trekked north to settle in the meadowlands just south of Gaernett and provided enough gold—strangely wrought, some say . . ." and his voice dropped in a stage whisper, storm-blue eyes under dark, straight brows quickly surveying the room, his broad hands describing delicate shapes of gold, adorning her with imaginary bracelets, armbands, and pectorals. He'd mimed a crown, tweaked at a reddish curl, and she'd slapped his hand away, laughing.

He'd pushed his hair back with both hands, picked up where he'd left off. "Enough gold to buy a herd of cattle. Not dairy cows, but *beef* cattle." His finger wagged under her nose to make sure she caught his emphasis. "And the grandfather ranged the countryside on other secretive trips, returning each time with a new bull or cow to breed into his herd. Some of the twins' aunts and uncles, the children of their grandfather and his three wives, intermarried, but the twins' father chose a woman from the town, as blonde and lithe as he was dark and lithe, but each equally silent, though the humor lines radiated from their eyes. The townspeople preferred not to mingle with them, so it was good they were used to silence. You know how standoffish those farmers can be, Doyce, just south and southwest of Gaernett. Good farmers, all, but they wouldn't trade you a spare word 'til they've tasted your coin." She'd nodded, just to keep him going, not that there was any way to stop him when he was in a tale-telling mood.

"Now, when the twins were born, boy and girl, the girl scarcely ahead of the boy, they were equally lithe but golden, the color of maple sugar, and with smoky blue-gray eyes the tint of burning autumn leaves." Oriel had savored the sentence, gratified by his choice of

words. "They spoke seldom, except to each other, and
with each other words weren't often necessary. They
both 'Printed the same day with two ghatten as like to
each other in their way as the twins were in theirs. M'wa
and P'wa were black, each with an identical white ruff,
a white forehead star and four white feet." He stopped,
interjecting in his normal voice, "Now remember, Doyce,
you can always tell them apart because M'wa's left front
leg has a high white stocking, not a boot, and P'wa's
right front leg has the high white stocking. Have you got
that? It pleases them so when somebody takes the time to
remember who's who." She had concentrated, nodded.

She nodded to herself now; she'd better remember
Oriel's story or she'd err when the twins and their Bonds
arrived. Oriel never could understand that many, herself
included, felt uneasy with the two pairs of twins in their
proximity. The four seemed to be but one pair, as if the
two Seekers and the two ghatti were each mirror images
of one another. To speak with Bard and M'wa alone was
to sense a lack, and the same was true when one spoke
to Byrta and P'wa. Rumor held that their mindspeech
echoed stronger, capable of penetrating greater distances
when all four rode near than when the pairs were far
apart. At least one concession to this closeness had already been made: when Byrta and P'wa started their circuit, the other pair followed the same circuit a day or
two behind them or journeyed a circuit that paralleled
the other's, so that although physically separated by
some leagues, they remained close enough to be together
in their minds.

Yet why did she feel so conspicuously excluded when
the two pairs of twins came together? It wasn't rudeness,
but a sustaining fullness and unity that did not require
outsiders—that, and the disconcerting habit they had of
speaking for each other. Direct any question to Bard,
and Byrta might answer, or at least finish his thought for
him, or vice versa. Whenever she spoke to either twin
she always struggled to keep them both in her line of
sight, never able to anticipate from which direction the
response would come. It felt impolite to be looking the
other way. Oriel laughed at her for that, teased her that
she was his little bird, trying to watch two worms at once

and ending up with neither. Just because *he* never had
any problems telling who was whom.

If Parcellus planned to go on a tear about the twins
tonight, teasing at them again, she wasn't sure she
wanted to hear it. Then she smiled despite herself. Unless, of course, they decided to retaliate as they had once
before when, with no word spoken aloud, they rose as
one, grabbed Parse by shoulders and knees, lugged him
out the door and deposited him in the water trough.
Per'la had followed, three paces behind the struggling
trio and three paces ahead of P'wa and M'wa, her expression rippling with embarrassment and barely suppressed
glee. "**Oh my, oh dear,**" Doyce remembered her mindspeaking to no one in particular. "**I *told* him, I warned
him. . . .**"

Doyce and Per'la shared a fragment of memory, and
even Khar's whiskers rippled in a recollecting smile. The
ghatta had been so silent, so brooding since last night,
but Doyce thrust the thought aside as hastily as she
pushed the empty stein away from her on the table. Rolf
returned with the fresh steins just as Myllard wended his
way through the crowd, a plate of stew in one hand, a
breadboard topped with a crusty loaf and a half-moon of
cheese balancing precariously on his arm. His other hand
gripped a shallow bowl of stew that he tried to extend
to her without losing control of everything else. She half-
rose from behind the table and clamped one hand on the
bowl, the other lifting the breadboard from his sweat-
slicked forearm. "Oh, Myllard!" She breathed deeply,
inhaling the aroma, the steam rising fast and hot enough
to feather a curl from her forehead. "Smells wonderful!"

He set the bowl on the floor in front of Khar, the
ghatta transfixed as well by the smell. "By the Lady,
enjoy and prosper!" And he darted off, waving his hand
in sketchy salute and mopping his face with his apron.
"Made with Fala's own two hands and served up by myself," the words floating in his wake. "Perfect on all
counts!"

Whatever Khar's worries and fears, they didn't seem
to affect her appetite, Doyce noticed as the ghatta fished
a delicate paw into the stew, hooking a piece of meat
onto the rim to cool. That was good. Khar looked up,

expression hidden by the steam, and flashed the half-smile that Doyce knew so well. **"Wouldn't hurt his feelings. Or insult his stew."**

"And maybe even enjoy it a little?" Mindspeech was a blessing with a full mouth.

"Maybe."

"Or then, perhaps Per'la or Chak would be interested in seconds?" Chak rumbled polite denials, but Per'la looked eager until she remembered herself. Whatever Parse's many flaws, he had probably broadcast a polite reminder on the intimate mode.

Without another glance in either direction, the two set to work, if work it could be called to properly savor and enjoy such a feast.

The worst of her hunger dulled, Doyce wiped her mouth with a napkin, using the moment to survey her surroundings. The ghatta had done so as well, eyes alert and inquiring as she watched the goings-on. Parcellus engrossed himself again in his finger-puzzle-toy, still unable to figure out its twistings and turnings, though any eight-year-old could have unlocked it in the blink of an eye. Rolf, with Chak comfortably draped across his feet, perched sideways on the bench, back to her as he retold the story of the reverse tide and the dead skipperfish to a local shopkeep and his elder son. Others played penny-darts, argued over weather and crops, did the hundred-and-one minor rituals of tavern drinking and telling, talk as warm and comforting as the food and ale.

She detected their presence before she saw them; the twins' entrance cut through the warmth and buzz as efficiently as a eumedico's scalpel through flesh. She pivoted around to greet them. Most eyes studiously gazed anywhere except at the doorway where the two Seekers and two Bondmates stood, surveying the company. Then better manners on both sides reasserted themselves: the twins smiled, or formed what passed for a trenchant smile with them, nodded, made brief hellos; the townspeople gave polite yet distant greetings and dove back into their conversations with relief, even if they could no longer remember the subject. Doyce concentrated on Oriel's instructions for identifying the ghatti, the long white stockings. So that meant M'wa on the left, P'wa on the right. The ghatti glided into the room, their lean black tails whipping the air with question marks, Bard and Byrta following.

"Greetings. Mindwalk." "If ye will," Bard started and Byrta finished the salutation. Doyce waved a piece of corn bread in their direction, her mouth full. "Have you" "told her about" "the trouble?" One question, split between them, addressed to both Rolf, now turned back on the bench, and Parcellus, finger-puzzle dropped and forgotten on the table. Per'la lifted a nervous paw, nudged it away from his elbow, and sat back, stretching her neck.

"Good evening, Byrta. Good evening, Bard." she spoke to each in turn, looking first one, then the other straight in the eye, praying that the other wouldn't initiate a conversation at that moment. "M'wa, P'wa, greetings, ghatti friends." The two black and white ghatti exchanged a glance, then the one on the right, the one with the long white stocking on the right foreleg, got up and moved to the left of its sib. "Oh, by the Lady, I missed again! I'm sorry, P'wa, M'wa. Now what's the trouble you mentioned? Has something happened?"

Treating the twins as one and the ghatti as one did save wear and tear on the nerves, Doyce reflected as she waited for their answer, except for the faintest, fleetingest look of sadness on all their faces, as if now and again the bonds of blood, love, and mindspeech bound them just a little too intimately; as if they wondered, and hated themselves for wondering, what it was to be part of but one pair, a Seeker Bond pair with two distinctly separate and unique partners, not the singular synthesis of Bard/Byrta/M'wa/P'wa.

Cut me and the other bleeds, she thought irrelevantly as she waited for them to continue, but Khar had leaped up beside her on the bench, muscles quivering, eyes narrowing and widening. She tried—and failed—to suppress a yawn of nervousness, turning her head to lick her flank and regain her composure.

"No, we've told them nothing yet," Rolf commented. "They'd ridden long and hungry. Nothing would have changed by telling them first. Besides, it was agreed that

we were to wait for you. That was the *official* decision,
let me remind you."

Parcellus nodded, voice surprisingly firm. "Bad news
always keeps. So will this until they've finished eating.
You're early." He rubbed at his nose with his handkerchief.

Byrta touched her brother's arm. "Aye, they're right.
Ill news always keeps. T'would keep even if there were
no telling, though we must. T'isn't wise, though, to let
this simmer any longer. Sheer luck they didn't hear the
gossip on the way in."

Doyce stiffened; Byrta had finished five complete sentences without sharing a single word with her twin. She
reached a restraining hand toward Khar to stop the
ghatta from licking at herself again.

M'wa looked up at the bench. **"We all have separate
voices. Even, sometimes, separate thoughts . . . if ever
you chose to hear."** A hint of bitterness tinged his tone.
**"But tonight we have agreed. The sorrow is so great that
one voice, one from each of us in each pair, will speak,
so you will hear us as individuals and concentrate on
our words."** He trembled, and P'wa leaned against him,
lending him strength and encouragement. Then she
pulled away, separate.

Byrta examined her hands, fingers clenched tightly in
the edges of her tabard, then glanced at the rest of the
tavern from the corners of her eyes, checking that others
drank, talked, laughed, ignored them. She freed her fingers, then clasped her hands behind her as if on report.
"They already know." She thrust her chin in the direction of Rolf, Parcellus, and the ghatti. "Myllard, too.
Others in town know bits and pieces, but not the whole
story. But after much debate, the Seeker General agreed
that it was our story to tell, for we were the ones who
found them." A tear poised in the corner of her eye, and
she dashed it away, impatient at the tiny drop of water's
power to interrupt. "Time enough for that later." Her
voice husked with tension, and she struggled to bring it
under control.

The Seeker General? What was Byrta talking about?
Except for Byrta, Doyce saw side-turned, averted faces,
no one else looking directly at her. The fine hairs on the

back of her neck began to rise and prickle, just as they had the night before.

"Doyce," Byrta swallowed hard. "Doyce, Oriel is dead. Saam badly hurt, a ghatt-shell without the mind-speech. We . . . we don't know what happened or how it happened."

The leftover stew on her plate grew ugly, she was sure of that, the fat and juices congealing in dead white globs . . . like flesh. A smear of pulped tomato hovered at the plate's edge, red as a gout of blood. Yes, quite ugly . . . no question about that. Doyce set her fork down with precision and leaned back, swallowing hard, willing her gorge not to rise. Ramming the back of her wrist against her mouth, she bit, not conscious of what she did.

Parcellus, Lady bless him even if She never had before, was sliding the body . . . no, the plate . . . out from in front of her. She opened her eyes and stared into the middle distance, toward the burnished counter with its candles reflecting off their pinked tin backs, the warm, intimate glow of oil lamps, the bustle, the people . . . alive, alive, alive, and Oriel dead! Ah, thrust all the suddenly staring faces, all the concerned faces, thrust them away, each mouth silently shaping the word "dead." Not Oriel, not again!

Easier to pretend another, a self-controlled Doyce watched Doyce, distancing herself from what she saw, heard, felt. Oh, dearest Lady, to be able for once to distance the pain of loss! If she stayed locked in this present moment, the now, could she not pretend the past had never happened, that the future would not unroll itself in this new pattern, that only this frozen moment deserved her total concentration? Better to watch, to lose herself in the wonder of each individual gesture, each sound, refuse to tally their cost, their meanings as a whole. Best to simply be, divorced from her outer being.

From a distant spectator's seat in her mind, she peered down at herself, the slight figure of Doyce with her cap of red-brown hair thatching the oval face with its slightly too prominent patrician nose, the hazel eyes now dark and dilated with fear. Interesting, how the wiry body held itself coiled, ready to spring away, escape, but found no place to hide; she was hemmed in, forced to concen-

trate on the activity around her, activity that abruptly
captured her interest, pushed everything away from her
cowering, frantic thoughts. Watch, don't think, the distant Doyce commanded—and she did. Time enough for
thinking later; for now she transformed herself into an
audience, assigned to sit and watch the drama. Make-
believe, it was only make-believe, wasn't it?

What missed cue made the boy at the bar pale to suety-
white, his mouth pinched with a muffled exclamation he
dared not utter, his eyes darting everywhere except down
to his hands as he fumbled beneath the bar? He pulled
up a dusty, squat bottle with a long neck and red wax
seal impressed on it, set it on the bar, knocked it over,
righted it, still without looking at his hands.

She watched with close concern, focusing with him on
his effort to extract the sticky cork, all the while not
looking at what he was doing. The small, rounded glass—
real glass, not pottery—was knocked over twice, once
nearly rolling off the bar, but the boy's hands, at least,
"saw" better than his eyes. It all appeared highly significant and necessary that she should scrutinize his actions,
deduce what would happen next.

When had Chak sprung to the top of the counter? Ah,
she'd missed that, intent on the boy. Chak threaded a
fastidious path amongst the damp ale-rings and the
steins, past a smoldering pipe in a cracked china saucer,
his dainty white paws negotiating the spills. "Sweet old
Chak, what would Rolf do without you?" she thought
idly as the boy backed as far from the counter and the
ghatt as he could and still keep his hands in motion over
the bar. Chak located a small, dry island and sat, twining
his tail around his toes as he leveled his head in the boy's
direction.

Myllard stood at the other end of the counter, dead-
still, drops of perspiration at his temples, only his eyes
winking from her to the boy and the patient ghatt, back
and back again, as if she somehow bore responsibility.
But she was not responsible for anything except sitting
politely through the end of this scene; she was the audience, not the director, not one of the actors. Nor had
she any idea who had written the script.

"Pour it," Myllard croaked, one hand shooting up to

twist at the tuft of hair over his left ear. The boy gathered
his courage and tilted the dusty bottle.

With infinite concentration, Chak collected the small,
rounded glass to him with a crooked white paw and
began easing his way down the bar, scooting the glass
along with him. The deep amber liquid trembled, threatened to slosh, but the ghatt persisted, gaining ground,
bar patrons pulling back, out of his path.

Rolf jumped to his feet and snatched the glass from
the ghatt. She could feel the tension in his rigid stance,
a match for her own. "Don't press your luck, old boy,
but Lady bless, there's one cool head in the bunch of us.
Now let them be." He took a few steps along the bar
and hoisted the bottle from the boy's limp grasp, said,
"Sorry," and nodded at Myllard in thanks. Chak jumped
down from the bar, landing hard and standing stock-still
for a moment, elderly bones jarred by the landing. Everything appeared normal, as if no ghatt had ever paraded across the bar, although the boy polished that
piece of counter with mindless compulsion, damp towel
swooping in widening circles as if to eradicate something
from his memory as well.

"Chak, you know full-well that's how rumors and bad
tales get their start," Rolf admonished. Then he sighed
and shrugged ruefully as he topped off the glass Chak
had retrieved with such care.

Tossing her head back as Rolf thrust the glass under
her nose, she dropped her hand from her mouth and
sniffed too deeply, barely avoiding a sneeze at the
strength of the sharp, biting smell. "Brandy," Rolf encouraged, tilting the glass to her lips, wetting them.
"Enough for all by the heft of it, though we'll have to
do without the pretty glassware." Chak levered himself
to his feet again, head cocked in query, hind legs
bunched for another spring. Rolf froze him with a sharp
command. "Leave it be! Do you want the boy to lose
his wits?" Chak sat, licked at his ruff and around to his
shoulder, head turned from the rebuke spoken aloud.

The smooth fire of the brandy trickled a pang of
warmth into her inner being, acted as a release, dropping
a curtain of reality between actors and audience. Now
she had no choice but to concentrate, assess, and reluc-

tantly become involved although she had no script to
follow, no idea of her cue. She pressed the brandy glass
against her lips, tongued the slickness of the glass, the
stickiness of the curved side where the liquid had slopped
just a little. She took a tiny sip, wondered why the back
of her wrist showed twin bite-marks, red and white crescents imprinted in flesh. Oriel always relished a well-
aged brandy, but she had never been able to appreciate
the complexities and subtleties of taste he could identify.
Brandy, enough for all, Rolf had said, enough for all,
but none for Oriel because Oriel is dead. Dead.

Dead. At least that's what Byrta had said, and Doyce
looked up for confirmation, hoping not to receive it. But
Byrta nodded once, captured the bottle from Rolf, and
gave it a defiant hoist, throat working. She thumped the
bottle hard on the table, the alcohol raising a hectic flush
on her cool, golden skin. "Oriel *is* dead," she repeated
as if to a child, "and Saam probably soon to follow. The
body wounds will heal, but without his mindspeech and
without his Bondmate, will he desire to live?" Bard
reached over, cupped a hand under Khar's chin, and
turned her face toward the light, his grip firm when she
tried to pull free. He conferred silently with M'wa and
P'wa for an instant, let his eyes question his twin. "I
know," Byrta replied. "I could feel that she knew,
couldn't you? It showed in her eyes as soon as we came
in."

Who had known? Khar? Doyce gazed down at the
huddled ghatta beside her on the bench. She had known,
she *had known*, she whispered fiercely to herself. *That*
was the burden the ghatta had carried with her since
last night. Unreasoning anger flared, burned through her
mind; she'd been shut out, deprived of the truth, the
sharing and the sorrowing. Lady take the ghatta to the
furthest reaches of . . . ! No, no, no, not and lose Khar,
too! Khar's amber eyes met hers without flinching.

"I knew. I knew but I didn't know *who*. Don't you
understand? I could feel it, but I couldn't sense where or
how or why. Only the dread, the dread! Evil twining
through the air! I kept straining, trying to read it, to
form the truth, but it disappeared . . . ! Everything disappeared, all the mindlinks fractured and in ruins. I

reached everywhere my mind could search, but no one
answered! No one! Oh, why didn't I try harder? I failed!"
The misery masked her face, her eyes sunken and shadowed, her fur suddenly lusterless and shabby. Per'la
shouldered closer and began to lick, working her way
around Khar's face. M'wa started on a flank, P'wa down
the back of her neck as if they could erase her sickness
of spirit.

"What happened to Oriel? How did you find him?
Where did you find him?" Doyce steadied her voice but
needed both hands to steady her glass—that, and her
elbows on the table.

Byrta leaned against her twin and took a deep breath.
"At the foot of the cliff that overhangs Wyllow Gorge,
just short of where it joins the river." She struggled to
continue, as if shamed by what she was admitting. "We
rode out so early, well before dawn . . . a wager, a silly
little wager with Oriel that we'd catch him outside the
walls before he got in. It . . . it wasn't the wager, so
much, we'd not seen him in a long time. Our circuits
hadn't meshed lately. We . . . missed him." Her voice
trailed off and Bard's long arm captured the brandy bottle from the table, held it out to her, smoke-hazed eyes
bright with concern.

She took a judicious sip, passed the bottle back to
Bard. "When the mindscreams started . . . P'wa and
M'wa became near-crazed with the pain, twisting and
yowling, batting at their heads. We couldn't 'speak them,
couldn't understand what was wrong. At first we thought
poison. When they went limp, fainted, we turned back
to Gaernett to get help for them . . . we didn't realize
others were affected, we didn't know what had happened, what to do! We feared their dying!" Her face
twisted at the pain of the memories.

Now Bard's voice picked up the tale, allowing his sister
time to compose herself. "M'wa came to very quickly,
but he still couldn't 'speak me. And no matter how hard
I reined the gelding back toward the city walls, he
wouldn't go, just kept galloping toward the cliff, M'wa
wobbling and weak on the platform as if begging him to
speed on. When we finally pulled up, 'twas clear there'd
been a vicious struggle all the way to cliff's edge, and

M'wa and P'wa slipped down the cliffside to see. That was how we found them."

"Rider, horse, and ghatt toppled off together." Byrta took a breath and retrieved the telling, as if by private signal. "Or that's what it was meant to seem. More tracks than theirs alone at clifftop. Oriel's horse held the faintest breath of life in him, when we'd scrambled down, but he faded away. Saam unconscious, bleeding from gouges and scrapes and a bad wound on his right hip. With the ghatti still weak, still unable to 'speak any distance to call for aid, we dared not move him 'til dawn when we could judge what we were doing. Oriel was dead from the fall, his head smashed in." She buried her face against Bard's chest to muffle the next words, but they heard them nonetheless. "His . . . his brain was gone!"

"No so surprising after a fall like that." So cool and controlled, so analytical over her friend and lover's death. Someone had to be, someone had to be. "It's not a straight, unbroken fall. He must have crashed and hit several times on the ledges, lost bits of skull and brain matter each time he hit. Those outcroppings are brutally sharp."

"No! You don't understand!" Byrta straightened, her usual flowing gestures choppy with anger. "I don't mean that it leaked out, that he was flecked with bits of brain. It was scooped out—clean as a melon! And we found further signs of a struggle down below. Especially around Saam, and a shred of black cloth snagged in his teeth. M'wa saw it." The ghatt's head bobbed once in mute agreement, and he went back to licking Khar.

M'wa finished Khar's ablutions and began to speak. **"My twin and I searched every spot we could reach, clifftop down. Trouble at the top, trouble at the bottom. No horse, no Seeker,"** he paused and sniffed emphatically, **"and most of all, no ghatt would seek his death that way to escape from danger. Our ways are *our* ways, and that is not one of them."** Per'la and Chak bowed their heads, eyes squeezed shut, as M'wa continued. **"Something, someone, made them take that leap."** And then a last sentence so low and vehement, so strictly ghatti-directed that Doyce strained to hear, sure that she must understand falanese. **"And when we find them. . . ."** No additional words were wasted.

Khar's eyes cleared and she listened. **"What of Saam?"** she stared at M'wa, awaiting his answer. P'wa and M'wa consulted between themselves before the ghatt with the long left white stocking spoke again.

"In body—fair. With rest and the medications, he would heal. But he will not be still. When Twylla tried to administer the sleeping draught, he struck at her! Mem'now blocked his blow, had to growl to make him desist!" No one, Seeker or Bondmate, had ever raised hand or paw to Twylla before, despite the pain, the mind-disorientation brought on by sickness or injury. Her very touch soothed the fretful. **"But he cannot mind-speak. We regained our powers slowly. He . . . not at all."**

The enormity of the loss was only beginning to sink in on the others, ghatti and Seekers alike. P'wa looked at her sib and coughed. **"Let me speak, brotherling."** He nodded wearily and the ghatta with the long white stocking on her right leg began to speak. **"We have conversed, Saam and ourselves . . . in falanese, our own tongue, but not through our minds. He can remember nothing, nothing but the loss of Oriel, and he knows not how or why. Only that he is gone and it is like to tear his very essence apart. The few words he speaks are forced, distracting him from the seeking for his Bond. Whether he will stay or go, I cannot say. If he seeks far enough, his body must follow after."**

"What is there to stay for?" Chak growled and placed a protective white paw on Rolf's thigh. **"Without one's Bond. . . ."** Rolf's eyes swam with tears and he cuffed the ghatt softly.

"May you travel, then, before I," he whispered. "The pain will be there for me, but my memories will help." The intimacy of his words resounded with unbearable pain to the others after the news they had heard.

❖

"Brandy?" Jenret cocked a suggestive eyebrow at the decanter the servant had left on the sideboard. He stretched back in his chair, brought his arms above his head and interlaced his fingers, in no rush for an answer. Much as the thought of the brandy pleased him, he had no eagerness about rising to retrieve it.

"Lazy," Rawn scolded, "**Fill your belly so full and there'll be no room for me on the pommel platform.**"

Mahafny sat arrow-straight, folding and refolding her napkin, thin fingers recreasing each fold. Lower lip caught between her teeth, she examined the napkin as if she'd never seen one before, then slipped it inside its ring. "A small one, perhaps. As long as you promise this isn't part of the ritual your father and uncle used to indulge in—brandy and cigars. The stench permeates everything."

Rocking onto the chair's back legs, he stretched his arms further, higher, then brought his hands behind his head, twisted his neck from side to side. "I think I can do without the cigars, and not just in honor of your presence." He leaned forward, the chair's front legs hitting the floor with a protesting thunk, and rose, heading toward the sideboard where the drinks tray sat. Strange, how familiar the room seemed, even though he'd been here only a few times before. It was the furniture he recognized, had known since childhood. Old pieces, the sideboard and a matching hutch, sturdily made but with a charm of caring workmanship and more than a modicum of inventiveness; most decorated in old, soft faded colors, stenciled with fruited cornucopias, sheaves of wheat, flowers . . . mustards, ochers, mullein greens, dusky roses, slate and navy blues. Wycherley furniture, long in the family, his uncle's, Mahafny's dead husband. The dining room chairs he well remembered for their discomfort, spindled backs always poking and paining whenever one dared relax backward. Certainly more effective with both children and adults than an admonishment against slouching.

"How much?" he asked over his shoulder, poising bottle over glass. Eyes closed as if she dozed, Mahafny jerked forward at the sound, arm sending a table knife spinning off the table. Rawn jerked upright, dignity offended as the knife cartwheeled and clattered beside his paws.

"What?" Mahafny's head bent below the table to follow the knife's flight. "Ah, Jenret, tender my apologies, please. The beast will think I'm ambushing him."

"I *told* you she doesn't like me!" Rawn sat perfectly still, tail wrapped tight around his feet, whiskers twitching as he glared at the offending knife.

Jenret gave the bottle a little shake, chinked the mouth against the rim of the glass to draw her attention. "Rawn thinks you're bent on foul deeds, basest murder, my dear aunt. I know it was accidental, Mahafny, but an apology might be in order. Now, how much would you like? Your humble servant awaits your command."

"And did I not ask you to tell him I was sorry?" Mahafny returned Rawn's glare, the ghatt pretending not to notice.

He exhaled, invoking patience. First Rawn's touchiness, and now Mahafny's as well. He wasn't used to playing the conciliator. "And I've explained to you before that Rawn does not care to be addressed at second hand when he's right here in the room. He's not invisible. Or deaf." He poured brandy for himself and set the bottle down to wait it out. "If you won't respect his wishes, my dear, humor me. Apologize to him directly."

He waited for her expostulation, her anger. He hated crossing her like this, but he hated betraying Rawn even more. Enough fools in the world when it came to ghatti, without his aunt joining their ranks. Just wait it out, wait it out, he counseled himself as he sipped at the brandy.

Without a word, without a look in his direction, Mahafny circled the table and came to stand in front of the ghatt. Rawn slanted his head back. "Rawn, I apologize for startling you. I had no intention of hurting you." Rawn's head dipped in gracious acceptance, then snapped up at the next words. "If I intend to do bodily harm, I am generally quite successful at it; therefore, this was obviously not an attempt." She stalked by the ghatt to the sideboard, reached behind the brandy and selected an earthenware bottle glazed in earth-browns and greens. "A little celvassy, I think, rather than brandy."

Jenret resumed his seat, cradled his glass. *"She didn't mean it,"* he mindspoke. *"She tends to be a bit gruff sometimes. Powerful stuff."*

Rawn hunkered down, front paws tucked comfortably inward against his chest. **"She meant it, every word of it."** His mindvoice sounded calm and even. **"I like her for that, if not for the sentiment. No 'I'm sorry I fwightened the fuzzy-wuzzy widdle kitty.' Refreshing."**

Bottling his laughter, Jenret half-rose for manner's sake as his aunt resumed her seat, celvassy in hand. "Rawn thinks rather more of you than he did before. You do have a way with ghatti, whether you admit it or not." He sat, tried to find a comfortable place against the spokes and spindles, failed, and leaned forward, resting his forearms against the table. "Beware the celvassy. You know how powerful it is. It's a wonder it doesn't self-ignite."

She nodded, serious, but didn't speak, picked up her napkin and unfolded it, refolded it, pleating and repleating it, fingers white against the bleached cloth. She opened her mouth to speak, then stopped, her fingers busy. Waiting her out, he examined the dining room again, admired the wainscoting, narrow strips of blondest birch, the plaster of the upper wall tinted a faint buttercream shade, all of it chosen as a backdrop for the few good pieces of furniture.

"Myllard would approve of a room like this," he mused, and the thought of Myllard spun him full-circle to his worries at the Ale House over the earlier events of the day. *"Are they done yet?"* he asked Rawn. *"Have they told her? How's she taking it?"* He took a fierce pull at his brandy, grimaced at the sting and fire; it wasn't meant to be drunk like that, and he knew better.

Rawn extended a paw, claws working, spoke simultaneously with Mahafny: **"Yes, from what I can pick up, she has been told . . ."** Jenret heard as his aunt said, "So, what do you know about that Marbon woman?"

"Strange you should ask, I was just thinking about her. The Seeker General gave dispensation for her to be told . . ." he searched for the word he wanted. "Informally, I guess you could say. To hear it from friends, amongst friends, not rushed into Headquarters and forced to keep a stiff upper lip. Given the seriousness of the situation, it surprised me—that and knowing that the Seeker General never overuses 'compassion.' Rather like you, for that matter." He made a face of apology. "That was uncalled for." And his dark brows bunched in consternation. "But how did you happen to know her name, know her involvement, even if only peripherally as Oriel's lover?"

Mahafny's hands stilled, napkin in a neat roll between them. "I know more than the name. I knew her well, once upon a time." The phrase distracted her. "Isn't that the way all the old stories begin?" she whispered to herself, then continued directly to Jenret. "I had the training of her as a eumedico some years ago. Before you were Chosen by Rawn."

A soft whistle escaped him, despite himself. "I never thought! Knew she had some training as a eumedico, but I never made the connection with you. Why'd she leave? That's a rarity."

She took a long sip of the celvassy, obscuring her expression behind the glass. She swallowed once, convulsively, and he blinked in sympathy. One savored celvassy in tiny, ritualistic sips; drink it down like water and you'd pay for it. Her eyes watered slightly, from the drink, he had no doubt. "A . . . crisis of . . . faith, I guess you'd say." The words came, each as measured as a ceremonial celvassy sip. "We all have them, now and again, but Doyce's was worse than most. Faith and spirit have been bruised more often than most with her through the years. She tries a new life each time, changes outwardly, though I'm not sure how much she's changed inwardly." She leaned forward, gray eyes intent on him. "You know what it's like to be bruised in spirit, Jenner."

The pet name from childhood flooded him with memories, memories he didn't relish recalling. Mouth open to protest, he stopped. No good denying what was true.

"Watch over her, Jenner . . . if you can. She needs a friend."

"I don't even know her well, let alone like her very much," he objected. "She has her own circle of friends. As do I."

Mahafny's gray eyes still fixed on his, pinning him, willing him to agree. "Well, you need an equal, if not a friend, and she's more than likely to be that—equally stubborn, and obstinate, even if she does it with a tad less flourish than you. There's honor and loyalty in you both as well."

She spread her hands, napkin knocked to the floor unregarded. "I'm worried, Jenret. Terribly worried. About her, about things I don't even know enough about to invite worry. All I ask is that you keep a friendly eye on her, aid her should she cross your path. Nothing more. Agreed?"

"I would anyway, she's a Seeker. But agreed." There was more to it than that; he knew it damn well, and it upset him more than he could consciously analyze. Well, let her have her silence if she must; he was inquisitive, he was a Seeker, after all. There'd come a time when he'd unravel this, find the pull-thread, with or without her.

❧

They stood in the farthest reach of the lamplight at the front of the Ale House. The moon hung heavy and ripe, one day to five of its satellites' prime, and an eerie halo surrounded it, verdigrising the silver-gold to silvery-green. "You don't *have* to go," Doyce repeated and stepped beyond the lamplight, the change so sudden she felt she'd stepped off a precipice; she shuddered, wishing her mind had selected another simile. The street lamps and torches hung few and far between as one reached beyond the city center, but she sensed the nervous energy of the ghatta at her side rather than seeing her. The ghatta loped ahead and seated herself just in front of the patch of light from the next street torch. She sat immobile, shades of black and white and silver in the weak light.

"No, *you* don't have to go. It can wait 'til morning," the ghatta commented. "Let it be until then."

She caught up with the ghatta and squatted down, cupping her face with her hands, fingers behind ears, thumbs tracing along the white chin. "I have to say good-bye. Now, not tomorrow with everyone else. Now. Why not go back to the room and wait for me?"

"Because then you couldn't 'speak with Saam." The ghatta's eyes pooled with bottomless dark sorrow, pupils dilated to the limit to catch every teasing bit of light, the normal cherry pink of her nose blossom white from stress.

"All right, then, let's both go and get it done with. Myllard promised to leave the door unlatched." She didn't want to say that she was glad the ghatta was along for other reasons—despite the fact she wanted nothing more than to be alone, protection was necessary. Foolish she'd been to rush off without staff or sword, but without them, even the most desperate cutpurse would still hesitate to attack a Seeker and Bondmate. A lone Seeker without the tabard looked like any other late-night returning reveler—fair game. The ghatta pulled free from her grasp and started ahead, twitching her ears in annoyance until Doyce's footsteps sounded behind her with no sign of hesitation.

Khar's senses twitched left, right, all around without a turn of her head. Every hair alive, drinking in each particle of activity or strange stillness around them. Doyce walked on behind her, aware that Khar was in charge for this journey and that all she had to do was follow. Follow and think, think and follow, as they wove through town toward Headquarters and the room where Oriel was laid out and where Saam waited, tortured in mind and body by his double loss of Bond and mindspeech.

Oriel Faltran had been eight years younger than she was, nineteen to her twenty-seven when she had arrived at Headquarters for training. He and Saam had already been there a year, with another year of training before they became Travelers, Circuiters. She had been so afraid, afraid of herself, for herself, and of and for the little ghatten Khar'pern, rummaging through the corners of her mind when she least expected it, tumbling her shuttered memories with all the abandon of a kitten loosed in a basket of yarn, unraveling her thoughts, retangling them, unknotting things she had hidden from herself for so long. If this was what it meant to be a Seeker, she wasn't sure she could handle it or withstand the constant contact. But to fail at this the way she'd

failed at so much else—her inability to be a dutiful, docile daughter; her career with the eumedicos; her failure
to save her husband Varon, her infant Briony, and her
stepson Vesey from the fire, while she had survived.
She'd prayed to the Lady about this new course that
she'd had no choice in selecting, but she was sure of the
price of success. It was always too high, and she a pauper
lacking the emotional coin to pay.

White-lipped, shaking so hard she could barely knock
on the solid oaken door of Headquarters, she had stood
there, the ghatten clutched to her chest while it batted
with feather feet at the locket around her neck, then
followed her thought with its mindwalking, probing and
working its way through her thoughts, forcing Varon's
face to flash unbidden before her eyes.

Her stomach heaved and her head pounded as the
ghatten made her remember the time when he had given
her the locket, his mother's, and shown her the portrait
inside, his baby picture. She had known then with a certainty that when they had a child, that was how the baby
would look. And Briony had.

Doyce knocked harder at the door, knuckles bruising.
Lady help me, what if no one hears, what if I have to
leave? The ghatten purred comfort against the base of
her throat, willing thoughts of contentment at her. It
wasn't enough, not by a long patch.

The door swung open a crack and a face peered out.
The face, she realized with giddy surprise, was attempting to
grow a mustache—she clung to that detail, determined
to build around it, swaying on her feet with weariness.
Deep blue eyes, storm-blue, medium brown hair worn
ear length, a pleasant, open face except for the silly
smear of a mustache trying to overcome adolescence.

"Got a live one this time," the voice sounded cheerful.
"Door's been creaking and groaning so much with the
rain change that we tend to ignore anything but a good
hearty knock. Fact is, that's what the knocker's for.
You've got to be more forceful," he bantered as he
pushed open the door and stepped out. "By the Lady,
what's wrong?" he queried as he caught sight of the ghatten at her chest. "Oh, that's the way of it, is it? Here,
give over." And with that he scooped Khar from her

quaking arms, cradling the ghatten against his shoulder
and clasping her with his free arm. "It gets better, it gets
easier, don't worry," he consoled. He concentrated,
brow creasing, almost looking through her for a moment.
"Don't worry, Saam will be here in a flash." And he
guided her through the door and into the entry hall.

A steel-gray ghatt swirled around their feet, golden
eyes full of curiosity and concern. She had never seen a
gray that color, she thought inconsequentially, almost a
blue-gray, with the sheen of carefully tempered, blued
steel.

"Novie, Saam. Take the wee tyke, can you? Take her
to the nursery." With all the joy of an adolescent obliged
to babysit an infant cousin, the ghatt gingerly picked up
Khar by the scruff of the neck and trotted down the hall.
The ghatten rowled and kicked her feet, then hung silent
as Saam shook her once. Doyce trembled as the little
ghatten's dismay and fear reached back at her, clinging
in her brain.

"You've got to learn to control, to guide," Oriel
chided. "They'll wear you ragged at first, until they learn
how to reach properly. They're so inquisitive that they
want to explore and learn everything. They don't mean
it, but they don't know any better. It's up to you to teach
her restraint."

Doyce pulled free of his arm, though she could ill do
without its support. "And why do you think I'm here?"
she snapped, and sagged against the wall and fell sound
asleep, her thoughts blessedly hers alone for the first
time in the octant since the ghatten had 'Printed on her.

And so Oriel and Saam had been the first Bondmates
she had met at Headquarters. In a closed society where
she wasn't sure she'd fit in, far older than the other Novies, or Novitiates, not wise enough to be at peer level
with the Instructors, she felt caught in the middle, be-
twixt and between, except for the moments when Oriel
and Saam made time for Doyce and Khar'pern. And they
had made extra time, guiding Doyce and Khar, making
them practice their lessons and exercises over and over

again. The first time she had been able to intentionally
mindspeak, *"Khar, do you want to go down by the
brook?"* And Khar had answered back, **"Now? Can
Oriel and Saam come, too?"** They had consciously communicated with each other!

Oriel had smiled at them both. "Very good, but try it
again on the intimate mode, not the broadcast mode.
Saam and I don't want to know everything you're saying,
do we?"

The ghatten had launched herself at the nearly full-
grown blue-gray ghatt and bowled him off his feet. **"Do
too!"** she crowed, and Saam rolled on his back, belly
exposed, paws waving in mock surrender.

"She's right, do too!" Oriel exclaimed and then kissed
her as if he were the elder, not she.

A friend, a companion, a lover, she had never expected any of this after Varon's death. But her relationship with Oriel had unfolded with a sweet harmony that
left her breathless. Each on their individual circuits after
both had finished training, leaving messages for each
other in towns they would pass through, hoping that their
leaves would match. Engaging in a little good-natured
finagling with some of the other Seekers to make sure
that they would. Their times together swelled rich with
sharing, or at least Oriel's sharing. Of late he had begun
to speak about what they would do in a few more years
when semiretirement came and they no longer both rode
circuit. Couldn't he just let it be, let things flow? To face
the end of a fourth life frightened her more than she
could begin to acknowledge to Oriel or herself. And she
knew the life Oriel so willingly offered her—after all,
she'd tried it and failed: Varon's and Briony's and Vesey's deaths proof-positive of that. She'd been avoiding
Oriel's question, avoiding thinking about the difference
in their ages, avoiding answering him.

The bronze statue held pride of place in the center of
the Headquarters' courtyard, old bronze with the patina
of years mellowing its surface, tempering the edges, mut-
ing the curves. The bronze portraiture of a young man
sprawled in comfort against a tree stump while a ghatta
stood with front paws balanced against his raised knee,
the expressions of both hinting at the revelation of some

hidden, private humor. Matthias Vandersma, founder of
the Seekers Veritas, and the first Bondmate of them all,
Kharm. She'd always counted it as luck that the ghatta's
name sounded so similar to Khar's.

As had generations of Seekers before her, she stopped
to touch the bronze ghatta's head and Matthias's elbow;
both spots satiny smooth and bright from years of surreptitious touches. There was no luck left, but she touched
anyway out of habit, the metal cool and sleek against her
fingers.

Now it was too late to answer Oriel at all.

And again Doyce found herself in front of the heavy
oaken door, come to say good-bye to Oriel, not to greet
him. She knocked, jarring her knuckles, in remembrance
of that first time. She would say farewell, just as she had
to so many others through the years: her mother, back
turned in rigid denial as Doyce had trudged off down the
dusty cart track toward Gaernett and her hard-won right
to join the eumedicos; the eumedicos who had ultimately
expelled her, who now when most saw her, crossed to
the other side of the street; Varon, Briony, Vesey, gone
beyond reach of farewells, explanations, apologies. She
thought she'd learned how to say it, to do it, to survive
it, but it seemed new each time.

The door swung open without a sound, Sarrett and
T'ss poised behind it, haloed by the entry light. Everyone
called them the most beautiful of the Seeker-Bond pairs
and, some whispered behind their backs, the coolest,
most restrained, only their exceptional looks on display,
emotions camouflaged. But Sarrett's white-blonde hair
hung disheveled, her eyes puffy and pink-rimmed, her
clothing rumpled. T'ss, so white that the paleness of his
skin stood out through his fur in contrast to his dark tiger
stripes, leaned against her leg, head slumped, blue eyes
listless.

"Oh, Doyce!" Sarrett cried out, and then began to
weep again, noisily, messily, pulling herself up short with
obvious effort and dragging a crumpled, sodden handkerchief across her eyes. "Sorry, sorry, Doyce." She swal-

lowed, laboring to choke the tears down. "It's just that we all miss him so, already. He's in the 'Tiring Room. I'll take you there."

She evaded the hand seeking her elbow. "No, it's not necessary. I know my way." The sharpness in her tone took her aback; she hadn't intended it, or mayhap she had. Sarrett pulled back, rebuked, and Khar rubbed hard against Doyce's leg, forcing mind contact.

"Think beyond yourself. Others loved him, too," the ghatta chided.

The words and tone stung uncomfortably. It was something Oriel would have said—had said—on another occasion. What loss had she been lamenting, holding it selfishly tight to herself as if others couldn't comprehend? She reached for Sarrett's hand. "I'm trying to be brave. It's not working, though. Would you go with me, at least to the door?" Sarrett's smile gleamed, genuine as a child's, something Doyce had never noticed before. She suspected Oriel had.

Oriel had noticed everything, she now acknowledged in retrospect: Rolf's and Chak's real fear of growing old, Parcellus's worry over his flightiness and his dependence on Per'la. And she knew why Byrta and M'wa had felt compelled to recite their stories solo without the aid of their Bonds and Twins: Oriel had been the only one who had cared enough to know M'wa and P'wa and to be able to tell them apart, to know whether Bard or Byrta had begun or finished a sentence and to allow each to speak complete thoughts as individuals, to know they were similar but not one and the same. And what had he noticed about her? she thought wistfully as she and Sarrett started down the hall, gray-polished marble floor reflecting a ghostly pair. T'ss and Khar followed after, touching at shoulder and hip, tails swinging low, heads low.

"Talk with me after, if you feel like it," Sarrett offered, leaving her at the door. "Are you sure you don't want me to go in with you?" Doyce shook her head, smiled her gratitude. She gripped the brass knob and clicked her tongue at Khar who turned, touched noses with T'ss in farewell, and then came to her side.

Eight-branched candelabra, tall as a man, lit each cor-

ner of the large, mirrored Attiring Room, but no direct
light shone on the bier. For that she gave thanks. She
sank to her knees at the foot, Khar beside her, motionless, tail lapped tight around her, eyes unblinking.
She tried to pray to the Lady, but no words came, no
familiar, comforting litany.

"I thought about letting you go, Oriel, but I didn't
mean like this," she whispered at last. "I hope I would
have gotten smart enough not to, but more than likely
my pride would have gotten in the way. Leave it to me
to take pride in my private shames, as if I were unique
in my suffering, the only one who ever had. And you'd
have said that pride was too strong a word, that I was
melodramatizing again. You'd probably have been right.
Regardless of what it was, I used it as a shield to avoid
commitment.

"But I promise you, Oriel, that I'll let your memory
laugh with a part of me, not let a part of me die to follow
you. I can't afford that any longer. And I promise you
that if I can find an answer as to why this happened, I
will, I shall, for my sake and for the sake of everyone
else who loved you. Not vengeance, even if that seems
called for, for that is not a Seeker's way, but a meaning
and a truth to answer and right any wrongs that have
been done to you. I swear to that."

"**. . . may you see with eyes of light in everdark, may
your mind walk free and unfettered amongst all, touching
wisely and well, may you go in peace,**" Khar intoned
beside her, completing the ghatti prayer for the dead. It
was the prayer given only by the Bondmate of a Seeker,
and Khar now spoke the farewell in Saam's stead.

The coldness of the slate floor crept through her knees
and into her legs, her calf and thigh muscles cramping.
She rose awkwardly, and raised her eyes at last to the
long, still figure on the bier, its head swathed in a crown
of white bandages, the broad, supple hands folded upon
its breast, and in the folded hands a velvet pouch containing his Seeker earrings and Saam's as well. They
would be buried with him. Oriel was attired in formal
Seeker Veritas garb, worn only for major celebrations
and high halidays or for Seekings at the Hall of the Monitor. Midnight blue pantaloons tucked into short leather

boots with folded tops. Deep forest green tunic covered
with the formal tabard, gold-broidered against the black
sheepskin, and the red waist sash tasseled with gold. His
staff lay at his left, his sword at his right. Someone had
spent time and effort polishing them, trying to remove
the scrapes and dirt, the gouges incurred during the fall.
Of course, Bard and Byrta had searched for them, had
found them amongst the debris. Never let a loved one
go unarmed into the next world. Despite the religious
training of the Lady-oriented culture they'd been raised
in, most Seekers exhibited a healthy skepticism about
journeying unprotected and alone to any unknown place,
including heaven. Sarrett had done the polishing, the oil-
ing and rubbing; she knew, had seen but not realized the
import of the less than perfectly manicured hands, the
smears of oil and whetstone dust, when Sarrett had
opened the door, lapis eyes swimming with tears.

"Lady keep you in Her bosom, Oriel, my love."
Doyce bent and scooped Khar to her chest, hiding her
eyes against the fur for a moment, then left without looking back. She had ten years of life with Oriel to remember, not this ending. Longer than she'd had with her
husband and children, she realized with a start. Did her
nightmares contain room for Oriel as well? She hoped
so, even that was a form of contact and continuation.

Khar pawed at her cheek, begging for release once
they stepped outside the door, and Doyce gave her an
abstracted look, unsure how she'd gotten there. She loosened her grip and the ghatta jumped down.

"Saam's in the garden." Khar trotted down the hall,
turning by the kitchen and continuing to the side entrance. She angled her head over her shoulder to make
sure Doyce followed, then stretched up and rattled the
door latch, nudged it with her nose. Dropping back to
the floor, she delicately fished at the edge of the door
with her claws, pulling it toward her. Doyce caught up
with her, eased the door open farther.

"Why isn't he in the infirmary? He's much too badly
hurt to be outside."

At first she couldn't see him in the dim nimbus of
light from the single lamp at the far side of the fragrant,
enclosed herb garden. Then ceaseless movement, a re-

petitive flickering motion drew her eye. Saam was pacing off a quivering figure-eight pattern along the far wall, legs stumbling like a drunk's. Four paces, then a pivot and turn and four paces in the reverse direction; a stagger and a shift of weight. Four more paces ahead, pivot and turn back until another stagger, leftward this time, completed the figure eight in its middle like the knotting of a bow.

Doyce stretched to unhook the lamp from its bracket and brought it over, careful not to swing it too near. She squatted and looked hard at the big ghatt. "Oh, Saam, Saam!" The ghatt continued to pace, finally registered his name and looked up, almost stumbling and falling as he lost the rhythm. The bandage on his hip had been scraped off as he rubbed against the wall; she swallowed hard when she saw the darker clot of blood around the edges of the raw wound, the downy pieces of fur and more blood at hip-height against the brick wall. "Oh, Saam!"

Puzzled, wary, the ghatt tested his memory against the word he heard. Khar pushed by and lightning-stroke swatted the ghatt twice with her front paws. Saam sat down, hard, but the third membrane across his eyes receded, and he shook his head. He raised his muzzle with effort and growled hoarsely. Khar sat unflinching while he gathered himself to attack. Panting a challenge, he controlled his shaking hindquarters and pushed off after Khar. She spoke a warning, soft and low as a mother ghatta speaks to her ghatten, and Saam stumbled into her and stood there, leaning against her, head down, whimpering sounds bubbling from his chest. Doyce knew that Khar was bearing nearly all his considerable weight.

Avoiding any sudden moves that could be construed as dangerous, she reached out and eased her arms around him, gathering him to her. Off balance, she collapsed with an armful of ghatt sprawled across chest and lap. Saam buried his nose against her inner elbow and inhaled, did it again, lips wrinkled back to drink in her scent. Khar moved near and with infinite delicacy began to wash one ear, then the other, on the limp ghatt. She spoke between licks in scarcely audible rowls and trills. Sighing, mumbling, Saam's eyes pinched closed and he

fell into a deep sleep. Doyce had tested the mindlink
several times as Khar murmured to him, but had touched
only blankness, confusion, and ultimately silence.

"**Can you rise without troubling him?**" Khar's concern
was evident. "**He should go back to the infirmary. He
was waiting for us, but he had trouble remembering why.
He scratched at Twylla when she tried to give him the
pain-killing grasses. He tried to tell her he had to stay
awake until we came.**"

"I don't think I can without jarring him." Doyce struggled to get her feet under her. If she could shift him
down from her chest and into her lap, perhaps she could
find her balance, but the ghatt was dead weight, sprawled
across her bonelessly. Or lifelessly! She panicked until
she felt the faint rise and fall of his chest.

"**No matter, I'll call. I told T'ss to stay about.**" Khar
nudged the big ghatt with her head, as she had when she
had been a ghatten craving attention.

Sarrett and T'ss slipped through the garden door. "Is
he . . . ?" Sarrett's voice trembled.

"No, just asleep," Doyce reassured. "Can you get us
up?" Sarrett, only slightly taller and more full-figured
than the delicate-boned Doyce, stood looking down at
the unwieldy pile of limbs, consternation written across
her flawless features. Khar and T'ss blinked at each
other, then T'ss moved himself with infinite patience
under Saam's right hip, where it jutted beyond Doyce's
chest. Khar paralleled his movements on the other side,
working her way under the arm that cradled Saam's
head.

With sudden resolve, Sarrett braced herself behind
Doyce, hooked her hands underneath the other's armpits. "Well, let's try. In two stages. First stage, shift him
down into your lap so he doesn't sprawl so much, see if
you can get a leg folded under you for leverage." They
accomplished that, the ghatti bearing more weight than
Doyce had thought possible, wedging themselves beneath
Saam, lifting him higher. "Second stage, count of three,"
Sarrett instructed. "Straight up. If you feel you're going
to fall backward, I'm behind you. Ready? One, two,
three!"

Doyce launched herself upward with the ghatt held

tightly in her arms, depending on Sarrett's tensile strength behind her. Once she found her balance, the burden was heavy but not impossible. She moved toward the light of the half-open door, Sarrett still steadying her while the two ghatti paced along beside them.

They negotiated the narrow back hallways and stairs to the infirmary and slipped Saam onto his folded blanket on the floor. Twylla entered, bright hair tousled as if roused from an unplanned nap, her short leg giving her walk a hesitating stutter, and went directly to the ghatt, feeling his pulse, thumbing back an eyelid. "I don't know," she confessed vaguely to the room at large, her hands already darting up and down shelves, selecting, rejecting various jars and vials, intent on her seeking. "We'll try, but it's unlikely, so unlikely. Even if we save his body—and that's not so difficult—I don't know how his mind will react." She ranked the bottles and vials on the table, chose, discarded some, rubbed an index finger over her front teeth as she considered.

The response came as one from T'ss and Khar: **"Just save his body. We will take care of the rest."**

Twylla's Bond Mem'now sauntered into the room, back from his rounds. **"We will take care of the rest. I've spread the word."**

The three ghatti ringed the sleeping Saam and stood, concentrating. Mem'now circled his yellow tiger-striped body around the sleeping ghatt, close enough to brush his fur, but not so close as to cause pain to the wounded animal. Mem'now purred breathily, and Saam's ragged breathing began to even out, rising and falling in time to Mem'now's steady rumble. Mem'now's eyes, half-lidded, watched.

Sarrett swung lightly into the saddle on her Appaloosa gelding and hooked her arm to help Doyce mount behind her. With T'ss and Khar trotting on either side, they rode at a slow, deliberate walk through the dark streets toward Myllard's. The moon and her eight disciples hung hazy and obscure to Doyce's sight as she rested her cheek against Sarrett's shoulder, sheepskin tabard wool-scented

and warm. A funeral march of sorts, she decided. Tired,
so very tired. Thank the Lady that Sarrett didn't feel the
need for chatter either. Putting Savoury into a mincing
walk that made no sounds on the cobbles in the courtyard, Sarrett slipped past the locked front door and
stopped by the path to the side entrance.

"The Lady with us all," she murmured as Doyce slid
down from Savoury. Doyce echoed the phrase, then surprised herself as she stretched to hug Sarrett's slim waist.
She dropped back, awkward and embarrassed, and
trailed a hand along T'ss's spine in farewell.

"Peaceful morn to us all," Khar's soft contralto echoed
in their minds, and no one dared question if it were a
farewell, a greeting, or a statement to come true as the
sun rose.

They tiptoed up the shadowed stairs together to the
third floor, Doyce blindly tapping with her hands to seek
out the steps, blundering clear of any potential obstruc-
tions in the dark. Khar chirruped and bounded ahead,
waiting at the top of each landing. A silvered crack of
light spilled from under the door of the chamber that
Myllard now saved for her, the one his youngest daughter
had laid claim to until she ran off with a peddler nearly
eight octants ago. She hoped no one had waited up for
her because she couldn't bear any more talk.

But Myllard, she realized as she unlatched the door,
had done one of his rare extravagances—left an oil lamp
burning for her. One didn't become a well-to-do (which
Myllard would have strenuously denied) innkeep by
needlessly burning oil or indulging in such excesses for
patrons never destined for riches. A note stood propped
against the lamp. "Enough hot water in the cistern for a
bath if you've the strength to pump it. No charge."

Khar looked suitably impressed and so did Doyce.
Myllard's was one of the few places other than the Monitor's Hall, the Hospice, and a few other well-appointed
establishments to boast even a modicum of indoor
plumbing. An outrageously pink porcelain flusher with
copper water tank was strictly for family use at Myllard's;
clientele used the privies with their terra cotta drainage
system in the yard out back. And two, yes, two enormous
porcelain shells nestled in wooden frames; one ensconced

next door to the family flusher, the other reposing in a chamber beyond that, ready to be rented out to those fastidious enough for a complete wash and with the wherewithal to pay for the luxury. And fastidiousness was something Doyce had learned from the eumedicos.

Creeping back down a level to the bathing chamber, Doyce began to pump, resting after every few strokes, massaging her arm, not conscious of her action. Khar perched on the rim of the tub and watched with interest as the hot water finally gushed out, careful that none of it splashed on her. Myllard or his wife, Fala, she suspected, had bequeathed her a small saucer of bath salts beside the tub, and she tilted them into the steaming water and kept pumping until a final gasp, a gurgle, and the absence of water told her the hot water cistern had emptied. Sandalwood scented the steamy air as she stripped off her travel-stained burgundy tunic and brown pantaloons, making a sound of helpless dismay when she realized she'd forgotten to take her boots off first and was fairly entangled. That was how weary she was.

Easing by cautious degrees into the hot water, she sat with knees drawn up to her chin. A knot caught tight in her chest, and she tried to loosen it, a small sound like a cross between a cough and a sneeze working its way past her constricted throat, and then she was crying, sobbing hard for Oriel, for Saam, for everyone she had ever known and loved and lost, and most of all, for herself. Blood flowed in lazy rivulets between her thighs, a bright strand of red fanning out to rosy pink as the water diluted it—so she wasn't pregnant. Not even that left as a way to remember Oriel. Khar balanced her way around the rim and licked a tear from Doyce's cheek.

"Hello?" The mindvoice brushed through the air, whisper soft as a baby tap on a silver chime bar. **"Hello? Does anyone hear me?"** The sound echoed bell-sweet to anyone who knew how to listen, who was awake to hear as a fingernail paring of dawn edged the horizon, eastern facades of building showing the barest lightening of night dark.

"Hello, I've caught your mindpattern. You're reaching over to the east quarter." T'ss's ears twisted back and forth, trying to focus on the pattern more explicitly. "Can you hear me clearly? I can read you, but I can't identify your voice yet, your sending's ragged." The stone steps stung damply against his rump and he shifted, wished for sunlight against his pale fur. A cling of early morning moisture jeweled his coat, set him shimmering in the faint light of the one torch lamp still burning. He had been waiting for some time, still and listening.

"L'wa here." The mindvoice answered him, stronger and more assured this time, the unspoken fear of further pain dissipating.

He gave an unconscious wriggle of relief, twisted nerve-stiffened neck backward until he heard a little pop, then dipped forward fast and hard. "Greetings, L'wa. How is the ghatten? Fine after last night's troubles, I hope. So very, very young to have been caught in that." He heard a murmured reassurance, a relieved sound. "So you're 'speaking from Headquarters? Mem'now asked you to commence the testing?"

"I volunteered. We must reassemble the patterns. I won't, I can't leave the little one, but I can do my part from here. Mem'now said when I 'spoke you that you were supposed to try to 'speak him."

"Well, wish me luck. Here it goes." T'ss concentrated, overrode a frantic desire to shy away from the possibility of renewed anguish, legacy of last night's disaster. He made a little mewling sound deep in his throat, then, shamed, tried harder, swept his mindspeech in a careful, concise overlay from one quadrant to the next. If L'wa, with so much to lose as a new mother, could try, so could he. He'd do it, do it for himself, do it for Saam. He pressed harder and harder, gasped in relief at the lack of pain, joy dancing through his mind as his distance increased, waiting to intercept the pattern he knew so well as Mem'now's. Ah! The edge of something, wait! He backtracked, then homed in on the familiar vibrations. "Hello!"

"Hello, yourself. A little imprecise, too scattered on the sending, but not badly done at all. It's frightening to try again when we've all been burned like that."

T'ss jumped, stiff-legged, back arching, then sat again. **"Mem'now! Have mercy! Don't shout like that, you know you always over-project! It still stings like a wasp's nest to hear anyone, let alone you. Where are you?"**

"Northern quadrant, nearly at the Ring Wall. Stay ready, I'm going to try a rondelet, see who'll pick up the repeats."

Mindvoices began to shimmer and dance, raindrop soft and hesitant at first as if after a long drought, then pattering harder, more certainly through the air, absorbed by thirsty, waiting minds. They bounced off T'ss, Chak's basso rumble from one direction, Per'la's languid tones from another. He drank in each one, traced their mindvoices, firefly bright, winking on and off across the city. Ghatts and ghattas moved with quiet purpose on night-dark streets, across wall tops, over roofs pointed and flat, testing position after position, sounding after sounding, restoring the mindnet patternings. **"Yes, here!" "Here!" "Hello!"**

Mem'now orchestrated, responded, directed round after round of response and answer as ghatti confidence built and swelled. **"Now, a mindmeld of three for distance, please. Are we up to it? We have to know if we've attained full reception, please. Volunteers? Myself plus two more."**

T'ss's mindvoice speared through the quickest, followed by another familiar voice. **"Me, as well, Mem,"** he heard Khar say from Myllard's.

"Let it be for now, Khar. You're due a little more rest." T'ss could hear the hesitancy in Mem'now's voice, overlaid with its usual courtliness. Ill at ease, he groomed. Khar had been the last out of the link with Mr'rhah when Saam's exploding distress had overwhelmed, overburdened them all to breaking. No one had yet heard from Mr'rhah, did not know whether she had lived or died.

"No! Now, Mem, I have to know now, have to know I'm ready, that I won't be caught wanting again." There was no quaver, no indecision to her voice, just a tired steadfastness.

"Fine, then. Three exhalations, then meld by seniority. Outreach as far as you can, starting in sunrise direction, then sweeping north and through the points. And begin."

As youngest, T'ss waited, tasted the blending of voice-strengths, then added his own. Easiest for him first as they explored east where he was stationed, then began the counterclockwise sweep around, not knowing when or where they'd find an answer. That was the whole point of the exercise. Extend, extend, he counseled himself, buoyed by the two voices around him, knowing his own buoyed the others. Extend, search! Search, listen! They'd swept north, swung toward the west, heard a glimmering, a teasing light of mindvoice, turned smoothly and hovered, testing again, hawklike on an imaginary updraft.

"Hello!" "Hello!" M'wa and P'wa's response overlapped, sounded like one word with an echo. **"Good! We've been waiting! Thought it might take four of you this soon."**

Mem'now's voice boomed like distant thunder. **"Greetings! Not bad odds, three of us to two of you. And your precise location?"**

The duo answered, **"Out beyond the Ring Wall, about a thousand meters out. Figured that was the best you could do, the best we could manage right now."**

"Well done. Make your way back now, don't want Bard and Byrta missing you when they rise." Mem'now began reeling in the mindmeld, a little warning chirrup sounding as he shooed first Khar, then T'ss free of the triple meld.

Khar's voice sounded faint to T'ss's mind, but he overheard her ask Mem'now, **"May we attempt one final exercise before dawn? We have to try to reach Saam."**

A breathy exhalation of dismay escaped Mem'now. **"Not wise, my lovely ghatta. Best to wait, let him rest. Let us all rest."**

"No, Mem, now may be the best time of all, while he's asleep, relaxed from the medication, not fighting and straining to mindspeak." Khar, quietly insistent, pressed home her point. **"We can't leave him like that, we have to reach through to him."**

"And if he does not, cannot respond?" Mem'now waited for her answer.

"Then we'll try again, today, and the next day, and the next and the next until someday . . ." her voice trailed off.

"And if that 'someday' never comes? Face the truth, Khar, face it now. There is a very real possibility he'll never mindwalk again." T'ss cringed at the response, but knew that Mem'now spoke the truth. He could do nothing else. Still, to give Saam up so soon angered the white ghatt with the black stripings, impetuous with youth.

He surprised himself into speaking. "Mem'now, T'ss here. Not trying is accepting. We may have to accept, but not without trying first. I'm willing." Other voices belled around him, some near, some faint and far. "And I." "I, too." "Willing."

Mem'now's voice rumbled, "Then let the seeking begin. Seek high, seek low, check for any mindspeech pattern you can't identify, that seems wavering, lost. Ready? Begin."

Mindvoices crisscrossed the city, searched high, searched low, sought for the lost, the lamed, the bewildered. Sought and found nothing, not a shred of mindvoice of an old, familiar friend, not a remnant of a mindpatterning forlornly waiting to be found and twined into the collective consciousness of their minds. One by one they faltered, bewildered at the lack.

"It's as if . . ." Mem'now hesitated, searching for the words. "As if his pattern is locked tight away within him. He's not wavering, wandering lost in search of Oriel, he's constrained. Just as one traps a bluebottle fly under an overturned goblet, watches it bumble and crash against the clear sides. He's totally locked away from us. And locked within himself. He can't get out any more than we can get in." He paused, considering an idea. "Unless we can repattern him. . . . It's never been done before, relearning the spirals. . . . Could it. . . ?"

But Khar, eyes stinging, murmuring apologies, took frantic exit from the conversation. "It's Doyce. She's dreaming wrongly again! I must go, now!" And torn between thoughts of Saam and her concern for Doyce, she broke the mindlink, hurtling herself into Doyce's dream.

❖

Effortlessly inserting herself into the sleep tale, Khar paused to find her bearings, but the dream flowed new, and she had no idea where she was, what was wrong. Except that something was wrong, or was going to be wrong; she could sense it. She poised herself for action, watched the dream unfold within Doyce's sleeping mind, pummeled by waves of pain and joy.

Oriel strode down a dirt road, more a cart track, really, dust puffing from his quick steps, clouding around his knees, rising to settle on his sweat-slicked skin. Clearly he was hot and tired, but his footsteps were eager. Khar heard Doyce cry out to him in her mind, but the dream-Oriel seemed not to hear, for he did not stop. He swung along, reached to scoop some pebbles from the roadside, and dusted one on his tunic, popped it into his mouth. The rest he scattered with an overarm throw, watching as they pattered down, one pinging off the trunk of a nearby tree.

"So thirsty," Doyce moaned in her sleep. "Poor Oriel, Oriel, my love." Khar's own tongue rasped against her dry mouth in sympathy.

A boy of perhaps twelve stepped into the roadway, wooden bucket of water sloshing on bare feet, and flung a full dipper of water in a circling crescent, rainbow scintillations of water droplets sparkling in the hot, bright sunlight. The boy wore an oversized man's carpenter's smock, sleeves rolled and rolled up thin forearms, shoulder seams hanging nearly to his elbows. He waved the dipper, beckoning an invitation.

"May I ease you on your way, sir?" the boy shouted courteously in Oriel's direction. Khar stiffened, hackles rising, as Doyce cried out, "Vesey? Vesey, lad, what are you . . . ?" Vesey? Khar growled low in her throat. Vesey wasn't supposed to be in this dream; he didn't belong here. Untruth! Not possible, Oriel and Vesey had never met, had never shared any part of each other's lives. She debated which one to expunge from the dream . . . they did not belong together like this!

A smile broke out on Oriel's face and he began to trot toward the boy, hands outstretched for the waiting dipper. Hating herself for doing it, hating to see even the dream-Oriel go thirsty, Khar gently paw-dabbed Vesey from the dream, tumbled him back to his own plane of truth within Doyce's mind, refused to allow him to min-

gle in this new sleep tale. She concentrated hard and
Vesey disembodied, no trace of him left except for the
droplets of water, dark disks on the dry baked earth.

Oriel looked around puzzled, then continued to walk
on and on down the road, his bulk growing fainter as the
distance grew. Doyce sobbed, brought the back of her
wrist to her mouth for comfort, then settled into restless
sleep, tossing and turning, sighing.

Propping her chin against Doyce's shoulder, Khar
stared at her steadily, watched the sleeping face, tracked
the thoughts in the sleeping mind. Disoriented, so tired,
so confused. But not while Khar was there to guard her,
to keep her safe, to make sure each part of her life stayed
precisely as it was supposed to, not a fantasy world where
various past lives improbably mingled. Now that she
knew what to watch for, she'd make sure that Vesey
never appeared in another Oriel dream, nor Oriel in a
dream about Varon, Briony, and Vesey.

✤

PART
TWO

✤

Some lingered under the thick, sheltering cypress, glad for the shade; others perched on stone benches, some alone in their Pairs, other Bond-pairs together, talking in undertones or sharing their thoughts. Oriel had been buried but not forgotten, not as long as there were Seekers and Bondmates to remember.

All were attired in formal Seeker garb: midnight blue pantaloons, green tunic, black tabard with red sash, the only difference being in the colors edging the tabard. Gold for Senior Circuit Riders, those with an octad or more of seniority; silver for the Junior Riders, those with less than eight years' service in the field; crimson bordered for those semiretired and working out of Headquarters; white for those fully retired and back into the world again; pale green for the Novies. And one, edged with purple and gold, the head of the Seekers, Swan Maclough, at the far side of the cemetery, causing a ripple amongst the Seekers as she paused here and there to lift a hand in greeting or exchange a word or two as she headed back to her offices. Mourning was done, but administrative details continued. The bitter reality and practicality choked at Doyce.

She swung her scabbard out of the way and rested her forearms on her knees, glowering at the pebbled path-

way, white-marbled chips framed by the close-cropped
grass. Rolf perched at the other end of the bench, back to
her, Chak at his feet. The twins, Bard and Byrta, slouched
on the late-summer lawn, back to back, supporting each
other, ghatti sprawled beside them. Parcellus wrestled
Per'la from his lap, muttering "ghatta-hair" in a subdued
voice. Clustered close enough to talk, no one bothered.
Little left to say, or Doyce didn't feel there was anything
worth saying. Their silence deferred to her silence. Khar
coiled at her feet, indulging in some desultory mindspeech with the other ghatti, but she resolutely tuned it
out.

"Now what?" At first she thought she had spoken
aloud, words mimicking her thoughts, then realized Khar
had spoken.

"Why should I know?" she asked with asperity.

"No?" Khar narrowed her eyes. **"Now what's going
on? Sarrett and T'ss are coming, and they don't look
well pleased. Hmmpf, T'ss isn't sending, either."** Doyce
turned and her scabbard splayed out from her side,
catching Khar's shoulder. The ghatta sprang away in dismay and swatted back at the scabbard vindictively, as if
wishing she dared administer the same punishment to
Doyce.

"Seeker General wants us all in her office in five,"
Sarrett halted, breathless, in front of the group.

"Can't mean us all," Parcellus worried, ticking off
names on his fingers. "Doyce and Khar, most likely.
Bard and M'wa, Byrta and P'wa, maybe." He began toying with Per'la's tail, waggling the tip between his fingers,
tickling her nose with it.

"I repeat: Seeker General wants us *all* in her office on
the double. All meaning specifically Rolf/Chak, Bard/-
M'wa, Byrta/P'wa, Doyce/Khar'pern, Sarrett/T'ss, and
last and definitely least, Parcellus/Per'la." Sarrett relented the metronomic precision of her recitation. "Sorry,
Per'la, you're never 'least,' just your Bondmate
sometimes."

"Up, then, ladies and gentlemen." Rolf stood and settled his tabard into place with a sharp tug, shifted sash
and scabbarded sword into precise position. Chak inspected his white feet with care, tidy-licked his ruff.

Crossing the path, Rolf extended his hands, one each to
Bard and Byrta, who took hold and sprang up lightly,
nothing disarranged. Not to be outdone, Sarrett offered
a hand to Parcellus who blushed as he set Per'la on her
feet and then looked up, unable to ignore the small hand
reaching toward him. He rose with far less grace, mortifi-
cation making him clumsy, stumble-footed, and Sarrett
sidestepped his lunge, reached out and smoothed a wisp
of his flyaway carroty hair into place with more care than
the occasion demanded. They formed a semicircle
around Doyce and the bench, Khar at its center. Rolf
strained, cleared his throat. "Come along, Doyce. You
know when the Seeker General says now, she means
now."

Doyce kicked a polished boot toe at the pebbles in the
path, picked up one and threw it as hard as she could.
Charted its flight to just short of the newly filled grave.
Why speak? There was nothing to say. But she'd go, no
choice to it. How much choice did she have? If she had,
she wouldn't like anyone, including Khar, including herself. Guilt spasmed the muscles between her shoulder
blades when she tried to throw her shoulders back. Apologize, she commanded herself, but couldn't bring herself
to do it.

They stood in an uneasy cluster outside the Seeker
General's windowless interior office, feet shuffling, debating whether to enter ahead of Swan Maclough. Rolf's
finger traced and retraced part of the inlaid pattern that
ran unbroken around the door and all along the outer
walls, both at ceiling height and floor level, a line of
coppery inset metal bent and notched in a repetitive
cubic design. Funny that he'd never paid much attention
to it before. Now he relished any distraction from the
matter at hand. "Enough." He clapped his hands once,
drew their attention. "Let's enter, get settled. Tight quarters, to say the least." He led the way inside.

The Seeker General's office had no business holding
seven Seeker Pairs plus an extra ghatt, Saam, occupying
the office alone and looking bleak and worn as he curled
atop a folded blanket on the Seeker General's paper-
strewn desk. The others found space through anxious,
subtle compromises in position as they fit themselves in

as best they could. Rolf wondered if it were incumbent on each Seeker General to add a piece of furniture to the office without removing anything that had gone before. Who had been responsible, for instance, for wasting needed space with those four pillars, one in each corner of the room and each topped with an innocuous free-form shaping in polished marble? Not exactly unattractive, just terribly dated.

The ghatti had the advantage: more out-of-the-way spots, high and low, designed for the fluid fit of a ghatt. The twins sat cross-legged on a low metal map cabinet, Sarrett and Doyce in the two straight-backed wooden chairs in front of the desk, though Rolf had to cuff Parcellus's shoulder to make him relinquish one. He scrambled out, miming silent apology with flashing hands, and perched on a leather hassock. Rolf leaned his thin frame against the wall to the right of the desk. He made a self-deprecating face in Doyce's direction as he pocketed a sweat-dampened handkerchief, and crossed his arms over his chest to wait.

At last the seventh and final pair arrived, the Seeker General and her ghatt Koom pausing at the door, then threading the maze of obstacles of people and ghatti until they reached the desk. She tugged her straining tabard over her short, no-nonsense broad form and sat, hands clasped across her stomach. Koom sprang up beside Saam, giving him a quick, friendly rub across the back with his chin.

"Tight quarters, but more private than one of the regular meeting rooms," Swan Maclough commented. "Too many young Seekers and young ghatti who haven't quite learned discretion."

Koom's yellow-green eyes swept the room, lingering on Parse, though the broad ghatt face remained impassive. **"And some older ones who still haven't learned,"** he capped her. **"Now, mindwalk if ye will."**

It gave them pause to hear him do that because the rules clearly stated that he should have denied himself such intimate access to her mind; he was not her Bondmate. Like Saam, newly bereft of his Seeker earrings, buried with Oriel, neither Koom nor Swan Maclough wore the gold hoop and ball, not any longer. Koom had

never 'Printed on Swan Maclough, a souce of wonder
and some small, quiet controversy to those who questioned Swan's continuation as Seeker General after the
death of her Bondmate, A'rah. The rules were explicit:
when a Bondmate died, the other retired from the company of Seekers. It explained one facet of their concern:
without Oriel, what place did Saam have?

Swan had been forty-two and A'rah twenty-two when
the ghatt had died, the same oct that Koom's Bondmate
Callan had slipped away from a wasting lung disease that
the eumedicos had slowed but had not been able to halt.
In his prime at only eight, the placid, russet-hued Koom
finished each assignment without hurry—until it dawned
on his naysayers that the ghatt had premeditated every
move to position himself two paces ahead of anyone else.

Legend had it that both Swan and Koom had sat in
the burial ground near the graves of their Bondmates,
thoughts swirling, unguarded in grief, but no invitation
given to mindwalk with the other. Except that they *were*
mindwalking, sharing the pain and loss, consoling each
other without volition. They returned together to face
the Tribune and convince them that they had meshed,
even without benefit of 'Printing. To their minds that
would prove the ultimate disloyalty to their departed
Bonds, but they had joined just as closely as some men
and women do without benefit of marriage ceremony.
And perhaps more closely than many legally married, for
they both envisioned the mutual loss if they left the Seekers. Too much to do, too many projects to organize and
plan, administer, advise on, for them to be shut out,
for nothing superseded their implacable dedication to the
Seekers. Nothing came before it. That had been ten years
ago, and it seemed possible that the Seeker General and
Koom could serve yet another ten years.

**"If this thing doesn't blow wide open in our faces,
destroy the Seekers' credibility and the Seekers themselves,"** Koom reminded Swan in private.

"We have a problem," Swan announced to the waiting
group. "A serious one, very serious, far more than you
may all realize." She anticipated their glances sliding by
over her shoulders, her ears, her lobes naked of earrings
since A'rah's death—ah, how she still missed him! and

with no disloyalty to Koom—any place but her eyes.
They weren't ready for this, but then she wasn't either,
and she had no choice. And very little hope. Neither
would they once they knew. Inaction meant the very
probable destruction of the Seekers. And without the
Seekers, who knew how much else might change if the
Truth were no longer the Truth with no one there to
read it right? But still, how much of the Truth to tell
them? Was it better and fairer to let them search it out
of her on their own terms? They were Seekers, after all.

Koom rippled his skin, impatient at her hesitancy. **"Do
it, stop maundering, get it over and done with so they'll
understand. Mysteries enough abound. They're not children. Then it's out of your hands for a time, but not out
of your direction. We can only wait and see."**

"As you all have gathered, there was something beyond the ordinary in Oriel's death and Saam's injury.
The ghatti are especially concerned by the rupturing of
the mindnet. That required an incredible force, and we're
still unsure whether Saam's extreme, near-terminal anguish and pain engendered it, or if it came from without
rather than within. Things occur that we're not always
meant to decipher—the Lady's doings remain part of a
larger pattern that we are not always privy to—yet this
is not the first strange thing, and seems to be part of a
veiled design that we but faintly begin to perceive.

"You remember Tabor Fairchild's and H'maw's deaths
this spring, battered lifeless when they were trapped in
that sheer cut by the flash floods. We assumed drowned,
but they suffered head injuries very like Oriel's. We put
it down to the tumbling through the flood waters, the
battering of the rocks, uprooted trees, the length of exposure before we could locate them." She forced herself to
breathe evenly, keep her voice dispassionate. "In retrospect, I now wonder."

"Then there was Khem, venerated by all, sharp and
wise at near thirty, until one day we found him wandering in circles, miaowing to himself. Vreni Geradus was
nearly beside herself when she tracked him down. Memory and mindspeech gone, no obvious wounds. Twylla
judged it a stroke of some sort, a short-circuiting of his
brain. Regrettable but not improbable at his age. And

he lay on his blanket like a newborn ghatten, his paws milk-treading, looking for something to nurse against, murmuring and mewling, until he curled up into a tight little ball and drifted off and died. Vreni still sorrows that she could never bid him farewell.'' She paused, the length calibrated to let them remember Vreni's anguish. The steeliness in her voice when she continued startled them all, herself included.

''But what you *don't* know is that after we buried him, the grave was exposed and the body stolen. I convinced Vreni and the Tribune that the fact should not be made public.'' She commanded their attention now, though they remained expressionless, wary. The ghatti twitched in discomfort, her words as biting as innumerable invisible flies against their skins.

''There have been other, similar cases involving brain injuries over the past few years, although we aren't sure how many. None have been as close together as these three cases, or so close to a pattern that we cannot detect the weave of. Oriel's death—and the manner of it—is already known, already being talked about, not just by us but by the rest of the city. The ripples, the rumors, are spreading beyond that.''

The twins wound their fingers together, mirror-imaged guilt. Swan gave a marginal shake of her head. ''No,'' her voice reproved them. ''No fault pertains. Stealth, secrecy, had no place in your actions. You were right to do as you did, especially with Saam to consider. Discretion is a nicety we can't always afford when a life is at stake.''

''But what do you want of us? Where is this all heading?'' Doyce spoke in a desultory, apathetic tone, then retreated back within herself without waiting for an answer, mouthing unspoken complaint. Rolf made as if to hush her, then contented himself with laying a restraining hand on her shoulder to avoid another interruption.

''Well, what *do* you want from us?'' he asked, still holding Doyce in check. ''We can't decide or agree until we know what you're after and what we're after.''

Koom mindspoke on the intimate band. **''Yes, you can order them, you have the right, but I wouldn't. . . . Don't let your tiredness and your fears push you to that.''**

He broke contact long enough to lean over and lick Saam, soothing the increasingly restless ghatt. **"I've been telling him everything you've said. Remember, he can't mindspeak or understand human speech, other than the few simple words and commands we all know of each other's languages."**

"Coincidences in all I've mentioned? I think not. Evil stalks us, mocks us. A crime has been committed and we must determine the guilty party, as it has always been the task of the Seekers Veritas to do. If we do not find out, a worse menace may await us. Oriel's death was the first overt act of which we are sure. What if there are more? But these crimes are not the *only* things we should dread." A pause, lengthening, as she strove to find the right words, her lips pressed tight to still her jangling nerves. "If we cannot seek out the Truth about what destroyed one of our own, what will the world think of us? At best we will be viewed as deceivers, frauds, as amusing road show mountebanks; at worst, as traitors to their honor and trust, guilty of gulling and victimizing and betraying them. What will a loss of faith in the Seekers Veritas mean to Canderis—whom can the people trust for the Truth, who will determine the right or wrong of things in lieu of us? The very fabric of society may be torn asunder!"

Her cry of the heart, despite the despairing calmness of her voice, left the others shaken, the full implications of her words already beginning to sink deep. The Seekers seen as charlatans, the ghatti hounded, hunted to death for having made dupes of the people. A Seeker could strip off the tabard, go into hiding, assume a new identity, but a ghatt could not.

"For near two hundred years we have been seen as . . . infallible, above reproach. A heavy burden but one that we have carried honorably and well. That is why we must find the Truth of Oriel's death . . . or never be trusted again. We must not abdicate the legacy that Matthias Vandersma and Kharm left us after their long search for acceptance, a way to fill a sorely needed role in our society."

Face bleached white, strained so taut the skull outlined itself beneath the skin, Rolf choked out an inarticulate

sound of protest and rage, but she shushed him relent-
lessly, watching for an emotion, any emotion, on Doyce's
frozen face, only the hazel eyes exposing a wary, banked
spark of comprehension. She'd feared Doyce incapable
of it, the grief so raw and new already mortaring itself
to the old sorrows and pains. And she knew too well that
the last time Doyce had seen an opportunity to expose a
group as charlatans, a group she had belonged to, she
had fled rather than do so. How would she react to this
challenge of proving that the Seekers were anything but
charlatans? Proving the tangibility of a seeming intangible such as Truth had more pitfalls than uncovering a
mere falsehood.

"Not ours to judge, never that, but always to seek
the Truth." Swan raked short-nailed fingers through the
white, shingled hair behind her ears, her naked earlobes.
"We must try to draw out this evil, determine its cause.
We must plan." Swiveling in her chair, she fixed Doyce
with her eyes. "Doyce, I want you to replicate Oriel's
last circuit, follow the exact route. Do as you would normally do on any circuit, but keep your senses open to
anything and everything. And that goes doubly for you,
Khar'pern Bondmate. Someone along the route may
know something, some little thing insignificant to them
but not to us. Even evil has to leave some sort of back
trail." The ghatta dipped her head once in agreement as
the Seeker General continued her strategy.

"Bard and M'wa, Byrta and P'wa, you'll follow behind, each of you two days after the other on Doyce's
circuit. You'll both be there to pick up any transmissions,
report back to us, aid Doyce and Khar if they should
need it." The twins touched each other's hands, then
raised right fists to hearts in salute, nakedly relieved not
to be separated any more than usual.

The others waited, tense but wary, to hear their roles.
"Seekers Rudyard and Brueckner, Parcellus and Sarrett,
you and your Bonds will remain here, combing the records for other strange cases or incidents involving Seekers, all the way back through our founding if it seems
necessary. Find out if there's a pattern or a clue we're
overlooking, or whether I'm a doddering old fool arching
my back at shadows and skittering leaves. Not everyone

in the Tribune agrees with me. I need support from
within or someone may try to take this beyond our control—and I'm not ready to admit defeat yet.

"If you need to, use T'ss and Per'la as runners, track-
ers, send them off to follow any leads you may find
promising, to gather any new information from other records that we may need. The eumedicos for one have
promised to open their files to us if it seems necessary
and relevant." Did Doyce know of Mahafny's relationship to Swan? She thought not.

Sarrett shook her head, desperately considering. "Doyce
is a better researcher than I am, you know that. That
was her specialty for years with the eumedicos and afterward. Give her a few strands and she can weave the
pattern complete." Her face pleaded with Swan
Maclough. "I'm merely competent. It would make more
sense to send me in Doyce's place and let her stay here
to do what she does best." And Swan hardened herself
not to respond to Sarrett's unspoken plea: Don't make
Doyce relive it league by league, knowing she's coming
closer and closer to where Oriel died at circuit's end.
Commendable of the young woman, but the wrong tack
to take. For once she'd make Doyce act, not stand aside,
regretting what she hadn't done or should have done.

Swan regarded her unwaveringly until Sarrett blushed,
tilted her head forward to shelter behind her long white-
gold mane. "You're too noticeable, my dear, and you
know it. Even on your ordinary circuits your looks attract
more attention than they should, through no fault of your
own. You ride in sunlight wherever you go, perfect, de-
sirable, and yet distant, unattainable. People don't chat
with you on the streets, in the taverns, the way they do
with Doyce. She's more ordinary and approachable."
She kept her voice sympathetic. "And besides, you show
more talent as a researcher than you think, as does Parcellus there with his love of puzzles. He doesn't have the
slightest idea of how truly good he is. But he will find
out, and you're going to help him and help us."

"That leaves me and Chak," Rolf's voice was neutral,
despite the fine sheen of nervous perspiration filming his
face. "Too old to ride and too old to research, I
suppose."

"Think that if you will, but you know it's not so. No, your places are here, learning, preparing to be a part of the Tribune. Charlton Sisset and his Bond wish to retire back to their village, although they won't do so if you do not accept. They know I need their support. Do you wish to accept?"

Chak and Rolf mindspoke, then they turned to the Seeker General. "It is an honor we had not expected, to be chosen for our governing Tribune. A great honor. We accept." And Sarrett, Parse, Bard and Byrta swarmed around him, hugging him, pounding his shoulders, stroking Chak, laughing, weeping, buffeting him back and forth until it looked as if both his frail trimness and his composure might break.

In the midst of the confusion and impromptu celebration, Doyce's words carried only far enough for Swan's hearing. "Yes, we accept as well. We've looked into your mind and Koom's. There is menace you give no name to, but the Truth you speak is clear. We shall seek and we shall find. When?"

"Two days hence."

Koom rested his chin across Saam's back. **"Those who Seek, find ... as you shall. Sometimes the Seeking hurts, but it is always worth it in the end."**

"What about Saam?" Khar asked.

"I don't know, but I believe a place will be found for him when he is ready."

Whimpering, paws flexing, Saam seemed to sense they were speaking of him, then he sighed in resignation and slept.

The infirmary lay hushed, the only sound that of a vaporizer hissing and misting to try to loosen the stubborn, harsh cough of a Seeker ensconced in one of the rooms down the hall. Saam curled on his blanket, chin flat on the floor, Koom and Mem'now sitting in front of him, though the gray ghatt barely acknowledged their presence. Saam was separate, the "other," unable to join in the mindspeech that flowed between Mem'now and Koom.

"**Don't press him so much,**" Koom urged, sliding a slantwise glance in Saam's direction. "**He's had an exhausting day on top of everything else that's happened to him. Swan said the tension was so thick you could cut it with a knife. Humans do have interesting expressions sometimes.**"

Mem'now limbered his spine, made himself taller, then taller still before he relaxed and sank back to his normal height. "**We have to press him to extend himself. Twylla compared it to a temporary paralysis; if we don't want his mind to atrophy, waste** away, **we have to constantly exercise it, repattern him, reprogram him from the very beginning. Finally, maybe his mind will remember.**" He dipped his head to Saam's level, coaxed in falanese, "Saam, I've a story for you, a ghatten tale."

"Don't want a story." One yellow eye half-opened, then closed in weariness. "What I want isn't possible, I want Oriel."

The two ghatti shivered at the naming. Koom, ruddy and solid as a brick, hunkered level with Saam. "I know. The wanting will never stop, but it will become less painful."

"Traitor!" Saam spat weakly.

Koom chose not to take offense, merely rubbed a fleck of spittle from his nose. "No, realist. Oriel is dead." The words tolled in the air, ringing with a finality that hurt. "But do you not wish to regain your mindspeech? Khar and Doyce are going to Seek the answer, the Truth as to what happened to Oriel, taking your place since you cannot go. What if they need your help?"

"I don't know. Does it matter? I don't know anything, I'm not always sure that I know you. I hear you say my name and wonder who you call. Who is Saam? Who was Saam?" The steel-gray ghatt half-rose, struggling, slithering off his blanket, claws scraping wild scars on the polished wooden floor. Yellow eyes burned. "My brain feels walled in and I am a stranger to myself! By the Elders, I do not know who I am! Who are the Elders?"

"**A chink of light,**" Mem'now spoke with a professional interest. "**One tiny chink and all may not be lost.**"

Koom shouldered against Saam, pushing him onto his blanket, forcing him to settle, making little soothing sounds. **"You have more faith than I, Mem, but I hope you are right. He is too good a ghatt for us to surrender without a fight."**

A breathy little purr burbled from Mem'now, his yellow stripes rising and falling, rippling in a gentle wave pattern. "Hush, Saam, hush. It will all come clear eventually, don't fret yourself over it, let it flow. Relax and listen, listen to what you once were like, what we all were like when we were ghatten. Listen and learn." And the Tale began. . . .

"It came to pass on a beautiful summer day that a ghatten set off to explore the world, though he never got farther than a broad roll of meadow crammed with all the delights a youngling could dream of. The sun spangled and sparkled and an errant breeze twisted and fluttered the leaves and grass, set them nodding in agreement at the perfection of the moment. The ghatten danced with joy, sprang and raced, tore from one side of the meadow to the other and back again, lord of all he surveyed as he twisted and pranced. Bees hummed and bumbled from flower to flower, and the ghatten sniffed each flower to test its scent, decide which he would prefer if he were a bee, then raced on to the next one. A beckoning creeper vine captured his attention, come-hither quivering in the breeze, and he stopped and crouched, hind quarters swishing back-and-forth and back-and-forth, as he chanted his skills as the noblest, cleverest hunter of them all. And then he sprang and pounced on the beckoning vine tip, growled to show it who was in command, cuffed it into submission, and dashed off again.

"Bounding, bouncing, spring-twisting in the air, he chased his own tail, spinning in gloriously giddy circles, until his spiraling course landed him near the one patch of shade in the meadow's center, a thickly-leaved elm, tall and densely dark with whispering leaves. And he chased his own tail in and out of the shadows and sun until suddenly his ears pricked at the sound of high-up, hooting laughter. Well, he sat and stared up, stretched back and back to see because he did not like the sound of being laughed at. No ghatt, ghatta or ghatten does, of course, for being laughed at is very different from being

laughed with, and the hooty chuckles he heard belonged
very definitely to the first variety and humiliation nipped
his skin like sand fleas.

"He stood, bristly with indignation, tail a spiky exclamation of his feelings. 'Who laughs at me? What are you
laughing about?' he rowled.

" 'Oh, to be young and foolish again,' came a voice
from above, harsh yet with a soft clatter. The ghatten
slitted his eyes to see and what he had taken to be the
stub of a dead, lightning-struck branch moved, rustling
feathers bleached gray as the dead wood, claws shifting
and scratching against the bark. 'Yes, foolish and fancy-
free in the summer sun.'

" 'Foolish!' hissed the ghatten. 'Owl, how dare you
call a ghatten foolish, how dare you call me that! I am
not foolish, the wisdom of the ghatti flows in my blood!
I can even catch my own tail! Can you say the same?'

"Another hooting laugh unscrolled itself toward the
ghatten, made him quiver and want to wash himself, but
he resolutely held his head erect, trying to catch the owl's
eye, except that the bird's head swiveled from side to
side. 'Well, can you?' he insisted. 'Can you catch your
own tail?'

" 'I don't believe I've ever tried, and I doubt I could
if I tried. But why would one want to catch one's own
tail? Mouse tails, squirrel tails, yes . . . a very useful
handle in the hunt.' He shifted, clacked his beak. 'But
to catch one's own tail, a pleasant foolishness of the
young. No harm to it, but no use either.'

"The little ghatten swelled with anger, a thready little
hiss of resentment sizzling the air. 'But I am *not* foolish,
I am one of the ghatti! I know the Truth, all ghatti do!
We are *very* wise!'

"The owl's feathers fluffed to twice his size, then settled as he uttered a thoughtful 'hoom-hoot,' and he widened his eyes to round disks. 'Little ghatten, would you
do a favor for me?'

" 'Why should I? All you've done is insult me,' the
ghatten called back, his tail lashing so hard he beheaded
a buttercup.

" 'Well, then, perhaps *favor* was the wrong word. You
wish to prove your acumen to me, to demonstrate that

you are not foolish. Do you not? Let me set you a task of cleverness and strength, knowledge and agility. Are you willing?' The owl squinted his eyes, waiting.

"Quick as a flash the ghatten spat. 'Yes, you feathered mocker, I will prove it to you.'

" 'Fine. Very well, I've seen you dance and prance, catch your own tail. Now, if you will, jump over your shadow for me.'

" 'Of course!' And the ghatten began to jump and leap, dash left and right, twisting and springing, until it appeared he might turn himself inside out. He paused, he sidled up to take it unawares, then corkscrewed through the air, but the shadow always tantalized him, partnering and mocking his every move.

"The ghatten collapsed on the grass, panting, sides heaving, legs trembly limp and weak. 'No fair,' he cried between sobbing breaths, 'It . . . won't hold . . . still!' "

" 'No, it won't, will it?' the owl responded. 'And you said the ghatti knew the Truth. What is a shadow?'

The ghatten hung his head in shame. 'It visits when I block the sun.'

" 'Is it real?' prompted the owl.

"The ghatten thought hard. 'I am not sure. It exists, I can see it, but it has no smell, no taste, no texture that I can touch. It grows with me as I grow, yet changes size by itself throughout the day. And Truth, as we ghatti know, is not always something you can see or touch or hear, it simply *is*. As is my shadow.'

" 'That is not a bad answer, you thought about it, applied your wisdom to it. Something you did not do when I presented you with the task.'

"The ghatten felt warmth suffusing his body, warmth beyond the heat of exertion and the heat of the sun. He bowed his head lower.

" 'Remember, little ghatten, Truth is your shadow, and you should never try to overleap it,' and the owl closed his eyes in sleep. . . ."

"Truth is my shadow," came a little echo-sigh from Saam and he slept. Mem'now sat, head bowed on chest in thought, remembering the old tale with fondness. **"Lovely, if I do say so myself,"** he mindspoke to Koom, then realized that the reddish ghatt sat with eyes closed, swaying slightly, sound asleep. **"And I do say so myself since no one else will. You're very welcome, glad that you enjoyed the tale."**

Koom bestirred himself, yawned hugely and winked at Mem'now. **"Ah, but I did. So very soothing—and edifying, of course. I listened through my dreams, the best way to hear an old and beloved ghatten tale. You told it admirably, as usual."**

Pride and doubt warred in Mem'now. **"Thank you, but do you think it did any good?"** He indicated the sleeping ghatt with the faintest whisker flick.

"Of course, old friend. But Twylla would tell you that one dose of anything, be it medicine or tales, is only the beginning, not the immediate cure. Tell him our tales, bit by bit, until they find a new home in his brain." He stopped, cocked his head. **"A long day for us all. I hear Swan wanting me now, so I must go. Take care of him, Mem, take care of him for his sake and for all our sakes."**

The two days passed, quickly for some, more slowly for others. For Doyce they lagged at leaden pace, but she strove to maintain a routine, her aloneness haunting her through sleepless nights. No, not sleepless, but exhausting, the slumber that was supposed to heal and soothe left her twitchy with nerves, as if even her sleep, her dreams, expelled her from familiar territories. She threw herself into the outward activities to mask her emptiness from prying eyes. Granted permission to stay at Myllard's rather than transferring to the dormitory at Headquarters, she embraced the privacy gratefully, almost greedily. Khar had chided her for her aloofness, but it felt simpler alone, without the press of the other Seekers and their Bondmates, their condolences, their attempts to convey a sorrow she dared not fathom. *They want me to set it aside like a beloved but worn garment, but I can't. I'm not ready to relinquish it yet, no matter how Khar glares at me. The ghatta's been remarkably silent with her thoughts, but then, in all fairness, so have I.*

She organized the supplies and necessities she and

Khar would require for the next circuit and even concentrated on a few tiny luxuries, easily carried, that made each circuit more civilized. A sturdy, blue-glazed water bowl for Khar to replace her old chipped one, a half-weight of the smoked fish they both enjoyed as a snack, sugar nuggets for Lokka. The evidence that one segment of her mind still functioned logically left her well pleased. She even remembered to visit Mintor's shop to discuss the deep green leather he had mentioned for boots.

He handled it as reverently as a baby, an incredibly flexible, supple piece of doeskin, dyed a deep, rich green, the green of a Seeker's dress tunic. "Thought of you when I first saw it," he confessed. "High towner pleaded for it when it come in, but I said no, you had first dibs on it. O'course ye don't *have* to take it. I *know* your boots, I should since I made'm, and know you don't need another pair far as needin' goes. . . ." He ran tannin-stained fingers across the leather, reveling in the texture and smell of it. "Those ye got on should last another few years, but for the fun o'it, for the pride o'it, thought mayhap you'd like an extra pair."

She didn't, not really, but the leather cried out to be made up. And she wasn't sure if she had it in her heart to hurt anyone right now. "You're right, Mintor," she admitted and watched his narrow, freckled face crease with delight. "You've got my measurements, so enjoy. No rush. Shall we say they'll be ready when I swing through after two circuits?" Think of normality, the *next* circuit, not *this* circuit, and by then perhaps she could work up the enthusiasm Mintor deserved for the creation she knew he would make. "Perhaps even a small tassel on the side? Nothing too gaudy, though, you know me. But what's the cost of all this magnificence?"

Mintor swelled with pretended offense, freckles camouflaged by the sudden color in his face, but that was part of the game, too. "You ask me what the cost will be!" He sprang on tippy-toe, tall enough at last to stare her in the eye, then dropped flat-footed with a percussive thump. "*You* ask *me* what the cost will be, as if it's ever been anything but strictly fair and justified and . . ."

She cut in. "Would you like me to have Khar ask you what the fair price will be? Profit price versus honest markup?" A ritual, this part of it, but the banter didn't come easily to her this time.

"Three goldens . . . and a surprise for you with the boots," Mintor parried, waiting for the bargaining to begin. Haggling amongst friends.

She knew it, but couldn't sustain it, not this time, not now. The price wasn't unreasonable; the high towner who'd seen the leather first would have jumped at the bargain. Her last boots from Mintor had set her back two golden, four silvers. "Agreed." And saw the little man wilt in disappointment, mouth down in preparation to protest her counterprice. Well, knowing Mintor, the surprise would be just a little more extravagant than he'd originally planned so he wouldn't feel as if he were cheating her. "Thank you, Mintor, and Lady keep you. I'll be by when they're ready, then." She turned and left quickly, even Khar caught by surprise.

"Doyce, Doyce, please!" Mintor scurried around the high counter after her.

She stopped outside, barely holding her ground, kicking Mintor's good, serviceable boot against the curbing, scuffing the toe, the cobbler wincing at the treatment. "What, Mintor?"

"It's just . . . well, it's just . . . that. . . . Never mind. And don't forget to stop by Rault's. He's been awaiting you." Mintor shifted uncomfortably from one foot to the other, hands twisting beneath his leather apron. Khar stepped onto the walkway and tilted her head back. He stooped 'til he was eye-level with the ghatta, something he didn't really care to do, neither the stooping that made him shorter than he already was nor the staring of the ghatta in the eye. He whispered rapidly, breathily, ignoring Doyce. "And we're sorry, tell her we're all heartsick about Oriel and Saam. She doesn't want to hear, but we all cared for them, too, because he cared about us." Khar stretch-bowed solemn thanks.

"We stop at Rault's." No question in the ghatta's voice, it was a statement.

"You stop, then. I've had enough shopping, enough of faces trying to see how sad my face is, how I'm coping. Prying so they can whisper to each other once I've left,

'Is she holding up, do you think?' " She kicked the curbing once more, viciously, and turned back toward Myllard's.

"Rault's is the other way," Khar persisted.

"Leave me be!"

"I would, but I can't. That's why we're bondmates. Once I chose, I chose. There's no turning back."

"There's no turning back, is there?" She forced herself to reach down and scratch the ghatta's neck. Khar twisted with delight, managed to insinuate herself beneath the hand so that her whole spine got scratched. *"Ought to leave me for a more companionable person."*

As trained as they were in the human mind and its convoluted turnings, the ghatti were not human but animal, and sometimes tended to take things too literally.

"Doyce!" Fright and shock echoed in Khar's tone. **"No ghatt or ghatta has ever left its Bondmate for another! Even the Seeker General and Koom have not 'Printed!"**

"Just trying to tease, my friend, and not very successfully if it hurt you. I'm a bear these days, admit it. Let's go to Rault's, but quickly and be done."

"My bear," the ghatta mindwhispered and wreathed herself around Doyce's ankles for an instant, then bounded down the street, tail quirked.

One of the oldest shops in the heart of the old marketplace, Rault Rasmussen's gem and gold shop had passed from grandfather to son to grandson, and Rault was no longer a young man. It also boasted the best barricades in the marketplace and with good reason: there was always someone foolish enough to think he could winkle a gem from the old man's trays or, better yet, make off with everything in the night. Not that the townspeople were thieves or suffered such poverty that theft was a necessity to sustain life; indeed, Canderis took care of its own through freely given gelt-gifts and through taxation. Yet everything Rault touched—the sparkling faceting of a gem, his hammer poised for a final breathtaking tap that would reveal the complexities of crystal far better than nature had; the lifelike details of his gold and silverwork—made his pieces cry out to be stroked, worn, admired. Sometimes the cry resonated so imperiously that it flooded people's minds, as if a prosaic business transaction of money changing hands sullied the vital force of the work. Other gem and goldsmiths dealt with theft, but not for the same reasons Rault did.

Ensconced within the tiny, cluttered shop, sipping gingerly from scalding-hot but fragrant jasmine cha, Doyce felt neither crowded nor claustrophobic, despite the forest of clustering iron bars and padlocks around her. Rault studied the teapot, its spout the frozen image of a ghatt stretched in a magnificent leap, muscular hind legs extended to spring from the body of the pot, forelegs stretched to form the spout. Another ghatt at rest, body C-shaped, formed the handle, head curled against forelimbs with its tail following the curve of its back legs; a tiny ghatten served as the knob on the teapot's lid, a ghatten sitting on its haunches, one front paw half-extended in readiness to pat at a nonexistent butterfly or falling leaf.

"I am christening it with tea, its first use. But I do not know about the handle," Rault confessed, mumbling through his bristly white beard. "Something seems . . . not quite right." He cocked a questioning eyebrow at Khar. The ghatta examined the teapot, sniffed it over, then shifted to the other side to examine it from that angle. She lay down beside Rault's hassock, her body creating a "C" which almost replicated the shape of the handle. Rault squinted and frowned, then brightened as both hands rapidly combed through his beard. "The hind feet are not right, that's it. They don't touch the pot properly. Thank you, Khar. That I can fix, I think, if I hold you in my memory. Still, memory fades." He reached behind him without looking, hand scrabbling on the workbench for a crumpled piece of paper. Smoothing it flat against his knee, he fished a charcoal stub from a pocket and began to sketch. "Yes. No. . . ." He frowned, wet his thumb and scrubbed at the paper, drew again.

Doyce slouched, handleless cup warming both hands, entertained by the beams of refracted color splintering and dancing on the wall where late morning sunshine poured between dark bars to strike the crystal pendants suspended from a piece of driftwood, aglow with mineraled leaves and blossoms unmatched in life. Diverted from her pose, Khar darted and skittered after a yellow disk of light shimmering and floating against the wall, then stopped short, disconcerted to discover its lack of substance. Rault creased the drawing paper into precise quarters and stowed it in the breast pocket of his blouson top, his cha-green eyes inspecting her for the briefest instant.

"Mintor said you wanted to see me." Doyce lifted the cup to her lips and blew at the cha, using the cup and its thready steam to shield her expression.

"I always want to see you and Khar," Rault reproved. "But, yes, there is something this time that I must do." He eased himself upright. It was obvious that his knees and hips were giving him pain.

"You need to consult a eumedico, old friend."

"Phah on them," he muttered. "Poke and prod, prescribe, think deep thoughts as if brushing at your soul. As if *they* knew what you were thinking and feeling instead of *you*. And then they try to tell you how you feel!" His voice vibrated with indignation.

"Even so, they do their jobs well for the most part and could probably ease your pain. If it attacks your hands, what then?" Doyce stated reasonably.

His age-spotted hands vehemently flashed the eight-pointed star. "Lady close her ears to such words! But you're right, I shall have to go and prevail over their pokings and proddings. But I'll stop off at the Lady's House first and leave an offering. Best to be covered both ways—insurance, you know." Leaning heavily against the security of his age-scarred workbench, he jerked open a drawer, taking out a small, blue velvet box. "For you," he offered, holding it out and limping back to sit down.

The box floated feather-light in her hands. Khar, insatiably curious, rose from beside the hassock and edged near, resting her striped head on Doyce's thigh. She rotated the box in her hands, testing the velvet for the seam which halved it and the tiny lumps that indicated the hinges. When she located them, she turned them away from her so that the box would crack open in front of her as an oyster reveals its pearl. And its heart and meat. Khar pressed harder, then gulped as she pinched her windpipe.

She nudged the lid up, not knowing what to expect. Two perfect garnets, one fractionally smaller than the other, nestled against white satin. Each garnet cunningly carved like a perfect, full-blown rose, each deeply, wondrously wine-red petal distinct and perfect. Each rose bloomed on a golden stem with a back guard so that it was clear they were meant to be earrings.

"For dress," Rault announced with pride. "You each wear the gold Seeker hoop in your left ear, but change the gold ball in the right ear for these. Elegant but not ostentatious. Perfect but subtle, and because I knew you both, I knew what he wanted."

"What who wanted? Rault, I can't accept these and I surely can't afford them. The coppers fair, the silver slim, and the gold fewer yet in my purse right now." She made as if to close the case and hand it back, but Rault stopped her with an impatient shooing gesture.

"The traditional plaint of the Seeker," Rault finished for her. "Oriel came in six circuits ago with the exact same tired plaint on his lips, but determined to do something about it. He said he'd leave it up to me what the choice would be, but that he'd pay me bit by bit each circuit when he came through. And so he did. It took me awhile to decide what to do and to find the right stones, but when he stopped by two cycles past, I showed him the raw gems and told him my idea, and he agreed. 'Everlasting roses,' that's what he called them. 'Everlasting roses for his everlasting love.' " Rault paused. "He was to pick them up this time."

She could scarcely see the roses, barely feel her fingers working to tug the gold stud from her right ear, but she struggled at it until she succeeded. Somehow she set the rose in place, but the old man had to help with the backing. She picked up the smaller rose, but it slipped from numb fingers and danced along the floor until Khar's quick paw stopped it. She knelt faster than the old man could, to spare him the indignity of the pain and to hide her tears. Her fingers burned slightly from contact with the rose, as if it held the power to warm her, and her right earlobe tingled as well. Khar'pern held herself motionless while Doyce removed her gold stud and slipped the smaller rose into place.

"They wanted you both to have them," Rault murmured. "They both knew beauty, not just outer beauty, but beauty or courage of spirit when they saw it. He said that he hoped it would remind you of the inward beauty you carry no matter what the years."

"Thank you, Rault," she managed, and leaned to kiss the gemsmith on the cheek, a shaking finger to his lips forestalling any more words. And somehow she gained the door, blindly gravitating back to Myllard's, unshed tears clouding her vision. Only Khar's persistent guidance, pressuring first one leg, then the other to move her right or left, eased her along her path, she didn't care which way.

Swan balanced on the stool, cradled the marble sculpture against her paunch and then hoisted it up, thumping it on top of the pillar. It had to fit precisely into the grooves and she gave it a cautious turn, then turned harder as she heard it latch. Two down, two to go. With a stabilizing hand against the pillar she stepped from the stool, missed the final step and felt her heel brush one of the copper urns, almost knock it over. She jerked forward and leaned both hands against the stool to recover her balance.

"Oh, flu-flar and fardle!" she muttered under her breath, head twisted over her shoulder to make sure she'd not destroyed her handiwork.

Koom gave a little sneeze-squeak. **"Is that an obscenity?"**

"Not precisely," Swan admitted. Her face flushed moist with exertion, and she longed to rub her hands over it. No, not until she'd finished and had thoroughly washed them. The chemicals were too dangerous. "I hate working with this," she grumbled as she dragged the stool to the next pillar, its sculpted top sitting beside it on the floor. "Everything is heavy and awkward and I'm too short. And too round. Not to mention the fact that this system is hopelessly archaic. There must be something more efficient if we only dared ask someone."

With a baleful look, Koom wandered near, but not too near the copper urns, then sat. **"Well, think how they** make me feel," he declared. "When you connect those things, it stings and smarts like a sea urchin if I let my mindspeech veer beyond this room. Thoughts hemmed in, barricaded, denied our outreach."

"Yes, and anyone who shouldn't have access to our thoughts is denied it while we're inside with this on," Swan mindspoke back. She carried the copper urn to the top of the step stool, careful not to slop the copper sulfate solution, then went back for the long, narrow clay pot and the sulfuric acid bottle. Pulling the stopper from the bottle as she'd been taught, between her middle fingers, palm facing up and away from the bottle, she felt the grating of the ground glass stopper as she pulled it out, continued to clench it between her fingers so that any acid on the stopper itself stayed clear of her skin. She measured the sulfuric acid into the clay tube, then restoppered the bottle one-handed. Only then did she set the clay tube into the urn, watching it sink and settle but not overturn. Next she inserted the zinc rod into the clay container. Almost there, almost done. She added a dusting of blue crystals onto the top of the copper sulfate solution.

"Besides, remember what happened to Crolius Renselinck and V'row?" She stood, waiting for Koom to acknowledge the truth of her words, even though the names were near one hundred and fifty years old. But the ghatti, as she well knew, did not forget.

"But Magnus deWit and Ru'wah had no intention of harming anyone, least of all Crolius and V'row," Koom protested. "They simply wanted to ensure a purity of purpose and vision to the Seekers Veritas, and they feared a slackening of the old ways under Crolius."

Swan looked indignant, stroked at the purple and gold edging of her tabard before she spoke. "And there's no harm in usurping power that has not been granted you? And when such a usurpment occurs, physical harm is often not far behind. Faction against faction, each believing in its own right." Her eyes softened as he wove his way over to her, muzzle twisting at the smell of the chemicals, stroked once against her calves, tail winding around her knee.

"I know, just as they did not believe us at first, that

we could continue as a Pair. If we had not convinced them. . . ." He leaned in place against her legs. "So peace, peace to us all, and to the sanctity of our thoughts at time. If Matthias Vandersma hadn't discovered early on from the remnants of the old spacer machinery that an electrical current disrupted Kharm's mindspeech, Crolius would never have thought of this device to protect against their overzealousness."

Unwinding the tail from around her knee, Swan started to go back to work, then paused, holding the tail in her hand. "It's worse, you know. Far, far worse than what Crolius and V'row faced." Her voice sounded distant, hollow with dread.

"I know, I can sense it." He knew the corridors of her mind too well, knew what fears lurked behind each door.

"And we don't even know what threatens us!" Swan mindspoke again.

Koom's head made an almost imperceptible movement, his lower jaw working. "You do not suspect Seekers and Bonds?" The thought left him aghast; he had found no hint of that within her until now, not behind any of the closed doors.

"I fear everyone and everything, myself included. Who knows, mayhap the most innocent breeze carries our mindspeech and then who hears?" She stopped herself short, an almost superstitious fear of saying more overwhelming her. "Let me finish this, and we'll take a break, a silent break," she amended aloud, "outside in the fresh air, away from these smells, my promise."

She picked up the thread of her concentration, held her other thoughts at bay until she finished. Now, up the two steps ever so gently, pick up the urn, keep it level, no sloshing, lift it away from you. Holding her breath, she gained the top step and turned with slow precision, raising the urn higher and higher to clear the top of the pillar and then sink into the hole that held it. On tiptoe she connected the wires to the binding posts, one on top of the zinc rod, the other on the top of the urn. That one had a spring connection that kept the wire from touching the urn until she depressed a switch. The reaction still went on whether or not she used the switch, but no electricity would be transmitted through the wires that decorated the outer office walls until then. Inefficient, a waste, she thought to herself, and not for the first time. Unsophisticated, but it works.

With a sigh of relief she almost scampered down the steps to heave up the sculpture which would go on top and hide the primitive galvanic battery. One more and she'd be done. Then, outside, away from all this for as much time as they could steal, though it would never be enough. The time would come when they would face the final meeting with Doyce Marbon and Khar'pern, as well-protected as she could contrive it but with no protection from her internal fears.

The farewells were finished the night before, as was the final, private meeting with the Seeker General. Doyce knew that Swan Maclough had let Khar and her sift through her thoughts, Swan's inner mindworkings; Doyce still had the nagging conviction that the Seeker General had not told her everything. Mindblocking was possible, but whether the older woman had done it on purpose to test her or simply to avoid things she could not even begin to face, Doyce wasn't sure.

A pro forma or, worse, had questions remained unasked that she was supposed to be aware of and voice, another test of sorts? She knew all too well about self-control and fear. Which kept the Seeker General from telling her the full story? Or, her spine iced at the thought, is the truth so fearsome that Swan Maclough is apprehensive I'll refuse the mission if I know? What she had heard and surmised so far already gave her nightmares.

"Khar, what are we missing?" She had 'walked the ghatta, hesitant to use the intimate mode in the Seeker General's presence.

Khar's tail twitched, the tip flickering back and forth in an angry tattoo. **"They don't expect us to succeed. They think someone, that we, have to try, but they don't believe we can do it. They're convinced something worse will happen, something terrible, but they don't know what. They want to warn us, but they don't even know where to begin."**

"Wonderful," she thought back. *"Two more sacrificial lambs. Why not stake us out somewhere and be done with it?"*

"You just slipped off the intimate mode like a Novie." Dismayed, Khar flicked her tail hard, thump against the wooden floor.

Strangely enough, Swan's tense mouth creased in a wry smile, cheeks dimpling deeply. "Not a sacrificial lamb, but a catalyst, something which causes different and separate things to interact or react in your presence, yet leaves you uninvolved, unchanged—for better or for worse—by the process. I don't know why, but you've always seemed like a catalyst to me, perhaps because of your past history."

"Not precisely a compliment." Doyce clasped hands between her knees, and rocked forward, then back, hands clammy with nerves.

"But by no means an insult, just an acceptance of the fact that unusual things happen around you, even if you've not always profited or grown from them. Such things have happened in the past, and that should be your guide, not to shut out or ignore those things in your background. And to remember that you shouldn't always try to make yourself 'responsible' for those happenings. A catalyst may 'cause' a certain action to occur, but it had no choice it was placed in proximity to those other things."

"And what things, unusual or otherwise, should I be looking for?"

"You know from your years of study and research during your eumedico training that no individual fact is precisely as it seems, that the linkage of facts, the large and small, relevant and seemingly irrelevant, weave the pattern, form the steps in research, an experiment, in a history, and determine the final outcome. You have the sort of orderly mind that can look back and say, 'We have a, b, c, something lacking, e, f, another something missing equals the answer, and you're able to sift through apparently unrelated, ordinary things to discover what the missing elements must be. That is, if you look deeply enough, honestly enough, avoid preconceptions, allow both logic and intuition their sway." Swan pressed the

heels of her palms below her eyes, then massaged the
ache in her temples. "It's a gift that not everyone has.
How it will aid you in your search, I dare not guess, but
with your range of knowledge from the eumedicos and
from your striving to find a meaning to life after your
family died, you have a far broader background than
most Seekers who join so young, so unformed by the
world outside that all they know is Seeking. It's all I
know, and some days I curse my narrowness, but it's all
I have to work with.

"And don't ignore Khar'pern, you've done that too
much of late. Your Bonding should have been one of the
best I've ever recorded; I thought so when I examined
you both after the 'Printing and at the end of your training, but I don't think your Pairing has lived up to its
potential. Why is that, I wonder?"

"We are true Bonded! We are a Pair, not like . . ."
agitated, Khar broke in, and Doyce half-leaped from her
chair, heard it topple and fall as she grabbed at the
ghatta, desperate to distract her, silence her before she
said something unforgivable.

But Swan continued, as serene as her namesake, before Khar could finish or Doyce interrupt. "Not like
Koom and me," she finished. "That's correct. But Koom
and I fit together in a more comfortable, more giving
way, despite our 'disablement' of not having a Bond.
You've never quite conceded yourself that comfort. But
then, Doyce, have you ever established that with anyone—your mother, with you so palpably convinced her
love was finite and unequally divided between you and
your sister; your fellow eumedicos; or your husband,
your child, your stepson Vesey; even Oriel? You nearly
go the distance, but not that final step. Someday you
may be forced to take it to see and fully live the final
design in which you play a part."

Laying her hands palm down on the desk, Swan rose,
then leaned forward placidly to peer over the top at the
woman still half-crouched on the floor. "Now don't go
to den under my desk. Yes, you may go, so stop squirming. I don't enjoy prying, but that, too, is my job at
times. Lady bless and keep you. Lady bless and keep *all*
of us, for that matter." She waved a hand in dismissal

and immediately set to work, tongue clicking, blunted, stubby pencil ticking the margin of a list, as totally involved with the tidy marking off of duties fulfilled as she had been moments ago with Doyce and Khar.

"Go in peace, go well," Koom's voice rumbled in their minds. "May you someday feel what we feel for each other. Then you will understand she is not being harsh, not prying."

"We understand," Khar responded with more civility than Doyce could muster as she tried to rise and exit with dignity. "We will succeed." And she wondered precisely what the ghatta meant by that: in seeking out the truth of what had happened to Oriel and the others, or in discovering the true depths of their relationship. A bleak hope that it might be both.

If the meeting with the Seeker General had served as a coda, this was a prelude, Doyce decided as she and Lokka trotted along Hight Street, pulling at the reins to test who was in charge. Doyce considered giving the mare her head, all the quicker to leave the capital behind. The Bethel's carillon had heralded the fair-weather promise of a rose-hued sunrise, and the streets were already barricaded by sagging carts, overwhelmed wagons and barrows, produce, complaining chickens being unloaded, barrels and tuns, baskets and bales, everything that the human condition needed to buy or could be convinced to buy stood ready to supply the many shops and stalls of the trade quadrant.

A beginning, but one more thread from the most recent ending remained to be tucked in place to prevent an unraveling of some sort, the way her mother had always rewoven the last thread back through the finished fabric, striving to make it lay flat, perfectly merged with the rest. Oriel is dead, nothing can change that. But my promise to him and by extension, to the Seekers, lives and I'll honor it. No running, no hiding, she commanded herself, shaking the reins for emphasis. Lokka protested, tossing her head and jangling her bridle; Doyce reined her in and turned to look back down the rise toward headquarters, at the training and burial grounds, the box hedges and wooded patches, pillars of white marble stark and clean against the green. And through the living greenery, a glimmer of movement, tantalizingly brief but enough to catch her eye. Someone using the burial grounds as a shortcut . . . or a hiding place. "Khar! What is it? Who is it? Can you judge?"

Khar stood on the sheepskin-covered pommel platform and stretched, back in a bowlike arch. **"Company,"** she noted conversationally.

"No one was to see us off. That was the decision."

"Your decision, not everyone's." The ghatta's whiskers twitched to test the morning air. **"Saam and the others. Wait for me."** She jumped down and sauntered off, picking her way fussy-footed through the damp and puddles left by the street sweeps. Doyce sniffed the sharp, clean aroma of a new day and freshly watered streets fast being overlaid with the familiar smells of humanity at work.

Five ghatti desperately strove to move as one: Chak, Per'la, T'ss, Mem'now, their bodies pressed tight around a steel-blue ghatt in the center, offering physical support and encouragement. Saam limping along, under his own power, but in obvious agony, breath hissing through his nose. Chak and T'ss staggered to the right, then dug their shoulders against Saam and levered him upright on his feet. Every few paces one or another leaned centerward to push their companion on course again. Khar joined them, bow-stretched with rump and tail elevated, then sniffed Saam on each side of his face. The big ghatt dropped weakly to the ground, panting with effort, the others collapsing around him in weary relief.

Doyce could mindspeak nothing of their brief converse, but it didn't surprise her. No point in trying, really. In deference to Saam's infirmity they spoke in falanese, the ghatti's other "silent" language—all whisker flicks and twitches, eye movement, tail signs, imperceptible motions. Khar listened, head cocked, sniffed Saam again in farewell and bounded back, leaping to the platform and facing straight ahead. Lokka's snort of disgust at the delay mirrored Doyce's own.

She saluted the group as Per'la reared back on her

haunches, forepaws waggling in the air as if after an invisible butterfly. She looked for all the world like the em-
bodiment of the silver ghatten that formed the knob on
Rault's teapot. Despite her claim of wanting no good-
byes, Doyce smiled, found herself waving in return to
acknowledge their leave-taking.

**"Saam wishes us well. Everything is still confused for
him, little left, but he would share what he could."** Khar
paused and licked a forepaw, rubbed it along her whiskers. **"I don't know what sense it makes, but it felt important to him. And he would not have us go without
knowing."**

Doyce traced a finger down the ghatta's backbone,
sliding along the sleek length of sunshine-burnished fur.

**"Dark, dark menace all around. Baneful eyes gleaming
like a ghatt's."** Khar recited, then changed to her normal
voice. **"Saam thinks he bit whatever it was, and he must
be right. Thunderous noises, although he isn't sure if
they were all around him or only in his head. But most
of all, the eyes, gleaming like that of a ghatt mad with
mate-lust, nothing stopping him. And a smell that bit
through his nose and choked him. A sharp smell that
sliced through the scents of sweat and fear and pain and
then overpowered every natural scent around him."**

"Mayhap it's a clue to you, but it still isn't much to
go on," Doyce ruminated as they reached the outer gates
and passed through. More carts and wagons formed a
patient double line outside, waiting to roll forward to
enter the capital. "But it seemed important enough for
him to want to share it with us."

**"There was more, but he couldn't sort the feelings and
the words. Only fussing himself, so I left. If there's more,
one of the others will send a message on."**

"Khar, do you . . . ?" She clamped down on the real
thought and substituted something less treacherous, willing the shutters in her mind to close. *"Do you think we'll
find what we're seeking?"* The question had really been:
Khar, do you love me as much as Saam loved and still
loves Oriel, as much as Koom loves Swan? But the corol-
lary was how much did she love Khar, enough to let her
see the deepest darkness of her heart and mind, the parts
she battened down by sheer strength of will to hide her

despair? She had begun to learn how in self-defense so
long ago, even before she became a Seeker, before the
formal training that allowed her to understand and to
withstand the worst of the little ghatten Khar's ceaseless
and energetic good-willed probing. Always pull back before it's too late, before you fail again or reveal the fail-
ings that lie within you. She touched the garnet rose on
her right earlobe, then touched Khar's smaller matching
one. Everlasting. Was love everlasting with no one to
share it? Could one preserve what one dared not use?
The ghatta stretched and rubbed her chin along her hand,
disrupting her thoughts.

"We'll know when we start Seeking." Her tone rang
playfully light, but with an underlying tension that
matched Doyce's own. Paw-dabbing at Lokka's mane,
the ghatta purred a message so that the little mare
wouldn't feel left out. The jauntiness came back into
Lokka's step and Doyce forced a whistling tune to match
it. The sun rose higher, the road stretched straight and
clear—at least for now—and they set off.

To follow Oriel's last circuit meant traveling roughly
west around the foot of the razor-shaped Leger Lake and
its two parallel but smaller sister lakes—the obviously
misnamed LeGrande and Lunette—then southwest into
the foothills and up the lower slopes of the Arnot Ridges.
The final loop of the circuit would carry them northeast
and then south in the direction of home. All told, a distance just shy of 150 leagues. The three previous Seeker
way stations had been minor courtesy stops and produced
no cases, so they had ridden on as expected.

Wexler, the first major town on this circuit, obviously
flourished, prosperous, pleased with itself and forever
smelling faintly of grapes, sweet, resinous, winy. A wine-
town with vineyards creeping down gentle, terraced
slopes on both sides of Leger Lake, Wexler basked in
the accumulated warmth that held off the late spring and
early fall frosts and gave the grapes the maximum chance
to ripen and mature. The town's wines traded everywhere in Canderis and beyond for premium prices; if

some of the winegrowers could have torn down their houses and installed another terrace or two of grapes, they probably would have. Who cared for a roof over one's head when the sun, the air, the earth, the water conspired to create wines so robust yet subtle, so variegated in their nuances that the gods themselves could never have grown tired of them?

The coopers held the townspeople's regard as the second most important, indeed, crucial occupation in Wexler, turning out oak barrels large and small, each with stout iron bands etched with grape leaves and sigils to denote the vineyard. Barrels aged and seasoned to provide the wine-makers with a helping hand toward the creation of an elixir that even a temperance-minded grandam would have to agree could hurt no one if consumed in moderation.

With the late afternoon sun bright in their eyes, they trotted into Wexler and headed toward the Chief Conciliator's office. Lokka momentarily lost her footing and blew in sharp dismay. "There's truth in the old adage," Doyce began, but Khar finished for her, **"In Wexler, look where you step. They have to put the grapeskins somewhere!"** Doyce giggled and Khar looked pleased with herself; only Lokka seemed not to see the humor in it.

To Darl Allgood, Wexler's Chief Conciliator for years, fell the task of deciding what punishment—if any—to mete out after a Seeker Pair sifted the evidence and read the truth. Be it civil, criminal, or even familial cases, the Chief Conciliator devised fair and fitting restitution or punishment, or remanded the guilty to the capital if he judged the gravity of the punishment beyond his scope. That, of course, could be interpreted as a sign of weakness—unless the Conciliator was addicted to playing politics and looking for notice and commendation from the High Conciliators.

Doyce swung down from the saddle and felt her foot skate from under her; she grabbed for the stirrup and found herself planted halfway under Lokka's belly, one leg folded beneath her, the other stretched straight ahead as if it had a mind of its own as to where it planned to go.

"Steady, Lokka," she sputtered as the mare shuffled in confusion and curiosity at the acrobatics beneath her. The ghatta jumped down and paraded under Lokka's belly, tickling her with her tail. Lokka twitched and stepped ahead, and Doyce landed on her bottom, still clinging to the stirrup. "Steady, fool! Khar, stop that this instant!" Damn, she could swear the horse and ghatta were laughing at her, could hear it inside her head. Khar walked around and sniffed, inspecting the heel of her outstretched boot.

"Grapeskin?"

And Doyce found herself laughing uncontrollably, hooting, holding her sides, tears streaming down her face. "Grapeskin!" she laughed, relishing what suddenly seemed the funniest word in the world. The unpremeditated laughter felt surprisingly good.

Attracted by the noise, the Chief Conciliator strode down the steps, and she realized with consternation that it wasn't Darl Allgood. Darl would have laughed with them even before he knew the reason. This one stood back, faintly defensive in his somber black pantaloons and white ceremony shirt piped with black, scandalized at the scene in front of him. Lifting his pantaloons fastidiously at the knees, he squatted and boosted Doyce from beneath the mare, making it into a production unwarranted by her smallness. Forehead level with his silver medallion of office, Doyce stood limp with laughter, laughter bubbling up again, and she swallowed hard, lifted her chin, bright hazel eyes meeting and assessing soft brown eyes with yellow around the iris, like a pansy. Timid eyes, obviously worried.

"Chief Conciliator? Where's Darl Allgood?" Not the most diplomatic, gracious greeting. She winced at her rudeness, immediately reminding the man of his newness, that she knew Darl, and that she didn't know him. Not a politic start at all.

She swallowed a final laugh, consigned it down to her toes and beyond, refused to check in Khar's direction. "My apologies, Chief Conciliator, a graceless misstep on my part." Let him interpret that as he would! "Allow me, I am Seeker Veritas Doyce Marbon, and this is my

Bondmate, Khar'pern. I don't believe we've had the pleasure of meeting?"

"Chief Conciliator Elgar Eustace . . ." he threw his shoulders back, puffing out his chest so that his medallion of office swung and bounced. She nearly didn't catch the rest of his sentence, as he perhaps intended she should not. ". . . the Younger."

Plague the pompous man who names a child after himself, she thought and stifled another giggle. The name betokened a certain familiarity, though she couldn't think how or why. A high-browed face, tiny, well-set ears . . . the pansy-brown eyes, and then, demons of recognition took over and Doyce gave way. "Not perhaps related to Tasman Elgar, now of Barleston?" Khar writhed with delight at the touch of feigned innocence in her tone, knowing full well that Tasman Elgar of Barleston was none other than Unk Tammy, notorious old mead drinker and the meanest card sharp, when sober, of Barleston and beyond. He could always be found at the Greenway—if not in the Inn, then in a stall, sleeping it off. Still, he had a deep fondness for ghatti and an inexhaustible round of stories, inexhaustible since he tended to repeat himself.

"Mm—er, uncle, my father's mother's brother, actually. Though we've not seen him in ever so long." The man did not own up to the relationship with any grace.

"A strong family resemblance." She stopped herself from continuing further in that vein, embarrassing him even more. "Are there any cases?"

"One. They've been waiting all day." Eustace swung his medallion between his fingers. "Troublesome lot they've been. Arguing amongst themselves since they arrived, no respect. They've practically turned the Seeking Chamber into a picnic area—hampers of food, cushions, dirty plates. And in *my* building." His dark eyes glowed with reverence as he waved a proprietary arm at the building now in his care and command, a two-storied edifice of cedar with its granite lintel carved with the seal of the Chief Conciliator.

"Well, we'll take care of that. What of Darl Allgood, though?" she pressed, taking her saddlebags off Lokka and loosening the horse's girth. She'd stay put, both from training and from the desire to crop the front lawn plot.

"Gone," he replied, still lost in admiration for his charge. "Oh. Gone to the capital. He's been called to the High Council, surprised you didn't run into him there. He hated to leave, city life's not his style, nor the games they play there, but his plain ways will do them good. I received my appointment two days ago." Honest pride and wonder warred with insecurity in his big brown eyes.

And no wonder. The selection of a Conciliator was serious business, the decision of a township or village to place their fates in the hands of a man or woman who would uphold the laws of Canderis and the local laws and ordinances as well. For a person so chosen justice could be no abstraction but a way of life, the rightness and wrongness of daily decisions reflected in the faces of the people one lived and worked with. Too rigid and a Conciliator failed; too easygoing and failure showed equally apparent. To judge evenhandedly was a monumental—and a lonely—task. Doyce felt a momentary surge of pity for this young man, selected by his fellows and the Canderisian High Council to dispense justice after the Seeker Veritas pair had determined the truth. Though Darl Allgood had never mentioned this young man, this Elgar Eustace the Younger, she had no doubt that he and his fellow townspeople had carefully watched him for years, along with a score of other likely candidates. For when election came, no names appeared on the ballot to vote for or against; each citizen voted from his or her own heart, writing in the name of the person they most trusted to pass fair judgment.

Still, his youthful pomposity annoyed her. He'd obviously wasted no time in readying himself. The Conciliator's apparel couldn't be whipped up in a few days, even by an experienced seamstress. The cloth itself was a subtle nub-weave only the capital could provide. The pantaloons required a double front pleat and an overlapping waistband clipped on each side with silver buckles, while the ceremonial shirt boasted a special inset front panel, seven diagonal stripes cut from the bias, the bias running in alternate directions from one strip to the next, and the absolute devil to stitch and have it lay flat. The sleeves, set into squared black-piped armholes, were ranged round with black broidery in a running leaf pattern to denote his territory. His was even a bit more elaborate than usual, she judged with a critical eye, admiring the perfect match of both shoulders. Even her own mother couldn't have done a nicer job.

As if reading her thoughts or simply self-conscious, Eustace stammered, "M . . . my mother and wife worked night and day to finish it. They believed before I did that I'd be selected, and they sent ahead for the cloth." A look of innocent wonder lit his face, and Doyce couldn't help responding to it. He'd evidently been too modest to consider himself a Conciliator. But like him? For that, she'd wait and see.

"Good for Darl, and congratulations for you. Now let's go inside and see what awaits us."

Something was decidedly wrong in the Change Room, the Chief Conciliator could feel it. Why did the curtain billow out like that? What caused that unseemly thump and bump? Not to mention that giggle again? How disrespectful, disgraceful, how utterly *scandalous*, he decided, and tasted the word in his mouth, sucking it like a lemon drop until his lips pursed. When he was sure it fit, he stuck his head behind the curtain, prepared to announce his superior sense of decorum and dignity and to reprove them for whatever unseemly behavior they engaged in. Was this really how a Seeker Veritas and a Bondmate behaved? His lip began trembling. It made him suspect for the thousandth time that he really wasn't ready, wasn't fit to be a Conciliator, would never be.

What he viewed behind the curtain sent him back to his childhood and teased a smile to his nervously disapproving lips. Struggling to wind her red sash over her black hearing tabard with its gold rim, Doyce tried to wrap and tie it while Khar lay on the floor, toying with the tassel. When Doyce swung the length around her waist, the ghatta followed helter-skelter, batting at the flying gold tassel.

"No, Khar! Stop it!" Doyce muttered and managed to tie the sash. Unperturbed, the ghatta discovered a new object of fascination in the leather tassels on her boots. They, too, swung enchantingly, and her paw developed a rhythm of swipe, wait, swipe, wait, swipe, swipe. "Khar," Doyce hissed in annoyance.

She bent and shoved the ghatta aside, but the ghatta flipped on her back and imprisoned hand and forearm, front legs wrapped around her wrist, back legs pumping furiously as if to disembowel an enemy.

Elgar Eustace judged that not a single claw protruded. He pulled his head from behind the curtain, loudly cleared his throat, and then stuck his head back inside. "Are we about ready?" Seeker and Bondmate stood at ease, a meter apart, looking as if nothing had happened except for the slightly twitchy, guilty expressions they both wore.

For no reason he could determine, the Chief Conciliator unexpectedly felt happy with himself and his job, more so than he had in the whirlwind days since his appointment. His wife and mother would be delighted about this leap in self-confidence, but he also knew that he wouldn't tell them about this particular incident. Unk Tammy might understand, but they wouldn't.

Seeker and Bondmate emerged at a stately pace, gliding, eyes inward-looking, and he knew they communed with each other. His instruction book, already dog-eared, had explained it in detail. Shoulders back, expressionless, he led off down the hall, followed by the pair. They entered the Query Chamber and the Seeker stopped inside the door, let the iron heel of her staff touch the polished hardwood floor three times. The beginning. . . .

As the percussive sound of the staff drummed through their wranglings, the room's occupants looked up at last. The Chief Conciliator stood with hands clasped behind his back and announced, "The Seeker Veritas Doyce Marbon and her ghatta Bondmate, Khar'pern. Be this your Choice or do ye Choose to await another circuit Pair?"

Anyone seeking conciliation had the right to wait for another Seeker Pair if she or he thought that Pair might be more easily persuaded to their side. A vain hope since

Seekers were entirely neutral, but it allowed people to believe they had some control over the situation. Doyce winked at Eustace to indicate a job well done, no quaver in his voice. She whispered out of the side of her mouth, "They may, you know, I've dealt with the defendant before." As if in recognition, the fat old man on the defendant's side of the room shifted awkwardly on his pile of gaudy plush cushions, obviously brought from home, and wiped his hands on a linen napkin before throwing it on the empty plate at his side. He waved a cheery greeting, pudgy, ringed hand and arm setting the full sleeve to billowing.

"Hello, Seeker Doyce, here we are again," he announced, stifling a burp. "I and my good-for-nothing sons."

"I take it that means assent on your part," Eustace reproved. "And on yours?" he continued, turning to two middle-aged men on the plea-bringer's side of the room. They consulted with brief intensity amongst themselves and the two women with them, hands waving, backs expressing rigid indignation, and finally turned.

"Agreed." The elder of the two gave his grudging one-word answer as if it pained him.

Doyce nodded and moved to the center of the polished floor to kneel while Khar paced four lengths beyond, then turned to sit facing her. Doyce laid the wooden staff beside her and unclipped her sword scabbard from her side, placing it in a horizontal line between herself and the ghatta, the hilt by her right hand, the sword drawn about a handbreadth from its sheath. A symbolic reminder that she, as well as the ghatta, could show her claws if truth were hidden. She nodded at Khar. "Begin, plea-bringer."

"I, Ivor Timor, and my brother, Tybor Timor, are being cheated out of our inheritance," the elder brother stated with even emphasis, though his manicured hands clenched and unclenched at his sides. The two women with them, clearly their wives, moaned in perfectly-orchestrated dismay, casting hostile looks at the old man and the buxom, cinnamon-haired young woman who tended to him, resettling his gaudy striped pillows, pouring him fresh wine, patting his brow with a crisp napkin.

Clearly a great deal of money had been spent to garb
the two wives in what they considered a dignified, well-
to-do manner, but the effect clamored of provinciality,
even to Doyce's less than fashion-conscious eyes. By
comparison the young woman radiated the vibrant glow
of lush summer gardens in her pink pantaloons, gauzy
white tunic, and embroidered rose overvest—daring
choices for her coloration. Such clothes cost far more
than Doyce earned on a circuit, but far less than the
other women's and with far better effect. Doyce ruefully
fingered the well-worn material of her own pantaloons.

"Your complaint seems premature since your father
definitely is not dead. Do you not inherit what wealth
he leaves behind once he has died and the disposition of
the will is made clear?"

"Well, yes, and no, you see, it's like this. . . ." The
younger brother Tybor spoke, only to be shushed by his
brother and the wives. His chagrined face held a modicum of sensitivity and humor and more than a little
weakness.

The old man, Hollis Timor, sat up, craning his neck
to not miss the action around him. She well remembered
Hollis Timor from several other cases: a shrewd, wealthy
wine merchant not above cutting things a bit fine if it
meant more profit for him. His mind clicked sharply
enough to count not just the gold pieces of profit, but
the coppers as well. Nothing seined too fine if money
could be netted. Still, he had never actually broken the
law, just stretched its intent. He had always taken her
Seekings and the Conciliator's rulings in good grace, as
if reassured that the system he tried to circumvent at
times still held firm.

"Yes, it's this way," Ivor broke in, smoothly recaptur-
ing his audience from his brother. "Dear Papa gave each
of us shares in the business when we came of age. Money
that we earned from the business was ours to invest in
our own enterprises. Now Papa is beyond himself, lost
in his dotage, withdrawing money and never reinvesting
it back into the business, as if there's no tomorrow." The
two proper little wives clasped hands over their mouths
in practiced unison, miming shock at what they'd heard.
She beamed a thought at Khar. *"And if there's money*

*being taken out with no reinvesting, they don't make as
much as before. There's no growth except from their own
investments, right? What do you read?"*

She depended on Khar to read the true feelings, the
true facts in each mind, treading paths of emotions, wist-
fulness, ought to's and should have's, seeking the truth
no matter how concealed in the human mind. Then, to
transfer the information to her without losing any of it
along the way, not discarding anything which might seem
irrelevant to the ghatta but not to a human. Finally, questioning if need be, but always through the Seeker,
through her, so as not to insult the fragile human ego
and brain by direct contact with a beast. Bad enough for
a human to know his mind was no longer sacred, but
even worse to feel it directly pierced by an alien thought.

Khar wrinkled her brow, nose twitching, not yet ready
to transmit to her, so Doyce continued aloud and alone
in her thoughts. "And since when has it become wrong
for your father, the owner of the business, to take a share
of what is his? Or is he usurping more than what belongs
to him?"

"Of course he is entitled to what is his." Ivor's silky
voice insinuated itself into the conversation, his high-
browed face bland and seemingly open. Where Hollis
Timor had been rough around the edges but canny, his
elder son radiated sleek assurance, his shrewdness part
of a careful education, not simple instinct. "But does it
seem *reasonable* that this once vital man, once the cleverest and wealthiest of merchants, should wish to bleed his
business dry, deny it life and growth, let it wither into
less than when he bought it so many years ago?" He
wrung his hands, then stilled them, as if he'd calculated
the number of hand-wringings needed for proper emphasis. "Surely a generous fixed allowance is justified, right
and honorable for a man in his dotage, but with my
brother and I to have the right to make all business and
financial decisions needful to carry our company forward."

"Khar, what are you Seeking?" Doyce mindspoke
again. For no reason she could fathom, a recurring vision
of fish, fish, fish all over, schools and shoals of them,
large striped fish, glittering tiny minnows, fishes of all

shapes and sizes and colors finned and flickered through her mind.

Khar licked her chops with a nervous pink tongue, yawned so hard her ears pinned themselves flat for a moment. "Fish," she responded. **"Fish, fish, fish. They're blocking. Everyone concentrating on fish! That's all I can read!"**

"What about the old man?"

"He's blocking, too, but not with fish. He's learned a few mind-shuttering tricks since the last time we saw him here."

She leaned to draw the sword another few centimeters from its sheath, the meaning obvious. "Well, Hollis Timor, how are you? And what do you have to say about all this?" Nothing to do but bluff and hope that Khar would finally break through.

"Certainly my sons have been loyal to my interests in my old age," he commented, clasping beringed fingers over his ample belly, thumbs tapping a tattoo while the emerald on his right thumb winked back at her cheekily. "More loyal and concerned than most would be in their place."

She caught an enticing hint of something hidden within that statement and wished with desperate intensity that the ghatta would hurry and clear a mindpath. She could almost touch the fish, the water lapping across her face as they swam before her eyes, and she pressed thumb and index finger against her eyelids to halt the vision. Khar must feel as if she were drowning in fish!

"But surely a man is entitled to what he has earned, what he has *honestly* earned." A self-deprecating ghost of a smile over his emphasis of the word "honestly." "It is his, *my,* right to do with it as I choose, especially after all these years, especially after having made provisions for the sons of the first wife to let them learn and strive and grow rich."

"Fish, fish, fish! Even the women think fish!" The ghatta practically wailed in frustration, tail lashing.

"Khar, who is the young woman with Hollis, his nurse?"

Halting in mid-lash, Khar's eyes widened. **"Oh, no. His new wife. I caught that the moment we walked into** the chamber, didn't you? It's so obvious you don't need mindspeech."

"Thank you, no, I did not." She gave an exasperated snort. *"So kind of you to happen to mention it. Now what? We'll be here all night if I have to keep questioning. I'm not a mind-reader, you know!"*

"I know. But I am. They block well, must have practiced it for octants . . . such concentration." Khar's expression showed a certain admiration. Few people had such an ability, and fewer could sustain it for long. **"I can touch Eustace . . . but he won't like it."**

Doyce thought on it. *"Well, make it light, a compulsion to do something or to speak, no direct converse, he's too green for that. But I don't know what good it will do; Darl would have known how to handle this sort of situation, but I'm not sure this one will. He's so innocent."*

"Don't worry. I've got it!"

Completely unaware, Eustace began toying with the medallion around his neck, seesawing it back and forth on its chain, twisting it, playing with it as he looked worriedly from one party to the other. Things didn't seem to be happening the way they were supposed to, and a burgeoning insecurity convinced him he was somehow to blame. With no warning the clasp gave and the medallion spun from his shocked fingers, clattering to the floor. Its jangle and skitter across the highly buffed, pegged oaken planking drew everyone's startled attention.

"Got it!" the ghatta beamed triumphantly. **"So easy, so silly!"**

"So tell me quickly—before we both inhale fish stink again!"

"The sons are lazy, do nothing for the business beyond keeping it running. They take their shares and salt them away, not even for their wives to spend. They never invest them back into the business or into a new venture."

"Ivor, Tybor, how have you invested the money you've earned from the business?" She molded the information into a question, striving to rattle them.

Tybor waved his hand for attention, eager to have his say. "The money's ours to do anything we please with, that's what Mama always told us. And you never know when you're going to have a bad year, so it's wise to accumulate savings . . ."

"Oh, shut up!" Ivor mouthed from the other side, a crimson wave rising up across his forehead and swamping his receding hairline.

"Tybor's wife is coming in, I've caught her pattern!" Khar chortled, white paws flexing with excitement. **"Oh, she's hopping mad at Ivor now for always bullying his brother! And she hates Hollis's new wife, she's livid that the woman has twice as many new things as she does even with all the money that Tybor's hoarded."**

"Sometimes everything you have doesn't seem enough, does it, Tybor?"

He nodded, relieved that someone had finally grasped his point of view. The old man made a derisive honking sound into a napkin.

"Hollis, you haven't introduced me to your new wife." She bounced the questions back and forth so that no one could prepare.

The old man turned baby-pink; she hadn't thought he had it in him. "This is Luchette, who has done me the honor of gracing my final years with her presence." The young woman reached for Hollis's hand and kissed it, the gesture natural, unfeigned; she loved the old man. A faint jealousy twinged at Doyce.

Hollis rolled from side to side to gain momentum and shoved himself higher against his pillows, holding out his arms in mute appeal. "I've tried, my dear, tried as you begged me to do in honor of my dead wife. But this is too much, they've gone too far. Read me, pretty ghatta, you've done it before. Are those others thinking of fish? Ha! Primitive measures, it figures. I could almost smell your brain waves frying fish all the way over here!" He caressed his wife's spice-red hair. "Clever little girl, her second cousin was a Seeker, she taught me a trick or two. Didn't think the others would be smart enough to even come up with fish."

The Seeking went more easily after that, although Ivor still remained stubborn about dropping his shield. At last Khar stalked over to him and stared him square in the eyes.

"Intimidating a witness," he blustered, but the shield gradually sank away.

"And so," Doyce concluded somewhat later, "Do we have this correct now? You, Ivor, and you, Tybor, are genuinely concerned about the business, especially with your father's new habit of withdrawing such large sums?" They nodded, faces long and sheepish. "And yet you have money of your own to invest to take the place of what's been withdrawn, money to risk the same as your father did so many years ago, and perhaps the challenge to reap the same or even greater profits than he did?" They nodded again.

"And you, Hollis Timor, feel that you are entitled to this money to spend as you choose?"

"By the Lady, I most certainly do! I *earned* it! For years I poured back every copper I made. Now there are things I want to do for Luchette, things I want us to enjoy together while I can. And a few old promises I was less than zealous about honoring. Our Hospice needs a new hall, things of that sort." He winked at Khar and Doyce.

Eustace spoke a fraction out of turn. "Then do you, Ivor Timor and Tybor Timor, care to drop this suit against your father to have him declared incompetent? With no ill will from either side?"

"That is correct." Ivor bowed stiffly, but Tybor rose, ignoring the looks of annoyance on his wife's and brother's faces, and crossed to his father's side.

"Sorry, Papa. Didn't mean to cause a fuss. Sorry, Luchette." Clearly the final two words came harder, but he spoke them and meant them. His smile flashed, and despite his weak chin there was no question that the smile paralleled Hollis's—like father, like son. "We're just going to have to tighten our belts as you and Mama did for so many years and plow back some of the money we've taken out. Should you care to invest some, we'd be honored."

"At what interest rate?" A sparkle of inquisitive avarice animated Hollis's face.

"Case dismissed without prejudice on either side," Eustace announced. His chain of office again hung securely around his neck, but he patted it with grave caution now and then as if afraid it possessed a life of its own. "But what was all this about fish?"

As the Timor entourage readied themselves to leave, with the combined efforts of Luchette, Ivor, and Tybor necessary to lever Hollis to his feet, Doyce started to sheathe her sword. By the Lady, what a vexing, petty case, and damnably near an embarrassing one! One that she'd cringe over when writing up the records at Headquarters. And not a thing to do with Oriel's death. The sword guard slammed home against the sheath harder than necessary. Pettiness, greed, envy still continued while Oriel was dead. None of this could help, nothing on this circuit would prove a thing. She would fail. She dusted her knees as she rose, tried to calm herself.

"Thank you, Khar," she 'spoke. *"You're a clever old ghatta."*

"Not old, but hungry . . . all those fish. . . ." She licked her whiskers, then stopped, angled her head at Doyce. **"And we're not done yet, we've leagues to go, plenty of places to seek the answers, the truth. . . ."**

A clangorous scuffle erupted in the outer waiting room. A child's voice rang out, piercing and high, "Is the Seeker still here? We gotta have the Seeker now!"

They entered in a tangle, childish arms and legs writhing and flailing, voices pitched sharp and echoing off the walls. Doyce attempted to count the number involved, but the bronze-rose robes, the color of a mourning dove's breast, swirled, rustled with iridescence, and the heads shifted too quickly. Five, she thought, four blond and one dark, his dun shirt and faded blue trews in dull contrast to the scholars' plumage. Eustace waded into their midst and somehow created order, or at least partial order from the chaos. Good for him. Khar's carriage was tense, her eyes huge, fascinated by the whole thing and faintly jittery. Ghatti seldom chose the company of small, rumpusing children on purpose.

The smallest blonde, an elfin child of perhaps five whose bronzed robe boasted pale blue bands at neck and elbow, looked the Conciliator up and down. "Is that the Seeker?" she asked, jerking a pointed chin over her shoulder in Doyce's direction. The three other blonds, a boy of perhaps seven, a girl of eight, and larger boy of about twelve kept tight hold on the fifth child, a wiry, thin, dark-thatched boy. Perhaps older than the others, she judged, but not as big as the larger blond boy. Dark circles ringed his eyes, and he glared around, unable to move. Robe ruckled up to his waist, the smaller blond boy had wrapped arms and legs around his chest and lower limbs, while his larger brother and sister pinioned his arms behind his back. The girl's scholar gown bore an edging of teal blue, and her older brother's of peacock blue. Two Matinels, one Prime, and one Tierce Scholar. Doyce chuckled at herself for forgetting that scholars were children first and students second. Fine, elevated thoughts never precluded rough and tumble activity.

"Yes, that's the Seeker. And what is this all about? This isn't a game for children," Eustace reproved as he stroked the little girl's flyaway hair into order.

"S'not a game! He killed my kitty!" The child verged on the edge of tears, tiny droplets poised atremble in the big blue eyes. "My kitty!"

Eustace rolled his eyes in mute apology at Doyce and Khar as he scooped up the sturdy little girl and perched her on his shoulder, out of mischief's way. Sandaled feet swung against his chest, leaving a smear of dust on the new white shirt. Doyce walked toward the quartet, standing like statues locked in their less-than-loving embraces.

"Let him go. By the order of the Seeker, you shall not do harm."

The dark-haired boy looked dubious about the pronouncement as did the smaller blond boy, reluctant to release his death grip from the other's waist. She put a hand on his shoulder, squeezed once to emphasize her words. "Let him go. Now, please." The blond dropped into a boneless heap on the floor, rolled vigorously to wrap his robe around him and sat up, clutching its lappets.

The dark-haired boy took his time, straightening his ripped and dirty shirt, concentrating on tucking it into his too-short trews. A delaying tactic, but it allowed him time to regain composure, so she said nothing. He raised his head finally, looked her square in the face without flinching, and Doyce winced at the dark plum of a bruise

puffing his cheekbone. The rest of him didn't look any
better served, come to that. "And you are named?"

The first try produced nothing. He moved his lips but
no sound emerged. The second attempt succeeded, force-
fully. "Claes." His arms and legs resembled withy poles,
thin and supple. Despite the dirt and bruises, the flush
of anger under his deep tan gave him an attractive look.
The eyes shone with wariness, watching, waiting for escape, a handout, a kick, for love, or whatever came his
way—he'd not be caught off-guard, no missed opportuni-
ties. The way he hooded his gray eyes as he surveyed
everything around him brought her stepson Vesey's face
into abrupt mental focus. He, too, had had such a trick,
watching and waiting to catch you out. How many times
had she seen that look? The boy spoke again more
calmly, "Claes," and stuck out a grubby hand with four
parallel scratches across the back, scabbed over now but
still puffy and sore-looking. Cat scratches from some days
ago, unless she missed her guess. She returned the solemn handshake.

"And you others are?"

The response came from the imperious little girl still
perched on Eustace's shoulder. The youngest she might
be, but the ringleader of this group. She counted them
off. "Tomas, Tellese, Toland, and I'm, I'm Tamar. And
he killed my kitty!" The pointed finger never wavered
from Claes.

"A serious charge against you, Claes." Eustace lifted
the little girl down, brushed at his shirtfront. "And do
your mum and dad know what's going on with you four?"
he added in the direction of the towheads. "You're for
straight home after lessons, and you know it, not for
hooliganing around whilst wearing your scholar's robes."
The four shook their heads, examined their feet. Khar
walked over and sniffed delicately at the youngest boy,
Toland; he tensed but held his ground, bare toes wriggling. Doyce suspected his shoes were tucked in a discarded satchel somewhere.

"All right. Claes, over here on this side, if you please.
You others, to this side. Khar, come back, and let's get
this sorted out." Doyce briskly indicated positions and
the children obeyed, the four sitting cross-legged, their

uniform robes and blond, well-fed looks barricading the dark-haired boy kneeling on the opposite side, poised to spring away at the slightest provocation.

"Tamar, you tell us your side of the story. Just as plainly and as accurately as your Edifiers in Matinels ask you to recite. Be true, be honest, for the ghatta will test your words and thoughts and know if you make up stories. She will do the same with Claes. The truth shouldn't make you frightened, should it?" She nodded reassurance in Claes's direction. "Now, Tamar, what happened?"

"I tol' you! He killed my kitty!" The little girl's face crinkled in dismay at the evidence of such forgetfulness on the part of a Seeker.

"That's what you've said, Tamar, but why and how?"

"The cat is dead," Khar whispered. **"The darkhair's mind told me that."**

"He didn't have a kitty of his own. He doesn't have anything of his own, not a mum, not a dad, not nothing. Can't even go to Tierce like Tomas." She confided to Doyce, excluding her brothers and sister. "I used to let him play with Ballen sometimes, but only sometimes 'cuz I felt sorry for him. I don't now!"

"Claes, is it true that you used to play with Ballen?"

"When I had time, when she'd let me, when she wasn't dressing him up in baby clothes." The boy's words came grudgingly. "But I didn't have *that* much time, gotta keep busy at the cooper's."

"And then what, Tamar?" Doyce pitched her voice low and dreamy, lulling.

"Then, one day, one, no, two days ago, I couldn't find Ballen when I came home from lectures. He didn't come for his milk, he didn't come when I called, he didn't come a'tall." A tiny finger sought her mouth to soothe her at the enormity of this betrayal. "He always comed before."

"She didn't treat him badly, other than the baby clothes. Never pulled his tail or beat him. She knew he didn't like the baby clothes, but she's the youngest, and there was no one else to play dress-up with."

"Why do you think he didn't come this time?"

" 'Cause he killed him." Aware at last that more than the repetition of the charge was required, she continued.

"Tomas found his body, buried down by the trash slope behind the cooper's, down where his rackety ol' hut is."

Tomas, the eldest, interjected, " 'Cause that's where he buries anything he's got he thinks is worth something. Usually it 'tisn't—we've checked."

Doyce shuddered at how many times the boy's few pitiful possessions must have been pawed over, tossed around by the curious, then left alone and exposed in their poverty, mute evidence that the boy owned nothing worth stealing.

"He buried the cat there, but it was dead when he found it."

"Stay with the girl for now," she instructed the ghatta. "Tamar, if Claes played with Ballen, he must have liked him. Why would he kill him?"

"On account of he didn't have one of his own and Ballen wouldn't stay with him. He tried it once't, but Ballen yowled and got out of his shed when he was working."

"Claes, is that correct? Did you try to keep Ballen once?"

The boy nodded, shamefaced. "He usta come an visit me. So I shut him in, see, to see if he'd like ta stay. But I was late comin' home that night, an I couldn'ta left him any food 'cause I didn't have none to leave."

"What happened when you found the cat?"

"Like I tol' them an tol' them, it was dead when I found it!" His voice soared high with indignation, then lowered as he fought for control. "All messy an bloody an its head bashed in. Didn't want her to see it like that," he twitched a shoulder in Tamar's direction. "Better she remembers what he was like, not what he looked like then. So I picked him up an took him back with me an buried him. But I never killed him!"

"What about the cat's head? Ask him more."

"Khar, he's right, later, no point in upsetting the others even further." The thought of Ballen's injury perturbed her more than she chose to admit to Khar or herself. *"Does he know who did kill the cat?"*

"No, no idea. There was no one nearby when he discovered it."

A wave of exhaustion swept through her, left her isolated and alone despite Khar's contact. But she had to continue, see it through.

"Tamar, we have read the truth in your hearts and minds. Claes did find the cat and bury it, just as he said, but he didn't kill it. He doesn't know who did. Perhaps it was an accident.

"Further, Tamar, you owe Claes an apology, and your brothers and sister owe him one as well for doubting him. Claes, you owe them an apology, too. Your intentions were good, not to hurt Tamar, but you should have told her right away that you'd found the cat dead and buried it. It was hers, and she had the right to know, even though it hurt."

Eustace started scooping children to their feet. "Now off with you, home. Tell your parents what happened or I shall, and no more picking on Claes. Make peace with each other outside." He gestured toward the dark-haired boy, still frozen in place. "Off with you, too."

He scrambled up, but Doyce and Eustace both cried, "Wait!"

"There's bread and cheese in the back room, in case you're short for tonight," Eustace offered. "Dare say sharing some wouldn't hurt me . . . or you either."

"Claes, come back for a moment, please. Khar and I have something we need to ask you."

He drifted back, one hand fisted against his belly as if the thought of food had been too much for him. His eyes were hooded yet again, sneaking sidelong glances at her, at the ghatta, at Eustace. The promise of food wasn't the food itself, and he jittered with impatience, fearful that the promise was all he'd receive. Pledges never filled empty bellies.

She wondered how to phrase the questions, how much to lead him. "Can you describe what the cat looked like when you found him? You said his head was all bashed in?"

"Worse'n that. Bashed in, all right, an partly missing. Weren't messy as it coulda been, though, since all the brains had been scooped out. Funny, not like ants an bugs'n crows'd been picking at, but almost clean an polished like."

"Scooped out clean as a melon," that had been Byrta's

description. Khar and Doyce remained outwardly silent
as they shared the memory of those words, but poor
Eustace puzzled over the turn the conversation was taking. "Was the ground strange in any way, scuffed up?
Were there other wounds on the body?"

"No, just laid peaceful-like on a tuft of sweet grass.
Couldn't have been hit by a wagon, he was too far from
the road." Thoughtful, he chewed his lower lip. "See,
nobody much even uses that path 'cept me an a few
people wanting to take the back path through to the eumedico's Hospice or beyond to the wainwright's. Course,
if you got something for the wainwright to repair, you
don't usually bring it by the back path, less you can carry
it. Not wide enough for wagons. If all's you needed with
him was a new hinge or spring for your wagon, it's the
shortest way down from the center of town."

Doyce fished into her purse, judging by feel for some
of the coppers, the largest coins but the least value. She'd
give him a silver piece but feared he'd have problems
explaining where he'd gotten it. A few coppers served
better and probably wouldn't be stolen off him as quickly
as silver. "Here, for you. Mayhap you'll find a way to
spend these."

Deftly scooping the coins off her palm, he hazarded a
lopsided grin. "Mayhap, and thanks." He held long
enough to scratch the ghatta thoroughly behind the ears,
then pounded off, bare feet echoing down the hall as he
headed for the bread and cheese. "Mayhap if I ever have
a cat, she'll be more like this one than Ballen!" Khar
puffed out her white chest for an instant.

*"Could you read any further between the lines of what
he said?"* she 'spoke the ghatta.

**"Nothing hidden very deep with that one. It's a won-
der it hasn't spilled to the surface before this. He used
the words 'just laid' though he didn't think why. He may
be right, though, that the cat wasn't killed there, just
placed there afterward."**

Eustace returned from following the boy out. "Fair
and square even before I came in. Loaf sawed in half,
cheese sliced in half, nice and neat. Not a crumb in sight,
though I think I know where those went."

Gathering up her staff and sword, Doyce nodded absently. "Somebody should have a care to that boy. If there's no family, why isn't the town responsible? He looks to be good material for Tierce, and you know the capital would foot the fees if the town's unable."

Eustace's lips pinched tight at the rebuke. "Sometimes they slide between the cracks, especially those who don't cry out for help. If they can scramble along, you don't always think about them, just the ones clamoring for attention. He won't slide by again, my promise on it to you."

"And to him, I hope. You've fresh eyes, Eustace, don't be blinded right off by seeing things as you think they should be seen. For all his goodness and care, Darl apparently missed this one; don't you, too."

"You're right. His mother was too prideful to ask for help before she died, and I should have remembered the boy would be, too, not just assumed he'd make it on his own. I should have realized he'd have no Tierce money, let alone coin for much else."

He busied himself folding together the slatted shutters on the windows, closing the place for the night. His uniform already clung to him with more ease and authority. "Will you join us for dinner tonight? We've a guest room as well if you'll honor us so."

"He wants to but doesn't want us to. Pleased to bring us home, but more pleased to have the evening to himself to tell his wife and mother how the first day went," Khar interjected before she could answer. **"I didn't pry. You can feel it in his stance, read it in his face."**

"A welcome offer, Eustace, but not this time. We've still a good amount of daylight, and it looks to be a fair evening. We'll ride halfway to Hussarville and camp. Start off early in the morning and be there for a full day's Seeking if necessary." Ducking back into the Change Room, Doyce exchanged her black hearing tabard for her sheepskin travel tabard and picked up her saddlebags. "Perhaps the next time, though, if you'd be kind enough to keep the invitation open?"

"Fair enough." Relief struggled with disappointment on his face; but relief won. "Hollis pressed me to tell you special to pick up a flask of the two-year-old golden wine called Neckar. Said it's going to be something wondrous, though most don't realize it as yet. His nose knows for sure. The price will soar as soon as they see him dealing in it, though he intimated he might set his sons about buying it. 'No one would ever suspect them,' were his words. Said you should act sure and grumble that it's adequate but not worth what they're asking. They'll come down." He laughed. "Trust Hollis on this. I may even stop off for a flask myself to celebrate surviving my first day in office."

"And you acquitted yourself well. The wine's a pleasant thought, Eustace, and a pleasant night to you."

♣

Leaving Khar in charge of Lokka, Doyce strolled down the street toward the shops. First the vintner's; then, if she remembered correctly, a butcher's shop stood cattycorner to that. Looking properly dubious at the joys promised and the price quoted on the wine, she reduced the price by eight coppers and stayed to chat, charting the course of the local gossip. Then, jingling the change in her hand, she marched to the butcher's. She selected a nice piece of liver, or nice according to Khar's taste, she hoped since she couldn't abide it, and watched them wrap it in oiled paper. Then back up the street to the mare and ghatta, exchanging pleasantries with late-day shoppers, hurrying homeward with laden baskets and bulging string bags to prepare the evening meal.

Something, someone was tailing her, she could just catch a glimpse out of the corner of her eye. An ice-cold finger of fear traced a path down her spine, and she quickened her steps, around one more corner and across three streets and she'd be back. Still nearly full light, though the shadows crept longer and deeper, velvet blacks and purple blue intersected by bands of light. Plenty of others about, no need to feel worried or threatened. No need at all . . . except for what had happened to Oriel, for what could happen to her. She pushed back the thought. Still, she wished she hadn't left her staff and sword slung on the saddle as usual. Most of all, she wished she hadn't left Khar behind.

"Someone's following," nerves twanging, she mind-spoke Khar, curled up in the shade cast by Lokka's belly.

The ghatta stretched with languid pleasure, rolled on her back and dug her shoulders into the dust, snake-twisting her spine. **"Just the boy."**

"Claes?"

"Hmhm. Followed you there and back. Thought you'd spot it before this."

"Obviously I've noticed a little later than I should have, oh noble and farseeing ghatta." She slipped the flask and packet into one of the bellows pockets on the saddlebag and strapped her sword around her waist, reassured by its weight. No need for it, not for just the boy, but it felt more comfortable in place. No margin to spare for complacency or foolish risk-taking on this circuit, not this time. Not on this circuit or any circuit ever again until they knew the answers. And without the answers, very possibly no more circuits or Seekers.

The boy darted from the building shadows into the light, rounded the corner of the water trough and slipped, skidding in a heap at her feet. He bounded up and disgustedly inspected the sole of his left foot. "Grapeskin." And wondered why the Seeker and even the horse and the ghatta seemed to be stifling laughter.

"Hullo, Claes, what brings you back our way?"

"Nothing much," he hunched his shoulders, thin shoulder blades nearly slicing through the worn shirt. "Just hangin' around. No place else I gotta be right now, less you mind?" His agile fingers played with the stirrup, turning it this way and that, examining it all over. "What's it like to be a Seeker?" He strove to sound casual but failed.

"Very special but very hard sometimes. Often it's exciting, but lots of times it's just like any other job, doing your best every day even on days when you don't feel like it. But people depend on you, so you must."

"And her?" He made a fluttering gesture in the ghatta's direction, head still tilted over the stirrup but eyes darting.

Khar groomed, her skin twitching to dislodge the bits of dried grass and dirt clinging to her from her roll. "She's what makes it special. She's a part of me and I'm a part of her. Sometimes I'm the brain and she's the hand, and sometimes it's the other way around. And sometimes when it's very, very right, we don't know which is which, we just *are*." But it hasn't been that way for a while, she reminded herself as she tightened Lokka's cinch.

"Don't it feel funny, having her poke around in your brain? I could feel her today. She didn't hurt, but it felt funny—not me."

Doyce swung into the sun-warmed saddle and slapped the pommel platform to entice Khar aboard. "You get so used to it that it doesn't feel like an intrusion any more, just another part of yourself."

"Oh." The boy stood, rubbing the back of his calf with a bare foot, pausing, trying to prolong the conversation.

She gave in, suddenly wanting human companionship. "You wouldn't care to ride along with us and point out where you found Ballen's body, would you? That is, if you're sure there's nothing else better you have to do?"

His face glowed as he swarmed up behind her, giving her waist an unconscious squeeze of excitement as the ghatta jumped in front. The ghatta seemed satisfied but disinclined to speak as they rode off, Claes semaphoring directions with wide sweeps of his arms as they went, preening in the knowledge that the villagers would see him in company with the Seeker.

Doyce spied the flag in the distance, three four-pointed stars in a triangular pattern, white stars on a cerulean blue field. The stars and, later, the three night lanterns meant "Come, at any time of the day or night, whenever injury or illness strikes, we are ready to succor you, give aid, to heal, to cure." So this was the local Hospice Hollis had spoken of helping. Ah, helping those who helped so selflessly. But it was the way the eumedicos created and nurtured that selflessness that she wasn't sure about.

The boy tugged at her elbow and pointed at a tussock of grass. "That one. No, over beyond that. See, where the grass is bent and flattened."

Khar dismounted, nose-twitching curiously, body hunkered low to the ground, whiskers abristle with the intensity she used for stalking an unwary animal. She circled round and round the tussock, working her way closer, then worked the spiral outward again, casting farther and farther away, intent.

Two voices clashed, Claes saying, "Is she speaking with you right now?" and another voice from behind, faintly amused, "Anything of interest?"

Lokka shied and skittered, and Doyce clutched hard at Claes's leg, holding him in place. Only the ghatta acted unconcerned, continuing one more loop on the spiral before she stopped and turned back. Doyce firmed up the reins and brought Lokka to a standstill before easing her around to face the new voice, Claes's thin arms now pinched limpet-tight around her waist.

"No, not really. Just exploring, I guess." She cursed herself for the tightness in her throat, the clenching in her gut, her reaction on meeting a eumedico, any eumedico. Old feelings died hard.

The eumedico, long white coat hanging open, thrust his hands in his pockets, cocked his head to one side, eyes bright with interest at the chance encounter. "There was a dead cat here last night," he said conversationally.

"Oh, really?"

"Right over there." Claes pointed. "I took him and buried him."

"Ah, that's good." The eumedico pulled a pipe from his pocket, fiddled with it, then stuck it in his mouth unlighted. "I came back with a shovel a bit later, but the body was gone. Always good to get things like that buried. Diseases can come from things of that sort, you know."

"Yes, we're aware." And watched the eumedico's eyebrows rise at her curtness.

"Good, so many still aren't, you know." He nodded and turned to walk back to the Hospice. "Must be going. If you need help, stop by, either of you. That's what we're here for." He made a point of ignoring Khar who had twice circled into his path, practically under his feet.

"They can read minds too, just like the ghatti," Claes's words tumbled over themselves with excitement. "How do they learn, do you think?"

"They study, they practice and train, just like the Seekers." Doyce perpetuated the lie again, hating herself for it. But she had sworn, sworn not to tell others the truth she had learned, that the eumedicos could not read people's minds. And the swearing was just one of the prices she had had to pay to leave the eumedicos. Better free and silent than daily living the lie, even if others found it a small price to pay for their training in healing.

"Nothing." Khar 'spoke bitterly. "Not a thing, except the faintest hint of a scent, but I lost that when the eumedico came. They always smell—sharp, disinfectant, so clean it kills anything interesting. Feh!" She sneezed.

"I know, even trust, even honesty. But for the good they do. . . ."

Confused, Claes tugged at her sash for attention. "I don't understand."

"You're not supposed to." And setting the mare in motion, Khar trotting along beside, weaving her way between tussocks, springing over some, Doyce headed back along the trail. "And where do I drop you off to find your way home?"

"Anywhere along the top of the bank over there. You're not staying the night?" He asked it casually but with intense interest.

"No, we've got to get along. Remember, I said even if we didn't feel like it sometimes?"

"And you don't feel like it, but you gotta." He nodded. "You can stop here." Doyce turned and clasped a forearm to his to swing him down.

How do you say farewell to a boy like Claes, someone you'll probably never meet again, but will always remember? "You know, if you need help, you can always go to him," was the best she could think of.

The boy took a few steps from the mare so that he could look up without craning his neck. "To the eumedico? But I'm not sick!"

"No, ninnykin, to Elgar Eustace, the Chief Conciliator."

"Oh, him. S'pose I could, if I needed help, but I don't, see." He stood with hands on hips, waiting to see if she understood. "I kin take care of myself. Have been for a long time, 'cept for today when I needed your help to make'm understand. Turn the favor back someday, my pledge." Hand thumped heart to seal the promise, then he turned and started away. "Bye!" He pulled a dry stem of timothy grass and tickled the ghatta with the fuzzy head as she bounced along beside him. The farther the ghatta went, the more forlorn Doyce felt. Lady bright, she chided herself, Khar isn't abandoning me, she'll be back. And perhaps, at last, she had a shred of a clue to mull over and ponder for the night. Was there a connection to Oriel's death in the boy's story of the death of the cat?

The wine was good. The fire was good. The night was good. She could feel it. She had set up camp beside a grassy verge that led into a brook meandering its way into Leger Lake. Lokka, after two double-handfuls of oats, a treat but not enough by her greedy standards, grazed contentedly nearby. Communing with the flames, Khar had tucked her body in a perfect mound, front feet folded inward, tail trimmed close to her side. From the self-satisfied inward smirk on her face, the ghatta had relished the raw liver. Doyce leaned against the saddle; stripped from Lokka's back it served as a convenient backrest. The wine *was* good. Hollis Timor had been right. She was, she decided, a bit drunk.

She took another sip, tried to reorder Claes's information in her mind, idly toying with it, letting the connections come as they would. The harder you seek for connections, the more they elude you, she told herself, trying to justify her lack of concentration. It felt so good to relax, and perhaps, at last, she'd sleep well tonight. She thought about the cat, Ballen, with its strange head wound, which made her think about Claes, which made her think of . . . Vesey?

"Khar, doesn't Claes remind you of Vesey a little, especially around the eyes?"

The ghatta squinted at the fire. **"I never knew Vesey. Long before my time. You know that."** The question had surprised her, left her uneasy at the connection.

Strange how she'd caused two very distinct and separate periods of her life to overlap. Doyce sat upright, perplexed, and shoved the stopper into the flask. "But you've seen him in my mind, haven't you? You know from those images."

"**That was your mind's Vesey, not the true Vesey.**"
The ghatta relented, but only a little. "**But from what I
saw, yes, Claes does . . . a bit. But he opens, I think,
more easily than your Vesey did.**"

"You're probably right about that."

One ear twitched and the ghatta snorted, batted at her
muzzle. "**Midges. Breeze died down.**"

Rolling onto her knees, Doyce began to dig through
her saddlebags, knowing by touch, by shape, what most
things were. She grumbled and dug deeper, then pulled
out a cylindrical object wrapped in a twist of coarse
paper. "Citronella candle. You don't appreciate the
smell, but you like the midges even less. Which will it
be?"

"**The candle.**" She wrinkled her nose as Doyce unwrapped the pudgy candle and lit it. "**Too bad their
minds are so small that I can't warn them.**"

"Out to save the world, Khar?"

The ghatta ignored her, expression contemplative. Setting the lighted candle between them, Doyce walked just
beyond the circle of firelight to stroke Lokka and palm
her a sugar nugget. Then she came back and sat down
again by the saddle, pulling off her boots and shaking
out the folds of a blanket. Too tired to wash tonight,
even though the plash of the stream sounded inviting.
Besides, the midges didn't need the invitation her bare
flesh would offer. Uncorking the flask, she took a final
sip of wine, restoppered it, and folded her hands behind
her head. Why was Ballen killed? Why had his brain
been taken? Why had Oriel's? Something to sleep on,
though not the most pleasant thoughts in the world.
Maybe her subconscious knew more than she did. "Good
night, Khar."

"**Sleep well, Bondmate.**" And Khar readied herself for
what the night-dreams would bring.

❖

The curtains gusted inward, flapping and bellying like
the sails on a ship, then hung limp as the rush of wind
subsided. Though the air smelled of moisture, so far no
rain had come, but then Mahafny heard the first synco-

pated patterings and plops, hesitant at first as if targeting their landing sites, then pounding more confidently. She wondered about closing the window, but hated to disturb the mass of papers on her lap, a full day's worth of reports from the Hospice. If she wasn't teaching, she was administrating; it seemed she did both more now than she healed. Leave the window be, she admonished herself, it's not raining in yet and probably won't. The wind's changing direction. And the fresh air feels so good. It was then that she sensed the watching, the feeling of not being alone, that someone's eyes bored into her back from the window. Her shoulders tightened and she set her jaw, moved the papers as casually as she could from her lap, shifted them to crown the untidy pile already on the side table beside her chair. Using the wide, flat wooden arm of the chair for leverage, she swung around to confront the eyes.

A white cat, amply inked with black on his hips, hind legs and tail, and with a black cap on his head and ears, sat on the windowsill, hunched against the rain, eyes imploring permission to enter. "Damn you, Peterkin, don't do that to me!" she exploded, nearly throwing a pencil at him. "Go stare at somebody else! You know full well I don't care for you, for cats in general, or for your ghatti cousins. Now shoo!" She waved the back of her hand at it, but Peterkin continued to regard her with reproachful dignity, becoming wetter, patches of fur sticking and clumping as the large raindrops bulleted him. The sight of him unnerved her. She went to close the window on him, hoping he'd go away.

He didn't, just continued to stare at her through the glass, mouth opening pinkly in a silent meow of complaint. Then the problem dawned on her, and she slid the window up. "Trude forget and shut you out?" Accepting that as a welcome, the cat slipped into the room, rubbed wetly against her shin in greeting. "That wasn't an invitation, beast, merely a logical deduction. Got shut out in the rain, did you?" The cat purred and sat, began to lick himself dry, twisting his head around and working down the length of his back. Mahafny shared the house and the servants with two other eumedicos; each had private quarters with joint kitchen facilities. Peterkin be-

longed to the other woman eumedico sharing the house,
Trude Voss, and she, Mahafny realized with sinking spirits, had the late shift at the Hospice tonight. She must
have left her window closed, giving Peterkin no access
to the house unless he tried to scratch at the back door,
but Cook had the night off as well.

She detoured wide around the cat and shuffled her
papers over to her desk, pulled out the chair and sat
down to work, but the unexpected presence of the cat
had shaken her more than she cared to admit. She could
boot him out into the hallway until Trude returned, but
Trude wouldn't be well pleased if her simpering little
pussykin Peterkin weren't kindly treated. Lady protect
her from cats and their kind; she'd owned a kitten once
when she was small, but had given it to her cousin Swan
after a few days, unnerved by the constant, assessing
stare, even on the fuzzy little kitten face.

Swan. And what was she going to do about Swan?
How could she possibly help? The papers in front of her
wouldn't stay in focus, the writing undecipherable as if
in an arcane language. She pushed them away into a
haphazard pile, not caring how they rearranged themselves, just needing the sanity of a clear, empty space in
front of her. Swan. She'd lied to Swan at that unexpected
meeting how many days ago now? The passage of time
might elude her, but Swan's story and her plea for help
still treadmilled through her brain, ceaselessly circling
and circling. No, she hadn't really lied to Swan, she'd
just hedged the truth, had to hedge it. The one explanation that burned itself into her mind was too preposter-
ous, beyond the pale, and she'd rejected it. But was it,
was it so impossible? It was impossible simply because
she'd failed to see it coming, refused to consider the
consequences.

Her long white hands scrabbled amongst the papers,
churned them, sifted through them, until her fingers
closed on the rectangular shape, a tooled leather case
hinged to reveal two portraits from so many years ago,
her dead husband and her daughter.

Too many years of thinking about it, fearing it, but
not acting; fearing and letting others take on her personal
responsibilities, letting others be accountable while she

had abdicated her duty. The cat Peterkin jumped on the desk, butted her arm with his head, then decided to burrow through the papers after a phantom mouse. She scooped him to the floor, absently noting his protests.

Well, time would tell if she were right, that and a visit north for her peace of mind. Because if she were right, time was a luxury she couldn't afford. How long had it been since she'd gotten out, gotten away? Too long, and now the thought of being constrained paralyzed her. She had to get out, to move, as if the very motion of traveling would stimulate her thinking. Prove to her if she were right or wrong.

She moved about the room, confident of the whereabouts of everything despite her clutter, choosing, discarding, packing swiftly. The leather case with its two portraits went into the very bottom of her bag, along with Terence di Siguera's genealogy files. The poor man had no idea how many years of genetic research had their beginnings in her purely ulterior motive. Oh, it had begun innocently enough and with laudable intentions: trace the ancestry of current eumedicos back in time to discover if any bore direct descent from the first spacer eumedicos, some of whom boasted the true mindtrance gift. But the birth of her nephew Jared and later, Evelien, her daughter, had changed the focus of her investigations, though Terence never seemed to wonder why or notice. He'd had no idea that he was corroborating her theory and her guilt with hard evidence while he searched for something entirely different in his branching diagrams. Two birds with one stone.

With a mental shrug she dismissed Terence from her mind. She'd stop at the Hospice, delegate duties, someone needed to be in authority during her absence, though certainly not Terence. The memory of the last time still haunted her. What to tell Swan? Stopping short, she considered the options. Anything concrete she said now would only increase Swan's anxiety. And if she indicated she followed on the track of something, it might raise false hopes. Perhaps a noncommittal note indicating that she would be traveling to some of the other Hospices to do some research, some record-checking. And perfectly true, no lie in that. And if, by chance, by fate, by hope,

by effort her path should cross Doyce's after so many
years, so be it. For Doyce had a place on those charts
as well.

Oh, Blessed Lady, let me be wrong in this. Please let
me be wrong. Because if I am right, I don't know what
I can do, how I can change things. Her knees gave as she
reached her old easy chair, never noticed when Peterkin
slipped onto her lap, just stroked him with a mechanical
rhythm. Praying to the Lady? An atheistic eumedico
praying? Well, if divine intervention would help, she'd
ask for it.

A door opened and closed down the hallway; she
heard it but didn't register its meaning at first. Trude,
home. She walked to her door, the cat cradled in her
arms, then opened it and set him on the threshold. Half
in and half out, he balked, twisted his head back at her,
and she gently closed the door, pushing it against his
bottom until he moved all the way into the hall. Through
the crack in the door she spoke, "Go Peterkin, tell Trude
you're home."

♣

At first she knew that the boy in the dream was Claes,
but then she began to doubt herself. The farther away
he walked, the more the angles and planes of his body
subtly changed and shifted, the hair lightened and length-
ened, and when he unwillingly turned to trudge home,
school gown billowing and tugging behind him in the
breeze as if to pull him back the way he wanted to go,
she could tell from the walk, it was Vesey.

Vesey the way he had looked on returning from school
each day, knowing he came closer and closer to home
and to the stepmother, Doyce, whom he would have to
face, make conversation with, say the proper words of
appreciation to for the snack she'd prepared, though the
thanks and the food daily lodged in his throat. He had
absented himself in spirit practically all the time, and as
much in body as was humanly possible, smoothly and
silently sidling to the periphery of any family scene, always edging out of the picture, effacing his presence.

With a start, she awoke, half-sat and awkwardly

tugged the blanket around her shoulders. She had slept, she wasn't sure how long and the wine had worn off. The memories alone would sober anyone. Why did her mind insist on reliving the past with such tenacity lately when the present remained to oppress her, more than enough to worry about? Still, when the memories struck her like this, nothing could exorcise them but the act of remembrance. She bent to stroke Khar at her feet. "Sleep soundly, little one, I'm going to stay awake for a while." She stroked and stroked along the curve of the spine, across the silken striped side until Khar exhaled a rippling little snore. The poor ghatta hadn't been sleeping well, either.

Vesey. The memories overflowed, tumbled out in no particular order about her previous life, her previous roles, her deficiencies. But that child had always mystified her, almost unnerved her with his uncanny ways. She had wanted to love him so much, to make things up to him, still felt guilty about her lack of success.

There had been a night when she had turned from the stove, Vesey at her elbow a moment before, only to find him gone, and she was unable to believe he'd vanished. Only much later, after she'd finished preparing the evening meal and had sat down to await Varon's return from his carpentry shop, she had thrown her head back against the comforting support of the rocker and looked up. Vesey lay stretched along one of the broad ceiling beams, sound asleep, one long, tanned arm dangling free, the other pillowing his face. She hadn't dared shout, or even speak his name, fearful that a sudden wakening might cause him to fall. Better to let Varon decide what was to be done or let the boy wake himself. But he had stirred, awakened, as if her very look had jarred his soul, and he had climbed down, yawning and stretching, walked by her without a word of acknowledgment, and gone to lift the lid on the casserole.

Well, she'd been warned, she certainly had been, that she was getting a handful of a stepson when she married Varon Bell, but people always relished warning someone. Mrs. Jopling had been no exception. Every town, even Ruysdael, had someone like Mrs. Jopling.

Doyce had settled in Ruysdael after leaving the eumed-

icos because it was at least partially familiar to her from
her youth, near yet not too near her old home. She had
visited her childhood home but once after leaving the
eumedicos, aching for a place to hide, someone to console her. But her mother had kept the big loom in constant motion all through her visit, pausing only once,
shuttle in hand, to say, "I was afeared it wouldn't work
out." The hazel eyes, so like her own, were faded and
bleak with regrets, whether for herself or for her daugh-
ters, one a cripple and one a failure, Doyce didn't dare
ask.

The position in Ruysdael had seemed perfect when
she'd heard they were in need of an apothecaire and a
ledger, someone to inscribe the daily life of the town, its
cautions and causes, its trade, its births and marriages
and deaths. In short, a recorder, someone who could
give permanent life to the town's recent past and present,
give it a needful, authorized reality, something to help
decipher its future patterns from its past. Her training
with plants and herbs, her knowledge of what combined
with which to alleviate the chills and pains of a cold, or
worse, were invaluable as well as an apothecaire. The
resident eumedico might not care for having a banished
member of his Ward in his town, but wouldn't hesitate
to recommend her skill and knowledge, for it would save
him time and effort.

She had been standing behind the counter at the apothecaire rolling pills the afternoon Mrs. Jopling had come
stumping through the door, whacking it hard with her
cane to make the brass bell leap in metallic fright, try to
shake itself free. She winced, didn't turn around, just
concentrated on rolling the pills, but shouted out, "Good
day, Mrs. Jopling." Mrs. Jopling paraded into the shop
the exact same way every afternoon, making the place
resound like a snare drum as she thumped her cane in
time to her unceasing flow of words. Yes, every town
had someone like Mrs. Jopling, the town busybody and
meddler. Except Ruysdael had managed the economical
combination of two institutions in Mrs. Jopling: gossip
and hypochondriac. "How are we today, Mrs. Jopling?"
As if she really wanted to know! But she would in short
order, no doubt of that. And she'd know about the fail-

ings, the slights and insults, of everyone in town, new
sins and old sins alike.

The cane rat-a-tatted the countertop, Mrs. Jopling's
personal call to arms. "You look at me, girly, you turn
and look at me when you speak!"

"No rudeness intended, Mrs. Jopling. Just let me get
these pills uniformly shaped so I've measured the right
dosage. Wouldn't want someone over- or under-
medicated, now, would we?" She continued her methodical work under the circle of light cast by the green-shaded
lamp, deliberation in every move. Yes, perfect, consistent size and dosage. She counted them under her breath,
scooped the pills off the marble slab with the silver flat-
edged spatula and funneled them into a container, coded
the label.

"Who they be for?" Mrs. Jopling wheedled.

She started to answer without considering, "They're
for . . ." and then stopped short. Merciful Lady, that
was how Mrs. Jopling obtained some of her gossip!
"They're for stock. No call for them yet, just making
sure I've advance supplies if needful. Saves wear and tear
if it should become busy or someone needs them in a
rush." She set the container on a shelf, as high as she
could away from prying bifocaled eyes, making sure the
label didn't face out. She turned at last. "Now what can
I do for you? Arthritis acting up again?"

Mrs. Jopling resembled a collection of dried fruit,
wrinkled and leathery dried apricot ears, figgy cheeks, a
datelike nose, and raisinette eyes, but nothing sweet or
nourishing hid in that dried, shriveled preservation of a
face. No candied cherry to the voice, either. "Of course
the arthritis is acting up. Didn't they teach you anything
at the eumedicos?" She sniffed for emphasis. "No, of
course not. Eumedico Fletcher stayed the course, unlike
you, and I don't think he learned anything either." She
leaned heavily on the counter, beckoned Doyce closer,
closer, whispered at her behind her hand, "And I'm a
bit costive today as well."

"I've just the thing for that, you'll even like the taste."
She turned to find the bottle.

While Mrs. Jopling felt some things required intimacy
of speech, her next topic wasn't one of them. The wasp-

ish voice buzzed and circled through the shop, waiting to sting. "Heard you're to marry that Varon Bell with that hellion of a boy. You're getting a handful of a stepson with that one, mark my words."

She measured the licorice-based syrup into a smaller container, concentrated on not spilling any of the stickiness on her hands. She didn't know the boy well yet, knew it would take time. "So what is it that makes him such a hellion?" And cursed herself for asking, as if she'd believe anything that old gossip told her. Her hand shook with nerves, and a tendril of dark, viscous liquid leaked down the neck of the bottle, a looping, black snake strand of a trail.

"That Varon's got his own problems, but the boy's got all of his mother's, may she rest in peace in death as she never did alive. You hear me, girly? There's something uncanny about the boy, as if he looks right through you clear to the inside and mocks everything he sees there. You feel unclean when he's done. And you feel," she groped for the word, "diminished, somehow."

They had both been so intent that neither had noticed the gentle ring of the bell, or the squeak of the door opening. The presence of a tall, broad-bellied man innocently intruded into the intimate fears that seemed to throb in the air. Kraay de Groote, the town's baker. He took two tentative steps backward, aware somehow of his intrusion, offering the politeness of distance while Mrs. Jopling rapidly fanned at her face with one end of her paisleyed shawl. He spoke at last, "Sorry, Mrs. Jopling, Miz Marbon, but you did say come about now so you could change the dressing." He waved his right arm to emphasize the bandage, justifying his intrusion. An odor of cinnamon and yeast, currants and sugar frosting emanated from him, a faint cloud of flour haloing each gesture in the sunlight from the window.

"Of course. You're right on time." She put her hand to her mouth, licked the spilled syrup off her fingers. Capping the bottle, she took her pen and wrote precise instructions on a label, took brush from glue pot and daubed, then flattened the label on the bottle. "Instructions are clear and simple, Mrs. Jopling. And don't try to outguess me on this, the dosage I've stated is correct.

More will not make you happy in the morning, believe me."

The old woman snatched the bottle, making a shushing sound, and wheeled out the door, cane heralding her retreat. "Tomorrow, girly, I'll tell you how it goes tomorrow."

"Old prune," de Groote muttered under his breath as the door swung shut. She nodded in agreement as she washed her hands, then came around the counter and sat the baker down to check the bandage on his arm. The silence seemed companionable after her last visitor, and lasted until she eased the old dressing free and applied a fresh poultice. He winced, involuntarily jerked his arm at the sting. "Meddler!" And this time his words were vehement. "Not you, her! She riles me no end. I overheard, didn't mean to, but she was trumpeting, and most times I'd say don't pay heed to a word she says, Miz Marbon." He gave a tentative touch at the large burn on the soft underside of his forearm. "People think a baker should know better than to get burned. She'll burn you worse than my ovens can, if you take stock in what she says, but this time, this one time, I think I'd take heed of her words. There's something about the boy that just doesn't sit right. Poor Varon won't see it, can't see it. Even the dogs and cats are wary of the child, though I've never seen him do a mean thing at them." He sighed. "If the ovens didn't always singe the hair off my arms, those hairs would prickle when that boy walks into my shop."

She finished rebandaging the arm, split the tail of the wrapping and tied it round. "I appreciate the confidence, Mr. de Groote, but he'd only an eleven-year-old boy. He's lost, lonely, still resentful after his mother's death. He'll come around with time and care and love."

Doyce sat rigid beneath the night skies, measured the wheeling of the constellations as she clasped the blanket tight to her, still achingly awake. Memories flew thick and fast, blizzarding like snowflakes presaging the winter of a soul, her soul, her hopes. They piled against her, drifted, changing patterns, no order to the time or place of them, they simply came.

She'd certainly not come to Ruysdael with any inten-

tion of marriage. It had been the last thing in her mind;
she had felt too frail and emotionally impoverished for
that, afraid she had nothing left to give after her rigorous
training and equally rigorous casting off by the eumedicos. But then she had met Varon Bell, and Varon had
convinced her she had something to contribute, mainly
because he was so sure that he himself lacked all hope.
They were both wrong.

"I killed my wife," Varon had stated the night he had
proposed to her in her tiny, ugly quarters behind the
apothecaire shop. The room served as partial payment
for her work; she couldn't afford to be choosy. "You
probably know that already, it's hardly a secret." Only
a force of effort kept his large, work-scarred hands
clasped in his lap, trapping each other to hold them still;
only the yearning to reach out and touch her showed
clear on his face. Yet his green-gray eyes seemed calm
and tranquil, as if, having said the worst, he rested content that he had said it.

She sat at right angles to him at the foot of the narrow,
swayed bed, picking at a darn in the coverlet, while his
broad frame overwhelmed the one easy chair the cramped
room could hold. "Yes, I knew that. More from the records than from what anyone said." No need to mention
Mrs. Jopling, that was a given. She'd listened but tried
not to hear. "I don't have time for many general conversations with people, let alone to indulge in gossip. Too
much to do just to spend the day in chatter."

He roused himself, his face creased in a subdued smile
that crept into his eyes. "You should try a little more,
you know. Your special grace is that you listen and care,
almost know what's going on inside people's minds."

Just like a eumedico. A bitter thought, but the man
hadn't said that to throw her failure in her face, hadn't
made the connection, and he sat, patient, waiting for her
to speak, so she did. "The records are marked 'Partial
transcript. Sealed by the Order of the High Conciliators.'
I know that much from the index. Why? That happens
very rarely."

"The Seeker Pair and the Chief Conciliator knew I
spoke the truth. They took the request for a verdict to
the High Conciliators at the capital and asked that the

majority of the testimony be sealed. Better the world not know what I knew." Varon's chuckle was short yet not mirthless despite the gravity of the topic, but his hands remained clasped, locked between his knees. "The record also states, 'Guilty: Extenuating Circumstances. No Sentence Passed,' I believe."

"You don't have to tell me this if you don't want to." She felt torn, intellectually curious about what had happened, but emotionally incurious, knowing that whatever she learned could not change her feelings for this troubled man whose large, competent hands could accomplish the most delicate joinings of wood . . . and of bodies.

"No, you'd best know why you're going to tell me 'no.' Don't want false pretenses between us." He shifted, let out his breath. "Else, my wife, Vesey's mother, wasn't like most people, not like most normal people, whatever that means. Those of us who laugh and sometimes weep, overcome pain, feel joy, who survive and heal ourselves through the love of others. Else wasn't like that. They said her father did terrible things to her in mind and body when she was a child. Taking out his own longings and fears and fantasies on her. And when her mother died, giving birth to a fourth son who didn't live, there was just Else and her two younger sisters left for her father to play his fantasies upon."

His eyes stared far away and long ago, beyond the tiny room with its faded, peeling paint the color of yesterday's porridge, its thirdhand furniture, beyond her. "I don't think any of us in town realized, had any idea. She went to school, did her chores, played with us all, laughed. But she learned to love pain." Face furrowed, he turned back to Doyce, his expression pleading with her to explain it to him, the complexities behind the reality of the words he'd uttered. "Can you imagine that? To learn to love pain as if it were love itself?

"And that's how she loved Vesey! I should have realized it; I saw it and felt it between ourselves sometimes when we made love, but I'm a big bear of a man, able to ignore the things she did to me. Thought it was just her way of showing her passion, her love, and I was righter than I knew.

"Came back early from work one afternoon. Forgot a chisel, left it at the house, but it was a beautiful spring day, so sharp and bright you could practically feel the grass growing at your feet, the crocus straining up and up all purple and orange, and I thought perhaps we could all go out for a picnic." Tears streamed freely down his face now. "Vesey was only seven, just seven, mind you." He was on his feet pacing, short sharp bursts of movement one way, then the other, a captive of the room and his recollections.

She yearned to say, Stop, it doesn't matter now, it's all over, it's all done, but Varon would have overridden her words, would have continued even if she fled the room. Not the Seeker General, not the High Conciliators, not the Monitor himself could force Varon to imprison the memories any longer.

"Only seven! Else was twirling around our bedroom, dancing, twirling, dancing, twirling, humming some jaunty little tune. Marking time with a wire bristle hairbrush in one hand. Oh, how the light sparkled on that wire, glittering like a scepter. Vesey perched on a stool in the center of the room, knees drawn up tight to his chest so that his little heels just barely touched the edge of the seat, arms locked round his knees and his head pillowed there. It took me a moment to see, to really see that he was naked.

"And Else kept twirling, humming, twirling by Vesey, and each time she twirled by she struck him with the brush, with the wire bristles. Twirl, hum, strike! Ruby pinpricks of blood on Vesey's back, his sides, his thighs, sometimes scarlet threads where it trickled down. He didn't move, didn't whimper, didn't cry, just sat as if he'd played that game before.

"I ran in and she smiled at me, the most beautiful dreamy smile, and she slashed me across the face with the brush." One large hand knuckled the scar along his cheekbone, came away wet with tears. "I grabbed her wrist and the bones felt so tiny, no bigger than Vesey's. She saw me but didn't see me—her eyes were huge, pupils so dilated you couldn't tell her eyes were cornflower blue. She just kept murmuring, 'My love, my love, my

love,' and slipped out of my hands and struck Vesey
again.

" 'Stop it, Else! Stop!' I begged her. But she just put
her finger to her lips and swirled by again and lashed out
with the brush at my eyes. I grabbed her and we struggled, and for all her tininess and dainty bones it was like
wrestling a demon. She kept screaming, 'My love, my
love!' over and over again, and when I slapped her across
the face, Vesey leaped off the stool and came at me,
pounding, kicking, biting . . . a little silent, deadly fury.
In my own house, my own wife and son!

"I cuffed him off, but he was on me again as if he'd
never felt the blow, arms wrapped around my leg, teeth
sunk into the back of my knee. I thought he was going
to hamstring me! I pried him free, and all the while Else
was raking both of us, Vesey and me, with that damned
brush. I threw him on the bed, hard, and he hit his head
on the post.

"That drove Else wilder. And yet it was strange, as if
each blow she gave me were a caress or kiss, as if she
were trying to seduce me then and there. I almost wanted
it, too." Tight-faced with shame, Varon made the admission, his back to her. "I . . . I've never felt an excitement
like that, could have taken her right then and there regardless of the pain.

"But the one thing I wasn't prepared for was feeling
her in my mind, turning me round and round and inside
out so that black was white and bad was good and pain
was love. I could feel her doing it, like the tightening of
a violin string to its proper pitch. It felt good, and she
kept whispering away inside my brain, telling me, showing me, other . . . things. And Vesey was there, too,
inside my head because of her, and she murmured, 'No,
I love Vesey, but he's just a child. You're a man.' Sometimes I was seeing her with my eyes, and sometimes I
was looking at me from her eyes . . . there was nothing
separate anymore.

" 'No!' I shouted. 'No!' And with each shout I tried
to pull myself back into myself, the me within me, the
me who was a gentle, good husband and father, a master
carpenter who carved and shaped useful, needful things
out of wood, who saw the possibilities and hidden poten-

tial in the grain, the knots, the secrets of each timber or
plank. And I concentrated on that, on pushing her back
within herself and me back into me. I shut my eyes tight
and forced myself with all my being. Until finally it
subsided.''

Varon faced her, stared at her as if seeing a stranger,
his voice flat, no longer reliving each moment of the
struggle. "Except I discovered that each time I'd been
shouting 'No!' with each pulse of concentration I'd tightened my hands around her throat. She hung limp in my
arms, but I could see the look in her eyes, a peak of
ecstasy we'd never climbed when we made love. I
clenched my hands one final time, and laid her down.
Then I realized that Vesey was conscious, had seen the
whole thing.''

The torrent of words ended. Varon sat, the old uphol-
stered chair protesting at the unexpected weight, and
crossed one foot over his knee and began to scrutinize
the sole of his boot. She rose, moving carefully, feeling
eons old, frail and aching in the face of such agony. An
ex-eumedico without words of wisdom or comfort, of
soothing or healing, just her presence. Shakily, surprised
at the depth of exhaustion she felt, she poured two cups
of red wine and brought them over, put one on the table
beside Varon and smoothed hair dark with sweat back
from his forehead, then leaned over and kissed him full
on the lips. "Yes, I will marry you." The sudden look
of light on Varon's face made him appear shriven.

She had understood all too well why the records had
been sealed: What had happened to Varon and Else at
the very end, the melding of minds—let alone the near-
stealing of his by hers—was not supposed to be possible
except for the symbiotic relationship of Seeker and Bondmate or the special and rigidly supervised trances the
eumedicos learned to delve into their patients to discover
the mental and physical causes of their illnesses. And the
eumedico's trance, she knew, was a fraud. They did not
have the vaunted powers they so carefully shielded from
the commonality.

What Else had been was a Gleaner, a mindstealer, rare
and flawed and dangerous. No one knew what caused a
person to become a Gleaner—whether the first inhabit-

ants had carried the trait with them unbeknownst or whether it was a mutation on this new planet, or perhaps was some imbalance set off by extreme stress. Some argued for a rare viral infection, and indeed, Matthias Vandersma and the first Seekers had been viewed with terror at the beginning because the populace feared the ghatti had infected them, just as rabies is passed from animal to human. The eumedicos were remarkably silent, kept their own counsel as to the differences between their gifts and the Gleaners' flawed abilities. Very few cases had been documented, and when such individuals were discovered they were dealt with swiftly and with the utmost care for fear of contamination.

Mindstealing, Gleaning, was one of the few offenses to invoke an immediate death penalty from the High Conciliators. Thus, while Varon had murdered his wife—and that, too, was a crime subject to the death penalty—he had done so in self-defense and had invoked inadvertent justice. She was sure the Seeker pair and undoubtedly the eumedicos they had called in had thoroughly examined the evidence and had advised the Chief Conciliator and the High Council that it was better if the world at large did not know all of the facts in the case.

So she had married Varon, sure she knew what she was getting into, sure that she could console and heal the stepson so scarred by his mother's love. And she had been partially right: the union was a good and true one, her love for Varon growing until it filled and sustained her, almost made her forget her failure as a eumedico. But no matter how she tried with Vesey, she failed, unable to love him enough to help. An armed truce was the most she could hope for, and the most that Varon could attain with the son he so hopelessly loved but who did not love him in return after witnessing his mother's death.

The birth of the baby Briony, a chubby, laughing infant girl with her father's square hands and Doyce's hazel eyes, had made them a family, with Vesey trailing them like a comet, swinging near, then away beyond their reach. He was good with the baby when he chose to be, patient and soothing, but distant, concerned yet uninvolved.

She could visualize them together, dark head bent over

light one, hooded, intent eyes locked on carefree hazel ones, boy giggle merging with baby laughter as she grabbed for his finger. And she would hope, would think, perhaps, perhaps, it will all work out in the end.

But it hadn't. Vesey was twelve, Briony nearly a year old, the day she decided to take an early supper down to Varon's shop and eat with him so he could work late and finish the hutch he'd promised. Nothing she hadn't done before, nothing unusual to leave the baby in Vesey's care for a short period. Briony slept in her cradle, clutching a tiny whirligig Vesey had carved for her. He had his father's skill with his hands when he chose to display it. Whether he'd apprentice or attend Tierce next term was arguable. The weather crackled sharp and nippy, and she built up the fire before she left. Winter would visit soon.

"Vesey, if Briony stays asleep, bring in some more wood, please," she requested as she left. "It's going to get even colder tonight and we want to keep the fire built up."

Vesey sidled to the far end of the room, almost beyond her periphery.

"Right." He whistled a tuneless song. "Don't think she'll come awake. All tuckered out."

So she had gone off, eaten supper with Varon, sitting on his workbench and swinging her legs, playing like a child with a curled wood shaving when she felt the constriction in her chest and gasped.

"What is it, Doyce?" Concerned, Varon grasped her by the shoulders, straightening her hunched body so that she could draw a full breath of air. But she couldn't, mouth open, fighting for breath—and still she couldn't. Then the band of steel around her chest eased, and she inhaled the wood-scented air into her lungs with hunger. Then she spasmed again.

Without knowing why, she knew it was Briony, something was wrong with Briony. "The baby!" she screamed and pushed out the door, running, cloak left behind. She fought to pull the damp, cold air in and out of her lungs and ran on, oblivious to the knifelike pain in her chest. Varon matched her stride for stride, unsure if he should stay alongside or outpace her and run ahead.

Early dark was already settling around them as they reached the house and she grappled with the door latch. Varon finally reached around her and slammed the door open, bouncing it against the entryway wall. Strangely enough, in the midst of everything, she had wondered how badly the knob had gouged the plaster.

The fire roared, too, too high, flames fingering upward, grasping at the mantle with its flowered tiles. Dark inside, curtains drawn, dark except for the flickering light and grasping shadows writhing on the walls. Vesey stood by the cradle looking dreamily at the baby. He held a pillow in one hand, placed it firmly over the baby's face, pressing down with masklike concentration, then lifting the pillow, pressing down, smoothing the white muslin casing, lifting the pillow up again. The baby lay motionless, silent. Vesey looked in their direction but his eyes comprehended nothing. The draft from the open, banging door made the fire jump even higher, scattered papers, billowed the curtains.

"By the Lady, no! Vesey, stop!" Roaring, Varon bowled Doyce aside as he rushed into the room. "Vesey, no!"

Vesey twirled around to the other side of the cradle and veiled the baby's face with the pillow. Varon's big hands closed on his son's arms and he lifted him bodily over the cradle, shaking him frantically. Vesey smiled and spat at his father.

A feeble cry, a thin, strained sound with little breath to spare. She heard Briony's cry but was rooted in place, kneeling in the entryway where Varon had knocked her as he'd rushed in. The sound offered a reprieve of sorts.

Vesey struggled, kicking at his father, digging his nails into Varon's arm, squirming and twisting like an eel. "Vesey, Vesey, child, please," Varon pleaded, holding his son off from him and straining to look down into the cradle at his daughter. Vesey's feet touched the floor for an instant, and with a burst of strength he broke free. Varon lunged and missed, and Vesey twirled away, humming.

"My love, my love," he sang as he grabbed at the baby and crushed her tight against his chest. He seemed almost to float above the floor, keeping a piece of furniture, a

table, a straight-backed chair, between himself and his
father as he dodged. Varon moaned, face blanched with
terror. And always the fire, leaping and crackling, the
shadows blending and melding as they accompanied the
dancing boy and baby.

She dragged herself upright against the door casing and
stepped into the room. Her chest pounded and she
couldn't speak. Vesey and the baby danced on, oblivious
to the leering flames behind them and Varon closing in
front of them. Varon snatched again at the weaving pair,
and the boy slipped under his arm. Pivoting back, Varon
slammed a hip into the table, knocking it over. She
charted the slow-motion glide of an oil lamp, bulbous
pottery body freshly filled that day by Vesey, as it slid
off and crashed on the floor, languid fingers of oil reaching toward the fireplace. Righting himself, Varon grappled again with the boy and found himself sliding in the
oil, rolling toward the fire. He pulled himself up short
and rose doggedly to his knees, eyes intent, measuring
Vesey's rhythms. "Come on, child, come on, love. That's
my boy. That's my Vesey. Give her over now."

Vesey stuck the pillow into the fire and pulled it out,
one end aglow. Feathers burst forth, flaming up in tiny
pinpricks of light, then falling black and shriveled. One
stayed alight as it drifted down and landed in the spill of
oil. The flames jumped greedily. Vesey ran through the
house, waving the pillow with one hand, fanning the
flames, the baby embraced to his chest with the other
hand. Varon dodged after him, leaping a line of flame
that trembled at his knee, tasting the oil, and suddenly
he was alive with flames, the oil on his clothes turning
him into a torch.

"Varon!" She screamed his name, released at last, and
ran for a blanket, anything to smother the flames.

He rolled on the floor, slapping and beating at the
flames. Grabbing the blanket from her, he snarled, "Get
Briony, get her out of his hands!"

Small blossoms of fire erupted through the house, like
a sudden profusion of spring flowers bursting forth after
a quenching rain. She followed the pattern they set forth,
but she couldn't spot the boy or the baby. No matter
which way she turned, he had been there a hairbreadth

before but was gone. Heavy, smoke-filled air teared her eyes, weighted her lungs, hampered her search.

The touch came so gentle, so tentative at first that she almost missed it. Faintly soothing, lulling, totally at odds with the rest of her feelings. *"Oh, Vesey loves, and Vesey loves. . . ."* The song echoed through her, coiled through her brain. *"Oh, Vesey loves Briony, and Vesey loves . . . Daddy, and Vesey loves . . . no, likes, yes . . . Vesey likes Doyce sometimes."*

"And Doyce loves Vesey," she thought as hard as she could, but she couldn't make herself believe it.

"No, oh, no, Doyce doesn't love me like Mama loved, Mama loved me."

Flames curled up and around the blue-checked homespun drapes she'd sewn with such care, ate at the wall, spurted up around the willow kindling basket, tasted the wood shavings and chips Varon brought home each evening for stoking the fire. The flames from the fireplace advanced unrulily into the room, rushing forth like children freed from school. Varon distractedly pounded at them with the blanket, his face and hands soot-streaked and puffy red from flash burns. "Find her, Doyce, find Briony and get out! Lady take Vesey to hell and gone with his mother!" he bellowed, pants and jacket still smoldering, still alight. "Can't see a thing, can't see to find them, my eyes!"

The house wasn't large: a kitchen, a living area, and a bedroom off that to the back, a loft area above where Vesey slept. But it seemed huge, as desperately daunting as an unknown land. Up the ladder to the loft, feeling her way as the heat and smoke thickened and turned ugly in her lungs, and there, outlined by the flames, was Vesey, catwalking one of the beams, Briony tucked rag doll-like under one arm. She edged after him, but he vanished, sliding down the central support pillar.

She heard and felt the hard, flat "whomp" as the fire reached the ten-gallon storage crock of oil, could sense the air shiver with delight, the flames' glee at finding sustenance. She dropped down and clung to the beam, held it by her fingertips as she readied herself to drop into the circle of flames. Varon stood surrounded, back against the wall, beating futilely with the charred, smoldering blanket.

Vesey stood in one of the few clear patches, bouncing Briony's tiny bootied feet near the edge of the flames, tossing her into the air. One little slipper sailed off and away.

"My love, my love." The message curled around her and within her, circling as voraciously as the flames, as suffocating as the smoke.

"Oh, Vesey! I'm coming!" she cried as she released the beam and felt her legs crumple under her, spilling her on the floor. It was the last thing she remembered.

Voices now, and hands, insistent, prying, tugging. She didn't want to be bothered, why did it matter? "I've got her! Anybody find the baby?" Coughing, choking. "Not yet. Varon's on the other side, I think. Don't know if we can reach him." Another voice, thick, phlegmed with soot: "Got the baby. What of the boy?"

She tried to speak, to say that Vesey was with Briony, had to be near her, but she couldn't. "Well, keep looking. And keep the buckets coming! Maybe we can reach Varon." Sudden yell of panic: "Back off! Get out! Roof's coming down!" And strong arms swept her up, swept her away into the blessedly cold, clear night air.

More voices: "Lady take you to her bosom, Varon, old friend. We tried." "I don't think the baby's alive." And a woman started to keen at the loss. "Is Doyce?" "Think so, barely."

Briony dead, Varon dead and, it had to be assumed, Vesey dead as well, completely consumed at the heart of the inferno. The neighbors had sifted through the ashes in the days that followed, trying to salvage anything that would start her on a new life, give her some remembrance or keepsake. They found the remains of Varon's body, but nothing of the boy's, except for a misshapen, half-melted piece of silver, its thin chain long gone. It had been the medal of the Lady that Else had given her son at his birth, a family heirloom. He had worn it around his neck like some sort of talisman.

She had known the Conciliator's hearing with the Seeker Pair present would be necessary after the fire. She didn't look forward to it, but it didn't matter, not

really. One more ritual obligation to go through, like the
funeral. What she hadn't expected and what had almost
completely unnerved her throughout her testimony was
the unwavering stare of the ghatt.

She gave her account slowly, clearly, hesitating only a
few times over the right word or phrase. Once she lost
the gist of what she had been saying and stopped dead,
confused, staring at the white bandages on her hands and
arms, wondering why she was here and what they wanted
of her. The Seeker prompted gently and sometimes
asked for clarification or amplification. And the ghatt sat
unmoving, watching her. It seemed to be looking into
her deepest being, assessing, weighing. Its large green
eyes, edged with a deeper jade around the slitted pupils,
neither condemned nor judged, but gave her the impression she had somehow been found wanting in the final
balance. Not a new feeling.

Dismissed at last, ground down with exhaustion, she
stood to leave and glanced back at the ghatt, pensively
rubbing its face with a paw. It struck her like a bolt.
Nearly ten years as a eumedico, yearning for the final
level of training which would allow her to reach out and
touch minds, but to no avail. The power did not exist.
Then the strange, momentary bonding with Vesey's mind
before he died. Now this ghatt, sensing her inward
thoughts as clearly as if her skull were a pane of glass.
"Lady save me, truly, from ever coming near another
ghatt," she prayed and could not control her sudden
trembling.

The ghatt stopped his washing, blinked rapidly. The
words pierced her brain directly, not through the Seeker-
intermediary. **"Do not be afraid. The sharing can be sacred. You will see someday."** She whirled in blind panic,
praying her legs would hold, and fled the room.

Doyce sat, blanket cowled around her neck, fists dug
deep into the material, arms crossed, pulling the blanket
tight around her. Not that cold out, not in the least, but
her memories ran cold, cold as ice, cold as ashes, fire
and freezing in her veins. Enough, enough for this night,

or what remained of it. How long had she been sitting like that, astray, restlessly wandering through the past? But once she'd started, there'd been no stopping.

The citronella candle still burned, but barely, beginning to gutter in a sunken pool of wax. Unclenching her hand from the blanket, she extended her arm, reached out to the sleeping ghatta, wanting the reassurance of stroking the warm, breathing body. Her hand landed a bit more heavily than she'd planned, and the ghatta jolted awake. Ah, she'd woken her too brusquely, a bead of moisture, condensation from the warmth of her breath, hovered at one pink nostril, the profile slack and sleep-ridden as she tried to pull herself into waking.

"Mzwurp?" Khar vocalized her protest, huffled slightly, managed at last to pry her eyes open. All four legs extended in a long and languorous stretch until her paws touched together, chin pulled in tight to her chest, then extended as far as she could. **"No sleep?"** She yawned. **"You haven't been sleeping? Then that's why . . ."** She didn't complete the thought so Doyce could hear; that was why she had slept so peacefully, so hard and so long, there had been no dreams from Doyce for her to guard against.

Doyce rose, unwrapped herself from the blanket, shook it out, the breeze threatening to overwhelm the candle flame. "Couldn't seem to sleep, though I'm tired enough to. Got wound up in the past somehow and had to unravel it. I don't know why, it never changes." She dropped the blanket, stretched as well, hands high above head, then on hips as she bent one way and another.

"Could you sleep now, Bondmate?" The ghatta walked over to the blanket, poked at it, hooked a corner with her claw to drag it back in invitation. **"There's still time before dawn, and no rule that you have to rise with the sun."** She crooned a ghatta lullaby through Doyce's thoughts, tempted and teased with images of rest, respite from the past.

Doyce swayed, rocking to the inner melody the ghatta crooned, cocooning her and sheltering her. "Don't know. So tired, so very tired, but sleep doesn't seem to help. Just as tired afterward." Despite herself, she fisted a yawn, then another one, rubbed eyes burning from lack of sleep. "The dreams can't be any worse than what I can and do remember when I'm awake, can they?" Kneeling, she smoothed the wrinkles from the blanket, then lay down. "Can they?" Her voice came plaintive, drifting as drowsiness at last overwhelmed her. "Can they?"

"No, love, no, not while I'm here. Now sleep, sleep." No, not tonight, not if she could help it, not by all the Elder powers she could pray to, and she'd make them hear her plea. **"Sleep, love, sleep."**

Khar waited, watched, listened to the night-world around her, busy, busier than the day. Owl wings' ghost-soft sussuration, death squeak, the scent of blood. Death came during the day as well, but at night it seemed more vivid, certain scents and sounds supplying images for the unseeing eyes. Crunch, snap, the sound of tiny, hungry jaws, shrew, she judged, munching at the brittle wings, chitinous body of a cricket sluggish in the cool of dark.

She sat sentinel-still, wondering if, when, what, Doyce would dream tonight, or whether her memories had been release enough to dampen the dreams? A possessive white paw tapped at blanketed knee, momentarily jealous of the Doyce-world before Khar, before the ghatta had become the center of it. But was she the center? Had she ever been the core, or did she simply rim Doyce's life, holding it in place when the center could not hold?

Careful, cautious, she prowled the sleeping mind, anxious, wistful for a hint that she centered in a pleasant dream. But Doyce slept, at peace. Why did humans appear so vulnerable in sleep? Whatever physical grace they possessed—and that was limited by ghatti standards—melted away in sleep to a touching awkwardness, defenselessness, leaving them susceptible to both inner and outer worlds in a way that even the exhausted slumber of a ghatten did not. Well, if Doyce slept that deeply, dream fragments familiar and unthreatening, perhaps she had time for a brief mindwalk.

She mindlinked out . . . out . . . even farther beyond, ever-vigilant. Too hard to shake the last disastrous experience from her senses, despite the practice with Mem'now and the others. Contact M'wa and P'wa? Possible, certainly. She searched for their signaling mirror-image mind-patterns, then floated by them untouched, ignoring the invitation, the desire to speak with those who understood. Out . . . out even farther, she allowed herself to be clasped by the echoes of the ancient mindvoices, ancestral thoughts, striations in the air like the strata of primeval rock. She spiraled once, twice, a third time through the layers, the levelings, reveled in the suddenly open path, the easy lift of the quarto turn, the spiral she despaired of attaining, and dropped back slightly, gasping. So close! So damnably near! Nearer than it had ever been before, more palpably achievable.

Still, a comfort in their stability, even a perverse comfort in her stability in the old spiral, she was what she was, knew her place until the Elders deemed her ready. **"Old ones, Elders, I am true to her, always true to her. Help me help her. I fear those dreams. They void the Truth. So far I've been able to reshape them, but if they become stronger than I? What then?"**

"Then . . . ? Then . . . then?" the voices echoed back at her, fragments of her fears, levels, layerings, and shadings of the past, past answers distorted but there if she could but hear them. "When . . . truth . . . ?" "Is found . . . found . . . found. . . ." "What . . . then . . . then, then?" "When . . . then. . . ."

No mockery to the echoes of the past, but no answers either. Still, comfort in feeling the touch of the past, and with that she spiraled herself down, down, savoring each slow swirl of echo, pure as water distilled from glacial ice.

Sky edged salmon-pink in the dawn in the east, wary as a trout back-finning in place before rising to snatch a waterbug. Beware, oh, trout! Does that waterbug conceal a hook? The line to snatch you out of your watery real-world and leave you gasping for breath in a nightmare-world? Khar shook her head, puzzled over the imagery that had entered her mind. It resonated like a fragment of a tale told to ghatten, but she had no memory of it. Was she to learn a new tale? Natural? Unnatural? Hook and line? Was there "bait" out there she was missing, that might hook Doyce and pull her away from her? Or were the Elders merely having her on, riddling her?

After yesterday's mindblocking with fish and now this, all she wanted was to see a fish in one place: on a plate in front of her! Not wriggling free to tantalize with watery illusion. Water distorted her vision, though it didn't the fish's. Distortion? What was distorting her vision? Nothing could distort her vision, she was ghatti, she knew Truth!

Khar returned to herself, checked Doyce's dreams again, and curled on Doyce's discarded tabard, nestled close for comfort. Not supposed to be on the tabard, she chided herself, but it felt so consoling, so rich with the scent of Doyce and the natural sheepskin smell. She gave a thoughtful, considering lick down her foreleg, let it veer off so her tongue rasped the sheepskin.

❖

The smell of burning reeked strong in Doyce's nostrils, something charring, ready to ignite. She opened her eyes in terror and the first thing that blurred her line of vision was a foot. A foot waggling slowly in front of her eyes. Pink paw pad, pink toe pads, white toes extended, flexed apart. The claws unsheathed, near translucent in the early sun, so that she could trace the rosy line within each where the blood circulated. A foot? Whose foot? A muffled slurp and the sounds of licking.

Rolling back, she gained enough distance to focus. "Khar?" she asked, sleepy, still uncertain. "What are you doing?"

"Leg o'mutton." Another slurp. The ghatta rested partially on her lower back, one foreleg planted beside her to lever her upper body perpendicular, her hind leg extended beyond her ear as the ghatta curved inward and explored a difficult-to-reach patch of fur near the base of her tail. She licked enthusiastically, snuffled, a juicy blowing sound.

"Khar, that's rude!"

"But necessary. Nice to be clean. You could use a wash, too." She crinkled her nose in Doyce's direction, snorted. "You were dreaming last night."

Unwinding herself from the blanket, she sat up, head throbbing. "Yes. How much did you catch?" The ques-

tion casual, to mask her interest and trepidation. Sometimes a ghatt could catch more of a Seeker's dream than
the Seeker could or would remember. The question was:
did she wish her memory prompted?

"About the same as usual. You know." The ghatta
considered a patch of fur on her white belly and attacked
with vigor, front teeth snipping away, pinching close to
the skin. "Got it!"

"You, the compassionate ghatta who wants to rescue
midges, have destroyed a flea? And remove your flea-
some body from my tabard this instant!"

The ghatta unwound herself and padded away, pausing
by the embers of the campfire to nose a scrap of paper
closer to the glowing coals. The leftover wrapper from
the liver, that was the charred smell she had noticed on
waking. Nothing more.

Heading down to the stream to wash, she felt absurdly
comforted to know that it was only the same old dreams,
her standbys. That she could live with, would have to
live with, as she had for years.

Another night, another tale. Mem'now settled himself
beside Saam with a murmurous greeting and thrust his
nose forward, inspecting Saam's hip wound, lips curling
back as he scented for infection, felt that the throbbing
heat had abated. Good, Twylla would be pleased, he
knew. She was an excellent judge of ghatti health, but
he, of course, was far superior, being one himself.

He toyed with which ghatten tale to tell tonight, picking and choosing through his repertoire. Despite himself,
he had to admit how much he enjoyed the tale-telling,
and wondered if he had become too pedantic, boring the
whiskers off Saam on a nightly basis. Still, when he lost
himself in ghatten tales, nothing could stop him. They
offered such marvels, and he envied Saam the pleasure
of hearing them fresh and new for the "first" time. Saam
had voiced no complaints, but every so often Mem'now
suspected his thoughts ranged elsewhere, somewhere
Mem'now could not go, and then he spun and embroidered the tale even more, trying to regain Saam's atten-

tion. If he could keep this up, he judged that they'd be ready to start on a Minor Tale very soon.

He eyed the two blue china saucers of milk nearby, already thirsty for his own. Even thinking about tale-telling could work up a powerful thirst in him. But thirst or no thirst, he had to make sure that Saam drank his down because Twylla had inserted a sleeping draught in it, had for a number of nights. Without it Saam prowled ghost-gray through the darkened infirmary, restless, unable to sleep, appearing in the oddest, most unexpected places at the most unlikely times. Mem'now had had to agree that Saam needed deep sleep to heal, both in mind and in body, and had helped with the deception, though he suspected that Saam knew about the drugging. The fact that he hadn't complained or fought it gave Mem'-now pause.

"Another tale, my friend," he told Saam, and the gray ghatt stretched, just a tantalizing hint of the restless power that his now-thin body had once concealed.

A little moaning sound leaked from Saam, his ears folded back like overblown flower petals. Uneasy, Mem'-now crossed and recrossed his front paws, refolded them until they tucked inward toward his chest. He glanced sideways just in time to catch Saam's slow wink. "Now I know how children feel about their Edifiers," he commented. "Is there a 'test' at the end of this, old friend?"

"No, you are the test, I think." Mem'now considered his statement, decided it fit. "But if you feel too tired, too pained, we can skip the tale for tonight, just drink our milk and try to sleep."

"Ah, not yet. You enjoy the tale-telling, and what pleases you gives me pleasure to give you. I will try to listen hard, my promise on that, though I may fail you."

Mem'now rocked back and forth, resetting his paws. "Yes, I enjoy the sound of my own voice, if that's what you're so politely trying to say. Still, I shall begin . . .

"It came to pass one very wet, rainy spring that a young ghatten grew bored with life in her crowded den, huddled together to avoid the showers and drizzle, the constant accompaniment to her boredom. Her sibs squabbled, someone's tail always slapping her face, paw-pokes in her ribs, constant roll-over crowding that left her precariously poised at the den's mouth, ready to be deposited into the damp outdoors in the midst of a sound and dreamless sleep. She knew her sibs' actions and reactions inside and out and knew her own as well, and they bored her mightily.

"And so our little ghatten decided to brave the downpours and dankness, to venture out into the world, for being wet, having one's fur clumped and sticky-damp could be rectified with brisk tongue application and good grooming techniques. Each day the ghatten ventured farther and farther from the nest, seeking not so much adventure as something—anything—interesting and different and new. She found it near a settlement of Newcomers, those strange beings who had journeyed from faraway skies and who presented such tantalizing potentialities, who resembled and yet did not resemble the Erakwa, and who, in their newness, offered fascinating viewing as did everything they had brought with them. She searched out a sheltered place beneath a grape arbor, umbrellaed by the broad leaves, sniffed the heady smells of quenched earth, growing green, plashing brook water, and most of all—the strange feather-fluffed, dusty aroma of the scratch-feet.

"Day in and day out she took up her position under the grape leaves, curled on the bark chips beneath them, and watched the scratch-feet. The grape arbor sprawled on one side of the creek, and the scratch-feet's abode sat on the other side, spanned by a plank upon which they paraded back and forth to reach the planted area of the Newcomers. The elder scratch-feet marched across the plank with grave dignity, high above the heads of the quacking web-feet who paddled below, but the younglings dashed back and forth, raced each other, necks low to the ground, yellow-scaled legs flashing, feathers soggy and bedraggled in the rain. She had viewed water dabblers, web-feet, in abundance in her world, shivered to the long-necked web-feet's lonesome cries earlier in the season when they migrated overhead, back to their ponds and lakes and streams, caroling the way to each other. She knew talon-feet, too, a silent, swooping menace to unwary younglings, and she recognized other varieties of scratch-feet as well, distant cousins who scratched busily at the earth for a living, but nothing quite like these. Against the rules of woodland silence they squawked and clucked incessantly, squabbled loudly amongst themselves, and at the first dawn or even earlier, the single male heralded the sun with an ear-splitting racket that threatened to make her forget her dignity and scoot to safety to escape the noise.

"Yet, singular creatures though they might be, these scratch-feet certainly didn't seem terribly practical to her ghatten mind. Big and heavy-bodied, with strong scaly legs with wicked spurs, and nearly useless wings. How she had chortled the first time she had watched them settle at dusk, flapping and flouncing awkwardly into the low branches of an apple tree, fluffing and settling for the night. Some wore pure white with fleshy red extrusions on their heads and dangling lappets beneath their beaks, others boasted an iridescent golden-red feathering, while the male paraded his finery back and forth, sashaying his green-black and red tail, rustling his gorgeous neck-feathers and fixing the world with a beady, burningly suspicious yellow eye.

" 'Here, chick, chick, chick,' the Newcomers cried and the scratch-feet came racing, crowding and shoving, pecking at each other to gain space to scoop at the scattered grain, plunging their beaks into discarded melon rinds or whatever was thrown their way. Unseemly behavior to say the least, no manners at all, she judged with ghatten superiority. She enjoyed the rumpus when a Newcomer chased a scratch-foot round and round the yard trying to capture it. As far as she could determine, the scratch-feet did not enjoy the game, for the scratch-foot always lost—if not that particular scratch-foot, another was captured in its place and trussed, taken to a chopping block and beheaded, wings beating more strongly in death than they did in life. Yet the strangest thing was that all the other scratch-feet showed only momentary agitation, quickly settling down to scratching and pecking for bugs and seeds as if murder had not been committed in their midst.

"And so, day after day, the ghatten continued her observations, for she obeyed the ghatti dictum of 'Watch, observe, and learn the truth,' and she intended to be the

very best, despite the dampness, despite the inconve-
nience of the rain dappling her fur, trickling down and
spattering her, even within the sheltering grape leaves.
She watched the younglings grow from tiny yellow or
black fluffed balls into rangy, half-feathered younglings,
most at the stage that she was herself, and saw them
become fully feathered, but still as stupid as the adults.
And each day the creek crept higher with the runoff from
the rain, encroaching farther up its banks, rising closer
and closer to the plank bridge that connected the scratch-
feet to their food place. The young scratch-feet ventured
into the shallows, splashed and scraped at the mud beneath, sent fountains of spray into the air as they chased
each other along the water's edge, battled the web-feet
for tossed corn kernels.

"Still the rains came until she swore the earth could
hold no more, and the ghatten continued her vigil—
watching, observing—until one day the rising water inun-
dated the plank connecting the two banks, leaving no dry
path from one side to another. And as the ghatten
watched, the Newcomer ventured forth from its dwelling
and cried 'Here, chick, chick, chick!' and the scratch-feet
came running, gabbling with excitement. The older, full-
grown ones stopped in consternation at the flooded
plank, milled around, clucking and squawking in agitation, flapping their wings but unable to launch themselves
to the other side and their food. But the younglings . . . !
The ghatten held her breath in shock. They dashed
straight into the water, swimming and paddling, cavorting
in the wetness, pushing the web-feet out of the way as
they scrambled up the bank and toward their dinner,
necks outstretched, feathers streaming.

"With that, the ghatten sprang up and away, back
toward her den, running as if all the dangers of the world
chased and nipped at her tail. She dashed through the
soaking, fat raindrops, splashed through puddles, dis-
lodged wet branches that slapped and grabbed at her, so
eager was she to spread the news of her discovery. Sodden, she arrived back at the den and mewled for her
ghatta mother, rowled long and loud to gather the others
of her clan.

" 'Oh, what I've seen, what I've seen!' she shouted to

one and all, then embarrassed at her appearance, groomed and sleeked herself to presentability. Soon the others gathered round, twitchy in the wetness but aching with interest. Green eyes politely downcast to the proper degree, she looked around her, amazed to be the center of attention of so very many.

" 'Well, youngling, what have you seen?' asked one of the elder of the males, her great-granther, worn and weary after many seasons of hunting and fighting, scar stripes on his face, half an ear chewed off in a desperate battle with a fox.

"The ghatten fought to control her breath, then blurted out the news. 'The scratch-feet have turned into web-feet, they're swimming! Paddling in the creek. It's clear at last! Just as a caterpillar transforms itself into a butterfly, so do the Newcomers' scratch-feet turn into web-feet! They've been transformed! Come see, come watch with me!' She made as if to run back the way she had come, eager to share her discovery with the others. What a percipient little ghatten she had been, how clever, how wise to wait and watch and learn! She swelled with pride. Let the others stay warm and dry in their dens, learning nothing new, content as they were, while she, she alone had braved the elements, made a new discovery!

"A sudden cough and warning bark made the ghatten squeak with terror, become airborne while she searched for a safe landing place and somewhere to run. 'Fox!' she yelped. 'Run! Fox!' And then she looked around her at the other unmoving ghatti, one or two trying to hide a tiny smile behind a face-polishing paw. The elder ghatt looked at her, barked again deep in his throat. 'Oh,' she sighed with relief, 'it's only you, granther.'

" 'Why, yes, so it is,' he inspected himself with care, craned his head over his shoulder, observed his tail, extended and retracted his claws. 'Only me, very definitely. I do not believe I've turned into a fox even though I just barked like one.'

" 'Well, of course you can't turn into a fox, you're a ghatt,' she replied with indignation. What did he take her for, a little silly?

"He rose stiffly, gave her a little nose-sniff and licked

her face, sleeking her eye whiskers back, removing the rain-beads. 'Learning a thing beyond your natural ways does not turn you into something else.' His breath whizzled hot but kindly in her ear, stirring the delicate hairs. 'Just as I have not turned into a fox, neither have your scratch-feet turned into web-feet, have they? They have learned something different, but they are still the same creatures. What have you learned?'

"She sighed. 'That truth is truth despite outward appearances, I guess.'

" 'Ah, good. Now, I would like to see these curious swimming scratch-feet. Are you coming?' And the elderly ghatt and the impetuous ghatten padded down the path together, ignoring the drizzle."

Still lost in the conclusion of his tale, Mem'now contemplated the middle distance, all but missed Saam's sudden rising and trotting to the doorway, ears cocked and listening. "What . . . ?" he asked, shaking himself out of his memories.

"Don't know," Saam answered over his shoulder, curiosity written over his face. "Some sort of flurry of activity, heading this way to the infirmary. Maybe you should go check, alert Twylla if it's necessary."

"Wonder what it could be?" Mem'now stretched as he rose, not as thoroughly as he would have liked, but enough to limber the kinks, and bustled out of the room.

With a tiny ghatti smile, Saam slipped back, nosed his milk saucer to the right of Mem'now's, reversing the position of drugged and undrugged milk. He hunkered down in front of "his" dish, then thought, and dipped his chin and a whisker in it, as if too eager to wait.

Mem'now returned. "You boast exceptionally sharp hearing. Child with a bee sting. They live closer to us than to the Hospice, so they brought the child here, wailing and crying. Twylla's pulling the stinger now, nothing to worry about." He came and sat in front of his milk saucer. "Thirsty, are we?"

Hanging his head, Saam contemplated his dish, not quite daring to look at Mem'now. Unfair, unjust to do this to an old friend. Still, he had to leave tonight, somehow he knew that with every fiber of his being. Nothing he could explain or justify, just that somehow he knew.

And if he told them, they would stop him. Nothing would
stop him now. Nothing! He hadn't a clue as to where he
must go or why, but he was going. The pull strained at
all his senses, faint but growing stronger and stronger so
that he could not refuse it or deny it.

He took a lap of milk, screwed up his face. "I don't
know what Twylla does to this milk sometimes . . . it has
the oddest taste, not bad, you know, but. . . ." He left
the rest of the sentence hanging, tasted the milk again,
then dipped away steadily with his tongue, hoping his
guilt wouldn't show.

"Oh, I don't know," Mem'now dipped his head to his
saucer and began to lick, less than dainty in his thirst.
"I really can't see anything different in the taste. Sometimes you perceive variations in taste because of where
the cows have been grazing, of course."

"Of course," Saam agreed as he drank, matching his
licks to Mem'now's as if engaged in a race to the bottom
of the saucer. They finished together.

Mem'now gave a tiny burp and yawn. "Drank too
fast," he reproved himself, yawned again. "A little nap
here with you before I go with Twylla on her rounds, I
think." He padded somewhat unsteadily toward Saam's
blanket, staggered when he formed a tripod balance and
tried to scratch behind his ear with his hind leg. "Share
blanket for a bit?" He yawned again.

"Please do." Saam sat, worked at removing the milk
droplets from chin, lips and whiskers. Mem'now flopped
down, drifted into a profound sleep, a ghatti snore whistling through his nose. "Farewell, old friend, sleep well."
And Saam jumped onto the windowsill, edged the shutter back as he slipped out into the night, every sense
alert to avoid discovery. "I'm coming." He said it to
himself as much as to someone unseen, unheard, reassurance for them both.

PART THREE

PART
THREE

The next seven days on the circuit proved routine, Doyce and Khar both agreed. Four towns: Barlesville, Ingelsby, Tarleton, and Taunton. Standard cases: neighbors disagreeing over a boundary line; a drunk and disorderly; a young, pregnant wife fearful that more than her husband's eye was roving. Nothing unusual, nothing inexplicable or threatening. The gossip in each town predictable standard issue, no enigmatic happenings or cryptic mysteries, nothing of the sort that might explain Oriel's death or give substance to Swan Maclough's fears. Nothing remotely related since the Seeking in Wexler, and her uncertainty chaffed her. A training ghatt had tarried long enough in Taunton to pass word that Saam had gained physical strength but with no return of his mindspeech. Then he had bounded off, full of himself, rushing back to Gaernett and his Bondmate, relieved and excited that he'd completed his messenger duties.

Swinging west out of Taunton, partially cheered by the news, Doyce squeezed her knees against Lokka and eased her into a gentle trot for a few dozen rods just to manufacture the pretense of a breeze. The late afternoon sun pounded almost as molten-heavy as it had at high noon; autumn might well be on its way, but the blazing sun hadn't accepted the season's verdict yet. Khar balanced nonchalantly on the pommel platform, then settled down to nap through the ride. Doyce felt sorry for her and Lokka, but they'd be in the shade soon, once they hit the main road running into Cyanberry. She dragged her sleeve across her sweaty forehead and finger-raked the clinging tendrils of hair off the back of her neck. Prickly heat rash if this kept up. The mere thought made her itch, want to scratch under her damp waistband. At least the inn at Cyanberry was good—not up to Myllard's standards—but a comfortable, clean place. Maybe there'd be time to get her clothes washed. And better yet, dried. One clean change left in her bags, and the thought of sliding them over a freshly scrubbed, talc-soothed body made her tingle.

More travelers headed back to Taunton than journeyed on to Cyanberry, but traffic flowed light in both directions. She tapped her heels against Lokka to speed her up and pass an oxcart loaded with green ears of unhusked corn tasseled with dried brown silk and children looking ready to spill over the sides at the least jounce. Two waved, and she returned the salute, easing Lokka to a slower pace once they had a fair lead on the rumbling cart and its dust plume. A welcoming line of shade and the smell of moisture wafted toward her, telling her nose that a stream rushed by farther ahead, parallel to the giant elms overarching the road.

She drew an idle finger around the edge of the pommel platform. Khar, eyes slitted, reached out and tagged her with a lightning paw.

"One," she 'spoke, face smug.

"Oh, you're going to be like that, are you? Keeping score?" An old and favorite game, and no matter their age, there wasn't a ghatt, ghatta, or ghatten who didn't love it. "Want to make a wager on it?"

"Fresh fish tonight?" The ghatta dissembled a look of boredom, but her tail tip waggled, giving her away. **"Three of my taps to one of yours?"**

Doyce laughed. "Generous odds, and foolish. I feel lucky, despite the heat. And if I win, you have to walk Lokka until she's cooled off. And watch the stableboy to make sure she's properly brushed and curried."

"Done! But I'll eat fish while you're supervising the stableboy."

They played on and off as they rode. Doyce set herself to wait until the ghatta appeared to be asleep and then tried side maneuvers. Or watched until a passing rider distracted Khar before she tried once more. But the ghatta anticipated each move, tagged her first again and again.

"Twelve, me. Two, you."

"And the commonfolk say ghatti can't count! Wouldn't they be surprised." Doyce felt disgruntled; she didn't really expect to win, she rarely did, but the score usually came closer to even. The ghatta was routing her. "We've still a few leagues to go, so look out!"

They continued playing, and Doyce concentrated, knowing that in theory she had the advantage: only she could attack, the ghatta could only defend. Whether it was because she was now wholly involved in it, or for some other reason, the score began to climb in Doyce's favor. The ghatta's moves came slower, each defense more perfunctory than the last. Another three tags and they'd be tied. Doyce considered that a victory.

She momentarily dangled the ends of the reins in front of Khar's nose to distract her. All's fair in love and war. Her right hand swooped from under the edge of the platform and she snapped the ghatta on a white paw. Tag! Emboldened, she essayed the same move again, sure that Khar would never expect she'd try it so very soon. A blur of white as the ghatta scored, and one flashing claw lanced the ball of her thumb.

"Ouch! Khar, no claws! No fair!" A fat drop of blood welled from the puncture, and she shoved her thumb under the ghatta's nose. "Look at that," she snapped.

A small feathering of a sigh floated inside her head before the ghatta answered. "Sorry. Didn't mean to, didn't mean to hurt. Just hot and tired."

"Well, so am I! Just because I was winning!"

"Sorry. I'll fix." And a pink tongue licked across her hand, the burrs on the tongue rasping, but not unpleasantly so, across her thumb. The ghatta examined it. "Better?" She licked again.

The images flickered in Doyce's mind, paralleling the

ones in Khar's thoughts. Colors quivering, sensations, emotions, kaleidoscoping into patterns. She laid her trembling hand on Khar's neck and traced down her spine. Her throat constricted. *"Do you remember?"*

The mindspeech hesitant, interrupted by Khar's breath, as if she were a child, falling asleep and struggling against it. **"Yes . . . no . . . I was little, little . . . tell me . . . tell me again."** A deep longing welled within the ghatta . . . not a Major Tale, not a Minor Tale, but hers, hers alone . . . and Doyce's. Just theirs.

Continuing to stroke Khar's back, Doyce began to order the events in her mind.

A delight of a late spring day, balmy, cloudless, every hue of earth and sky so vivid they might have been freshly mordanted by the dawn, the sun enlivening rather than fading them. Varon's sister Glenna pulled Doyce, protesting, to the door. "Come on, it'll do you good. Look at it, how can you resist such a day? If Lytton can agree to take time off, even suggest it, how can you refuse?" For an instant the role of matron and mother disappeared as she dance-stepped beside Doyce, who regarded her dispiritedly.

Despite her mother's and sister's pleas that she at last return home where she belonged, her refusal had been instinctive and adamant. She could not go back—and she could not go forward, not yet, so she had chosen to stay with Glenna and her husband Lytton and their children since the fire, since the deaths of Varon and Briony and Vesey. Not a moment when the enormity of her loss didn't pierce through her heart, chilling her, making a glorious spring day as drear and lifeless as the frozen gray-white winter. Even her part-time work as ledger didn't arouse her mind, make her think of other things. She penned the entries, cross-listed them, sent monthly summaries to the capital. Each mark of her nib, each stroke of ink on paper made her aware she tallied human lives, crossing them out one by one, again and again.

"Glenna, I've work to do." Hard-won patience in her tone.

"Nothing that can't wait a day. To all be out together, going somewhere new, it's a treat. The whole family together!" Glenna cajoled, sliding an arm around her waist. "It's something we've never done before, something we've never had the chance to see. Please, Doyce, think of it, seeing a ghatta with her ghatten! The children will never forget it! Neither will I!"

That was the last thing Doyce wanted to see, the memory of the Seeker and his ghatt Bondmate questioning her, querying her about the fire and the deaths. The ghatt's eyes on her . . . and she trembled despite the warmth of the day, drew comfort from the circling arm around her.

The reverse of it was that Glenna and Lytton had offered her such kindness and concern, asking nothing from her she wasn't ready to give, making space for her in their lives as well as in their house, treating her with unstinting kindness. Maybe that was part of the problem—everything they did was so discernibly conscious and conscientious. Given her grayness of spirit, her unexpected outbursts of tears and moping, she wondered how many others would have continued to try to include her in their lives. Glenna's request was so spontaneous, so generous, that an effort must be made to reciprocate, and she would.

With a small but genuine smile on her lips, Doyce turned. "Well, we'd better not keep Lytton and the children waiting, then, had we?" Glenna linked a sisterly arm with hers and, laughing, tugged Doyce toward the wagon where Lytton sat, the three children piled in the back on fresh-smelling straw.

"Doyce, welcome!" Lytton's deep voice rang out. "Up with you both." Doyce shook her head and boosted Glenna onto the high seat.

"I'll sit in the back with the children. More space for everyone."

Lytton clucked to the heavily built, gray workhorses and they plodded off, harness bells jingling a raucous tune. Glenna squirmed round in her seat, talking over her shoulder at Doyce. "Isn't it wonderful? Just think, if Lytton hadn't met that man—what's his name, Lytton?—

in town yesterday and done him that favor, we never would have had the chance."

"Dexton Phelps," Lytton answered the prompting. "I had some extra seedlings, his didn't come on so well. No need to charge for what you plan to cull." A sunburned arm came back automatically and forced the six-year-old to a sitting position in the rear of the wagon. "Down, Marek, don't stand and bounce. You'll bounce out on your head."

Marek, blessed with his father's sturdy build and his mother's dark coloring and inquisitiveness, pulled himself upright again to lean precariously over the wagon side and watch the wheels turning. Doyce snagged his waistband and dragged him back. "Do you know him well?" she asked, trying to think of something to contribute to keep the usually shy Lytton talking.

"No. Seen him around since he and the ghatta finished their service and came back to take over the farm. Knew his cousin when we were boys."

"Just think, coming back to run the farm, just like anyone else, and him having been a Seeker and everything." Glenna was plainly awed. Most people had limited contact with Seeker-Bond pairs; meetings were likely to be on a formal basis, rather than an informal one, and many lived out their lives with no need to consult the Seekers.

"They all have to retire sometime," Doyce commented. Although she had had but one experience with a Seeker, she knew more about them and their ways from her stint as a eumedico. The Seeker-Bond mental communications had fascinated the eumedicos although they had little hard data to support their hypotheses. Not until she had left the eumedicos had she understood the fascination and the urgency behind their inquiries. She had read what records existed in the eumedico archives and later transcribed the Chief Conciliator's case reports in town during her stint as a ledger before and after Varon's death. "They have lives to live for years after their Seeker days are done."

"Well, he's the only Seeker our town's ever had. That's quite an honor."

"Can't be more'n thirty-five," Lytton added, with a

surprising turn of loquaciousness. "O'course he was unusual in that he'd just started a family before he was
Chosen. Married real young—in a burning hurry, if you
catch my drift. Little boy, and a little girl on the way
when the ghatta picked him, and him scarce eighteen.
His cousin said Dexton didn't know whether to laugh or
cry when it happened, nor his wife either. But once a
ghatt's 'Printed, there's no going back and saying, 'Sorry,
I can't.' "

"What happened with his wife and children?" Glenna
tugged his arm, scandalized by the thought of a man
deserting his wife and family.

"They stayed behind at the farm, got a hired hand,
and Dexton visited them when he had leave." Lytton's
grin stretched toward his ears. "Couldn't have been too
bad, had another two children. One more than we've
managed!" His sunburned neck went redder, ears crimson, as he threw his free arm around Glenna's still slim
waist. "Though not through want of trying!"

Doyce clasped her arms around her knees, embarrassed at overhearing Glenna's and Lytton's easy intimacy, and she watched the children tumble like puppies
over each other, burrowing in the straw and popping out.
The sound of the wheels and the steady plodding of the
horses' hooves counterpointed by the bells soothed her.
She thought she spied a blue-black satin cloak by the
edge of the road, undulating in the faint breeze. Barn
swallows, she realized on closer inspection, two score or
more, daubing at a puddle of mud left from last night's
brief shower. They busily packed mud in their beaks and
then flew off to mortar their nests. One sailed over, its
white throat and buff waistcoat, its elegant V-shaped tail
knifing the air. The wheels sang, "Going to see the
ghatta, going to see the ghatta." She dozed and sank,
buoyed back to the surface by sounds of chatter from the
children, deeper adult voices in harmony.

"Come on, Doyce, we're here." Glenna's voice cut
through her pleasant drifting, silver knife slicing the
golden cord of sleep. Unfair, so long since she had slept
really well, without dreams or memories. "Doyce!" And
the children tumbled over her to run across the yard

while the youngest waited patiently, thumb in mouth, for
an adult to lift her down to touch the ground.

Hallos rang back and forth across the yard as Dexton
and his elder son, a boy in his late teens, came out of
the barn. Twins, a boy and girl of about ten, burst from
the house toward their father, while a girl of perhaps
sixteen, carnation-colored dress casting a splash of color
against the white of the house, raised her hand in a wave
and continued inside with her bucket of water.

Wiping his hands against his trousers, Dexton walked
toward the wagon, shook hands with Lytton. "So you
made it, decided to make a day of it? Chores have to
wait on a day like this. Your visit's a bona fide excuse."
He smiled all around, nodding pleasantly. A rich, well-
modulated voice, a typical Seeker-trained voice. "This is
my eldest, Piet, and the twins are Marya and Martin.
You'll meet my wife and elder girl at lunch, if you'll
stay."

Leaning against the wagon tailgate, Doyce drank in
the freshness of the scene. The twins warily circled her
nephews and niece, herding them together as if they
feared them to be recalcitrant sheep, ready to break and
run in any direction. Knowing the children, especially
Marek, she had to admit it was a distinct possibility.

"So, come into the barn and see the ghatten. Sischa is
still a little excitable and overzealous about watching
them, so move slow and easylike. Don't try to touch
them, only myself or Piet, here, can." He led the way
into the barn, sliding a wide door open on its track to
admit more light.

"How many ghatten are there?" Glenna wanted to
know.

"Two, and both seem strong and healthy. A husky
tiger male and a smaller female, but she's got the perfectly matched stripes, and wee white feet with a dab of
white on her face and more on her chest and belly."

"Only two?" Lytton sounded doubtful. "Any barn cat
can drop six without blinking. And have them in with
your shoes the next morning."

The farmer threw his head back, crowed with delight.
"Don't let Sischa hear you say that! She wanted the
wife's blanket chest in the worst way. And no matter

who I pleased, someone was bound to be upset." The boy's face darkened, scandalized at comparing a ghatta to a barn cat. "Ghattas don't breed as well or as easily as their cousins. A litter of three is rare, and to have more than one in a litter live gives luck to us all. This is Sischa's second and most likely final litter. We're blessed to have two survive this long."

"What do they seem to die of, then?" Doyce's medical training reasserted itself. Any eumedico needed some familiarity with animal illnesses, both as to how they might affect humans, and sometimes because, like it or not, eumedicos were the only trained personnel nearby to treat an animal in an emergency.

"Don't rightly know," Phelps confessed. "It's not necessarily that one seems weaker than its littermate and dies, or that some illness sweeps through the countryside. You just get up one morning and go out to check, and one's dead, and the poor mother crouched over it, mourning."

Hazed darkness inside the barn, duskiness made darker by the square of light from the door, until their eyes adjusted to the dimness. The smells of dust and hay, fresh milk, warm cattle, flats of seedlings waiting to be set out. A chicken scratched busily near the door, and Marek darted after it until one of the twins, the girl Marya, pulled him back into the group.

"There, in the stall to the right. Now go gentle and quiet-like, children, just as if it were your mama with a new baby." Dexton swung the smallest of his visitors, Tess, up into his arms for a better view.

The ghatta Sischa had molded a compact nest for herself in the straw. Stretched indolently on her side, the ghatten nuzzling at her, she raised a wary head, one front paw flexing, claws flashing in and out. She was white, with irregular patches of butterscotch yellow in mosaic clusters around her body, her eyes a spring apple green ready to swallow Doyce with their awareness. She didn't think she was being probed, her mind searched, but those eyes engulfed her, as if deeply concerned as to what sort of person stood before her. Doyce considered the question and felt herself wanting to please the wide green eyes rather than be found a disappointment in some obscure way. What a silly thought, to want to please an animal.

She squatted for a better look, amazed by the ghatta's size and look of confident power. Sischa turned her head away and swatted lazily at the male, impatient to nurse more, then licked the smaller female.

"What are their names?" Glenna whispered.

The boy, husky voiced but not quite at full manhood, answered, scornful of such ignorance. "They don't have names yet. We can't name them, they name themselves when they 'Print."

Rounded belly swaying, stiff-legged with indignation, the little male rushed at his sister, butting her with his head. His spiky tail quivered with the injustice of not being allowed to nurse any longer. The female squeaked, her small, milky gray-blue eyes wide with betrayal at the unjustified attack, but held her ground, uttered a baby growl. The male ghatten might be bigger, stronger, but in a contest of wills, the little female had no intention of yielding.

Without thinking, Doyce reached out to give the little male a placatory stroke. She froze, hand outstretched and clamped tightly in the ghatta's mouth. She'd struck quick as a snake. Sharp teeth pinched her palm, pressed deep into the thin skin on the back of her hand; if she moved, even flinched involuntarily, the teeth would puncture, score her hand on both sides as she pulled free.

"Easy, girl, easy!" Dexton cajoled, and Doyce wondered if he addressed her or Sischa. "Steady now." Her hand locked in the vise-grip, Doyce felt the ghatta pressuring her hand up and over the male toward the female. Then the pressure suddenly slackened and, limp with shock, her hand dropped on the little ghatten, the striped female. The ghatten rolled onto her back, gripped Doyce's hand with all four paws and pumped her hind legs back and forth against the base of Doyce's thumb, instinctual knowledge of disemboweling its prey. The tiny claws slithered but didn't really hurt, but the sharp puncture at the ball of her thumb by the keen, tiny new teeth did. She yelped and jerked her hand, the little ghatten clinging like a bramble so that she was forced to reach up with her other hand and cradle her from falling.

Something rustled in her mind, an unformed voice

striving for words. **"Khar?"** the voice said, then with
more delight as it tried it out again. **"Khar . . . pern."**
The last syllable on a breathy, exhaled note of contentment, almost a purr. **"Khar . . . pern, Khar'pern. Me,
Khar, me, me, me,"** the voice trilled. The ghatten licked
with dainty precision at the drop of blood on the ball
of Doyce's thumb. **"Khar'pern,"** it cooed, and the little
ghatten fell asleep in her cupped palms. Doyce marveled
at the perfection of stripes, almost a circular bull's-eye on
each side, the lighter gray-buff legs with their matched
black stripes, the tiny white feet, the smudge of white on
the muzzle setting off the pink nose, and carefully laid the
ghatten back beside its mother, somehow hating to yield
her.

"You've been Chosen, Doyce. She's 'Printed on you
and you alone. Congratulations, you'll be a Seeker
soon," Dexton said. Piet's eyes filled with tears, and Dexton hugged him roughly. "Don't take on so, lad. If it's
to be, it's to be. You can't force the Choosing." He
glanced around, apologetic. "Sorry, the boy had his heart
set on the female, but it's up to her to Choose, not the
other way round. Rare to have two Seekers in a family
anyway. Sometimes I think the ghatti want to make sure
we don't become inbred."

Unmindful that Lytton and Glenna reached out together to support her, Doyce stood shakily, rubbing dubiously at her thumb with its two neat punctures. "But I
don't want . . . I can't. . . ." she spun around, outflung
arm pointing to Piet. "Let him, then, not me! I'm not
ready to. . . ." Be myself, let alone a Seeker, she cried
inside.

"No, it's done." With a brisk, dismissive clap, Dexton
signaled the viewing's conclusion. "Now let's go to the
house for a drink. We've cause for celebration. I didn't
think them so close to 'Printing or I wouldn't have invited
visitors. Let fate take its course, and mayhap it did.
Sischa seemed to know." He shooed them toward the
house, Doyce still supported at each elbow by her sister-
in-law and Lytton.

They sat around the kitchen table, Dexton's wife pouring mugs of sparkling hard cider. "But what does it mean
to be a Seeker?" Doyce miserably clutched her mug,

beads of moisture condensing on the gray glazed sides, weeping on her fingers, her throbbing thumb.

"That you'll find out soon enough. You've got about two octs' time, I'd say, before they're fully weaned. Then you can take her and go to the capital, to Seeker Veritas Headquarters and discover for yourself. Telling won't prepare you, you have to experience it firsthand. You'd best come around each day and play with her so she won't feel abandoned and you can begin to sense what it's like."

Glenna's and Lytton's faces reflected awe and, Doyce had to acknowledge, more than a bit of relief. She knew they thought it would be good for her, a solution to her depression and brooding, a new life to be built. And their life back to normal.

"To have a Seeker in the family," Lytton's words came slow and musing. "Now that's an honor, Lady be praised."

An honor? But she couldn't help remembering the warm, sweet weight of the ghatten cupped in her palms. Khar'pern, Khar, the name she'd fashioned for herself. A name and a being and a mind that had merged with hers now and forever. Was she worthy of the distinction of being Chosen? She would do her best by Khar, but her best hadn't always been good enough before. It will be this time, and she surprised herself by the fierceness of her vow. *It must be, it has to be, for both of us.*

"And that was how we met," she concluded, tickling her finger along the ghatta's foreleg. Khar purred sleepily, breathily, thoughts flickering in and out.

"**I chose . . . I chose,**" purr, "**you.**"

Yes, you did, Doyce thought, and so far we've both survived it. The ghatta slept, and Doyce continued to pet her. Then, for no reason at all, her fingers veered to touch the gold trim on her tabard, outward proof to the world at large that she was a Seeker. It reminded her that a dress tabard still in its tissue wrappings remained in her footlocker back at Headquarters. She smiled at the thought and at the tabard's utter uselessness. Lady knew she'd never need that one with its purple and gold trim; only the Seeker General was permitted that. But the black wool was her mother's finest weaving, an extravagant gesture, the embroidered trim-work her sister's, as was the awkward, cramped backhand of the short note. "Ma says do it right this time, Doyce. We love you no matter what."—Francie.

✤

The Cyanberry Inn, its two low stories clapboarded in cedar mellowed silvery-soft by time, could never compare with Myllard's establishment, but it presented a comfortable sight all the same. Tickling the ghatta awake, Doyce gave Lokka her head to take them around to the side of the stables. Khar mumbled protest, sleepy still, logy, faintly disoriented, jumping down with a murmured complaint and faltering when she hit the ground.

"All right?" she whispered as she dismounted and led Lokka into a free stall, stripping her tack and forking down some hay. She'd send a boy out later to brush and water the horse, give her a generous measure of oats. Doyce stretched with unrestrained pleasure, relishing the shiver of cooler air caressing her moisture-laden skin, then whistled to the ghatta to follow her inside. Khar seemed slightly more awake; making an uneasy back and forth prowl of her surroundings, although her eyes still looked inward, hazed with sleep. A large male barn cat, nondescript tiger except for a mightily tattered ear, followed in the ghatta's wake, sniffing and making excited quivers of spine and tail, trying to decide where to spray.

Juggling saddlebags, sword, and staff, Doyce lost her grip on the polished staff, felt it sliding under her arm until the ironshod end struck the ground. Khar jumped, then looked around her, bemused. The barn cat startled and fled, spitting a snarl over his shoulder.

A half score of townsfolk lounged at trestle tables outside, nursing mugs of ale, talk lulling and low. Doyce smiled and nodded to acknowledge various general greetings and entered the inn, piled her baggage on the bench by the door. Not as fresh as outside, but the cool dimness overlaid with the tang of years of ale smelled pleasant and heady with promise of a cool draft. No one inside except her and the barmaid that she could see as she walked to the counter and stood waiting. Khar flopped at her feet, then got up and roamed from spot to spot, sniffing under benches, poking her nose here and there, back twitching as if working to spook herself for no good reason. What ailed the ghatta?

"Dark ale, please," she said to the young woman standing behind the counter, back to the door as she wiped the regulars' pewter mugs, each with a name engraved on the side, and hung them on their individual hooks. In the various times she'd been here, she'd never seen anyone so diligent at The Cyan. Or for that matter, as neat and clean, the young woman's dark, smooth hair caught back out of the way with a pink kerchief, white apron crisply ironed, even the ties in back showing the neat press. Perhaps The Cyan was coming up in the world, losing some of its earthy charm, itching to become as polished and prosperous as Myllard's Ale House. She'd twit Myllard about the up-and-coming competition when she got back.

"And a bowl of fresh water for the ghatta?" The lilting alto voice inquired as the young woman gave a final buff to the last tankard and hung it back amongst the ranks.

"Please. And a thank you from us both." Momentarily lost in admiration of the dull luster of the tankards, Doyce jerked to attention. "Claire, is that you?"

"Yes, as long as you don't mention this to Papa." The young woman spun around with a welcoming grin. At the sound of her voice, Khar trotted over and stretched her forelegs up to the girl's waist, craning her neck as she waited for her ears to be scratched. The girl, for it was truly a girl of perhaps eighteen, rubbed behind the ghatta's ears with industrious affection, fingers digging for the right joy spot.

"But I thought . . ." Flustered, Doyce halted, uncertain how to continue diplomatically.

The girl arched dark eyebrows with a look of comic woe. "That I'd run off with that no-account peddler and would come to no good?" Her laugh was rueful as she tucked a few errant hairs back beneath the kerchief, resettled it so that her widow's peak came clear. "Well, yes and no and maybe to that. Has Papa relented yet?"

Doyce shook her head, sorry that her response couldn't be more positive. "Not precisely. Willing to take you back with proper humility shown, of course. And abject apologies."

Myllard's daughter to the core, as stubborn and determined as he. Her determination had captured the heart of a handsome young peddler with barely enough stock to peddle, but filled with the same determination as his newfound love. A wanderer and an absolute risk in Myllard's point of view. A chance to see new vistas and an opportunity to create a new future with the man she adored from his daughter's point of view. And when Myllard had refused them permission to wed, she had run off with her peddler love. Never did an ale house or inn lack for ladders.

Doyce glanced at her critically, compressed her lips to quell an exclamation of dismay. Claire was glowingly pregnant, early days yet, but definitely pregnant. "And the yes and the no and the maybe?" she ventured, trying to sound offhand, praying she hadn't been abandoned by her peddler.

"Well, I'm pregnant." Defiantly, Claire laid her hands across her still flat belly.

"Yes, I know."

"Oh, Khar, you told her!" She bent and rubbed under Khar's chin, momentary bravado sliding into abashment. "No secrets while you're around."

"Khar didn't tell. It's obvious to another woman. Your complexion, the look in your eyes, the slight shift in your walk. Don't blame the ghatta. But what are you going to do about it?"

Sudden comprehension flooded Claire's face and she giggled, velvet-brown eyes filled with merriment. "Oh, Khar didn't tell you anything. I'm sorry. No wonder you looked so upset and disapproving. Everything's right, honest as rain. Wyatt and I are married, true, with papers to prove it. And still as in love as ever, if not more. If we can raise the money, Wyatt can buy into his uncle's store and settle down. But we have to have the money soon. That's why Wyatt's out traveling, peddling as much as he can as fast as possible. We took what little we had and used it to stock up so he'd have the very best to sell.

"I knew Eli Zenger needed help at The Cyan, so who better than me? Oh, he crowed a bit when he found out who I was; I felt I had to tell him to get the job and a little more in wages than Eli planned." She shook her head at the memory. "He still likes to bring it up, rub it in, but he's not bad to work for, not really."

Doyce sipped at her ale. "And the baby's due . . . ?"

Claire raised an admonitory finger to her lips, glancing around to make sure everyone remained outside. "That's something Eli doesn't know, nor Wyatt either. Otherwise they'd both be stubborn and never let me be here. No matter that my mother worked just like this while she carried me."

"And look what came of it. Trained as an innkeep from the womb." Doyce laughed. "Still, let me give you a 'script for something strengthening and the coins to pay for it."

Claire protested, tried to back away from the counter, but Doyce caught her arm, held her in place. "Call it a wedding gift from Khar and me since we had no chance to do otherwise." She closed Claire's hand around three silver pieces.

"On those grounds, fine . . . as long as I don't have to name my firstborn after you or the ghatta." Something creaked and rumbled like dull thunder beneath their feet. She spun away and grabbed her cloth, darted toward the kitchen. "Eli! And I've work to do."

Debating whether to take her ale and sit outside or lounge in the soft dimness of the taproom, Doyce leaned her elbows along the polished brass rail, fingers laced around her mug. Khar wandered to the open door, back again, and halfway back the other way before flopping on her side, tail twitching and snapping.

"All right?"

"Mmph. Just can't seem to settle . . ."

"Go out, then, wander a bit, stretch your legs. That way mayhap we'll both have a good night's rest."

Puffing, swearing under his breath, Eli Zenger, The Cyan Inn's owner, rolled a new barrel of ale up the ramp from the cellar, maneuvered it through the trapdoor and propelled it in the direction of the bar, more hindered than helped by an elderly, seedy-looking man tottering on pipestem legs and looking as if he'd already tapped the barrel. He blundered back and forth, in and out of the barrel's path, stumbled, nudged the keg off-course, misdirected it again as he tried to right it. "Just stay

clear, Cal. Straighten up behind me, if you must," Eli
panted, no time to look to see if Claire were working.
The old man nodded, made elaborate pretense of rearranging the stools and benches pushed aside during the
keg's progress and watched Eli set the spigot with a concerned eye.

"Not too hard, now," he admonished, pushing close,
practically under Eli's arm. " 'Twon't do to rile it anymore. 'Tis all shook and churned after its journey. Let
it settle a bit." He licked his lips, swallowed hard.

Eli eased the spigot home and cautiously turned the
handle while he held a mug under the spout. Foam, white
and creamy, gushed forth along with a thin trickle of ale.
He clamped the spigot shut and took a sip. "It'll be fine
after it rests."

The old man brightened. "Aye? Then let me have a
taste, just a drop, after all that work." The raw, anxious
look in his eyes, his trembling mouth and shaking hands
revealed that it had been far longer than the old man
liked between drinks. Most every ale house or tavern or
inn had at least one of his ilk, a sad old sot with no
money or family but a desperately long thirst.

"You've not earned your keep yet for today, Cal," Eli
responded patiently. "You know the rules. If you want
alms, go beg, and not in my inn. If you want work, stay
here and do it without complaint. I don't run a charity."
He looked harried but pleasant, firm but fair, and the
lines etched around his eyes came from laughter and unstinting observation. He'd watch every copper because
he had to, not out of miserliness. And even when he
didn't have to watch, he still would out of habit. That
was what made a good innkeep.

"So what'm I to do, heh?" the old man whined, running twisted, large-knuckled hands through stringy white
hair. The result still resembled an abandoned bird's nest.
"Near wore out from getting that keg up here in one
piece, but if there's more, I'll try—though I don't know
where I'll get the strength."

"Aye, Cal, supervising's hard work." Eli raised the
trap on the counter and stepped behind. "Claire, you
need any help in the kitchen? Cal's willing," he called
toward the back.

Claire's response came too quickly, as if she'd been listening. "No, not yet. Let him bide for a bit, Eli, I'll need help later when the evening crowd comes in."

Eli raised sandy eyebrows at Doyce, making a pretense of noticing her for the first time, though he'd been well aware of her since he'd come up from the cellar. He'd spotted the Seeker tabard right away, his eyes narrowing, and had looked to check on the ghatta and what she was up to. Doyce was relieved Khar had finally gone outside to indulge her restlessness.

"Another ale, miss?"

"Yes, I'd appreciate it." She leaned across the bar and spoke in an undertone. "Any objection if I offer your old man an ale? And one for yourself, of course."

He considered, looking her over, taking his time as he rolled his cuffs down over well-muscled, freckled forearms. A small, compact man with a slender, foxlike face, broad across the brow but pointing toward the cleft chin, he handled himself well, aware of each move as if he'd boxed in his youth. The flattening at the bridge of his nose, the scar tissue around his eyes suggested he had. "For myself, yes, and thank you. And since I've never known old Cal to refuse a free drink, I'll draw three for us, but go ahead and ask him."

Doyce moved to where the old man sat, back against the wall, eyes half shut, head nodding. Not a healthy man, she judged as she put her hand on his shoulder to rouse him. Not just age, but hard times and poor eating habits, the lack of care a result of drink, from the smell that rose off him, a compound of stale beeriness, woodsmoke, perspiration and, she sniffed again to be sure, the sharp, pungent smell of eumedico disinfectant. Strange, she'd have bet her life the old man would never willingly venture within twenty leagues of a Hospice.

She shook his shoulder, faintly repelled by the greasy stiffness of the canvas shirt beneath her fingers. "Sir, may I offer you a drink?"

"What . . . ? Oh, miss, thankee, miss," he made a chortling, raspy sound in his throat, turned his head to spit but thought better of it. Rubbing at rheumy eyes with grimed knuckles, he leaned his head against the wall, focused on her Seeker tabard, and his face turned expressionless. "Oh, er, never mind, never mind. Don't really need it, see? Got work to do, got work, don't you know?" And pushed by her at a rapid hobble, throwing an angry, spiteful look over his shoulder as he went out the door.

Eli finished topping the second mug and pushed it toward her along the counter, setting the empty third mug back on the shelf. "Now that's a first, something I never thought I'd live to see the day," he admitted, head tilted a bit to one side, waiting to see how she'd react. "My apologies," and raised his own full mug to hers. "To the Lady's health and to ours."

Doyce claimed her own mug. "It happens sometimes, those that don't like Seekers. The ghatti remind them of what they try to hide from themselves."

"But few of Cal's ilk who would refuse a free drink to make their point." He saluted her again with his mug and sipped. "Well, Cal was right about one thing: there's work to do. I should check the kitchen. Will you be staying for dinner and the night?"

"Yes, if you've the room. And someone to see to my mare, other than Cal," she added, still stung by the man's refusal. She hoped Khar wasn't wandering wherever the old man had gone. Although the ghatta would instinctively sense his dislike, she didn't want their paths to cross. No sense to give provocation without reason or need. She cleared her mind to try to sense Khar, but felt nothing, the ghatta busy about her own affairs.

"My pleasure. Any special requests for dinner tonight? We've some nice fresh fish, plump for grilling."

"You're read my ghatta's mind, then. And mine as well." And they laughed.

♣

Washed, clothed in her last clean outfit, an old yellow cotton tunic, thin and soft from many washings and wearings, and equally old gray corded pantaloons, Doyce relaxed at a table at the far end of the room, away from the bar, finishing her dinner. Khar still rambled, and Doyce resisted a twinge of worry, wishing the ghatta back with her. Still, Khar enjoyed prowling around in the early night hours, so she tried to pay it no heed.

Dark grill-marks scored the tender, translucent flesh of the plump fish. Picture-perfect vegetables: summer squash, tomatoes, giant red slices layered over with circlets of raw sweet onion big enough to adorn her wrist. A small saucer held a piece of cooling fish for Khar, though she'd begrudged the sharing just a tad. Claire sat across the table from her, stealing a few moments from her tasks, eyes darting to keep track of whose mug would need refilling when she set to work again.

Smug satisfaction on her face. "Your clothes should dry by morning. I had them hung outside, but we'll bring them in by the fire before it gets damp. There'll be time to press them first thing in the morning."

"Perfect! It's the one thing I can't stand about doing circuits. Not having all the clean clothes I'd like, or the means to wash them properly. Too many years as a eumedico preaching cleanliness—and practicing it, too."

Claire's laughter bubbled, she shook an admonishing finger at Doyce. "Too many years around finicky, fastidious ghatti. That might have something to do with it as well. Papa always said your room was neater when you left than when you came, and then Mother'd get embarrassed. If she knew you were coming, she'd spend half the day dusting and polishing in nooks and crannies you never thought a room could have!"

Doyce had the grace to look flustered, and she was. "I didn't know I was that bad. I'm sorry . . . all that extra work I've caused your mother. Frankly, I'm always so glad to be there and not on circuit that I never realized."

"She relishes every moment of it, loves having you and Khar and the other Seeker-Bond pairs there. And Papa's theory is that no one would dare steal or cheat with all of you there." Claire patted her arm reassuringly. "Mother's especially fond of you and Khar. You've always reminded her of her younger sister. You're family as far as she's concerned, as far as we're all concerned."

Touched, knowing she could never free the words caught in her throat to thank Claire for such unexpected, unmerited affection, Doyce tried to refashion the subject elsewhere. "You and your parents have always liked the ghatti. Strange, though, how some seem to take an instant dislike to them. Old wives' tales of an absentminded scientist and an experimental lab cat who escaped, or someone's bad experience—apocryphal, at best—at a Seeking. Mainly, a senseless dislike of gentle beasts."

"You mean like old Cal?" Claire's look was shrewd. "Eli told me what happened. Probably didn't tell you why. Don't think he knows, come to think on it. He hasn't owned The Cyan all that long. Bought it with his ring winnings, banked them up, took the blows and then got out while he still had a brain, as he describes it. He's got too much invested in this to waste much talk on Cal."

Doyce stirred sugar into her cha. "While you aren't too busy, despite all the work you have to do?"

"You can work and listen at the same time. I know what it means to have someone listen to you and care about you. You used to for me, every time you came. Everyone needs that, so you have to make the time."

Twenty years younger and so much wiser than she. So often the listening seemed a conscious effort, a burden of caring and involvement, not the easy spontaneity of the girl/woman across from her.

"You may have heard of Cal? His full name is Calvert Tipton. Perhaps from the ledgers or your Seeker records?" When Doyce indicated no, she continued. "He used to be a Seeker."

Surprised, Doyce's head jerked up, hazel eyes narrowing in consternation. "How long ago?"

"He must have retired long before I was born, oh, nearly three Eighths ago." Claire picked up Doyce's fork at its balance point and rocked it back and forth, tines touching the plate, the handle tapping the table. "At least, but sometimes it's hard to judge from his ramblings. At any rate, retirement didn't sit well with him. He didn't want to stay at Headquarters and help with the training, some sort of tiff or feud, and he couldn't seem to settle down to anything worthwhile. A little of this, a little of that, and he'd be dissatisfied. Said that even his ghatt, Aroo, didn't give him as much comfort anymore." She tinged the fork against the edge of the plate, let it find its balance point again.

"He'd wander from one town to another and somehow pick up bits of gossip or rumor. He said 'somehow,' but I think the ghatt transmitted the information." She spared a glance at Doyce to see how she reacted, but Doyce kept her face closed, a neutral expression of polite interest. "Well, it's possible," Claire insisted. "Isn't it? And I don't think the ghatt went searching people's minds for anything terrible or bad, but he transmitted just enough embarrassing things so that Cal would have a sort of hold on them. Not exactly blackmail, but enough for him to get an ale or two, some food, whatever he needed to keep body and soul together."

"It is, of course, against all the rules and strictures." Doyce's voice remained level, but angry thoughts swirled. To degrade a ghatt to that state, and the ghatt might well have done it, out of love and devotion, protesting, yet trapped in the need to protect and share. "And you're surmising things from an old man's ramblings that may or may not be true."

Guiltily, Claire nodded and continued to play with the fork: up and down, right and wrong, good and bad, a simulacrum of the scales of justice.

"But the ghatt Aroo finally died and Cal had no one left, no family and no friends, and certainly no way now to barter for his sustenance. He offered himself to the eumedicos then, said they could do what they would with him. Is that true, Doyce? Would they do things to him? And what?" Brow furrowed, entreaty clear in her large brown eyes, Claire paused, expecting, craving reassurance.

Doyce took her time framing an answer. Distasteful memories rose, twisting at her stomach in mockery of the good supper she'd consumed. What to say, how to phrase it to an outsider, and how much to say? With a grimace she snatched the fork from Claire's fingers, still unwittingly playing with it. "Stop toying with it. Look, consider it as a balance, like the fork. Something bad or unpleasant on one side weighed against a greater good for more people. How do you measure it? What justifies it?"

How had she justified it? "At times we would discover something new—a new theory, a new approach, a new 'script that might alleviate someone's suffering, cure a disease, prevent a death. Then we . . ." she corrected herself with savage emphasis, "*they* had to test it.

"Did they have the right to try it on innocent people under the guise of helping them when they might be hurting them even more? Sometimes we, *they,* did, but not without asking permission to experiment, saying that it might work or that it might make things worse. The patient made the decision as to whether to try it. But sometimes more tests, more experiments were needed beyond that, and they would ask for volunteers. Mostly from amongst the eumedicos." She unconsciously rubbed a scar on the inner side of her left elbow, souvenir of one such trial. "And sometimes they found volunteers from outside. There's always someone poor, hungry, with no hope left except for what the eumedicos offered. And sometimes, if it were really dangerous, there was a handsome reward—if they survived to collect it. That's probably what Cal meant."

"It doesn't seem fair!"

"No, it isn't," she shot back, embittered by the memories and irked at Claire's innocence. "But neither is it painted in black and white, no life is, just shades of gray." So many hues she couldn't begin to count them sometimes, while Claire, still young and untried, saw things in their polarities. "Does Cal still go to the eumedicos?" She tried to keep the question nonchalant.

Claire fought back tears, head bowed low, and whispered, "Yes, I think so. Sometimes. He comes back and that's when he rambles on about the old days, about himself and Aroo and the things they did, the cases the ghatt searched out, the way their minds melded." She pushed her bench away from the table, face drawn. "I . . . I've got to get back to work. I've tarried too long."

Swinging her feet up on the vacated bench, Doyce watched Claire weaving her way back and forth, carrying pitchers of ale to replenish empty mugs, brandy for the prosperous merchants traveling through, wine for some of the courting couples. Each time she passed by she refused to meet Doyce's eyes, her head held high, cheeks burning. It would pass, Claire would be herself by morning, she hoped, but the young never found it easy to learn of something cruel, an injustice so far removed from their range of experience that they could not imagine how others could condone it.

Lady knew, she had hated those experiments for all of her years as a eumedico. No pleasure in causing further pain, but she had to concede the good that came of it. The dissection of a body suddenly dead from some unknown or poorly understood disease, that she had coped with marginally better—the carefully labeled samples, the tissue cultures, the slides stained for viewing. The dissection of . . . ? She swung her feet down hard, back rigid with certainty. *That*, that was what they, what someone had done with Oriel's brain, with the brain of the poor cat Ballen! Someone was dissecting their brains, but for what? Yet the cold certitude of her rightness seeped into her flesh, chilling as formaldehyde. The smell Saam had mentioned? Formaldehyde? Ether? Trembling, she took a sip of ale without tasting its flatness, and tried to think.

Blast that ghatta, where was she? What would Khar make of the story if she'd been there at her feet to hear it? Let Khar mull it over, and then tomorrow they should consider sending a message back to Swan Maclough and the others. She never had sent word back about the cat, just as well since she hadn't had all the pieces in place at that point. Was it worth having Khar 'speak M'wa and Bard, and have them relay to Byrta and P'wa, and back through the others on the circuit? How long would it take to transmit if all the ghatti were in range? She began to work backward on her fingers. Alternately, she could send Khar ahead to the Way House in Roxborough to pass a written message to one of the young ghatti in field training to carry, if she felt uncomfortable about broadcasting her thoughts to too many. Still, what was the precise message to be?

Darts thunked against the red and yellow cork target as two courting couples challenged each other in a game. If they could toss darts as well as they laughed and loved, they might even hit the target instead of the pine backboard. Only their love scored a bull's-eye. She flinched as one dart took wobbling, erratic flight and narrowly missed piercing a bystander's ear. He jumped back with a yelp and jostled Claire, balancing a tray jammed with full ale mugs. She swayed and dipped, graceful on her feet in a complex dance and kept the mugs upright, contents barely sloshing.

Take it as an omen, she counseled herself. Balance, rationality, in the midst of erratic thoughts. But still, why would an ex-Seeker voluntarily offer himself to the eumedicos for experimentation? No love lost between eumedicos and Seekers; grudging respect at best. But all Seekers knew that the eumedicos did not have even a shadow of what they were blessed with—the ability to read minds, even through an intermediary ghatt. Did Cal have a place in the puzzle? Did the eumedicos? She wondered if Swan had any recollection of Calvert Tipton.

Calmer but no less confused, Doyce stretched, ready for more thought, if not for bed. She collected the saucer of fish and slid from behind the table, headed for the stairs and her room. Let the ghatta return soon and they could discuss their options and sleep on it. Then, most likely, send a message through M'wa and P'wa. Mindlinked together, they could reach Swan and Koom directly. Some interesting conjectures, unexplained coincidences, but nothing that fully explained what had happened to Oriel and Saam. Not yet. She longed for the others: Bard, Byrta, Rolf, Parcellus, Sarrett. I pray thee well, by the Lady. And the ghatti, too, especially you, poor, dear Saam. She raised her hand in good-night salute to Eli behind the counter, looked in Claire's direction but received no answering farewell. She turned for the stairs. But the cold malice of someone's glance hit her square between the shoulder blades, made her stumble at the first step. She twisted her arm back, momentarily expecting to find a dart dangling there, the pain so piercing. But the ominous presence had fled, leaving her convinced she imagined things. No one at The Cyan Inn had reason to hate her or hurt her.

The smell of sulfur and the bright flare as she struck the lucifer and touched the woven wick of the oil lamp made Doyce shiver at the isolation, alone in the tiny island of light. Not good to be vulnerable in the dark, not after her last sensation of fear downstairs moments ago. She fiddled with the wick and forgot to shake out the lucifer, burning her fingers. Blast! Hot! Sucking finger and thumb, she fitted the chimney onto the lamp base and looked guardedly around the room, whitewashed walls, dark beams, a narrow bed with a dark blue and maroon woven coverlet, and an ewer and pitcher on the stand by the bed. A darker shadow loomed amongst the shadows at the foot of the bed, she drew her arm back, ready to fling the lamp in its direction, then cursed herself for overreacting.

"Khar, how did you get in?" The ghatta's sides heaved, and when Doyce held the lamp near, she could see that her eyes were glazed, the nictating membrane partially cloaking them. "Khar, what's wrong? You gave me such a start! Why didn't you 'speak me?"

"**Window,**" she stated with an effort.

With the lamp nearer and steady now, she gave an inward groan, realizing the signs. How could she have missed it, she should have known far earlier. Even the tomcat in the stable had sensed it. "Khar, you're in heat, aren't you? And about twenty days early, too. Why didn't you say something when you felt it coming on? We could have stopped it then and you wouldn't be like this."

"**Didn't think . . . it was. Too early. Just didn't . . . listen to my body,**" the ghatta panted. "**Close window so I can't get out.**"

Doyce tugged at the leather wallet bag attached to her belt, snapped the side pocket open. She had the dosage wrapped in a paper spill, simply brew the decoction and get Khar to swallow it and she'd calm down. It would just be that much harder and longer since they hadn't caught it in time. Hurriedly, she shuttered the window.

Ghattas came into heat two or three times a year, but long ago the Seekers, in conjunction with the eumedicos, had devised a 'script that rendered them infertile. A contraceptive that kept them from feeling the raw hunger and desire of recklessly pursuing a mate regardless of the emotional and physical turmoil that rendered them useless during this time as a partner for their Bondmates. The ghattas took the 'script voluntarily, so concerned

with their Bond and their calling that they wished it to
come first. Only when they desired a litter to continue
their species did they refuse. Ghatts, too, took a related
'script that rendered them impotent, that relieved them
of the burden of prowling for willing females, doing battle amongst themselves to win a mate. A few of the
ghatts became addicted to their 'script, wheedling more
than necessary; they were easy to identify from their
overly placid dispositions and plump, cushiony looks,
their sedate walk.

Pouring water from the pitcher into a tiny glass beaker,
Doyce shook the gray powder into it, cursing as it floated
without dissolving. She balanced the beaker atop the
lamp, precarious on the petaled top of the chimney, and
waited for the water to boil. Could they even travel tomorrow with Khar like this? And that let out sending
a message back through the route to Bard until Khar
recovered. Rummaging around, she found the glass pipette in its slim mahogany case, and used the rod to stir
the mixture. Boil, she commanded it, and at last it
obliged, or nearly so. Further pacing impatience as she
waited for it to cool. Then, finger over the top of the
pipette she controlled the column of liquid in the tube
and bent over Khar, slipping it into the corner of her
clenched mouth as she lifted her finger to release the
liquid. It would take longer this way to ensure Khar swallowed it all, but she didn't trust the ghatta to be able to
sit up and lap from her bowl, she was shaking too hard.

At last she droppered all the fluid into the ghatta and
felt her shuddering abate, although the terrible, feverish
burning remained, consuming her body with an inner
fire, burning with the physical longing for what she had
chosen to miss.

So much for her idea of a bed tonight, she decided as
she shook out her bedroll on the floor. Best to let Khar
sleep undisturbed. She stripped off her tunic and pantaloons and hung them on the peg beside her staff and
sword and prepared to settle down.

"No. By me, please." Khar's mindspeech sounded
weak but steady.

*"But you're so hot and tired, love, and it's warm out
tonight."*

The ghatta persisted, **"Please. Need to touch, I need you close."**

Doyce eased under the sheet and reached to turn down the lamp. Khar's feet skimmed her back, each paw pad hot and harsh and dry. With a deep sigh of contentment, the ghatta fell instantly into a drugged sleep. It took Doyce much longer. Folding an arm beneath her head, she prepared to wait for sleep or the morning, unsure of which might come first, but willing to wait and see. In truth, what else was there to do?

The light rapping on the door melded with her dream, a part of it, no doubt, as was the voice calling, "Doyce, Doyce," with a hint of exasperation. She pulled the pillow over her head, groaned. The same tone Oriel used when he tried to rouse her to the fresh wonder of a new day.

"Don't care," she muttered, muffled by the pillow. "Never met a sunrise I've liked. Let it wait."

"Doyce, come on! Wake up, the tray's heavy."

Untangling herself from the covers, Doyce sighed and shook her head. So, she *had* slept. Funny that she should wake up like that in the middle of a dream, just as the dream voices called to her, so coaxing and cajoling. What had they planned to tell her? What would have happened next? The old terrors she knew inside and out; this new one with Oriel at its center had yet to run its course. Down at the foot of the bed Khar lay, sleepy golden eyes half-lidded but watching. She reached down to caress the ghatta and felt her cooler against her palm, her muscles relaxed, no longer tense and quivering as she'd been last night.

"Better?" She rubbed the ghatta's ears and tickled along the chin line.

"Much. Still weak but better. Almost fine." She rested her head in Doyce's cupped hand, luxuriating in the touch of the searching fingers scraping along her chin. **"Now get door?"**

The voice came again and the door handle rattled.

"Doyce, I swear I'll eat every bit of it myself if you don't get up." The clatter of crockery shifting on a tray.

"Claire? Is that you? Sorry, sorry, I was deep asleep. Hold on, I'll be right there." Doyce tumbled out of bed, debated halfheartedly about pulling her clothes on, but decided shift and shorts sufficed 'til she'd washed and eaten. Thumbing back the iron latch, she opened the door a crack to find Claire balancing a breakfast tray and tapping her foot in annoyance, just as her father Myllard so often did. Steam from the tray curled airy tendrils around her heart-shaped face, and the morning sun from the stairwell window flooded in behind her, highlighting the few long strands of hair escaping from her kerchief, warming the yellow primrose design on collar and cuffs, turning the edge of her crisp white apron transparently gauzy where it extended beyond the outline of her body.

"Good morrow. Lady bless your waking," she recited, face bent downward toward the tray, still not looking Doyce in the eye.

"And Lady bless you, too, Claire," Doyce responded, pulling the door wide to shield her half-naked form and waving the girl inside. "Did I detect a note of irony in your voice, though?"

Claire hesitated, then continued to arrange the tray's contents on the table. A steaming bowl of porridge, a plate of fresh biscuits, butter, ruby jelly, cheese, a small pitcher of milk, and a double-handled cha pot with two matching mugs. Finally, a small, empty bowl. "What do you mean?" Still glancing downward, she concentrated on shifting things a fraction this way, a fraction that way. "About last night, I'm . . ." Misery flooded her voice.

Doyce realized that what she had taken to be banter was working on two different levels: her straightforward one about her notorious problems with waking, something that Claire and her family had chided her about time and again, and Claire's fixation that everything said related in some way to their conversation—and her embarrassment—from the night before. "You know I'm a bear straight out of bed," she mock-grumbled and gave the girl a quick hug. Oh, the power of the young to think that everything said and done pertained directly to them. The focus would change with years and experience.

"Now, what's this about breakfast? Are you joining me? Do you have time? And then we'll discuss last night if you want, though it's not necessary."

A quick, relieved smile danced across Claire's face. "I've time. Eli's given me a half-haliday until mid-afternoon." She plumped down on the unmade bed and stroked Khar. "As to breakfast, more cha, yes. But nothing else. You know a good cook always samples as she goes along." She motioned Doyce to the stool beside the crowded little table. "Now eat."

"A great cook doesn't have to sample everything she cooks because she knows it's perfect. Look at your mother." Doyce poured cha and handed a mug over to Claire, poured one for herself. "If she sampled each and every one of her creations, she'd be a more than ample woman. Myllard would have to widen doors, reinforce floors." She broke open a biscuit and buttered it, contemplated the ruby jelly and decided on self-control—wait to try it on the next biscuit.

Getting into the spirit of the morning, Claire grinned and her eyes at last met Doyce's. "Ah, but you said a 'great' cook and I said a 'good' cook. If I reach Mother's greatness, I won't have to sample. Besides, I'll have Wyatt to do it—just as Papa does for Mother! Until then. . . ."

Doyce bit into her biscuit. "Well, if this is any indication, you're well on your way there." Pouring milk over the porridge, she began to eat in earnest. "A half-haliday, bless Eli. What are you going to do with it?"

"Visit with you until you're ready to leave. Then go to the open-air market and wander around a bit. Nothing much to buy and little enough to buy it with, since I'm saving every copper, but perhaps some fingering yarn for knitting." She turned shell pink and stared down at her yet trim stomach, one hand cupped there protectively.

"Perhaps we'll join you, if we may? Khar's still a bit unsteady and weak. Unexpectedly came into heat last night and we didn't catch it as early as we should have. We're not expected in Kissena until tomorrow afternoon, so I thought we'd travel in two stages, part late this afternoon, the rest on the morrow."

"Oh, poor Khar, poor baby," Claire crooned and lavished more affection on the ghatta. Khar, with a keen sense of the dramatic, flopped from her sitting position into a limp mass on the bed, striving to look pitiful. "Oh, I nearly forgot. I brought a bowl for you so you could have some milk, Khar. That is, if your selfish Bondmate hasn't used it all on her porridge!"

Chastened, Doyce surrendered the bowl and the half-full pitcher of milk to Claire, who poured it out. "Don't feed her on the bed, Claire, You both know better."

"But she's so weak!"

"She's a little weak, but fast approaching the pink of health. Don't spoil her, Claire, or she'll be even more insufferable than she is." With wounded dignity, Khar held her head high and jumped off the bed. With a critical eye Doyce appraised her movements, no major leg tremors, merely caution. "She's mending fine, a little more rest and she'll be perfect."

"About last night," Claire sat down again, turning her cha mug pensively in her hands, then abruptly thrust it out for more cha. "I overreacted. It just seemed so horrible and unfair to use an old man like that."

Doyce said nothing. After a moment, Claire continued. "I don't like that it has to be that way, that there are the poor and the hopeless and the helpless. That some sink so low that what the eumedicos offer seems a salvation of sorts. And what the eumedicos do, I suppose it's necessary. Isn't there a phrase, 'No progress without pain'? If I were ill, or Wyatt, or Mother or Papa, I'd want to know that the eumedicos had tried every possible way to help. It's just that it's so. . . ." She shrugged, still bewildered by the conflicting thoughts, trying to reconcile them yet leave her own self-respect intact.

"I know. The greater good, the lesser evil, which is which? I know that any time I helped with the experiments, or was experimented on myself," Claire's eyes went wide with shock and she pressed a hand to her mouth, "that the subject was treated with respect and honor. They never try to cause pain, though they sometimes do. And remember, most of us go on living our lives, never bothering to volunteer, nor ever thinking it might be necessary, just leaving the task to someone else." Doyce buttered another biscuit, thick-spread the

ruby jelly—cherry, she judged—on it and wished she
hadn't. The talk reminded her of last night and her jarring revelation about what had been done to Oriel; her
stomach spasmed and she put down the biscuit.

"Still, I'm sorry. I wouldn't have hurt you, been rude
for anything. I haven't upset you again, have I? You look
so distant all of a sudden."

She pushed the thoughts aside for later. "No, I'm fine
and you're forgiven. Now, shall I get washed and dressed
so we can head for market?"

Claire bounced up, resilient and relieved. "Fine. I'll
check to see if your clothes are ready so you can get
them packed." She headed toward the door, then stopped.
"Oh. If you aren't going to eat that biscuit with the jelly,
perhaps I will after all. I just seem so hungry these days."
She snatched it up at Doyce's nod and, munching, went
out. "I'll meet you downstairs in a little while."

"Going to be a big, husky baby boy." Khar checked
her milk bowl to see if any more had materialized. She
nosed under it and edged it along the floor toward Doyce
and glanced an appeal, tongue-tip protruding, petal-pink
as her nose.

"That's all, I'm afraid. And you never got your fish
last night, poor thing." Doyce poured the last drops of
milk into the bowl. The dried remains of the fish sat in
their saucer by the lamp. "How do you know it will be
a boy?"

"Just do. Can tell sometimes." Her face radiated smug
self-satisfaction, eyes half-closed.

Doyce paused storklike, one leg in her pantaloons.
"And will it look like Myllard?" she teased.

Khar considered the question with grave deliberation.
"A little. Plump and bald and pink."

"You are hopeless! A charlatan amongst ghatti!"

Although double-burdened—Doyce, Claire, and Khar—
Lokka managed a spritely pace, just as excited as everyone else by the color and bustle around her as they approached the Market Square. She arched her neck and
essayed a prance until Doyce clucked disapproval, bring-

ing her under check to avoid the dashing, shouting children; stall owners hectoring each other as they arranged their wares, stepping back into the street, oblivious to riders and pedestrians alike while they admired their displays and disparaged a neighbor's, then stepped back and made a careful adjustment or undetected misadjustment, if at all possible. Potential buyers, Claire and herself among them, already poured down the narrow streets toward the square. Some had journeyed far, dressed in their best clothes or their one workaday outfit, lightly powdered with travel dust; others only from the opposite side of town; but all sounded happy, expectant, and eager to buy, for the market convened but once an octant. Claire craned this way and that to peer beyond Doyce's shoulders, one hand knotted so tightly in Doyce's waist sash that she wondered if she would be bisected. Even Khar sat at attention, captivated by the bustling activity and sense of happy urgency. The jingling coins started their siren song of "buy, buy!"

"Look, over there!" Claire waved enthusiastically until a large figure in a billowing wheat-colored robe cinched at the waist with a length of hemp stopped his sweeping of the steps of the local Bethel and waved back. "It's Shepherd Harrap. I'll ask if we can tie Lokka by the temple steps. I'm sure he won't mind."

Doyce concentrated on navigating Lokka through the crowds and to the steps of the Bethel, the Lady Temple where almost all in the area came every Achtdag to honor and pray to the Lady, to recite the mysteries of the Eightfold Trusts, and feel themselves a part of the larger community of heaven and earth combined. Doyce seldom attended now, but the unexpected twinge told her she missed it, the sense of peace and quietude, the implicit faith in the rightness of whatever happened in the sight of the Lady. Yet how could the Lady have countenanced Oriel's death? Or the fiery demise of Varon, Briony, and Vesey? Find the rightness in that and she'd consider believing once more.

Although small compared to many others she'd seen, Doyce admired the Bethel's architecture. Four white marbled steps, then a wide landing, then four more steps led up to the massive double doors of dark, well-oiled

teak inlaid with the symbols of the Eightfold Trusts the
Lady had bequeathed to her disciples and ultimately to
her followers. The promise of perfect peace to each be-
liever, both on earth and in the Afterward, was a goal
to strive for, and the Lady never frowned on those who
tried their best yet did not succeed. If not this day, perhaps the next; if not this life, perhaps another.

Sheltered in an alcove above the door stood a statue
of the Lady, her eight graceful arms outstretched in ever-
welcome, carved with great love and only somewhat less
expertise by a local carpenter. The Bethel itself was con-
structed of limestone aged to a creamy yellow-tan, while
long, narrow windows, arched at top and bottom, ran
along both sides of the building and were fitted with forest-
green shutters folded snug as grasshopper wings over the
windows to keep the coolness of the interior at bay from
the rising heat of day.

Shepherd Harrap dropped his twig broom on the top
step and bounced down to greet them, leather sandals
slapping against the marble. About fifty, Doyce esti-
mated, with mild, dreamy blue eyes, guileless with the
love of his Lady. His breadth of shoulders and chest and
a hint of a paunch made him appear shorter than he
was. And anything but soft, she discovered when corded,
powerfully muscled arms plucked Claire from the saddle,
setting her down without a jounce. Claire dropped an
affectionate kiss on the tonsured spot on his head as he
legged a mock bow.

"Oh, Harrap, I've the morning free, thanks to Eli!
And this is my friend Doyce," she added as Doyce dismounted and reached out to clasp his hand.

His grip held firm but with no intent to crush, as if he
grasped a fragile hatchling. "And my Bondmate, the
ghatta Khar'pern," she said.

"Ah, the little sleek one hasn't felt well, has she?"
The rich melody of his baritone voice thrilled Doyce, a
voice which would make him the responder in the mystery chants. He scooped Khar from the pommel platform, the ghatta startled and ill at ease before she
decided to settle against his chest. He deposited her on
the first step with loving care and Khar licked her fur

into place from the rumpling, basking in the attention she'd received.

She regarded the man with revised interest; Khar wouldn't have accepted a familiarity like that from many strangers. Also, a more perceptive remark than she'd anticipated from the Shepherd, a man she expected to be more beguiled by the inner mysteries and contemplation of the Lady than in tune with the mundane around him.

As if blessed with eyes in the back of his head, he gave a guilty start as another Shepherd, this one wearing the golden pectorate as All-Shepherd of the Flock, the head of the Bethel, stood at the top of the steps, one arched, sandaled foot pointed like an accusation at the abandoned broom. Harrap hitched his robe up to his knees and dashed up the steps, reclaimed his broom, and began sweeping with vigor, dust surging around his ankles, his being turned inward as he chanted the perpetual cycle of prayers. The tonsured spot on his bent head glowed ruddy. The All-Shepherd returned inside and Harrap slowed the broom as he muttered out of the corner of his mouth, "Just tie the mare over to the side, there, and I'll keep watch over her."

"Thank you, Harrap." Claire blew him an airy kiss.

"Have we caused him trouble?" Doyce asked in concern.

"Harrap's so truly good that no one can be mad at him for long, no matter what. It's just that sometimes he takes the unity of heaven and earth a little too literally for Shepherd Nichlaus's taste. Nichlaus'd rather see him concentrate more on the glory of the Bethel and the Lady and not strive quite so much for oneness with the world around him."

"Everything to the greater glory of the Lady," Doyce managed with weak piety as she took Claire's arm and started toward the stalls packed along the other three sides of the square and lined across its middle, exuberant with gaudy banners and hand-lettered signs, impromptu displays. For some, the merchanters, this served as a full-time occupation, whether in permanent shop or temporary open stall; for others, it provided the opportunity to sell or barter an overabundance of some crop or handicraft.

Baskets, large and small, utilitarian and decorative

sweet grass; woven rush mats; leathercraft frivolous and
everyday sturdy; curve-beaked, yellow-green songbirds
atwitter; rakes and hoes; fresh meat pies with crescent-
slitted, egg-glazed tops. They wandered in a happy daze,
stopping here and there to exclaim at whatever struck
their fancy. Doyce hesitated by a tray of obsidian pieces,
carved into pocket-sized mirrors and slim belt knives.
The raw power of their carved decorations stirred something within her. Not the usual market goods, not by a
long shot.

When she looked up from the ornaments to praise the
seller for his skill, she caught her breath in wonderment.
An Erakwan! In the midst of a Market Day fair! Eyes
black as the obsidian trinkets caught her own. Rare for
one of the elusive first peoples of Methuen to be seen at
all, let alone to mingle with the descendants of outworld-
ers, invaders, conquerors of their land, if not of their
peoples. The Erakwa and the original spacers and their
descendants had never warred, fought no pitched battles,
no campaigns to determine supremacy. Instead, the Erakwa simply faded away, remained in seclusion in the
deeply wooded mountains, slipping northward across the
river into Marchmont during the summers and drifting
southward to Canderis as winter approached. They too
had suffered from the Plumbs the first settlers had
placed, but the Erakwa had blamed no one, had demanded no retribution.

To be so near, especially in a setting like this, almost
paralyzed her with a sense of his otherness; she had on
occasion glimpsed one still as a fawn in the midst of the
forest, but even then had never entirely credited her
senses. The clacking of ornaments brought her back to
herself; the Erakwan had rattled his tray to catch her
attention. A shy smile dimpled one cheek; he looked at
ease but not at home in the square, his coppery skin
decently clothed in a minimum of Canderisian garments,
his waist cinched with a woven leather belt from which
hung a worn but intricately beaded pouch.

"No." She shook her head, signifying her regret.
"They're beautiful, and you have much skill, but I cannot
buy today." The dark eyes saddened, but he picked up
a curious ornament, cunningly carved like an animal

she'd never seen, and rested it against his lips. Cheeks
puffed, he blew once, and a note echoed out, pure and
overpowering with its clarity: a whistle. He smiled again,
as if at a secret they shared, and started to hand it to
her to try. Then his face abandoned all expression, closed
off tight as he spied Khar escorting Claire back from a
few booths away. One hand dipped to his waist pouch,
clutched it to absorb the comfort of his earth-tie, while
the other hand waved her off with a brusque, chopping
motion. She took a backward step, then another, Khar
closing the distance between them, curiosity plain. The
wary beauty of his expression vanished, a masklike im-
placability and suppressed anger replacing it and she felt
as if she'd been physically assaulted, pushed backward
by an invisible hand. She backed further, turned, at a
loss to know what she had done to provoke him. Or
Khar, for that matter. The ghatti and the Erakwa were
both original inhabitants; she as an outsider she could
understand.

**"They always close their minds from us, from our
touch. Trying to read them is like scratching on glass."**
Khar whisperspoke, craning her head over her shoulder
as they retreated. **"Someday I would like to 'speak one
of them. No ghatti has ever succeeded, but there would
be honor in trying."**

Doyce shook herself as if breaking free of a spell and
turned after Claire, losing herself anew in the multitude
of objects around her, the familiar, the workaday, rather
than the exotic. No hope of gaining the whistle now,
even if she had the money to pay. Somehow she had
offended him and lost something she thought she was
meant to have without knowing why. Earth eater, earth
taster, the strength and endurance of the earth in their
very stride—a Ninth Mystery of a Ninth Trust. Beyond
the Lady's ken, but not beyond Her love, she hoped.

They moved on. Fine linen, coarse linen; nails and
hinges and ironwork; lamp oils; laundry soaps in rough-
cut bars; cow balm; early greensaps and late pears near
bursting through their pink-gold freckled skins with juice
that attracted eager swarms of wasps; fresh baked bread
and figure-eight twisted rolls studded with raisins and
dredged in cinnamon sugar; broidery flosses and ribbons

and yarns. By these last they stopped, and Claire began fingering first one and then another.

Khar sat at her feet and reached a tentative paw to bat a dangling tail of yarn. The crowds were hard on the ghatta, crammed in at knee level with no one looking down to notice her presence. Feet intent about their business, random flying feet, feet with a mind of their own. Khar had yowled once in protest when someone trod on her tail, and now Doyce carried her through some of the more crowded spots, Khar's haunches balanced in the crook of her arm, her forelegs over Doyce's shoulder. Khar held her place by digging her claws into Doyce's sheepskin tabard, one of the things for which it had been designed. But the ghatta proved more of an armful than her slight frame could comfortably manage, and Doyce set her down whenever she could.

Claire perused a fine apricot-tinted wool, touched an end against Doyce's cheek to test for softness, and cocked her head, waiting. Doyce pursed her lips in thought, then finally shook her head no. "What about this, then?" and passed her a skein of pale yellow, light as a petal. Out of the corner of her eye Doyce caught Khar again batting at the dangling yarn like an untrained ghatten.

"Khar, stop that this instant," she reproved as she bent over, hands on hips. The ghatta ignored her and grasped the yarn in her teeth, pulling hard.

" 'Is one!" Her mindspeech echoed the fact that her mouth was full. " 'Erfect!"

Doyce untangled the strand of wool from Khar's teeth and surreptitiously wiped it on her sleeve before Khar could take another bite at it. "Claire, look what Khar's picked out. She's convinced that it's perfect." Following the yarn back to its main skein, buried under others on the table, Doyce found the source at last. "I think she might be right."

Blue, a blue that changed and glowed with each feeble comparison she thought of—the delicate shade toward the start of sunrise, the first tiny star-shaped bluet of spring, the tremulous mist-hazed edge of distant mountains—all that and more. The sheerest outer fibers of the yarn seemed to borrow from whatever color was nearby, a touch of violet, rose, a deeper blue, moss green, the delicate faded yellow of Doyce's tunic, the amber of Khar's eyes.

Claire stroked the yarn with reverence. "Oh, yes," she barely breathed the words. "Oh, Khar, Doyce, it's what I've dreamed of, but I didn't know you could spin a dream."

The stall owner edged around the table, proprietary hand laid on the yarn, nostrils flared as if she could scent their coins. "How much for four skeins," Doyce asked, since Claire still seemed rapt in contemplation, holding the yarn up to catch the sunlight, turning it this way and that.

"One silver, six coppers," the old woman stated, rapping her knuckles with flat emphasis on the stand as if to count out the sum. "There be but two women in the hill lands who spin and dye such as that. Not much comes our way."

"Too much," Doyce replied with genuine regret and turned to briskly escort Claire from the stall. Claire's jaw dropped in protest, but Doyce shushed her, clamped down hard on her arm to silence the cry of entreaty she could feel building inside the younger woman. All part of the game, even if Claire'd momentarily forgotten the rules. The stall owner let them retreat one step further than Doyce felt confident about, then gave a harsh, begrudging cry to reconsider.

They haggled back and forth, Doyce hindered by Claire's adamant refusal to relinquish the yarn a second time. At last, with one silver and two copper agreed upon, both sides felt pleased with their bargain. Tucking the packet under her arm, Doyce whistled up Khar and led Claire from the stall. Their purchasing finished, they strolled back toward the Bethel, stopping once to buy two meat pies and two mugs of ale, planning to sit on the steps and eat.

Doyce perched one step higher than Claire and set the mugs down. Claire broke off a corner of her meat pie and placed it in front of Khar, who patted it this way and that, waiting for it to cool. Resting her elbows on the step behind her, Doyce stretched out her legs and absorbed the scene around her. Shepherd Harrap sat on

a leather-seated tripod stool to the left of the large double doors, and an elderly woman clothed all in black,
head draped with a black scarf, sat beside him on a similar stool. He held her hand, listening, head cocked to
catch each word, patting her shoulder as she broke into
sobs. The soothing sound of his rich baritone voice,
though not the words, floated down to them.

When she looked back, Khar sat bolt upright, almost
lifting off her front paws, intent, meat pie scrap forgotten. Her ears twitched and turned, the hoop and rosette
glowing in the light, and her whiskers rippled and flexed
as she sniffed, testing the air.

Doyce herself could hear something faint and far away
but closing fast. She sensed a difference in the bustle and
hum of the square and surrounding area: a distant but
irate shout, an outright scream, a rumble as if something
had been knocked over, and the pounding of horse's
hooves. The sounds edged closer, jumbled but louder,
ricocheting off the closely packed stone buildings, then
swallowed by the canvas tents and stalls.

"**Trouble**," Khar announced. "**Ghatt in it.**" She began
to weave her way through the crowd, jumping up to walk
a ledge, springing higher to a low porch roof.

"Who?" Doyce queried as she trotted to where Lokka
was tied to yank sword and staff from their saddle
sheaths. She buckled the sword in place around her
waist, settled it to draw properly, and gripped the staff,
loose but ready, in her left hand. Shadowed by the
Bethel, she hoped no one noticed her precautions,
prayed they weren't necessary as she moved back into
position.

"**Don't know. I sense fear, but he isn't speaking. Concentrating too hard on escaping.**"

"Claire, go up with Harrap. Now!" She pulled Claire
to her feet and gave her a push up the steps. The Shepherd hadn't noticed anything amiss and still spoke, melo-
dious and low, with the elderly woman.

Claire grabbed up her bundle of yarn and protectively
cradled it to her chest. "What's wrong?"

"I don't know, but go! Probably a rumpus of some
sort, a street brawl, so just stay clear."

A ghatt, orange and black and white in no discernible

pattern, ran full tilt through the throng, dodging under feet, between legs, over baskets, and beneath tables. His tongue protruded from his whitened, foam-flecked muzzle. Clearly he'd been running long and hard, was near to the end of his endurance.

Close behind, a man on a horse cursed and maneuvered his panicky mount through the crowd. The horse's eyes rolled white-edged as he tossed his head, trying to shake the cruel pinch of a hard-held bit, but the rider spurred him and cursed again, leaned down from his mount to shove aside two merchants with a sideways swipe of his staff, then hauled the horse around in the direction the ghatt had run. With mounting horror, Doyce took in the tabard, the twisted face: a Seeker straddled the horse, a Seeker named Georges Barbet. The ghatt had to be Parm, then, but why, in the name of the Lady, would Georges try to ride Parm down like that? Had the world gone mad, metamorphosed overnight while she slept?

"Georges!" she called, throwing herself into the melee at the foot of the steps. "Hold! What ails you?"

With a savage jerk he reined in and the startled horse reared back, then sprang forward as he dug spurs into already bleeding sides. "I'll kill him! By the Lady, I'll kill that ghatt!" His dark eyes gleamed wild, sparked by a searing rage so deep she couldn't begin to fathom what fueled it.

Mouth dry, her nervous swallowing loud in her ears, she pushed after Georges, though the path he'd cleared now overflowed with people rebounding and caroming off each other, uncertain in which direction to move. Whose side was she supposed to be on? A blind man could have picked out their trail: smashed crockery, overturned tables of bruised fruit, bright ribbons crushed and dusty underfoot, people picking themselves up and brushing themselves off, mouths agape.

"Khar, what is going on!" she mindspoke, desperate to understand. She couldn't see the ghatta but knew she had to be somewhere near. *"Are they both mad?"*

"Black heart! Black soul!" Khar wailed.

"Whose, damn it? Georges or Parm?" Neither was possible. Doyce forced her staff horizontally across her

chest, clearing her path in the direction of Khar's voice. She lurched, bowled over a self-important little man in a rich blue weskit just picking himself up from his first headlong dive to safety. No time to apologize.

Now Parm retraced his route, spinning back into the heart of the chaos, generating even greater havoc as he landed in the middle of what he'd already upset. Doyce whirled back, running hard, shoving, flailing her elbows as she tried to gain a lead on the ghatt, desperate to anticipate his route. The press of sweating, panicky bodies, the confused mingling with all order or pattern disrupted made it well-nigh impossible, fool's fancy. No one knew which way to turn, where to run.

As far as she could judge, the ghatt didn't know either. Still, his best chance of escape, if escape were his goal, lay in the crowds, the close, winding, packed streets. He could eel his way through, lose himself in shadows, nooks, and crannies where a horse and rider could never follow. The greatest danger lay in a clear, straight, unobstructed path of escape. Incredibly fast for a sprint, a ghatt couldn't sustain a full-out pace for more than three hundred meters. Much beyond that and a horse and rider were superior, sure to win out.

Doyce ran smack into the small, self-important man in blue whom she'd swept off his feet only moments earlier. He grabbed her hard by her upper arms to steady himself, fright and frustration clear on his face, and they essayed a ritualized dance of passage, intricate, desperate footwork in a confined space.

"This way! Back to the steps!" Khar's voice homed in on her although she couldn't see the ghatta's location. Out of the path of trampling feet, she hoped, as the little man stepped hard on her instep. She gritted her teeth at the pain, snapped her forearms up inside his grasp and broke his grip, and was off and running, limping. She thought Claire had reached the relative safety of the steps. She cast her mindspeech back in Khar's direction. *"Are they both mad? Whose side are we on?"* The Market Square seethed and twisted with knots of shouting people, pushing and shoving, belaboring each other as they tried to clamber over counters and collapsed canvas stall walls, pushing and boosting each other. She doubted the

townspeople would ever look kindly on Seekers or Bondmates again. And to top it off, she didn't know whom
she was fighting for—or against.

**"Georges is mad. Something cracked inside his head.
Parm can no longer serve!"**

"Impossible!" She heard the words but couldn't believe them as she shoved and pummeled her way toward
the crowded steps. An elbow drove into her midsection
and she returned the favor; managed to turn her head to
avoid another elbow crashing toward the bridge of her
nose. The world was not a safe, sane place; Oriel's death
had proved that, but this sudden instability, the random
absurdity of this mad, directionless rushing, the hysterical
crowd, left her mind whirling to escape the import of
Khar's words. A ghatt served until death took one or the
other of the Bondmates. There was no turning back. And
Georges, mad? No ghatt or ghatta would have 'Printed
on an unstable person, one who would prove unworthy
of the offered Bonding.

With a gasp and a final hard shove, she scrambled to
the first landing on the Bethel steps and paused to look
back, winded, blessing the advantage of added height. A
middle-aged farm woman, face scoured red by weather
and anger, swatted her on the shoulder with her net bag
of purchases as if she held Doyce personally responsible
for the confusion. Maybe she was, she had no way of
knowing. As credible as any other explanation she could
think of.

Parm rounded the corner, back into the heart of the
Square, horse and rider struggling behind. He sprang,
banked off the top of a handcart loaded with eggs and a
brace of trussed, gabbling hens, scrambled on, leaped a
fallen child bawling dismally, and landed on a table of
cutlery, sending knives, scissors, and razors spinning in
deadly circles. His path zigzagged, but he gained ground,
the havoc he'd created swamping the horse and rider in
his wake.

Sides pumping like bellows, eyes intent on his goal, he
hurtled up the steps past Doyce. Georges Barbet had
finally abandoned his horse and ran close behind, bulling
his way through the crowd that now showed enough
sense to try to pull away from him and clear a path. As

his boot slammed the first step, his empty eyes looked straight through her, made her feel invisible. They registered blankly, glazed over, devoid of any human emotion she recognized. He moved like an automaton, a vile wrongness in trappings that should have been right. Despairing, she planted herself in his path, brought up her staff, knuckles clenched white, and braced herself for the impact. She couldn't restrain him without using force and didn't know if she could bring herself to hit a fellow Seeker. Now was the time to find out. Khar chose that moment to reappear and dart between Barbet's legs, tumbling him back into the Square.

At the same instant a yell and a crash crescendoed from the top of the stairs by the Bethel doors, and she wheeled, distracted, in time to see Shepherd Harrap and Parm collapse in a tangle, Harrap's arms windmilling for balance as the tripod stool kicked out from under him. One hamlike leg swept up and scythed over the widow he'd been praying with, and she swayed and crashed on top of Harrap with the stately, implacable grace of a felled tree, Parm sandwiched between them.

The widow bolted up with surprising agility, black veils swirling and flapping as she fled without a backward glance, a keening wail unraveling behind her. Harrap and Parm struggled, rolling and wrestling, the ghatt either locked in an embrace or captured. The ghatt yowled frantically, high and lonely, and Harrap roared colorful variations on an earthy vocabulary that had no business near the Lady's House or coming from one her Shepherds. Harrap's robe had ridden up, exposing a large, plump, white buttock. The total irrelevancy of her thought transfixed Doyce; the age-old question that generations of children whispered when they felt daring: What does a Shepherd wear under his robe? The answer stared her in the face, and her giggle degenerated into a choked-off moan. A new moon on the Lady's horizon! Indeed, a full moon! Lady forgive!

Shaking her head, whimpering snorts of laughter spurting out of her, she started up the steps, placing each foot with deliberation, buying scant time to think, to control herself. Khar walked alongside, tail erect. She dared spare a thought for Barbet's whereabouts but trusted the

crowd to contain him; someone would have to pay for
the damage, and he was closest to hand. Harrap had
managed to sit up and tuck his robe under him for mod-
esty's sake; a large goose egg swelled over his left eye
where he'd hit something on his way down. Parm
sprawled across his lap, one of Harrap's meaty arms pinning him in place. The ghatt's sides rose and fell quickly,
his ragged breathing audible as she reached the top step,
took in the absurd tableau.

With deliberate intent the ghatt painfully twisted his
head and sank his teeth into the fleshy palm pad below
Harrap's thumb.

"By the blessed butt and tits of the Lady!" Harrap's
heartfelt intonation of the oath silenced everyone in the
crowd. He caught the ghatt a buffet behind the ear, then
raised his hand to suck at the wound. His face slackened,
then tightened, all color blanched from it, his terror pal-
pable as shudder after shudder racked his body. "By the
Lady, no! No! Not inside my head like that!" he
whimpered.

"Parm has 'Printed!" Khar trembled with a strange
exultation.

"But that's . . . that's impossible!" The world spun
around her, then slid to a nauseating halt, crashed at her
feet. She let her staff slip from nerveless fingers and a
part of her heard the metal tip chime against the marble,
a peal of doom. *"Parm's imprinted on George Barbet?
He can't change! It doesn't work that way! It doesn't
work! It's never happened before! Not even to the Seeker
General and Koom."*

"It has now." Khar stalked forward and greet-sniffed
Parm's face. **"And you'd better help Harrap before he's
convinced he's lost his mind or been invaded by demons."**

In all the histories, in all the legends, in all the nearly
two hundred years of recorded ghatti-human bondings,
some as strange in fact as they were in fiction, nothing
like this had ever occurred. Except now she bore witness
to it whether she believed it or not. Believe, her mind
shouted at her, Khar can't lie, it's true. I don't know
how, but it's true. She cradled Harrap's large hand, totally limp, in both of hers. It felt no more icy, no more
clammy than her own. "Harrap! Harrap! It's all right.

Believe me, it's all right!" His superficial, rapid breathing and unfocused eyes made it clear he labored from shock.

A thready piping of a thought crossed her mind, transmitted with difficulty. **"Mindwalk . . . if ye will."** With no one else to offer the traditional greeting, Parm offered it himself, voluntarily throwing open his mind to mesh with hers. Khar nudged her hand to make her react.

"Parm, what have you done?" Her tone severe, she thumbed back Harrap's eyelid, then pressed her fingers against the bull-like neck to test his pulse.

"Explain later. Didn't mean to hurt him. Will he be all right?" The ghatt blinked several times in rapid succession, his throat flexing with a nervous, dry gulping noise. She felt a sudden and equal thirst. **"Is the other one gone?"**

"Who? Georges Barbet? I don't know," and she realized she truly had no idea what had become of Barbet since his fall; things had happened too fast. *"Khar, go check, would you?"*

"Don't have to. Didn't you hear him leave? He rode out of here as hard as if all the powers of darkness chased after him." The ghatta turned somber at the thought. **"Not good he got away like that."**

"No use crying over spilt milk, and there's enough of that in the Square and everything else at the moment. Seeker General isn't going to like the damage claims on this incident." Doyce motioned to two of the bystanders. "Here, get his stool righted and elevate his feet, can't you? And mind the robe. Stop standing around gawking and give me a hand."

The heavy teak door slammed open and the All-Shepherd Nichlaus swirled out, his lean face suffused with anger. "Who dares disturb our Lady's peace like this?" He stopped short, inspecting Harrap and the dappled orange and black ghatt on his lap. His voice bit with glacial contempt. "What is the meaning of this, a ghatt and a Shepherd sprawled on the steps like common drunkards? You profane a holy place with these . . . these antics! Send that ghatt away this instant!"

"It's too late for that," Doyce addressed him, feeling an overpowering weariness at her own words. "Far, far too late for that and for I don't know what else. The ghatt stays, I'm afraid."

Khar sauntered over and considered the Lady's Shepherd, her head craning one way and then the other. She swirled around him twice, coming closer and closer with each silken sweep, and ended by twining herself hard against Nichlaus's shins, first one side of her furred length, then the other until he stepped back, revulsion clear. With a seductive twist and roll she threw herself on the ground in front of him, digging one shoulder and then the other into the spot where he had stood. Nichlaus stood woodenly, robe clutched up to his bony knees, trying to pretend not to notice.

Little did he know, Doyce winced, that Khar's face wore the exact same expression of distaste. She had applied one of the most intimately damning of ghatti insults to humans, the purposeful touching and apparent affection, then the contemptuous shoulder roll, as if rolling in something spoiled and rotten. To anyone who knew ghatti well, the gesture and the intention reeked with unmistakable contempt. A few appreciative snickers filtered from the now subdued crowd, and the All-Shepherd spun around, stung by the laughter and, his robe hissing around him, stalked inside.

"Self-indulgent, Khar," she reprimanded. Claire knelt beside Harrap, bathing his face with a cloth dipped in a basin of water she'd miraculously rescued from somewhere. Doyce chaffed his wrists, thinking furiously, trying to plan what to do next about Harrap and Parm. Not to mention the absent Georges Barbet. Curse it all, she had no 'script suitable for calming him. Considering his size, the dosage would have to be massive. Blast the eumedicos, never a one around when they really needed one.

"Oh, I don't know about that. Now, everyone, back to your stalls, your shopping. There's still a good part of the day left and pleasant times to be had if you all work together to put things to rights." The voice personified cool authority with a leavening touch of good humor to it, a voice that she had heard daily for nearly ten years of her life. And one that she had never ceased to miss since leaving the eumedicos. Mahafny Annendahl, her teacher, her taskmaster, her mentor, her friend during those long, arduous years of training. One of the few who had wished her well when she had left in disgrace.

Time stood still, then reversed itself with sickening speed, nearly crushing her with the weight of memory. So many years she'd striven to scale the summit of her new life, leave the valleys of her despair and failure behind, and now the sound of a single voice sent her avalanching down the incline of years, nearly flattening her with the burden of remembrance. . . .

♣

She lay curled on the bed, knees drawn up, pillow crushed tight against her face and chest, barricading her from the spartan quarters, just wide enough for cot and desk, the ordered shelving of leather-bound tracts on anatomy and pathology, neurology, obstetrics, her dog-eared pharmacopoeia, the precious microscope with its mirrored reflector, the burner and alembic—used more for making clandestine cha than for experiments. The muslin pillowcase clung to her cheek, the fabric drenched in tears, her face and eyes raw from crying, sinuses flooded, nose streaming. The handkerchief was a wadded, wet ball, capable of absorbing no more. She let it drop off the edge of the cot, pulled the pillow tighter against her face, her hot, moist breathing reflected back at her, stifling her.

A light knocking rattled the door and she tensed, or perhaps she heard the wind. An open window at the end of the corridor could produce the same result, goblin rattlings when the breeze changed or a storm veered through. Besides, no one had ventured near since she had left the wards in disgrace, running, stumbling, throat scoured from the screams she'd swallowed down to avoid disturbing the other patients. Even then, even then, she hadn't wanted to upset them, to imperil their healing or their hope. A creak of hinges, the complaint of floorboards told her someone had entered her room, moving with light assurance as habit and training dictated. Never reveal your anxiety by rapid movement, agitation, running. Anxiety is as contagious as any disease. She had broken that rule today, but at least she hadn't shouted. She clutched the pillow tighter, molded her face into its damp bulk, lacking the strength to care who stood beside the bed, though she could sense the presence.

A hand pressed against her shoulder, forced her to roll back while peeling the pillow away from her face, fresh air tickling and drying the moisture. She kept swollen eyes closed, hard to breathe on her back, her flooded sinuses draining down her throat, gulping to cope with the overflow. "Doyce, what's wrong? What is it?" An arm slipped behind her back, brought her unresisting into a near-sitting posture, pressed a clean square of cotton into her hand. She used it automatically. She knew the voice, had prayed to hear it earlier while there was still time, still hope—Mahafny Annendahl, her teacher. But Mahafny had not been making rounds the last few days, had turned over her teaching duties to Terence di Siguera, her second, while she had escorted some trainee to the Research Hospice in the north. Gone, just when Doyce needed her support the most.

"He died," she declared, voice clogged and thick. "He died! He was a nice old man who died when he didn't need to! If we'd acted aggressively, we'd have had a chance to save him." She hunched forward, mopped at her face, kept the handkerchief pressed to her forehead, veiling her eyes.

A shift in the bed, a tilt of the mattress toward the right told her that Mahafny had sat down. "Surely you've had patients die before, this can hardly have been a first." A neutral tone, not a question, simply an understated reminder of reality.

She brought herself fully upright on the bed, forced her back against the wall for support. "Of course I have. But I knew what was wrong, don't you understand? And di Siguera didn't even listen to me until it was too late. Even if he didn't believe me right off the bat, why didn't it show clear in the mindtrance?" Her fisted hand drummed in frustration against her knee. "Why . . . didn't . . . he find it?"

Had it been only three days ago that they'd brought Edam Sellicote in? She remembered that it had taken the combined efforts of his two sons and a nephew to literally drag him to the diagnostic clinic. Three were necessary because Edam had been protesting and digging in his heels all the way, despite his weakness.

"No need, no need ta worry. Don't know what got into them to make'm so concerned," he wheezed as di Siguera examined him, listened to his heart, inspected his throat and glands, poked and prodded at the man while Doyce stood at his shoulder, jotting notes. "Touch o'the bloody flu, that's all it be. Aches and pains in me back and chest, arms and legs jellylike, or they'd never have dragged me in like a lamb. A powerful scratchy throat, then ye feel like someone stoked a furnace inside you 'cept you be too busy shivering and shaking to be able to heat up proper. Sorta like being in the sauna and the ice tub all ta'oncit."

One of the sons, bandy-legged and burly chested, already ruddy with tan from the spring sun, maintained his grip on Edam's shoulder, pinning him to the examination stool. "Now, Da, mayhap it *is* just the flu, but we got a busy spring aheada us and you know it. You out sick any length o'time and we can't keep to schedule. We be booked solid for the next octant and ye know it."

Edam cuffed at his son's hand. " 'Course I know it! I told Avram zactly how many to book, how many we'd agree to take, din I?"

She waited for di Siguera to ask what Edam Sellicote did for a living, ready to note it for the records. A person's occupation could be important, provide a leading clue as to the illness or type of injury. But di Siguera acted abstracted, distant, his thick fingers with their mossy dark hair on the back still ranging with care over the old man's body. She hated to disturb the eumedico's trance, his inner communing with the patient, but decided to risk it. Any eumedico deep into the trance rarely noticed outside interruptions unless they bordered on the cataclysmic. Best to complete the record. "And what is it you do for your living, Master Sellicote?"

His round head with its scattering of sleeked back hair tilted up to beam at her, complexion walnut-colored from years of outdoor activity that even a winter indoors couldn't fade. "I bayint one'o the best sheep shearers around. We travels the entire spring slipping the little

woollies outa their winter jackets, we do. Neddy and
Kevin, my boys, works near fast and clean as do I. My
nevvy, Avram, does the bookin', the weighin' an tallyin',
minds the finances.

Neddy thrust his arms back, brought them together to
crack his knuckles. "Aye, we do just fine, Da. But we
need three healthy men to meet the schedule. Kev an I'll
shear by lantern light if we must to finish this job and
let you rest, but we need you bad." He threw an explanation in Doyce's direction. "They holds patient and still
for ol' Edam here, and he peels those fleeces off slick
and smooth, all in one piece and without airy a nick to
the sheep or the fleece." Doyce nodded her comprehension. Her mother had depended on superior yarns for
her weaving, and a fine, undamaged fleece enhanced the
value of the wool.

Di Siguera interrupted, his olive complexion sallow
and drawn. The trance drained the eumedicos, she knew.
"You're right as to influenza, but I want you checked
into the infirmary for a few days' observation and rest.
What I don't want is to have his turn into pneumonia."

For no reason she could put her finger on, the diagnosis nagged at her, too superficial and obvious. Still, she
could keep an eye on Edam Sellicote for a few days,
reassure herself that di Siguera hadn't missed anything.
Though she wasn't initiated in the trance state yet, perhaps she'd notice some symptom, some little thing that
would convince her. Besides, the obvious diagnosis was
so often the right one, and who was she at this stage of
her training to second-guess?

And so she charted the old sheep shearer's progress
on each of her rounds, stopping to chat, to listen, if nothing else. She enjoyed speaking with Sellicote, glad to
listen to someone who enjoyed nature and the work he
did. She had also discovered they knew a few people in
common and that he had heard of her mother, admired
her work. "She weaves slow and true, they say, and any
fabric ye buy from her will wear longer than you do,"
he'd chuckled. "Best buy it while ye be young to get the
most use of it."

At first he'd appeared a bit better on her night rounds,
but by the next day her doubts increased. His lips and

nails had taken on a bluish cast and the fever returned, kept rising. His chest rose and fell too quickly, his respiration rapid and shallow, and worst of all, she found subcutaneous edema in the chest and neck area. She made a little tsk-ing sound before she could stop herself, but went no further. "So where were you shearing the past oct or so?" she asked, hoping for distraction while she took his pulse.

Edam smothered a cough, groped on the side table for a mug of water. "Neustadt, Dejemmal, and Salton." The word "Salton" came out "S . . . s . . . Sal . . . ton," as he tried to override the cough reflex. "H'ain't been there nigh on to twelve years. They had to give up grazing sheep there when they had a 'thrax outbreak. Put down every horse'n cow, sheep'n goat, burned the earth, turned it over just to be safe. Anything to contain it. Lovely, lush place, too, the woollies look so right on those rolling green hills. T'were the sky green, the sheep'd be the puff clouds. Glad they think it safe to try again."

" 'Thrax?" she queried as she tucked his arm back under the covers, saw the little rippling motions of the sheet as he vibrated with chills. "You mean anthrax?" Her mind clicked back and forth, digesting this new piece of information, discarding other pieces, waiting to test this new alignment and fit. And worst of all, it did, practically all of it. Something that made sense to anyone country-raised rather than city-bred like di Siguera. She chatted a little more, then wheeled off down the long, wide passage between the rows of beds, walking steadily, not letting her white coat flap after her, betray her excitement. Where in the name of heavens had di Siguera hidden himself? Probably in his cubbyhole of an office, waiting for her and the other trainees to come back with their reports, rather than making the rounds with them, supervising, correcting, amplifying. When it came to ways to subtly slack work, Terence di Siguera had mastered them all, managing to indicate far more important yet highly illusory tasks at hand. Yet Mahafny seldom found fault with him.

Doyce poked her head inside the door as she knocked, not waiting for permission to enter. Di Siguera manhandled a large and dripping sandwich, mouth whale-wide as he strove to cram it between his jaws, eyes squinted shut in happy anticipation. It made her realize her own hungry rumblings—late afternoon and he had finally found time to eat; she'd had nothing since sunrise but for a cup of cha, cold, and swiped from one of her fellow eumedico trainees when he'd abandoned it to respond to an emergency. The final cold mouthful, dense with settled sugar, had given her a jolt of sorely needed energy, now long-gone.

"Terence," she interrupted, smelling the stacked beef, the sweet peppers and lettuce dripping with oil and balsamic vinegar, mouth watery with shared appetite. "I know you've thought of everything, but did you deduce any trace of *Bacillus anthracis* when you tranced?" She pushed on hurriedly, terribly aware of the strong jaws chewing, distorted cheeks bulging with the effort. "Woolgatherer's Disease," she amplified. "Pulmonary anthrax. Terence, you heard him say he shears sheep for a living." She rushed on, "And he just mentioned to me that he'd sheared in Salton. They had a severe outbreak about twelve years ago. Just started running sheep again. You know how long the spores can live on in the soil even if all the animals have been destroyed." She ground to a halt, waited, wishing fervently she dared steal the other half of his sandwich, or better yet, have him offer it.

He swallowed hard, gave a tight little smile of satiated enjoyment and shifted the plate nearer to him and away from her as if aware of her thought. "Surely it's unlikely. I caught no trace at all when I read him. Just a nasty case of influenza." She detected the faintest drift of worry from him, intangible yet there like a cloud slipping across the sun and then moving on. His voice droned on as oily and slick as the herbed oil glistening on his mouth and chin. "Surely it's long gone by now, twelve years should be more than enough. I'm still afraid of pneumonia, though."

"Couldn't we try some *penicillium*, though? If it is pulmonary anthrax, it's the only thing that will stop it, especially if we start it now. And if it is pneumonia, it won't hurt for that either."

He toyed with the sandwich, considering, shook his

head with a pained decisiveness. "No, you know how hard it is for us to extract *penicillium* from the broth, to retrieve enough of any great strength. I can't authorize wasting it on something that will run its own course, that we can control with expectorants and decongestants, a febrifuge. He's a strong man, he can fight pneumonia if it develops."

"But he can't overcome pulmonary anthrax without *penicillium,* it's fast and fatal!" She wanted to bluster, tantrum until she got her way. "Mahafny Annendahl would authorize it," she snapped and then realized her error, wished the words back, wished to swallow them.

He tilted back in his chair, the springs creaking, his expression bland. "But Annendahl's not here, and she's left me in charge. Is that perfectly clear?" He didn't look angry, but he sounded tired and defensive. "You know it's too precious to waste. We have to use it so sparingly." She could hear the pleading in his voice. She'd seen him pushed before, seen him turn obdurate and hard, refusing at last for the sake of refusal. He was a strong second to back Mahafny Annendahl, but a weak first on his own.

She backed slowly out of the room, hands gripping her opposite cuffs to keep anxiety at bay. "Well, when you check in on him later, please keep it in mind as a possibility." Nothing more she could say, no one else she could appeal to unless she went over his head and over Mahafny's head to the Staff Senior. She would if she had to, but she hoped she'd prodded Terence to act, even if only at his own speed, on his own terms.

But by the time di Siguera had acted, Edam Sellicote was in shock and had slipped into a coma; the *penicillium* had been wasted, used too late. She had pulled the sheet over his blue-cast face and stormed from the ward, back to her room to rage and hide from her failure.

"He should have known," her voice puzzled, fist measuring out the cadence of her words. "How could di Siguera have overlooked anthrax, given the man's medical history? Tell me that!"

Clothes travel-stained, skin drawn tight around her eyes, Mahafny stared at the far wall, not yet ready to answer.

Doyce scrambled off the bed, forced her way in front of Mahafny, tried to break through the shell of fatigue that surrounded the older woman, cloaking all response. "If I could diagnose the disease without trancing, why couldn't he!" Until a thought so heretical swept through her that she fell backward, managed to perch herself on the desk. "Terence can't achieve a true mindtrance, can he?" Mahafny sat rigid. "Can he?" And the final puzzle piece locked in place. "Can you achieve a mindtrance?" She flung the words out as a challenge, but they weren't meant to be; she was begging, pleading for the acerbic voice to chastise her, convince her of her error, her lack of faith.

The ghost of a smile flittered across the eumedico's face, but never touched any higher, gray eyes like clouded ice. "Well done. You've finally figured it out. Did it come to you in a shattering bolt of revelation or have you suspected all along?"

Each word came hesitantly as a step on cracking lake ice, too thin to sustain the weight of knowledge she bore, each word further fracturing her brittle composure, until she would plunge through, bereft, drowning in chill certainty. "I didn't . . . mean to. . . . Of course you can . . . have I ever doubted your skills?" She reached out, desperate for the consolation of flesh against flesh, and Mahafny brushed her arm away absently as if it were a distracting fly.

"You would have been instructed soon, been informed that the 'mystery' contained no mystery, but why the ritual was deemed necessary. It would have served as the culmination of your training, the final, still center of the maze of learning." She sighed, a long, drawn-out sound of anguish. "I'm sorry it had to happen like this. But you've always quietly doubted so much within yourself that perhaps this doubt was not unnatural."

"Then only Gleaners can . . . ?" The question had been surprised out of her, though it wasn't the question she had meant to ask. She dared not finish, not when Mahafny's assessing look flayed like a whip, as if to lash the very thought from her head, analyze what else she knew. Where was safe ground? "But, why? Why the subterfuge? Why perpetrate a lie? And all the other eumedicos as well? If you lack the power, I doubt that any of the other Senior Staff have it either."

"Perfectly correct." Confirmation brought no joy. "We live a lie to help others as much as we possibly can."

The taste of blood on her lip brought her back to herself, forced her to concentrate on what Mahafny was waiting to tell her. "Explain it to me. Please, I beg you, I have to understand, not flounder in another lie."

Mahafny walked to the door, cracked it open to check who roamed the halls, then closed it soundlessly, pitching her voice low so that Doyce was forced to lean forward, feeling trapped in some sort of illicit intimacy. The whispered words came tripping light and fast, ready to shoot by her if she relaxed her concentration.

"You ask why." Mahafny twisted her head back and forth slowly, almost wonderingly. "Do you have *any* conception of what it was like when our ancestors came to this planet and unexpectedly found themselves stranded here? They came from a world of high technology, demanding as a God-given right the most advanced resources a society of that caliber could provide. They—our forebears, the doctors, the medics, the technicians—reveled in being thought of as omnipotent, all-knowing, all-wise, and they insured that their patients viewed them that way. But as the medicines ran out, as the hypersensitive life-support machinery, the laser scalpels, the image resonators died—things we can only dream of now and barely comprehend their workings—we had to fall back on something."

The words hissed in Doyce's ears. "We had to create *something*, a mystique, if you will, to offer people security, hope, confidence. If a patient doesn't trust you, you've already lost half the battle. We've been over that time and again."

Doyce attempted a smile, failed. "One of the cardinal rules." But the words fell on deaf ears, the first time she had ever seen the eumedico ignore a pupil's response.

"It is possible that a few of the first doctors, especially some of the psychiatrists, boasted telepathic powers. Any space contingent usually carried a few people with various psionic powers for empathic purposes with indigenous life forms. But the Plumbs destroyed so many records that we are not sure if any of our doctors did or not. I've done hundreds of genealogical charts tracking the descendants of those doctors, curious to see if any of them transmitted such abilities to their offspring." She shook herself as if awakening. "That's another story, I'm sorry. Maundering again."

"But what the psychiatrists taught us to do, the heritage they gave us—that you strove so eagerly to possess until today—was the ability to attain a trance state, and to convince everyone that we could visualize the cause of a particular disease or the extent of an injury while we were in the trance.

"We relearned skills that had been forgotten or ignored because of technology. We built our laboratories to the highest standards we could attain, ludicrous imitations of what we'd lost, knowing that at best they resembled the antiquated labs of hundreds of years past. And finally, we realized that if you listen, *truly listen*," she slapped the desk twice, causing Doyce to jump, "to the patient, the patient will give you the diagnosis. And with no technology to bolster us, we had to learn how to become hypersensitive to every fragile clue the body and mind of the patient could provide us with, and then utilize that information and trust in our intuitions." She stood in front of Doyce, arms folded across her chest. "Do you begin to understand? Now do you understand what we lost and what each new generation of eumedicos tried to substitute in its place?"

Doyce pushed herself off the desk, brushed past Mahafny to seek safety and distance at the far end of the bed, then realized she had cornered herself. These revelations jeopardized her, whether in mind or body, she couldn't judge, but she longed to escape, yet compulsively wanted to hear more. Would a question let her step to solid ground or would the ice again crack beneath her feet?

"You said I would have learned eventually, that I would have shared the secret, shared in the lie. What happens if a trainee refuses to accept it, refuses to live a lie? Decides to denounce you as frauds?"

"Very few even consider such a thought, let alone attempt it. The people we train are dedicated to saving human lives, even if it comes at the expense of their own integrity, through living a lie. I remind you that on Olde Earth doctors selflessly aided patients suffering from the plagues of the time, even if it cost them their own lives, a greater sacrifice than we ask you to make. And I will tell you that no one becomes a diagnostic eumedico who doesn't have the best training, as well as sensitivity and intuition honed sharp to determine what ails a patient."

"What about Terence di Siguera?"

"You've hurt yourself in this, Doyce, and Terence as well, I'm afraid, though it's all for the best in Terence's case. I had hopes for that man—when he's on target, he's incredibly sensitive and acute. But he tends to fade under stress or tiredness, something that can't be allowed to happen. No, another place will be found for Terence, out of harm's way. There are always those who train with us whose strength fails or who lack that intuitive knack, that sixth sense. They either leave early without completing training—we see to that if we possibly can—or they are shifted to some other area of endeavor within our community. Pure or applied research, anatomical studies, even surgery for those with a knack for the knife. I'd hoped Terence would learn to steady himself, keep on an even keel, but it's clear he hasn't. I think he'll be more than happy to devote all his time to some genetic studies he's been working on with me."

She pushed her shoulders into the corner, twisted back and forth as if burrowing deeper, but her back remained tight against the wall. No escape. "And . . . what about me?"

"Yes, what about you?" Mahafny asked, and Doyce searched hard for some unspoken warmth, ready to embrace her with the open, caring arms of shared complicity. Except that she had to choose for herself. The tears started down her cheeks again, amazing that she had any moisture to spare.

"You are a good diagnostician, you have the skill to listen and assess, make the connections. Are you willing to give up part of yourself to become a full-fledged diagnostic eumedico or even continue your research in herbal medicines if you can't bear to face the patients with a deception that must become a part of you, until that falsehood becomes as automatic as sleeping or breathing? Can you do that?"

"And if I can't manage that? If I can't accept any of it any longer? What then?" Traitor! her mind screamed. And more than her treachery, she feared death, feared the shining slim scalpel sliding between her ribs, the air-filled syringe plunged into a vein. Would they—did they—kill to preserve the mystery?

Her face must have shown transparent, revealing every fear that dashed across her mind. Mahafny smiled, a genuine smile of amusement, and the gray eyes flickered with empathy, not the cold, cloaked guilt she had carried into the room. "No, Doyce, we save lives rather than taking them. It *is* part of the creed, you know." She looked thoughtful, far away for some moments, then seemed to reach a decision. "And you cannot accept either alternative I've offered?"

Dumbly Doyce shook her head, unable to speak. At last she managed to croak a response. "Not . . . in my heart. It would gnaw at me like a canker from within, until I'd feel an empty shell."

"Too fine a moral sense can be more debilitating than any disease. You'll always be disappointed in yourself and in others. And you'll have selfishly stolen from others in need all the good you could accomplish here."

"Please, don't make me." She stood up tall, straight, refusing to cower in the corner any longer. "Is there another way, please, tell me."

Mahafny opened the clothes cupboard, tossed down the worn bottle-green carpetbag, the more recent canvas tote she'd acquired. With a booted foot she toed the expensive leather eumedico bag from its place by the desk, the bag that Doyce had saved for so long, to the center of the room, jumbling the narrow space between bed and desk. "Then I expect you should pack and leave. Discover something else to do with your life. But remember this, it does not end when you walk out the door. You must make—and keep—one promise, and I mean that with all my heart. You must never tell another living soul what you have learned here today. You do not have to live the lie by remaining a eumedico, but you must keep that lie on your sacred honor. When we formally

convene tomorrow morning to cast you out, you must
swear never to tell why. Do I have your word?"

"You have my word. Your lie is still a burden, but at
least I don't have to live it with my every breath." And
then the tears flooded in earnest, and she collapsed on
the bed, crying for everything she would lose by giving
up the eumedicos, for whatever scrap of dignity she'd
retained, and for any number of things she couldn't even
begin to explain.

And through the night Mahafny stayed with her,
rocked her, held her close as she sobbed, stroked her
hair, whispered endearments and encouragement. Though
she wondered once as sleep claimed her where Mahafny's
mind really dwelt despite her physical presence. "Evelien
didn't cry when I left her today," she murmured once
into thin air, but Doyce didn't care what it meant, because Mahafny held her safe, safe in the arms of her
teacher, her love.

❖

"Yes, Doyce, it is I. And no, I don't read minds, as
well you know. It's just that your face is so transparent
sometimes." A faintly tanned hand with long, thin fingers
tidied Doyce's hair back from her forehead, fingertips
a brief kiss at the hairline. The touch promised peace,
understanding, a chance to yield the burdensome responsibility. "Now, I believe you need some help here." The
slightest hand gesture served as a command. "You gentlemen over there, four of you, if you please. Can you
assist the good Shepherd to his quarters?" Her still dark
eyebrows quirked with the faintest trace of condescen-
sion. "I assume he has quarters nearby?"

Two husky farmers and a stonemason, from the looks
of his dusty, heavy canvas clothes and leather-looped
chisels and mallets hanging from his tool belt, volunteered. Joining a reed-thin lay brother, they strained to
lift the just beginning to stir Harrap and carry him in the
direction the young man indicated with a jerk of his chin,
his breath and concentration needed for more important
matters as he strained under the unaccustomed weight.
Parm staggered up and walked slowly behind, ears and

tail at half-mast, never letting the Shepherd out of his
sight.

"Shall we accompany them, do you think?" Mahafny
commented.

The procession wound its awkward way through the
cramped side gate, Mahafny uttering brisk instructions
and running commentary as they maneuvered through.
Doyce, Khar, and Claire, still clutching her basin, her
package of wool secured in the bib of her apron, trailed
at the end of the procession. Claire's dark hair hung
loose in exuberant waves, her kerchief long gone in the
melee, or so Doyce thought until she realized that Claire
had sacrificed it to bathe Harrap's face. Resourceful of
her.

The stonemason muffled an oath as his tool belt caught
and hung on the door casing, yanking him back like a
hooked fish. He shifted his grip on Harrap, eased backward and swung his hip free, nodded to continue forward. The low, thatch-roofed building whose narrow
doorway they had crowded through appeared to serve as
some sort of communal dormitory, luckily deserted at
this time of day. Built of the same limestone as the
Bethel itself, it washed them with a blessed coolness, the
air unmildewed but overlaid with a lingering aroma of
myrrh. Groaning in concert, the four men lowered Harrap onto the cotlike, coarsely blanketed bed nearest the
door, unwilling to carry their burden any farther. Five
other beds lined the room, three to a side, each with a
stout, scarred wooden chest at its foot and an unadorned,
octagonal Lady's Shield pinned on the wall over its head.
The young lay brother mopped his brow with his sleeve
and spoke in an undertone with Mahafny, gesturing with
butterfly hesitations to emphasize his words, his hands
the most fluent and lovely thing about him, far more
expressive than his solemn face, still in the throes of late
adolescent acne. He came as close to a bow as his Order
allowed and left.

"I'll examine him, perhaps sedate him as soon as the
young man fetches some fresh water and my 'script
case." Doyce felt entrapped in Mahafny's gaze, the cool
gray eyes, the long eloquent neck with its twist of silver
hair rising above it, caught near the nape with a wood

and leather clip. Putting her hands into the pockets of her long white eumedico's coat, she rocked back on her heels, examining Doyce from top to bottom as frankly as if conducting a physical. "Perhaps it might be less distressing if you and the two ghatti were elsewhere when he comes around? And if the young lady would stay and assist further?" She raised her chin in Claire's direction to indicate her preference.

Doyce knew the polite tones, the rising inflection at the end of each utterance, the "perhaps" at the beginning, stood as Mahafny's equivalent of a command. She expected obedience, in truth, assumed immediate compliance with each directive. But now Doyce doubted her readiness to obey as pliantly or as quickly and as unquestioningly as she had done in the past. Too many years separated them and their relationship: pain, growth, and change, for better or for worse. She had changed through the years, learned to take control of herself to avoid the hurt; whether Mahafny had changed remained to be seen. Yet no matter what she told herself, Mahafny still retained enough power to make her feel obscurely guilty, unsure of herself. That was how the older woman had always treated the eumedicos-in-training, making them feel beholden yet gratified that she had befriended them and guided them. And no one could say that she did not genuinely care for and, in some instances, love her charges, but Doyce wasn't her charge any longer. Not here, not now, not with the world turning upside down beneath her feet again as it had done once before so long ago in another dormitory hall. Now she had a right, a sanctioned duty to seek the truth, not obscure it.

"No, I know Parm will feel more secure if we remain close by where he can watch, be sure that Harrap fares well." She surprised herself with her firm steadiness as she met the abruptly frosty regard of the eumedico's eyes, expertly masked chagrin at the contradiction.

"I don't see the relationship. Why does the ghatt require the presence of a Shepherd of Our Lady?" The scornful lift of her dark brows and her phrase, "I don't see the relationship," had been enough to cow hundreds of eumedico trainees through the years.

"Perhaps you don't," golden-sweet as honey, Doyce

tasted the enjoyment of the phrase, "but the ghatt has just 'Printed on Harrap. He's worried, fearful of losing his new Bondmate. And the ghatt's name, by the way, is Parm. My ghatta is Khar'pern."

Mahafny came down hard on her heels, hands fisting in her pockets. "Impossible. Absolutely. It can't have happened," she said with meticulous, level emphasis. "I know of no precedents, no cases. . . ."

"Yes, precisely. Nor do I. But past history—or lack of it—bears little immediate relevance to our concern with Shepherd Harrap's condition. Perhaps you could see to him now? The brother has brought the water and your 'script case." Motioning Khar and Parm after her, she withdrew to the far end of the room to give the eumedico and patient a discreet amount of privacy.

Parm hoisted himself up on the vacant bed, too tired to spring, and stretched his length along the rough brown woolen blanket. Looking down at him, Doyce decided he'd do as the most strangely marked ghatt she'd ever seen, as if some mad, blindfolded painter had mixed a palette of tabby orange and black and a bit of white and daubed at random, a speck here, a splotch there. A white chest and chin, but half the ghatt's face was orange, or mostly so, the other half black, but even the line of demarcation faltered and floundered across his face. White thumbprint-sized markings on one side plus one white hind leg. Rare for a male to carry such coloration, and the few who did were invariably sterile. For the most part Parm bore his motley proudly, jaunty as a jester in his ragtag coloring, a perky, knowing expression and a sporty walk a part of his being.

Now, however, he looked woebegone, fur matted in spots; in other areas clumps of fur stood straight, patched with the residue of his race through the Market Square— raw egg, beer, custard, something else Doyce hesitated to identify, though Khar's derisive sniff confirmed it. Whiskers wilted with dejection, Parm's ears stayed tucked low, pinned back against his head.

"By the gift we all hold sacred and by the truth we Seek, what happened, Parm?" she mindspoke.

The ghatt shifted, twisted himself on the bed. **"It's Georges . . . we cannot Bond anymore."** He hesitated, and the voice in her mind cracked with pain at the admission. **"He . . . he is not Georges!"**

"What do you mean? Of course it's Georges, who else could he be? Are you mad?"

Georges Barbet was Georges Barbet, a quiet, unassuming yet basically proficient Seeker, a man with a hidden but barbed sense of humor to match his name. When he chose to sting, he made his victim very uncomfortable. She had known him for some time, an acquaintance rather than a friend, the majority of their chance meetings and occasionally similar leave times had been on a superficial but correctly pleasant basis. They'd played a number of hard-fought card games when he'd discovered her weakness for Tally-Ho, but conversation had been minimal in deference to the need for careful point counting. Parm was the gaudiest thing about Georges, as if the ghatt had symbolized some deeply suppressed aspect of the man.

"Something in him has turned wrong. He hides from my mindtouch . . . and I can feel the blackness growing within him!" Parm's tongue darted in nervous licks at a spot of stiffened egg yolk on his leg, and Doyce gave him a moment to groom. **"So black . . . the badness inside, the seed sprouting, just as when we must destroy a ghatten because it is not good."**

"But if he wasn't good, how could you have Chosen him, 'Printed on him?" No sense, no sense at all, or sense that she was missing? She twisted at a strand of hair, wound and unwound it, perplexed at missing some secret that shouldn't have been a secret at all. *"And what do you mean about destroying ghatten? Ghattas don't kill their ghatten, they're not like some barn cat devouring her litter!"*

Ghatt and ghatta side-glanced each other, communicating beyond Doyce's ability to mindwalk with them.

"They must sometimes." Parm stared down at Khar. **"Tell her! She must understand this!"**

Khar's head drooped low, vulnerable and beseeching as a supplicant. She paused, reordering her thoughts. **"Sometimes a ghatta sees within her newborn that which is not right, that which is not true. Not a weak or sickly body, but a mind wrong bent, that would cause great**

damage if allowed to survive. To allow such a mind to
'Print with one of yours would cause destruction, a black
seed growing into a warped black vine that strangles all
it comes near. It was so with my first litter. . . ." Her
amber eyes dilated, pupils black against the deep gold,
Khar cast a yearning look toward her Bondmate, craving
understanding and forgiveness. "And so I killed them."
She shook herself. "What Parm is trying to say is that
he knows of that blackness, and that same blackness is
now within Georges."

Knuckles white, wound so tightly in the lock of hair
that she expected it to pull free, Doyce let her mindspeech scream, *"But how could you have Chosen Georges
if you knew!"* Would a black-souled ghatten corrupt an
innocent person or choose a Bondmate with an equally
black soul? Could an evil person corrupt an innocent
ghatten, bend its mind to evil? Her mind spun, trying to
sort the permutations, the possibilities, more than she
could chart. And how was Truth subverted then? *"How
could you . . . ?"* And didn't know how to finish the
sentence.

"Because he was true when I 'Printed on him!" Khar
nodded once as if to affirm the statement, and she had
to trust her, had no choice. "But ever since our trip
through the Northerlies three circuits ago, he was changed.
He went away one night, he said for cards and said he
must go alone, that the others would be afraid I read
their hands. And when he returned, he had begun to
change. It kept waxing stronger and stronger, burning
inside him. He kept staring at me and I knew he wanted
to claim my mind! As if he would devour me and the
me-ness inside me! Bondmates share but they do not
consume!" The ghatt panted in dread at visions that he
would not share. "The Bond was broken."

"It is true," Khar interjected. "I felt it in him as soon
as he entered the town. Faint at first . . . then stronger,
more lethal, clawing at any thought within his reach. I
have never felt that before . . . except . . ." She froze,
the fur along her spine rising. "Except for . . . the night
Oriel died and Saam was hurt . . . when I felt something
so horrible but so faint that I could not believe my mind
read true."

Doyce sat numbly, thoughts squirrel-wheeling around and around, gaining no ground the harder she thought, ceaselessly circling. *"Did . . . you notice anything like it last night at the Cyan Inn?"* She poised herself for the answer, breathing fast, waiting for confirmation.

"No, no, I don't think so." The ghatta's eyes slitted in concentration. **"No, but I was far gone into my time when we arrived. I stayed outside all the evening until I reached the room. What do you mean?"**

"I don't know, but for a moment at the inn, amidst the laughter and the comfort and the camaraderie, I felt . . . something just as I started up for bed. Animosity so sharp I stumbled. It was probably . . . nothing."

But it had been. For a brief instant it had pierced sharp as a suddenly unshuttered lantern beam lances night-vision, destroying it. Then nothing, as if it had never been. Who had been in the taproom at that moment? How many people, some she knew slightly, some by sight only, and others she'd never see again? Where had it—if anything—come from? Or was she so on edge, so suggestible, that Khar's and Parm's stories together made her recast and remold things into a foreboding signaling?

"Doyce," Mahafny's voice called her to attention, beckoned from across the room. "He's coming to now. If what you say is true, I think you should be here."

She stood, pressed her knee against the side of the bed to brace it, and then turned. "I am a Seeker Veritas as you well know. I speak the truth, but I don't know where it will lead us, Mahafny. I only hope the Lady herself knows."

Walking down the main aisle to Harrap's bed, she reached out and captured an unwilling hand. "Harrap, Harrap. You must listen to me now, we have much to discuss."

Harrap's restless eyes avoided hers, searching around the room. She knew what he searched for, what he fervently prayed not to find. With a low whistle she called both ghatti to her, Khar pausing while Parm tumbled off the bed. "Harrap, his name is Parm. Give him no other; he chose it for himself."

"I know." The fluty whisper bore little resemblance to Harrap's normal baritone. "He *told* me." Reaching down hesitantly, broad fingers splayed, Harrap allowed his palm to touch the ghatt's forehead. A deep purr rolled from the depths of Parm's chest, but Harrap jerked his hand away, and the ghatt stopped, neck stretched upward, head seeking the caress again. Harrap reached back gamely and jerked away equally as fast.

"Parm, you're pushing too hard, let him be for a bit," Doyce begged, knowing the ghatt mindspoke on the intimate mode, chattering magpie fast and furious in his eagerness to communicate with his new Bond.

"Just telling him that I am his and he is mine, that we are a Pair," Parm protested, radiating hopefulness at the recumbent man who regarded him with wide blue eyes, one hand pressed tight to his mouth like a frightened child.

"Yes, and ghatt-dancing and ghattawauling through his brain into secret places he never even knew existed."

The fringes of his tonsured hair whipped back and forth as Harrap shook himself, hoping to cast off the voice the way a large dog shakes himself to shed water. "Go gently, little friend, little Parm. I think I hear you speak but know it can't be real. The exalted hear from the Lady in their hearts, but I am only a simple Shepherd, not worthy enough for that, though I've listened hard."

Rearranging the contents of her medical bag, Mahafny cleared her throat, but continued her organization. "He's not a demon, Harrap, nor are you mad or blessed with visions, hearing voices. It is the ghatt you hear in your head."

Doyce hadn't expected Mahafny to speak, to throw herself in on her side. She had counted on the eumedico to argue, to continue to protest that it was impossible, or that if it were possible, that it could be cured as if it were some sort of disease. The challenge she'd set herself dissolved before her face. Obscurely, she questioned if she wanted an ally or, more particularly, this one. It destabilized the relationship she knew and that she could at least see objectively after so many years.

"Transparent, Doyce," Mahafny chuckled, but no amusement lightened the sound. "But that that is, is. You know that and Harrap, I'm afraid, is beginning to know that. One must acquiesce to facts, but I remain intrigued. I've certainly never heard of a second Bonding. A total anomaly. Could this be replicated in other instances?"

"Doyce, what is going on? I don't understand," Claire broke in, and she started in alarm, forgetting that the girl remained, so locked was she in the triangle of Harrap and Mahafny and herself, and the triangle of Harrap and Parm and herself. Claire's presence came as a sudden, extraneous element and she sorted frantically through her mind as to how much to say, how much to tell her. Best to let her involvement remain peripheral if she could manage it.

"Claire, do you think perhaps you could find some wine for us all?"

Her look of protest more eloquent than a shout, she restrained herself. "Ever an innkeep's daughter," came her wry response, all bitterness checked. "But only if you promise to explain things to me later."

Harrap sat propped upright in bed now, arms thrust behind him in pillared support. Parm crept onto the foot of the bed, one orange ear and one black ear just visible over the mound of the Shepherd's feet. An orange/black nose appeared, tested the reception and withdrew in haste. "How often does he speak?"

"As often as you want, frequently more than that, and sometimes never when you truly crave it." Khar gave an explosive sneeze at Doyce's rejoinder. "You have a hard road ahead of you, Harrap, but a worthwhile one. First, you'll have to travel to Headquarters for training, and then . . ."

"But I can't!" he broke in, a bead of sweat jarred loose by his agitation rolling down his face tearlike. "I am a Shepherd! That is my vocation, that is my vow—the Bethel claims me to serve our Lady in any way She sees fit! How can I serve the Lady and be a Seeker? To have a ghatt at the center of my world, we who vow to have no other being or thing ahead of Our Lady!" His words rushed into each other, his eyes swimming with tears as his hand sought the solace of the medallion at his chest. "Must I choose one or the other, perhaps lose the Lady's blessing?"

Mahafny sat on the edge of the next bed, her usually

erect shoulders slumped. "I know it seems late in life to make a change, but it may be necessary. I do not think the ghatt will demand that you stop loving and revering the Lady; am I correct, Doyce?" Doyce nodded, then nodded with more conviction. "But it may be in more challenging and more subtle ways than before." Her voice dropped, becoming almost inaudible, so faint that Doyce questioned her hearing of the final words. "To face a choice at this stage, when the time of questioning seemed past, is it a blessing . . . or a curse?"

Doyce risked a tentative stroke to the twisted crown of silver hair and wondered, for the first time, what private regrets crowded Mahafny's mind.

"Harrap, I've little time, for I must be on my way about this circuit for other reasons. But let me begin to explain, to train you a little." Doyce prayed that the confidence in her tone showed, that that much of the eumedico training remained with her. "I'll have Khar transmit a message to request that a Seeker-Guidancer pair ride out immediately from Headquarters to teach you some basics, offer encouragement, to help you decide your path. You and Parm together have much to think about over the next few octs and octants.

"Now first, I want you to let Parm touch your mind again. Gently, Parm," she admonished. "No, Harrap, don't try to block it, I can see it in your eyes, not yet. You don't know how to block it and you'll only strain your sanity. Just accept the voice for what it is, a voice."

"I will be gentle, I will not pry," Parm reassured. The ghatt's eyes brightened and his head popped over Harrap's feet. Harrap, Doyce suspected, had made an effort to mindspeak, not simply let his thoughts be read. "Because you are good, because you are my Bondmate," the ghatt purred, rubbing his head and chin against the blanketed mound of Harrap's feet.

Catching Harrap's attention, Doyce continued. "Parm is using surface mindwalking with you, rather than the deep mindwalking you felt before when he became overexcited. Surface is for simple conversations between you, deep mindwalking for Seeking Truth when we judge our cases. They do not pry with any particular enjoyment to discover inner secrets, but out of a charge to Seek the

Truths. Ultimately Parm must engage in this with you to
know you inside and out, as well or better than you know
yourself. The ghatti carry that responsibility with great
care and pride not to break the trust. Our skills as Seekers do not range as deeply as theirs, and while we can
read them and speak them to a certain level, our abilities
will never allow us the deep mindwalking of the ghatti
. . . or approach the specialized gifts of the eumedicos."
The lie came effortlessly, although not painlessly, as she
paid lipservice to the old credo, refusing to reveal Mahafny's secret, the eumedico's secret to outsiders, but Mahafny only inclined her head, her eyes half-closed in
meditative thought.

"I, too, came to be a Seeker later in life than most,
have had other pasts and personal ambitions that I wasn't
sure I wanted to yield in favor of this. But Parm has
made his choice, and you have both branched onto a
path you never expected to take. In all honesty, we've
no road maps or guides to a Bonding of this sort, and
while we can assist you, much of what you do will be
creating new paths of knowledge for us all. You lack a
sure footing at this moment, but we are all here to guide
and reassure you as much as we can. And others will
soon be here to help even more.

"I must go for a little while, but I promise I'll be back.
Arrangements must be made, messages sent, things decided. Mahafny, will you stay with him until Khar and I
return?"

"Of course. Harrap, whether you wish silent companionship or someone to talk with, I shall be here. Although," and she paused, her eyes holding a glint of
amusement which Doyce remembered only too well, "I
wonder what the All-Shepherd Nichlaus will have to say
about a lone man and woman together in the Shepherd's
sleeping quarters, chaperoned by a ghatt."

Harrap let out a roar of laughter that rollicked Parm
on the bed and left the ghatt tremulous with delight.

The final chant floated mistlike through the night air,
and Parm's fur trembled and rose with the unearthly

beauty of the sound. Voice upon voice swirling in and
out of each note, one leaving, another beginning, then
two sounding as one, the echo of counterpoints. If the
ghatti mindnet were audible to human ears, he thought,
it would resemble this. The last notes faded away, but
the resonance remained, tingling the hairs of his inner
ear. He shifted and settled, curled himself into a tight
ball and wrapped a paw around his nose and over one
eye. Phew! Still smelly! He'd licked and rubbed and
licked some more until he'd thought the bristles on his
tongue would wear away, leave him smooth and slurpy
as a dog. Ugh, what a thought! Harrap didn't notice the
smell, he was confident of that; humans didn't have very
sensitive nostrils, despite their size.

Harrap lay beside him, stiff and unbending as a log.
He quelled the desire to race up and down the wide
figure, to startle him and find himself airborne from the
booming laughter. He didn't dare—not yet. Perhaps
soon, and perhaps . . . never. He had taken on responsibility for guiding and training a fully formed human
mind, not a malleable youngling of their species. Now
what was he to do? Well, the rightness resided in Harrap
and he had determination and patience. No matter that
many laughed at him and his looks, he knew what he
was made of and the mettle of the new Bond he had
Chosen.

He gave a minute ghatti sigh of distress into the soft
fur of his inner leg. It wasn't fair to Harrap, so good, so
kind, and so baffled by what had happened. But what
other choice had he had? In all honesty, Parm felt
equally bewildered, sure that he was just but wondering
if he'd gone about it the wrong way. The Elders had
remained silent to his desperate cries, and when he'd felt
the emanation of goodness from Harrap he had literally
taken his life and run with it, away from Georges toward
the sensation he felt, beckoning stronger and stronger as
he raced through the Market Square toward Harrap. But
what was a Shepherd, this kind of shepherd?

A hand crept from under the blanket, trying to move
as stealthily as a mouse. Parm's uncovered eye watched
it creep down and halt, then the fingers waggled and
brushed the curve of his flank. *"Are you awake, little*

one?" The mindvoice twittered and broke, a startled bird flushed from cover.

"Yes, my Bondmate. I am always eager to hear your voice." He gave a little stretch and wiggle that managed to slide his head under the man's hand, felt his ears being scratched.

"We must get new earrings," he purred, **"a pair for you and a pair for me to show we belong."**

The hand stopped scratching, held steady just above his head. "Earrings? But the Lady insists that we employ no adornment beyond our medallions. It is not fitting to bedeck oneself like that." One finger prodded the hoop in Parm's left ear, moved it back and forth. "Though I do admire it."

Parm tried not to rush the words, not to overwhelm the man with his 'speaking. **"I would wear a Lady's Medal for you, if you wanted me to, if it would make you feel better."**

Muffled laughter made waves through the bed, rocking and soothing the ghatt. "I don't know what All-Shepherd Nichlaus'd think of that idea. Best not to try it."

"But I would," he protested, **"I would wear that, I would do anything you wanted of me!"**

"Even leave me if I asked you to, little Parm, little mindbadger burrowing through my brain?" The baritone voice echoed solemn and serious through the bleakness of night.

Parm choked, made a little wailing sound, and mewled. Then wordlessly, he slunk on his belly toward the foot of the bed, ready to slide off and be swallowed by the darkness. Cast off! Oh, by the Elders, no! Unwanted, disowned, doomed to wander without mindmate! Cursed, unfit to share a human brain! So wrong, wrong to try this! His front paws reached the foot of the bed and he readied himself to slip to the floor, run out the door, and hide deep in the woods until he died of loneliness, rejected by humans and his own kind for his failure. Reckless hands seized him around the middle, hoisted him into the air, and crushed him breathless and bruised against Harrap's chest. Never had pain felt so good.

"I don't care what the Lady thinks, but I don't believe she can think badly of you, for you're one of her creatures," Harrap roared. "If Nichlaus tries to send you away, he sends me away as well! You are my Bond, and I—for whatever you'll do to me, with me, for me—am yours. But, oh, little one, go slowly, because I am so very afraid of the unknown. And you certainly are that."

Trilling so hard that his mindvoice dragonfly-fluttered, then floated steady on an updraft of love, Parm answered, **"But not unknown for long!"** Yet a thought nagged at him. **"What would the Lady ask of me? I do not know what you call religion, how you worship or why. But I would embrace it if it would please you. Explain to me how and I will try!"**

Harrap's cheek sandpapered against the soft, short hairs behind his ear, then came to rest on his crown. "Well, let's see." Harrap considered, then continued, "First we have to have you tonsured."

The ghatt squirmed, cracked his head under Harrap's chin. **"Tonsured?"** He glared upward, unable to see any farther than the meaty underside of Harrap's jaw, his throat. **"Tonsured! They laugh at me now because of my markings!"** Then he subsided, settled, heart steeled to the indignity of having his crown shaved. **"But if it is what you wish, then do so."**

"Ah, poor little Parm, you'd suffer any indignity I offer you. Just as we do for Our Lady, putting others' needs first above our own. We vow to have no other being or thing ahead of Our Lady, but perhaps She will permit you to walk beside Her. Mayhap you are one of the Lady's mysteries, sent to me to decipher, and mayhap you are simply you. But for better or worse, we are together now and until the end."

"Not going to shave head?" Parm whisperspoke.

"No, no tonsure, and perhaps, when I've thought about it, an earring or two for me, if it means so much to you. We'll see. Now sleep, little one."

And Parm fell asleep on Harrap's broad chest, lulled by the gentle rise and fall of the Shepherd's breathing, feeling safe at last.

PART
FOUR

A long night and promising to be longer still, Doyce knew as she knuckled the graininess from her eyes. Lucky Khar to be able to sleep on the pommel platform, rocking unconcernedly to Lokka's stride, while she, Doyce, played pilot and lookout. The afternoon had grown tormentingly long, the evening longer still, a drain on mind and body.

"**Am too watching. Even with my eyes closed I see more than you.**" Khar thwacked Doyce's wrist with the tip of her tail in reproval.

"Good, then you can use your tail to tickle me awake." Doyce gave a deft tug at the twitching tail. "Now, have we done everything we should have? When do you think Bard and M'wa will reach Harrap and Parm?"

Khar resettled herself on the sheepskin padding, pulled her tail from unresisting fingers. "**Soon, probably before daybreak. They've been given permission to cancel the circuit, so they can cut cross-country.**"

Doyce had had Khar mindspeak M'wa to report the situation to him and Bard; M'wa, in turn, would transmit the story in its entirety to Byrta and P'wa, who would transmit it back to Headquarters, though what the Seeker General would make of the day's astounding events she

251

would have dearly loved to know. Georges Barbet's defection; a second Bonding, all too fantastical for words. The Seeker General desperately needed hard facts, not suppositions, but these hard facts did nothing but engender more confusion. She'd downplayed what she'd told Khar about her previous evening's thoughts regarding Ballen and dissection. Rationality, daylight logic told her she had jumped to unwarranted conclusions with insufficient evidence. At any rate, at least they could send a Seeker-Guidancer pair to work with Harrap and Parm. Until then, Bard and M'wa would remain at Harrap's side, and Mahafny had promised to stay on, although Doyce fought her uneasiness at the situation. Why she should feel distrustful she wasn't sure. Just a prickling unease that somehow a eumedico should play no part in this. Or, she struggled with the thought, tried to face it squarely, am I jealous?

"Of what?"

She forced herself to try to pin it down, to give an answer that would be true and make sense to the ghatta. "Because Mahafny belonged to my previous life, and I deserve to be beyond her sphere of influence now. Or . . ." she paused, thinking, feeling the wind tumble her hair, staring off and beyond at the eight satellite moons waxing and waning in their stately dance around the Lady Moon. Harrap would reassure her that the answers would be there. "Or . . . because I don't want to share her. I don't know anymore."

"Mmph. Some of one, some of the other." Khar's tone was noncommittal.

Doyce changed the subject rather than waiting to see if the ghatta would probe any further. "Do you think Claire is mad at us, or more likely, at me?"

"She's not well pleased, but her curiosity will hold until we see her again."

Claire had not relished Doyce's further instructions to take Lokka back to the inn so she could perform her afternoon's and evening's duties for Eli, but had admitted she had little choice. She needed the job. Only the promise that she could bring Lokka back into town along with Doyce's gear later that evening to say good-bye had placated her. And a good thing she had returned, because in her excitement she had forgotten her yarn.

"I still don't see why we had to push on tonight."

"I don't know. Obstinance, mayhap. I just felt we had to reach Kissena by morning. Tired, but I couldn't have slept anyway, could you?" Although she felt dreamy and lulled by the ride, sleep still eluded her. Suddenly she sat bolt upright in the saddle, knees squeezing Lokka tight, panicking Khar who, in turn, nearly spooked Lokka. She soothed and apologized to them both.

"But what was Mahafny doing in Cyanberry anyway? She doesn't travel as a eumedico any more, she's Staff Senior at the Healing Hall at the capital!"

Looking put out, Khar resettled herself, rewrapped her tail, and kneaded the pommel platform. "A little late to ask that now."

❖

The scream harrowed the air with passionate despair and utter hopelessness, hung for a long breath, puncturing the very earth, drilled through the faint, false-dawn breeze with a piercing intensity that racked mind and body. Then a convulsive shattering of sound and a leaden curtain of silence slammed into place, suffocating thought.

Every hair on her body prickled, her flesh crawling as adrenaline coursed through her, arguing for action, any action. But nothing was possible until she controlled Lokka. The mare reared skyward, and Doyce dug into her stirrups, forcing herself straight, aware of Khar pinned between her and the platform, only to feel the mare slamming down stiff-legged, trying to buck them both off. Using every iota of strength she possessed, leaning back on the reins so hard on Lokka's soft mouth that she grimaced in sympathy, she clamped her legs tight and managed to hold Lokka steady. The mare quivered and blew as if she'd run a long race.

"What was it?" she gasped, daring to ease the reins a fraction.

"Quick! Quick! We must follow!" Khar's rigid form stood nearly twice its normal size, her fur needling out all over her body, her tail crooked and her ears pinned tight to her head, mouth wide in a snarl.

"Where, damn it? You still can't see a thing off the main road! Where are we going? Calm Lokka first!"

"I will guide Lokka!"

Muscles straining, body canted forward until it appeared the ghatta might take reckless flight over the mare's head, Khar seized control, mindspeaking Lokka into a careening gallop. Doyce held on grimly, ducking whipping branches and draping vines that tried to noose her head, praying all the while the valiant mare wouldn't trip and fall. She was galloping full tilt, Khar exhorting her, and Doyce hadn't the slightest idea of their direction, except that they had left the main road. False dawn, but still pitch-dark in the hardwood stand that hemmed the two-track road they had followed before veering off into a planting of long-pin pines, the air sharp with the smell of resin and the ground treacherously slick with old needles. All her energy and control evaporated, sapped by the sinking hour between dark and first dawn. She crouched in the saddle, thrust an arm to deflect a branch that she sensed more than saw in the murkiness. The branch whipped by, slapped and stung, scraping the length of her forearm.

Lokka broke from the stand of pines and rocketed across a grazing meadow, oblivious to the dangers of chuckholes and rocks. A small cottage and barn glowed gray-white in the distance, like leftover pieces from a child's toy town, abandoned for the night.

"Too late, too late," Khar moaned, and the flood of agony overwhelmed Doyce. **"Too late from the very beginning!"**

Lokka clattered to a stop outside the barn, chest pumping and light brown coat slicked dark with sweat. Khar sprang clear as the mare took a last stumbling step, and Doyce swung herself after, clinging to the pommel platform for balance as she hit the ground. The place looked forlorn and deserted, dead quiet in the early, creeping light, not even a cow lowing in anticipation of the milking, nor the early, uncertain bustle of chickens, or the lithe shadow of a hunting barn cat returning home. Belting her sword around her waist and grabbing her staff, she went toward the partially open barn door. It was then the shadow moved.

Doyce lurched to a stop, legs locking except for the tremors that coursed through them, but the ghatta stiffened, then walked ahead, ignoring the old man and the equally elderly ghatt propped against the wall. **"They are not the problem. Come."**

She hesitated, then swept the lantern from the ground beside them without asking or apologizing. The old man acted drunk or in shock, never looking in her direction, one hand ceaselessly stroking the ghatt, lost in his own private thoughts. Edging to the threshold of the black rectangle of emptiness that stood out against the white siding of the barn, she paused for Khar to catch up with her, afraid to step through into the unknown. Much as it shamed her to admit it, she hoped the ghatta would enter first.

"Together?"

She nodded, exhaled through clenched teeth as she held the lantern high and to the left, away from her, and raised her sword on the diagonal to shield her body. Khar glided low and stealthy, then they both stepped inside.

Heart banging, breath fast and ragged, she felt as if she were reliving the terror of their earlier headlong ride, and her stomach roiled, sour with fear, threatened to reverse itself. Poised like a javelin about to be launched, the ghatta rippled with an unending, monotonous growl, hair standing in bristles along her spine. Holding the lantern higher, swinging it in cautious arcs, she strained to see, vision drowned in darkness and shadows.

The smell bludgeoned her very being, an odor comprised of the sickish-sweet smell of clotting blood, blood in abundance, as if she had wandered into a shambles, an abattoir; the reek of perspiration, sweat engendered by terror; and the raw, pungent odor of loosened bowels. Even her eumedico training had not prepared her for this prodigality of blood. She forced short, niggling gasps through her open mouth; waiting for her sense of smell to numb itself to the stink. An uneasy cow stamped and grunted, its eyes rolling as she swung the lantern back.

One guarded step, then another, and she saw beyond the cow's stall a human leg jutting obscenely pale in the

light, stocking ruckled down around the ankle, foot
twisted in an improbable direction. Pooled blood, rapidly
sinking, darkened the packed dirt floor. Clutching hard
at the lantern and her sword, she tightroped one foot
ahead of the other, navigating around the darker patches.
Finally she peered over the partition of the stall.

A man lay still, face in a rictus of agony, an angry,
oozing crushed spot jelling his right temple. She counted
other body wounds aplenty, parallel slash marks that
puzzled her, and deeper, gaping wounds, the obvious
work of a swordsman intent on obtaining as much suffering as possible from his work before killing. He lay in a
pool of blood, one hand still locked tight on a pitchfork,
the shaft broken off halfway. A fat, bumbling fly, one
of the last of summer, slow-witted, sated on blood, and
desperate for a warm place to finish out its time, bounced
and butted at Doyce, slamming into her shoulder, her
cheek, the lantern. Its mindless, whining drone buzz-
sawed through her, made her want to scream to drown
it out.

Khar's monotone growl rose in pitch and intensity,
breaking into a cry of devastation that spanned an octave
on one tortured breath. Spinning left, Doyce tilted the
lantern higher, trying to locate the ghatta as her scream
filled the barn to overflowing with lamentation. Khar's
eyes reflected eerie green in the lantern light, and she
followed the luminescent twin beacons.

In the unsteady circle of light Khar crouched over the
body of a tortoiseshell ghatt, twisted, torn, bloody, its
neck at an unnatural angle, one ear nearly torn off, lips
peeled back from sharp teeth. It, too, had not died an
easy death. She bent down and had the doubly sickening
sensation of realizing that it was a ghatta; a tiny white
ghatten with gray and black patches lay inert under the
ghatta's foreleg. She stroked Khar unthinkingly, smoothing the bristling fur, and the ghatta whirled, teeth bared,
aiming a reflexive strike before she mastered herself.

Desperate not to inhale the fetor, Doyce rationed herself a thimbleful of air, hungry for more. "Khar, it's
Wwar'm and Asa Brandt. I didn't know we rode that
close to their farm, you didn't tell me where you were

leading." The words, inconsequential at best, dropped lifelessly around her.

Asa, recently retired with Wwar'm; she had attended their farewell fete two years ago. How could she not have recognized the strawberry blond hair? Easy, she knew, for Asa had been so alive: energetic, bubbly, warmhearted, suggesting perfectly sensible and absurd things in the same breath. A clear blue sky and a bright yellow sun offered occasion enough for Asa to scoop up Wwar'm and indulge in a dance of joy. No more, she thought, no more.

Khar swallowed in agitation, throat muscles straining with the effort. Her mindspeech sounded hoarse, as if her actual growls and screams had strained that as well. "Wwar'm! Why!" And then she cocked her head and sprang into the farthest corner of darkness, a jumble of burlap sacking tossed by the wall where harness and various leather straps and leads were hung. She could smell the oil; Asa always took good care of things.

Breathing a prayer to the Lady, Doyce followed, until Khar's growl of warning pulled her up short. Then she heard it, a tiny, thread-thin wail of terror as Khar hooked a guarded paw into the topmost sack. A little yellow tiger ghatten lay beneath, eyes pinched shut, body quaking, tiny claws spread wide to defend itself. She reached out for it in an agony of compassion, and Khar batted her hand away, hard. The reaction shocked her.

"No! It's ready to 'Print. The shock made it come early. Don't touch!" Khar nuzzled him and received a pawful of needle-tipped claws across her nose. She tried again and the ghatten squalled, his small heart hammering frantically against his rib cage. One survivor.

"In your 'script pouch . . . larissa, mungwort, a pinch of mull bark? Do you have it?"

"I think so, I . . . yes." She mentally reviewed the necessaries she carried in her saddlebags. "An infusion?" The ghatta nodded. "But how can we get him to swallow it? And what will it do?"

"Put him to sleep until we can get him to a nursing ghatta."

"Doyce!" The unexpected touch on her shoulder galvanized her, nearly sent her exploding straight up into

the loft. She pivoted in a defensive crouch, ready to
strike and kick. Where had she left her sword? Starting
to dive toward the ghatta's limp body she cursed bitterly,
Fool! In the midst of danger more danger and death
stalked, and now she and Khar would accompany Asa
and Wwar'm and the unnamed ghatten, one barely alive
and one dead, on that journey. "Doyce! It's me, Bard!"
And strong arms snaked her upright, held her tight until
sagging limbs gained control. "Didn't you hear me come
in? I spoke."

Doyce pressed shaking arms against Bard's chest, let
her head tilt against his shoulder, relieved that he taken
firm control of the lantern. In her hands it would have
wavered like a drunken lightning bug. She blurted,
"We've got to do something quickly. There's a ghatten
still alive, and Khar says it's ready to 'Print."

He cradled her with both arms, blocking out her sight,
but her mind still saw the bodies, the blood. Had Oriel
looked like that when Bard and Byrta had found him?
"I'll take care of it," but his voice faltered. "Now come
outside and sit down. I might as well tell you now: Asa's
wife and daughter are dead—inside the house. M'wa is
still checking the grounds. Who are the old man and the
ghatt outside? I feel as if I should know the ghatt, at
least."

Formless little muttering sounds fumbled themselves
on her tongue, senseless except that they gave voice to
her fear. Ready to babble, she could feel it, so she compressed her lips hard, pushed off from the safety of
Bard's chest and the familiar wool-scent of his tabard,
and wove an unsteady path toward the door, now suffused with pale daylight. "I . . . I don't . . . know. Didn't
. . . take time for intro . . . ductions." She pushed harder
at the words, made them break cover from where they
lurked. "Khar said . . . not to mind them."

Bard chewed at his lip, struggled to sort through his
thoughts and memories. Then he slammed fist into palm.
"I've got it! That's Ma'ow. One of the oldest ghatti I've
ever met. That old man isn't his Bondmate, but I'd guess
he's the father of his Bond, Nathan Cummins. I think he
rode circuit about the time Swan did with A'rah, before
Koom. He used to visit our father and mother. That's

how Byrta and I knew we wanted to become Seekers. He was one of the few people who would stop and visit with us. Really visit, not just pass the time of day, ask the weather." A hint of yesterday's memories brightened his face, his teeth flashing in a fleeting but wide grin. "I thought Ma'ow looked familiar, but his whole mask has turned snowy now. *He* remembered. That's why he winked at me, the old rascal. He knows my memory isn't as good as his."

Outside now, Doyce lowered herself to the ground, back against the barn wall, thankful to soak up the morning sun. The old man and the ghatt slept, or at least dozed fitfully. Sleep, to let us forget the terrors we have witnessed; sleep, to create greater terrors from the soul's dark fears. A bane and a blessing, she decided as Bard walked to the house to heat water for the infusion.

"Wouldn't have gone in there, was I you, but ye did anyway, didn't ye?" the age-clouded voice boomed in her ear, matter-of-fact yet regretful. "No, 'tis a terrible, terrible sight. Knew it was something bad when we set out, but not like this. Should have been Nathan's duty by rights, but what with him laid up, side stove in and back kinked up after fallin' through them rotted shingles, what could I say? He told me, 'Poppa, something bad is happening, Ma'ow can feel it, and you've got to go in my place with him.' Well, I tell you I didn't know it'd be like this!" The rambling voice paused for breath, and Doyce heard the glugging sound of a bottle or jug. She rubbed at the scrape along her arm, fingers finding and smearing blood. That, at least, was real.

He sat cross-legged by the door, a hearty-looking but white-haired man, well into his seventies, supporting the ancient ghatt in his lap. Khar sniffed his face, and the ghatt turned his age-whitened muzzle toward Doyce, looking in her direction with eyes filmed by cataracts, milky-blue in the light.

"A drink? There's little left, but I'll share. You'll need it after that sight." He gestured with the tan stoneware bottle and Doyce reached forward, smelling the familiar scent of rum mixing with the warm, moist reek of blood emanating from the barn. Astonishingly, the thought of a drink made her swallow with an almost sacramental anticipation, and she stared back at the ghatt as she hefted the bottle.

A whorled tiger somewhat like Khar but with nowhere near the white on him, only a tiny chest patch, and thirty at least, an exceedingly venerable age. He wheezed, gave a cough, and mindwalked, his mindvoice still resonant and vital despite his years as he offered the traditional greeting and then continued.

"Welcome, younglings, though it's little welcome we all find here. As Bard knows, I am Ma'ow, and this is the father of my Bondmate, Nathan Cummins." His grizzled head wavered with old-age tremors, and it was obvious he was forcing himself under control, dismayed at his body's lack of resilience. **"Too old for this, but when times are dire, we must all respond."**

The first swig of rum left her eyes tearing and her throat on fire, but the second slid silken-smooth. Doyce sat cross-legged in imitation of the old man in front of her, waiting for the return of his bottle, but too polite to ask for it back, anxious head cocked to count her sips. She passed it back.

"What happened? I don't understand. That scream, like nothing I've ever heard, the terror inside, and now we sit here drinking rum and chatting. Khar, what happened? Who did this?"

The ghatt responded before Khar could. **"You have seen for yourselves. It had to be done. And if you, so young, can explain such madness, I will listen, learn. If not, so be it, for I cannot explain such savagery."**

The early light set sun motes dancing and crazy-weaving in the near distance, the sun reflecting off clouds of dust. Travelers so early? Danger or help? Whoever they were, they rode hard and fast. The old man had drifted asleep again, mouth half-open, head lolling against the wall. With a wordless apology she retrieved his rum bottle, took another sip, set it down. She pushed herself upright, letting her legs slide her up the wall until she stood, sword in hand, thankful that Bard had brought it along with him. More trouble, perhaps, although in her heart she thought not, or one or more of the ghatti—Khar, still inside, M'wa or Ma'ow—would have alerted her. Still, best not to be caught lacking again; the nagging memory of her unprofessionalism, the pathetic near-dive across the dirt floor a few moments earlier, made her burn with shame, adding its heat to the false warmth of the rum.

The separate cumuli of dust mingled as one and Doyce waited, chanting a calming sequence to herself. Strange that with the early morning sun, the freshness of the day, the sounds of a distant cicada just beginning to warm and saw away, the wheeling of doves leaving the barn cote, that everything could appear so normal, falsely secure. Yet in the house with Bard, two bodies; and in the barn watched over by Khar, more bodies, blood-drenched losers in an incredible battle. Appearance and reality. And worst of all, she had no idea what had befallen them. Something to do with Oriel's death or, worst thought of all, something to do with her, her presence in the area? Her vision blackened, swamped with darkness; what had Swan called her? A catalyst? Had her bumbling search for the truth behind Oriel's death unwittingly caused more death? The nervous perspiration collected under her arms, behind her knees, around her waist where the sash held the tabard tight. She knew the scent of her own fear. Coincidence, chance that she rode nearby. Not her fault. Not! Please, not again!

Balanced tall over its high-springed single axletree, a bright canary-yellow cart pulled by a dappled gray pacer wheeled into the yard, the driver judiciously flicking the whip to direct its course. And tight behind but to the left to avoid the dust, galloped a man dressed all in black, riding a lean-limbed black stallion and with an imperious coal-black ghatt thrusting forward on the pommel pad. The cart cut a tight semicircle, rocking as it went, and Doyce had no time to mark who drove it, but she knew full-well the black-garbed man's identity: Jenret Wycherley.

Of all the would-be rescuers the Lady might provide, why him? Not to mention his ghatt, Rawn. Did Jenret dress to complement the ghatt or had the ghatt Chosen Jenret because of his attire? Lady only knew, but both of them annoyed her with their carousing ways, not to mention their studied arrogance, overbearing superiority, and, in all honesty, their impeccable professionalism.

Jenret paused in front of her now, soft-brimmed hat

rolled loosely at his side, black trousers and tunic still showing a crease despite the hard ride, his black sheep-skin tabard flecked with the faintest trace of road dust. He was unconsciously rectifying that with his free hand even as he stood facing her, studying her, she decided, the same way a scholar views a particularly duplicitous piece of information. One lock of dark hair winged over his brow toward his deep blue eyes fringed with dark, curled lashes.

The voice, when he finally spoke, took her aback, always surprised her: a pure, clear tenor, nearly too soft and light for a man so obviously masculine yet downright pretty. She'd bet the voice had spurred him into fights to prove his manhood. "We set out as soon as we heard Khar's danger cries in the night. No hope, we suspected, but we pressed on despite. I'm pleased to see it's not you in danger, but what seems to be the trouble?"

"In the barn." She jerked her chin over her shoulder, acutely conscious that he made her feel a trifling child, rumpled, messy, with a bloodstained knee to her panta-loons, the dust and grime streaking down her tabard, a dribble of rum marking a sticky path down her chin. Fretful, she rubbed at the scrape on her forearm and winced. "Just don't startle Khar."

"Of course not. Thank you for informing me." And he and the midnight-hued ghatt strolled into the barn. Doyce cocked an ear at the retching sound, suddenly choked off, and felt faintly ashamed, but not enough to cancel the tiny shard of pleasure that stabbed at her, a traitor to her better intentions.

Turning back she examined the trim two-wheeled rig as it swung around again, the patient driver subduing the gray's desire to race. Some horses were born to run, and the excitement from the urgent, headlong pace made this one eager to continue, exulting in perfectly cadenced freedom, now checked short.

Still, the driver demonstrated persistence and obvious skill; the high two-wheelers were notoriously precarious to balance if road or weather proved rough or the horse untrained. Other than those who drove them on Fair Racing Days or the young, intent in equal measure on hell-raising and courting, only the traveling eumedicos consistently favored the high-wheelers.

A small shiver of anticipation iced the thin trail of sweat down her spine. "No, it couldn't be Mahafny. There's no way. . . ."

But it was Mahafny who leaped down, followed, on the other side, by the Shepherd Harrap, face paler than his robe, teeth clenched hard enough to bulge his jaw muscles. She'd bet golden eights he'd never reached a destination with such lightning speed in his life, with or without the blessed Lady's intercession. Parm followed after, misjudging the jolt and sway as the carriage springs rebounded with the abrupt release of Harrap's considerable bulk. Parm collapsed in an ungainly tangle of limbs but ignored the embarrassment and hightailed it straight inside the barn, his orange and black motley blending sunlight and shadow as he disappeared.

"You're all right?" Mahafny asked, slightly breathless, pale gray eyes raking over her. "What's wrong? Parm went frantic, nearly unstrung. Harrap realized that something terrible was happening, but Parm's explanation rushed gibberish fast, so nightmarish in Harrap's mind that he couldn't absorb it all. I don't know how Parm managed to guide us here."

Harrap's broad face creased with a smile of relief. "And the little ghatta is fine, too?" Doyce nodded affirmation and he rushed ahead, barely waiting for her response. "But what was Parm so desperate to tell me? What's wrong? And who is that old man smelling of rum? And the ancient ghatt so like Ma'ow, Nathan Cummins's? That's his father, isn't it?" The barrage of questions ran down as Harrap waited for enlightenment. Mahafny stood still, her appraising expression having noted the blood on Doyce's pantaloons, the ripped shirtsleeve, her shaken appearance, and the drawn sword still clutched in her hand. Doyce caught the intent of her gaze and flinched, lowering the sword so that its point dragged in the dust.

She managed a succinct explanation, and Mahafny and Harrap exchanged shocked glances, then entered the barn, Mahafny drawing a small white square of gauze over her nose and mouth, securing it behind her head by its tie strings. Harrap, even paler than before, pulled forth the Lady's octagon hanging around his neck and carried it in one large fist, holding it aloft as if to let the Lady's love and benevolence shine forth, better late than not at all.

Harrap returned almost immediately, eyes clenched shut, tears seeping down his cheeks, chest heaving as if he'd run an endurance race. "I couldn't . . ." he gasped, "couldn't even finish Our Lady's benediction. Such savagery! Such smells! Have to try again. Must give them peace!" Spying the rum bottle, he grabbed it and shook it, draining it off in a giant gulp. Doyce raised her eyebrows but said nothing as he started to trot back and forth, gaining momentum to carry himself back inside. As he rushed the door he asked, "And who is that handsome young man inside with his head between his knees?"

✤

The rest of the morning rippled with blurred images, but still, despite her wishing she could will it otherwise, certain scenes stayed in sharp focus, frozen forever into a separateness, framed by fears that forced her to peruse them again and again, no way to avoid watching them replay themselves in her mind:

Khar clutched the little yellow-striped ghatten by the scruff of the neck, rendering it immobile in the time-old grip of a mother ghatta. He squalled and kicked, frenetic with fear, then hung limp. Khar rolled her eyes in Doyce's direction and she inserted the pipette, managed to drip some of the diluted milk and herbal infusion into the ghatten's pink mouth while he choked and sputtered, then swallowed. A thin stream ran off his chin, soaked his ruff and belly. Khar at last deposited the ghatten into Bard's cupped hands, and he carried him outside, nestling him beside the old ghatt asleep in a patch of sun. Ma'ow stirred, then pillowed his massive head across the ghatten's back in protection and fell asleep again with a deep sigh.

Mahafny and Harrap had taken charge of preparing the bodies for burial, carrying Asa's inside the house to join the bodies of his wife and daughter. Gently they sponged them, straightened their limbs, closed the gaping wounds, smoothed the tangled hair. A labor of love for strangers destined for a journey to join the Lady, with only strangers to see them on their way.

Mahafny had called Doyce into the room where Asa lay, his body naked and a sheet drawn up barely to his hips. "Take a look at the wounds, Doyce, and tell me what you see."

Aware of herself, of her every reaction, Doyce viewed it all, examined, felt Mahafny's strong, thin hand pinched tight around her wrist, forcing her to concentrate, to see the how, the why, the wonder of individual bones, muscles, sinews, ligaments, their connections and interactions, what disease or injury does or does not do to the human body, its ways of compensating and coping. The old lessons, so hard-learned, rang in her head, as did Mahafny's new commands.

"Look. There. And there." Mahafny gestured to gashes on the chest and stomach, lowered the sheet further to show the near-disembowelment. "What do you make of it, Doyce?" Patience in her words, patience but the expectation of the correct answer the first time. No fumbling or mumbling or guessing from a prize pupil.

Moving closer, Doyce narrowed her vision, changed her angle, checked from another direction. In several locations, four deep lacerations, gashes roughly parallel to each other. Deeper as they extended downward. The surrounding skin sometimes puckered, torn with puffy ragged edges, unlike the clean sweep of knife or sword that she identified elsewhere on the body. The marks lower on the belly, deeper from a powerful force, crisscrossing each other as if the attacker had sought a new vantage from which to rake. If Asa hadn't been wearing a heavy leather belt, the claws would have touched his vitals almost immediately.

Claws? Doyce tilted her head back, willing her face blank, and met Mahafny's challenge. "Claw marks. Like a giant cat's, a wildcat or a lynx."

"Or a ghatt." Mahafny shook her unresisting arm in cadence with her words, her hand an icy band imprisoning Doyce's wrist. "Or a ghatt!"

"Like a ghatt, but it couldn't be a ghatt," Doyce heard herself reply with a calmness that she forced. "A ghatt would never do a thing like that." Not unless it fought for its life, or . . . fought to take someone else's life. But Wwar'm would never have done that to Asa.

Mahafny swung her around, away from Asa's body, and took her face in both smooth, cool hands, and Doyce savored the touch against her feverish cheeks. "Perhaps, perhaps not. And a ghatt never Bonds a second time with a person. So we all thought. Things are changing, Doyce, changing in strange ways. You made me see what was seemingly impossible. You must be open enough to do the same."

With a backward toss of her head, Doyce broke free of the cool, restraining hands, but not from her thoughts, and left the room. Impossible? Possible? Or something beyond what any of them could imagine, but imagination must have some foundation in fact, somewhere from which to spring, just as nightmares feed on hidden fears.

She rested her head against the windowpane, wished her thoughts had the same clarity. She turned her head back and forth, not caring that she smudged the glass, taking a peculiar delight in clouding something else, and saw Jenret, shoulders slumped, walking down the roadside to flag the first passerby. The news would have to be carried into town to gather family and friends, to relinquish the burden of the dead to those who knew and loved them. Jenret, still impeccably garbed, lock of hair pushed ruthlessly back into place, but strangely silent all day, fighting within himself over the havoc he'd witnessed. Unwilling to look squarely at anyone yet. She hadn't expected him to take it this hard. It should have been a small triumph for her, but it suddenly gave her no enjoyment, no gratification. Not this time, not now.

Earlier, Bard, Jenret, and the ghatti had patrolled the grounds, working over every centimeter of the barn's interior before the bodies had been moved. Bard, economical and thorough with every movement, Jenret cautious and distant, hanging back at first, then taking the lead, casting across the stained and gouged earthen floor for any signs. Too many had trod in and out already, obliterating clues. But they had scouted some footprints foreign

from their own. Two different pairs of boots, one with
run-down heels, the other nearly new with their sharply
defined edges, and scuff marks from soft-soled boots,
more like moccasins, perhaps the flexible, high leather
lace-ups that woodsmen wear. And when Doyce had entered reluctantly to hear this news, she had found Jenret
braced on a stool, face burrowed deep in the comforting
tan flank of a cow, methodically milking her. No one
else had remembered to ease her discomfort on this of
all mornings. How deft his hands were. Astounding, in
fact, that someone she considered the epitome of a city
man should know how to milk.

Finally, sitting uncomfortably around the once hospita-
ble kitchen table, drinking scalding strong cups of cha,
they discussed what little they knew. The old man, Nathan Cummins's father, now joined them, sobered by
dint of cold water and a long walk, his arm slung over
Harrap's shoulder, the Shepherd dragging him along until
his feet finally began to pace on their own. Hot, strong
cha served to revive the rest, for they now realized that
none of them knew precisely what, if anything, he had
seen on his arrival with Ma'ow.

The garrulity of liquor having deserted him, Cummins
Senior, a retired hostler—they had learned his occupation but not his first name—would rather have been long
gone from here. Doyce sympathized with his woebegone
expression, knowing she too would rather be elsewhere.

"Ma'ow and me come bursting into the yard with the
wagon and team. I'd been whippin' for all I was worth.
Ghatt'd yowled all the way like a steam whistle hooting
and screeching, but then he fell silentlike. And just as
we pulled in, three men came running out of the barn
toward the wood. One acted bad hurt, the old'un, I'd
say, because one of the others had him propped up,
looped his arm round his neck. Other one carried something in his arms close an' precious, looked like a white
fur rug against the dark of his clothes, all'n black like
the gen'mun here." He swallowed cha in a mighty gulp
and rolled his eyes at the heat, beads of sweat forming
on his balding pate and forehead.

He took another mouthful, sucked air through parted
lips, his grimace making it clear he preferred it laced

with rum. They wished theirs were as well, but the rum was gone and Asa kept none in the house. Asa never needed liquor to be drunk on life; even at Myllard's he had quaffed Fala's fruit punch or water.

"Ma'ow tried to light off after them, but his legs give out. And I was afeared it was his heart again. Didn't know what Nathan'd do to me if I come back with the ghatt dead. So I stayed by him a bit, then got the lantern and slipped real softlike into the barn, unshuttering the light just a crack. Could feel the ghatt with me, reading me, even though he wasn't there beside me. You know what we saw." He hunched his shoulders and stared at the table, as if the plain, homey comfort of the wood would erase the sight, dabbed a finger at the wet ring from the cup, unconsciously making patterns. Doyce poured another round of cha for everyone, and they all stared into their cups, as if the swirling leaves would pattern the answers they sought. Seek. Seeker.

Unexpectedly, everything within her united, her brain reconciling itself with her body, the strange detachment gone. She held out her hand, fingers splayed, stared at it front and back, pressed her lips to the steady throbbing line of blue at her wrist that indicated life. Knew what she did, why she commanded the hand to move, to act, not react. Everything glowed new-minted to her, the pine tabletop, silvered gray and smooth from many scrubbings, yet veined with a harder grain, like pond ice with wind ripples frozen within. She ordered her hand to grasp the cup with its rose patternings of improbable birds and tropic flowers, lift it to her lips so that she could inhale the scent.

The four men, so different: Bard, with his smooth, unlined maple-sugar skin and smoke-haze eyes sharing the kitchen space companionably yet gravely; she'd known him longest yet knew him least of all, just the surface. Pray that she would have time to rectify that, to know him and his twin as individuals as Oriel had. Harrap, broad chest and paunch straining his Shepherd's robe, striving hard to give comfort yet in need of solace himself, still terrified from his unprecedented Bonding with Parm; old Cummins Senior, involved by accident and good-neighborliness, body wound tight with the need to extricate himself and his son's precious ghatt to go home, duty done. And Jenret, deliberate and correct but remote, shielded as he struggled to decide whether to continue as a distant observer or return to the world his body so precisely inhabited, a choice she knew too well. Come back, you can't escape it this way. Objectivity cannot cancel the pain, honest emotion can make it bearable, she wanted to say. But the unspoken words evoked a dangerous intimacy of feeling and he stood as a stranger to her.

Finally, Mahafny, looking more open, more human, more perturbed and troubled than she'd ever seen her. What had brought Mahafny here, pushed her to the point that these past two days had awakened her to the fact that her stable, scientific world of disciplined order could crumble as rapidly and unpredictably as any other human's life did? A wave of pity for them all swept over Doyce. But no, pity indicated superiority, and she was anything other than that, anything and everything but.

"Where are the ghatti?" she asked, her question unpremeditated but bursting ahead of all others.

Bard set his cup down. "Out burying Wwar'm and the ghatten. They insisted on doing it themselves, I don't know where. It seemed right to let them." He looked to her for agreement and anticipated her next question. "The other little one is doing as well as can be expected. He's tucked in the hamper by the stove. Ma'ow says there's not another nursing ghatta within leagues, though Nathan's hound whelped three days past. It's not perfect, but it's the best we can do if she'll accept him."

She spread her hands, palms upward in supplication. "Lady knows what he'll be like after he Bonds, if he Bonds."

"If he has the strength to survive this, perhaps one of the best you've ever had." As if realizing that she of all people had no right to be an authority on ghatti, Mahafny rushed ahead. "Human or ghatti, breeding always tells."

Khar, M'wa, and Rawn marched through the kitchen

door, their bodies protectively flanking a fourth ghatt. Registering their presence, the group swung around as one and Doyce gasped. Encrusted in dried mud up to its belly, its coat ragtagged with burrs and leaf and stem fragments, the ghatt in the middle wavered on its feet, emaciated, ribs poking out, its spine a necklace of bumps down its back. Saam! Saam, exhausted but alive after what had clearly been a long and arduous trek.

She threw herself out of her chair, knelt to hug him against her thighs, casting her mind out and waiting, craving the sound of his mindspeech, but she heard nothing. No communication, no voice. She slid down a smooth, impenetrable wall of silence, no cracks or holds of recognition to sustain a hesitant grasp.

"No, he still can't," Khar interjected. **"But he felt something was wrong over an oct ago and started traveling. Slipped away from Mem'now in the night. He can't explain what or how he knew, just that he did, and that he had to come as if he were dragged at the end of a rope. He says he's sorry to burden you, but could he have a bowl of milk?"**

Jenret dippered milk from the fresh bucket he'd brought in, and, much to Saam's dismay after he had drunk, Bard scooped him up and deposited him in a washtub where the ghatt stood belly deep in warm water left from the kettle.

"It's the only way, can't have him licking it all off and filling himself with mud," Bard apologized to the room at large as he scrubbed and rinsed. Eyes pinched tight, whiskers flat against his screwed-up muzzle, Saam balanced on tiptoes to raise himself as far above the offending water as possible, stoically making no move to escape. With the exception of Rawn, the other ghatti shared his expression of discomfort, and Doyce remembered stories she'd heard that the large black ghatt had been trained as a fisher ghatt.

"Now what do we plan to do about all this?" Jenret's frustration hammered at them, and everyone turned. "Go back as a delegation and inform Headquarters? Too many things have been happening too rapidly: Oriel's death and disfigurement, Saam's loss of speech—yes, Doyce, I attended the funeral, though you didn't see me.

What condolences can you really offer at a time like that? I left as soon as the service finished. But I heard the gossip then and in town over the next few days, if it's gossip to share your fears about things that make no sense happening to those you love, and Oriel was loved by so many. The whole town whispered the secret, and the part of the secret that grew, expanded with each telling, said that we Seekers were stymied by what had happened to one of our own.

"Then Parm's new bonding with Harrap and Georges Barbet's defection; and now this, the cold-blooded murder of three people, one an ex-Seeker, and two ghatti. I don't know if they're related, but isn't it uncanny that they've all occurred in such a short time and in such proximity to each other? We really aren't that distant from where Oriel died, if we aimed straight at it instead of following the circuit perimeter." Jenret sat rigid on the edge of his seat, ready to pounce and attack anyone who disagreed with him.

Mahafny cleared her throat. "Without dealing with the cause, which we can't know, but concentrating only on the relationship—if there is any—I fear I can tie one strand together." She reached gingerly into the pocket of her white coat, now stained by the long ride and the morning's labors. "I apologize for not mentioning it sooner, but it slipped my mind in the press of things." Pulling her hand clear of her pocket, she displayed a sharp, lethal-looking instrument on her palm, and the others craned to see better.

Staring at it critically, Jenret commented, "It doesn't look near big enough to have inflicted the wounds on Asa and Wwar'm. Sharp enough, yes, but not easy to wield in a fight. Whatever it is, it's meant for more delicate work."

"It's a trepanning instrument," Doyce stated levelly, gauging Mahafny's unruffled expression, trying to read her intent. "Where did you get it?"

"What's a trepanning instrument?" Puzzled, Harrap stretched a tentative finger toward the gleaming instrument, wary of the edge.

"It's used to open the skull to relieve pressure on the brain or to reveal a blood clot." She answered without looking at Harrap, refusing to take her eyes off the eu-medico's face. "Now where did you get it?"

The older woman's mouth twisted in a frown. "I found it when I went into the barn the first time. When I knelt to examine Asa I nearly sliced my knee open. I didn't think, just picked it up and popped it in my pocket."

"It's not from your own surgical kit?" The distrust welled up inside her. What business drew Mahafny to Cyanberry yesterday, only to become involved with Harrap and Parm? Why had she rushed here to bear witness to the deaths of Asa and the ghatti? Why was a eumedico so irrevocably enmeshed in Seeker affairs and troubles?

"Doyce, enough!" Jenret commanded. His black-clad arm sketched an elegant sweep that brought Mahafny back within the compass of people around the table. "Then, madam, I take it this instrument could be used to . . . remove a brain?"

"No, but it would help expose it, beginning the process."

"Then it seems likely that the three men Cummins here saw running away hadn't finished with their task. If he and the old ghatt hadn't arrived when they did, the bodies would have been further desecrated." Standing, his dark presence riveted their attention. "Is there more we should know?"

With an underhand toss, Mahafny flipped the trepanning instrument onto the table where it landed with a thunk, everyone's eyes involuntarily following the motion as the shining tool came to rest. "Doyce can tell you about the other possibility."

Damn her, damn her beyond the furthest reaches of the Lady's starry realm, Doyce exploded savagely but silently. The wonder teacher, ever full of new and striking insights, capable of expanding the boundaries of their meager knowledge! And treading now at a boundary where she didn't belong!

"Well, Doyce?" And worse, Jenret taking his cues from Mahafny, model student to the model teacher.

"Some of the wounds on Asa's body and on Wwar'm's were atypical. Not consistent with the apparent instrument or instruments used—a sword or knife." Her words were reluctant and, she hoped, somewhat obscure.

"**Girl, say what you mean. We know already.**" Everyone except Mahafny and the old man started and stared at Ma'ow, curled beside the hamper containing the ghatten. "**I've lived a long, long life, too long by our counting, and now I've had to live to see this. . . . There is a rogue ghatt loose, allying himself with humans no better than he. I sniffed his sign on the doorjamb as soon as we arrived. The others smelled it, too.**" The ghatt spat weakly, and the other ghatti shifted and twitched.

Body low in deference, Khar hesitated, then spoke. "**Was it wise, venerable one, to tell them? It is something we must avenge ourselves.**"

"**It is too much alone. You are too young, you have not spiraled high enough to understand how much is at stake. Evil flowers in both races, ours and theirs, and it will take both Seekers and Bondmates to destroy it.**"

With growing despair, Doyce released her breath. She had seen, had known, and denied her senses. And if one evil mind existed amongst the ghatti, could others be hidden as well? Insane to damn the entire breed because of one flawed mind, like saying that one human thief or murderer sullied and discredited the whole human race. But humans did not view the ghatti as they viewed other members of their own race. Swan Maclough had worried about the ghatti being viewed as frauds, discredited, no longer trusted to know the Truth, but it boded even worse if a ghatti could pervert the Truth, destroy and kill in conjunction with its Bondmate. The danger of dishonor, disbandment—and death—had increased a hundredfold if the public learned of this perversion. Her course was clear now—find the truth or die trying, not wait for it to find her on this parody of a circuit.

The others sat without stirring, waited for her to speak, to confirm Ma'ow's words. "You were right, Mahafny, the ghatti verify your suspicions. I apologize for doubting you. And I'll tell you all this much more: Khar and I are *not* riding back to Headquarters, we're going to ride after them. The trail can't be that cold, and once we find them. . . ." Her hands convulsed, wringing at empty air.

Not the cold trail after Oriel's death, not the mindless repetition of a circuit, feeling like a clapperless bell,

needing to be struck by outside forces for a chime of
recognition. She felt a tocsin of anticipation and danger
pealing in her blood. Honor—hers, the Seekers Veritas's,
Khar's, the ghatti's . . . and Oriel's. *I cannot run away
and hide this time. It's not simply my involvement, there
are too many others I hold dear. Find Asa's and
Wwar'm's killers and I'll have Oriel's as well, the answer
I promised Oriel I'd find. Not to suffer in ignorance but
to know the truth.* "We leave now!"

"But not alone; right, Bard?" Jenret loomed dark beside her, closer than she liked, his presence shadowing
the wild singing joy of solitary danger. She retreated a
step to regain her strength of anticipation but held her
ground. "There were three of them and one ghatt, although one of them may have been hurt. You don't know
where you're traveling or how far or what you'll face,
and you must not face it alone if you're to succeed. And
succeed we must."

"But the Seeker General gave *me* the charge! Oriel
was my friend, my lover! Saam is Oriel's Bond and my
friend as well. I'll take Saam with us if he will, but that's
all I'll drag into danger, no others! I can bear no responsibility for other lives, only my own." She stoppered her
shout and rubbed nervous hands along her temples,
twisting her hair back behind her ears, and then, low and
warning, "Not you, and not Bard!"

Bard's neck corded with tension, his face tight-drawn
with some inner conflict. "Jenret has the right of it, you
must not go alone. The Seeker General's charge to find
the truth involved six Seekers, and I am proud to be one
of the six.

"But I must go back to Byrta, I must! When you first
had Khar call me to succor Harrap and Parm, I had
already had a message from Byrta. Not through M'wa
and P'wa, but directly." Embarrassment and pride twisted
his features into a lopsided grimace, but growing pride
smoothed his discomfort at the intimate revelation. "You
know we are twins, that we are so close as to be one
sometimes. I heard her cry, shared her pain when her
horse shied at a partridge that broke cover and she was
thrown. Her leg is badly broken. When she heard the
news, she insisted I ride ahead to Harrap, but I promised

to return as quickly as I could! I could not even reach Harrap before I raced here! I am being pulled farther and farther away when she needs me most!" Supple golden-tan hands swept outward to encompass his thoughts. "I could not anticipate that I would be a part of this, but what could I do! I must serve! I will serve! But now I must see her—even for just a little while—and then I will catch up with you. Her pain courses through me as if it were mine!" Mute appeal as he begged their understanding.

"I know, Bard, I know. No other reason could keep you from my side. You both loved Oriel, too. Go see to Byrta, make sure she's well, then ride like the wind to Headquarters and give them a full report, ask their advice while I ride on. Have the Seeker General caution all the ghatti about what they transmit over the mindnet, for we don't know who might be listening." She trapped one of Bard's agitated, thin hands and held it tightly for a moment to emphasize her concern. "Give Byrta my love."

Jenret prowled and poked through the cupboards, doors creaking at his touch. He jerked them open sav-agely, twisting the knobs as if snapping the necks of quail. Most yielded to his touch, balking him of his anger, but the last door creaked and stuck, and he yanked at it, felt its resistance as winged vibration, beat-ing, beating, echoing through his hands, up his arms and neck until it reached his temples, no escape until he fi-nally slammed it against the wall. The internal quivering that had assailed him since early that morning began to subside, absorbed by the sympathetic vibrations of the door. It eased him toward normality; he gathered food, supplies, scooped various items against his chest, into the crook of his arm, preparing. "That's one you've disposed of very providentially, Doyce, but you haven't disposed of Rawn and me." A lock of dark hair had sprung loose again, making him look like a rakish brigand bent on bending her to his will by brute force or charm, which-ever proved needful. "You can forbid me to join you, but you can't stop me from following you. And one morning you may wake up and discover that you are following me!"

The arrogant rattling of the door set her off, screwed her anger a notch tighter. Had he always gotten his way as a child, a rich, spoiled, arrogant brat, heir of one of the richest and most respected merchanter houses of Canderis? And now a Seeker as well, and if truth matched even a fraction of the tales and boasts she'd heard and the few times she'd seen him on leave, a seeker of pleasures—women, wine, gaming. She'd passed him one night prowling when the pleasures at Myllard's had proved too tame, strolling the streets suave and sleek and considering, sword cocked at his hip, alert for activity, eyes measuring the women he passed as Rawn padded beside him. She'd heard Jenret's high, cultivated voice ordering the best wine, the most costly any inn had to offer, then his disdainful sniff when it did not meet his standards. This was the Seeker she was supposed to welcome with open arms as a partner on her quest?

Yet for all his flaws, his dissolute ways, he possessed a cutting intelligence that she could not deny. Worse, she could envision him at her side, a partnership of minds. What unnerved her, chilled her with a deep distrust was his erratic oscillation between pleasure and duty. Would he stay true to the task at hand, or tire of it as quickly as he did any other whim? Her ambivalence took her aback. No, not ambivalence, I have to measure the facts, think of the consequences.

She studied him and for a moment thought she had penetrated the mask, the careful shielding, to the pain within. So much hurt buried within the black-clad facade, need so like her own she tried to disbelieve her intuition. Something more lay buried there deep inside to help her, complement her strengths and weaknesses.

Her response surprised her, came unbidden to override her rational concerns and fears. "Come, then. It's easier if no one has to eat the other's dust." His sudden smolder of hope and excitement, the quick damping down to hide the flame of need, caught her off guard. This search meant something to him, something he refused to publicly acknowledge. Sifting through the supplies Jenret had gathered, she shook her head, disapproving of a few choices, conferred in a quiet undertone and sent him to search for other necessities. Best to get him out of her sight before she changed her mind again.

"What about us? We want to go with you as well." Harrap's deep voice trembled, with emotion or fear, she wasn't sure. Parm pressed tightly against his knee, radiating physical support as well as intimate mindspeech.

"No, Harrap," she picked her words, not wishing to wound. "You and Parm and Mahafny had best return to town. You've still much training to undergo and decisions to make beyond that. I'm sure Bard and M'wa will transmit another message to alert the Seeker-Guidancer pair to hasten there and continue your training. You've made great strides, but you aren't a full Seeker yet. The offer is well meant and gratefully received, but far too early."

She turned to involve the other woman in her complicity to protect Harrap's innocence and hoped she'd meet no resistance. "Mahafny, you'll drive him back to town, won't you?"

"Of course. And then I've business of my own to attend to. I'm sure our paths will cross again sometime in the future, Doyce." Putting a consoling arm around Harrap's shoulders, the eumedico began to clear the table of cups, straightening and cleaning in tribute to Asa's wife who had bequeathed a meticulous kitchen to her unmet visitors.

"We must leave soon, all of us. Let's make ready."

✤

"So they're coming with us." Khar wound her way through the pile of supplies, sniffing and poking. "Interesting."

Doyce rocked back on her heels from her kneeling position, face clouded. *"Khar, what have I done, asking them to accompany us? Why didn't you stop me? We can't get along with each other, I know it."*

"Stop you? You were caught up in something beyond yourself . . . and maybe between yourself and Jenret." The ghatta's mouth curved as if she smiled, but then Doyce always thought that ghatti mouths turned that way naturally, revealing their endless amusement at the human world. **"Besides, it was interesting to watch you both."**

She knew no way to erase that feline smugness. *"Then you think it wise for Jenret and Rawn to accompany us?"* Please let the ghatta agree with me, convince me that I'm not second-guessing myself.

Khar stuck her head inside the open saddlebag, popped out again. **"Wise may not be the exact word, but prudent, yes. Highly prudent."**

"Why?"

"Because you need help, and for once you've acknowledged that you need help, been willing to share the burden. Ma'ow reminded me that we ghatti cannot do this alone, and neither can you."

Still stubborn, Doyce insisted, *"But I wouldn't have been alone, not with you and Saam. He will come, won't he? I should have had you ask him, I'm sorry."*

"He insisted on coming even before you spoke, beat Jenret and Rawn to it, much to Rawn's chagrin."

She began to slide various packets in the saddlebags, trying to work and think at the same time. *"Then you think it will be all right? That we'll get along?"*

"Whether the sum is greater than the parts remains to be seen." Khar looked over her shoulder, through the open door in the direction of the kitchen. **"But then, you've always told me that we ghatti can't count, let alone do sums."**

"Khar, stop teasing. This is serious," she protested. *"Deadly serious."*

"Of course it is serious. Serious enough for me to be thankful to have others around to protect us, and we them. Just as we strive to protect the Seeker-Bond community as a whole. Do I make myself clear?"

"Eminently, my dear ghatta. And thank you for reminding me."

Khar ducked her head into the other saddlebag, checked Jenret's pair. **"Speaking of reminding, do you think Asa kept any smoked fish? We're running low. Saam likes it."** She added the last as a confidence, head tilted, amber eyes demure.

"Not half as much as you do, you little beggar. But I'll check."

❖

Jenret curried the horses, both his black stallion and
Lokka. After the brushing, he'd let them have some
more water, he decided, but not too much or they'd slosh
like the very devil. "You, there!" He slapped his stallion
on the shoulder, hard but affectionately. "We've a lady
joining us and I don't want any trouble out of you, you
hear me?"

Rawn sprang from the water trough to the stallion's
back, draped himself there. **"Why should he bother
Doyce? She's a Seeker, not a lady,"** he asked, face almost level with Jenret's.

*"Ninny, not Doyce, Lokka. We don't need Ophar de-
ciding on a romantic interlude in the middle of everything."* The stallion tossed his head as if he knew they
were talking about him. *"Remind him in no uncertain
terms. No, remind him in certain terms, very vivid terms,
of what I'll have done to him if he lets passion rule him."*

Rawn drew himself up, discomfort clear on his face.
"Not nice! Not nice at all! You wouldn't?"

He relented, ever so slightly. *""You don't have to tell
him I wouldn't really do it, but you can still remind him
of the possibility. I want his ardor cooled."*

**"When I finish explaining, his ardor won't be just
cooled, it will be iced."** Rawn hesitated, chose his next
words as ginger-cautious as a bear trying to flip a porcu-
pine. **"I understand why we must go, but I am not sure
if you truly comprehend your own reasons. Do you?"**

*"It seems patently clear to me, but if it isn't to you, then
please feel free to read my mind."* Jenret stood at ease,
face expressionless, waiting for the black ghatt to probe.
"Well?"

**"Superficially acceptable, but there's more, isn't there?
Things that you prefer not to admit. Do you wish me to
remind you?"**

Jenret leaned his weight across the comfort of Ophar's
broad back, buried his head on crossed forearms. "No,
thank you," the words came muffled. He saw things all
too well, had seen things far too lucidly since he had
entered the deceptively quiet barn. "Let me work it
through myself."

He had been squatting on the floor, one hand gripped tightly to the back of his neck, pressing it between his knees, forcing it down. Bright spangles of light exploded before his eyes, turned into a blood-red wash that swept to blackness when he tried to raise his head. Stay down, he urged himself, stay down or you're going to pass out cold. Worried, Rawn butted against his knee, threatened to overturn him, then sniffed at the lowered head and moved off, exploring while he kept an eye on Jenret.

Blood, he didn't know there could be so much blood, that it could spread with such profligate liberality. He had had his share of fights before—sanctioned and un-sanctioned—a few official ring bouts and numerous tavern brawls, some that he'd instigated himself when the anger rose in him too hot to control. The anger always terrified him, made him fear bursting into another dimension, another being, and he had seen the results of that, and the reverberations of that past time still resonated through his life and the lives of the rest of his family.

But the killings he had witnessed before, so long ago, hadn't had blood in abundance like this. His mouth filled with saliva, he swallowed, prayed he wouldn't vomit. No, when Jared had killed the two servants there had been practically no blood, though the twisted shells that remained reminded him of the body he saw here, a man trying to escape himself, escape the pain. And this new death, the wantonness of it, reinforced his need for atonement, to do something to make it right, just as he must have done something to make it wrong that day so long ago when he'd goaded Jared, taunted and teased, until Jared had spun around and lashed out with his mind—not at him, not at his little brother—but at the two servants who had come running to separate them in response to the shouts. Jared had toyed with the servants, a small boy twisting at their minds, wrenching the essence from them, the charge of their fears energizing him, driving him further, fueled by their pain, until the two servants had dropped lifeless, contorted, puppets with the cut strings of their sanity in Jared's hands. And Jenret had hidden in the wardrobe, the smothering weight of his father's winter cloak across his face, frail protection from the wrath he saw outside. How could an eight-year-old boy have such power? And if Jared had such power, did it lurk inside him as well? He tried to reach inside his mind to see, but forced himself back. If he found it, what would he do with it? Would he master it, or would it master him?

"Uh, uh, uh, uh, uh," he didn't realize the little groaning sounds had found their way between his compressed lips until he felt the hand on his shoulder, bringing him back to the present. The pressure shifted to his neck, and he felt himself being inexorably pressed downward, lower yet.

"Jenret." And he groaned in relief, recognizing the voice. It was Mahafny, his aunt. "Jenner, kneel, don't squat. Drop your head lower." He obeyed, felt the strain on his thighs and calves diminish. The blackness receded minimally and he risked opening his eyes, taking a side-long glance.

He tried for humor, knew it fell short. "I'd ask what you're doing here, but I hate impeccable explanations." A weak gesture with one hand. "Have you looked around?"

"Enough to know it's too late. If you think you'll be all right, I'd like to further examine the body. I take it the poor man was a Seeker? At least the dead ghatt over there indicates the probability of such a relationship."

"Yes," he swallowed hard, raised his head a fraction, waited to see if the faintness returned. "Certainly unexpected, but perhaps not unanticipated, given the givens. Not that poor Brandt anticipated his own death."

The faintest hint of scorn touched her words. "But you Seekers should have anticipated the possibility of another death, is that what you mean? Well, you aren't mind-readers or mindstealers."

The final word set him trembling. How could she flaunt it in his face like that, if she knew what he had been remembering, reliving? "Leave it in peace, aunt. We've enough to worry about right here and now."

"That's true enough, but you're the one who can't leave the past in peace. And perhaps I can't as well. We'll see."

He started to rise, felt her hand gripping him above the elbow, ready to break his fall if he fainted again.

"You know that Doyce Marbon is outside, don't you?" She gave an almost imperceptible nod. "Is that what brought you here?"

"Yes and no. I'm putting the past to rest, exorcising it, as our friend Harrap would say."

"Who? Oh," comprehension dawned on him. "You mean the Shepherd who charged in and out of here? Where did you collect him?"

She fixed him with a gimlet look. "I don't 'collect' anyone, as you so quaintly put it. Not Harrap, not Doyce, and not you. Just remember that. You're not specimens." He turned, unresisting, with the pressure of her arm. "There is one favor I'd like to ask, though, that you don't say anything to Doyce about our relationship, at least not yet, not now."

He couldn't see her face, only the top of her silvered head. "I don't see why it matters."

"Mayhap it doesn't, but I'd prefer to let it rest for now. Will you? She might feel as if we're united against her in some way. Let her react to each relationship as she knows it, not throw any new permutations at her."

The fact that he couldn't see her face worried him, but still, he had to trust her, believe in what she asked. "Fine." The one word sounded brusque in his ears, but she accepted it as sufficient.

"I want to look at the body again. Are you up to it?"

Without answering, he turned and led the way.

He jerked himself back to the present, felt the rough texture of horsehair under his fingers, against his cheek. What had possessed him to insist on accompanying Doyce? Lady knew, he didn't especially care for the woman; she was stubborn and unyielding. He stopped, revised that—not unyielding or she would never have agreed to let him join her. Or had she simply made the best of a bad situation, him being the bad situation? He rather liked her mind, but her looks certainly didn't live up to his standards, more like a little gray heron with her slim body, the way her neck and head sometimes jutted forward, searching and still, awaiting an unwary minnow. No, he preferred a woman with more beauty and grace, more rounded curves, the sweetness of a full-blown rose.

"Herons, roses. What marvelous comparisons," Rawn gave a husky chuckle. "Will you try caterpillars next?"

"Why caterpillars, my friend?" He asked the question out of idle interest, more concerned about what else remained to accomplish before they left.

"Because they turn into butterflies."

"Spare me your ghatti aphorisms, Rawn. There's no butterfly inside Doyce Marbon, of that I'm sure. A nice little moth at most. Now, can you get them moving? It's almost noon."

❖

The sun slid toward its zenith behind growing cloud cover when Jenret and Doyce, both mounted and with their respective ghatti in position on their pommel platforms, bade the others farewell. Saam perched on a postern platform on Lokka, his seat hurriedly cobbled from Wwar'm's old platform which they'd located in the barn. Lokka twisted this way and that, turning herself in a circle to verify the newcomer who rode on her back. Saam had greeted her nose to nose before he'd jumped up and settled himself, but Lokka still craved reassurance as to exactly whom she carried.

Clouds scudded in from the mountains to the north, and the air hung heavy, seeded with unshed rain, the humidity as oppressive to humans and animals as it was to the sky. Bard had already departed, his lean form arrowing along his gelding's neck as if he would outrace his mount to his beloved twin, relief plain in every stride that took him closer to Byrta. Harrap and Parm, Mahafny, and the old man Cummins and Ma'ow stood nearby, Cummins with a tiny, towel-wrapped bundle awkward in his hands. The bundle contained the drugged ghatten.

"Don't worry, sir, he'll sleep for a while longer," Jenret assured the old man. "Just give him to your son when you get back and he'll know what to do. Don't worry, he won't 'Print on you." He grinned in boyish delight and doffed his hat, holding it close to his heart in promise.

Doyce ached so to be gone that every dawdling moment tormented her. Mahafny, ever perceptive, made the smallest, slightest of shooing gestures and smiled in sympathy.

Finding her voice as she heeled Lokka, Doyce cried out, "Lady bless you all and thank you, my friends. May we meet again in better times!" And she and the mare sprang from the yard toward the wooded copse where old man Cummins had pointed out the direction in which the nightstalkers had retreated. Jenret wheeled his stallion and waved, and in a few strides they had settled comfortably shoulder to shoulder with Doyce and Lokka.

"May they not bear the scars of what they've seen and learned." His eyes were somber as he spoke, more to himself and Rawn than to her, she decided.

The swift departure proved ironic only a few moments later. Rigid with impatience, Doyce and Jenret sat their horses, reins slack, while the three ghatti cast back and forth just beyond the wood's edge, prowling the undergrowth, sniffing here and there to pick up a scent, anything to mark their course.

The girded branch of a poplar testified where reins had been ripped free in haste, but few tracks showed clearly. It was equally possible that they'd departed along the hard-packed road, already the recipient of early morning traffic, including a herd of sheep, or that they'd bolted into the woods.

Voice rowling high and low, Saam scented the trail first, Rawn and Khar rushing to confer with the shadow-gray ghatt. Doyce suspected that Saam's handicap, his loss of mindspeech, left his other senses sharper, more attuned to nature and his own personal world instead of sublimated in the all-important human-ghatt interaction. Jenret shifted, skittish at the delay, ready to swing down.

"What is it?" he called, his sharpness jerking Rawn to attention. The muscular black ghatt looked less than pleased at the interruption.

"Just wait, can't you? Give them time to decide for sure." Doyce studied her hands, toyed with the reins against the pommel platform, rather than stare down

Jenret's restiveness, not let it exacerbate her own. If he's
more impatient than I—and with less reason—we've
landed in a fine fix, and I've packed patience in short
supply after all this time. Can't he tell how edgy I am?

**"If you both go on like this you'll be like two mirrors
endlessly reflecting and reflecting and reflecting back on
each other. Pity us ghatti caught in the middle."** Khar
spared a thought in her direction, then went back to her
conference with Saam.

She took a calming breath, held it until her lungs
burned, and exhaled until she felt empty. It didn't precisely calm, she decided, but it gave her something more
immediate to think about. The darkness of the woods,
deep hunter greens and soft charcoal blacks, green-grays
and harsh blacks, tall firs and large-boled oaks crowding
close and dense, snarled together, left her uneasy. Why
anyone would want to live this close to a wilderness, she
couldn't guess. She'd cut through its outskirts more than
once when pressed for time, but she hadn't relished the
experience, the brooding oppressiveness that weighed
her lower and lower as if she crouched over Lokka for
protection from some unseen force older than anything
she'd ever known. If they had to journey deep into the
High Firs, she wouldn't be well pleased. Few ventured
far into the High Firs, the ancient guardians of the Tetonords. Logging and hunting proved safer and easier
elsewhere. Only the Erakwa leaving the southern borders
of Marchmont after their summer's hunting moved through
with swift unconcern, finding trails and familiar scenes as
easily as a resident of the capital navigated the maze of
twisted, narrow streets that comprised the old quarter of
Gaernett.

The ghatti returned, wending their way through the
undergrowth without riffling a branch or leaf. With a low
greeting cry Khar vaulted to her platform, followed a
moment later by Saam.

She circled and settled. **"Saam says they came out of
the forest but left by the roadway. We think we can
follow, now that Saam's shown us what to feel for."**

Rawn stretched up and around, paws on Jenret's shoulders, and butted him under the chin. **"Aye, but we'd**

**better try to outrun the rain or even Saam will lose it
entirely."**

"Then let's ride!" And Jenret proved as good as his
word, precipitously abandoning Doyce as he pricked his
horse with his heels, the stallion's muscles bunching and
surging as he hurtled up the soft, loamy bank to the hard-
packed roadway.

Poor Lokka, daydreaming, was hard-pressed to scramble after them, and Doyce restrained herself. No need
to push too hard. Better to drop behind for the moment
and build up speed on the roadway.

"Don't worry." The faintest feline smugness sweet-
ened Khar's tone. **"Remember, we have Saam with us."**

*"It's not a contest, Khar. We're both after the same
thing—we all are."*

"Mmph. Yes, but still . . . we wondered."

Leave it to the ghatta to prick your conscience, read
your mind. She just hoped that Rawn was doing the exact
same thing to Jenret. She leaned over the ghatta, pressing her in place on the platform and stretched herself
against Lokka's neck. *"Tell Saam to hang on. Let's close
the gap!"*

They rode achingly hard for the afternoon and into the
night, traveling through three villages, stopping only to
rest and water the horses and to ask a few questions. No
one had seen anything of note. They tried a short detour
onto a secondary road that Saam indicated, but it swung
around the verge of a small, sedgy marsh area and then
rejoined the main road they'd been following.

Doyce wondered who'd be the first to call it quits for
the night. The moon and her satellites rode high, though
misted over, and the rain had held off, but a creeping
ground fog writhed and twisted around them, tattered by
the horses' hooves, hampering visibility. Only the ghatti's
sharp vision had saved the rapidly tiring horses and their
riders from several spills.

"Can we pick up the trail in the morning?" she asked
Khar.

The ghatta conferred with Saam in falanese. **"Yes, I'll
tell Rawn."**

"No, don't," she insisted too sharply. *"He'll tell Jenret
and then he'll know. . . ."*

"That we all need to rest?" Khar finished for her. "You said it's not a contest. Besides, there are ways, never fear. I'll have Rawn tell Ophar."

"Who?" Doyce lifted herself in the stirrups to test her leg muscles' response. They worked—but complained.

"The stallion, silly. Did you neglect to ask his name?"

The two horses began to slow until, bit by bit, as if by mutual consent, they walked.

"I think the horses are tired." She pitched her voice low and discovered it was almost swallowed by the mist.

"Aye," Jenret grunted a reluctant concession. "Wouldn't want to finish them on the first day out."

"Perhaps we should stop for the night. Saam thinks he can pick up the trail come morning."

"My thought as well. If this cursed mist isn't confusing me, there should be a stream up ahead. Used to hunt and fish here as a boy, but I don't think they've moved the stream since then."

"Unlikely," Doyce agreed, pleased by his attempt at humor.

They rode a little farther in silence until Jenret abruptly disappeared off the shoulder of the road, his form floating darkly in the mist, and then engulfed by it. She gasped in disbelief just as she heard him yell, "Over here!"

"Show-off," she muttered and turned Lokka to follow.

Gamely launching herself into misty nothingness, Lokka landed without a misstep. The darkness seemed absolute, but she could hear the gentle plash of water and the rustling of willows. Khar and Saam hurled themselves down, into what, Doyce had no idea. She paused, then followed suit, dubious about what she'd find underfoot, but the earth felt firm and grassy, neither soggy nor yielding to the touch. So she wasn't standing in the invisible stream. She jumped as the voice came at her shoulder.

"Strip Lokka's tackle and I'll take her down for water." Doyce did and then set herself to searching her saddlebags by touch until she located the small rectangle, carefully padded in cloth. Packrat she might be, she decided with a burst of triumph, but it did pay to be prepared! The wrappings concealed a small, collapsible candle shield, each of its four paned-glass sides hinged

to fold flat. She struck a lucifer, gladdened by the small,
cheerful flame the stubby votive candle gave. May the
Lady forgive her for using it in a place other than it was
intended for.

Snagging her bedroll from her gear, Doyce spread it
and then sat to consider the easiest, quickest meal, assessing the contents of first one pack, and then the other.
The three ghatti materialized around the candle, purring
excitement, eyes reflecting the dancing flame. Khar, with
her white muzzle and front, was the most clearly visible,
while Saam appeared wraithlike, and Rawn was darkly
invisible except for glowing eyes. "Dinnertime?" she
feigned innocence.

"Aawr! Rrow! Oh, yes! Quick!" No one had ever
faulted the ghatti for not having healthy appetites.

She piled handfuls of dry trail food into three equal
portions, each ghatt holding back until the others were
served. The nuggets consisted of ground wheat and corn,
dried liver, brewer's yeast, fish oil, and shredded esch-
beel leaves, something like spinach, she thought. While
a steady diet of it spelled monotony, at least to her mind,
it was nourishing, and none of the ghatti spurned it, at
least for short periods of time. Three heads bobbed down
as one and the ghatti began to gulp away. "For heaven's
sake, chew it a little at least! You'll all have belly aches
tonight!"

Khar's head never lifted as she pursued the last elusive
nugget, nosing and sniffing through the grass. **"Didn't
plan on being awake to feel it. More?"**

"That's more than enough to nourish and sustain a
working ghatt or ghatta," came Doyce's rejoinder as she
cut bread and cheese and sausage for herself and Jenret.
"Of course, there might be a bite of sausage for dessert,
after we've eaten."

The three sighed as one, swallowed audibly and gen-
teelly backed away to content themselves with grooming
until the proffered treat materialized.

This time she saw Jenret before he spoke and handed
him a slice of bread laden with meat and cheese. Asa's
wife had baked the day before, and the bread was still
crusty, lightly charred at the bottom, moist within. He

took it and juggled it one-handed as he sat cross-legged
on the other side of the shielded candle.

"The horses are watered and tied so they can graze.
Don't you want a fire?" The last came indistinctly
through the mouthful of food Jenret wolfed down. She
cut more without asking, piled the bread high, and he
snatched it with contented greed. She'd forgotten how
much more it took to fill a man. But then, Oriel, despite
his bulk, had been a finicky eater.

"I brought water back, too. We could make cha."

"I'd be asleep before it could boil." She groaned as
she pulled her knee tight to her chest, then thrust it
straight. The candle flame barely illuminated his face and
his hands floated like pale, disembodied moths against
the dark of night and his clothing. Why did he always
wear black?

"Sore? At your age you have to be careful about that
sort of thing."

Doyce surged to her feet, ignoring the pain, and the
ghatti started, ears laid back as they glared around.
"Old? Yes, I am, and not about to lie about it! But I'll
outride you and outlast you, you black-shirted, fra-
granced fop, and just you remember that!" She paced,
strides rigid with anger, stopped with her back to him,
staring into the night, saying nothing more because she
dared not. She'd allowed him to score without really trying, and her overreaction humiliated her. He'd struck
sparks off her like a piece of flint.

"Touché! It's said that with old age there's a lessening
of one's sense of humor—I guess it's true." Cool amusement in his laugh. "If it's any consolation, I'm thirty-
two, nearly your age. So let's save the feistiness for later
when we may need it."

Inwardly cursing herself for flaring up, Doyce sat back
down and tugged off her boots, taking comfort from the
well-worn leather. The release of pent-up hostility had
felt good, even though she knew it was misdirected. Oh,
for a decent night's sleep to loosen tension, let her regain
her perspective. But not much chance of that, not lately.
She'd sleep for a thousand years if the world would only
let her. Folding her tabard for a pillow, she wriggled into
her bedroll and turned to blow out the candle, then

spoke. "When you get to be my age you get cranky if
you don't get enough sleep . . . and have loved ones
murdered and maimed and find more bodies along your
path." It was as close to an apology as she could
approach.

"I know." Then, quieter still, as if it had been dragged
out of him. "I'm sorry. 'Twas meant to tease."

"I know. Good night."

"Sausage!" Two voices cried in her mind while the
third one rowled aloud.

"Oh, damn, Jenret. Slice them some, would you? I
promised and I forgot." Laughing, Jenret complied, and
satisfied purrs mingled with the willows' dialogue with
the stream.

❧

Byrta shifted on the straw pallet, reached to finger the
bandaged splints that encased her leg from her foot to
above her knee. It felt as if she'd been embraced by a
picket fence; it itched already, and she focused on that
minor indignity rather than on the pain that shrouded
her like a second skin. With a sleepy hand she searched
for a straw, anything she could slide beneath the bandages and scratch with, muttering, "There ought to be
enough of them around, we're in a barn, aren't we?"
and then gave up and dozed.

Perched on a hay bale, knees drawn up, arms folded
tight around them, the urchin-child looked from Byrta to
the ghatta, P'wa, sitting by the pillow, then back again.
Light from the lantern hung on the nail from the loft
beam cast long and short shadows, bars of light and dark
across the figure on the bed as the girl watched. Tiny,
white teeth nibbled at her lower lip. She was nine, and
small for her age, and the size of her responsibility filled
her with awe. Wally had gotten to ride the sway-backed
old mare to fetch the eumedico, but afterward, her father
had said it was her task to watch over the Seeker for
anything she might need. She even had an old chamber
pot at the ready, just in case. She might be only nine,
but she'd trained three on it already, and three more to
go. The thought made her sigh, just enough so that the

ghatta noticed her movement. It flicked an ear, setting
its ear hoop swaying, and the child wished she had jew-
elry of her own, but her Da said they were all his crown
jewels, and that they needed no others.

It had struck her as strange that the Seeker wanted to
stay in the barn, rather than the house where it was more
comfortable, but she had worried it through until she
thought she understood. In the big house you were never
alone, never had enough privacy, bustle and bedlam ga-
lore, though. The more she thought on it, she didn't
blame the Seeker for her polite insistence on staying here
until the eumedico decided she had stabilized enough to
move her to the Hospice. Besides, the Seeker said that
her brother knew to find her here and would be coming
soon. Then she'd be able to watch two Seekers and two
ghatti, both twins, so the lady had said. The Seeker
stirred, gave a grunt of pain, and raised herself on her
elbows, stared around, unsure until she saw the child's
smile.

Bare feet scuffing the straw, the child marched to the
makeshift table, an upended wooden fruit crate, that
held a mug of water and pills in a saucer. The saucer
was her contribution, chipped, but still pretty with its
flaming red poppies, sole survivor of a long-gone set and
hers alone now. "Think ye should have the pills agin?
It bay'int long after dark—moons have just risen." She
reached out a hand, circumspect in front of the ghatta,
and brushed the woman's forehead with her wrist. "You
be feverin' still," she scolded.

"Take the pills and send the child along to bed," P'wa
advised.

"But they'll be here soon," Byrta protested, managing
a smile in the girl's direction as she mindspoke P'wa.
*"And those pills leave me wooly-headed, half-here and
half-where I don't know. I don't want Bard to see me like
that."*

**"But they ease the pain, don't they? Take them. Let
the child get her sleep as well. You know she won't
budge unless she thinks you're tucked in for the night."**

She made a grumbling noise, then halted as the child
skittered at the sound. Scooping the pills from the saucer, she tossed them into her mouth, the child anticipat-

ing and handing her the mug, water slopping in her
hurry. "Thank you, Lindy. Now why don't you go into
the house and get some sleep with the others?"

The child hung back, stubborn about abandoning her
duty. "What if your brother comes while ye be sleepin'?"

The thought of Bard made her smile. "I'd know—
awake, asleep, or dead."

Nimble as a grig, the child hopped up the hay bales
and turned down the lantern until only a firefly speck
remained, then dropped to the floor. She left with a whispered "good night," pale braids swaying and bouncing
to her skip-steps. She knew what she'd do, no bed for
her yet, she'd make the Seeker a custard despite the
lateness, give her something nourishing but pleasant to
eat, to share with her brother when he arrived. Mam
wouldn't begrudge the eggs and milk and sugar, she
knew, though she'd begrudge the noise this late if she
wasn't mouse-quiet. And the ghatta would probably like
to lick the bowl, she decided.

Byrta drifted off as the pain diminished, sighing a little
at her inability to keep her eyes open. P'wa, as well,
napped in relief, then awoke and decided on a meander
around the barnyard to stretch her legs. She, too, had
been swept off the horse when it shied, and while she
landed with more grace than Byrta, the landing had
bruised, made her stiffen later with the enforced sitting
and watching, the worry. She twisted her tail, even that
hurt, then slipped through the door into the pleasantness
of night.

The child, Lindy, placed the last custard cup in the
pan of hot water and startled, sharp ears catching the
sound of a horse being walked slow and stealthy toward
the barn. She grabbed up the empty mixing bowl, ready
to rush out to welcome the Seeker's brother and the
ghatt, when she realized the rhythm of the sounds indicated not one horse, but two. Puzzling it over, she eased
the door open just enough to let her stand, eye to the
crack, and strain to see. But the horses were riderless;
whoever they belonged to was already in the barn. She
nibbled at a braid-end, rubbed the tip across her lips.
And then something struck her as very odd, wrong, left
her clutching the bowl so hard she came close to halving

it like a walnut. Neither horse had a pommel platform on the front of the saddle. If not the Seeker-brother, then who?

An explosive growl detonated darkness outside, and she sensed more than saw the fluid motion of the black and white ghatta racing toward the barn. She could detect the ghatta's shame at her momentary desertion and measured her own against it. Hadn't Da told her to watch over the Seeker? The child flung herself after the ghatta, casting a longing look back at the safety of the kitchen, the upstairs where her parents and brothers and sisters slept the sleep of the righteously exhausted after a day's mowing.

"Bard?" Byrta half-woke as a hand touched her shoulder. But the hand pressed her backward, as did the hand on her other shoulder, pinning her to the mattress. Yet another hand slapped a moist rag over her mouth and nose. The sickly-sweet smell made her cough, gag, and she awoke in earnest, dread rippling through her, jangling at her pain. Not Bard! Who? Where was P'wa?

She heard the ghatta's command, knew she came at a dead run. **"Hold your breath! Don't breathe!"** The mindvoice resonated with desperate urgency, closer now, in the loft above her, she thought. **"Go limp! Then spring!"**

She obeyed, then twisted with catlike strength, swinging her good leg to the floor, dragging the other after it. No time to think about Bard now, though he would feel the abrupt fluctuation in their link. Her unexpected move made the hand holding the rag slide from her mouth, clout her behind the ear, and she drew a quick breath, then lost it as her bad leg hit the ground. The pain rolled through her in waves, grabbed at her stomach, and the combination of the sickly-sweet smell and the pain made her head swim. Hands grabbed back, pulled at her, taunting with their power, their easy manipulation of her as if she were a puppet. An internal voice threaded through her brain, ordered her to be still. Anger soared—no human, no one but Bard could, should, invade her mind like that!

P'wa dove from the loft, slammed into the back of one of the shadow figures, and the chain reaction sent Byrta shuddering and jolting against the makeshift table. She forced her fingers to close on the crate, slam it against the other dark shadow dragging at her. Brittle crackling sounds, sharp snappings, but little damage, she judged. Still, it bought time. P'wa lashed with her claws, shrieking ghatti invectives at the top of her lungs. She felt a separate shock of pain, more indignity than pain, as P'wa's tail was trod on, through pure chance, pinning her in place on the floor.

"Keep your foot there! Put the ghatta out first," a voice commanded. Byrta feinted with the crate slat that remained to her, and feinted again, drawing the figure left, luring him away from P'wa, jabbing with all her strength at the midsection.

"Leave'm be, you bullies! Be off with ye afore my Da comes or you'll be sorry!" With a groan, Byrta sent the stroke wide as the white, scowling face of little Lindy popped in front of the dark figure. The child was brandishing a—Byrta shook her head, tried to clear it—a bowl? But the dark figure laughed and tossed the child out of the way, sending her into a stumbling crash onto the ground, bowl breaking. Then the figure kicked once at Byrta's splint-cased leg and the pain closed up and over her, and she plunged down a long well of darkness and pain.

Fat white candles cast flickering light from every wall sconce in the room; oil lamps balanced on shelves, the leathern record books eased aside to make room. Still, it seemed shadowy and sad to Sarrett, though she knew that the Hall of Records had seldom seen so much light. Usually it was occupied by day by the Master Scriber, a retired Seeker whose duty it was to transcribe from the travel notes all the cases a Seeker heard during a circuit. Then they were verified, signed by the Seeker and the Seeker General as to their authenticity, and finally filed. Three or four Novies, Seekers-in-training, assisted on a rotating basis; it served as good background for the cases they would ultimately hear. Sarrett had enjoyed her tour of duty here not so many years ago. Sometimes a scholar or Conciliator came, asked permission to do research or to examine records for precedents before passing a verdict, but all in all, it radiated a sense of tranquillity and peace, smelling of ink and parchment, dust, leather bindings, and now the sharp aroma of the scented oil and the smell of burning beeswax.

A flurry of sneezes threatened to gutter the candles on the table, and Parcellus sniffled a damp apology, hands fluttering in pocket after pocket to find his handkerchief. Per'la minced across the table, tapped him on the nose with a soft paw, and then languidly subsided across an open Record Book.

Shaking her head, her pale, white-gold hair gilt-traced in the candlelight, Sarrett tossed her own handkerchief to Parcellus. He flashed a smile of thank you, eyes watering, and honked loudly, not the most pleasant of sounds.

"You aren't allergic, are you?" She prayed for a negative answer. "The mold spores, the dust, they affect some people that way." If so, she was in for it. How long could she listen to Parcellus sneeze? One day had been more than enough already. Oh, for a common cold, even if she caught it, too. T'ss curved his way around one of the stacks, gave her bleak look of sympathy—and sneezed as well, eyes wide in surprise. "Lady bless," she said automatically; she'd given up saying it for Parse, one could utter the words just so many times and she couldn't afford the distraction.

"Don't know, could be. I'm allergic to lots of things— milk, strawberries, pollen. The medicaments the eumedicos give me help . . . some." He whoffled into the handkerchief again, then got back to business, dragging Per'la off the book he'd been perusing.

"Thank the Lady you're not allergic to ghatti, think what a life that would be."

He deposited the ghatta on the floor, gave her a gentle shove to join T'ss. "I am allergic, always have been, though it's gotten better as I've gotten older. Poor Per'la, to have to put up with me. I've nearly sneezed her off the bed many a night." He raked flyaway red hair back from his face and looked serious, pale complexion even paler and more sickly in the flickering light.

"Now, explain it to me again. You're right, we can't just go searching at random through two hundred years of history. I'd be old and gray and you'd run out of handkerchiefs to give me. There has to be a more efficient way."

"There is, staring us right in the face." She tapped at the blue leather-bound book by her right hand. "It's all here. You can't just transcribe cases and file them on the shelves, someone has to know where to locate them. I don't know why it took me so long to remember, just thinking that if we dove straight in we'd somehow find something faster. Anything to help Doyce find out what happened to Oriel.

"Anyway, there are chronological files and subject files; each one with a brief annotation of the incident or case and a Circuit Number to look up for further reference to the complete report. Each file has the same annotation, but sometimes seeing it in another grouping gives you different ideas. I can start with the chrono file, read it from now backward in time, and you can do the same with each of the subject files. If anything strikes either of us as significant, we can check the full reference for more details."

"Sounds better than what we've been trying so far," Parcellus agreed. "But how long do you think this will take us? I'm worried about Doyce, too. Anything we can find to show the Seeker General might help."

Closing the heavy leather volume in front of Parcellus, Sarrett added a new one on top. "I know. I'm nearly as frightened for the Seeker General as I am for Doyce. There's something Swan Maclough isn't telling, and I think what Doyce is doing, or trying to do, is only the tip of it. Why she won't tell, I don't know. I've never seen her look so old and afraid."

With a sigh Parcellus opened the volume at the back and began to skim the recent cases first. "Land disputes, boundary disputes, wouldn't you know it? Not likely to be here, is it?"

Picking up an equally heavy twin to Parcellus's book, Sarrett opened the cover. At least she could read from front to back since each chrono book covered a year's cases. "I don't know," she said resignedly. "It could be anywhere, encompass anything, some obscure connection. It may be more than one thing or incident that we're looking for. Part of it does seem to revolve around injuries or illnesses to Seekers and Bondmates, perhaps people other than Seekers. Why not put that aside and try something more along those lines first?" She pulled a candle closer to her and shoved the oil lamp in Parse's direction. At least he couldn't blow that out as easily. It gave her minor hope.

Muffling a sneeze in the crook of his elbow, he drew the lamp closer. "I'll stay with the boundaries for a little while. Who knows? It all has to be done sometime, so I might as well stick with it." He rested his chin in his hand and read in silence for a long time, scribbled a note or two, and read more.

Sarrett hooked a foot around the leg of a neighboring chair and drew it over without looking up, propped her feet on it. Pages turned, the ghatti prowled, stalking shadows, gauging the erratic flight of a moth trapped outside the windowpane, wanting to reach the lights. The candles burned shorter; the world outside grew still as night settled more deeply.

"But what *are* we looking for!" Parse muttered once, slapping his hand flat on the table. The sound made her jump.

"Whatever we can find that will help, my friend, so let's keep at it." She laughed, felt the rising nervousness of the sound. "After all, we've only two hundred years to search through, as you so well reminded me!"

Bard fisted a yawn, wondered if it were possible to swallow his own hand, and M'wa yawned in sympathy. Actually, he had to admit, the ghatt wasn't being sympathetic so much as he was miserably bone-tired as well. Still, it didn't matter how exhausted they were, at last they rode in the direction they longed to go—toward Byrta and P'wa. The ghatt with the long white stocking on his left foreleg purred, and the humming happiness that coursed through Bard at the anticipated reunion was not dissimilar.

Pain still emanated from Byrta, dragged at his well-being as if they shared a common chord stretching across the leagues. But the pain was not as severe as before, when he had felt the crack and splinter of her leg when her horse had thrown her, a spurt of agony that had come close to making him black out, the empathy so great that he had grabbed at his own shin, convinced that bone stabbed through flesh. Strange to reach down and touch a leg perfectly whole. But the harshest pain of all had been her feverish insistence that he ride away from her, not back toward her as his heart pulled him to do.

Caught in the twisting throes of a drug-hazed slumber, Byrta's unease communicated itself to Bard in the distance, made him push on a little faster though he knew it was foolishness. She was fine, he reassured himself, just disoriented. M'wa yawned his agreement. He sang under his breath, in their own private language, a tune to soothe, knew it wove through the night until she quieted, drowsily echoed a few bars of the refrain, flat on the eighth notes as usual, he noted.

M'wa's head tilted, testing the air, then he gusted a satisfied sigh and settled back on his platform, **"They've moved her to shelter."**

Wavering in the saddle, Bard chuckled. *"I know. She told me ages ago. Didn't you notice me wince when they moved her?"*

"Well, P'wa was busy supervising." M'wa sounded miffed. **"She's never seen so many children in her life. Swears the farmer raises more of them than he does crops."**

"She'll feel right at home, then," Bard responded, remembering their years of growing up, the hoards of cousins, intermingled bloodlines. And the two of them, Bard and Byrta, always in their midst, yet always alone, set off by their tawny coloration, their twinship, the communion that no one else could sense or even seem to understand when they strove to explain it. Together even when they were apart, and yet sometimes wishing to be apart when they were together. Were they whole without each other or merely halves, he'd often wondered, and which was the stronger half?

"I know, I know," the ghatt singsonged to himself as

much as to his Bondmate. **"A long, long, long, long day,"** and with each repetition the ghatt stretched his spine. **"Try it,"** he cajoled.

Balancing against the canter, Bard raised himself in his stirrups, stretching to pluck a disciple moon, until he collapsed back into the saddle. "Lady bless," he started to say aloud, and then realized that he was alone with M'wa, could say what he wished, what he felt, as he had been raised to pray by his grandfather, all wrinkled knobby knees and elbows, ribs like sprung barrel staves, dark skin etched with ashy dust from tracking the cattle, loincloth twisted and knotted like a clout, the earthen amulet swinging round his neck. "Divine Harharta, hear my plea, and I will honor it with fresh blood thricefold when I reach cattle worthy of sharing their vital fluids. Keep her safe, comfort her against the night, another night that we are apart." He felt better after that, after the stretching and the true-hearted prayer.

They rode, ever closer to their hearts' desires, comfortable, compatible in their shared bonds, both near and far, judging their progress by the rising moons. And then, a brief sensation of . . . something . . . tugged deep within Bard, insinuated itself through his veins with an eerie urgency. He started in the saddle, scanning to discover the source. But it had receded, evasive as a nighthaunt from his grandfather's tales, though it left Bard chilled with fear sweat.

The tip of M'wa's tail lashed, metronomic twitching, but the rest of him was statue-still. **"Did you . . . ? What was . . . ?"** the ghatt asked, uncertain as if awaking from a dream.

Licking his lips, Bard strove to compose an answer, one that he could believe in as well. But what was there to explain? The sense of violation was gone. *"Mayhap Byrta's having a nightmare?"* he suggested. The answer didn't satisfy, but it was the best he had. Without noticing, he urged the tired horse faster still.

The second intrusion serpentined through them both, contorting muscles, swamping their senses, snaring with a sinister, compulsive seduction, as did the voice lashing through his brain. But the voice sounded nothing like his twin's. "Byrta!" he shouted. "She's in peril! I'm coming,

Byrta!'' There was no need to shout it to the skies, but he prayed that she heard above the strange dinning within his own skull.

Lips drawn back in a feral grin, Bard drove his horse on through the night. The mindvoice would not take her from him! That he would not allow, not if he had to follow to the lands of the dead and beyond to win her back. M'wa screamed an unearthly yowl. **"P'wa! Beware the cloth! Unclean! The bad smell! The smell that Saam . . . . Too late!"** he spat, yowled in frustration.

Bard spared a thought in M'wa's direction. *"To the death?"*

"Yes, but theirs first!" And Bard gave a wild, ululating laugh, head thrown back to the moons, throat straining with joy at the blood lust that honed his instincts to the pitch of his grandfather's grandfather in the Sunderlies. This was blood he would drink before he offered the gods their sacred portion!

"Almost there! Knives flashing! Now!"

And Bard skidded his horse on its haunches, was off and running, naked sword in one hand, short knife in the other. He was dimly aware of bobbing lights in the house nearby, of frightened shouts, running feet, confusion, but concentrated only on the pounding berserker joy of blood lust flowing through him, his focus narrowed to the desperate calling of Byrta's heart and soul. He never saw the child crouching in his path, somersaulting over her as she wailed in terror, hands scrabbling through the straw to gather and reunite the broken fragments of her bowl. . . .

Bard elbowed himself up, subsided at the sight of two pitchforks aimed at his chest. M'wa shifted one way, then the other, trying to insinuate himself in front of the tines circling and jabbing at his Bond. **"Stay still!"** The muted sobs of a child made a monotonous background sound that ground at his nerves. **"Everyone's alive! But everyone's upset!"**

It held an uncanny reminiscence of the terror he had witnessed early that morning in the barn with Doyce, as if one evil for the day had not been enough, and he must see the twin of it.

The pitchfork hovered near his throat, and a burning

brand seared his face and eyes, the hot brilliance making
him squint in pain. "Lars! Watch that damn thing!" a
voice snapped. "This here's a barn, full of straw! You
want to set it alight?"

"I'll put it out soon as we're sure, Da. Yeah, this one
must be the brother, came from the same pod, all right."
The torch pulled away, and Bard dared finger the lump
on his head. Knocked out cold. Byrta limped into the
circle of light, mirroring his gesture as she pressed her
own hand against her head. She had been out cold as
well, whether in sympathy with his wound or whether he
had lost consciousness because she had, he wasn't sure.
A scent of evil still prevailed around her, a miasma, ma-
lefic fingering, tainting everything within its reach, although it was dissipating rapidly.

"Byrta, we must warn Doyce . . . ! It fingers at your
mind . . . starts to tear it free." He struggled to sit up,
gasping, head pounding. And then he felt his jumbled
thoughts stripped away, everything he had seen and done
this night erased. He struggled to cling to his thoughts,
but he couldn't remember anymore, couldn't remember
what he wanted to tell Doyce, and from the blank expressions of his twin and the two ghatti, knew that they did
not remember either. Baffled, he hit the heel of his hand
against his forehead, praying to jar it loose, but there
was nothing there to free . . . it was gone. He cradled
his head in his hands and moaned.

Only delicate fingerings of mist remained when Doyce
awoke, Khar curled warm against her belly and Saam
aloof at the foot of the bedroll. The sight of him there,
as if he existed on the bare sufferance of others, hurt.
She boosted the complaining ghatta to her feet and disen-
tangled her legs, pulling on her boots. Early morning
birds whistled and sang, and a pheasant hen drank by
stream's edge, beady eyes flashing as it tilted its throat
back to let the water roll down.

Saam stared at it and made guttural chickering sounds
deep in his throat, his body quivering, and looked to

her for permission. Every muscle trembled to attack and pounce.

"No, Saam. Leave it be. We'll eat soon enough." It struck her again how much wilder, more feral Saam seemed without his ability to mindwalk. Ghatti rarely hunted except to avoid starvation. The few ghatti who lived beyond the deaths of their Bondmates sometimes returned to the wild, and she wondered if—and when— it would happen to Saam. To lose him, too, would be unbearable, the severing of one more tie to another Doyce that she still remembered all too well, the Doyce who had loved Oriel.

Gathering enough windblown wood for a small fire, Doyce set about making breakfast, amused that Jenret still slept soundly although Rawn had sprung up when she had, stretching elaborately fore and aft and going off to attend to personal needs. Humming under her breath, she rubbed her hands in front of the fire, then set two custard apples near the coals to bake, waiting for their yellowish-tan tough skin to turn a deep golden brown, the interior baked to a honey sweet, creamy consistency. With cha brewing in her battered tin kettle, she edged slices of bread topped with cheese close to the fire to warm and melt. They'd run out of bread before it became stale, and wish for more, she knew. No oven and no time to bake. Besides, she had no talent for yeast breads, could barely manage an edible journey cake. The last slice almost flipped upside down when she felt the eyes on her.

Hands unsteady, she exhaled slowly through her mouth to center herself, then repositioned the bread, striving to appear natural. Sending her mind spinning out on the danger mode, she searched for Khar. None of the ghatti roamed within her line of vision.

"Here! What?"

" *'Ware! Upwind from you. Alert the others!"* She toyed with the fire, feeding a few twigs deeper into the center, reaching around the gray-ashed coals at the edge to turn the apples. That gave her an excuse to raise herself off her left knee and bend her right leg under her, ready to spring. One good-sized branch burned well; if she could grab that and thrust. . . .

Jenret's eyes flew open, but he remained relaxed, one
arm curled under his head. He, at least, could see behind
her, and she watched to gauge his reaction. Rawn had
'spoken him awake. The only acknowledgment of danger
came when his eyes fixed on a spot behind her and to
her right. At least she knew which way to pivot. A drop
of sweat hung heavy and clammy at her hairline. She
could feel it poised, ready to run.

'Stay still! Coming around!"

A branch cracked in the undergrowth behind her and
Jenret threw his blanket aside and sprang up, shirtless,
chest bare. With one sweeping arc, his sword whistled
free and he was tossing his staff in her direction. She
caught it left-handed and whirled, staff in one hand,
burning brand in the other. Two ghatti, one striped, one
pure ebony, bolted in from opposite directions in a pincer
move, their motions a fluid blur. She scanned for danger,
eyes desperately raking back and forth, high and . . .
low. Relief left her giddy, yet still appalled by what she
saw.

Saam crouched low by a tanglewood bush, a limp,
bloody rolapin hanging from his mouth. Its long ears
draggled against the ground like furred mullein leaves.
He growled deep and low in warning, the meaning as
clear as if he had snarled, "This is mine!" Rawn and
Khar stopped short, then Rawn began a slow advance,
belly low, not in subservience, but creeping to the attack.

"Khar! Stop him! Stop them! Talk to Saam, remind
him why we're here!"

Jenret cursed and yelled at Rawn, but Khar had already run ahead, shouldering her way in front of the
black ghatt. He stopped, reluctant, holding his ground
but not retreating. Khar stood within a leap-length of
Saam, and his growl rumbled higher, tenser.

Then the sound ceased and his eyes dulled, his body
slackening. Khar raised one foot, then brought it forward, little hesitation steps easing her closer, not slinking
but proudly erect. Doyce's breath caught. He looked so
wild! Dropping the rolapin, Saam shook his head vigorously, a look of bemusement on his face. He gazed off
slantwise, away from the two ghatti, and licked a paw,
then rubbed it against his bloodied muzzle. Khar stepped

a few paces nearer, then stopped, waiting for Saam to
look at her. When his head-turn acknowledged her, she
wheeled back past Rawn, toward Doyce and Jenret.
Saam stared down and began to scratch dirt, shreds of
dried grass, twigs, over the dead rolapin. Then he followed after Khar, giving Rawn a wide berth and main-
taining a respectful distance from the ghatta.

"**Saam says he's sorry.**" Khar's words came with formal stiffness. "**He didn't mean to scare.**"

Rawn, usually silent amongst outsiders, spoke. "**Well,
he did. Did mean to or didn't mean to—still had the
same result. I want him gone.**"

Jenret whistled the black ghatt to him and gave his
ears a thorough rubbing in hopes of restoring his good
humor, but the ghatt pulled back, unmollified. "**His
sense of purpose wavers. I can follow trail as well as he,
maybe better. We don't need him.**"

Saam slumped disconsolately by the fire, near the
other four but still at a painfully calculated distance of
propriety. Reaching down to give Khar a hug, Doyce
whispered, "What are we going to do? Are we losing
him, do you think?"

"**I don't know.**" Khar's tail twitched at the tip, irrita-
tion showing only there. "**I just don't know. He doesn't
know why either. Something came over him just now,
sang in his blood. He feels some things that we can't.
Rawn doesn't want to believe, but it is so. He is more a
ghatt, less a Bondmate, and the gulf grows.**"

"But there must be something we can do? Can we
trust him?"

"**Yes. Stroke him, he feels shameful, disgraced. Breakfast?**" The last on a rising, eager note. "**Always helps!**"

Doyce suspected that breakfast was designed to help
Khar and Rawn more than Saam, but she refrained from
saying so. A happy ghatt was usually a hungry ghatt, and
Saam looked neither. A sharp charcoal scent warned her
that her own breakfast scorched, the bread a dark brown
on the bottom and the melted cheese running and dripping. At this point, the custard apples bubbled and
hissed, ready to explode. "Go wash up and be quick,"
she admonished Jenret and hoped he'd obey. She wanted
a moment alone with Saam.

The blue-gray ghatt, still scruffy from his ordeals of the past few octs, examined the ground, feigned disinterest, but Doyce could feel his worried yellow eyes following her, just as before they had bored through her with blood lust. *"Khar, I want to talk to him alone, don't translate for him."*

"Don't know how much he'll comprehend."

"I know, but I've got to try." Moving toward the fire, Doyce removed their breakfast, talking softly to herself and, she hoped, to Saam. Ghatti understood verbal speech, or at least more so than most animals, but the special combination of verbal and mental communication afforded them full comprehension. Saam might understand only simple commands and tones of voice, or he might understand more. She had no way of knowing, or of knowing if he could still sense the truth behind her words.

"Saam, beloved ghatt. Saam, beloved Bondmate of my beloved Oriel." A slight ear twitch and head jerk at the sound of a familiar name, but more so at the sound of Oriel's. She knelt and stroked his head, her other hand lifting his chin. He flinched, tried to pull back from her touch; the action made tears well in her eyes. Never had he pulled away from her before. "Saam, I love you and I need you. You are good, Saam. Good. And I need you. I need your help so much to find out who hurt Oriel and you, who hurt Asa and Wwar'm and her little ones. You can Seek. You must Seek." The word made him thrum with nervous energy. "And no more wildness like that, no more! Do you hear me!" She wagged a finger in front of his nose.

Rhythmically stroking the length of his body, she sighed at the thinness, stroking again and again, watching the dead hairs float off into the air. With a ragged breath the ghatt visibly relaxed, eyes half-closing and a wisp of a rough purr breaking and catching in his chest as if it had been too long since he'd tried.

"Poor old Saam, poor old ghatt. But a good ghatt. One of the best. Saam will help his friends Seek." How much was reaching Saam? No choice but to wait and see, and she prayed that no one's life depended on it, least of all Saam's.

"Breakfast ready? I'm starved." Jenret stood beside her, pale face and hands glistening with droplets of water, nature's ephemeral diamonds, dark hair sticking up in wet spikes at his crown. His tunic neck buttoned crookedly, donned in haste. Blast the man, she thought, he's done it again. She gave Saam a final farewell stroke and 'spoke Khar, curled up tail over nose, on her bedroll.

"Why didn't you warn me he was back! I can't stand him sneaking up on me like that!"

"Moves near as silent as a ghatt," Khar noted with approval, widening her amber eyes and staring owl-like over the fluffed tip of her tail, using it like a fan to mask her smile.

Doyce handed up some of the singed bread and cheese to Jenret, poured cha to cool, and stuffed a bite of her charred breakfast into her mouth before she rose to portion out the ghatti's food.

"Oh, cust-ables!" came the long, drawn-out word behind her.

"Cust-ables?"

"Cust-ables," he repeated cheerfully. "That's what we used to call them when we were little."

"We who?" She put a double handful of trail food in front of each ghatti. Saam wavered, but at last dipped his head and began to chew methodically, eyes pinched shut in concentration.

"Oh . . . well," he hesitated and picked up his mug as if hoping to divert her into pouring more cha. "My . . . my brother and I. Many children call them that. Didn't you?" He had brushed by the personal to the general and then thrown the conversation back at her. As if he didn't wish to reveal anything further.

"Fur rubbed the wrong way?" Khar questioned.

"Mmph." The heavy, dark stubble of his beard after only a day unshaven made her wonder what he'd look like with a beard. Elegantly distinguished or piratical? Well, that would be answered soon enough. Assuming he didn't irritate her so badly that she crowned him with her staff. Like a stubborn mule—first you have to attract his attention before he'll even notice the carrot. And what was his "carrot?"

"So why are you with us, Jenret? A sense of adventure

or something more?" She smoothed the pique in her tone until it sounded more businesslike, impersonal. After all, she was his senior in age—as he'd so carefully pointed out—and a full Senior Seeker with only somewhat less seniority. And she had a charge to fulfill: the Seeker General had instructed her to seek out evidence, to follow it through. He had not been so instructed.

Stung by her tone, Jenret's face hardened, became masklike. "Hardly adventure. But I am a Seeker, and this concerns me as well as you. It concerns *all* Seekers and Bondmates, remember that. Our own have been killed and we must know why. That is enough of a reason for my presence and Rawn's."

Something more lingered behind his words, the same strange longing she had glimpsed before, but she could tell he had no plan to share it. Nor did she, perhaps, deserve to hear. For every step forward they made in trust, each took two steps back. Her mouthful of overdone toast and cheese stuck in her throat, scraping its way down, an insult to its careful baking. She gulped a mouthful of overhot cha to compensate, and her eyes watered. The heat, she told herself. Still, he had no right to insinuate himself into a situation where he wasn't wanted or needed just because he wanted it his way, calling it duty. She knew what duty meant and the self-sacrifice it required. She'd let him play on her sympathies, a momentary lapse she could ill-afford. What had ever made her think that like called out to like?

Delicately wielding the point of his knife, Jenret punctured the tops of the custard apples and handed her one, sweet steam spiraling from it. Jenret ducked his face into the steam and slurped with noisy pleasure. "Is the ghatt going with us?"

"Who, Saam?"

"Yes, him. I'd feel safer if he'd stayed behind."

"And I'd feel safer with him than letting him free on his own. Besides, he has even more at stake in this than I." And implicit in that statement was that she had a greater stake than Jenret and Rawn, but she knew he had caught the implication.

Ears flaming red, Jenret rose and wiped his hands on his pants legs. "So be it. But keep him under control

. . . if you can. Now, let's ride. Time enough we've
wasted this morning over false alarms."

They broke camp with brisk efficiency, two solitaries
in unexpected harmony—or at least no outright discord
over who took on what task. Boundary lines, invisible
but real, directed what they would or wouldn't do or say.
She felt them, had helped draw them herself, despite her
initial invitation to him. Saam cast about, darting ahead
and back, fanning out to one side or the other, head in
the air, then close to the ground as he sniffed for a
deeper scent. Three men and a ghatt rode somewhere
ahead, perhaps still riding, perhaps gone to ground, hidden while they quarreled. Did they think themselves safe
from pursuit? Would they strike again soon? What did
they hope to accomplish? She understood as little of that
as she did her resentment of Jenret.

They were mounted now as Doyce awaited Khar's
translated instructions from Saam. Black-clothed rider,
black stallion, black ghatt nearby, a dark parody of the
mysterious menace they chased. Jenret reined in beside
her as she pointed out their direction.

His face unsmiling, he asked, "So what did you call
them?"

"Call what?" The man was making no sense.

"Cust-ables! When you were little!"

Despite herself Doyce grinned and clipped her heels
into Lokka's flanks, shooting ahead down the road.
"Custies!" she shouted back over her shoulder. Jenret's
face remained solemn, and then she ranged too far ahead
to see the smile that crinkled his blue eyes, sparked them
to a brighter hue.

❖

This day hung overcast as well, the air gravid with
unshed rain. The only breeze that ruffled sweat-drenched
clothes and hair came from what they created as they
cantered along. An occasional shaft of sunlight speared
down through the overhanging clouds and stabbed deep
into the flank of the earth, only to disappear, swallowed
whole.

Neither Doyce nor Jenret spoke any more than needful, both lost in their own private thoughts. Nor, Doyce decided as she started to speak, was there anything to say. Nothing to keep it light and cheery, to pretend they played at a morning's ramble. She knew now that their path pointed toward the Greenvald River which divided the lower, more habitable stretches of the High Firs from their darker, overpoweringly dense cousins who guarded the Tetonord range. The Greenvald snaked through in a wild unpredictable torrent, wide and rushing with a force that kept inhabitants of each side of the river as separate and distinct as the armed boundary of two conflicting nations. Deutscher on the west bank boasted the only safe crossing for leagues, and owed that not to nature but to manmade compromise that paid its own inadvertent dues in life and supplies to the ever-hungry river.

The closer they came, the grayer and more overcast the sky appeared, bearing down with the weight of all-encompassing armor, until by late afternoon the gray-green light ineffectually forcing itself through the dense trees barely illuminated the road. Saam's impetuous scream of outrage and his headlong leap from Lokka's back left Doyce rigid with apprehension. Had he turned wild again or sensed some lurking danger?

"What is it? Why didn't you warn me?" she protested to Khar as she swung Lokka to a standstill and watched Saam dash off the road's shoulder and disappear into a thick copse of oak saplings and alder brush, their leaves, some already turning with the season, lank and still in the heavy air. She fingered her sword grip and put Lokka into a tight circle while she checked for danger. It could be anything, anywhere. She felt her throat constrict at the enormity of the thought.

But Khar charged after Saam, with Rawn arrowing in front of her, a body length ahead. **"Not danger,"** she flung back, **"but something!"**

Bringing Ophar around toward Doyce, Jenret dismounted and peremptorily threw the reins at her, dashing after the ghatti before she could form a protest.

Khar's 'speech jittered with impatience. **"Come look! We need you!"**

A distant cannoning of thunder prickled the hairs on the back of her neck as she slid from the saddle. No need

to tie the horses, both were trained to stand when the
reins were dropped to the ground. "Stay," she whispered
to reassure Lokka and slapped Ophar's shoulder before
she scrambled and scraped her way down the bank to
join the others. The thunder rumbled again, closer, and
the air pressed deathly still.

"What is it?"

"A body!" Jenret called back as she crashed through
the undergrowth.

She stopped short, avoided tripping over Jenret's bent,
dark-clad form as her eyes tried to adjust to the murkiness inside the stand of trees. Rawn and Khar sat on
either side of the body, looking with fastidious interest,
but Saam burrowed and snuffled through the dead leaves
and fern bracken. She bent to study the face of the
thing—the body—that lay crumpled in front of Jenret.

"Dead?" She didn't want to touch it until she'd looked
around.

"Aye. And recent, too. It's still faintly warm, still flexible." He prodded it in demonstration as a less than
pleasant smell floated from it, cutting through the dried
leaf, mulch scent. The features had frozen in pain and
the taut lips shown pale blue, almost gray in the lack of
light. Jenret tugged back the leather jacket to reveal a
makeshift padding of bandages around the chest and midsection of the grimy, wizened form.

She bent closer, then halted in amazement. "It's Cal.
At least that was the name I was told, and I know his
face."

"Well, from the looks of it, Asa and Wwar'm didn't
die without at least giving back nearly as good as they
got." Jenret found a twig, used it to separate and shift
the sticky, blood-encrusted bandages. "Looks as if Asa
pronged him with the pitchfork at least twice, and those
are Wwar'm's contributions." He pointed to the deep
claw marks, so like the ones she'd seen on Asa's body.
"But how do you know this man?" The misgiving in his
voice made her wonder what doubts he harbored about
her.

"I met him briefly at The Cyan Inn. Offered to buy
him a drink, but he refused when he saw that I was a
Seeker." She faltered, the realization of what she was

about to say shaking her. "The tavern maid said that he
. . . he used to be a Seeker himself." She reached to
touch a leather thong around his neck, then pulled back
the silver disk which had swung behind his shoulder.

"A Seeker? We'll discuss this later. Now let's go!
Don't you see, if he's here, the others must be close by!
They couldn't have abandoned the body too long ago
from the looks of it." He was halfway back to the horses,
confident she followed behind.

"Unless they left him here to die," she shouted after
him. Tarrying a moment to slip the leather thong over
Cal's head, she stuffed the disk in her pocket and then
rushed after. Why did she tamely follow instead of
searching further? But Jenret had the right of it: what if
they pressed so very near and then let the murderers slip
away? The thunder growled again, closer and deeper yet,
and the air blurred and shifted as if she peered through
water rather than air.

"Should we say something for him? He was a Seeker."
Khar kept pace with her, amber eyes troubled.

*"I don't know, Khar, I don't know. Maybe later if it
seems right. Now come on. Where's Saam?"*

**"Back already. And he doesn't like what you have in
your pocket."**

*"Well, he's just going to have to dislike it for now be-
cause we don't have time to discuss it."* She scooped up
Lokka's reins and savagely jammed her toe into the stirrup. *"Mayhap there's someone who'd cherish it and his
memory."*

"He won't ride if you carry that."

Vaulting up, Doyce slapped the pommel platform to
bring Khar to her, then reached into her pocket. "Jenret!" she called. "Catch! Don't lose it! It's Cal's Lady's
Medal." The silver disk arched through the air like a
comet, its leather thong trailing behind. Jenret snatched
at the glow of silver and nodded before he turned and
galloped away. She wished she'd had time to examine it,
but it certainly was nothing more than a Lady's Medallion, an older version of the one that Vesey had worn
and the remains of which she carried in her pocket.

As soon as Doyce felt Saam land on the back platform,
they followed after Jenret, just as the heavens split asun-

der and emptied themselves on riders, ghatti, and horses
alike. And on one corpse, receiving its first bath in years.

They pounded along, not sparing themselves or the
horses as the road churned itself into a river of mud and
brown, swirling water. No hope of spying a pothole or a
projecting root or stone until they hit it. But Deutscher
loomed around the bend, Duetscher and its strange ferry,
a dangerous but effective route across the tumbling, roiling river sounds she heard booming ahead, its steady
grumblings and mutterings dulled and muted by the
pounding rain.

If their foes had already crossed on the ferry, they'd
have no hope of catching them; the ferry couldn't func-
tion in this storm. If they still waited to cross, they had
a chance. She understood Jenret's urgency better now.
Headstrong he might be, but he wouldn't swerve from
danger, known or unknown. Pressed tight to Lokka's
neck, her body screened Khar from some of the pounding rain, and she spared a thought of pity for Saam, claws
sunk into the rear platform, completely exposed. Still,
there was no choice, and she urged Lokka faster, trying
to pull alongside Jenret to avoid the water and clods of
mud flung back by Ophar's plunging strides.

Jenret must have harbored the same worries about
their options, their chance for success or failure as they
swept into town and down the slickly treacherous trail
that now funneled water like a chute toward the riverbank. With a shout of dismay he pulled Ophar up and
shielded his eyes against the rain. "Halfway out!" he
screamed as the rain battered his words to crash and die
against the water. Hands cupped around her eyes, she
squinted hard, straining to make out a slightly darker
speck on the water, something foreign to the wild, dissonant partnership of river and rain, possessed of the same
elemental force yet still at odds. The darker patch tumbled and bobbed as if on a leash, casting up a white
flume of water like a lashing tail as it heaved and struggled against the river's monumental pull.

As if on command, a flash of lightning cleaved the
sky, a blue-white tracer illuminating looming shapes and
shadows, bobbing specks of whiteness—faces aboard the
ferry—the sodden gray bulk of cargo, three horses, and

the tented shape of the canvas shelter at the ferry's center.

She had inspected the ferry once before, snugged tight against the lee of the bank while it loaded, but had never watched it in operation. And ferry was a misnomer for it as far as she was concerned, about as safe as sticking candles on a shingle and floating it off down the rapids. Faced with the all-consuming, constant fury of the river, the townspeople of Deutscher had been wise not to try to tame or conquer it. The best they could hope for was a sickeningly swift ride which might or might not buck them off before they reached the opposite bank. She knew why gambling held no appeal in Duetscher: why bet on cards, dice, or the swiftness of horses when a river crossing offered the ultimate high stakes: life or drowning?

The ferry was primitive, no more than a flat log raft with both ends warped into identical rounded prows to glance off rocks. On each side of the raft two massive iron rings were pinned deep into the logs, and from these stretched heavy rope cables joined to an even larger iron ring welded to a frame enclosing a set of pulleys that ran on wrist-thick twisted cables across the river. Three or four times higher than a man could reach, the cables were attached to a pulley system set in pylons on either side of the river. The Duetscher-side pylon had a windlass set at its base.

Traveling from west to east, from Deutscher to the other side, the raft shot on a diagonal across the river, the current carrying it to the landing point downstream. The cables kept the raft from being swept away, but the current carried it along. For the return journey from the far bank back to Deutscher, the windlass provided back-breaking labor as men struggled to turn the giant cranks to precariously winch the raft upriver against the current, working from low to high point so that the raft never broached, but instead angled its deliberate way back home.

Despite the fact that the ferry was halfway across, the dock stood deserted, no ferry-tender in sight. A tiny hut the size of an ice-fishing shanty perched on the bank just above the dock, but Doyce couldn't tell if it was occupied

or not, the dim shadow of a shuttered window isolating
it from the pounding rain. With a shout of dismay, Jenret
jumped onto the planks and dashed toward the crank,
threw his full weight against it, trying to turn it over and
halt the raft's downstream run.

"Help me winch it back!" he shouted into the pounding rain, as if his command would be heard and obeyed,
but by whom she didn't know. Without waiting for a
response, he eased the stopper bar free and began to pull
against the force of the current and the plunging weight
of the raft. His muscles bulged, fighting not to yield the
slack the raft needed to run with the current.

Knowing her weight on the crank would mean little or
nothing, she sluiced the rain from her eyes and cast
around for what she needed. Rope—a mooring place had
to have coils of rope scattered all around. Where, damn
it? Khar sped past her, looking like the most sodden,
miserable beast she'd ever seen, but she had no time to
sympathize.

"Over here, on the barrel!" Khar leaped to the top
of the piling to elude the swirling water threatening her
footing.

Damnation! Why wasn't there anyone to help? Giving
a shout in the direction of the hut, she splashed on,
squinting against the driving rain and acutely aware of
the dragging wetness of the sheepskin tabard plastered
against her body. Jenret's must be hampering him as
well. If she could reach him with the rope and have him
secure the crank, then all she had to do was make sure
the other end was knotted to Lokka's or Ophar's saddle
horn. That should hold the raft, freeze it in midstream
until they could summon help to winch it back to shore.

The rain-sodden rope refused to bend into knots, but
she fumbled with cold, moisture-slick fingers and finally
clove-hitched it to Ophar's saddle horn; it would have to
hold, no time to try to better it. She spared breath for
another shout, yelled at the top of her lungs and swore
that the rain washed her words away. Then she ran, falling, running again, uncoiling the rope from her shoulder
as she descended toward the dock and Jenret.

A blade of light stabbed at her eyes, caught her attention as two shapeless figures came tumbling out of the

hut, bellowing shouts of dismay and warning. Distracted, Jenret half-turned, lost his concentration at the crank.

She heard as much as saw the darker shape of Jenret being bodily lifted and flung backward, his fight with the winch handle lost as it tossed him up and across the rain-wet planks. Freed from restraint, the handle spun round and round with a thwap, thwap, thwap, and the unleashed raft shot forward to its haven on the other side. No way to halt it now.

Dropping the useless rope she ran to Jenret's side as he struggled to rise, balanced groggily on hands and knees, head bowed low. He collapsed and slumped face forward into the swirling rainwater, ankle-deep as it sluiced along the planking, rushing too fast to drain between the cracks. The winch handle must have slammed him in the ribs or in the face when it broke free, enough to knock the wind or the sense out of him and let him drown. Grabbing for his head, her hand hit something furry and warm, heat radiating through soaked fur.

"Me," the miserable voice identified itself, "Rawn. Hurry, he's heavy!" Rawn, the color of darkness and the driving rain, crouched under Jenret's head, supporting his unconscious Bondmate, holding his mouth and nose above the rushing water with his body.

Deciding drowning presented a more immediate concern than any injuries, she grabbed him by the collar and shoulder and heaved him onto his back. The uncertain flicker of a lantern highlighted a bloody, puffed nose and a rapidly closing, swollen eye. The ferrymaster brought the lantern nearer, rain sizzling against tightly-sealed glass sides.

"Got'em there, too," he noted, swinging the light for emphasis. "Thought he'd missed with his face. I c'd 'ear the thud when'e took'em in the ribs. Handle musta flipped up fra there." The ferrymaster and his son stood bulky and stolid in oiled slickers, watching as if this presented the most interesting entertainment they'd seen in recent days. " 'E can't, can't nobody stop the ferry when she's shooting like that, not wid the extra flow."

"Well, give me a hand getting him inside somewhere dry—and be careful," Doyce grunted, still struggling to hold Jenret's head and shoulders clear of the water.

"Oh. Ah. Inn, Bosquet," he commented to his son,
and the two reached strong hands under Jenret's arms
and hauled him upright, none too gently from the moan
that creased his lips.

Eyes still pinched shut, feet moving automatically, Jenret muttered, "Got to stop them. Must stop them!" He
struggled to pull free, nearly fell.

"Oh. Ah, boy. Not stoppin' nothin' on the river ta-
night. No way ta reel nothin' in as you done see'd."

Wishing sourly that the ferrymaster had imparted that
shining bit of wisdom before and not after Jenret's losing
battle, Doyce floundered in their wake. The damp,
dispirited procession wound its way up the bank and
waded against the current of water swirling down the
street, dodging floating branches and human debris, a tin
bucket, bouncing and bobbing, stove kindling.

"Wet as the river but nearn't so rocky," the ferrymaster murmured in what she took to be consolation as she
gathered up the horses and followed, trailed by three
equally wet ghatti. Khar and Saam sprang clear of the
water with each step, as if hoping that dry ground would
magically appear where they landed; Rawn waded along,
paddling once when he lost his footing, stoic in the water.

Pushing through the inn's door, a denlike dimness engulfed her, the pent-in blue haze and reek of tobacco
smoke, the tallow scent of wind-extinguished candles,
rancid grease, and the warm, yeasty smell of fresh and
stale beer. Woodsmoke wreathed the fireplace as the
gusting wind wrestled it back down the chimney. Eyes
stinging, Doyce peered around the room as she motioned
for the men to bring Jenret all the way inside. He
coughed once, sputtered a faint curse that turned into a
groan that made her grimace in sympathy; coughing with
broken or bruised ribs gave exquisite pain.

The inn—she wasn't sure if it deserved to be called
that—made her heart sink. Shaggy unfinished logs, bark
stripped clear in spots by idle hands, formed the walls,
a few cured skins pegged along the outer sides. From the
rank smell she suspected something still inhabited some
of the skins. As candles sputtered to life against the
sulfur-blue flare of lucifers, she made out split log
benches and tables with random tree trunk sections serv-

ing as crude but solid stools. If rustic implied a sort of
country, homespun charm, this inn made wilderness living a homey proposition. The few inhabitants appeared
to be trappers or woodsmen by their garb, but the innkeeper, despite his towering height and coarse woolens,
had two things in common with his brethren everywhere:
his white, ale-stained apron and the harried ability to
thread his way through jostling crowds without spilling a
drop of ale.

"You given up ferrying for fishing, Lester?" he boomed
out, and the men at the tables laughed and elbowed each
other, then went back to the more serious business of
drinking.

"Aye. If'n on'y they don' make'e throw'em back fer
bein' undersize." The ferryman threw his head back and
brayed with laughter, pleased with his own witticism.

"You got horses outside?" the innkeeper asked Doyce
as he shifted Jenret's weight from the ferrymen's grip
and propelled him toward the fire.

"Two horses outside and three very wet ghatti inside
by the door. Have you beds for the night?"

"A Seeker and a Seeker-lady in one swoop!" An erup-
tion of widemouthed "haws" and coughs left her face
spattered with moisture, part tobacco juice, part saliva.
It was better outside. "Looks like you netted well, Lester. Near as well as we done already." With barely a
glance over his shoulder, he spat, let loose a bellow
toward the back of the room. "Selig, it's not a fit night
for man nor beast, so git yourself out there, you won't
notice it! Git those horses sheltered and dried and fed."

Shadows at the far end of the room seemed to ripple,
swim through the smoke and murk, as two figures de-
tached themselves from the darkness and rushed forward, one of them tripping over a log-end stool and
sending it flying from his path. The bulk and movement
looked all too familiar, and she blinked in dismay. It
couldn't be.

Jenret managed a weak bark of laughter. "Company!"
And Doyce nodded in grim agreement as Harrap and
Mahafny made their way to them. Parm's high trill invited the other ghatti beside the fire where he toasted
himself on the slate hearth.

"Harrap, what happened to you?" she blurted before
she could stop herself. The weak wash of candlelight
couldn't hide the fact that Harrap was now attired in
strikingly, violently purple pantaloons, his robe kirtled
up around his paunch, and a green jacket with red cuffs
and facings straining across his massive chest. She
pressed her hand against her lips, swallowed hard to sub-
merge the laughter bubbling to escape.

Jenret couldn't do it. "Did you rob a marching band?"
he inquired between whoops and pain-racked coughs.

Harrap turned his leg this way and that, admiring the
swirl and rustle of the fabric. "There's not much choice
in my size ready-made." The blush on his guileless face
matched the jacket's trim.

"Nor was the man who yielded them up terribly
pleased to do so, even with adequate recompense," came
Mahafny's dry comment. "He mentioned several times
about it being very cold without them." Mahafny, too,
was dressed far differently than Doyce had ever seen her,
her white lab coat absent, replaced by a new outfit of
supple, well-tanned doeskin with a plaid, heavy cotton
shirt beneath the loose-cut tunic top.

"Ask him about the coat!" Parm's thought tickled and
teased the air with the equivalent of a ghatt chuckle.

"Do we want to?" Doyce whispered to Jenret, now
standing on his own but with the wall supporting his
back. He threw out his hands in mock surrender.

"Well, yes . . . the coat, you see," Harrap rushed the
words out. "A bit flashy some might say, but then . . .
it's warm. Buttons tight around the neck, once I ease the
buttons over. And it fits quite well, don't you think?"
He pirouetted back and forth, arms out, so they could
admire it. After years of plain, utilitarian wheat-colored
robes and hemp belts, Harrap peacocked in his newfound
finery.

Mahafny prompted, "Yes, but tell them how you obtained it."

"Oh, yes . . . well . . . a small game of chance with
one of the Monitor's messengers on leave. A fine,
friendly little game."

"And when Harrap caught the man cheating, he sat

on him until he gave up the coat!" Parm burst in, plainly delighted with his new Bondmate.

Jenret strove for a chiding tone but failed. "You, a Shepherd of Our Lady, robbing a man of his pantaloons, gambling for a fancy coat. Neither the Shepherds nor the Seekers will welcome you after this!"

Drawing himself up straight, Harrap radiated a sense of seriousness and determination, nothing ridiculous about him. "Sometimes things are necessary, wrong as they may seem. The greater need decreed that we should come after you and help so that you wouldn't face these trials alone." He jerked bushy eyebrows in Mahafny's direction and continued in a stage whisper, "Ask her about how we got here!"

The comment left Mahafny unruffled. "A little horse trading seemed in order. I'm sure the stabler will find my gray and the two-wheeler a generous trade for the two mounts I selected. Finding one capable of carrying Harrap for any distance was no easy task."

Jenret slid down the wall, legs jackknifing beneath him. Doyce heard him land with a thump and turned, conscience-stricken, reaching to stroke back the wet hair. "No," he said in answer to her unspoken question, leaning his head away from her touch. "Just wet and sore and more weary than I thought. And so discouraged. We were *that* close!" he exploded, fist slamming the floor.

"What happened? Are you hurt?" Mahafny knelt and thumbed back one eyelid, then the other. "Harrap, get my kit—and some more light." With firm but light fingers she explored the mass of bruises puffing Jenret's cheekbone and eye, letting her sensitive, trained touch confirm what her eyes couldn't see.

"Lost a battle with a winch handle." Jenret sucked in his breath but held steady under Mahafny's touch. "We almost caught up with them—two of them crossed on the ferry, the ghatt, too, I think. The third's dead—back aways off the road."

Harrap pressed closer, face pale. "Your doing?"

Raising his palm in a pacific gesture, Jenret shook his head. "No. Before we arrived. He was wounded from the fight."

"Well, they're gone for now, then. Did you take hurt elsewhere?"

"When the handle broke free it caught him in the ribs," Doyce interrupted, aware that Jenret would offer the eumedico less resistance than he'd offer her, despite her training. She suspected he would have fought her attempts at ministration, preferring the pain and discomfort to exposing his vulnerability. The relief she felt surprised her as well: the thought of running her hands over his chest and upper abdomen attracted her and angered her at the same time. All eumedicos learned to suppress emotions of that kind; when had she lost the skill? Curiosity, she thought, only curiosity. Not as muscularly built as Oriel had been with his dark tanned skin and his breadth of shoulders from years of early apprenticeship to his blacksmith uncle. Nothing like the white marble flesh and the silken shift of muscles she'd seen that morning and could still envision beneath the black garments.

Doyce turned her back hurriedly as Harrap arrived with an oil lamp and a reflector spotted with grease and rust, and Mahafny, with his help, began to peel off Jenret's clinging wet tabard and shirt. She wrinkled her nose at the wet wool smell. Wet wool reminded her of wet sheep, and wet sheep of wet . . . ghatti. How could she have forgotten them?

Approaching the bar, she asked the innkeeper, "Have you a dry sack or two, please?" With several in hand, none too clean but dry, she began a brisk rubdown. While ghatti could stand the cold, the damp and wet left them notoriously vulnerable to chills and ague. Rawn might be more used to it, but Khar was not, nor was Saam, especially given his recent stresses. Khar and Saam huddled close, woebegone, and she murmured endearments to them. She did Rawn with the same thoroughness but harder, exactly what the muscular midnight-hued ghatt craved, a rumbling purr and half-lidded eyes proving her right. She'd thought Rawn a pure, solid black, but in the light of the fire she discovered a tiny patch of white, no more than six or seven hairs, far down on his chest.

"Well, what do you think of our company?" Khar asked between licks, her pink tongue searching and busy.

"Ugh! Have to groom forever!" Her mindvoice shifted to include everyone, giving Doyce a chance to consider the question. **"Rawn and Saam wanted to swim out after them."**

"I don't know, but I don't like it. Harrap wants to help, but Mahafny's presence bothers me." With a handful of sack, Doyce wrapped her palm around Rawn's tail and pulled outward from base to tip. Rawn's tail twitched in anger, whether from her action or Khar's last comment, she wasn't sure. She juggled back to the outward conversation. *"That would have been foolhardy. You'd have been swept along like wood chips, tossed wherever the current carried you. With luck you'd have been swept ashore downstream. Without luck, you'd have drowned."*

"Would have made it if Jenret could have held the raft." Irritated, Rawn's tail flicked, scattering a few jeweled drops of water. **"Don't know about him,"** he stretched his neck in Saam's direction, **"but I could have."**

She wanted to speak more with Khar but couldn't muster the strength to separate the conversations. Khar had not indicated whether she approved or disapproved of their visitors, and she wondered if that were on purpose. Finding a dry part of the sack, she continued rubbing, letting the mechanical gestures take over.

Parm bounced twitchy-footed around the tableau, licking at first one ghatt, then another, unsure where to begin the cleanup. He squeaked, skittered to another spot every time he trod in a patch of water. **"Aren't you going to ask how we knew to come here?"**

Parm's thoughts seemed to dance in all directions. The multi-colored ghatt found almost everything in life vastly diverting, as if determined to derive as much entertainment from life as people did from his crazy-quilt appearance. He stretched on his hind legs and rasped his tongue against her cheek, shoving back a strand of wet hair, gave her a considering look and licked again until he was satisfied.

"Well, aren't you?"

"No," replied Khar, Rawn, and Doyce in unison.

"Later," she soothed, scratching his chin. *"When everybody's listening. How goes it with Harrap?"*

Parm's chest puffed with pride. "I did right! It will take time, because he is still fearful, still draws back sometimes. But he is a good learner, with much wisdom of his own."

"But what of Georges? What will become of him? What really happened?" Knowing that Georges lurked somewhere gave her one more worry.

"I do not know. I wish I did, but the Bond is dissolved. I can no longer feel him. Always I will remember our early days together, but later . . . the growing wrongness . . . it burned, burned at my heart and vitals like a spear impaling me. I could not convince him he lied to himself or find the source of his lies, no matter how hard I looked within him. It was leave . . . or die." Parm stared into the distance, through and beyond the snapping fire, thoughts far away. Then he gave himself a violent shake and began to groom Saam with delicate concentration, stroking each clump of wet fur into place, his final words a lonely whisper, barely reaching her. "Saam knows what it is like to meet the badness."

When she rejoined the others, Jenret sat, tightly cocooned in bandages from his armpits to his waist, as Mahafny deftly tucked in the tail-end of the bandage. Harrap made his way back from the counter, four mugs of mulled rum engulfed in his huge hands.

"I asked Walcott," he nodded in the direction of the innkeeper, "to put the tiniest drop of brandy in four bowls of milk. Do you think that's all right?" he asked, expression anxious. "The poor ghatti need to warm their bellies, too."

"Always the good Shepherd taking care of his flock." Doyce smiled at his earnestness. "I don't suppose you have any dry clothes so that two other members of your flock can dry from the outside in as well as warm from the inside out? Our packs are in the stable and I, for one, am not about to venture outside until the rain stops."

Looking up from her handiwork, Mahafny returned her smile, and Doyce found herself pettishly wanting to say 'It's not for you.' "My next thought exactly. I suppose everything in the packs is drenched anyway."

"An early and unexpected laundering," Jenret confirmed. "Except without the soap . . . unless Doyce's squirreled that away in her saddlebags as well. I think she carries a complete general store in there. Collapsible lanterns, cust-ables, who knows what else."

The borrowed clothing felt warm and dry at least. Doyce, wearing extras of Mahafny's, overlong in leg and sleeve but not overlarge otherwise, smothered a laugh at seeing Jenret in one of Harrap's generous robes. It wrapped around him twice but exposed his shins and bare feet until he leaned back against a table and tucked his feet under him. Taking a hearty sip from her mug, Doyce decided she was developing a taste for cheap rum as the trickles of warmth coursed through her. Mahafny sat with an enigmatic smile on her face, self-possessed, self-contained, and she pondered how anyone could manage such serenity. Did she make a constant effort at self-control, or had it become second nature to her? The older woman looked at ease amidst these rough surroundings, a part yet not a part of it.

"Sometimes we see in others a potential that we refuse to acknowledge in ourselves." Mahafny met her gaze for an instant, then looked deep into her mug.

But the last thing she could feel in herself was serenity, self-acceptance. "Why are you here? How did you know to come here, that we would be here?" It went beyond mere coincidence. The planning and gathering of suitable travel gear, the trading of the pacer and rig for two horses—that bespoke advance intent and insight, but whose, Mahafny's or Harrap's? Harrap boasted more facets than she'd originally envisioned, but she doubted that he had instigated any of this. It bore the eumedico's signature of thoroughness and attention to detail. But why involve herself?

The chiding tone in Harrap's rich, deep voice shamed her as effectively as a scolding. "Mahafny and Parm and I talked on the way back. We feared to see you set out with just the two of you and the ghatti against such evil. Mahafny and I are both older, and we've seen much of the world, although we may have let it pass us by. Still, our wisdom combined with yours may be necessary to defeat the horror that we face.

"Don't blame Mahafny, I can see it in your eyes. I broached the idea and she did the planning, along with

what I gave her of Parm's advice. After all, he was canny
enough to ask old Ma'ow where he thought those," he
paused and forced his mouth around the word, "killers
would flee. And to ask about shortcuts that only those
from the area would know to reach here. If you hadn't
arrived, I don't know what we would have done next,
but Parm would have figured something out."

"But this isn't your battle," Doyce insisted, rubbing
the bridge of her nose, feeling the weary frown knotting
her forehead. How could she make them see, make them
turn back for their own safety? Harrap was too pure and
good a man for this. And Mahafny . . . for whatever love
and respect she had borne for the woman from their
earlier relationship, enough still existed to make her fervently wish the eumedico clear of this struggle. That,
her mind nagged, and the fact that it seems so utterly
convenient that she'd reappeared like a fairy godmother
and asserted herself over me again after all these years
of separation.

"But it *is* our battle." Mahafny extended her hand
along the table, reaching yet not quite reaching out to
her. The hand quivered—palsy, age, fear? "Harrap is a
Seeker, will-he, nill-he, and bears the spirit of Our Lady
with him wherever he goes. It makes him a double-edged
sword against the evil we search for. And I, well, I am
not a Seeker as you well know, and that may lessen my
esteem in your eyes. But I am a eumedico with octads
of service in finding and eradicating the evils that invade
men's bodies and their minds. We have been rigorously
trained to detect the falsehoods of the body, to look beyond seemingly healthy flesh to the cancer within, beyond the seemingly placid, fever-free brow to the turmoil
contained there." The silver-haired head balanced erect
and proud on the thin, graceful neck, cool gray eyes luminous and intense as she waited for Doyce to contradict
her, expose the falsehood behind the eumedico vow that
she espoused. And Doyce knew for a certainty that she
could not. And that Mahafny counted on it, testing her
oath, her resolve.

"Jenret?" She hated herself for depending on him, for
making him voice her rejection of their aid. She had not
wanted him either, but now she needed him as an ally.

If it came from them both, perhaps the others would listen, would turn back to safety, to the sanity of the worlds they both knew.

He had observed the interchange between Mahafny and herself too closely, with a secret sympathy equally divided; she had no clue which way he'd turn. "I say yes. I would have welcomed Harrap's weight on the winch tonight. But ask the ghatti. They have a stake in this as well." Still a chance, a chance, but a slim one, and she refused to open her mind to Khar, to influence her decision in any way. She would not beg for Khar's support.

"Khar'pern? Rawn? Saam? Do they join us or not?" Her words husked tight in her throat, her eyes blinking back moisture that she denied, that she prayed wouldn't run and betray her. Not this on top of every other indignity she'd faced and overcome.

Ghatti faces and bodies flickered and twitched, explaining the situation to Saam to make sure he had captured the nuances of human speech. Leaving Parm to hold their space by the fire, they glided to a halt in front of Harrap and Mahafny. The three briefly examined Harrap, satisfied by what they found, but two stalked around Mahafny, staring at her from all directions, sniffing her with implacable thoroughness. Saam leaped to the table, yellow eyes glowing with the intensity of his querying, Khar's whiskers tickled at the back of the eumedico's neck, testing, questing.

Composed, breathing evenly, Mahafny returned Saam's stare with fortitude. She broke eye contact first, not surprising since few could sustain steady eye contact with an unblinking ghatt. Still, knowing Mahafny, it would have been like her to make Saam blink first. That's score one for Mahafny, for normal behavior, Doyce mentally chalked it. Saam, two.

"Do I pass?" the eumedico inquired, one hand rubbing the back of her neck to erase the sensation of tickling whiskers.

"Yes," from Rawn. "Yes," from Khar. A meow from Saam.

"Yes. I've been outvoted," Doyce thawed the words frozen in her throat. It was obvious that Khar sensed something reassuring about the eumedico's presence;

she'd put her trust in that, but she didn't have to like it. "Welcome's run a bit thin at this time of night, but you have joined us now, for better or for worse."

Jenret's robe billowed as he stood. "I for one will offer a warmer welcome on the morrow, though this one is heartfelt. Are there beds in this place? I don't think the storm will ease before morning, and we've no hope of crossing until then."

"Beds there must be," Harrap's brows caterpillared with worry, "but I never got around to checking. I hope there is room enough so that our slumbers may be seemly."

Harrap's wish was not to be: the inn contained one long, narrow attic space with beds dormitory-style, not unlike his old lodgings at the Bethel. However, the two men took beds at one end of the room along with some other guests, and the two women retired to the other end with the ghatti split between. Heat radiating from the chimney rising through the center of the room did little to dispel the chill, and the restless wind searched for shingles to pry loose, but the low-eaved room offered a sense of peace compared to the storm gusting and howling outside.

Doyce sat upright in bed, struggling to pull a comb through her wavy, tangled hair, still damp from their ride in the rain. Khar stretched across her legs, pinning her in place, and she bunched the woolen blanket around her waist to hold in the heat. The mattress felt hard and damp, made her shiver. Saam curled at the foot of the bed, as close to the edge as he could get without falling off. Holding a lock of hair straight out from her head, she flailed at the snarled end with her comb.

"Go easy, or you'll have Harrap's tonsure," Mahafny scolded as she remade her bed to her own satisfaction. "Here, give me that comb. You've no patience left, that's clear." She pulled the tortoise comb from Doyce's grip and propelled the younger woman a quarter turn away from her so that she could sit behind Doyce.

Easing the comb in and out of the tangles with short, expert movements, Mahafny clucked in disgust. "When did you comb this last? Your Lokka gets curried more often than you do your hair."

"Hasn't been much time lately for the niceties." Much as she hated to admit it, the combing, the rhythmic stroking felt good, relaxing, and some of the tension flowed from her neck and back. She stifled a yawn. "Maybe I should pay the stableboy to do it when he's finished with Lokka."

"Not unless he can borrow sheep clippers. Now hold still, this end is going to have to be trimmed, there's a permanent knot." Reaching into her pocket Mahafny pulled out a tiny pair of surgical scissors and set to work snipping. "Thank the Lady you wear it short now, so this won't be missed."

"Do you always carry your scissors in your pocket?" Doyce asked, feeling herself go taut again, knowing Mahafny felt it as well. The scissors seemed a grim reminder of the trepanning instrument the eumedico had found on the floor of Asa's barn and had pocketed.

"No," the older woman answered shortly. "A bad habit of old age and more than likely to puncture my pocket or my fingers when I reach in. I put them there after I'd finished with Jenret's bandages." She sat silent for a moment. "Doyce, I know you're not well-pleased to have me here. You've made it patently clear in every look, gesture, and word. I'm sorry, but I am somehow a part of this, despite your preferences or mine. Just be assured that I know the difference between then and now and give me the benefit of the doubt now as well." With that, she administered a brusque pat to Doyce's back and moved back to her own bed.

"Call it a truce, Mahafny. There've been too many cataclysms in my life of late." Confused, she slid down in the bed, savoring the patch of warmth the eumedico's body had left in her mattress.

"Do you think he'd sleep with me?"

Doyce found herself bolt upright, blanket clutched to her chest. "Who? Harrap?" she asked, shocked, trying to keep her voice low. Now what was the eumedico thinking?

A snort of laughter answered her. "No, goose! Saam. You looked crowded with a bedful of ghatti."

Quaking with laughter, Doyce buried her face in her pillow, choked, finally managed to respond. "I don't think so, but it's up to him. If he feels like it, he'll shift over."

Sleep came, but it took longer than she'd anticipated. Every time one or the other of them started to drop off, the other would break into giggles, blessed release after the tensions of the day.

♣

She slept, a smile still quirking her face, dimpling one cheek. Khar nudged closer, tight into the hollow of pillow and neck, backbone against backbone, fitting the bumps. She tucked white paw over nose to warm her breath, fell into the shallow sleep that let her keep watch if need be. . . .

Meadow, sun, tiny wildflowers, not showy, but sweet. Tiny purplish-blue flowers, each one rising up like the teeth of a double-sided comb, seed pods like miniature bean pods. White star flowers, five petals off a long, vase-shaped calyx, plump at the bottom. He picked these one at a time, then smashed the base against the palm of his hand, head cocked for the faint "pop."

"Vesey," the voice cried. "Come on, hurry up!" And the boy turned and ran toward the sound, broke the coupled hands and placed himself between, jumping and prancing, tugging back and forth between the restraining hands.

Briony sat in the middle, propped against the lunch basket, arms waving, giggling, head thrown back to watch the figures towering above her. Bare feet kicked and caught at the blanket beneath her. "Come on, Vesey," Varon's voice boomed. "You lead." Varon and Doyce and Vesey encircled the blanket, hands clasped, feet whitely bare in the long green grass.

Pushing Varon ahead of his outstretched arm, pulling Doyce at arm's length behind him, Vesey began the chant, eyes fixed on the baby as he began the circle. "Oh, ring-around, ring-around, ring around the rosy, ring around the rosy . . ." he sang, pushing faster and faster, making the circle spin. Varon laughed, trotting ahead, Vesey at the end of his arm. They capered around and around the baby, her head thrown back.

"Ring around the rosy," Vesey roared, then quick as a terrier after a rat, spun himself in the other direction, pushing at Doyce, rather than pulling her. Doyce stumbled but managed the turn, dragging Vesey behind her, Varon kite-tailing after him. "Ring around the rosy, ring around the rosy!"

"Ring around the rosy, pockets full of posies," Vesey warbled, high and breathless, "Ashes, ashes, we all fall . . . down!" And as Varon and Doyce fell in an obedient heap on the ground, collapsing around the blanket, Vesey broke from their grasps, jumping skyward, arms outstretched with a shrill shriek of glee that he'd fooled them all. High, childish laughter bubbled from him, laughter that left him weak-kneed, bent over double, holding his stomach, staggering this way and that, until he finally tripped over himself and rolled onto the blanket, laughter still whistling and bubbling in his throat, eyes streaming. "All fall . . . down!" Varon fell on top of him, began to wrestle him into submission, both of them laughing and rolling. "Ashes, ashes!" screamed Vesey.

"We *all* fall down!" Varon finished. "Fooled you!"

Doyce's smile broadened as she dug her shoulder into the thin pillow and drifted deeper into asleep. Khar registered the end of the dream sequence and came alert, surveying her surroundings, listening to the breathing around her, some hushed and regular, others noisy and snorting. The eumedico made the tiniest of smacking sounds, then subsided.

Khar knew without looking over her shoulder that Saam no longer slept at the foot of the bed, could sense him alone, huddled by the chimney. With a sigh for the lost warmth, she slipped off the bed and padded over, giving a tiny warning trill of her presence as she went. Then stopped short, waiting for further invitation or refusal. Always before he had been her leader, she the happy follower, acquiescing to his demands, though he made few on her. Now, she sensed with unhappiness, their positions were somehow reversed, the loss of mindspeech lessening him, making her superior at this moment. Regardless, she would not intrude unless he wanted her, though her heart ached to comfort him.

The barest of whisker flicks invited her forward, and she came, settled near but not too near. He paid no attention to her, lost in his thoughts. "Oriel!" He gave a breathy purr, seemed to speak to himself. "I taste your touch on my fur and I rejoice!" He licked at his flank, licked again, at last looked at her, yellow eyes haunted. "But there's nothing left now—every remnant, every flavor and smell and sound of him has fled!" A frail mewl like that of a lost kitten. "Everything is gone from my head! It's all gone wrong! What's happening to us?"

Rawn and Parm glided across the floor, settling without a word at a calculated distance behind Khar, their unease as evident as if they shouted it. Saam glared in their direction. "Too many, too close."

She could feel Rawn's anger building. He shifted, a flurry of claws working at the wood of the floor, and spoke in stiff falanese. "We've no choice. We may be solitaries, not pack animals, but we have no choice in this except to continue to intrude on each other's space. We must stay together for the sake of our Bonds."

"It is hard," Parm soothed. "We sniff and hunt like dogs giving chase, we who take pride in observing and then ambushing the truth, alone, each to his own."

"Then let us go our separate ways and ambush them." Rawn's lips drew back in a snarl, fangs gleaming. "Jenret and I can stalk them, trap them."

Parm shook his head. "We do not know what manner of evil we face. Fighting our own separate, personal battles will not succeed this time, don't you see? We must be like the links in a mindnet, working together, supporting and bolstering each other for the added strength. Any time we come close to them, I feel weakened, the pain and evil disrupts, claws at my senses."

Saam spoke. "I am so confused! Nothing feels right any more. Even Doyce makes me feel . . . uneasy," he confessed. "As if there is a badness not in her but a part of her somehow. Jenret as well. Yet that came only as the storm struck."

With a hiss of dismay and anger, Khar backed away, drew against Rawn for comfort. Betrayer! she wailed in her heart, betrayer of the beloved of your beloved!

"I know. I feel it, too." Parm admitted. "They are not

bad, not evil within like Georges. *This* I would know."
His words emphatic as he drew closer to Saam. "But it
is as if they carry some unwitting badness with them, not
within them. I do not understand it, but it is so."

"What are we going to do!" Unmistakable agony
shook Khar's voice. "Doyce is my beloved, my Bondmate, I would know if there was something wrong." But
in truth, she knew something was wrong within Doyce,
the strangeness of her dreams clawing at her for so long,
no matter how she hunted, tried to find the key. But the
others didn't, couldn't know that, and she would not
admit it, not and shame her Bondmate and herself.

"You cannot silence Truth, it's just that we can't hear
it yet. We all have to listen harder, inside ourselves and
our Bonds, and all around us," Parm exhorted.

"Couldn't we try to contact the Elders?" Khar pleaded.

Rawn gave a snort. "Not likely in this storm, not with
the lightning, and you know it. We'd lack control. Besides, I fear giving a signal to someone or something else.
We must wait, be vigilant."

With careful tread, Parm crossed to Khar, hunkered
in front of her until his forehead rested against hers.
"Doyce has been having bad dreams, hasn't she?" Sympathy radiated from him. "I can feel a confusion building
in her, not badness, but confusion, as if she cannot believe what she must, a lack of trust in her instincts."

Khar searched for the words, wanting to explain, not
wanting to reveal how Doyce sometimes seemed to shut
her out, exclude her. "The sequences are mixed, one
past overlaps on another, mingles without reason. I try
to chase away the wrongness, that which does not belong,
but still it happens. Tonight there was no problem, the
dream was of only one past, true and right."

"Do you remember what the Elder Amm'wa once
said?" Parm tilted an ear in her direction, waiting for
her response. After a moment, he continued. " 'I slip
through the tall grass and not a blade stirs. I am a part
of all I survey and yet—not. But the mouse I stalk will
soon be a part of me.' Have you tried without, not just
within? I think that is how I failed with Georges. Try to
understand the pattern, not right it, and perhaps you will
find its source."

"Maybe." Khar sounded unconvinced. "What else can we do about the Truth we seek?"

Rawn's whiskers flicked. "Stalk it when we can. Until then, follow, support each other's instincts. This closeness is not our way, but we have no other at the moment. And pray that our curiosity won't be the death of us." He made a small, sardonic falanese laughing sound.

"And try not to irritate each other by that closeness. I am sorry," Saam's eyes swung from one to the other. "I am not me, my me-ness shifts and slides, though I try to hold it in check."

"I know. If I had lost as you have lost . . . I do not think I could. . . ." His voice suddenly gruff, Rawn halted. "Let us go back to bed, if not to sleep." He brushed a terse comfort-touch along Saam's length as he retreated to the far side of the room.

Sarrett had lost track of the days—and nights—they'd spent in the Hall of Records, wading through the minutia, the trivia of hundreds upon hundreds of past cases of once-crucial import but now quaint relics of long-past times. Even the more recent cases the Seekers had heard on circuit, her own and Parcellus's amongst them, bore the distance and remoteness of another life.

Despite Housekeeping's best efforts at replenishment and tidying, the room was cluttered with the lonely-looking stubs of burnt-down candles, plates with cheese parings and petrified bread crusts, an apple core shriveled brown and dry. The only positive thing she could identify was a mound of fresh white handkerchiefs stacked beside Parcellus, near at hand to contain the erratic pattern of sneezes which burst forth at the most inopportune times. Twylla had confirmed that allergy, not a cold, left Parse in a simmering state of explosion, and had done what she could with further medicaments and the handkerchiefs. But the medicine left Parse drowsy and he refused to dose himself, saying that if she could stand the sneezes, he could live with it.

As if in response to her thoughts, Parcellus looked up at her with pink-rimmed, watery eyes and gave a dainty sneeze, positively anticlimactic after what she'd experienced. Neither Per'la nor T'ss twitched a hair but conserved themselves half-waking, half-asleep, chins tucked against chests with snub-profiled dignity. Despite the dust and boredom within and the beckoning beauty of the outdoors as fall approached, neither ghatti had ventured far, as if they waited for their Bondmates to find the answer to a secret they already seemed to know. But then, ghatti always looked so knowing, except when it came time to admit who had snagged the final piece of bacon from her plate this morning.

Well, if they could be patient, so could she, but it wasn't easy. Sarrett twisted her hair into a heavy white-gold swag and coiled it around her head, let it cascade free. The more days and nights she worked, and this night was no exception, the more disheveled Parse's carroty hair became, flying out from his ears and nearly straight up from his crown as if he'd sustained a lasting fright. Yet his dishevelment ran in inverse proportion to the neatness about him, and Sarrett wavered between admiration and pique at the contrast.

Parcellus's half of the table showed stacks of Record Books aligned with military precision, every needful thing near to hand, sheets of foolscap inked with spiky, angular writing in even lines; her notes boasted marginalia large and small, doodles, angry cross outs flaring across the page like flags of defeat, tiny bird tracks of secret hopes. Her stacks of books jumbled together, some in cozy, cluttered piles, others tossed aside in dismay as promising lines of inquiry dwindled, faltered into some perfectly reasonable explanation of no use at all. She'd never given Parcellus his proper due for his methodical, single-minded search for the answers which might enlighten the Seeker General and help Doyce's quest for the truth.

With a start she realized that Rolf and Bard stood in the shadows at the door, waiting for someone to notice them rather than startle the others. Why hadn't T'ss alerted her that they were there, and then she realized that the constant pressure against her calf came from T'ss, black stripes against his white fur blending light and shadow. Per'la, too, was trying to alert Parcellus without 'speaking him, paw hooking first one clean handkerchief, then another, from the pile so that they floated off the table's edge like giant snowflakes.

"Parse, visitors. Back to the present on the double, close the book." She levered herself up against the edge of the table, tired, glad for the chance to stretch and move. How long since she'd taken poor Savoury for a run?

"Not visitors, friends, I should hope," came Rolf's response as he and Chak entered, Bard and M'wa a diffident pace behind.

Parcellus waved greetings, then grabbed a handkerchief just in time. Peering out over the white cotton, his eyes smiled welcome and with a final sniffle, he asked, "How's Byrta coming along, Bard?"

Bard's face glowed and M'wa arched and rubbed against his shin, slim black tail kinking. "Better, much better, thank you for caring. Now that Twylla has her in the infirmary, I feel much more confident, and M'wa feels better because P'wa isn't worried sick any longer. The healing will be long, but Twylla promises she'll ride circuit again. And tell me in advance what the weather will be when her leg aches! I only regret that the Seeker General would not let me return to Doyce's side."

And the regret was genuine, because he knew there was something he had to tell Doyce, warn her about, but he had no earthly idea what it might be. He tried again to remember, face crimping with the agony of the effort, but it was no use. Just the faint malicious echo of laughter inside his brain each time he tried, then a teasing blackness. It made him want to beat his hands against his head, wrestle it into submission. With an effort, not wanting to alarm, he let his eyes rove around the shadowed, cluttered room, taking in the stacks of leather record books, the crumbled papers and debris of days of work. He managed to make his voice normal. "Don't you have anything to eat in here?"

"Ate it all ages ago." Parse considered, then looked to Sarrett for confirmation. "It was ages ago, wasn't it?" She nodded in agreement. "Sometimes I forget how long we've been working," he apologized.

"No need for that," Rolf said. "Bard, bring in the

basket. We brought you a little something for sustenance. Knowing your habits, Parse, we thought it might be necessary, but we were counting on Sarrett's good sense about regular meals."

Bard flourished the lidded basket, eyed the crowded table and decided to borrow another smaller one from the other side of the room. Cold chicken, crisp pears, steaming biscuits, and a flagon of white wine appeared as if by magic. Per'la's head disappeared into the basket to see if there were anything more, then sighed with contentment.

They ate and drank, made companionable by the shared meal, although Sarrett found herself being cautious with the wine and noticed that Parcellus was as well. Glorious to relax, disastrous to become muddleheaded. They chatted, inconsequential gossip, but she could see the lines of strain etched deeper on Rolf's face. His new position as a member of the Tribune advising the Seeker General was no sinecure, and she wondered just how much of her unnameable burden Swan Maclough had laid on Rolf's shoulders. If only they had some answers for them!

As if on cue, Rolf stared off into space, then reached down to play with Chak's ears, rumple his fur. "So how goes it?" His voice balanced between commendable neutrality and polite interest; she watched his hands twitching with anxiety as he stroked Chak.

"If we're the hounds set off after the rolapins, then the rolapins are laughing their heads off," said Parse, a gloomy, dismissive wave of his hand indicating nothingness. "Round about and round about and round we go until we're fair dizzy with it."

The silence hung on, the food lost any semblance of flavor or appeal, the lights dim and groping. Surprisingly, Bard broke the silence. "And if Parse's nose gives out," he indicated the red, raw nose, enflamed and tender from repeated sneezes and wipings, "we still have Sarrett's more elegant one to track the information." Eyes wide and innocent, he continued, "And did you know, miss, that there's ink on it?"

Grabbing one of Parse's precious handkerchiefs, she wet the corner with her tongue and scrubbed in earnest, trying to see her reflection in the polished silver candle stand. Then stopped as she realized her foolishness; Bard, always so self-contained and solemn, had caught her out—there was nothing there, no smudge, no smear. How unlike him to play the trickster! T'ss chuckled in the back of her mind, laughed with her rather than at her.

Bard began to pack and straighten up, leftovers wrapped, plates stacked, the flagon and two glasses left on the table if they should require more later. "Rolf, let's be going. Time for bed and they want to get back to work."

They made their good-byes, and Sarrett and Parse tried to settle in, making little, unconscious gestures and movements that brought them to the brink of the uncharted paper ocean they must dive into again.

Parcellus picked up his pen and made two neat checkmarks against his list. "I can't glean a thing from all this, not an absolute thing. I know what we don't need to know, but I don't know what we need to know."

"What did you just say?" Sarrett felt the far-off glimmer of an idea tugging at her brain. Gold or dross, which was it? "What did you just say!"

Peevish yet patient, he repeated himself. "I know what we don't need to know, but I don't know what we need to know."

"No, before that—quick!" Standing now, hands clenched, holding her breath, waiting for the word to see if it would glint as brightly this time. Please, oh please, by the Lady, let this be, don't let me be wrong, don't let me have given him unreasonable hope, she prayed.

"I said I can't glean a thing from all this . . ."

Still blissfully unaware of what he had said, Parcellus was more than aware that Sarrett had flung herself at him and was kissing him. He returned it enthusiastically and waited for enlightenment. T'ss's and Per'la's eyes widened, then narrowed knowingly, their bodies relaxing as if unbound from some inner tension of knowledge self-controlled, self-contained until the correct key turned the lock. Bondmates were truly strange beasts, they reflected. Always needing the proper cues for everything. . . .

✤

The storm had spent itself during the night, wisps of stringy clouds darting erratically across pearl-gray sky as the wind sheepdogged their heels, nipping them away from the swell of pale blue at the horizon's edge. Clearing fast, and the river flowed powerful and strong, still swollen with the previous night's downpour. The ferry had been winched back into position on the Deutscher side of the river, carrying with it two early morning travelers and one pack horse.

After a hurried breakfast, Doyce, Jenret, Mahafny and Harrap awaited their turn to cross in the other direction.

"Will it hold all of us?" Harrap worried, counting on his fingers. "Four humans, four horses, and four ghatti?"

"And two ferry-tenders. And cargo. And anyone else in the vicinity who wants to cross over." Then, with just a touch of wide-eyed innocence, Jenret added, "You can swim, can't you, Harrap?"

"I used to . . . but. . . ."

"Swim? Get all wet? Oh, no!" A desperate Parm twined himself around Harrap's ankles, nearly toppling him.

"All ghatti can swim. We just don't like to." Khar spoke with excessive patience. "And we won't have to if you don't bounce around once we get out there."

Loaded on the raft, with Harrap and Parm stowed in the center like so much excess baggage, Doyce felt a kindred sympathy with Harrap as the raft began to pitch and toss its way down-current, tethered by a cable that looked as flimsy as a spiderweb now that she rode the raft. Clinging to a guard rope with one hand and with the other planted hard on her hip, she tried not to dwell on the fragility of the matchbox raft as she let her legs absorb the motion like springs. Her stomach didn't want to stay on an even keel, and she ardently wished she'd never heard the word "breakfast," let alone eaten it. Jenret and Mahafny reclined at ease amongst the boxes and barrels of cargo, chatting. Doyce fixed her eyes on a spot on the far shore and tried to lock it into her vision for stability. With shock, she found herself focusing intently on the spot she'd chosen.

"Khar, what is that? Over there."

The ghatta, crouched on the deck with claws sunk into the rough overplanking, looked puzzled. **"Where?"**

She gestured. *"No, further downstream. The forest line just above that huge boulder where the waves crash white."*

Scrambling onto a box and then onto the next higher one, Khar pointed herself into the wind, spray flying around her so that she slitted her eyes, riveted. **"A rider, no, two. And . . . a ghatt with one!"** Hackles rising, she growled deep in her throat and Saam sprang up beside her, the blue-gray of his coat shimmering sharply silver on the edges where the sun and spray misted it.

The raft lurched, dipped sickeningly, then its prow darted up, slicing through the view ahead. As they dropped back with a flat-bottomed smack, there was only forest and swift-running water to see, the trio vanished without a trace.

"It was them, wasn't it?" Doyce asked in a whisper.

Khar wove her way to her side while Saam continued his vigil, scanning the high riverbank, undercut and ravaged by racing water and churning winter ice. **"Saam confirms it. I will tell the others."**

"But why?" she asked Saam, knowing the hopelessness of an answer. "Why would they wait, stay this near when they must have known we were right behind them?" she asked the others as Jenret and Mahafny, Harrap tottering behind, made their way to her.

"They should be leagues ahead of us by now. That would have made sense." Jenret scanned the shore for further signs. "It will make following easier, but damn it all, why?"

Mahafny balanced between Jenret and Doyce, a hand on each to keep her equilibrium. "Exhausted, most likely. And with the rain they may not have been able to ride ahead. The ferryman said there are houses on the other side of the river. Or," she considered, "there may be another possibility. Something that I, for one, am not sure I like to contemplate. Perhaps they mean for us to follow them and don't want us to lose them."

"Why would they want us to?" Lips white and compressed, Harrap eased around the last barrel in his path,

practically hauling it with him for security. He'd clung
with a death-grip to each convenient object, hampered
by Parm's refusal to budge from his side—wherever Harrap stepped, Parm was underfoot.

"I don't know, but we'll soon find out." Face set, Jenret strode along the wet, slick planking to check on the
horses.

"What made you say that, Mahafny?" She gripped the
older woman by the upper arm for mutual support and
gave an imperious tug to turn her from contemplating
the empty shoreline. It hadn't been Jenret who had said
that, someone with experience in hunter and hunted, but
the eumedico, surely a woman with no experience in this
sort of life and death hunt. Doubts and dark suspicions
churned in her head, always there, impossible to dismiss.
Why did she still distrust—even after last night? And if
distrustful, why had she let her come—but the ghatti had
overruled her. Did Mahafny, too, carry a whirlpool of
secrets swirling within her, her doubts and fears waiting
to suck her down? How had she expressed it the other
night? Something about looking beyond the placid brow
to the turmoil contained within?

"I don't know why." She reached out her slim, elegant
hand and began to pry Doyce's tense fingers loose, giving
no indication of the pain they caused. "But I can feel it.
Can't you? I think Saam can as well. Look at him. No
facts to fit it or explain it, but somehow you just know."

With a final shudder and a splashing wave that broke
over them, the ferry jammed its prow against a piling
and one of the tenders leaped to shore, dragging a stern
line to pull the ferry parallel against the bank. A worn
trail paved with flat river stones led at an angle up the
bank, heavily gullied and muddied from the rain's runoff.

"She's still running high. Gonna hafta git yer feet
wet," he shouted to his passengers. Jenret untied Ophar
and led him gingerly across the planking strip he'd helped
shove out, the stallion shying once as he plunged into
the icy, hock-high water.

"Come on, we'd better disembark Harrap," Mahafny
commanded, crisp and practical. "At least if we lose him,
he won't sink like a stone. Those pantaloons should hold
enough air to keep him afloat."

Despite herself, Doyce grinned. And given Harrap's
woeful expression, Parm perched neat-footed on his
shoulders, but fidgeting with fear at wetting his paws,
she could envision Harrap billowing down the river,
Parm perched on his paunch and chattering all the way.

She grabbed Harrap's left arm and Mahafny the right
and they propelled him down the gangplank, Harrap
hunching over to hoist his purple pantaloons above his
ankles and the lapping water. Jenret extended a hand to
help haul the Shepherd onto the trail, his mouth moving
in silent prayer, and Doyce and Mahafny returned to
gather the other horses and their gear.

"We'd best be moving quickly," Doyce shouted back
to Jenret, straining to make herself heard above the rushing water.

He paused long enough to give her an impatient nod
of agreement. "I know. Bring Harrap's gelding across
next so we can get him mounted and ready."

Saam, Rawn, and Khar had already sprung across
without so much as dampening a paw and raced up the
bank, loping smooth and sure in the direction where they
had spied the shadowy horsemen and the ghatt. Panic
clutched at her throat as she watched the steel-gray ghatt
running free, and she prayed that Saam would wait and
not rush headlong into the forest in chase. She had no
idea if she could predict the ghatt's behavior any longer,
and without him, the tracking would be more difficult
and time-consuming.

Mounted at last, they picked their way across the sodden bank toward the woods where the three ghatti had
raced. Doyce cast a glance back and waved at the ferry-
tenders, suppressing a shudder at the thought of riding
the raft back across the river against the current. Strung
behind her on the path were Jenret, Mahafny, and Harrap, Parm aboard a pommel platform—Ma'ow's old one,
she guessed—spinning like an overzealous weathervane,
engaged in a running commentary with the Shepherd. If
she didn't know better, she'd judge the ghatt lacked a
serious bone in his body, an eternal jester determined to
live up—or down—to his particolored markings. Still, he
had been astute enough to ask the enfeebled Ma'ow in

which direction they should strike out to follow their most likely trail.

Clumps of grass plastered wetly underfoot, the ground spongy and oozing so that each time one of the horses lifted a hoof, a dismal sucking sound emerged; their deep, indented tracks filled with water after each step. A series of stagnant miniature ponds, each glistening in the sunlight, marked their trail behind them and ahead of them. If only all the tracking were this easy, a string of tiny lakes from here to the Lady knew where, like a chain of water droplets on a spider's web, but who knew what the center of the web held? Who spun the web and would they catch or be caught?

Farther ahead the ghatti had stopped short, making agitated circles around something on the ground. Saam and Rawn appeared the most disturbed, shoulders high, sidestepping in disgust, but she couldn't catch the drift of mindspeaking from any of them, not even Khar, as if they argued amongst themselves.

"What have they found?" Jenret urged Ophar ahead, crowding Lokka to the side. "If Saam's got another rolapin, I'll send the beast back on the raft. Better yet, make him swim for it."

Irritated, Doyce jerked her arm, motioning him to quiet down, and kneed Lokka forward, not an easy task given that the horses were restive, nerves taut after their water crossing.

Khar's voice cut through, prim and distasteful, the words spitting out. **"Absolutely disgusting. Only the very young or the very ill . . ."**

"Or the very brazen would not conceal it," Rawn finished for her. They looked with ill-disguised contempt at a pile of scat on the ground, simply lying there with absolutely no attempt made to scratch over it or bury it as any self-respecting ghatti would do.

Threading Ophar amongst the ghatti, Jenret leaned down and poked his staff at the heap. "Fresh, too. And they're right, just lying there for all the world to see. Why leave an obvious marker like that?"

"As an indication of what they think of us." Doyce whistled Khar back to her platform and patted Lokka's neck as she waited. "Saam, come on, let's go!"

"An unusual token, to say the least." Jenret ranged Ophar alongside Lokka, and the mare rammed the stallion affectionately with her shoulder; Doyce's knee collided with Jenret's. "So blatant," he continued, yet seemed unaware of the body contact, though Ophar veered off, rolling an anxious eye at Lokka. He held himself stiff in the saddle, trying to keep from swaying in time to Ophar's stride. Ribs must be hurting him badly, she judged. Indeed, he even seemed to have chosen the comfort of an old and worn wool shirt in red and black blocks, the first time she had ever beheld him in anything other than immaculate black; that is, if she didn't count his appearance in Harrap's second-best cassock. She examined his right cheekbone and eye critically—still puffy and purplish with streaks of yellow and green.

"Did Mahafny give you anything to put on that this morning?" She swept her own hand along her face to indicate her meaning.

He shook his head, cautious not to twist his body. "Told her it wasn't necessary. It'll be fine."

"Don't be a martyr. The salve will bring the swelling down that much faster. You might enjoy seeing out of both eyes instead of having one squinched up like that. Harrap will be happy to sit on your ribs while we apply it, if you're going to be stubborn."

"Unfair to Harrap. He of all people shouldn't be the butt of our jokes." His lips twitched around the beginning of a smile.

Ignoring his comment, Doyce picked up their previous topic of conversation, worrying it back and forth. "I haven't really had a good look at the strange ghatt—have you? It's always been too shadowed or dark, just a strange pulsation of whiteness. As if he's looming out there like a figment of our imaginations."

"Or our nightmares." His laugh broke short and sour. "What was it about our ancestors that made the ghatti want to delve into our minds, share our secrets, offer us the gift of truth, no matter how painful? It's a wonder Matthias Vandersma didn't go stark mad that first time, thinking his thoughts were not his own. The absolute nightmare with no waking. I've thought I've had those nightmares—though through no fault of Rawn's, long ago, long before his time—in the nursery with my brother." He drifted off, then picked up his train of thought again.

"Don't you wonder what the ghatti were like before . . ." he waved his hand to encompass them both, their tabards, ". . . before us. This one looks almost as if he were one of the original ancestors from the wilds. The things from which legends are made." He tucked a shoulder as if to dismiss his fantasy, yet unable to let it go. "What uninformed parents tell their misbehaving children to beware of—or the ghatt will pluck the liars and fibbers from their beds in the dark depths of night."

The horses' hooves made sucking sounds against the earth, but the farther they advanced into the woods, the sound modulated into a steady, spongy squishing noise that seemed almost soothing. "Did you believe that?" she asked.

"Yes . . . and no. I'd comfort myself in bed at night after a whipping by pretending that this wondrous wild ghatt would come sweeping through the window and claim me as his Bond. We'd leave my brother behind and range wild and free around the land doing good, battling foes, helping the helpless find the truth, just as Matthias and Kharm, the first Bondmates of them all, did. Oh . . . I don't know . . . all those madly impossible things children invent for themselves when they're oppressed or depressed."

He spoke into the distance, as if he relived another time where the memories weren't all pleasant, of that she felt sure. "Was he older or younger than you?" Her words floated out light and easy as thistledown lofted high on the summer air.

Still turned inward upon his memories, Jenret responded, "Older by two years, and I feared and worshiped him more than any other human being in the world. . . ." He jerked ramrod straight and winced, whether at the pain in his side or the memories in his mind, she couldn't judge. She tried for opacity, oblivious to the searching, frightened look he raked her with, and then his eyes went shuttered and cold, making her rue her intrusion, however innocently she'd meant it. Prod-

ding Ophar into a trot, he pulled ahead, pointedly alone.
"Tell the others to move along. The footing underneath
is fairly dry."

"Prickly." She swung her arm in a beckoning circle at
Harrap and Mahafny, motioning to them to pick up
speed as she urged Lokka ahead.

"Then don't poke and pry or he'll curl up tighter."

She ducked a low-hanging branch, knocking it aside
with her hand and a waterfall of droplets pelted down
her leg, dappling the gray trousers with black splotches
of moisture. *"So there's no soft underbelly exposed?"* She
picked at the damp material. *"I wasn't trying to do that.
He just took it that way."*

"And now you know. So don't." Khar sat tall on the
platform, narrowing her eyes, then opening them wide,
casting the air currents, pink nose twitching.

*"I'm never going to understand him. That's all I was
trying to do."*

"There's time. More than we might like."

Dark horse and rider ranged nearly out of sight, blending with the wet, dark tree trunks, only the occasional
brightness of Jenret's red-patched shirt flashing, winking
at her like a cardinal exploding out of the bushes.

"I suppose you understand everything about him." The
words burst out of their own accord, sarcastic and cutting. *"You and Rawn have been exchanging notes. Filling
each other in on all the details, haven't you? Well, I don't
like it. What we know of each other is private, between
the two of us."* Why did she have the urgent need to
shutter herself just as Jenret had moments before? She
reached a contrite hand to the curve of the ghatta's back.

**"And what's between Jenret and Rawn is between
them. No, I don't know, but I have some ideas, just as
you have, just as he must have about you. Let it alone,
let it come by itself. Stop prodding."** Doyce jerked her
hand away.

Saam murmured behind her back and Khar turned
sideways, listening. **"Faster and more to the north. Saam
says we're drifting off their track, following where it's
easiest instead of staying on their trail."**

" *'Speak the others, then."* And with resignation, she
turned Lokka toward the even denser forest to their

right, the High Firs—toward the north, toward the dark,
toward the danger.

❖

They had ridden for four days now, pushing themselves as far as possible despite increasingly early dusks
abetted by the towering stands of hardwood and firs
blockading any sun once it began its low westward creep.
The trees soared tall and straight, stretching toward the
light, making them weave their way amongst them as if
they wandered through the columns of an ancient ruin,
searching for answers to long-ago mysteries. The gloom
left her with a continual uneasiness that veiled her other
perceptions with the same vague anxiety. Why would
anyone willingly choose to live amongst such disheart-
ing surroundings, she had wondered more than once, or
was she simply blind to a rough, remorseless grandeur
indifferent to the longings of daily life, its petty hopes
and fears, its need to control what it could not understand? The Erakwa felt no disharmony in these surroundings, and although this land existed within the formal
bounds of Canderis, it seemed a private world beyond
her understanding.

She gave a snort of exasperation at her maundering
thoughts and tried to see with fresh eyes, to find some
beauty in the land around her. The colors, perhaps? The
colors of twilight, sometimes muted gray-blue, sometimes
soft greenish-gray fingered with mauve, tinted the perpetual order of the day, broken by occasional clearings,
some natural, a few man-made, where sunlight streamed
down, and the sight of blue sky and white clouds held
an intensity beyond bearing, so unnaturally pure did it
seem even after so short a time without it.

Sometimes the stumps and burn marks in the center
of a clearing made it obvious that the spot was man-
made, whether by Erakwa or trappers or loggers, she
couldn't surmise. Still, she had experienced enough
travel to calculate that they gained ten or twelve leagues
a day, although not always in a linear direction.

She continued her reverie as they paused at one such
clearing for a quick meal and to rest the horses. Their

oat supply dwindled, the horses demanding more to eat
after their labors and the grazing too thin for satisfaction,
let alone sustenance. This site at least offered the variety
of some meager yellow-tinged grass and scrub for foraging. Harrap seemed especially oppressed by the gloom,
and he threw himself out of the saddle, flinging his arms
wide with delight at the brightness, the lack of shadow,
and his face wreathed with a smile.

"The Lady be thanked for offering us this respite!" He
circled in a joyous, impromptu dance of praise, red-lined
coattails flying, and Parm capering at his feet.

"Too brief a one, I fear, so all the more welcome."
Mahafny swung down and loosened her horse's saddle
girth. "And I, for one, am going to spend our break
sunning myself atop that pile of rocks over there. Anything to bake some of this cursed dampness and depression out of my bones."

Harrap tossed a companionable arm over Doyce's and
Jenret's shoulders, pulling them close. "It's hard on her,"
he confided. "Harder than she'd like to admit to herself
or to any of us. At least I have the padding for such a
sustained ride, but she doesn't."

"Nor do you have quite as much as you started out
with, I suspect." Jenret slapped him on the back. "You'll
be the slimmest Shepherd-Seeker in town by the time we
return. We'll all be slimmer if I don't see if I can hunt
down a rolapin or two for tonight's dinner. Best go easy
on the supplies until we know where we're headed.
Doyce, do you think you could convince Saam to do
some hunting with me? I don't want to arouse the wrong
instincts in him, but we could use his help."

"Are we no nearer, then? No closer to our goal?"
Harrap's agitation was evident.

"No closer, but no farther away, according to Saam
and to the signs we've seen." Doyce tried to be honest.
"How far, how long we go, I don't know. Until the end—
wherever that may be. We knew it wouldn't be easy,
Harrap. We've only begun, for all we know. But we'll
gain on them yet, finally meet them face to face. And
when we do . . ." She let the thought hang unfinished,
unsure herself what completion meant.

"And when we do, what then?" The Shepherd's face

mirrored his inner conflict, furrows rolling up his brow
to his crown, eyebrows meshed in worry. Each of them
had privately considered their options before, worrying
at them, tentatively scrutinizing their own consciences,
flinching at the recognition of unworthy or faulty motiva-
tions. Doyce knew her own feelings, their fluctuations,
their ebbs and flows, felt with all her heart that she must
find and stop these killers. But stop them at what price?
How? Yet they had seldom spoken of it, each engaged
in his or her own solitary struggle to decide. Truth, vengeance? Did the two coincide or were they incompatible?

Clouded with fatigue, she shuffled her feet and rubbed
her hand across her face to erase her thoughts, then wriggled fingers through her curly hair until it bristled. "I
don't know, Harrap. It's something we're going to have
to face, must talk about, I think, before the thinking
drives us mad. But what if we don't agree on the
answer?"

"The answer's plain and simple!" Jenret interrupted,
his face suffused with color, eyes fever-bright and hard.
"This is no time for weakness or indecision. Not after
what they've done, not after what we've seen!" He bore
the look, the fervor and intensity of a young crusader,
privy to personal visions of Honor and Right. Or a young
avenger poised to wield justice, and the incandescence
of his gaze made her feel ineffectual, cowardly, but sane.

Exchanging troubled glances with Doyce, Harrap
touched the young man's shoulder, bringing him back to
the present, his eyes blinking as if shocked awake. "I
have Served the Lady for more octads than you've lived,
Jenret, and even She acknowledges stages, levels, changes;
that there is no immutability or perfection or perfect right
other than Herself. The radiance of Her illuminating vision strikes each person differently. We have much to
decide and I, for one, will welcome Mahafny's counsel
when she's rested and we've stopped for the night."

With Jenret earth-bound once again, Doyce dared
speak. "About the hunting . . . we need fresh meat. If
not rolapin this deep in the woods, squirrel, perhaps, or
whatever." They had all heard the sounds of game on
occasion, though the woods looked too inhospitable to
support any sort of wildlife. The clearing, with its brush-

wood and saplings, berry bushes and wild grasses, might
well have enticed small creatures dependent on the cover
and food they provided. And small creatures often enticed larger predators. Whether they were edible, or considered the Seekers and the Bondmates to be edible, she
didn't want to consider in detail, not after some of the
night sounds she'd heard. "See if Khar wants to go along
with you and Rawn. I'd rather keep Saam away from
temptation, if you don't mind."

Khar, unsuspecting recipient of an expertly placed
goose from Doyce's toe, squeaked indignation and jumped,
then walked stiff-legged in Rawn's direction, not deigning
to look back.

"I'll get you for that!"

*"I know, and I'm sorry, but would you? Besides, you
didn't seem to be listening."* Doyce kept her mindspeech
as repentant as she could. *"I'd rather Saam didn't go."*

"All right, all right. But keep an eye on him." She
waved her tail in slow curves. **"And I was thinking as
well as listening."**

As momentarily embarrassed and out-of-sorts as the
ghatta, Jenret turned to Ophar's side and unpacked a
short bow from an oilskin case on the saddle. Not many
Seekers carried such; she realized that he was as truly at
home in the outdoors as he'd intimated. Unable to meet
anyone's eyes, he busied himself with digging through his
saddlebags for his quiver, then stalked off after the ghatti
without a backward glance.

"Still young in certain ways, and sure that black is
black and white is white. But he carries some private
burden as well," Harrap observed to himself, waving at
the unseeing back.

In agreeable silence they both turned in the direction
Mahafny had taken, toward the cairn of boulders, mossy
and gray, some almost elephantine in size. The sun sparkled off minute flecks of schist and mica embedded
within them, glistening veins of quartz, the boulders
stacked and staggered like a weary giant-child's abandoned marbles. Mahafny concentrated on working her
way higher, climbing toward the invitingly flattened surface of the topmost broad stone, about five meters above
the ground.

"Want to go up and join her?" Doyce asked.

Harrap shook his head in amused resignation. "If I manage to climb up, I'd still have to get down. Going down tends to be faster, but infinitely more painful the way I accomplish it."

Mahafny had reached the base of the topmost flattened boulder and stood, hand shading her eyes, spellbound by something beyond their line of vision. Still staring over her shoulder, she eased one leg over the far side of a rock, shifting her weight as she started downward. She gave a scream, sharply bitten off, holding herself locked in position, one leg awkwardly extended.

Harrap groaned in dismay and began to run. "Don't tell me she's broken it!"

"Worse than that! Snake, I think! I never thought to warn her!" All too likely with those warm, sunny boulders, the rock crevasses. "Don't move too close too quickly!" Catching up with and passing Harrap, Doyce pounded along, wishing with all her heart that she hadn't insisted Khar hunt with Jenret and Rawn. Khar, with her graceful fearlessness and quick footwork, could mesmerize a snake until Doyce arrived to dispatch it. Worse, she knew with a sick certainty that any snake in this region was likely to be highly poisonous, a single envenomed bite paralyzing and killing prey many times its size.

But Parm, lazing in the grass by the horses, was already running a hodgepodge, rapid course toward the rocks, his black and orange fur flashing bizarrely bright against the gray stones as he dashed and tumbled and bounced up and over each obstacle. Yet every move landed surefooted and swift, a jester tumbling and stumbling to entertain . . . and distract. If only Parm could buy her time to climb the other side of the mound and see what held Mahafny pinioned against the rock.

Stumbling as she ran, Doyce unhooked her sword belt with clumsy fingers and slung it bandolier-style across her shoulder and chest. Better to have it up and behind her for a clean draw from above. Also better not to be hampered by an entangling scabbard capable of tripping her amongst the rocks.

The boulders appeared deceptively easy to climb, but each was stacked or piled either too far from or too close to the next to make for a sure step. First one stretched, then minced along, sought precarious balance on what appeared a solid, steady stone, firm as the ages. She bit her lip and forced herself to slow down, to move soundlessly. Hurrying would accomplish nothing if she fell or frightened the snake into striking in surprise.

Beneath her scrabbling, straining fingers, the lichen and moss on the rocks resembled miniature forests with tiny trees, some palmate, some firlike, in rust and tan, grays and emerald greens and blacks, one with touches of scarlet so tiny against the somber tones that the flecks appeared like fruit on minute trees. And all covered with ants, tiny foresters and harvesters engaged in busy foraging. Over one more boulder and she would face Mahafny, able to look down at whatever held her transfixed. She wiped the sweat from her face with her forearm and scrubbed her hands down her pants' legs, ignoring scraps and abrasions rawly scored on fingers and palms. From a distance the rocks hadn't looked so difficult to surmount, but now she wondered if Mahafny weren't part mountain goat. But no, she had ascended with the same care and planning that she gave to everything—until her attention had been diverted.

Harrap, she could hear, had halted partway up the rock mound and now spoke in low, measured tones, a repetitive chant. And Parm had stationed himself just above her and to her right, now stockstill except for an almost imperceptible weaving of his head, poised and waiting for her, muscles coiled to spring. Something sinuously smooth brushed between her legs and she throttled a scream, heart pounding, not daring to look down. Her foot tottered on a stone, the rocking noise thumping with her pulse, louder than an avalanche. Cursing, she forced her foot back on the stone's fulcrum point and Saam popped up beside her elbow. She clenched her teeth. "Get back down, you fool!" But with a supple curl of living gray against the inanimate gray, Saam flowed up the slanted rock face toward Parm.

With a gasp, Doyce levered herself over the last boulder in her path, eyes locking with Mahafny's while the eumedico mouthed "Snake!" She peered down from her perch to where Mahafny's foot dangled a handbreadth

above the flat surface she'd been stepping toward, and
where a snake, thick as Doyce's arm, coiled and swayed.
It observed them through slitted, beadlike eyes, its diamond patterns neat and precise, black and bronze and
verdigris etched sharp against a deceptively duller background of brown-gray scales. Mintor's bronzework sprang
to her mind, but no artist could capture the fluid form
of this living terror. Its arrow-shaped head was poised,
ready to strike home in living flesh. Harrap's steady
chanting carried from the other side, and the snake
swayed in time to it, captivated by the rhythmic, repeti-
tious rise and fall of his tones.

"No!" Harrap's voice broke, the pattern destroyed.
"Jenret, wait!" And with the explosive crack in his voice,
everything burst into motion. Mahafny's other foot
slipped, the smooth sole of her boot scrabbling against
the stone, unable to find purchase, forcing her dangling
leg downward to take the weight-shift. And the long,
deadly elegance of the snake snapped forward, whipping
home to the target of her calf.

Parm hissed and launched himself, every hair on his
body erect until he puffed to twice his size, tail crooked
like a sickle. He caught the snake a glancing blow with
his paw, partially deflecting its strike, and he skittered
by, spinning in the cramped space and striking at the
snake again, entangled by one fang in Mahafny's leather
pants' leg. The sword leaped out swift and smooth from
its sheath, and Doyce clutched the weapon in a two-
handed grip, desperate to strike but with no room to
maneuver. Mahafny, both feet on solid rock now, arms
outflung behind her for balance, stood motionless, face
white but composed, staring down.

Claws hooked into the snake's throat, Parm threw it
back and away, its coils shuddering and reweaving, gathering itself for the next strike, but as it raised its head,
Saam struck once, twice, a third time, each blow snapping the snake's head against the rocks.

"Back, Saam! Now!" Doyce grunted and concentrated
every fiber of her being in a short, arcing stroke, all her
strength centered in her wrists, pivoting the sword grip
close to her breastbone so that only the blade itself swung
glinting and hard at its target. Saam bounced up and

away a hairbreadth ahead of the sword, and the blade
sliced home, severing the snake's head and slamming
hard into the boulder behind it. Steel rang against stone
and echoed. It could have been Saam's head in that exact
spot.

Relief washed through her in waves, her knees quaking, her wrists scarcely strong enough to hold the dangling sword. Have to hone it, work hard on the nicks, a
morning's work at least, she thought randomly. Her grip
on the sword slipped, slick with sweat. She wondered
why Mahafny had slid into a crouch, legs tucked in, head
buried on her knees. So undignified, so unlike her. Saam
and Parm poked at the still writhing body of the snake,
darting in and out, claws lashing with lightning speed.
The severed head had fallen away, down between two
stones where it could no longer do any damage. A droplet of venom glinted on the rock.

The eumedico raised her head, pale gray eyes dilated
to black as their glances met. It brought her back to
herself and beyond, shaking her to see Mahafny's self-
control disintegrating. They both smiled tremulously,
tentatively.

With a muffled expletive Jenret heaved himself over
the crest of stone behind Mahafny. "By the Lady!" He
bit off the rest and swung himself down beside the older
woman, drawing his sword and skewering the still-
struggling body of the snake on the point. He snapped it
away, like a child launching a windfallen apple from the
point of a withy stick. "Did it strike you?" He grabbed
Mahafny by both wrists, dragging her upright.

Stung by her forgetfulness, Doyce rushed forward,
kneeling to examine the punctured doeskin, venom still
beading it, and rolled the pants' leg up. The leather was
soft and yielding, but so trimly cut to the leg that it
shifted upward with difficulty. One small puncture wound,
a dark ruby droplet of blood welling from it, stood in
stark contrast to the whiteness of the eumedico's leg.

"Belt!" Doyce commanded, and Mahafny unbuckled
her belt from around her waist before Jenret could grasp
what she wanted. With a deft twist, Doyce wrapped it
around Mahafny's leg just above the knee, forcing it to
bite hard and deep into the flesh. "Hold it in place. Like

so." Quicker this time, Jenret took over while she reached into her boot top for her knife. "Ready?" She didn't wait for assent and, with two quick slashes, carved an X into the flesh at the puncture spot. Blood welled and she squeezed hard, milking the wound, then pressed her lips to it, sucking and spitting out the blood and whatever venom remained at the site. Every move, every action came back to her as if it had been only yesterday that she had left off training with the eumedicos. She squeezed and sucked until Mahafny dropped a restraining hand on her head.

"Enough. The worst of it is out now or already in my system." Doyce nodded and motioned for Jenret to release the tourniquet. She scoured her lips with the back of her hand, desperate for a drink of water to sluice out her mouth.

"Harrap! It's all right!" She turned toward Parm. "Have him run back to the horses and get Mahafny's medical kit." She stroked the black and orange head, checking for wounds. "Neither of you got bit, did you?"

"No. Ooh, wasn't it big, though?" Parm gave a vigorous shake to recompose his fur.

"And bigger with each telling you'll do, I'm sure." Doyce's voice held real admiration. She searched for Saam, but the big blue-gray ghatt had already wended his way down the rocks, past Harrap and on his way about his own business.

Banked coals glowed ruddy at the campfire's heart. Now and again Harrap or Jenret fed it judicious tidbits of seasoned wood for its comfort, a low, orange-red glow that did little to push back the darkness of the night or the denser dark of the forest, a black sentience that oppressed, watching, mocking their encroachment within the trackless boundaries. Mahafny shifted, lips thinned with pain, but voiced no complaint.

Doyce checked the compresses, eased them back to palpate the swollen leg, and waited for a response.

"Numb, still," the eumedico confirmed, "but it hasn't

crept any higher than before—about halfway above my knee. And yes, I'm still feverish."

Doyce reached for a fresh compress soaked in groundroot, willow bark, and tinterret. Not the ideal combination, but the best they had. She tossed the cloth from hand to hand, letting excess water drain away.

Jenret shifted by the fire, restless, his ribs aching again, but he steadfastly refused a pain-deadener. He had carried Mahafny down from the rocks and had persisted in carrying her all the way, even when Harrap had rushed to help. Indeed, he had acted afraid to let her go once they had descended. The early stop and rest proved a godsend for them all, she had to admit; they'd been traveling too long and hard, fear nipping at their heels, harrying them all the way. She hadn't plumbed the depth of her own exhaustion until now, when even wringing the compress and molding it to Mahafny's leg took a major effort. The tiredness made her feel swaddled, wrapped in batting like some treasured ornament or relic, protecting her overwrought nerves as it obscured her senses, clouded her reasoning.

Doyce draped the compress, checked its coverage, and collapsed beside Harrap, accepting the battered tin cha mug he pressed into her hands. His broad, peaceable smile warmed as much as the cha. "Sugar?" He ducked his tonsured head in a conspiratorial whisper. "I always carry a bit about me. Sweet tooth, I confess it."

"Please!" Even such a small luxury as that roused her gratitude tonight. The momentary homeyness left her unprepared for the Shepherd's next remark.

"Can we catch up with them after this? And most importantly, if we do, how do we resolve this madness?" He swung his arm wide in an encompassing gesture that included them as well as their elusive, invisible quarry.

Jenret stiffened, then forced himself to lean back, drubbing a dry, broken branch against the ground, eyes fixed on the fire. Hands clasped around her good knee, Mahafny regarded it as well. Only Harrap's trustful yet troubled eyes met Doyce's. For better or for worse, she had been elected to speak. Or at least to speak first, she silently amended.

"**Then speak little and wisely until you've sounded them out,**" Khar counseled.

Teeth pinched in the soft flesh of her inner lip, Doyce bit hard against tears ready to run. Hellfire and damnation, all she did lately was leak tears, she who had trained herself to stay so sternly dry-eyed. Maybe the tiredness made her more susceptible, pushed them closer to the surface, an underground spring betraying its presence. She bit harder; it wasn't fair, having to speak first. She hugged the dissonant thought to her for warmth, stoking her anger. With a deep breath she thrust it from her as an unworthy emotion. *"I will, Khar. I promise,"* she 'spoke. *"Thank you for reminding me."*

"**No, it isn't fair,**" Khar continued, having scooped her earlier thought as well. "**But they feel you deserve the right to go first, because of Oriel. You must speak for him, for Saam, for Asa and Wwar'm, and who knows how many others with no voices to tell their tales. The heavier the burden, the more honorably it must be borne.**"

"Well?" Harrap prodded. "I don't know what we face . . . not for sure, but I must know what we hope to accomplish . . . that it is right, fitting, proper. Or . . . or I can't go on!" He wadded his fists against his thighs in helpless anguish. "I'm being torn in two directions! One way I know, the way of Our Lady. The other way, your way, I'm still seeking. Sometimes it runs fainter than the path we follow, or say we're following—and I fear I cannot reconcile its end with what I know of the Lady's teachings."

Doyce stood alone in front of the fire, its flickering light dappling her legs, her arms wrapped around her to try to ward the inner cold and fear she felt. "We were all raised in the ways of the Lady, Harrap, even if perhaps not all of us worship Her, or at least not formally now. But what the end promises for us or for those we seek, I can't offer you an ironclad guarantee. Not and be sure I speak the truth."

"But murder for murder? That's what Jenret indicated earlier today."

"Pain for pain, blood for blood, murder for murder, if that is what it takes to expunge them from this world!"

Low and cold, Jenret's words lanced with a ritualistic, incisive clarity.

"No, Jenret, to understand, to learn, perhaps to cure and control, if that be Harrap's Lady's will." Beads of sweat clung at Mahafny's hairline, catching the fire's flash and flare like opals. She pushed herself straighter with her arms, a small grunt of pain escaping as her leg shifted.

Doyce tried to mediate. "Any one of these ways may be our answer, Harrap, or a combination of them may prove to be our course. I'm sorry, but I don't know any more than that because I don't know what we'll discover when we reach the end." And what she resolutely refused to say was: *If* they reached the end, whether some of them or all of them or none of them. No more promises to make, she didn't dare try to live up to them, couldn't. Tired of standing like a mute sentinel, she abruptly folded her legs under her and sat, hugging her knees for comfort, defeated by her own thoughts.

"But in all honesty, we don't even know who or what we're seeking. That's what you've admitted. Parm says the same. Who are these people? What are they?" Harrap plowed ahead, determined to search for answers, or at least ask the questions. "What do we know—really?"

"Yes, Doyce, what do we know? Perhaps you could tell us?" She felt Mahafny's words were intended as a goad, a command to recite and analyze as she went along, to make quick and accurate deductions. In short, to diagnose. To give the aches and pains, related or unrelated, the fevers, the fears, a name, a status, see it as a whole, and with that, with a coherent knowledge of the ailment, to treat it. She threw Mahafny a rancorous look and opened her mouth to respond, but Jenret interrupted her. She subsided, rested her cheek on her knee. What caused the extent, the depth of his anger, what hidden aches, what wound healed over yet perhaps infected within, spurred him to react to this situation as he had?

"That they killed—in cold blood and without quarter— Asa and Wwar'm and their loved ones, for reason or reasons unknown. That some perverted, unnatural connection exists with the ghatti, something unheard of in all the years of Service of the Seekers. That, most logically, these same people, or others of their group, killed Oriel and nearly killed Saam. That they will shame and humiliate us, invalidate and destroy the Seekers Veritas, and sacrifice other innocents if we do not destroy them first!

"It is self-defense, it's as simple as that! A Seeker does not serve as judge and jury, but he has the right—anyone has the right—to defend himself from death and danger!"

"Three facts, or seeming facts, and one multiple assumption. Doyce?" Though she might be in pain, Mahafny missed nothing, unperturbed by Jenret's outburst, awaiting Doyce's response.

Doyce wet her lips, started to speak, then paused. "Before I—before we—analyze, I should introduce some additional facts, related or perhaps—not. But I would be remiss not to consider all the . . ." she found herself wanting to say "symptoms," knew Mahafny heard her whisper it, then continue, "evidence."

"First, and perhaps I'm stretching a coincidence into a connection, when I rode Oriel's circuit, I heard the story of a cat who had disappeared and died. The boy who found the cat's body said that the brain had been scooped out; Byrta used a similar phrase when she spoke of finding Oriel's body and seeing the head wounds: 'clean as a melon scooped of seeds.' "

"Where did this incident take place?" Jenret's normal light tenor croaked harsh as a crow.

"Near the Hospice at Wexler," she responded and then froze, mind reeling, making a rapid, distinct connection with the trepanning instrument found in Asa's barn. Not just Mahafny, but any eumedico would have access to trepanning instruments and the knowledge of how to use them. Did the others have any idea? She risked a glance around the circle. Mahafny's head dipped once in acknowledgment.

And then her brain reeled, grappling with new associations. Were eumedicos involved? And if they were, then why, why, oh, by the Lady, *why* was Mahafny here with them? Why had she shown up when she had? Why had she hurried to catch up, cajoling and convincing Harrap that they must join them? And when Doyce had mastered her emotions and dared look Mahafny's way again, the eumedico gazed at the night stars, serenely innocent.

"Perhaps only a coincidence about the cat," offered Harrap. "What else is there we should know?"

"Oh, aye, I'll go on, but while I do, Jenret, tally how many head or brain injuries have befallen Seekers the past few years, either human or Bondmates, and ask yourself if there could be any other explanations than the stories we've accepted." That would give him something to chew on and perhaps remove the question Swan Maclough had planted in her mind days before, a question that had gnawed at her since. Oh, to run a search through the records back at the capital. Not for the first time she cast a wistful thought back toward Parcellus and Sarrett, wondering how they fared in their research and how the others all fared.

"Hear this, then, Harrap, and the rest of you. The man we found dead just outside Deutscher, the man who rode with those we've been trying to catch, once wore a Seeker's tabard."

Harrap cast the sign of the eight-point star, whether to ward off evil or to give peace to the dead, she dared not ask. Nor would he be sure if she did. Even Mahafny appeared disconcerted, Jenret tensely alert, remembering that he hadn't listened to her when she'd announced it before. She had their attention now.

"Yes, Calvert Tipton had been a Seeker, or so goes the story I was told. And after his ghatt died, he was poor, alone, and at last took refuge with the eumedicos, allowing himself to be used for experiments in return for shelter and food. Had you heard of this, Mahafny?"

Mahafny's hair drank in the firelight, helming her in silvery light with bloody underglows. Her eyes narrowed in pain as she stretched to change the compress on her leg. Harrap clambered up to help, wringing out a fresh cloth to replace the old one. "No, I had not heard of this instance, of this man, specifically." She eased herself back, shifted at the discomfort. "But it's not unheard-of, you know that full well yourself, Doyce. There are always those willing to help us in hopes that we can help them."

The cavalier dismissal stung. "An understated way of

putting it. Perhaps you should explain in detail what you mean so that Harrap and Jenret can understand."

With a bitter sigh, Mahafny began what sounded as if it were a set recitation. "To be a practicing eumedico, to be able to help and heal, means constant attention to new ideas, new facts, new experimental procedures. Without this there would be no advances in our skills or our ability to save lives. Sometimes we seek permission from a terminally ill patient so that we can experiment, not so much in hope of saving that life, but in hope of making a discovery that will save another life.

"But all of our theories and ideas mean nothing if we cannot test them. Often the experiments are painful and fraught with danger; many fail. But we always need volunteers, and volunteers are few and far between." She stopped, shook her head as if she'd lost her place. "Except that sometimes we hear of one like the man Doyce mentioned, Calvert Tipton, alone in every way. And then perhaps we can strike a bargain: the use of his body, his time, in return for whatever it is that he needs to sustain him—food, shelter, money."

"And a good time was had by all!" Jenret's voice snapped whiplike as he cut off Mahafny's story, intent on his own thoughts. "Doyce, there was Tabor and H'maw that time in the flood, a few years back. And the ghatta and her ghatten who were stoned to death, oh, an octad or so ago, up near the northern border. When they went to bury the bodies, they were gone. And Carolus and his ghatta, from the fumes after that strange chemical fire. And Khem, but that could have been old age just as easily."

"And Khem's grave was vandalized, his brain stolen." She watched him digest that piece of news. "And Oriel. And Saam. And Asa and the ghatti dead, even if the killers lacked opportunity to do anything further."

"Summation, please. Working hypothesis."

Despite herself, Doyce admired the eumedico's courage. She rose, clasped hands behind her back, voice steady as her thoughts jumped ahead, marshaling disparate facts, abrupt intuition limning the shadowed spots, startling herself with the rightness of her response. "That the goal involved is mindspeech, how it works, how it operates, the discovery of this to be determined by examination of the brains, whether from dead or live specimens, of those trained as Seekers, human and ghatti, and of related brains—regular humans and cats, distant cousins of the ghatti. A cat's brain is strikingly similar to a human brain, especially the limbic system, the center of emotions and sensations—that is well-known from standard dissections. Until now, the capabilities of ghatti brains have never been explored, but considering their intense mind interactions with humans, it's likely that their brains resemble ours even more closely, especially in areas of cognition. In short, whether this goal involves the acquisition of mindspeech for those who do not possess it remains to be seen.

"Further, that the person or persons involved have a relationship within the community of eumedicos, on what level—witting or unwitting—we cannot ascertain at this time. There also remains the possibility, somewhat more remote, of a relationship within the Seeker community, although currently available data—including Calvert Tipton's death and Georges Barbet's madness—indicates a relationship detrimental to any Seekers so involved."

"A good beginning, but anything more to postulate? Such as who the prime movers might be, who else might have a vital interest in such matters as mindspeech, or where this is taking place, or why?"

So crisp, so icily confident, Doyce marveled at Mahafny's self-control, realizing that only she and the older woman knew the fraudulence of the eumedico's vaunted mindtrance. Did Mahafny think she'd expose her? How deeply was she involved? Doyce resolutely examined the idea from all angles before she answered. "Perhaps. But one thing more. Jenret, would you retrieve the medallion I asked you to hold for me? The one we found on Cal. I'd nearly forgotten about it." So like the medallion Vesey had worn, and her surreptitious fingers touched her pocket to make sure it was safe. Wild goose chase? What had made her think of the medallion now? The faintest, most elusive connection tweaked her brain, and the harder she thought on it, the deeper it hid. She gave her head a little toss to clear it.

Surprised at the request, Jenret rolled to his knees and

began rummaging in his saddlebags, digging deep and, at first, seemingly fruitlessly. Harrap held the hem of his robe to capture the untidy odds and ends pulled into view. "You're blocking the light, Harrap," he groused as he pawed through his possessions. At last, with a grunt of satisfaction, he pulled the medallion from the folds of a wadded-up shirt and held it aloft by its leather thong. It glinted sharply, like ice struck by sun, in the firelight.

"Looks rather like mine." Harrap craned his neck for a better view.

"Mayhap. Toss it over, Jenret." As it sailed toward her, she was again reminded of a comet set on its course through space, perhaps someday slicing through the atmosphere close enough to damage or destroy, or harmlessly flaming by.

She plucked it out of the air by its leather thong as it started its downward curve, thong trailing behind; somehow the thought of touching the silver repelled her—sheer silliness. Besides, she allowed ruefully, not much choice if she wanted to examine it. Small solace that Saam wasn't near, since it had unnerved him so much before.

To the casual eye it did very much resemble a Lady's Shield, Harrap had the right of that: a Shield very much like the one that he, the Shepherds, and many other believers wore, very like the misshapen remains of the one she carried in her pocket, mute reminder of Vesey and Varon. This too was octagonal, each of its eight sides faintly curved, nearer to a circle in shape than a strictly geometrical octagon. The convex side bore signs of etchmarks, the symbol of the Lady, no doubt. Turning it this way and that in the dancing light, Doyce caught her breath, felt her heart lurch and pound. A trick of the firelight, her tiredness, perhaps, and the wearing down of the design, almost obliterated in spots, but the symbol did not appear to be that of the Lady. She rubbed it against her sleeve, then peered at it again, willing her eyes not to deceive her into seeing what didn't exist, couldn't exist.

But it did. A crude delineation of a human brain, its segments outlined: cortex, cerebellum, pons, medulla. The very image of a page in a medical text or—worse—

very like the emblem she had chanced upon in the old
records, closed records that she had been given permission to search once, nearly another lifetime ago, because
of the curious paths her life had taken. "So I'll grant
you permission," Swan Maclough had said, scribbling the
order on a slip of paper, impatient hand dripping sealing
wax on it. "Let you see how you were recorded by the
Seeker after your family's death." And she, restless and
unnerved by this account, each word a reliving of a time
she wanted desperately to forget, had strayed through
the other pages of the leather-bound record book with
its iron catch-lock, only to find an obscure reference to
an earlier volume and record, one she had located before
the Recorder had returned, mindful of her need for
privacy.

The key had stuck, frozen by old oil and a hint of rust,
but at last she'd worked it back and forth, felt it catch.
A transcribing of an old case, shut away for some fifty
years: a case detailing a group of outcasts, of Gleaners,
those dangerous mindstealers who had hidden their secret ability, had found others like themselves and had
banded together, hoping that their individual talents
would meld and increase with numbers. They had just
begun a tentative test of the extent of their powers and
their ability to control them when they were found out—
and destroyed.

They had sounded a frightened group—or so she read
between the lines—fearful of their strange skills and
more terrified yet of discovery by outsiders. They were
correct; the townspeople had banded together and am-
bushed them, but not without loss to themselves: five
killed outright, seven sucked mindless as the frantic
Gleaners defended themselves with their most lethal
weapons—their minds—in a battle with no quarter given.
The identifying symbol they had used amongst themselves bore the same shape as the one she held in her
hand. After all, how many people would look closely at
a Lady's Shield—except for those who knew to look for
a difference? Out of sight in plain sight. She had closed
the book then.

Icy-fingered, she flipped the medallion over and saw
another design scratched onto the back. Clearly much

newer and done by an even less skilled hand, it repre-
sented a cat—or a ghatt. Puzzled, she rubbed her eyes,
thinking hard, wondering at the connection.

Jenret stood by her shoulder, staring down at the medallion. She handed it to him without comment, glad to
have it away from her and curious as to what he would
make of it. His response electrified her with its un-
expectedness.

As if it were a thing unclean he cast it into the heart
of the glowing embers, and then began to feverishly stir
new life into the fire. Snatching at their small stock of
dry wood, he recklessly began to rebuild it, making a
conical stack of branches that the flames began to writhe
through like a chimney. He remained crouched close
until satisfied that the fire had caught, soaring into the
night air like a beacon.

"Gleaner! Let them see that!" He quivered with revulsion, wiping soot-stained hands on his thighs as if to wipe
the brief contact with the medallion from his fingers. "If
I'd known I carried that with me!" He kept rubbing,
unaware, as he stared into the fire.

"I feared as much." Mahafny made the reluctant admission. "I suspected it, but at least I, we, now know
for sure."

"But how would you know? Either of you?" With a
rising unease, Doyce sidled near Harrap, glad of his comforting bulk, although the Shepherd appeared mystified
by what he'd seen and heard. He fingered his own Lady's
Shield protectively, silently defying anyone to rip it from
his neck and cast it into the fire.

"A cup of water, someone, please," Mahafny asked,
and Jenret sprang to do her bidding, kneeling beside the
eumedico, his arm cradled behind her back to prop her
upright while she sipped. Dark head dropped close to
silvery one, and Doyce heard the indistinct thread of conversation, lost in the crackle of the fire.

"Shall I tell them, or will you?"

"For better or worse, let me begin, Jenret." Her voice
sounded clear but papery-soft, close to the edge of exhaustion. "Jenret is my nephew by marriage. His father
and my husband were brothers. There is, Lady help us,
some sort of 'taint' in the family or—at least by the terms

ɪost of the world uses so easily—it is considered a 'taint.'

another place, in another time, with other training, it
ɪight be construed as an incredible gift: the ability to
ɔomprehend people's thoughts. Telepathy is the old—
ɪd far more correct—name for this gift. In most cases,
vithout training and guidance, the ability is misused, a
ɪanger to those who possess it and to those in proximity
ʏ anyone possessing this trait."

Jenret offered her another sip of water, then pressed
ɪe cool metal of the cup against his brow, his head bent
ɪ shame. He swallowed hard and lifted his face to theirs
ɪː he set the cup down. "She means the ability to
ɪlean."

"Jenret's brother Jared exhibited the ability at an early
ɪge." Mahafny touched Jenret's knee with soft insis-
ɪence, bringing him back to himself. "No one understood
ɪe problem at first, or how to cope with it. And since
ɪe was young and totally untutored in his ability and in
ɪastering his emotions, he nearly killed Jenret because
ɪf his jealousy. Later, two others, two servants, were
ɪilled before Jenret's father finally allowed himself to
ɪdmit that there was some terrible difference about his
ɪlder son. Something that to him grievously compro-
ɪised the family honor.

"He attempted to make reparation in the only way he
ɪould conceive of doing. He killed Jared, but not before
ɪe boy had burned his mind completely clean and blank
ɪuring their struggle. Perhaps it was just as well in the
ɪnd. . . ." She patted the black-clad knee again and Jen-
ɪet pulled back, distancing himself from the compassion
ɪn her touch, as if undeserving, guilty in some strange
ʋay. "Perhaps just as well, for the note found in his
ɪ ɔom indicated that he also planned to kill Jenret to en-
ɪure that the seeds of this ability were not passed to
ɪnother generation."

Jenret pressed the cup into the earth, twisting it, rais-
ɪng it, and placing it next to the first indentation, making
ɪnother interlocking circle, then another, but his voice
ɪarried firm as he picked up the tale. "And so my father
ɪves on, with a quizzical, open smile and a mind as blank
ɪs a newborn baby's. When he sees me on a visit I could
ɪe a servant, his son, or someone completely alien to

him, but then, everything is alien to him now in the empty room of his mind. That was the legacy my brother bequeathed me. That—and more."

Motioning for another sip of water, Mahafny swallowed and continued. Despite her rising horror, Doyce once again admired the eumedico's self-possession.

"But Jenret's brother wasn't the only one so afflicted by this, this curse, talent, taint, call it as you will. As I mentioned, my husband and Jenret's father were brothers. And so it was that we discovered much later that our daughter Evelien also carried this trait." With a lift of her head in Doyce's direction, she spoke as if they engaged in a private conversation. "You met her a few times, Doyce, while you were near the end of your training. Remember, she had just begun as a trainee."

She started to deny it, that she didn't recollect, then stopped short. "The slim, intense one with the long, dark braid of hair? I vaguely knew you were related, but I didn't realize she was your daughter. You never introduced her as such."

"Just so. She preferred not. Few eumedicos have a family, for children demand attention that their patients need. But I was determined to have both. I soon discovered I didn't have the time or the patience to raise her alone, not and do it right, so I left her with Jenret's mother. Still, when she finished her Tierce at sixteen, she was determined to become a eumedico.

"Not through any love or admiration for me—Lady knows, I didn't warrant it, not after deserting her, even though I left her in the best possible care after her father's death. It was more a crazy-quilt, mixed-up kind of love and hate. Perhaps not that unusual in any adolescent under any circumstances. That was when I noticed it, or began to realize, but almost too late." Hands spread in mute appeal to forestall any comment, she rushed the next words out, and Doyce wondered if Mahafny spoke to her or to herself now. "Quick-tempered, quick to love, emotions flowing hot and cold, and enthusiasms, too, jealous . . . so much like me when I was young and impetuous. And at first I thought our empathy bespoke kindred blood and kindred spirits, despite our separation. But then I began to sense her transferring my thoughts, surreptitiously trying them on for size, measuring those that fit and those that didn't and casting them aside. Oh, it was subtle, very insidious, she was old enough when she began to realize her power, not like Jared, so that for the most part she didn't do irreparable hurt to anyone or to herself. And being raised in a household that had already been maimed by a Gleaner's power may have helped her damp down her talents, increased her self-awareness because of the sheer need for self-preservation. But she was more than capable of spite and hurt—and that's when I made arrangements to send her on, before things became any worse. She was insanely jealous of you, Doyce—and of our relationship."

The words dropped at her feet, waiting to be embraced as truth. And in remembrance of those days, the good times, the caring times, she rushed to ease the look of supplication in Mahafny's eyes. "But surely the relationship of mother and child carries different, stronger bonds—beyond what we had. We shared something very special," and swallowed hard at the unbidden memories of their love, "but not what she shared with you."

Mahafny shook her head, pitying, and Doyce realized that she had missed some subtle nuance that the eumedico saw all too well. "No, she wanted you. Because you wanted me, and she wanted to have whatever I wanted all for herself, even if later she decided to spurn or reject it. She shadowed you everywhere. When she realized she couldn't sway you, she readied herself to strike at you."

With diplomatic delicacy Jenret interjected himself into the intense conversation, and Doyce felt a flicker of gratitude for his sensitivity in trying to shift their talk away from forbidden territories. "And so you escorted her to the Research Hospice, the one for pure or theoretical research. She's still there, isn't she?"

"I think so. I hope so, although I haven't had direct word from her since then. I had a twofold objective in sending her there: to help her learn to master herself, and to give others the opportunity to learn what to make of her special talent, and in so learning, perhaps to help other unfortunates master it before it destroyed them. And to give us the gift we have sought for so long, the talent we've pretended to possess. I receive—or received

until recently—twice-yearly reports from the director.
Now the silence worries me. Even colleagues passing
through have said nothing, look surprised when I ask,
don't seem to know who or what I'm talking about."

"That must have been at least twelve years ago."
Doyce shook herself loose from her thoughts, from the
effort of tracking back through the years. "She must be,
what, twenty-nine by now?"

"Yes. And you know where the Research Hospice is,
don't you, Doyce?"

Tracing at an eyebrow, still lost in the unraveling of
time, Doyce sifted through her memories. She certainly
had heard of it, but mostly through rumor and gossip. A
secretive place, shrouded in mystery. Only the very best
of a very special kind of eumedico-in-training and a few
outstanding older eumedicos who had surpassed themselves in their profession, pushed it to new heights,
gained admission. Come to think of it, she had met only
two eumedicos who had left that rarified world of pure
theory to rejoin the real world, the daily numbing round
of patients, some to be helped, some to be eased, and
others to be lost despite every effort. She had never felt
the faintest desire to be transferred there, though it sup-
posedly constituted the ultimate advancement for any eumedico. Without really thinking about it, she spoke. "It's
up in the north, isn't it? Up near the Marchmont border.
Very isolated and remote . . ."

Two watched her with comprehension and pity; one,
Harrap, watched with pity but very little understanding
of the import of what he had heard.

Reflected in their faces she saw what she had refused
to see, and finished the sentence in a rush. ". . . and
that may be precisely where we are heading, where our
rendezvous will take place. You think Evelien is involved
in some way? You can't possibly believe. . . ?"

"It seems possible. Or rather, not impossible. She may
not be involved, but Gleaners are, and eumedicos, from
the evidence we have—and she is both. When Jenret met
me for dinner one night after Oriel's death, he told me
about the incident and mentioned you in passing, merely
as a name. I knew the name. I also knew of your marriage and its end. And I didn't like the sound of what

had happened to Oriel. While I kept my suspicions to myself, I warned Jenret to be alert for anything which seemed out of the ordinary or dangerous on his circuits. And I set out for the Hospice to see for myself—and to try to watch over you as well, not sure how close I'd be able to get to you. I didn't know how easily you'd accept my presence after all this time, how much you begrudged your oath. And I was right about not expecting a particularly warm welcome in your new life."

Doyce bowed her head in unspoken acknowledgment of the words as Jenret spoke, eager to pick up the story. "She never explained precisely what she wanted me to keep watch for, though, and somehow that aroused my suspicions more than anything else. When you seldom speak of something, as we seldom speak of Gleaners in our house, the unspoken carries greater weight than the actual words. Somehow everything comes to relate to it. Still, I had no evidence, not until tonight, just my fears."

His voice thickened as he wrestled with his thoughts, then continued. "All my life I've lived in terror of Gleaners, even before I had a name to call them, of what they've done, what they can do . . . whether I carry the seeds . . ." his thoughts drifted away, lost in memory, ". . . watching my mother try to cope, run the mercantile as if Father were still in charge, playing an elaborate charade so no one would lose faith in the House of Wycherley, struggling to remain true to the memory of the man she married. I vowed then, I vowed. . . ."

Harrap interrupted, voice sonorous and pure-toned as a bell calling the faithful to worship and be not afraid. "And so, we think we know where we are going or where we are being led. We have some inkling of why this is so. Perhaps even an idea of who may be involved, although that is still tenuous. But still we have no idea of what we will do when we arrive." Flinging his arms wide in an all-encompassing gesture, he smiled, the smile of a child, or of the pure of heart, too pure to fear or even fear the feeling of fear. "And we will do what must be done, trusting ourselves and each other until then and beyond. And the answer will come. Lady's will be done."

The taut muscles in her face and neck relaxed themselves, and Doyce managed a small, genuine smile of relief. The others' expressions echoed hers, uncertain at first, but gradually smoothing at the sound of a trusting voice, sure in its faith even if they hesitated to lay their burdens down. The answer *would* come; it must.

"And so, to bed," Jenret shook himself as if to let the ghost memories fade and spoke, in complete charge of himself and the others once more. "Harrap, will you take first watch? I'll take the second, and Doyce the final leg. I think Mahafny had better rest the night through."

"Two ghatti on and two off for each shift?" Doyce waited for confirmation, only too aware of how tired she felt. Typical of Jenret to assign himself the worst possible shift, breaking his rest into two short halves so that the others could gain a longer, uninterrupted slumber. She could argue him for it, but held back. Let him give what he chose to give; he needed to do it. And she was so very exhausted. She forced her jaw closed in the midst of a bone-cracking yawn.

"Yes, but where are they anyway?" Perplexed, Jenret scanned the camp, searching for the blend of fur and shadow. "Khar's been here all evening, curled tight as a clam, but where are the other rascals, especially Saam?"

The yawn broke again, she couldn't swallow it. "Out scouting. And I have a sneaking suspicion that Saam may be teaching Rawn the finer points of stalking. Parm's probably along for the fun of it."

"Well, have Khar round them up. I'm for bed."

Mahafny's voice broke into their quiet companionship, a touch of chagrin frosting the sleepy tone of her voice. "Lady knows how I forgot. You know why I got bitten today? Why I didn't pay any mind to where I planted my foot? I caught sight of something, someone, just then. At least . . . I thought I did." Dubious, she paused, mulling it over. "Seeing faces in the forest, a mindtrick, no doubt. Like finding faces in the clouds." Then, decisively, "There was no one there."

"Well, if our companions—seen or unseen—have waited for us this long, they'll probably be waiting in the morning, but all the more reason to set a guard," Jenret answered, rolling himself into his blanket, shoulders digging back and forth as he twisted into a position of easement and muttered a good night to Harrap.

On the other side of the fire Doyce bundled her blankets around her, twisting and turning as Jenret had, trying to settle in. *Should have taken the time to grub a bit, carve out a hollow for my shoulders and hips.* Savage as a miniature spear, a twig stabbed through the blanket at her right shoulder blade and she dug behind her, routing it out and discarding it, then falling back on her left thigh—only to feel the dull lump of a stone she hadn't spotted in the dark. She started to chuck it away viciously but restrained herself and laid it aside. Despite her exhaustion, sleep felt very far away: everything said and unsaid, the looks, pauses, hesitations, the misjudgments cycled through her brain. Khar nosed her, patting and testing at the cocoon of blankets, wistful at the missed warmth since she was due on guard.

Doyce reached out with her mindspeech. *"You've been silent tonight. Why didn't you speak, why didn't you help?"*

"It was something you had to resolve amongst yourselves, just as we ghatti sometimes have to amongst us. I listened."

"Well, so what do you think?"

The ghatta twisted her neck, licked at a spot between her shoulders. **"That you all told the truth. Or told the truth as you see it and believe it—as much as you know. That's still the problem—we don't know enough yet."**

"So how do we obtain the knowledge we need?"

"That's another tomorrow. And I have to go on watch now. I've been lazy all evening, as Jenret pointed out."

Doyce hoisted the blanket over her ears, snuggling the scratchy wool around her neck to cut the cool of the night. *"Well, you'd better take care. . . ."* and fell instantly asleep.

Khar roamed the night silence with Saam, their sleek moves slicing the ground mist without tattering it. They prowled several meters apart, together yet alone, neither impeding the other, aware of each other's cautions and starts, double-checking scents and sounds from one another's reactions. The woods always smelled interesting, different scents to each pine or fir variety, all sharp but each individualized. A headier, richer scent of rot and decay, of needles and leaves decomposing in gradations, the musty, moist smell of an overturned tree trunk, shifted and rolled in a search for grubs, earth and punky, exposed side shimmering pale against the dark. Bear smell garlanded around the log and the surrounding earth, and over the bear stink she could taste-scent fish and honey, acrid ants. And the familiar scent of those they followed still tainted the air with a faint green effulgence, neither stronger nor weaker than before.

Saam ghosted to her side; they stood cheek to cheek to communicate, eye whisker flicks, vibrissae rub, ear semaphorings, all in keeping with the silence. "I will keep watch alone if you wish to track her dreams," he offered. The tiny warm stream of nostril breath touched moist against her face.

"You think I cannot do both at once?" And now she angered, despite herself. It was hard to concentrate on both when she began following the path of Doyce's dreams, too easy to misjudge a footing and reveal herself either in the real world or the dream world, and she couldn't afford exposure in either place.

He backed a discreet distance, sat, licked one paw, then the other, concentrating, eyes lowered. Finally he tried again, "If we both do what we each do best . . ." and he drifted off, ". . . and I cannot help you with that." She knew what the admission cost him, and respected him because he had phrased it that way, rather than flaunting the greater acuity of his physical senses, thus putting her on the defensive, shaming her with his superiority. She rubbed her chin across the hump of his shoulder blade, conciliating. "How did you know she was dreaming again?" His insight gave her pause.

He gave a little shrug-twist, as if her rubbing tickled. "She makes the air swirl around her when she dreams, the dust motes dance, my fur feels staticky, my ears tingle with a sound too high to hear." He wrinkled his nose in puzzlement. "Don't you feel it, too? I just can't read it."

"Ah," she mouthed the sound without sound. "What

if I stalk her dreams from here, watch this spot right here? You cover the rest?"

"Fine. I will stalk alone as well. Good hunting," and he ghosted off.

Curled between two tree roots, Khar let her mind range free, sought the patterning and set herself to wait. Parm had counseled her to wait and watch, not try to correct, and tonight she would see what that brought. Given everything that had already happened tonight, she expected Doyce's dreams would be more chaotic than ever, maddening to a tidy ghatta who wanted to re-arrange and reorder. Humans tended to react to stress by conjuring up a fantasy of truth and untruth, oil and water that would not mix to her mind. But it let them play out their fears—or worse, strengthened them. She netted a tiny, unobtrusive place in the dream for herself, batted at it to set it to rights, ready to seine a fish, to view what she had seen before as knots holding the net, instead of trying to unravel them. . . .

"Five, ten, fifteen, twenty . . ." Doyce pillowed her eyes against crossed arms, felt the soft inner skin of her forearms dragging against the rough bark of the giant red maple she leaned against. She knew that people massed behind her, could hear them shifting and shoving, impa-tient, trying to clear as far away from her as they could, muffling their sound against her singsong counting. A branch cracked underfoot, and she heard a sharp exple-tive begin, then choke off. The change in air movement told her that some swarmed by her silently, charting a new direction, confident that she couldn't search every-where at once, that someone could always slip home while she ran a fruitless chase after another. Although she couldn't see the faces, she knew that everyone from her past and present was laughing, running from her, hiding. "Ninety, ninety-five, one hundred! Ready or not, here I come!"

She wheeled around, paused, held a hand over her eyes to block the sun. How far did she dare run from "home," leaving it undefended? Or had everyone scat-tered so far that she had no hope of tagging them? A shadow moved, wavered in a direction counter to the breeze, and she darted toward it, dashing helter-skelter, hoping to flush as many from their hiding spots as she could. Faces flashed and spun by, faces she knew, faces she could barely place, so long ago and far away.

"Tag!" she sang out, and tapped the shoulder of an elderly woman with a face that looked made of wrinkled, dried fruits. But she wasted no time in remembering the name, whirled back toward the tree and tagged another, a man, this time, hitting him so hard he stumbled and fell. He skidded on one knee, threw her a reproachful look as he panted. "Sorry, Rolf!" But she didn't have time to be sorry for any of them if she wanted to protect "home."

It seemed to last all afternoon, countless figures fleeing and shrieking with laughter as they dodged her, her breath ragged in her throat, an overpowering thirst gripping her. How many more still out there? She risked a quick look at the tree, a milling cluster of people on the right side, those she'd tagged; perhaps five or six to the left, those who had journeyed home free. Limping back, pressing her fist hard against the stitch in her side, she saw Varon standing to the left, holding Briony, smiling and pointing in her direction.

And somehow she knew that she had at least one more person to find. "Varon," she shouted. "Know you're not supposed to tell, but is Vesey still out there?" Mayhap he was on the right side, hiding from her as usual, but she couldn't remember having tagged him.

Varon put his finger to his lips, made the universal hushing sound, then, eyes dancing, made the smallest gesture behind him. She was off and running, holding her side, squinting into the setting sun, scarcely able to see. Her breath whistled through her nose and she couldn't stop the little "uphing" sounds that pushed out of her lungs. He'd hear her coming, have to, or smell the sweat of exertion on her while he stayed cool and still in some secret place.

She quartered the meadow, grass trampled flat from running feet, quartered it again, moving as far as where the woods began, and retraced her path halfway back to the tree, pretending indifference. After all, he deserved to make it "home," but he should have to run to earn it. She whirled, quick and sharp, hoping to have lured him out behind her. Nothing, absolutely nothing, as she shaded her eyes again to peer toward the woods. But something, definitely something glinted a short way off. She lost the glint as she moved forward, had to track back and forth to find it again, then snatched downward at the matted grasses. Vesey's Lady's Medal! The thin chain had broken while he ran.

She waved it trophylike in the air. That should lure him out! "Finders-Keepers! Losers-Weepers!" she sang out, breathless with triumph. "Come on! You want it back, race me home!" And without looking, she turned and ran toward home base, the great overshadowing maple filling her vision, mahogany red leaves touched with deep green, its roots sinking deep into the earth, limbs soaring toward the sky and beyond . . . past and present united, welcoming shade and rest with those she loved beside her.

Khar waited, waited to see if the time had come to draw her net tight, not sure of what lay within it, but sure that she had trapped something of interest. Now to understand it, the seeming and the not-seeming, the truth and the not-truth.

❖

The shaking went on, inexorable, irritating, as she struggled to revert to the dream. The air stung cold, smarting as a slap, and she pulled at the blankets, straining to settle them tightly around her. She couldn't find them, and the shock of the night air on her body made her gasp and roll over, hands scrabbling as she chased the comforting scratchy wool.

A hand rested on her shoulder, twitching her to and fro. She grabbed at the wrist, pinned it in place. "Tag! I've got you now, Vesey!" she shouted as her eyes shot open, realized she clutched Jenret's gloved hand. Her fingers uncurled one by one, unwilling to admit her mistake. "Wha . . . ? Oh, Lady . . . not Vesey—you. His laugh so near I swore . . ."

She dragged herself into a sitting position, doubled over for warmth, then rubbed the crook of her arm against her eyes, ran her fingers through her hair as a rough comb. Anything not to have to look at him, at the perplexed expression on his face, the way he cradled his wrist where she had grabbed him. With a low groan she stood and jumped in place to set the blood flowing, her feet stiff and clumsy in her boots. "All right. I'm awake. I'm on duty."

The fire looked freshly tended, and Jenret thrust a metal mug of cha into her hands. She flinched at the sudden contact and nearly dropped it as the metal sides throbbed with heat, her hands throbbing in unison. "Ow! No gloves!" she protested. "Take it back for a moment, quick!"

He grasped the cup one-handed. "Vesey? Who's Vesey?" Dark smudges circled his eyes, his face gaunt and strained under the dark wool-knit cap he'd pulled down over his hair. How he had managed to cold-water shave every other day she couldn't imagine.

"No one, no one important," she evaded, but the untruth was something he didn't deserve. "No one . . . that you know," she managed, "just someone from long ago, another life, another world." He stood still, holding the mug, sympathetic but wordless, as if certain what she said was only a partial answer and he would bide his time until she found the words.

"Just give me a moment and you can turn in." She felt guilty making him wait as she swung up one of the waterskins, pulled the plug and squirted a stream of water on her handkerchief. She scrubbed her face with it, shivering as errant trickles ran off her cheeks and coursed down her neck, startling the words from her. "Vesey was my stepson, Varon's son from his first marriage. I guess it's not surprising that I dreamt of him after our conversation this evening. He was . . . he was a. . . ." The word wouldn't come, it strangled her. "He was *only* a child, but he was a. . . . And I couldn't stop him, couldn't save him, couldn't save anyone . . ."

"Gleaner." Jenret finished the sentence for her.

She wound the wet cloth around her hand, unwound it, glad of something to do, something to see other than the compassion she glimpsed on his face, shaded with concern. "I can't always control the nightmares from those days. Why can't I dream about Oriel? Why is it always about Varon and Briony and Vesey? Why, can you answer me that?"

She didn't want an answer, didn't expect one, grateful at least for his unvoiced compassion, but he surprised her by speaking. "Because to deny them or try to hide them would be a lie, a lie about something that made us who and what we are. But not the whole part, not by a long shot. Remember that when you remember your dreams."

Her smile wavered, she could feel it flickering, but it was sincere nonetheless. Lady help them both, but she was robbing him of sleep by keeping him up like this. "Quiet tonight? How's Mahafny doing?"

"Quiet. I'd say she's doing well enough. Resting, not restless, and I think the fever's easing." He handed back the mug when she rewrapped the wet cloth around her hand. "Peaceful without as well. No fuss, or nothing that the ghatti have reported. I'm going to turn in. Sorry to leave you with the worst part of the watch."

"You've had that. Smack in the middle."

He gave a quick head toss, as if ready to argue, but it turned into a confidence. "Perhaps. I always hate that final stretch before the sun rises. As if I'm afraid that someday it won't, or something absurd like that. Just like you I start thinking about all the things that are done and gone and will never rise again."

"Then don't. I'll promise to let them go if you will as well," she whispered. "Go to sleep now. I'll be on watch."

"I know." With a sinuous grace he whipped the knit cap off his head and tugged it over hers, then pulled up her collar to meet it. "Stay warm."

"I will," she reassured, knowing that they both knew he meant, "Stay safe."

She marched along the outer boundaries of the firelight, always looking outward, amazed anew at the varied shades and densities of blackness, the subtleties and variations one learned to gauge rather than seeing a uniform pitch dark. Too easy, too seductive, and too dangerous to sit in huddled converse with the fire. Then one's eyes adjusted to the light and not the dark, and the dark, the beyond, was what needed watching. A good rule to learn early and abide by. The cha warmed her hands and stomach, and she no longer felt sluggish.

"Three glider squirrels, one fox, one deer. Two owls, one hawk. Saam and I are coming in. Rawn and Parm will be out on guard. That's probably all the movement you'll see. But I doubt that." The last sentence sounded distinctly smug.

"Well, I saw you before you 'spoke me."

"You were supposed to, silly."

"It's not that difficult unless you smear dirt on that white muzzle and chest of yours. Not to mention your precious feet. Ever thought of advancing backward?"

"Hmmph!" The ghatt slid up beside her, appearing out of the patchy ground fog and darkness like a conjuring.

"Stay up for a moment, will you? I want to check on Mahafny."

Sliding her knife out of her boot top, she tiptoed to the sleeping figure, one leg elevated on her saddle. Easing the blanket back, Doyce crouched and examined the bare leg and foot. Hard to tell in this light, but she judged the swelling had receded, and the color looked more normal, the purplish-rose flush leaching away. With delicate balance she scraped the point of her blade along the sole of Mahafny's foot and saw with relief the curl of toes at the sensation. Good, the numbness had gone, or nearly so. Retucking the blanket, Doyce rose and began to walk the bounds she'd set for herself.

"Thank you, little one, you can go to sleep now."

"No, I'll stay up with you. Mayhap doze a little. I have thinking to do."

She cast along the demarcation of light and dark, nerves twitching; someone unaccounted for. *"What's Saam up to? Where is he?"* She hadn't noticed if the big gray ghatt had come off-duty or not. She almost decided to risk a sidelong glance toward the fire, but controlled herself to wait for Khar's response.

"Over by the fire, taking a bath."

So, she had felt something but hadn't realized it. *"Did he find anything?"*

"Yes and no. They're all around, so close it seems as if we could touch them. The scent pervades everything. They've crossed over and over their tracks so that you

can't tell the old from the new or which leads where. Worse than a yarn tangle. And that other ghatt keeps leaving markers for us on the trees. You should see Saam's and Rawn's hackles rise then."

"Maybe he's trying too hard to pick up the trail." She paused, then forced the words out. *"Khar, does he think about Oriel much?"*

The ghatta delayed, licked a paw with meditative slowness, spread it wide to nip at a space between toe and paw pad. **"Thorn. Yes."** A longer wait for the next words. **"As much as I think about you, about us."**

Overcome, Doyce squinted through dark stillness where trees blended into night, and night into rock, and the ground fog draped itself over all like an airy silken shawl. Always the darkest, heaviest part of the night when hope and life so often slipped away, forgetting the eternal promise of the newly refreshed sun.

And in that period of dark and loneliness was time to think, perhaps too much time to think. Of Oriel. Of Varon and Briony and Vesey. And of all the others left behind or lost. Jenret had the right of it; this was the worst time to think about all the old things and loved ones done and gone, never to rise again. And of what she would do when she met those Gleaners face to face. Ah, they'd cost her dearly through the years, a price too high to assess. Too much time to think things through and still to find no answer renewing itself like the sun. She slipped her hand into her pocket to fondle the misshapen piece of silver that had been Vesey's medallion, but her fingers drew no comfort from it. It felt curiously cold and dead, unwarmed by her flesh, as if it had withdrawn into itself. Nor did it warm for as long as she held it in her clenched fist during the rest of the night.

✤

PART
FIVE

✤

Dusted, straightened, and tidied, with fresh candles burning and oil lamps polished and filled, wicks trimmed to avoid smoking, the Hall of Records at last looked as clean and organized as it had before Sarrett and Parcellus had begun their research. A thorough dusting, sweeping, and airing had also helped control, if not conquer, Parse's allergies.

The one disorder came from the gaping holes on the shelves where leather volumes had been removed to the Tribune Meeting Room, awaiting the Tribune's perusal. At least twenty massive volumes, including several locked records, had been carried there by Sarrett and Parcellus, their pages marked with annotated slips of colored paper fluttering like miniature flags. Nothing for it now but to wait.

Sarrett stalked back and forth, mindlessly whistling a single shrill note; her Bondmate T'ss appeared edgy as well, back rippling, tail tip flicking. Having salvaged a puzzle-toy from his waist pouch, Parcellus fingered it this way and that—he'd found the solution early that afternoon but couldn't find it again for the life of him. The single shrill note cheese-grated at his nerves and he skimmed the puzzle across the table, blew his nose, more

out of habit than need at this point. His back to her, he
missed Sarrett's wince at the sound.

They had turned over their findings to the Seeker General and the Tribune early that morning; late evening
now approached, and their nerves felt frayed and raw.
Twice they had been summoned to explain some fine
points and details in their findings, to rebut an argument,
and it was clear that no agreement would be reached
easily—or soon. Swan Maclough and Rolf stood ready to
act, but Andwers Rendell and Dovina Marskyll, the
other two Tribune members, were cautious, conserva-
tive, and concerned, but shortsighted to the potential disaster ready to overtake not just Seekers but the whole of
Canderis if the Gleaners gained a foothold. They argued
deadlocked, the solution as achingly distant as the answer
to Parse's puzzle-toy.

"Heels cooled sufficiently?" Parse inquired of his pacing friend. Per'la's teeth showed in a huge yawn as she
rolled over on her back, exposing her stomach for a
tickle.

Pulling up short, Sarrett shot him an indignant glance,
then managed a rueful smile at her frustration and pent-
up energy. "Mayhap walking cools down horses, but it
isn't working for me. I just keep getting madder and
madder. *When* are they going to reach a decision?" With
a toss of her hands, she began walking again, tracing a
finger along the spines of the books she passed. The
muted sound made Parse think of a stick dragged against
a picket fence, a child's reproach to boredom.

"When isn't as important as what decision is reached."
Per'la wriggled and stretched as Parse tracked an exploring finger down her cream-colored belly, then grabbed
without warning with all four paws as he tickled too hard.
He yelped and she tossed his hand away, continued as if
she'd never been interrupted. **"Andwers and Dovina are
hidebound in their ways, but not nearly as hidebound as
Rull and Nef't. Two such stubbornly correct ghatti I've
never met in all my born days."**

"Not that you aren't stubborn?" T'ss chimed in. **"Just
sweeter about it, eh? Still, you're right—let them argue
another day and a night as long as they reach the right
decision. Let's just hope it doesn't take that long."** He

rested his chin along outstretched forelegs, gave a gloomy exhalation.

"But how much longer can Doyce and Jenret go without help? They have no idea what they're facing, what we've discovered! They're in more danger than they ever thought!" Despite himself, Parcellus rose and began to pace, almost bumping into Sarrett with his random, hurried movements. He mumbled an inarticulate apology, face flushed from the near-contact, though Sarrett paid him no heed. "I don't think Rolf can stand it much longer either. He looked so gray and worn when he came to call us the last time. It's preying on him; he's a doer, not a speaker."

Sarrett stopped short and Parcellus did bump into her, treading on her heels. Panicked, he threw himself backward as she whirled. "Well, then, why can't we be doers?"

"Do what?" He mopped at his face, trying to erase the worry creases.

"Ask the ghatti, my friend, see if they agree with me." Quick and decisive, Sarrett began to bundle odd scraps of paper, flipped through a stack of notes for the map sketch that Parse had made several days earlier. Mouth ajar, Parse jiggled back and forth from one foot to the other.

The two ghatti craned their heads, inscrutably staring into space. T'ss butted shoulders with Per'la, and she purred back. Parse essayed a complete circle around them, did another, waiting for enlightenment. Per'la nonchalantly licked behind T'ss's ear, and he closed his eyes in appreciation.

Parse halted, hands on hips, foot-tapping with impatience. "Well, lovely ghatti, what? I ask you, *what* am I supposed to ask you?" He cast a scowl in Sarrett's direction, but she affected not to notice so he concentrated again on the ghatti. "What?"

"Be a doer," Per'la said and T'ss finished, **"Not a speaker."** And both ghatti bounded toward the door without a backward look, tails high and crooked, heads tilted expectantly. **"Be a Seeker!"**

"In other words, Parse, we go after Doyce and Jenret and the ghatti ourselves—without waiting for the Tribune's decision." The knowing, enigmatic glance she tossed at Parse made him all too aware of how much it mimicked the ghatti's expressions and how slow the three of them made him feel sometimes. Sarrett finally took pity. "We know where they have to be headed, even if they don't yet realize it themselves. The sooner we leave, the more chance we have of warning them. We'll have to ride hard for the Research Hospice in the Tetonords. How long do you need to ready yourself?" Flourishing her papers in front of Parcellus's still-red nose, she tapped it lightly, then brought the papers back and stuffed them in her waistband. "After all, you drew the map yourself."

And so he had, although he hadn't caught the implications as clearly as she had, the opportunity for action rather than the nail-biting frustration of enforced waiting. Oh, to be that quick and clever. Well, he could prove himself, too, could plan and organize. "The horses are well rested, the ghatti certainly are, though we aren't. Adequate food and supplies are the main necessity." He began to tick off items on his fingers, brow furrowed in concentration, determined to forget nothing. "Trail mix for the ghatti, oats, bread, cheese, dried meat, waterskins, brandy. . . ." Thinking hard, he gnawed at a thumbnail. "Can we winkle extra bandages and medications out of Twylla? More than we'd usually carry—I'd feel more secure."

She nodded approval. "T'ss, go see what you can do about that without giving anything away." The white ghatt with the startling black striping shot off on his errand.

Sitting now, scribbling a list, Parcellus strove to make his warning casual, "You know, we could be stripped of our tabards for this, for disobeying the Seeker General. . . ."

"I know. So be it. We ride."

"We ride," he agreed, quirking the smallest of grins, hoping that it looked suitably knowing and feline. "Besides, Swan Maclough never said we couldn't go. Perhaps she just never got around to actually telling us we could."

"Hairsplitter!" She gave him a mock buffet. "I've no doubt you're right. Just an oversight on her part, she's

had so much to concentrate on lately." Grabbing a stack
of clean handkerchiefs, she piled them high on the table.
"And don't forget these."

Absentmindedly cramming them into pocket after
pocket so that he bulged in unlikely places, Parse leaned
back, dismayed. "What about Rolf and Chak?"

"Leave them a note—and hurry! They're arguing so
loudly again that I can hear them all the way up here,
like a swarm of bees about to hive. Now's the perfect
time to leave."

❖

The folded note with its spiky, incisive script balanced
against the lamp when Rolf hurried into the room, his
whole body quivering with fatigue and barely checked
anger. Yet another quibbling point to clarify. . . . Chak
stopped, his tail lashed once, then was still.

**"The've gone. I thought I felt someone drift by me
before, but I wasn't sure. Couldn't afford the distraction
of seeing if I could reach beyond the shielding the Seeker
General's got on."**

"Where have they gone?" Rolf ripped open the note
with uncooperative fingers, tried to hold the sheet steady
and distant enough so that his farsighted eyes could
focus. The few sentences were enough to make him
crumple the note, toss it with a fury he'd refused to let
loose 'til now. "Oh, those blessed idiots! Couldn't they
have waited—they still don't know the full implications
of what they've discovered! Now we've got to convince
the Tribune to save them as well!"

"In for a penny, in for a pound." Chak cocked his
head, dug behind his ear with a hind foot. **"This should
stir up things nicely for our side, don't you think?"**

"Perhaps." He retrieved the tossed note, forced back
his dizziness, and brushed the paper smooth against his
thigh without thought. "If Dovina and Andwers don't
decide the Seeker General put them up to this. Come
on, let's go back. I suppose it's too late to stop them,
they're outside the gates by now, aren't they?"

"Most likely." Best to be noncommittal, Chak decided, glad his Bondmate lacked the skill to read his

mind. Let them have their head start, and would that he and Rolf were riding with them. And then he resounded with the cramping numbness snaking down Rolf's left arm, the clenching pain in his Bondmate's chest, and with every bit of strength within him let out a frantic mindscream for Mem'now, for Twylla to come running.

❖

"There *must* be a shorter way, something more direct." Harrap sounded aggrieved as he shifted his bulk in the saddle, plucking at an uncomfortable seam that chafed his inner thigh.

"There is. Unfortunately we're not on it." Mahafny's tone stung, forbearance barely held in check.

Reining Lokka around, Doyce eased the mare between the two riders, hoping to avoid an argument. No one was in a good mood, herself included. Four more days of riding, four more days of unending, unbreaking dim forest, soaring black trunks barring the sky, branches cathedraling far above their heads. Monotonous food, adequate but never quite filling enough. The same with sleep. And mountainous inclines, barren single-file paths, and impossible downslopes that left the horses sliding, desperate for a firm footing. Shifting talus. If any Plumbs still survived, they ought to be here—and cursed herself for the thought, as if thinking it might make it come true. Plus one night of icy rain, a stinging drizzle close to freezing in needle-sharp spurs that bedeviled horses, riders, and ghatti like a cloud of biting, invisible gnats. And that was a bare accounting of physical discomfort; nothing had been said aloud of the malign force drawing them in its wake into the unknown.

"What Mahafny means is that . . ." she placated, touching Harrap's arm.

"Don't assume what I mean. You've no right to make assumptions of that sort!" With a sour twist of her mouth, Mahafny scrutinized Doyce and she felt herself wilting under the glare. Mahafny continued. "We're coming in through the back way, the back door, so to speak. There's a good, serviceable road to the east of the Hospice, but we aren't east of it. We've been moving from the west to the northeast, so we'll arrive at the Hospice long before we arrive at the road. Assuming we get there. After all, it's just a matter of a few mountains, a raging river or three, unsavory weather, wild animals lurking, and continual worry and fear over whether what we're seeking rides ahead of us, behind us, around us, or has vanished into another country by now! Not impossible given that Marchmont's border isn't that far. Just a normal, run-of-the-mill day or oct or, Lady help us, octant or year for a Seeker. Aren't you glad you're a Seeker now, Harrap?"

Hunched forward on his horse, his once jaunty scarlet-faced jacket the worse for wear, damp and soiled, braiding unraveling, Harrap blew on his chapped hands, kept his eyes downcast. Jenret held the lead position, within earshot, but from the rigidity of his bearing, striving to ignore the squabble behind him.

"I think you omitted inadequate leadership." Lamenting the impulse that had pushed her to the Shepherd's side, Doyce spoke. Glutton for punishment, she reproached herself, but the words sprang out, floating in the air like a perfect target.

To her surprise, Mahafny did not take aim at the words. Instead, she thumped her tired horse with her heels and broke into a canter to overtake Jenret. Even then she didn't stop, but drew past him to take the lead.

Harrap opened his mouth, and Doyce snapped, "Just don't give me another of your platitudes, that the Lady's will be done, or whatever. If you want to talk, fine. But spare me that."

He started to speak again, stroked Parm and cocked his head, then tried once more. "It's not that easy for any of us, but it's been harder on her. She has no one to confess her thoughts and fears to, no one to give her consolation, to take her as she is."

"I told you to leave religion out of it!"

"**He isn't speaking of religion**," Khar reproved her. "**He's speaking about us, our relationship.**"

"Oh." Reins slack, Lokka continued forward, Doyce sitting woodenly, color flooding her face. Hands twitching, she grasped the reins and managed to throw a meager apology in Harrap's direction. "Sorry."

"I know. You and Jenret tend to take it for granted. I almost take it for granted, but not quite yet." Parm stretched on the pommel platform and rubbed against Harrap's stomach until the Shepherd scratched his chin, lost for a moment in a silent conversation. "But the relationship we have with our ghatti is a source of comfort and release for the things you can't or don't dare say to your fellow travelers. The things she finally said to us. Not that she means them, but that she felt them, and they were poisoning her mind as badly as the snakebite poisoned her body. Think of the anxiety she feels that Evelien may be involved."

They rode on, tired but in amiable silence for the moment. Finally Doyce asked, "So what now?"

Harrap considered. "So we enter by the back door."

"Not that. What about Mahafny?"

"As I said, let her enter by the back door as well. Metaphorically speaking. She can't come back and out-and-out apologize, or isn't likely to. So let her do it her own way, let her enter by her own back door." His eyes were wide and baby-blue, utterly without guile or meanness in them as he surveyed her, and Doyce felt chastened.

"Did anyone ever tell you that you're a very wise man?"

He beamed, buffed a button against his sleeve. "The ghatti don't pick fools, do they? And neither do the Shepherds, although they require a different wisdom than the rest of the world's."

"I'll try to remember that."

"Ah, but you'll forget." He wagged a finger at her. "But I'll remind you every so often."

Up ahead Jenret signaled a halt and called to Mahafny to stop and come round. They had descended the last boulder-strewn, overgrown trail winding down the final ridge and were back on level forest floor again. A small clearing here, not unlike others they had passed through before on their journey; not unlike the one where Mahafny had confronted the snake.

Without knowing why, Doyce sensed that this particular clearing was man-made, though she didn't know what made her jump to that conclusion. She could see evi-

dence of old fire around the perimeter, where it had
radiated from the center burn spot. The dark ash color
of the ground and the scarring of the bordering, twisted
trees gave evidence of fire only, but whether set by
man or nature's lightning, she couldn't judge. Perhaps
a purposeful burn-off, perhaps not; too much time and
a modicum of regenerative, healing growth had blurred
distinctions, at least for her limited woodlore. Regardless
of who created it, nature reclaimed it: spindly white pine
shot upward around the boundaries, the first "young-
sters" she had seen, obscuring the scarring which marred
the bark of the parent trees, while a few hardwood saplings, oak from the look of the leathery brown leaves,
and low, shaggy berry bushes, long past fruit-bearing,
dotted the once clear center.

Mahafny lingered at the far side of the circle, dismounted but head bowed against her horse's saddle,
arms hanging limp and dejected. Then she turned, throwing back her head and shoulders, and walked past Jenret,
tossing a noncommittal comment in his direction. Passing
Saam, she bent without breaking stride and patted his
head. The other ghatti stretched and twisted, smoothed
ruffled fur, and made tentative, exploratory moves at
whatever caught their interest.

The suddenness of the bird call cut through the random
creaks and moans and whufflings of the horses and riders, so sharp and sweetly piercing as to make them all
look skyward, craning their necks. Shielding her eyes
against the brightness, Doyce cast about, waiting for the
call to be repeated, but heard instead a whisper of sound
slicing through the air with the deadly precision of
scythes at harvest.

Out of nowhere, the shaft struck quivering, a hairbreadth from her foot, and the next arrow slammed Harrap
full in the chest, sending him toppling, arms backstroking
and a roar burgeoning from his throat.

"Gleaners!" Mahafny screamed as she rushed toward
Harrap.

The air shivered with the soft, sussurating sound of
arrows, arrows that seemed not to find their mark, unless
their intent was to herd them all toward the center, away
from the horses. Dodging this way and that, with no one

within striking distance of sword or staff, indeed, no one
even visible, Doyce fell back, always scanning the perimeter of the barbed circle. Jenret did likewise, one arm
trailing a thin line of blood where he'd been pinked by
an arrow, a touch too clever in his dodging and weaving.
They stood back to back now, she could feel his body
heat, with Harrap's body and Mahafny's kneeling form
at their feet.

"Gleaners? Have they finally attacked us after all this
time?" Doyce eyed her segment of the circle, intent on
searching out one solid form, one person with whom to
do battle.

"No." Jenret's tone held a certain admiration as he
marked an arrow's spent flight and carved it in two with
his sword. "Not Gleaners. Gleaners hardly need to use
arrows. Erakwa." He bit back laughter, coughed to cover
it. "I do hope they found the Gleaners before they found
us."

Plastering themselves flat, the ghatti worked their way
outward like the four points of a compass, bellies tight
to the ground, moving soft as a summer sunrise, so that
one had to look twice to realize their progress. Once
they reached the boundary of the trees and broke free,
the Erakwa would have something to reckon with. Doyce
mindspoke, calling out love and encouragement to Khar
and wishing that Saam could comprehend as well. Then
with rising guilt, she broadened her 'speaking to include
Parm, now bereft of a second Bondmate.

The piebald ghatt paused long enough to give a jaunty
twitch of his tail and respond. **"He's fine. I hope he gets
me a Lady's Shield after this is done!"**

She sagged against Jenret for support. "Did you hear
Parm?"

"Did I hear him? Who couldn't? Any Seeker within a
two-league radius could read him loud and clear. Mahafny, what's the prognosis on your patient?"

Pulling Harrap's jacket back across his broad chest,
Mahafny struggled with the buttons and risked a glance
up. "Incredibly lucky, but with an honorably ugly and
painful contusion underneath his medallion. Fit to die
with the rest of us at any time now."

Harrap's chuckle rumbled low, his voice strained.

"With a bedside manner like that, I'm bound to improve. What can you spare me in the way of weapons? I've the Lady-blessed right to protect myself but not to take life."

Jenret's answer was short and to the point. "Clods of earth. Stones. My staff. Beyond that, your bare fists will have to do."

Scrabbling at the dirt, Mahafny had already gathered a pile of pebbles, each about the size of her thumb. "You're sure it's Erakwa? But why? They've always been peaceable from everything I've ever heard. They tend to back off and disappear if confronted, not fight."

"Well, Gleaners wouldn't need arrows, not with their special talent, so it's likely to be Erakwa. Besides, the fletching doesn't resemble any I've ever seen hunters use. We're on Erakwa land and have been for days, the trail we're following leads right through. But I haven't a clue why—you're right, they're gentle folk. They don't believe in the concept of 'owning' land, not as we do, so we can't be trespassing." Without taking his eyes from the forest, Jenret handed Harrap his staff as he continued to mark the flight of the few random arrows which still came their way.

When the whistle sounded again, Doyce felt herself transfixed anew by its clear, liquid beauty, but with an added menace twisting in her stomach. What did it signal? She remembered the Erakwan in the Market Square cupping his hands around his whistle, lofting that one clear note to the sky. What happened now? She watched the ghatti freeze at the sound, then resume their soundless creep. The arrows had stopped. Whether they had run out or the whistle had commanded them to cease, she didn't know, but the field of shafts, some red, some black, their fletching glistening, swayed like some exotic field of grain ripe for the mowing. That no one had been seriously hurt seemed a miracle, even without the sounds of Harrap's muttered thanksgiving in her ears.

The whistle sounded, this time on a descending, rather than an ascending note, and now she could discern faces within the forest around her. A shadowed profile here, a glint of eyes there, a glimpse of coppery shoulder further over, then nothingness, the forest seemingly empty of human habitation.

Upright, his weight on the staff, Harrap balanced beside her and Jenret, the three forming a defensive triangle. Mahafny stayed crouched, her pile of pebbles at the ready.

"How good are you these days?" Jenret asked the eumedico as he transferred his sword to his left hand so he could explore his wound with the other.

"From here to halfway to the trees, extremely accurate. But that brings them a little too close for comfort." Mahafny fumbled at a pouch tied to her belt, brought out a rawhide thong with a leather patch at its center. "Of course, with my sling, the distances doubles or triples, and without any great loss in accuracy."

"Don't tell me you still carry that?" Unable to stop herself, Doyce laughed out loud, letting herself slip back to more carefree times when she'd watched Mahafny knock pine cones from trees with her sling. "And believe me, she can hit anything she chooses."

"I know." Jenret's shoulder brushed hers, the touch a comfort, solid and real. "She taught me on a visit one summer."

All the time they'd been talking, Doyce had kept her mindspeech open and receptive, awaiting word from the ghatti. Jenret and Harrap did the same, she knew. Other than murmured thoughts of caution as the ghatti slipped outward, she had heard little of moment. They seemed as perplexed as the Seekers as to how the Erakwa had crept so close without the great cats noticing. Rawn sounded especially grumbly and put out by it, as if his professionalism had been found wanting. Parm, as usual, viewed the whole thing as a delicious lark, but Khar remained silent, a puzzling development to Doyce's way of thinking.

From this distance Khar's stripes and whorls of black and tan and gray blended into the drying grasses and near-leafless bushes.

"Six, no . . . seven, ahead of me. They keep moving, shifting back and forth. They move more easily than sunlight."

Seven? Not too bad, if that were all, but she wouldn't delude herself, not with the thicket of arrows hedging them in, and their simultaneous directions.

"Ten ahead of me," Rawn growled. " 'Nother ten or eleven ahead of Saam, he says."

In contrast, Parm sounded deflated when he responded: "Only eight, no, seven." The chiding that Harrap gave him wasn't audible to the others, it was too personal, but they suspected the ghatt had been lectured about envy and greed. "I know. We should have listened to Saam. Not been caught like this."

"I take it Saam knew?" With the three back-to-back, Doyce caught a glimpse of Jenret's profile, saw the long, dark lashes dip against his cheek when he spoke.

"Apparently." And no longer had any time for speech as the three ghatti mindspoke as one.

" 'Ware! Coming through!"

The cessation of arrows had lulled them, a momentary false peace, an eye of calmness in the storm, but now the very trees shook with explosive life and movement, writhing as if to expel the Erakwa from the womb of their woodland home. Coppery, near-naked bodies, gleaming in the late sunlight, fragmenting, moving with such smooth speed that the eye could scarcely discern one from another. They swept in a molten wave toward them, bodies merging into one solid wall of flesh with grimacing, painted faces and arms menacing with hatchets, clubs, short spears.

"Stay together! If we separate, it's easier to cut us down!" Jenret shouted as he parried the initial blow. Mahafny bounced up, her sling whistling around her head as she let loose the first stone, and an Erakwan fell, an incongruous look of surprise on his face as his jaw dropped slack and his eyes rolled back.

The ghatti sprang to their feet, dashing through the charge, tripping some, leaping fiercely onto Erakwa backs, wheeling and slashing with their claws. Parm used one bare back as a vaulting point and sprang in another direction, claws whipping across the face and eye of one Erakwan. The man howled in pain, blood welling down his face, and Parm screeched, too, first with astonishment, then with confidence. Khar and Rawn both rebounded from one charging body to the next like two furred, demented demons, striving to distract and damage as many as possible.

Horrified, Doyce saw an Erakwan pluck Rawn from
the back of one of his fellows and dash the ghatt to the
ground, smashing at him with his war club, but the black
ghatt spat defiance and twisted aside at the last possible
instant, disappearing into the melee of legs.

Saam didn't fare as well. Grimly clawing at the back
and shoulder of a heavily muscled Erakwan with blue
chevrons painted like surprise marks over his eyes, Saam
set his teeth around the neck bone, working to pierce it
and slide a fang between the vertebrae to puncture the
spinal cord. The Erakwan flailed ineffectually, unable to
reach or unseat him. Busy with her own defense, Doyce
turned in time to glimpse a war club wielded by another
warrior catch Saam along the shoulder and send him
crashing earthward in a heap. It was the last thing she
had time to notice as more and more Erakwa rushed
within striking distance, and she parried and thrust, hacking wherever an opening presented itself.

Mahafny dodged back and forth, throwing now rather
than using her sling, and finally, laying about her with a
large rock as the bodies pressed tighter against them,
hemming them in, making them collide with one another,
misjudge their strokes. Jenret went down on one knee,
bodies pressing him backward with no room to wield his
sword. Severing a spear shaft with her own sword, Doyce
kicked an Erakwan in Mahafny's direction with a yelp of
warning and the eumedico promptly thumped him behind
the ear. Harrap's massive arms swung his borrowed staff
with a metronomic regularity until a low-swung club
slipped under his guard and he crashed down with a bellow, five Erakwa on top of him, grappling to pin each
limb. With the comforting bulk of Harrap gone, Doyce
sensed that Jenret had never regained his feet, leaving
her back unprotected.

To have come this far and fail at this point! The
thought galled her and she swung with renewed but hopeless fury, on the brink of overbalancing herself. She had
no breath left to curse and saved it for another stroke,
no longer bothering to choose a target with care; she was
bound to hit someone in any direction she turned. Too
many of them! Too many! She lunged to full extension
and a hand snagged her wrist, and more hands grasped

her from behind, pulled her roughly to the ground as Khar screamed, changing course to spring to her aid. Then yet another pair of legs blocked her view.

"No!" She screamed at the top of her lungs and projected in mindspeech as well. *"Go! Back away! Now! All of you!"* If she could send the ghatti off free, they could seek help or perhaps devise a rescue plan. Saam and Parm limped in rapid retreat toward the forest, and Rawn broke his stride, wheeling back to intercept Khar and turn her. He slammed her with his shoulder to force her to change direction, and the ghatta lashed sideways at the solid black shoulder, already scored with blood, and hissed at him, charging forward with a rebellious growl. *"Go!"* Doyce mindscreamed again. *"Khar'pern! Run, love! Escape!"*

But the ghatta ran on, oblivious to anything but Doyce, her mindspeech a roiling frenzy of wrath and alarm, the near-palpable sensation of the fear of loss overriding everything else. Khar never noticed the gaily decorated war club that smashed the back of her head. She collapsed and rolled, tongue lolling, half on her side, half on her back, the vulnerable white of her chest exposed for a killing spear point. A small circle of Erakwa gathered around her, first one, then another, gingerly prodding the ghatta with club or spear. One, clearly one of the leaders, raised his painted war club, studded with a spike of antler, ready to crash it down on Khar's unconscious head.

Without knowing how she managed it, Doyce struggled to her feet, her wrists lashed securely behind her with rawhide. She bulled free of the grasping hands, aware of tearing pain but not caring, and charged the circle head-down, scattering bodies as she slammed through. She gauged the club's downward swing as she dove over Khar's body. Then there was only jarring, numbing pain as the blow landed.

❧

Pockets of shadow and brightness eclipsing and expanding, elongating and shrinking as torches moved back and forth amongst the horses and Guardians. Rolf squinted in the unrelenting glare, narrowing his eyes, then strained to see as the torch moved to one side. Fifteen in the squad plus their sergeant, wide and hard as burled oak in his formfitting leather gear, helmet resting secure over close-cropped grizzled hair. The sergeant nodded, not really seeing him, more concerned with gear, rations, travel readiness. He paid special and personal attention to the tack on Swan Maclough's bay, callused, large-knuckled fingers checking every buckle and seam.

"We should be able to catch up with them," the Seeker General said, her bay twitching, nervous under the probing hands of the sergeant. "Balthazar and his men know the north like no one else. And we have the advantage of fresh mounts as we go along. They won't, so while they tire, we'll be able to gain on them."

Rolf tilted his head to take in the mounted figure of the Seeker General, indigo cloak wound around her, Koom on his platform gleaming ruddy red in the torchlight. He wouldn't, please, wouldn't beg, Lady help him, he wouldn't, but he had to try again. To have failed, collapsed before he could race back to announce the premature departure, heart flittering as irregularly as an agitated songbird beating at its cage when the cat creeps close. Angina, Twylla had said, but a portent of worse to come if he didn't ease up. Chak coughed, bringing him back from his self-pity.

"I still think it advisable that I accompany you. I must go!" The naked appeal in his voice shamed him but he pressed on. "You need another Seeker with you. By rights it should be me." His heart didn't flutter now, he could feel its trip-hammer thudding at his temples, his throat, at every pulse point.

"I've sixteen already," she pointed out, reiterating the obvious, Rolf knew, trying to make him acknowledge his presence as unnecessary. "You're needed here. Someone has to keep Dovina and Andwers in line, keep them from informing the Monitor yet as to what's going on. I've this escort as a favor only; you know it isn't strictly legal for me to have commandeered it." Swan wet her lips. "And if for some reason I shouldn't return, I'm hoping that you'll be elected in my place. I've left sealed documents

for the Monitor—should they prove necessary—and one
of them asks that he name you Seeker General Pro Tem
until an election can be held." She reached out a hand
and brushed his shoulder, not daring to let her touch
linger, to communicate her affection. "And after the
stress you've been under recently, Twylla feels rest is
advisable."

He pulled back, afraid even her casual touch would
register his inadvertent stiffening, his resentment. Stress?
Balderdash, she'd been under greater stress and for
longer, not to mention that she must have fifteen years
on him! He could keep up, Chak could keep up, they
would if they had to crawl every centimeter of the way!
The veins in his forehead pounded, flecks of black and
gold spangled his vision, and he forced himself to breathe
slowly and steadily, to face the unpalatable truth. Being
a reasonable and logical man, he had to acknowledge
that part of what she said had validity: the Tribune must
remain intact to govern the Seekers in her absence. Let
Andwers and Dovina sound a hasty alarm and who knew
what would happen? But his friends rode out there—
especially Parcellus and Doyce, Per'la and Khar. Abandon friends and you have none left, he whispered to himself, holding the thought tight.

"There is a way," Chak interjected. "Just be more
forceful, but with subtlety." And the image Chak projected made him giddy with excitement. Could he do it?
He might be younger than the Seeker General, but he
wasn't a young man nor, he had to admit it, a well one,
either. Nor was unprovoked violence his way.

Raising his shoulders in seeming acquiescence to the
Seeker General's words, he smiled and wordlessly moved
off as if the debate were finished and he had been convinced. As he turned, he tapped one of the Guardians
on the arm to attract his attention. "A word with you,
if I may, about the Seeker General's needs on a forced
ride such as this." The young man came politely, toying
with the leather and bronze helmet in his hands as he
followed Rolf into the dark throat of a passageway between buildings.

Like a shot Chak darted between the Guardian's legs,
clawing at his cloak from behind; the young man stum-

bled and looked down to see what pinned him in place.
With every hoarded piece of strength in his body Rolf
smashed clasped hands behind the Guardian's ear, sending him crashing to the ground. Then as Balthazar, the
sergeant, called for the laggard, Rolf stripped off the
unconscious man's breastplate and leather arm guards,
fingers trembling with exertion and excitement as he
fought with unfamiliar buckles and straps, the throbbing
in his temples a joyous accompaniment. He scooped up
the fallen helmet, jammed it low over his forehead, and
rushed out, hugging Chak tight to his chest under the
hastily donned cloak, and flung himself on the one free
horse while the other riders milled about, ready to be
off. Once they escaped beyond the revealing torchlight,
who would notice?

He jerked his horse into position after the others, weak
with relief. For some reason this Guardian had tied his
bedroll to the pommel of the saddle rather than lashing
it behind. An impromptu platform for Chak. Still, he
kept the cloak flung over the ghatt to keep him hidden.
What Guardian would be accompanied by a ghatt?

"This cloak has not been washed recently," Chak muttered and sneezed.

*"Neither has much else from the smell of it. But don't
complain, it was your idea."*

Hooves, pounding and pounding through the night
until they rang louder and more constant than his heartbeats. Leaning forward with exhaustion, wavering in the
saddle, Rolf rode at the tag end of the squad. How many
leagues had they covered from night until near dawn?
Chak clung for dear life to the bedroll, still draped by
the offending cloak.

Balthazar dropped back until he rode level with Rolf,
paced him in silence as Rolf struggled to draw the hood
of the cloak farther over his helm. Lady help him if he
had to speak, he hadn't a clue as to what timbre of voice
the young Guardian had possessed, high, low, shrill,
gruff?

"Night's not that cold, think you'd be a mite stuffy
like that," Balthazar observed.

Rolf muttered some noncommittal sound, neither denial nor agreement.

"Doesn't it bother the ghatt?"

Rolf jerked upright in the saddle, jaw unhinging in disbelief. Discovered already, Lady help him, what a fool he'd been to think he could disguise himself! Now the ignominious sending home, back to do his duty.

The sergeant reached to twitch the cloak back from Chak. "Had a bet you'd try something. Could see it in your face from the beginning when she said you wasn't going. Didn't seem fair like. So we drew lots as to who'd be the one tapped if you tried anything. Ferris was a right good sport about it." He gave Rolf a comradely smile. "Sure and you didn't think it was *that* easy to overcome a Guardian?"

Hope as fresh as the air fanning his tired face and head, free of the hood and helm for the moment, rushed through him. "You don't plan to send us back? We thank you. But I'm not sure I'd want to be you when the Seeker General finds out about this deception."

"Stay back, stay out of her line of sight and in another day or two, it'll be too late. Any man's entitled to try his hardest to protect what he holds dear." He passed a canteen across and the rhythmic sloshing of the water sounded beautiful in Rolf's ears. "Hold on to your hopes, that's what makes a good Guardian." And with that the sergeant urged his steed back to the head of the squad.

Rolf worked the plug out of the narrow spout with his teeth, managed to squirt a dribble of water into Chak's mouth until the ghatt coughed, then swallowed noisily. Then he drank, throat working in relief as they rode on, still exhausted but resolute.

Blackness, velvety soft. She blinked, experimented again to be sure. Yes, her eyes were open . . . the colors darted and swam back and forth when she closed them. Hard dirt tamped firm by years of animal and human feet, an enclosed, acrid smell from continuous habitation, smoke, cooking fires, curing skins, rancid fat. She shifted, rolled onto her back, ignored the wave of pain as her other shoulder and the back of her head made contact with the ground. Hands puffed and swollen, still

bound behind her, and her head throbbed with slow,
steady rolls of pain. Waves of pain, and with it the potent
sense of desolation and loss. Khar! Khar! Dead, lost,
gone. Alone again.

But the steady swells of pain began to vary, alternating
its rhythm so that two distinct and separate flows attacked her from opposite directions, counterpointing
each other. Her own pain and pain on the very threshold
of her mindspeech. Wavering, flickering in and out,
sometimes merging with her own heart's beat and her
own throbbing pain, sometimes distinct and separate.
Sometimes as an "other," sometimes as one.

She allowed herself a smile of exultation, tears sliding
down her face, moistening matted hair. Khar lived!
Alive, she could feel it! Doyce called out with her mind,
but touched only unconsciousness, a blank receptivity
without boundaries that she had never encountered before. She let her mind reach out and enter, encountered
a series of blurred images, saw herself featured in many
of them. She pulled back and withdrew, instinct telling
her she trespassed on an intimacy that Khar had never
offered before and was now powerless to stop. Still, it
didn't matter. Khar was alive and near.

With effort she rolled back onto her good shoulder
and jackknifed until her thighs were at right angles to
her body. Her hands, tied at the small of her back, gave
little leverage, but she managed to raise herself onto one
hip. Behind her, faint shimmers, a murky flicker of light,
bobbing, sputtering, hissing, more noise and shadowy
motion than illumination. She pivoted on her bottom to
find the source, digging her boot heels to turn herself
around.

"Ah, welcome back. It doesn't burn too brightly, I'm
afraid. It's just a wick floating in a dish of liquified fat."
Mahafny, steady and as bracing as a cool wind over rain-
swept fresh earth. "Wait. Sometimes if I blow on it, it
burns brighter."

She did so, and the flame jumped tall and pure, outlining her face, cheeks rounded with blowing, cameo-carved
against the dark. Her silvery hair hung loose, straggling
around her face, and the sight disconcerted Doyce. Mahafny disdained untidiness or carelessness of appearance.

Mahafny, her hair not wound in her elegant chignon. A wonderment and a puzzle, nearly driving her thoughts of Khar from her pounding head.

"You're gaping like a gaffed fish, Doyce. If you're going to say something, do so. If not, stop opening and closing your mouth. It doesn't inspire confidence as to your mental capacity after a blow on the head."

"What . . . what about Khar? Where is she? Where are we? Harrap and Jenret?" It took effort, but she mouthed the words, made the sounds. She operated on two different planes of consciousness—or unconsciousness—one very much her own and aware, the other deepmelded with the ghatta's pain, and the possible entry into the heart of an unknown and uncharted union.

"Khar's over beside me, resting on your tabard." Mahafny's words rushed, jumbled in her ears, though she heard the eumedico speaking distinctly, no attempt to soften the impact of her message; it was not her way. "I don't know, Doyce, if she'll survive. She took a bad blow the first time, much harder than the one you took trying to save her. The Erakwan managed to deflect the worst of the blow at the last instant. He had no intent to kill you. Though why they strove so hard to take us alive, I don't know. We weren't as restrained as they—some died.

"They unbound me for a little after they brought us here, let me check on you both before they tied me again. Her head's swollen, I can feel more flex and movement to the cranium than I'd like. There may be pressure building inside. If it doesn't subside soon. . . ." She trailed off, rested her chin against an upraised knee.

Doyce hitched herself across the floor, hesitant as to what the darkness hid between her and Mahafny. But no obstacles impeded her fanny-dragging, and at last she sat beside the eumedico, who bent again to blow on the lamp wick. Khar's still form leaped into view, flame and shadow dappling the black, buff and gray striping, making her seem to shiver and move in the light, but the only real movement came from the rise and fall of her slow, shallow breathing. Awkwardly, Doyce bent and brushed her face along the ghatta's flank, rubbed her

cheek against the satin fur, then pressed her ear down
to listen for the heartbeat.

"She refused to leave with the others when I ordered
her to. She came back after me!" Her voice climbed
high and wailing, quivering with self-accusation. "It's my
fault, she wouldn't go! She knew how much I need her!
She's the only one who ever came back for me, to stay
with me! Mother let me go, you let me go, Varon and
Briony, Vesey, Oriel! Every one of you deserted me,
wouldn't stay when I needed you most—everyone except
Khar!"

Mahafny fought back a strangled sound. "Hush, Doyce,
hush. No, no, never alone, always around you people
who've loved you, who love you, if you'd let yourself
feel it and return it. Harrap and Jenret. And me—again.
The only way I could save you before was to let you go.
There are three more of us right here who love you—if
you'll let us."

Snuffling, throat constricted with the effort to imprison
her sobs, she pulled herself upright, grateful for the life-
line of control Mahafny threw her way. But dignity cost
more than she could afford, as she forced herself to wipe
her bleary eyes and running nose on the knee of her
pantaloons, no other alternative. Unsanitary but effective.

"Are Harrap and Jenret all right?" She gulped, tried
hard to level her voice.

Mahafny shifted from one hip to the other and blew
at the wick, a golden shaft of light piercing the dark
before it faded. "Well, as I said, they were alive when
last I saw them. They're being held in another hut. Without the ghatti to transmit for us, I don't know any more
than that."

"Then Rawn and Saam and Parm did escape?"

"Again, I hope so, I believe so. But I've not had word,
and if they'd contacted one of the others, I think Jenret
or Harrap might have risked having them try to 'speak
me while you were still unconscious. If only Khar would
come to."

Yes, if only Khar would regain consciousness. If only,
if only. She cast her mind toward the ghatta, but again
touched nothing beyond random thoughts, the ebb and
flow, the spinning toward the vortex of a communion she

didn't recognize. She sat, mind keyed, waiting, hoping, but there was nothing. Except Mahafny waiting at her side, silent, compassionate.

After what seemed an eternity of emptiness, Doyce looked up. "If you turn your back to me, mayhap I can untie your bonds. My fingers feel like sausages, but it's better than sitting and doing nothing, better than just sitting and waiting."

"And waiting for what, I don't know. If it will keep you occupied, fine, though I don't hold much hope." With that Mahafny obligingly turned her back to Doyce.

Tight-knotted leather thongs, each knot smooth and hard as a nut. No edges that she could discern as she let her clumsy fingers grope, numbed and balky, blind to solving the unyielding puzzle.

"A bit like surgery, tying a knot one-handed in a spot that you can't see," Mahafny commented, wincing as Doyce fumbled and reworked her way over and around and under the intractable bonds.

"I suppose. But usually if you tie sutures, you're not called on to untie them. You get to cut them later." She spun on her hip to face the eumedico. "Mahafny! I don't suppose there's any chance you've been forgetful lately?"

"Doyce, I'm not the one who's had a blow on the head."

"Your pockets, Mahafny! Did you forget and leave your scissors in your pocket again?"

The eumedico chuckled. "Yes. And I've two punctures in my thigh to prove it!"

Doyce scrambled, forcing awkward, tied hands in the direction of Mahafny's pocket. Who had ever thought a pocket could be so elusive, but with her hands locked behind her, the eumedico's pocket floated tantalizingly close yet impossible to reach. How could her fingers have become so fat and stupid? A chance, she begged, just give me a chance to do anything rather than sit and wait for Lady knows what. Wrong, dammit, wrong angle! And she jammed with blind, heavy-handed frustration at the pocket's slit.

"Just wait a moment!" Mahafny protested. "Don't rip the clothes off me. Here," she struggled to her knees.

"Let's make the path a bit straighter and easier to negotiate."

And with that her hands blundered, snagged, then slid into the pocket and her fingers touched metal. "Ouch! Got them!"

"Warned you they were sharp. Now, for pity's sake, I hope you can tell the difference between my wrists and the rawhide."

The work went finically slowly; the scissors sharp but small. The thin blades and the short handles gave her little leverage; Doyce found herself holding the blades apart, slicing with one blade or the other to make tiny incisions. To hit the same strand in precisely the same place took time and concentration, especially since she couldn't see a thing. More than once she nicked and slashed herself where she'd inserted her own fingers under the strips of leather she worked at to protect Mahafny's wrists. A long flap of loose skin dangled annoyingly on her knuckle where she'd sliced at the wrong thing, but luckily there was little pain.

"Wait. They didn't do as thorough a job when they retied me. I think I can snap it now." Mahafny sat straight and composed herself, only the thinned mouth and corded neck and shoulders attesting to the struggle behind her back. "Nnmph! Ah, got it!" She brought her hands in front of her, each wrist braceleted with the remains of her leather bonds. "Give me a moment to flex my fingers, and I'll set you loose."

But Doyce's face set in shock as a hand jerked back the curtain covering the doorway, and an Erakwan woman ducked through the low entrance. Elderly, that much was clear from her iron gray hair, tight-plaited behind her, and her toothless mouth and sagging breasts, for she was bare from the waist up. But her naked arms and legs below her short leather apron skirt were muscular and hard, no soft, loose excess flesh of old age. And the knife at her side looked honed to a killing thinness from a lifetime of daily use.

She balanced a white birch bark slab for a tray and on it she carried a bowl of what smelled like food, a water gourd, and a saucerlike clay dish with herbs steeping in boiling water, wafting an intense, enlivening smell of the outdoors through the hut. Her free hand held a better lamp, underlighting her face and penetrating to the ceiling of their dwelling.

Doyce froze and prayed Mahafny would keep her hands immobile, not reveal by an involuntary movement that they were unfettered.

But the old woman scrutinized one, then the other, and chuckled. "No matter." She nodded her head at Mahafny's hands. "You safer in here dan out in woods, dat you seen. Folk more dan'rous than Erakwa out der, hah?" A heavy but decipherable accent. "You t'ink leave, silly, now. Mebbe later, we 'cide what do wid you. You need eat, and t'ings for sick anmul. Doan know why I save, but I try. Mebbe reason I not know." And with a swift grace she bent and placed the tray at Mahafny's feet, her metallic-brown skin shiny soft in the light, an odor of animal fat, warm and richly sweet, emanating from her body.

With a practiced movement she backed out the door, her foot hooking behind her to nudge the skin covering the entrance. Never once did her dark eyes leave them, frank, intense, assaying, but good-humored. She chuckled again as she left, a skittering sound like a squirrel kicking and rustling amongst dry leaves. "S'eep now. Wait for day."

Mahafny balanced the water gourd to Doyce's lips, then took a sip herself. "A welcome of sorts, I'd say." Removing the scissors from Doyce's lax fingers, she began to slice away at her companion's bonds.

Hands free at last, fingers protesting, throbbing and tingling at the unrestrained rush of blood, Doyce chafed at her wrists and sniffed the saucer, considering the blend of scents. "I think I recognize most everything in it. Cinnamage and marsh star to reduce swelling. Harrabalm for fever, something else familiar but that I can't place. Worth a try, I think. Not poisonous."

"How are you going to get Khar to swallow it?"

The nicks and cuts oozed, bled, as she clenched her fingers, aware of her clumsiness. "I'll have to dip a piece of shirttail in it and drip it into her mouth; she'll swallow, even though she's unconscious."

Drop by drop, she did. Some of the liquid spilled,

missed its mark, and Doyce cursed each precious drop
that soaked into the earthen floor, but continued. After
a while, Mahafny eased her aside and took over, and
Doyce sampled the food that had been left. She couldn't
identify it, but it was filling and required a concerted
effort to chew, each mouthful expanding spongily as it
mixed with her saliva. Some sort of dried meat pounded
together with berries, nourishing to travelers or hunters,
and easy to transport.

While she chewed, she examined her surroundings.
Longer than it was wide, the hut's walls and ceiling
blended into a crescent, bent saplings arched overhead
and lashed together, then covered with slabs of bark, the
inner side of each piece a silky gray. No windows, a small
smoke hole at the top that revealed the inky night; a low
door at either end. She eased toward the door at the far
end of the hut and squatted beside it, teasing the leather
flap aside with a wary finger. A war club slapped the
flap back into place with finality. She sucked at a bruised
knuckle.

"House arrest, you might call it." Putting the strip of
cloth back into the saucer, Mahafny checked the ghatta's
pulse and rose, stretching widely. "Your turn again."

Doyce sat and began to drip more of the mixture into
Khar, holding the corner of her mouth open with one
hand. She resolutely forced herself not to try to make
contact with the ghatta, not yet, not until Khar could
somehow indicate the necessity. The pain's cadence
danced partner to her own, and a change in that would
alert her to any change in the ghatta's condition.

"She's probably had all she should." Mahafny took the
scrap of cloth from Doyce's hand. "Take the rest yourself. You've had a bad knock on the head as well."

Rocking back on her heels, Doyce smiled, her head
pounding in reminder. She had tried to convince herself
that the pain she felt was all Khar's, but part of it re-
soundingly remained her own. "As you have reminded
me time and again, humans and animals do not have
identical physiologies or identical tolerances for the same
drugs; thus animal experimentation is valid only up to a
certain point."

Mahafny held out the saucer to her. "In this case the

relationship may be closer than we realized. Certainly the Gleaners seem to think so. Now take the medicine."

"And I'm too tired to care one way or the other. I'll take it." She grimaced as she swigged down the dregs of the Erakwan tisane and grabbed the water gourd, sloshing her face in her hurry. "Phew! A sure sign of efficacy—bitter!"

"Rule number one," Mahafny intoned with mock solemnity.

"If it tastes good, it won't work. I remember." She slid over beside the older woman, their shoulders touching. "Now, one final thing before I try to sleep. I'm going to open my mind and see if I can reach any of the other ghatti—they've got to be out there somewhere."

With a restraining hand on her knee, Mahafny hesitated. "You're not afraid of whom else you might reach? Is it wise to broadcast too widely?"

"Don't know. I'll damper it down if I feel the faintest tug of something or someone I don't recognize. I know Parm's and Rawn's speech signatures well enough. Saam's, too—if it mattered."

She sat silent, hands outstretched, palms up on her knees. Keep the spine straight but not rigid, the balance within as well as the balance without. Deep, steady breaths to center, to regulate herself, to send her mind aloft as far as she could, eager for kindred touch and conversation. She pressed harder, farther outward than she ever had before, but sensed nothing, either good or ill. Just mocking emptiness interspersed with the normal night sounds beside and beyond her. Some might call it peaceful, but she yearned for contact, communion.

With a sigh, she reeled herself inward. "I don't know where they are. Not a touch," she confessed. "You get so used to it, you know. And when it's not there, it's like being bereft of something . . . an amputation."

Silver and pewter in the light, Mahafny nodded in understanding, not analyzing but accepting, and Doyce relaxed.

"There are blankets over there. None too fresh, I suspect, but I hope no vermin. Now go to sleep. I'm going to blow out the larger light."

Woodsmoke and dried sweet grass, a touch of dampness, perfumed the blanket, not a bad smell by any means, she reassured herself as she wrapped it around her. Easing herself as close to Khar as she could manage, she fell asleep, one hand warding the comatose ghatta.

❦

" 'Lo? Hello, Doyce?"

Insistent as an insect the voice buzzed and bored through her head, droning against her pain. Wary, unsure of where she was, she hunched upright and tried to concentrate, blanket shawling her shoulders. A bare pinprick of light, a badly burning lamp, met her eyes and she remembered, mentally touched the steady waves of pain from Khar, and clamped down hard on her lip.

"Doyce? Sorry, sorry. How's Khar? Oh, woe! Anyway, Harrap said I should 'speak you, even if you slept. Sorry, sorry."

Parm, dithering away as usual. How near she couldn't judge, but despite his dithering, he was concentrating, arrowing a single concise thrust of mindspeech directly at her, no leakage to invite intruding thoughts.

"Where are you? How are Harrap and Jenret?"

"Oh. They're fine. Still tied up, but they're fine. Except for the bruises. And the sprained knee. And they've got sand fleas in their hut! Ooh! And then. . . ."

"Where is their hut?" Despite herself, Doyce fairly shouted at the flustered ghatt. Thank the Lady for mindspeech so she didn't rouse Mahafny, let alone the whole camp.

"You're at the southern end, they're to the west. They've got lots more Erakwa guarding them 'cause when Jenret tried to break free, they. . . ."

"Worse than a silly ghatten!" Rawn's voice broke in, hoarse, tired. "He didn't have any more sense than Parm here, but he's learned his lesson and none the worse for wear. We three are here, back at the attack clearing, about a half league south from your camp. Trying to get closer when it quiets down more. Once we get the lay of the land we'll try to figure out something."

Parm sounded his treble next to Rawn's deeper voice. "Saam says to say hello. Oh, and Lokka, too. I got the horses rounded up and away when we couldn't do anything else." His chest-puffed pride in his ingenuity was deflated by sadness at not having been able to accomplish anything more.

"Well, there wasn't," he continued, as if reading the subtext of her thoughts.

"He can be clever," Rawn's grudging commendation made Parm's mindpattern caper and glow. "We snagged the bridles off, at least, but I don't think we can get them on again if we have to."

"Never mind. We'll manage. I think you've all done wonders," Doyce encouraged. *"What do you sense from the Erakwa? Do you have any idea how we're going to get out of here?"*

"They're clustered 'round the campfires—very hard to read, mostly shuttered from us. The young ones sometimes let a random thought escape. What little we can pick up doesn't sound good, but it's not all bad." She wondered what Rawn was hiding from her. "We're trying, we're trying to figure a way out, but right now everyone's bone-tired and sore. . . ." He lapsed off, embarrassed. "Oh." For a moment he sounded so like Parm dropping one of his "oh, and by the way's" that Doyce wanted to chuckle. "You didn't feel the brush of something earlier, did you?"

"No. Such as what?" What had she missed while asleep, the drug making her sleep more soundly and dreamlessly than usual. She concentrated hard, trying to read between his words and images, wondering what he refused to tell her.

"Well, nothing. Never mind. All for now, we've got work to do. Sleep well."

"Lady bless, Harrap said to say. Bye!" Parm's cheeky tone echoed, and their voices faded. Comforted, smiling to herself, Doyce rolled over and fell solidly asleep.

Morning. Milky-pale daylight seeped through the smoke hole in the roof and slender chinks of light startled the eye, horizontal here, vertical there, where bark slabs had curled loose or hadn't overlapped. Fuzzy light, more a quality of lessened darkness, around the hides hanging over the two doors. Daybreak sounds and smells, birds, a scolding, angry jay, people rousing, fresh fires being kindled, food smells rising, the murmur and padding feet of half-awake people passing on morning business. But the hut itself remained in cool and silent semidarkness, cavelike.

Exhaling long and loud, Doyce shivered and sat up, sore to the bone and wondering again where she was. The sight of Mahafny erectly seated, silver-star hair combed and caught up in a twist, yet strangely, without her white coat, threw her back in time to the Hospice training school.

"Ooh, late for rounds," she groaned. What tickled round the periphery of her brain, enticing, demanding a weak but emphatic entrance? She brushed at her face as if to clear the cobwebs inside. But another voice still echoed inside her head.

"Doyce, Khar's awake."

And with that, everything came back with such certitude that she could hardly believe she'd forgotten. The fruitless chase, the Erakwa, the capture, Khar. She scrambled on hands and knees to her folded tabard where Khar rested. The rhythmic waves of pain she'd shared the night before had receded but still lapped through her, along with an enfeebled consciousness.

"How is she?" she asked, and mentally projected the thought as well.

"Here. Oh, hurts to think!" And then with greater urgency, front paws scrabbling, eyes focused cockeyed but desperate, **"Oh, need to go! Need to go!"** The front paws scrabbled again, but the hind legs did not bunch and respond to bring her to her feet.

"She needs to relieve herself. What are we going to do?" Doyce asked, one hand massaging the ghatta's shoulder blades as she looked around, wondering what to do.

"Well, get her off your tabard first," came Mahafny's practical rejoinder. "Much as she—and we—may not like it, I'm afraid it's going to have to be inside."

A surge of humiliation flooded her brain as Khar protested. Inside like an unhousebroken ghatten. Not to be able to go outside and away in privacy. She scooped up the ghatta, cradling the limp hindquarters against her chest.

"I found an old bone during the night, jabbed me every time I rolled over until I dug it out," Mahafny said. "I think I can loosen the ground a bit over there. I don't know about you, but frankly, she's not the only one who has to go."

Scratching, hacking, digging, the older woman softened and churned a segment of hard-packed earthen floor about two hand spans wide. Doyce eased the ghatta into a sitting position, one hand still under her chest to support her. The sigh of relief was audible even to Mahafny as the tang of urine filled the air. "Thanks. I'll cover it once I put her back."

A draft of morning-freshened air knifed through the dank confinement as the leather curtain over the door snapped back, making them jump. Their visitor from the previous evening, the Erakwan woman who had brought them food, crouched in the doorway, frowning.

"Fah!" She wrinkled her nose in disgust. "No wait go ou'side. Bad." The ghatta, struggling to sit upright, caught her attention. "Oh. Unnerstan'. Sick one. Good sign den." Jerking her head toward the door, she continued, "Mebbe you wan' do same—but ou'side? One, den od'er."

"Mahafny, you have until I count fifty, so don't linger!" As badly as she had to go herself, Doyce yearned for a few moments alone with Khar'pern. Bless the Lady that Mahafny seemed disinclined to waste time politely debating who should go first.

She made her mindspeech as intimate and caressing as possible, though she wanted nothing better than to shout her anxieties. Reining in her emotions to avoid a sensory overload, she strained not to share the roiling fears within her. *"Khar, can you 'speak any of the others? Are the other ghatti close? Or at least Harrap or Jenret, they're nearby."* To have to use the ghatta like this when she was so sick shamed her, but what choice did she have? And whatever information she gained might help orient her when she was allowed out to relieve herself.

"Hurt, hurt," the ghatta whimpered a plaintive, little

lost sigh. **"You hurt, too? Can feel it."** Her obvious concern tore at Doyce.

"Yes, love, but not as much as you, and most of the hurt I feel is yours. But the others?"

"Can't 'speak far, my thoughts wobble. Hold me, please."

Doyce cupped a steadying hand under her chin and placed the other on her brow, the ghatta trembling in pain at the contact.

"Ah. Touched Jenret." Her eyes half-closed, concentrating. **"West, about . . . about seven huts away from here. I think it's bigger than this hut, lots of men guarding it. He says not to give up, that they'll figure a way to escape. And,"** the ghatta wrinkled her face, the dark stripes above her eyes crowding close, bewildered, **"do you have any flea powder in your famous saddlebags? Does that make sense?"**

"Yes, don't worry. Tell him to have Rawn or Parm 'speak me as soon as they get in touch again."

With effort, the ghatta focused, the shiver of effort tingling Doyce's fingers. **"Harrap says Lady bless us three."**

"Yes, Lady bless us three and the others out there as well. Now rest, dear heart." As Khar's eyes drifted shut, Doyce slid a cautious hand to the back of the ghatta's head, fingering the head wound. The swelling had subsided somewhat, but what did the paralysis mean? Would it last, or was it only because of the pressure on the brain? Yet they were lucky, both blessed even if she remained crippled. If Khar had lost her ability to mindspeak as Saam had . . . both of them to be locked inside themselves with no way to share their thoughts?

As Mahafny shouldered aside the flap to enter the hut, Doyce wasted no time in brushing by her. Outside at last and blinking in the sharp, thin light, eyes watering, she resolutely ignored the Erakwa captors gathered around her at a calculated distance.

"This way?" She motioned to the elderly woman awaiting her, and without stopping for an answer, turned and walked with the sun at her back, toward the west, and toward the direction of the hut holding Jenret and Harrap. How long would her luck hold?

With a show of mock impatience, the woman grabbed her arm, slowing but not stopping her for another few strides. "No, no. Dis way. Not walk t'rough cen'er of villidge. Od'er way quicker." And now the hand on Doyce's arm locked in place, implacable and restraining as a mother holding back a stubborn child from danger.

She tugged once, testing, then yielded with marginal good grace. Let them think she simply didn't know which way to take. Her few paces in the "wrong" direction had allowed her a cursory survey of the village, and the glimpse of a hut farther toward the center, heavily guarded, where Jenret and Harrap must be held. The village's size surprised her. Perhaps forty huts or more, if her quick scan had been accurate, with some huts far bigger than others, large enough for extended families. The browns and silver-grays of the bark enclosures, some edged with the green of moss, blended naturally into the landscape without a rough betraying edge. The woods crept close on the northern and eastern sides, but she'd seen cleared, possibly cultivated land along the western margin.

Propelled by firm shoves, she forced herself to march docilely east toward the rising sun, squinting against the glare as she strained to make out details. Grateful, she opened her eyes wider as the forest rose to shield some of the intense brightness. A harder shove pushed her toward a clump of chest-high scraggly bushes with crackling brown leaves, half-denuded, and she realized that this was all the privacy she'd receive. Still, better than nothing, considering that Erakwa surrounded the bushes. Sighing in resignation, rigid with embarrassment, she dug a hole with a stick and then squatted in quick relief. Exactly how Khar had felt.

The walk back was slower, less urgent, but still too short; it gave her only enough time to notice that everyone, old and young, male and female, tried to pretend she wasn't visible, or worthy of being seen. Their covert appraisal told her otherwise, as did the bristling sensation at the back of her neck. She tossed a hurried glance over her shoulder, then stared straight ahead. She and the others were an undoubted curiosity, but not necessarily a welcome or pleasant one. Behind the carefully blank, neutral faces and sharp obsidian eyes she detected fear as well as hostility, more a doomed, angry acceptance than aggressive instincts, and that puzzled her. As if they unwillingly accepted something they'd had no choice in; strange for the victors of the encounter.

The urge to run, to flee, swept over her just as many hands thrust her back inside the hut. She struggled, dug her heels in, then stumbled forward through the curtain, hating the smothering drag of the leather against her face. She stood panting, fists clenched, quaking in helpless fury as the eumedico watched without speaking. Nothing to do but wait until their time came, whenever that might be.

She settled, curiously formal, with her back half-turned to Mahafny, who sat with legs curled beneath her, one hand on the ground for support. "Well, they haven't retied our hands, so they can't believe we're too dangerous," she commented. "And we've been marginally well-treated, sheltered and fed, at any rate. The woman cared enough to try to help Khar, and it seemed to work. I wonder what they've planned for us."

Doyce interwove her fingers, cursed her unsteady hands for betraying her. "I don't know, but I still don't think it's anything good. There's activity in the center of the village—as if they're getting ready to hold a meeting." She couldn't explain her haunting feeling about the eyes, the looks, wouldn't, not and burden Mahafny with additional worries.

"Of which we're to be the main topic of conversation, I suspect. Not the possibility of an early winter, or whether the hunting has been good, or anything as mundane as that." Mahafny's voice was bleak but controlled.

The skin covering the door lifted, golden sunshine spilling through, their visitor a blocky shape against the light until the flap fell. The old woman, and again she carried food for them.

She sat, dark eyes thoughtful and assessing, and seemed to reach a decision as she hoisted herself up and pinned back the door flap so that light poured in. Then she shooed them into the patch of sun, clucking and muttering as she busied herself with ladling food into shallow bowls. Steam danced, carrying with it a nutty, sweet

scent. Both Doyce and Mahafny accepted with a nod of
thanks. The wooden spoon in each dish was flat, more
paddle than spoon, but they both set to eating without
hesitation. Despite the Erakwan's knowledge of herbs
and forest things, Doyce found she had no fear of poisoning. Whatever it was, the gruel tasted good, with a granular texture enlivened by dried blueberries swollen plump
and sugary with cooking. It felt warm and satisfying in
her stomach.

"So," the old woman commented. "So. Now mebbe
we talk. Me Addawanna." Her hand swallow-swooped
to her chest and away as she introduced herself.

Mahafny set down her half-finished bowl and mimicked the gesture as she repeated the name several times,
spoke her own distinctly, and then added Doyce's name.
Doyce's name came easily to Addawanna, but the eumedico's name seemed to have one syllable too many for
her. She frowned, rolled it over on her tongue. "Ma-
HAF-ny. Ma-HAF-ny. I go fast, it be Maf'ny." She
wagged a playful finger in the eumedico's direction. "I
go fast, you still answer Addawanna."

"You speak our language very well," Mahafny responded diplomatically. "How did you learn it?"

"Is hard langwidge. Too many words sound'n same,
mean diff'ent. Not many 'nough words to mean od'er
t'ings, 'portant t'ings." She slapped her knee with her
open palm, the sharp crack emphasizing her dislike of
the limitations. "I learn long 'nough ago when peoples
trabeled nort' in summer, to what you call . . . what?
. . . Marchmon'? Why you t'ink dat sep'rate land? Der
no mark on groun' saying 'Dis Marchmon' dis side' and
'Dis our land dat side,' and even if was, it madder?"

Twisting and looping a braid, she strove with the concept of invisible boundaries. But then Addawanna settled
back, her eyes taking on a reminiscing squint. "Young
den. Young and, oh," she conspired a merry wink, "look-
in' for all sorts t'ings, you know? Meetin' a man der,
your race, he know some my words, I learn some his.
Nights shorter 'den in summer, and we busy, busy, but
we not busy, we learn.

"No go back much. Der side, dis side. Ni'er want us
back and forth so easy. Not want us e'der place. Not

right. Both sides ours much as anybody elses. *All* ours
share first."

"Sometimes our governments decide things we don't
always understand," Mahafny guardedly picked her words.
"I know that in the old days travel between the two
countries was freer, more easy. I journeyed there myself
once long ago. But then with the new trade compacts
and with a new Monitor in charge . . ." she trailed off,
aware that her explanation sounded inadequate and almost incomprehensible to someone who didn't have
Monitors or trade agreements or the fear of invasion and
conquest, or at least the fear of invasion from others of
their own race. Land enough there might be, but not
enough for the newcomers to share, even if neither side
used all that it claimed.

"So. You no know e'der, really," she shook her head.
"If ol' woman like me not know, and wise woman from
od'er race not know, how anyone 'spect to know? Or
just pretend? Puff chests and pretend wise and knowing?
But that nod'in in prob'em now, not here."

Addawanna stared at the ghatta, speculating, watching
her striped sides rising and falling with each breath. Hating to do it, Doyce brushed Khar's side, captured one
front foot and shook it to wake her, or at least to bring
her to a light doze so that she could be called to action.

With infinite slowness, Addawanna reached toward the
ghatta and Doyce held her breath. A gnarled finger air-
traced the circular striping on her side, not ruffling the
fur. "What sort an'mul dat t'ing? It good? It bad? What
it do? Neber trap nod'in like dis. Dey tell of dem in de
o'd tales."

Could they have lived in the woods so long and never
have had any real contact with the ghatti? Possible, if
the ghatti didn't want to be seen, but the Erakwa boasted
incredible woodlore. Or had there been some sort of mutual avoidance? Doyce wanted to push the hand away,
but restrained herself. The touch had been that of someone who liked animals. "I should hope you've never
trapped any. It's a ghatta, a female ghatt. Her name is
Khar, short for Khar'pern." The ghatta purred in her
sleep.

The woman laughed, imitated the sound and the final

syllable. "Pern, pern! She big for khatt. You got big mices where you come from?"

Was the Erakwan woman teasing her? "Not cat, ghatt—or ghatta for the females. They don't catch mice."

"Den what good dey be? Big beast to be lazy."

One step at a time, she counseled herself. How much was the woman ready to accept? How much would she accept? How much before another war club smashed down upon the unsuspecting, silky furred head? If not wielded by Addawanna, by someone else in the camp. And did the ghatti have anything to do with their being taken captive—she recalled the Erakwan's face that day in the Market Square when he'd seen Khar—or had they unwittingly trespassed across some invisible Erakwa boundary of sorts, a demarcation between their world and the Erakwa world?

"They can understand intuitively," she hesitated and reached for a less abstract word. "They can understand in their hearts if people speak or feel false or true. They know if someone tells the truth or lies, or even if a person thinks he tells the truth but hides the truth from himself."

"In der hearts? Or in der heads?" A shrewd question. "Can dat Pern-khatt tell, now, if I speak right or wrong?"

"In their heads they hear and understand what isn't said out loud but thought. But their hearts tell them if it's true or false." She simplified a little, feeling it safer. "Khar could tell if you were speaking false or true if I asked her to, but I haven't asked her to listen because I think you speak true."

"Ah. But you no know fer sure," Addawanna admonished with a flick of her hand. "She no hear ev'yt'ing alla time?"

"Well, yes and no. She hears everything all the time, but she doesn't always listen."

The woman scowled. "Addawanna no un'nerstan'."

"You do it, too. When you're in a crowd of people, with everyone talking at once about different things. You hear it, but you don't always listen, you listen to what interests you, to what you want to hear. Besides, the ghatti don't think it's polite to listen to people unless it's

necessary, unless it has some bearing on finding the answer to a problem. Then they listen to what you say and
to what you think so they can discover who is right and
who is wrong. They stalk truth instead of mice."

"Dey no snatch your t'oughts away and leave you
em'ty?"

"No, no, absolutely not!" Doyce snapped, indignant
at the slur to Khar. Where would the woman conceive
an idea like that? And then with a sick certainty she
knew. Gleaners. The Erakwa must have had some sort
of fateful contact with the Gleaners. How else to explain
the unexpected attack? But what would lead Addawanna
to think that the ghatti had some relationship with, or
an ability similar to that of the Gleaners? Addawanna's
bright eyes searched her, raked over her, and she forced
herself back to the more immediate problem of gaining
the woman's trust. "If Khar did what you said, I wouldn't
have any brain left at all, would I? Do you fear seeing
what it's like?"

Addawanna rocked back and forth, one fist drubbing
her knee, her lips pursed in thought. The pounding accelerated, then stopped, and her dark eyes sparked defiance. "Try! Addawanna too o'd have any t'oughts wort'
stealing!" A wide smile slashed across her toothless face,
then she became instantly serious, on guard.

"Khar, wake up. You have to wake up, I need you."
Doyce begged and shook the flaccid forepaw again.
Scythelike claws flashed gleaming crescents, caging her
fingertip without a puncture.

"Am awake." Her voice came peevish, muzzy with
sleep, but not as weak as before. **"Am too awake. I
heard, but you shouldn't have said that without asking.
No ghatti has ever 'spoken an Erakwan before, their
brains are too prickly, like nettles, make you itch all
over. We tried to Bond once, long, long ago, and when
we bit there was a spark and a flash like lightning. We
don't know why they don't want to share minds, but we
respect their feelings."**

Doyce's heart sank. *"I'm sorry. I never thought. Now
what are we going to do?"* Being shown up as a liar
wouldn't help their cause.

Khar twisted her head, side-glanced at Addawanna.

"She doesn't feel as bristly as most, not like the one in the Market Square. I'll try. I've always wondered what they're like inside, we all have."

"All right. Are you ready?" Mahafny crossed to Addawanna and stood, holding her hand. "Now, think of something you'd like her to know—true or false—without saying it out loud and let her read the thought inside you and see if she can judge the truth, the truth that is within you."

The Erakwan gave a terse nod, and smoothly, effortlessly, the ghatta transferred her question into Doyce's mind. She breathed a sigh of relief. She answered, "No, she's not my mother."

Addawanna smiled again, but then her face froze, her hand knotting against Mahafny's until the eumedico gasped in pain. "But sometime, sometime you wish she was," she said wonderingly.

Damn the ghatta, Doyce thought with a surge of frustration, she'd read the deeper subtext of her silent answer and transmitted it directly to Addawanna without so much as a by-your-leave.

"Well, it's true."

"*Fine. Do you always tell everyone everything you know about me?*" she mindspoke back.

"Wait! She's trying again."

"Too easy. Try harder one now, no be lucky guess. Now you tell what I t'ink and tell it be true or makin' bel'efe." She had pulled free of Mahafny and sat stiffly, right hand clenched white-knuckled on a leather waist pouch, dark eyes narrowed, alert as a hawk as she stared at the ghatta.

The ghatta made a little whining noise, her skin twitching. "Oow! She's prickling! Ouch! Tingling, can't read!" Panicky, Doyce reached to stroke the ghatta, trying to reassure and encourage her. A snap and crackle of static leaped from the ghatta to her outstretched hand, enough to make her flinch at the shock. "Thank you, that cleared the prickles!" Khar sounded absolutely as surprised as she was. "It's as if they generate a flow of negative energy."

Doyce struggled to remain alert but relaxed, ready for anything the ghatta might transmit, no matter how un-

likely. Would Addawanna play devious, think a lie to try
to fool them? And then, despite herself, Doyce's mouth
curved in a reminiscent smile, as if she, too, had lived
through the stream of images Khar began to transmit,
faster and faster. She gave herself over to the sounds,
the smells, the sensations. . . .

"His name was Nathan—Nakum. No, that was the
name you gave him, Nakum, back in the meadow with
the white star flowers weaving their perfume from stem
to stem until the whole meadow was garlanded in it, and
in the smell of the tiny wild strawberries crushed under
you, until you were striped with their juices. . . . That,
that was where you conceived your daughter, wasn't it?"
Even after more years than she knew, Doyce saw the
images as vividly as if they had happened a moment ago
and she a voyeur on the scene. "And then, you'd chase
each other down to the stream. . . ."

"No more. 'Nough! Happy-sad dat you see clearer dan
me." An abrupt chopping motion cut Doyce off, and
she sat, still enmeshed in the next sequence of images,
disappointed as they flickered away from her. Khar had
halted as soon as the command was uttered.

Addawanna touched her right earlobe with strong,
gnarled fingers, setting a small, purple shell pendant waggling and twisting. "From Nakum, like yours from your
love." Doyce touched her own garnet rose in automatic
response. "You lose, too. Like od'ers here lose. Not one
of dem! One of us!"

**"It seemed right to give something in exchange. Worth
it, I think. They believe we are Gleaners, too."**

"Go now," Addawanna rose, fingers kneading at her
waist pouch as if she derived some comfort or strength
from it or its contents, whatever they might be. "Not
much one o'd woman can do, but try. Mebbe dey lis'en.
Mebbe it work." She bent to leave, then cast an indignant look at the ghatta. "I no fergit!"

"What won't she forget?"

**"That I'm hungry. You got to eat, but nobody brought
anything for me!"**

And Addawanna was as good as her word, for even
as they settled themselves back on the dirt floor, striving
to find a comfortable position, a teenaged boy slipped

inside, bearing a bowl of broth. His grin and the set of
his eyes, though not their color, a hazel-gray, convinced
them of his kinship to Addawanna. He stared hard at the
ghatta, his face intent, eyes wonder-struck. Excitement
hummed through him until, trying to appear impassive,
he turned and bolted from the hut.

The morning wore on, leaving them tense and bored,
alternating bouts of calm with nervous pacing and jumpi-
ness at the slightest noise. None of the other ghatti had
contacted them, and Khar lay asleep, conserving her energy, injured body striving to heal. An occasional tiny
snore whistled through her nose and her ears twitched at
the sound, then she would drift into a deeper slumber.
Doyce didn't have the heart to wake her. She and Mahafny roughly tracked the passage of time from the shifts
of light that poured through the smoke hole. No one had
returned with another meal, although the sun had now
reached and passed its zenith.

Bouts of talk intermingled with long silences, until
their individual silences and thoughts became too heavy
to bear and one or the other broke the stillness with a
sudden spate of chatter, only to let it dwindle and die.
For the fifth time, Doyce marched around the perimeter
of the walls, swinging her arms, forcing herself to take
measured strides. Nine across, then left turn, twenty
paces, then left, nine more, then left again and down the
final leg.

"Doyce, will you stop that? I'm getting dizzy watching
you."

"Oh, sorry. I just get so stiff sitting still." Out of stubbornness, a compulsive need for completion, she finished
the last leg of her go-round and stopped in front of Mahafny, tried to think of something to say or do as she
hooked her thumbs into her pockets.

"What have you got in your pockets?"

"I don't know. Why?"

"Why not? Maybe it's not the most exciting of games,
but we might find something useful—or at least pass the
time."

Feet planted wide, Doyce matched her actions to Mahafny's words and began to rifle through her pockets,
tossing the contents on the ground. A comb. A pencil
stub. Two lucifers. A piece of twine. A pink crystal,
something she'd picked up and carried simply because it
was pretty, though she couldn't remember for the life of
her when or where she'd found it. The melted medallion
that Vesey had worn and that she had carried with her
ever since his death. That went back into her pocket. A
few pieces of dried plums, wrapped in a twist of paper.
And finally, from her breast pocket, Oriel's leather day
book. How many days since she'd looked into it, had
read it as she tried to match her journey to his final
circuit? Her own day book lay waiting in Lokka's saddlebags; she'd been remiss in keeping it current and wondered if she'd ever have the chance.

She tossed it onto the packed dirt beside everything
else. Her final journey seemed to be following a very
different script, although the end result might be identical. She shivered.

"Is that all?" Mahafny protested, weaving the string in
a cat's cradle pattern on her fingers. "I thought Jenret
said that you carried anything and everything with you."

"In my saddlebags, not my pockets. Besides, I've provided entertainment and lunch. What have you
contributed?"

The contents of Mahafny's pockets proved equally un-
promising, either with means of escape or food.

"No folding shovel. No sacred ritual object of the Erakwa to make them worship us as gods. No secret weapon
ready to deal death to hundreds while leaving us safe,"
Doyce melodramatized as she parted her hair with her
newly rediscovered comb. How long since they'd both
had proper baths, not counting the numerous times
they'd been rained on? "The folding shovel is in my saddlebags, though."

"Wonderful. And perhaps Khar can instruct the horses
to tunnel in and rescue us." Doyce broke into a hoarse
crow of laughter, but Mahafny made an urgent shushing
sound and sprang to her feet in one economical movement. Khar had already snapped out of sleep, raising
her head and upper body, ears flicking back and forth.

"They've stopped debating and reached a decision, I think. They're coming this way!"

"Addawanna's with them. She says trouble . . . trouble ahead, but be brave, we can survive it. She says something more, but I don't know what she means . . . strange people waving things at us." The ghatta's voice wavered off into a jaw-cracking yawn of nervousness as she riveted amber eyes on the door.

Eight men filed into the hut, four on either side of the doorway. Ranging from young manhood to middle age, all were strong and well-muscled, though each exhibited bruises, ghatti claw marks and other wounds from their encounter with the travelers the day before. Initially they all resembled one another, coppery-bronze bodies, broad cheekbones, almond-shaped dark eyes, and black hair cropped just below their ears, though two wore their hair long and in complex braids. Except for the youngest, each boasted an intricately-beaded waist pouch similar to the one Addawanna wore and which they had assumed held the various simples and necessities that everyone carried. Somehow the lack made the youngest conspicuous.

The more Doyce looked, the more their individual features stood out. A stronger cleft chin and deeper set eyes on the one immediately to the right of the door. A broad, tender-looking bruise stretching diagonally from left pectoral to below the rib cage on one of the older men. The hint of a dimple on another's cheek, a jittery twitch making it visible—the craftsman from the Market Square that day, the one who had disliked Khar's presence so much. Had he journeyed back to warn that she was in the vicinity? Or had he been in search of her? They all attained separate identities and then merged, blended together again as an implacable one: the enemy.

"They're more afraid of us than we are of them. Don't press them or they'll overreact."

"Why?" Doyce queried.

"Don't know, but they especially don't like me." Khar sounded hurt. **"I can feel it, though I can't read much else. They all surge with energy, smart like teasels except for the youngest one."**

Addawanna shouted from outside the hut, "You come out now, slow-like. Bring an'mul wid you."

Doyce and Mahafny moved to the ghatta and each picked up the corners of Doyce's tabard, lifting the ghatta between them. She cried once with pain at the sudden shift and sway beneath her, and went still, eyes wide and questing. Then they ducked out the door and found themselves herded toward the center of camp, their eight guards ringed as closely as they could without touching the women.

"Harrap and Jenret are there already. They're arguing, but they stopped when I told them we were coming."

The late afternoon sun was thin on warmth, and Doyce shivered at the difference between the outside air and the stuffy closeness of the hut. She missed the heavy warmth of the sheepskin tabard over her shirt and short, boiled wool jacket. She risked a look up and over the heads of those near her, trying to surmise the two men's position, but couldn't see them, hemmed round with a crowd of Erakwa, weapons poised. At random intervals, someone from the outer fringe of the circle would peel free, rushing off on some unstated business, and another would join the edge so that a constant eddying and drifting occurred around the outside, but the nucleus remained solid and unmoving.

She craned her neck again and stumbled, Mahafny hissing, "Concentrate on where you plant your feet or we'll dump the ghatta out."

Mumbling a generalized "sorry," she guiltily concentrated on her footing, stretching the tabard corners taut, matching her pace and pull to Mahafny's. Without realizing it, they had penetrated the outside of the milling circle, drawn farther into the core, the edges immediately overlapping until they were consumed by it. Eyes cast down to watch her footing, she saw swaying legs and shifting feet, some bare, some encased in moccasins, earth with remnants of beaten down, withered gold-green grasses, and at last a pair of booted and a pair of sandaled feet. She obeyed without thought as Mahafny instructed, "Down now. Lay her down."

Only then did she trust herself to look up, up beyond the ghatta, beyond the naked legs clustered around her like golden beech trunks.

Jenret and Harrap greeted them, stripped to the waist, elbows and wrists bound behind their backs. The bruise on Harrap's breastbone stood out in livid contrast, and more bruises bedecked his upper body, arms, and face, but his smile beamed unchanged: innocent, welcoming, delighted to see them.

"Lady bless, we're most all here, then. Where that Parm has gotten to, I don't know, but I hope it's not into more trouble. And the little ghatta, how fares she? I felt her tickling my thoughts as you came along."

Although she wasn't sure what rules or strictures might constrain a Shepherd from embracing a woman, nothing could stop Doyce from hugging him. His bulk felt comforting and warm, so much so that she hated to let him go.

"A bad blow to the head's left her a bit dicky in the hindquarters, Harrap, but if nothing else happens she may make it."

"If nothing else happens, we'll all be lucky. Good to see you, regardless." Jenret spoke with difficulty out of a swollen mouth. "No, the other side this time," he muttered as Mahafny ran a swift, questing hand over it, then touched the makeshift bandage tied round his upper arm. "It's more the knee I'm worried about. Can't put full weight on it. Kicks out the wrong way when I need it," he confessed.

"So you'll have to hop off when they let us make our farewells." Mahafny knelt and began to probe his knee, knowledgeable fingers testing muscles, ligaments, tendons as he swore and tried not to pull back.

"I'm afraid it's more complicated than that," Harrap began and Jenret shot him a rancorous look. "Well, if they're going to have to watch, and it appears that's why they've been brought here, they might as well know what they're going to see," he finished reasonably.

"You see that group over there—women and children, and old men and young alike?" The Shepherd jutted a stubbled chin toward the wide, open pathway that led to the camp's center. "Notice what they're carrying: rocks and tree limbs and antlers and clubs and hatchets. They'll line up on both sides soon, and our way to freedom lies right down the middle between them all. It's called a gantlet, and we're to run it. If we can reach the far end alive, we've earned the right to depart. Their promise on it. They don't like us, but they've decided we're not evil, thanks to your friend Addawanna over there, but they're still angry that we killed some of their people yesterday."

"But that's impossible to survive! Nobody could survive that!" Doyce shouted. "That's like giving you no chance at all!"

"It's a chance, and a fair one, by their sights. They'll untie our hands before we start, and if we grab anything to defend ourselves with as we go along, that's part of the rules as well."

"Except that I can't run more than a step or two without my knee buckling, so Harrap's got to run twice as fast to make sure one of us escapes and can escort you both out of here," Jenret muttered, intent on the gathering crowd. "They promised that much."

Harrap butted his shoulder against Jenret's, tears of consternation in the Shepherd's eyes. Who to leave, who to try to save? "I've told you I'll hang back, shelter you as much as I can, pull you along with me."

"And lose your own chance for freedom and theirs as well?"

Mahafny inspected one face and then the other. "And I take it if neither of you finish this, this thing, that Doyce and I stay on?"

"Yes." Harrap gave an exploratory pull at his bound wrists and subsided. Despite the outer sheathing of fat, his arm and chest muscles stood out in stark relief.

"What if I run in Jenret's place?" Doyce pounded at Harrap's shoulder for attention. "I'm fast enough for a short stretch." She already bounced on her toes, ready to sprint at the first sound.

Jenret turned his back to them, surveying the group lining up in readiness, yells of anticipation and anger rending the air. " 'Fraid not, my love. By invitation only." He whirled back to face them and his knee buckled. "Damn! Rawn! Where are those ghatti? Can Khar pick up any word?"

Khar mewed a negative, and sat as upright as she was able, dragging her useless hind legs across the tabard. **"Nothing. Not a thing!"**

"Well, we'd best do what we can to stabilize Jenret's leg." Mahafny surveyed what was available and shrugged. "Doyce, it's bound to be tough and the devil to cut, but can you manage some strips from your tabard? Here, I've still got my scissors. And give me your belt while you're at it."

Doyce hacked away, fingers cramped and pinched by the effort of forcing the tiny surgical scissors through the heavy fleece and leather. She stopped, rubbed at the angry red indentations on finger and thumb and went back to work. Khar twitched a hind foot out of the way as the scissors came closer.

"See! It moves! Not much yet, but a little!" The ghatta sounded plainly gratified, and with good reason.

Hope flared high for a moment, but then Doyce damped it. *"That's wonderful, but don't push yourself too hard or too soon. Besides, don't let the Erakwa know you can move until you have to."* Lifting her head, she realized that she had a helper: the lad in his early teens who had visited the hut before, the young Erakwan with the gray-hazel eyes who so resembled Addawanna.

He held the strip of leather and fleece taut and to one side, giving her more room to maneuver the scissors. The light hazel eyes seemed to ask for her permission, and at her short nod he reached a tentative finger and touched the ghatta's front paw. Khar gave a tiny purr of amusement and batted back, shifting her weight to balance, but not a claw flashed. "Purr-fur," he rolled the "r's" with a flourish. Looking sidelong at Doyce, his hand crept toward a white hind foot, then he nodded to himself and withdrew without touching, his eyes meeting hers, then shifting away conspiratorially.

"Doyce, hurry up with that last piece! I think they're about ready." Mahafny struggled to wrap and bind Jenret's knee, lashing the joined belts over a padding of strips from the tabard. With luck it would immobilize the joint, allowing Jenret clumsy but relatively solid movement. "Well, it will either support you or cut off your circulation. How does it feel?" She tugged harder on the end of the belt and drew it snug, watching Jenret's face to see when she should slacken it.

Hesitant, Jenret took a few practice steps in the mea-

ger space allotted by their captors, tried a sharp pivot
on the bad leg and stayed upright. It was awkward and
unwieldy; his entire leg had to swing in one straight,
unbroken line for him to take a step, but it held firm.

"Better, much better." He bent to graze Mahafny's
cheek with a kiss. "I think they're about ready to take
us to the starting line." He laughed, then his face twisted,
the features of a scared little boy showing through. "If I
don't make it to the finish, stop by and explain to
Mother. And take care of that one, too." He raised his
chin in Doyce's direction and a quirky delight brightened
his face. "She's a pure weathervane for pointing toward
trouble, but she makes life interesting!"

They stood at the starting line now, arms untied, waiting for the chieftain's staff to fall and begin the race.
Doyce judged the course to be about two hundred meters
long, a quick sprint under normal circumstances. But
this, this was like running into the maw and down the
gullet of a giant, fanged beast. Erakwa, young and old,
male and female, lined both sides of the path, deathly
silent but intent with anticipation. And armed with any
weapon that came to hand. A little boy of no more than
four struggled with a windfallen branch nearly as big as
he and had already jabbed two of his neighbors with it.
Farther down on the opposite side, a young woman with
raggedly hacked hair and an ash-stained face streaked by
tears grimly hefted a more serviceable—and dangerous—
club. Raw anxiety ate like acid as Doyce recognized one
of the new-made widows, courtesy of Jenret's sword during the battle. She clutched hard and felt Mahafny return
the pressure, hand ice-cold.

Against the sea of coppery skin the two pale, naked
backs, both sheened with nervous sweat, one broad and
sheltering, the other slighter but well-built and powerful,
looked incredibly vulnerable. Harrap shouldered himself
onto Jenret's weak side, ready to drag him upright if the
younger man faltered or fell. All movement froze as they
readied themselves to spring forward as soon as the chieftain's painted staff reached the end of its tortuously slow
descent. The old man's arm quavered in the air, frail
wrist shaking the staff, making it tremble and hesitate in
its downward course, dangling the temptation of a false

start. Every eye locked on it as it jerked and quivered,
and slowly, slowly descended. Doyce moistened her lips
and began to pray.

"Now, now, now, now!" The voice was mild but menacing with its precise and careful articulation. "We can't
have that. Wantah, stop that. Did you think I'd let you
play with them just because I let you capture them?
Whatever did you think you were going to do, trade dam-
aged goods to me? This wasn't part of our bargain." And
the chieftain drew back, not dropping his outstretched
arm but bending it so that the staff's tip returned to its
starting point, and his opaque eyes dropped in ill-
concealed loathing. "No, not after I've led them this far
with such solicitous forebearance."

Doyce broke free of Mahafny's grip, whirling to look
behind her, aware in one corner of her mind of her feet
tangling, the crash to one knee. The quality, the timbre
of the voice rang teasingly familiar, although the articulation was not. The sight, despite years of training as a
eumedico, made her blanch. A survivor of a major catas-
trophe, that much was readily apparent.

A tall man, long of trunk and long of leg, dressed in
tight black leather, but unlike Jenret's garb, there was
nothing elegant about it, simply utilitarian. He sat a deep
chestnut stallion with black mane, tail, and stockings.
The whiteness of his hands and face and throat offered
chill contrast to the dark shirt, and much of the whiteness
of flesh consisted of pale, shiny scar tissue; it flowed
down the whole right side of his face and neck, ropy and
twisted in spots, smooth and glistening in others with the
luster of satin. The right ear was nubbed like a blighted
ear of corn, barely there, and the lashless right eyelid
was glazed with scar, while the mouth on that side fused
and curled at the corner, thus explaining the man's need
for careful enunciation. The nose had escaped damage
except for a splash of scarring along one side.

The scarring ran down his neck and as far down into
the open throat of his shirt as she could see. Indeed, she
suspected it ran down the whole length of his body on
that side, for the hand on the right curled clawlike, the
thumb still working opposably, but the fingers welded
together, several end joints missing. The right moccasin

looked overly stubby and short as well. Young, old, she
had no inkling, but on the whole she opted for young
from the unmarred hand and the unscarred portion of the
face she could see. That, and the voice. But the horror of
his appearance became commonplace next to the white-
furred apparition that materialized out of nowhere to rub
seductively around his horse's hocks and then spring up
in front of the man. A ghatt, the white of bleached
bones, with black stockings, a black muzzle and deep
pink eyes, the color of the ripe heart of the passion fruit
from the Sunderlies. The total reversal of normal coloration increased its horror. It half shut its eyes and
yawned once in their direction, patently clear that boredom was the least thing on its mind. Its long, lashing tail
writhed like some white, deadly, snake. The scarred hand
reached out and imprisoned it long enough to make its
command known, and then dropped it. The very tip continued its insolent flick.

"Well, little mindmate, what do you think?"

The ghatt rilled deep in its throat, and Doyce shivered
in unison with its cry. Despite its broad, nobly shaped
head, its wide chest and slim flanks, its perfectly set ears
and intelligent eyes, she felt she had never experienced
anything so innately evil in her entire life. It simply *was*,
not through choice or will, but by its mere being, a
wrongness pulsating from within its own heart and brain.

She cast about wildly for Khar, desperate for a sense
of contact, for a rightness of being, and saw only the
empty tabard. Empty, no nesting, weak ghatta there.
And if not there, where? She pushed blindly at the chests
and shoulders surrounding her, mind spinning crazy patterns of fear. Not anywhere near this, this *thing*, she
prayed. She sucked in a breath, started to mindspeak,
almost not daring to trust herself.

"Hush!" The one word struck with force, shaking her
on her feet. Urgent, demanding, and utterly final. She
could feel Khar sever their communion as if the umbilical
between minds had been cut clean, a total separation,
and Doyce prayed for the ghatta's escape.

"What?" The man shook his head as if to clear it. The
white ghatt and the scarred man regarded each other,
clear puzzlement on the part of one and incomprehension

on the other's part. "But I thought *you* said something. Well, never mind, then." The ghatt sat still, pink eyes even more intent.

"It's nice, of course, to have you all together now, my four stalwart, faithful followers, tagging after me for so many leagues, and their four equally faithful ghatti, so committed. Of course, capturing *them* was quite a coup." The claw of a hand rose in a casual half-salute, half-wave of command.

At the signal four men trotted in from the forested side, each pair carrying a stout pole over their shoulders. And from the first pole hung Rawn and Parm, feet lashed together, heads dangling, tails limp, and from the second pole, alone, Saam. Each lolling head exposed the vulnerable throat, ready for slashing. But most pitiful of all was the limp crescent each body created, from dangling tail across the long broad arc of the back, then the sudden drop and course of the extended neck and head.

"Four, damn you! I said four! Where's the other one, the little bitch, the ghatta!"

With a sobbing moan, Harrap pushed his way toward the ghatti, Jenret in his wake, swinging his stiff leg and cursing in a low monotone. At yet another signal from the rider, Erakwan after Erakwan tackled the Shepherd, clinging with dogged determination to whatever part of his body offered itself to their grasp. He moved slower and slower, as if wading though ever-deepening water, until at last he was dragged down a good ten paces ahead of the lighter, slimmer Jenret, who punched and kicked and fought his way down. As Harrap toppled beneath the wave of Erakwa, they heard his last despairing, desolate shout of "Parm!"

Now, before it's too late to distract him, before you choke on the fear rising in you, before you and everyone else are helpless, paralyzed by fear of, of, this *thing*, this being, and his equally macabre ghatt! Face contorted, frenzied fists pumping the air, Doyce screamed, "What have you done to them? You can't treat Seekers this way! Are you mad? What have you done with Khar? Where is she? If you've captured us all, why isn't she with the others?"

The face, so whole and handsome on one side, so horrifically scarred on the other, turned and regarded her performance with interest. "Ah, yes, you. Dear little Doyce, so many years, hasn't it been? Since you last took an interest in me, that is. I suspect you take more of an interest in that ghatta than you ever took in me. But then, I now know what that's like, don't I, Cloud?" The disfigured hand toyed with the white ghatt's ears, translucent in the sunlight.

"Ah well, losing her is unfortunate, but no matter, really. I did assume that you managed to spirit her off since my men couldn't find her. After all, I gave them *explicit* commands, and they know better than to disobey me. Even inadvertent disobedience requires . . ." he rolled the words with sensuous pleasure, ". . . corrective measures. Even my direct interest in them is more than they often like . . . but then . . . they've no choice. As you'll soon find out, won't you, Doyce?"

"Who are you? How do you know my name? And how do I know you? I've never seen you before in my life." Heart hammering, Doyce stood, hands clenched behind her. Not that it fooled him, not in the least, she knew it, and knew with sick certainty that he relished seeing her tremble.

"Oh, no, that's not quite true." She sensed a more than mild enjoyment in his correction. "You've seen me before. Not like this, of course. But you used to take quite an interest in me . . . once. And I'd like my medallion back now, my dear stepmother."

"Vesey?" The world windmilled around her, swooping and diving, rising and sinking, until she thought her stomach would rebel. Her eyes blurred at the swirls of blue sky, brown earth, green forest, the earth's colors muddling themselves into the dire hue of fear. But the black and white of the dark-garbed man and pale ghatt stood out in stark, searing contrast, untouched by the whirling in her brain.

"Vesey?" Belief and disbelief rose and fell in the same swooping pattern. "But you're dead! The fire . . . consumed you. We couldn't even find a body to. . . ." And comprehension dawned, petrified her until all she could do was stare, helpless, at the good half of his face, the face that did resemble a younger, handsomer Varon, the

voice that had tickled her memory with its timbre and
quality.

"No, you couldn't, could you?" The tone offhand, almost conversational. "But the headstone beside my
mother's was very touching. Too bad, though, that you
had to bury her murderer, my father, on the other side.
And that squalling brat of a baby on his other side.

"Now, the medallion! Give it here!" The insistent
voice struck lightning-hard at the core of her being. And
she let herself crumple to the ground, drawing the safe,
soft blackness around her for comfort and escape. The
image of Khar flickered, then blurred. If she didn't know
where the ghatta was, and he didn't know . . . then, well
. . . she must be safe. And no one could track either of
them in the darkness, she prayed.

Cradling the Appaloosa's right forehoof in his hands,
Parcellus jerked his head and grunted to indicate the
loose shoe, two nails gone, a third loosening. Sarrett hovered beside him, teeth chattering, nose red and dripping,
arms wrapped tightly around herself to ward off the cold.
She shuffled her feet to warm her toes, felt only numbness. Lady bless, but the higher they rode into the Tetonords, the colder it became, as if the laws of nature
and the seasons had accelerated their cycles to match
the extremes of towering, foreboding peaks and sheer,
boulder-strewn slopes they traversed with such excruciat-
ing care.

Frankly, nature had intruded more than she liked or
understood. She thought about the events of the last
three days and her heart sank yet again, though she'd
sworn it couldn't fall any lower. First, the shortcut that
hadn't been a shortcut. They'd argued about that,
whether to chance it or not, and she'd won out, so anxious to press on. "Terrain's got to be worse," Parse had
warned, tracing his finger along the map. "Stick with the
main road, it may not be much of one but it's all we've
got."

"But we can save nearly a day," she'd protested, and
remembered her wheedling tone, "Please, Parse. Trust

me on this one." Well, trust her he had, and look where
it had gotten them. The middle of nowhere, or close
enough to it. And then to have Finian bolt with half their
supplies . . . damn all anyway! It had all seemed so clear
and uncomplicated, absolutely right in the cozy library,
like some childhood tale of noble rescuers.

The thought of the wolves still spooked her almost as
much as they had Parse's gelding, Finian. The ghatti had
alerted them to the wolves' presence, warned that they
were running a doe, and they had stumbled onto their
kill, the doe crashing down, entrails ripped and steaming,
but still clinging to life. The wolves had drifted off like
woodsmoke, growling and snarling in their direction,
loath to leave their kill but uneasy near the riders. Parse
had sprung down, planning on putting the deer out of its
misery, when one of the wolves angled closer, canines
bared, tongue lolling, yellow eyes predator curious. The
nearness, the feral wolf smell, the scent of blood—with
a scream of panic Finian had reared and bolted, Per'la
tossed into the air, scrabbling and twisting to right herself
as she'd landed. They could hear the sound of the horse
careening through the trees, crashing and galloping back
the way they'd come. They'd spent half a day calling and
searching, but the horse had vanished.

Since then they'd ridden double, but the trail snaked
too steep and rough for Savoury to carry the weight easily, so they'd shared the walking turn and turn about.
Sometimes both walked to give Savoury a good rest.
They'd all but gained the road they should have remained
on to begin with—and now this. Sarrett looked around
with growing despair. Per'la and T'ss lay curled up on
the gear stripped from Savoury, their coats fluffed with
the cold, tiny plumes of breath white in the air.

"Shoe's not going to hold much farther. We'd best
walk her until we reach the next village." Parse pulled
out his map, uncreased it against Savoury's side, dirty
finger marking their route. "At this rate, we should reach
it tomorrow morning. Not this evening as we'd hoped,
but there's no choice now that we can't ride." Parcellus
sneezed and Savoury twitched at the indignity of the sudden spray. "And this is a cold, definitely. Not an allergy.
You needn't have shared your cold with me." He hadn't

complained about losing Finian, but he grieved inside, prayed the horse was safe. He'd not complained, cried "I told you so," or betrayed by a word or a gesture his dismay at their situation, just gone on as best he could. But the cold made him pettish at last.

"Would you rather have slept alone and tried to keep warm by yourself? That was a freeze, not a light frost last night. We had every blanket left on top of us plus the ghatti—and you have cold feet!" Sarrett snuffled miserably, hated the bickering, hated herself for having gotten them into this mess, for not having apologized. Parse relented enough to hand her one of his handkerchiefs, increasingly precious as the supply dwindled, gone along with the better part of their food on Finian's fleeing back.

"How can Doyce and Jenret keep going in this weather?" she wondered. "And how can we possibly catch up with them like this if we go at a crawl? The ghatti can't seem to raise them, the mountains distort their mindspeech, they haven't a clue as to where they are now. We've got to reach them and warn them what they're up against! To blindly tackle Gleaners . . ." she trailed off, swallowing hard and refusing to finish her thought, though she could see her apprehensions mirrored in Parse's strained expression as he envisioned exactly what she did—friends and compatriots as walking, empty shells, minds snatched and discarded like so much chaff tossed into the wind. While they limped along like the blithe innocents they were, thinking to offer assistance. It galled her that they were two babes in the woods, literally ready to make themselves a bed of leaves.

Dusting his hands on his pantaloons, Parcellus unslung his canteen from his shoulder, unstoppered it and took a sip. "Here, it's still warm. Er . . . at least it's not stone cold." The last of their cha.

"Well, I am." Pale gold hair straggling from beneath her red tam, she shook her head. "If they don't have a smith at the next village, perhaps we can buy horses and stable Savoury there until we come back. How much money did you bring?"

Slapping his head, jaw dropping, Parcellus clutched at

his waist pouch. "Lady bless and keep all fools—including me—I forgot to bring . . ."

"Any money," she finished for him.

"Well, he remembered everything else," Per'la consoled, snuggling tighter against T'ss, her wide peridot eyes even wider and rounder with indignation over the slur against her Bondmate. **"And he knows when short-cuts aren't shortcuts,"** she added with a ladylike private hiss in Sarrett's direction.

Sarrett let herself collapse in a heap, holding her aching, stuffy head in both hands. "And what I have won't go far, we've spent some of it already on food."

"Riders coming!" T'ss and Per'la both sang out, springing to their feet. They danced and boxed in mock combat, excitement barely held in check. T'ss whirled after his own tail, then stopped short, gave his spine a lick as if he'd planned that all along.

"That's something to be thankful for, but why such joy, my purrling friends?" Parse asked.

"You'll see. You'll see. Just wait!"

"Either bandits—in which case we've nothing much left to steal—or rescue for the rescuers. Well, since there isn't much else we can do, we wait." Untying her bedroll, Parse shook it out. "Come on, Sarrett, up. Get this under you. Too cold to sit and wait on the bare ground like that." Smoothing the blanket, he sat, drawing Sarrett under his arm. Per'la and T'ss threw themselves across their laps, all feline grins and knowing superiority.

By the time the riders swung into sight, Parcellus's and Sarrett's roles were reversed, Parse asleep with his head on Sarrett's shoulder. As the first three trotted around the western curve of the trail, all she could see were their silhouettes' dark outline against the vibrant orange-gold of the setting sun. The crest on the helmets cut sharp and bright as a flame-edged sickle.

Guardians! The helmets meant Guardians. Her heart dropped stone cold toward her growling stomach as she calculated the reception awaiting them. Roughly shaking Parse awake, she wondered if they were on business of their own or if their business was finding them, ordered to bring them back after their precipitous—and unauthorized—departure. To be fetched back now. . . .

T'ss and Per'la made elaborate stretches, rumps high and forequarters low, extending each hind leg in tandem. Per'la shook herself, long, silky hair flying free and then neatly settling into place, for all the world like a coquettish maiden plumping her flounces.

"Company! Koom and Chak are here!"

"What? They can't be here. Why didn't you tell us they were coming?" She began to primp as well, tucking loose strands of hair back under the red tam, pulling her rumpled jacket down, smoothing her tabard with chilled fingers. The full import of their statement began to sink home, making her worry about the Guardians nothing compared with the trouble about to break loose. She stabbed her elbow into Parse's ribs to catch his attention and realized she'd jabbed him harder than necessary because of her own frustrations.

He looked ready to jab her back. "And since it's unlikely that Koom and Chak would be traveling alone, that means the Seeker General and Rolf are with them." He'd obviously put two and two together faster than she. She should have expected it.

T'ss groomed his ruff, caught up in the primping as well. **"Well, naturally,"** he reproved, surprised she hadn't made the immediate connection. **"Chak and Koom said not to mention anything further."**

Parse rubbed his ribs, all sleepiness gone as he edged around Sarrett and began to fold and tie the bedroll, packing their gear. More riders swept into view around the curve. "Dear Lady, did Swan Maclough bring the whole Guard after us? We're in for it now! And we never even managed to reach Doyce!" .

Sarrett counted under her breath as more dark figures were highlighted by the sun's backdrop. "No, hardly the whole Guard. But too many just to retrieve us; perhaps enough to go after Doyce and Jenret and do some good. Do you think it's possible?"

The Seeker General halted her bay beside them. "Well, prodigals, you've made a good start but a poor end from the look of things. How lame is Savoury?"

Sarrett stood stiffly, almost at attention, refusing to meet the Seeker General's eyes. "Loose shoe. If that were fixed, she'd manage."

Clanking in his ill-fitting armor, Rolf joined them, taking the bridle of Swan's horse so she could dismount. Parse stood transfixed by his strange garb, the bronze and leather helm sinking over his eyebrows, his face even more angular and pasty gray below it. The heavy wool Guardian's cloak, the breastplate and arm guards made him appear the exact opposite of military.

"Enlisted or drafted, Rolf?" Parse asked, tremulous with suppressed laughter and nervous apprehension.

Sarrett ignored the banter as the Seeker General swung down, Rolf catching her waist though it took each of them balancing the other for her to gain her footing once she touched ground. Her face had lost its noncommittal mask for the moment, and Sarrett felt the weight of her tired, strained expression, saw the new worry lines and the old ones deeper and more pronounced. Better to know and get it over with, she decided. "Are you sending us back?" Koom's face wrinkled in warning and T'ss echoed him in her mind, cautioning her not to push too hard.

A narrow smile, strained at the corners, creased the Seeker General's face. "Mercy, no, not as long as you're all right." She shook her head as if counseling herself. "I've discovered some things that even I can't command—such as love and friendship. That kind of defeat I must learn to take gracefully. You've as much likelihood of obeying me as your friend Rolf here. He was told to stay behind. Would that I had friends as loyal to me as you three are to Doyce and to Oriel's memory.

"Now come along. We changed mounts at the last Guardians' station and picked up a pair for you when Chak alerted us you were up ahead. Parse, if it's any consolation, Finian's stabled there. They found him about half a league from the station, so we realized you'd hit trouble."

Parse's face lit up with relief. "Thank you! But where are we going?"

"The same way you've been headed, the same location, though I hope without the sort of detour you attempted." The Seeker General motioned to the sergeant to supervise the changing of mounts, and the grizzled man exchanged a companionable wink with the older

woman as if they shared a long-standing private joke.
"Of course, if we fail," she continued, "you may all three
find yourselves permanently drafted by Balthazar here."

Thumbs hooked into his belt, Balthazar looked them
over, cool and considering before he spoke. "Mayhap I'll
become a Seeker, then, rather than cope with disobedi-
ent troops." Rushing to forestall Parse's impertinence before it left his lips, Sarrett jammed her elbow into his
ribs in exactly the same spot as before and his nervous
giggle died unborn. But this time he jabbed back.

❖

Her legs hung lead-pipe heavy, dragging from her hip
sockets. Something or someone was sending bursts of
dynamiting pain up and down her spine at regular racking
intervals, and her hands were swollen again, immobile
behind her back, unable to push her body upright. On
the good side, the comforting smell of horseflesh and the
heat of the beast radiated against her chest and face.

"Lokka?" Doyce whispered, not sure if she wished the
little mare into the hands of these people or not. Still,
the reassurance of the horse's presence was a minor
blessing of sorts. "Lokka?"

The mare broke into a curvet, jouncing Doyce even
more painfully. "Whoa, girl, whoa, gentle down." Fire
lanced through her body as she commanded spasming
calf and thigh muscles to grip Lokka's barrel and ordered
her own back upright. To her amazement, it came, and
since that did, her head followed, although she'd lacked
faith about the natural progression working. She tilted
her head back, limbering neck muscles, rolling her
shoulders.

Itching to wipe the sleep crust from her eyes, she
looked around, wished for an instant that she hadn't
come to, but there was no choice. Lokka dance-stepped
again, tossing her head from side to side for attention,
trying to nuzzle her rider, now erect and balancing, despite the fact that her feet hung stirrup-less, tied at the
ankles with a band that ran beneath the mare's belly.
The mare halted and turned her muzzle toward Doyce's
knee until a rider pounded up behind them and slashed

at Lokka's soft nose with a short whip. Doyce clapped
her with her knees and urged her forward, murmuring
consoling pet names, wanting to stroke the stinging
muzzle.

Nightmares she'd had before, in her sleep and waking
ones as well, but none approached the one she found
herself in the middle of right now. And then the answer
made her guts clench, warp with panic. The dreams!
He'd been shaping her dreams, her nightmares ever since
Oriel's death! But why? And how had he found her?
Bitter bile burned as it cascaded up her throat, and she
threw her head to the side just in time, the stream spattering the rider on her right who cursed and pulled his
horse wide.

Vesey! Vesey, not dead. Who had somehow escaped
from the fire which had killed Varon and Briony and left
her near-mindless with grief and remorse. Vesey, with
the childish, unformed abilities of a Gleaner, already lethal at that stage. Now the child had reached manhood
with who knew what powers tapped or untapped at his
disposal? And unless she missed her guess, powers that
had been molded and trained in a very special direction
and for a very special purpose. Amplified and molded
from his own losses and hatreds, or molded by others to
fit their needs and his?

He rode at the head of the line, black-clad back
straight, right shoulder hunched higher than the other.
The strange white ghatt wreathed himself around his
neck and shoulders, stared back at her with its throbbing
pink eyes before slithering down like a wisp of steam—
or a cloud, its name. The only ghatt she'd ever heard of
with a human word for a name, a name not chosen from
its own private language. Cloud, a commonplace word,
yet menacing now.

Mahafny rode directly behind Vesey, bound similarly
to Doyce, except that her hands were lashed in front of
her for stability, although she had no control over the
reins of her horse, held by the rider beside her. She
risked a glance over her shoulder and relief surged
through her as she spied Jenret and Harrap bobbing
along, bound as well and with riders on each side of
them. But where were the ghatti? A pack horse with

wicker panniers on each side might hold the answer. And still no idea as to where Khar was, except that Doyce gave thanks the ghatta wasn't a part of this group.

About sixteen all told, she thought. Four of them and twelve of the others that she could count. On occasion, she caught the flash of a body at the forest's edge, paralleling the rough track they followed. Erakwa serving as Vesey's outrunners, legs carrying them as tirelessly as the horses did the group surrounding Doyce. It couldn't be possible, but it was. They seemed to absorb strength and endurance from the very earth they rushed across so effortlessly.

But no need thinking about what you can't understand, she chided herself. The real puzzle seemed to be that the Erakwa had not appeared happy to see Vesey and his group or to do their bidding. An uneasy alliance, if alliance were the right word. Indeed, they acted cowed by his presence, a reaction she could well understand. Near dusk now, not long before all she'd be able to see were Lokka's ears in front of her, if she were lucky. No more glimpses of the Erakwa then.

"Where are we headed?" Wondering if she could coax the information from the man who rode at her right, the one she'd nearly thrown up on. He had a generously hewn face with rough-molded features, a bevy of pockmarks across his chin and lower left cheek. Unlike some of those riding with Vesey, he lacked their bland, placid looks, his deep-set dark eyes reflected intelligence and worry. His sober jacket marked him a cut better than the others, as if he might be next or second-in-command to Vesey.

The dark eyes deliberated whether to answer or to continue riding in silence. With the shift of a chewed lucifer stick from one side of his mouth to the other, he finally responded. "Hospice. Where'd you think?" Not a hint of malice or meanness in his words, merely a faint surprise that she could believe it might be elsewhere.

"How far is it?"

"Near two days' ride, full two at a normal pace. We'll rest in a bit. We rode straight through to reach you at the camp, and the horses are weary."

"You, too, I'd think."

He spat the matchstick with an explosive sound. "Some, yes. Me, *him*," he nearly capitalized the word, "and the new one he's just coaxed into the fold, love to know what glory he promised him. Others, it don't matter, they don't much feel anything good or bad. Wouldn't mind if we ran 'em right into the ground. They'd not notice."

A strange description that left her pondering; she rode on in silence, unaware of the sidelong looks the man cast at her. Once, during her training as a eumedico, she had known a man who fit his words. A gifted artisan, a potter who made formless lumps of clay sing with the fluid lines and shapes he brought to them. But he had suffered from extreme bouts of depression and rage, smashing his creations, doing damage to himself and to his family during those bouts, which extended over longer and longer periods of time, until sometimes there were no gaps, no interludes of good humor, creation, or pleasure in life.

His distraught family had brought him to the eumedicos for treatment. Every kind of drug, both natural and chemical, had been tried with no success until finally the eumedicos recommended surgery as the only solution. And so they had operated on his brain, severing certain connections, and he had survived.

But not as the man of before, not the man of depressions, or the complex artist whose spirit lived in his creations, bonded from fingertips to the graceful curves and glazes of the pottery. Now he was placid, even-tempered to the point of doltishness, obediently following any instruction or directive without thought or heed, a living automaton. Faced with a lump of clay, he cast it into beakers or mugs or crocks, whatever was requested, and every piece came out serviceable, ordinary. Objects, not embodiments of genius.

Once they had left him making crocks and forgotten to collect him in time for dinner and beyond into the evening until they realized his bed lay empty. They had rushed out, white coats billowing mothlike in the evening air, combing the grounds, the outbuildings—only to find him still in the workshop, unfired crocks stacked, tilting off every shelf and counter, crowding across the floor, a miniature earthenware army blockading the door. His eyes burned red-rimmed with fatigue, face and body masked with a second skin of dried powder, fingers shriveled from the moist clay, the last pots streaked with tiny lines of blood like decorations. Had they done right by him, she had always wondered? She had wondered what they had seen in his mind to make them do the surgery, but now she knew precisely what they had "seen"—nothing. The first chink in her eumedico armor.

As if fearful that he'd said too much despite her silence, Doyce's captor jerked Lokka's lead rein and moved them forward at a faster pace, bringing them closer to the front of the line. But almost imperceptibly, they began to drift back, the space widening between them and the leaders.

Gauging that the man wanted yet didn't want to talk, Doyce controlled herself to wait for the right moment. She counted her heartbeats, something to concentrate on instead of the cramping of her feet and legs, muscles tightening like ratchets against the pull of her ankle bonds, the pinch at her wrists, and the faint throb of her head and shoulder, almost an old friend by now, given the length of time it had been with her.

"So," she said to no one in particular. He made a similar sound, almost in exhaled relief, and waited. "So. Do you have a name?" she asked.

"Ya. Guess there's no harm in your knowing." He reached out with a broad palm and stripped a handful of needles from an overhanging pine branch, then opened his hand, watching them sift downward. "Towbin. Towbin Biddlecomb."

"I'm Doyce Marbon."

"Ya. Know it. You be related to *him*." Again, the almost inadvertent emphasis on the word "him."

She frowned, shook her head. "Not by blood, no. I married his father after his first wife, Vesey's mother, died."

"And a right pretty pickle you got yourself into, I'd guess."

"You could say that," Doyce acknowledged. "But why are you and the others with him?"

The sudden flex of jaw muscles made it clear Towbin wasn't happy the conversation had taken this turn. He

fumbled the reins and started to tug at Lokka's lead and
Doyce feared he would speed them up again, draw closer
to the lead for safety or anonymity.

There was pain and sorrow, a haunted look in his eyes
that craved her understanding, begged her compassion.
"Because of my wife. Ah, Lady bright, I love her so!
Fool for love, they say." His eyes softened, gentled at
the thought. "They promised to help, to cure her.
They're not, they're using her," the words came tumbling
out. "And'll use her worse if I don't bide by their rules.
You see, she's a . . ." And then his face drained white,
twisted with pain, beads of sweat popping out along his
temples and hairline. He swayed, eyes pinched shut, then
righted himself as he cast a baleful look at the head of
the line, a tiny tear clinging at the corner of each eye.
"Right! Never forget who's in control." He clasped his
head with both arms as if fending off imaginary blows,
groaned, then whimpered, "Sorry, sorry, sorry!" like a
small child pleading for forgiveness. "Mayhap it's better
to have your brain sliced and rearranged or sucked
clean," he concluded to himself, and Doyce strained to
catch his words. Towbin said nothing more during the
rest of the ride, his face averted and anxious.

She gave the camping arrangements that night a rating
as rudimentary but adequate—as long as she ignored the
limited food, piercing cold, ignominious bondage, and
the high, childish laughter of men with partial brains, still
a better, purer sound than the shrilling giggle emanating
from Vesey at the far side of their camp area. Gnawing
ruminatively on the stale half loaf provided her, along
with some hard, mold-spotted cheese best described as
antique—and not as a compliment—she tried to conquer
the feeling that her flesh wanted to crawl away as if it
planned to abandon her, flee separately. Every time
Vesey laughed it wanted to escape a little farther. Not
without the rest of me, you don't, she told herself.

Mahafny sat a little way off, hands still bound in front
of her as Doyce's now were, eyeing her similar piece of
cheese, then tossing her shoulders and gamely taking a

bite. Though they sat near one another, they were not close enough to speak without being heard by the others, nor could they narrow the distance without alerting their captors. She'd tried it already. Both she and Mahafny wore rope around their waists that ran up to the binding on the wrists, and was then tethered to one of the placid but very solid individuals who sat close by, backs to them, but facing a glowing fire. Perhaps later, she thought, if they both took care, they could creep closer and talk.

Harrap and Jenret sat on either side of a fallen log, chained to it by manacled wrists. The first man to dismount at Vesey's signal to halt and make camp had taken a long iron spike with a broad flanged head and driven it through a link of the chain and into the log with the butt end of a hatchet. How they planned to free them in the morning preyed at her nerves, plagued her with visions of them carrying the log wherever they went, dragging between the two like a corpse.

In the early confusion of dismounting and setting up camp, she'd managed scant time for a few words with Jenret. Untied at last, Mahafny's legs had played tricks on her when she'd dismounted. Crumpling to the ground, she startled her horse and caused a flurry of distraction until Towbin had cuffed some of the placids aside and hoisted her upright. Still astride Ophar, Jenret kneed the horse beside Doyce as she stood, or rather, leaned against Lokka while she exclaimed and tried to put weight on one foot, arch cramping, toes curling toward the sole of her foot, impossible agony within the tight confines of her boot.

"All right?"

She nodded and concentrated on shifting her foot, increasing the pressure to make her toes expand and spread, looking downward, pretending he wasn't speaking.

He gave a low, gravelly chuckle which turned into a cough, face reddening above the dark stubble as he tried to conquer it. "Good Lady bright!" He sounded breathless. "Next time I'll volunteer to run the gantlet. It has to be easier. Is that really your stepson?"

"Yes, that's Vesey."

The dark circles under his eyes emphasized their bright

blueness, and the fear that lodged there. "Then Lady help us all, because I don't know what we can do against him. Cornered and trapped with or without the bonds!"

And with that Towbin sprinted over and grabbed Ophar's bridle, the resentful stallion jerking his head as he led them away. For the first time she saw Vesey's other lieutenant, the one who had ridden beside him all day, only his back in her view. A ripple of shock and revulsion surged through her. Unbelievable! She'd shouted his name without thinking, "Georges! Georges Barbet!" as he approached and seized her by bound wrists, pressing a dirt-smeared hand along the back of her neck as he steered her forward. She'd never seen him this dirty and unkempt before—yet his face glowed with an expression of luminous exaltation—as if whatever burned so brightly within left such external concerns as cleanliness in ashes.

She strained to talk over her shoulder as he shoved her along. "Georges, how did you get here? Have you joined Vesey? What in the merciful heavens is going on?" Wasn't he going to speak, respond? The words died in her throat until all she could manage was "Georges? Oh, poor Parm. . . ."

The name made his mouth twitch in a jerky parody of a smile. "Oh, yes, Parm." The words sounded thick, as though he'd become unused to speaking aloud, but then he began to regain a conversational cadence. "Oh, yes, poor Parm. Stupid ghatt! Not to know, not to understand that it could be greater than ever before. To flee like that when we could have attained so much more, once I'd found the way to explain things to him." He paused, eyelids fluttering as if he dreamed, "He was the only bulwark I had at first, and we needed each other so. . . ."

"Well, then explain to me," she cajoled, hating the damp touch of his hand on her neck, wanting to fling off the over-familiarity.

"So long ago when I was a child, hearing voices, hearing voices in pain from inside, needy for help, and not knowing what I could do to help them, though I could tell what was wrong. Mum always said not to worry about the voices, that it was natural we could hear them, we were descended from eumedico stock and should be proud of our skills, tender with them to others because someday I'd learn to be a eumedico and everything would come right. Until then I should, I *must* keep quiet about what I could hear because people didn't understand, and hated what they couldn't understand—us.

"I didn't understand either, and it was such a relief when Parm chose me, because at least I knew where his voice was coming from and what he wanted of me. He made the other voices seem more distant." His fingers pinched up just behind her ears. "Only the two of us in my thoughts, almost like being alone. And I didn't want to be a eumedico—the pain, the blood, the agony. Not after all I'd heard in my mind. No, not that, being a Seeker was better."

"Then why change, why stop?" she gasped. "Parm ran away in sheer terror, afraid not just for his life but for his mind."

"But don't you see?" Barbet sounded petulant. "We needed him with me. They wanted Oriel and Saam to experiment on, but not me and Parm, we're too valuable for that, what with both my abilities. There are at least fifty of us who can hear voices, read minds, people at all levels of skill, and what the Seekers have relates to it somehow. The eumedicos will help us find out, they do Vesey's bidding, *must* because he and the eumedico who can mindspeak make them toe the line, just as Vesey keeps the rest in line. There's so much to learn before we reach the culmination of our abilities! And once we do, we can go forth and remake Canderis as it should be! As it was meant to be! A true sharing amongst all minds!" His voice rose. "And you've no idea what Vesey offers, what he does inside your brain, the feelings, the sensations! Agony at first, a ravishment, then a rapturous bliss exploding within you!"

They had halted where he indicated, and he'd kept his hand in place, squeezing at a pressure point in her neck to force her to spin around and face him. "The sensations!" The haunted look on his face turned sexual, and his hand began a long, tantalizing slide around her neck and crept toward her breast, toyed with a button along the way. His eyes darted ferret-fast and nervy with lust as he shouted invective and instructions toward the two placids with Mahafny, his hand still in a stealthy creep. She backed a half-step, and his narrow, fine-boned face, the features now pronouncedly wizened, swung in her direction, as if just realizing her presence. With deliberation, he grasped her shoulders and molded her tight against his body, kissing her, his tongue lingering in her mouth like a slug. One hand shifted to her breast and began working it like a doorknob. She wrenched her mouth free and spat, wishing she dared do it in his face. And the most chilling thought of all was that she served only as convenient vessel since his beloved Vesey was not available.

"Later," he crooned. "I'll be back later to make you understand. No, stay still while I get your hands tied in front of you. Too bad, if they stayed tied behind, it'd make it easier later."

It was taking a chance, but she didn't care. "I rather think Vesey may have other plans for me, and I doubt they're similar to yours. Should we check, do you think?" Every muscle in her body vibrated with loathing and exhaustion, but she cherished the momentary glow of triumph, warming herself on it. Not like this, not now, not ever with Georges if she could help it.

"What he doesn't know won't hurt him!"

"And you think he doesn't know everything you do? In fact maybe you should wonder what—or who—made you act like that just now. Go ask Towbin how he got his leash tugged earlier. I daresay you know the same feeling yourself—or you will soon. And then how long before that exquisite pain and new knowledge in your brain leaches to nothingness—like those placids over there? Why should you be different? This isn't a game of Tally-Ho with Vesey, where you count points, calculate odds, chalk it on the board."

He scowled, but the skin around his eyes stretched taut with apprehension. She wondered if she'd struck home at all, made him ponder what lay beyond the now, on whom the next experiment might be tried. "Later," he mumbled, but this time it was less a threat and more a compromise to save face.

And now she was sitting here, hands tied in front of

her, wondering if it were safe to eat a piece of bedraggled cheese. Why not? After all, what were the odds? If Mahafny could eat it, so could she. She wrinkled her nose, peeled the rind with her teeth and nibbled a tiny chunk, considered spitting it out, but as its sharp taste mellowed on her tongue she decided it wasn't really that bad.

What she desperately craved—yet didn't—was the opportunity to speak with Vesey, but her desire swung back and forth like a pendulum. When, not if, was the question, because she surmised that he, in his own way, longed for it as much as she. She managed another, bigger, bite of cheese, then brushed bound hands against her side pocket, relief trickling through her as she grazed the lump that meant that the misshapen medallion still lodged there. So, he hadn't taken it from her yet, hadn't had Towbin or Georges search her pockets to reclaim his treasure while she lay unconscious. If he'd waited this long to reclaim it, what could one night more or less matter to him? But serving as its custodian might offer her added protection against Georges.

Her continual worry for Khar hemmed her closer and closer, the pressure of her absence routing Doyce's other fears. She yearned to try to contact the ghatta but dared not for fear it might alert Vesey to Khar's whereabouts, assuming she lived, was any place near. The conscious and continual restraint of an old, familiar habit wore at her heart and mind. Nor did she dare try to contact the other three ghatti, stone silent, drugged into a stupor. As if reading her thoughts—what a stupid thing to think, she berated herself, of course he was, with or without permission to mindwalk—Cloud drifted over and stood observing her.

Almost without volition she opened her mind to receive his thoughts. Realizing the stark danger, she snapped up barriers, reeling with the protective backlash, then damped them down bit by bit as she regained control. The pinkish-red eyes throbbed in intensity like a pulsing, open wound, and she willed herself not to be swallowed up by them.

Just as her defenses started to crumble and cave in, the ghatt gave a head-splitting yawn that squeezed his eyes closed, then craned his neck from side to side, regarding her with mincing little sideways glances. Interesting, she had at least forced him to yield some sort of grudging respect, whether for her or for the medallion.

Instead of words, an image jolted her mind, an image of a white ghatt with black muzzle and feet and carnelian eyes stalking a bird. Capturing it, it began to play, tossing it, shaking it, growling through a mouthful of feathers, batting its trembling form from paw to paw, always there to thwart its pitifully elusive gestures. Finally, bored, the image ghatt stalked away, ignoring the broken, bloodied body's anguished fluttering before its tiny heart burst.

"**Like to play,**" the ghatt crooned. "**Yes, such fun.**" He angled his neck, preened himself. Then, almost as an afterthought, "**Vesey likes to play, too.**"

The last bite of cheese lodged in her throat, its pungency melting down her gullet so that she swallowed convulsively. Oh, please, don't let me see any images of Vesey's play, she begged her brain. Self-control, self-control, block the conversation, end it, you *have* to be able to do that.

"**Oh, you can, you know.**" Cloud walked away, tail waving in sinuous S-curves. He stopped, sniffed, and backed up to spray a protruding rock. "**My mark. Mine. But you can't stop him from reading you. He has been, all this time, you know. He's had his mark on you for a long time.**" He stretched his head back for a final look. "**A good thing for you that you really don't know where that stupid bitch ghatta is.**" An obscene snigger and image seared her mind as she mindblocked a fraction too late.

How could she have been hungry earlier, she wondered as she stared blankly at the uneaten bread and cheese, fighting against the rising nausea that clenched her stomach muscles tight. The bread and cheese got thrown over her shoulder, better to let some animal or bird have it—unless she'd served up unwitting bait to lure some other innocent to Cloud. Activity, walking, was what she craved, to escape in any direction, walk until she could break into a blind run, until she could fly, flee. She tried an experimental tug at the rope connecting her to one of the placids, and he turned, gave her a half-wave of greeting, a blank, bovine smile on his face. She tugged again, harder, and this time a frown marred his bland features. He ran astonished fingers over his face, as if imprinting the unfamiliarity, then waggled an admonitory finger at her, looking in surprise at his moving hand before it wandered back to his food, a plate of some sort of stew. She smelled with clarity the separate components of potatoes and carrots and beef and gravy, the last things she wanted assaulting her nose. She turned away, hunched her shoulders as if that could blockade the smell, and saw Jenret and Harrap, pinioned to their log, using it as a pillow while they spoke in undertones to each other.

Cloud's words replayed themselves through her mind. Ominous and yet not in the least unexpected. He didn't need the ghatt to transmit thoughts from one human to another. Vesey could read thoughts and leave them intact, not merely snatch them away in the usual crude Gleaner fashion. Unprecedented, never done before, despite the eumedicos' years of pretense, not to mention efforts to discover why and how it happened. A skill that the eumedicos had once had, after all, and not lost if Georges were to be believed. It was simply that those who possessed these skills were not eumedicos. Had Vesey learned by himself or had he had help? Had the fire wrought some sort of change in him?

She sat, gnawing the back of her wrist, thinking, calculating. Depending on the skills of those who followed him, fifty were enough to hold off any army, control any country the size of Canderis, twist good intentions or bad ones. Were there others scattered through the land as well, unallied with Vesey or unaware of their powers until his clarion mindcry drew them to him? No way of knowing until it was too late. And if Vesey were sane, then she qualified as mad.

Then, something she didn't want to think of but had to, based on her eumedico training and on the last obscene image Cloud had taunted her with: how often would a trait like that breed true from generation to generation, or was Vesey unique? Damn the eumedicos to the furthest reaches of hell if they thought this a nice pristine experiment, able to be controlled or destroyed at their whim? Vesey was living proof of that. Microscopic slides didn't begin to hint at the reality. Eumedicos! She glanced in Mahafny's direction, sighed—still impossible to move close enough to share her thoughts and fears with the older woman, and she felt bereft, alone.

A commotion in the camp's center by the fire distracted her as a horse and rider appeared out of the night, flanked on either side by an Erakwan, one a full-grown man, the other a slight youth whom she thought was Nakum, Addawanna's grandson. Nothing but dark center and light-fused edges since horse and rider positioned themselves between her and the fire, staring into its flaming heart.

The neat, economical dismount, no excess motions, tweaked at Doyce's memory, reminding her of someone, and her ears caught the rise of light, dismissive, feminine laughter. The two Erakwa drifted away, back to their forest and their own camp, and the boy—Nakum, she *was* right—contrived to slip past her as they left. The faintest wink in an otherwise studiously impassive face, the cupping of right hand over left arm, crooked to his chest as if he held and stroked it with his free hand. Could it be possible . . . ? No, not with the Erakwa's feelings about ghatti.

The woman, yes, clearly a woman now that she had shifted to the other side of the campfire, greeted Vesey—always a cautious distance from any flame, she had noticed that throughout the evening—and then bent to talk with the placid who anchored Mahafny's rope leash. He nodded, an eager head-bobbling, and rose, reaching for a torch. The two walked in Mahafny's direction to where the eumedico dozed, unaware of visitors.

The thrust of the lighted torch and a sharp-spoken word woke Mahafny and she clambered to her feet, ungainly for the first time Doyce had ever witnessed. Overnight she had begun showing her age and more, tired, gaunt, worried, on the raw, tattered edge of self-control. Doyce gasped as the younger woman shifted, and the torch illuminated both faces. For the face reflected Mahafny's mirror-image, if a mirror could subtract thirty years and present a smooth, faintly supercilious expression accentuated by dark, winged eyebrows and a smooth coiffed chignon of dark hair.

"Hello, Mother."

"Hello, Evelien." From whatever scant inner resources she hoarded, Mahafny drew herself straight, reflecting her daughter's pose, shoulders back, defiant chin-set. Her voice, when she spoke again, held no tremble of fear, and Doyce mentally applauded her. "I'd ask what brings you here, but I fear I already know."

"You don't know even the half of it, Mother; you never have, even in your wildest imaginings of scientific breakthroughs and glory for the eumedicos, the glory you thought lost and gone so many long years ago." Her voice swelled with an evangelical fervor and suppressed triumph.

As if rousing herself from deep thought, Mahafny managed a bleak smile. "No, I daresay I don't, but I presume you've come to enlighten me. Or have you come merely to gloat?"

Evelien's words tumbled over themselves in her eagerness. "It's been too many years for that. I cured myself of that desire a long time ago, when I realized that I could live without caring whether or not you noticed my existence, could thrive without your approval." She stood, challenging, clenched hands on hips, as if trying to lay old ghosts to rest.

"But not without my love, because you've always had that, no matter what you thought. Because no matter what you were or what you weren't, through no fault of your own, I've always loved you."

"Perhaps you have, Mother. You always were one to stick with outmoded fashions rather than changing with the times. With your scientific ability, your training, your mind, you could have had *anything* you wanted if you'd been willing to take the final step to reach the top. You could have headed the Research Hospice here, leading the way in pure and applied research, discovering new breakthroughs. But you wouldn't dare the final step, too human, too frail, so I did. I control and direct them all now. And I've learned more than you and all those dreary eumedicos on their dreary, daily rounds could ever hope to discover!"

"I'm sure you have, but to what use have you put it?"

Again her words crowded together with a hectic animation, as if she were seeking approval. "You've seen Vesey, you've seen and talked with him. What do you make of him—of his gift!"

"I'd say that further research and investigation are necessary before I make a determination." The winged brows shot upward. "Perhaps you claim his ability as well?"

"No . . . not yet, not fully." The admission chastened Evelien. "Just glimmerings at times. It will take even more years of training before I can begin to approach his ability and power." And her look of self-chastisement was banished by a lustful smirk, sated with self-satisfaction. "But wait until you see our children and the abilities they will have as their rightful heritage! Even now I carry his child! There's no doubt from my studies, based so helpfully on yours, that the child will inherit that ability; the gene's recessive. So often it's masked. When it is, the most you can hope for is someone with Seeker abilities or the paltry empathy of a eumedico. Cousin Jared and I were sheer chance that two separate marriages managed to match recessive genes. This was planned to make the most of what Vesey and I both have."

"Perhaps your studies are incomplete, inconclusive. Have you thought on that? Have you ever wondered why so few of you are born? Or live to maturity? Nature often rectifies its own mistakes. Perhaps you should think on that." No loss of control, no emotion breaking out of bounds, but Doyce watched aghast as Mahafny raised bound hands and deliberately slapped her daughter across the face. "I pray to the Lady that I not live to see the day you pervert your child's innocent talents—if it lives."

Rigid with anger, color rushing to her stinging cheek, Evelien spun on her heel to leave, the placid stumbling out of her way. "Don't worry, Mother, you may not have to."

Mahafny abruptly sank to the ground, silvered head cushioned on folded wrists. Warily, Doyce crept toward her, testing the amount of play left in her leash. Good, the placid controlling the other end had shifted, moved

back from the fire and ceded her a few precious lengths.
She reached feather-light, afraid to startle, and laid her
hand on Mahafny's shoulder. She could just reach.

Quivers as regular as waves riding in to shore rolled
through the eumedico's body. When she cringed from
the contact and raised her head, no tears marred her
cheeks, but her face looked as if it were made of eggshell
porcelain, crazed with fine lines, ready to shatter at the
faintest touch. Doyce held on hard, willing her touch to
quell the shivers that traveled up her own arms like a
lightning conductor, absorbing them into herself to dissipate them.

Without conscious thought, Doyce felt herself carried
back in time to her last night with the eumedicos, the
night she knew she would leave because she had learned
the secret, learned it and refused to perpetuate it as a
eumedico: eumedicos could not mindspeak their patients,
but must always adhere to the mystery. Now the mystery
stared her in the face. How she had cried, frantic at the
loss through that long bitter night, only Mahafny by her
side, holding her, patiently trying to ease the tight-wound
mind and body in any way she could, the kisses, the
stroking, the furtive loving, knowing it gone forever after
that night. And now, in this dark, chill forest, people
existed who could do what the eumedicos had claimed,
but at what crushing cost to the world?

Mahafny's words, fluttery as a night moth, brushed her
ear. "Beware, be very careful. She's beyond both of us
now, and your Vesey is far beyond her in his powers. I
love her still, but Doyce, do whatever you have to do,
whatever you *must* do to stop her. And to stop him."

"I will, I will," she promised, as if the litany of words
had power to comfort and make it come true.

"So this is what the search for knowledge brings," Mahafny whispered to herself, and the elegant stalk of her
neck bent lower, the tears streaming free at last.

Doyce continued to sit, outstretched hand on Mahafny's shoulder until her arms ached and grew numb while
her mind spun round with thoughts. At last, she pulled
her bound hands to her chest, curled up and tried to
sleep. What wry comfort to know that any more dreams
she might have were courtesy of Vesey and not her own
strained imagination.

PART
SIX

PART SIX

Nakum trotted to Addawanna's side, matched his pace to hers, puffing as he strove to keep up. Thumb hooked under the strap, he heaved the sling over his head as his grandmother bent her neck to receive it. With a clucking sound she settled the sling sack against her waist and kept running, Nakum valiantly trailing in her wake. "How feel?" she hissed over her shoulder.

"No make any sounds, inside head or out," he answered, breathing a little easier now that the burden had been shifted over. "Awake, eyes so big, but no speak."

"Not khatt, how you be feelin'?"

Lacking breath for more words, he grasped hard at his pouch, the newness of it, the honor of it enough to overwhelm him, making him want to dance, to sing. Earth-born, earth-taster, earth-strength! And as he clutched the sacred pouch, his strength flowed back, not as much as he needed but some, enough to keep him going. "Better," he allowed. "Harmony take time, time to flow and grow."

"True. Few be honored so young. Still need grown yourself, no jest strengt from Earth." She tried to keep her face impassive, not let it beam with the pride she felt, but she knew he could sense it, basked in it as much as he did the honor of the pouch-gifting. "You go, join

459

od'ers behind for bit, slow-slow guard behind. No shame bein' young, learnin' gift. 'Sides, I want mindtalk with dis khatt, see she speak me."

"I go. Come back la'der, take purr-fur again." Nakum turned and began a slow jog to the rear of the line, rather than waiting until they caught up with him. Long boyish legs jumped and lashed the air once in joy, then settled into a steady, ground-devouring pace.

Addawanna's braids swung as she shook her head, watching him run, then she turned her attention to the sling sack. Making a tickling, scratching sound along the bottom, she traced up to the mouth of the sack. A white paw flashed out and tapped her. "You, Pern-khatt, we carry you dis far and you no talk us?"

Pointed ears, one with a gold hoop, the other with a garnet rose stud in the tip, and a pink nose poked out of the sack, sniffed the air in all directions. **"You wish me to touch your mind? You won't sting me?"**

The Erakwan woman looked puzzled, gave a nasal sound of disgust. "Why Addawanna hurt? Bring dis far, no leave you wid man who snatches thoughts. Dat be easier dan dis."

Khar twisted around, tried to look up at the woman's face. The constant bouncing and jouncing hurt her head, made her back and hips ache. She despised her weakness. **"But before, didn't you see the sparks, see my fur stand on end? When that happens I can't read you, not when you defend yourself like that."**

Loping at a ground-eating pace, Addawanna thought, clasped at her pouch for concentration.

"Raow! Ooww! Stop!" The ghatta's eyebrow and muzzle whiskers, the edges of her ears, glowed and pulsated with a sparkle of blue light, crackling and jumping. The light began to radiate down her spine, zigzagging, illuminating the inside of the sack.

Thunderstruck, the Erakwan stopped short, dropping her pouch as she pulled open the sack with both hands, stuck her head inside. "How do dat?" Her face looked suspicious. "No do again! Light gib us away!" She tapped a reproving finger on the ghatta's nose and jumped at the surge that leaped to meet her. Then she began to laugh with no sound. "I know," she said, triumphant at her discovery. "You be caught in earth power, earth flow! You like lone, tall tree in meadow when lightning look for place to strike-zap!"

"Well, whatever it is, it hurts!"

"Ya! Good fer you, make khatt strong, no tired, like Erakwan." The thought seemed to amuse Addawanna as she began to run again, but then her expression sobered. "What we do, what you goan do stop all dis? We no help jest 'cause we like."

"I don't know yet. I have to think." The ghatta struggled in the sack, twisted to a more comfortable—or at least a less uncomfortable position. Carried along like a helpless ghatten! But she didn't care, would accept any indignity, as long as she remained near to her beloved, and she knew that Doyce rode just ahead, trapped by the dream-man, the dream-man that she had cuffed from Doyce's dreams because he had no place in some of them, had usurped a place beyond the one he deserved. She rested her chin on the edge of the sack opening, felt the steady jounce as they covered the ground, and began to worry the problem.

She had known with a visceral instinct the moment Vesey had appeared on the scene, known the truth before Doyce had. And had known without knowing how or why that she must escape, must sever herself from Doyce for both their safety. Their survival for the time being lay in separation. Crawling on her belly, stumbling, limping, one hind foot curled and bent so that she walked on the top of her foot, not her paw pad, she had slipped between Erakwa legs while everyone stood frozen, distracted by the coming of the dream-man. Without warning, arms had scooped her up, and she had begun clawing, writhing to escape until she had recognized the scent of Nakum, a fear-scent as desperate as her own.

He dodged, hid, ran, clutching her to his chest, the new, beaded pouch hanging from his neck crushing into her side. "Not find, not find!" His breath came in spurts, heart pounding as he kept chanting under his breath, "Not find, not here! Not here, not find!" She felt marginally safe, the crooning setting up a fragile protective film around them, shadowing them to near-invisibility, though she could feel the impulses snapping, crackling, radiating

out from the pouch he wore and knew she dared not try
to 'speak him, no matter how friendly he felt. They had
hidden in a dense windblow until Addawanna had found
them. Now they ran with the group that escorted the
dream-man and Doyce and the others, cautious word
going up and down the lines to be ready, be alert, that
perhaps now they could break Vesey's hold on them.

Thinking came hard, trying to overcome the rhythmic
swaying of the cocooning pouch, the desire to close her
eyes and sleep. But she had pieced it all together at last,
shamed by her gullibility, her innocence in assuming that
she could sense, could know the truth. Her Bondmate
had not lied to herself, but had been lied to by Vesey's
crafty recentering of each dream around himself. Oh, he
had been circumspect after that one dream where he did
not belong, took only true dreams and tainted and
twisted them, loosening doubts and fears. But she had
found his bolt hole now and would watch and wait. One
thing more she must do, must attempt, before she rejoined Doyce for better or for worse, for life or for
death. Whether it would work or not, she had no idea,
but she would try. **"I will contact the Elders!"** she mindspoke the words to Addawanna.

The Erakwan woman chuckled. "Ah, good, you done
t'inking? Be long time but Addawanna know you t'ink
of somet'ing. Be sure, but not so sure when! Who be
Ed'ers?"

**"Ancient ones, both living and dead, the wisest of the
wise. Ancestors of ancestors, who forget nothing of our
memories, our history, that which makes us ghatti."** She
hooked her claws into the sack opening, pulled herself
out further. **"We have to stop, please. I can't do it if we
keep bouncing."**

"Mm, mm, umph," Addawanna sounded reluctant.
"No good stop, best move like breeze, always stirring,
never seen."

"Please," the ghatta begged, pressed her forehead
against Addawanna's arm in a friendship touch.

Decreasing her pace, Addawanna moved out of the
line of her brethren who ran with her, waving them on.
They ran without looking back. Addawanna swung the
sling sack to the ground and Khar crawled out, wobbly

and dizzy with the sudden solidity beneath her feet. The ghatta gave a long, shuddering sigh.

Addawanna stroked her head, down the striped sides. "Be hard reach des Ed'ers?" She cocked her head for an answer, keeping her hands well away from her pouch. "Dey a'ways lis'en for you? What if od'er one hear you cry for help? What den?"

"They always listen, but they don't always answer." Khar acknowledged, licked down her flank rather than look the Erakwan woman in the eye. She gave a minute twitch and shrug, resettled the fur along her spine, spiked out of place by the friction from the sack. "As to what happens if the dream-man hears me . . ." she left the thought unfinished.

"Den Addawanna gib him somet'ing else to notice, if he notice at all." She sat cross-legged, her back to Khar, and continued talking over her shoulder. "Dis pouch, it strong, not strong as he bein' strong, but can distract, hide a bit. I sit here like so, hold pouch tight, like shield, you t'ink hard to Ed'ers. Bed'er all round, you t'ink fast, Pern-khatt!"

The name touched the ghatta, made her realize her responsibility not only to Doyce and to the ghatti, but to this woman as well, a woman from a race mindblank to the ghatti until now, but now offering a heartfelt alliance that endangered her as much as them. "Ready!" she sang out and sensed a sheeting of pale blue light rising up, shielding her as Addawanna clutched the pouch with both hands, concentrating on drawing the earth-flow up and out through her until Khar feared she glowed like a beacon. No time to worry about that, not now.

She let her mind soar up, up, struggling until she felt her mindthought catch the updraft of power as a hawk turns effortless circles in a rising thermal current of air. Yes! Into the power, climbing the first spiral. "I will sing for you, Elders," she chanted. "Sing the mindsong loud and clear without missing a note, make the mindpattern complete and whole—with or without your aid! I come here not to beg, not to ask your aid unless you freely choose to give it, and then I will accept it as my due—for I am ghatti and now I see the Truth!

"Yes, I allowed it to hide from me before, thought that

the Truth only resided within when it lurked without, menacing. **Truth is all around us and within us; I was blind before, but I am not now! I do not know if I contain the wisdom to destroy the dream-man, the one who would destroy minds, would destroy Truth, but I will try! I will sing for you of Truth and of the love I bear for my Bond, so listen, oh Elders, listen!"** And the ghatta sang the pattern brave and true, as she spiraled upward and upward, not drawing breath until she finished.

"When Truth is . . . found . . . found . . . found . . ." came the echoes back at her. No mockery in the echoes, just whispers, whispers of the past. No answers, no promise of aid.

The ghatta Khar'pern sat up straight, ears twitching, twisting to catch any possible word. Then she gave a grim little ghatti smile. **"Very well, then. I have sought and I have found only myself to depend on. It may not suffice, but I will not know until I try. And you cannot stop me from trying."** With slow unconcern, she spun herself back down the spirals, took pleasure in each sweeping glide of Truth revealed, hugged it to her tight, returned to the present, saw the blue glistening around Addawanna falter and fade.

"I have communed with the Elders, Addawanna, and I thank you for your help." The prickling didn't seem as fierce to her this time, perhaps she was becoming accustomed to it.

The Erakwan woman slumped, let the pouch drop into her lap while she wiped sweat from her face. "Dey answer? Dey help?" she asked, the metallic glow of her coppery skin dulled and lifeless.

The ghatta considered her response. **"Yes, they answered."** And so they had, telling her that only she could save Doyce. **"You are tired."** Her heart ached for the strength the Erakwan woman had so willingly given to protect her. How could they continue on now? And the selfishness of the thought shamed her, but Doyce was her overriding concern.

Addawanna rose on unsteady feet, shook the sling sack on the ground to reveal the opening. "No be too bad. Strengt' come back fast. Use pouch for ou'ward power to guard, no strengt' for me. Use pouch way sup'ozed be, Addawanna fine." She managed a faint, tired smile. "Jes' no talk Pern-khatt while hold pouch now—den you know prickle like neb'er know afore!" She shook the opening of the sack. "In, in, quick now!" Khar dove into the sack and turned herself around, popped her head back out the opening.

Pounding along on moccasined feet, Nakum caught up with them. "Smell power in air," he chided. "Hope od'ers," he gestured toward the trail, "not sense. I carry purr-fur for while, let you rest. You take Nakum place behind, I run ahead." And with a heave and a jounce he swung the sling sack into place and was off, running, overtaking others of the rearguard in his path. The ghatta began to consider her strategy.

The tugging at waist and wrists awoke her, insistent as a fisherman reeling in his line. She fought to throw the hook, ready to dive into the safety of sleep, into rushing waters of escape, but was inexorably reeled to the surface again.

"Good morning," her placid made the words a beamish singsong. "Get up now. We're going home."

Grabbing the end of her tether, Doyce hauled herself to her feet. "We're not going anywhere until I've relieved myself. Nature does call."

"Oh." He stood, mouth half-open in thought, head lolling on the thick neck. "But we have to go. Now! Come on!" He tugged her along toward the horses, not looking to see if she followed.

Doyce skipped ahead a few steps to gain some slack, got a handhold, then stopped short, heels dug into the ground. The rope snapped taut, and her captor halted in dismay and gave a hesitant tug, for all the world like a child discovering his pull toy snagged in the rug. Soon a harder tug would follow, and she braced herself. "No! That isn't nice. *He* won't like it, *he'll* be mad, and then I'll be in trouble! It hurts, hurts!" His voice wailed upward with the last few words.

"Towbin," she called, "come do something about this!" She strained to maintain her balance in the tug of war, felt a foot slip treacherously. As soon as the placid realized that all he had to do was exert his full weight she'd be finished. Harrap and Jenret watched, still linked to their log while one of their captors worked a small pry bar to lever out the spike holding their chain in place. Jenret's attentive face and quirked eyebrows told her how much he was relishing the scene she'd created.

Towbin strode over, the eternal burden of second-in-command written on his face, duty sparring with common sense. Vesey waited at the far end of the clearing, mounted and ready to ride, Cloud frolicking around his horse's hooves.

"What is it? We've a long way to go before we reach the Hospice, and the weather doesn't look promising." He paused and jerked his head in Vesey's direction, whispered, "And *he's* more than ready to leave. Don't thwart him or we'll all pay for it."

Pity, anger, exasperation left her waspish. "Well, we can all be on our way 'home' as your friend so nicely puts it, if you'd be kind enough to provide us females some scant privacy and a chance to relieve ourselves. I assume even the wondrous Evelien needs to do that on occasion?"

Towbin smiled in sudden comprehension. "Not used to having women with us. And the Honorable Evelien returned to the Hospice last night. Sorry, but make it quick."

First Mahafny, drawn and silent, then Doyce, did so, and Doyce thought of the same scene the previous morning when they'd been held by the Erakwa. Captivity, regardless of the captors, promised a level of indignities she hadn't even begun to imagine. It made her wonder if the Erakwa still served as lookouts, out-runners for this last leg of their journey? Somehow she didn't think their service willing, not from their reaction to her group and their fear of Vesey. But then, Vesey had power—literally—to command, and the Erakwa had been forced to learn that lesson somewhere along the way.

Fastening her trousers, snugging her belt in a notch, she saw Cloud materialize at her feet, insolently kicking dirt over the urine-soaked patch of earth.

"I saw you. Vesey saw you."

Forcing her mind not to respond, she skirted around the ghatt and trudged back to the placid, tapped Towbin on the shoulder since he studiously stared the other way, and headed toward Lokka. The yearning to have Khar by her side slashed sharp as any knife-wound, and she banished the thought from her mind. Why wish her fate on the ghatta?

The voice lanced her mind. *"No, Doyce. Frankly, I doubt that you'll ever see her again. Too bad for you, of course, and too bad for me—I'd have dearly loved watching Evelien dissecting the bond that you two have made. You should see her with her scalpel and probe in hand, the triumph of discovery glowing in her eyes when she dissects a new circuiting connection."*

Her head jerked as if slapped, and she could feel the blood draining from her face in panic at the casual skill with which he probed her thoughts. The misshapen medallion in her pocket seemed to burn like molten metal through the fabric to brand her hip, then cooled as icy cold as she felt.

"Later, Doyce, later. I'll reclaim that which is rightfully mine later, never fear."

Towbin shared a grimace of sympathy as he gave her a leg into the saddle, then lashed her feet together again.

The air hung heavy and damp with chill, the sky slate gray with unshed, wet snow. She could smell it on the air. Early in the season for it, but not impossible, not this far north. The very highest peaks on the next ridge already wore a pristine shoulder cape of white on the sheltered sides. It might or might not linger long, but it signified the first brief kiss of winter, tucking the earth to sleep, a fitting shroud for her as well.

The granite ridge they'd started across was barren except for lichen and occasional stunted, twisted spruce with a look of wind-whipped misery, their needles scant and tattered from continual battering against the bare rocks by mountain winds, an eternity of flagellation with no penance in sight. Again she thought of the Erakwa, of the gantlet, of how they could blend with the very earth, even here. How they seldom revealed themselves and yet always stayed abreast of the horses, hidden yet ranged all around them, their tireless, coppery legs pumping away, attuned to some perpetual earth rhythm she could not detect.

The sheltered slope they now aimed toward bloomed richly luxuriant by comparison, with gnarled, sturdy trees, the lower trunks stripped bare from the weight of past snows and the desperate foraging hunger of elk and mountain sheep, but a lively green nonetheless, as if adversity spurred their growth in this relative pocket of safety. She longed to linger.

She rode, miserable, nails turning faintly blue as she clutched the pommel for security, then raised her hands and fumbled with numb fingers at the top button on her jacket and tried to tug her collar closer and higher. Lady knew, she despised the sensation of her legs dragging like useless appendages, rope pulling snug at her ankles, chafing and wearing the good, serviceable leather. Mintor would never have to worry about finishing her green boots, and somehow, now, in the midst of everything, she longed for them with all her heart—their promise of a future in which to wear them. With an effort, she stopped thinking about the boots, concentrated on poor Lokka, ragged and rough groomed, a bit gaunt, perhaps, but someone had obviously had a care to her in the night. That, at least, was something to be thankful for.

Growls and squalling sounds tearing from the panniers at increasingly regular intervals overwhelmed the steady clop of the horses' hooves. It sounded like music to her ears for it meant the three ghatti had regained consciousness. She cast her mind out to 'speak them, but could make no sense of anything, their minds roiling, still muddled from the drugs. That they were still bound she had no doubt, or their rapier claws would have shredded the panniers like wet paper. No effort had been made to exercise or feed them, but then, there was no way to docilely walk a ghatt hell-bent on revenge. That Saam and Rawn and Parm still lived offered reason enough to rejoice, although it didn't begin to compensate for the pang of loneliness she felt for Khar, abandoned or dead somewhere.

A scream raw with rage and frustration echoed from one of the panniers, and Georges Barbet rode beside the uneasy pack horse, wielding his cudgel against the bas-

ket, drubbing it like a drum until the horse panicked and
veered. He laughed and dropped back into place, but
his face spasmed with guilt as the basket heaved and
shuddered, the lid threatening to spring free before the
ties stretched but held.

They rode higher and farther north, past a glacial lake
dark and dead gray as tarnished silver. "Bottomless,
that's the legend," Towbin muttered at her, and she shivered with a jolt that disturbed and broke the pattern of
regular shivers which ran through her body. An easy way
to lose an enemy, sunk forever in those depths, but that,
she decided, presented too easy, too humane an ending,
and put it out of her mind. Morning stumbled toward
noon, although there was little enough to see of the sun
to prove it. The land lay encased by a domed sky-bowl
swirled with pearly gray and whites, sometimes a pearly
tracery of pinks or lavender like the nacreous interior of
a sea mussel. The sun sporadically reconnoitered the
cloud cover but could find no one place fragile enough
to break through.

They rode, and still they rode. She willed her mind to
wander blank as the sky, watching the action eddying
around her through her own private haze. If an idea, a
plan, broke through, it would be as welcome and unexpected as the sun. On a whim, she kicked her mind into
action, looking for something to stir her interest and
involvement in the scene around her. Then an idea
floated her backward in time to the childhood game she
and her sister had played on the long, endless ride to the
twice-yearly weavers' mart, the wagon laden with bolts
of her mother's woven cloth, the ox plodding and slow.

"You count the red cows on the right, Doyce, let your
sister count on the left," her mother had exclaimed, sick
unto death of the whines and squabbles behind her.

So she counted Erakwa, hoarded both sides to herself
to see how many she could spy, but their woodlore and
skill let them weave in and out of the forested edge beyond the trail like smoke-wraiths. But patience she had,
and time enough, and nothing else to do. At rare moments she rewarded herself by catching the glint of an
eye or flash of a leg, a shadow too still to be cast by a
tree, and by luck, the staring, perfectly outlined profile

of an Erakwan, turning so that two dark, glittering eyes marked her passage.

Once they tarried long enough to water the horses and pass hasty dippersful to the prisoners, but neither she nor the others were untied or allowed to dismount, although she tried to cajole Towbin to let them. "Be thankful we've stopped moving," he commented and passed on with the dipper. Vesey remained aloof at the head of the procession and looked back over them all, eyes gliding past her as if she weren't there, but she knew she was lodged in his mind. Barbet stayed tick-tight to him whenever he could, and their perverted relationship soured the water she'd drunk. The scars on the right side of Vesey's face glowed, reflected the subdued light, while everything else around absorbed it, swallowed it whole.

They continued on, even the horses weary and lacking their customary surefootedness; Towbin and Barbet whipping their steeds back and forth, up and down the line, exhorting, cursing, prodding prisoner and placid alike. She ducked a poorly aimed blow from Barbet and decided she didn't care, frankly, she didn't care at all, not a bit. Nothing mattered now. Whatever awaited her awaited them all at the end, and with eyes heavy, she slumped over Lokka's neck. The warmth of steaming horseflesh curled itself around her, and the honest smell of sweat lulled her toward uneasy but necessary sleep. She grunted as the pommel platform cut into her ribs and she shifted, twisted from side to side. Why worry about sleep, she decided groggily, when she could wake into a nightmare whenever she opened her eyes.

She groaned in dismay when another horse shouldered hers, jolting her into wakefulness. Why had they halted? Why did everyone stare, transfixed by a sight beyond her line of vision? Disoriented, she twisted her head, felt her body sliding sideways in the saddle until strong hands gripped her upper arm, dragged her upright until she found a firm seat. Whatever had attracted their attention, at least one person seemed unmoved by the sight, more interested in her well-being than in anything or anyone else.

"We're here," Harrap said in her ear, his bound hands

still clenched around her arm. He nodded toward the right. "The end of our road."

"Harrap, I'm so sorry," she blurted before she could stop herself. "You're too good and innocent for all this. . . ."

He released her arm, kneed his horse away from hers so that he faced the same way as everyone else. "Nothing to be sorry about. We each choose our own paths from the infinity of paths the Lady offers." She followed his glance, unable to credit what she saw looming in front of them. "We may have chosen imperfectly, but we chose as best we could. No shame to that. Making the choice is as important as following it through—it's refusing to choose that's a sin against the Lady and ourselves." He chirruped to attract his tired horse's attention, stepped him farther away. "I'd best get back before we're seen speaking."

The shell-like cloud dome had shattered, but the sky still lowered grayly, clouds with the density of carven marble creeping in solid, slow formations marshaled by the rising, knife-edged wind. Late afternoon, the short pause before the sun sank for the night, and now the light it cast forth spotlighted a large, low building nestled against the lowest south-facing shoulder of the soaring peak ahead of them. So near, very near, and if they could have flown, the distance would have been as nothing. But they had yet to negotiate the final path that zigzagged back and forth, scaling and rescaling a fraction of the same steep grade, and each time creeping farther and higher toward the final goal—the Hospice.

It sat bathed in light, crouching massive and un-adorned, with dark slits of windows that looked from this distance like bars on a cage. Built for utility, for the rigorous pursuit of scientific discovery, not for grace or comfort. Sharp peaked roofs angled to avoid holding the weight of winter's continual snows. Chimneys sprouted up, squat and square in their ugliness, like giant pins thrust through the building to keep its precarious place on the mountain's slope. One large round chimney soared high from the building's center, a cloud of steam writhing from it to meld with the scudding clouds. Easy to identify as the central chimney for the boiler, designed to keep water constantly boiling hot for sterilization, the utter cleanliness required to facilitate accuracy in so many experiments.

The setting sun thrust a soft, hesitant haze of color against the brutally plain building: roses, violets, and lavenders, tenuous touches of dull gold washed soft against the harsh vertical lines now blending into the blue-grays of mountain bulk shadow-dusk. Its momentary enhancement and sudden, plangent beauty tugged at her heart until she contemplated what awaited them there. Not that she knew precisely what awaited them—except that they would never survive it. Vesey and Evelien would see to that.

Everyone but the prisoners had dismounted, scurrying, stripping the mounts of their tack, sending them off with new placids who had swarmed up from the lower stables as soon as they had ridden into view. Towbin's practiced hand twitched Harrap's mount to the side, the reins passed to a lackwit. Setting to work to untie Doyce's ankles, he reached up at last and grabbed her waist, pulling her down.

Doyce sagged, then straightened. "Don't tell me we have to walk up? Or crawl in penance?" A lame jest, more like prophecy in fact, and the idea had a certain poetic rightness to it. Ignominious it might be, but the thought of ending the journey under her own power rather than trussed to her horse seemed more dignified.

"Not quite. Or rather, not yet," Towbin chided as he struggled to unknot her wrist bonds. "Now don't try anything foolish. I'm responsible for your good behavior. Besides, there's no place to run."

The others were being untied as well, standing and stretching and flexing, coaxing life back into stiff extremities. With covert glances at each other, at their captors, they tried to assay the meaning of their halt.

"Look! Isn't that Evelien riding down from the Hospice?" The crimson of her cloak had darkened to a deep blood color in the dusk.

Towbin squinted and gave a curt nod. "Aye. Vesey wants you all for a small meeting down here before you go up." In wordless apology he patted her shoulder as she tucked a shaking hand under each armpit to force

warmth back into blue-nailed fingers. She found herself
liking the man, caught by circumstances almost as much
as she. "There'll be a bonfire, too, belike, and a chance
to get warm and rest."

Her glance strayed back to the trail and the moving
figure, a maroon shadow now. "Why aren't we going
straight up?"

Towbin spat and his voice dipped low, choked with a
smoldering anger. "Mayhap there are some things even
he doesn't do up there, that *he* thinks are better done
down here, out of sight of the rest. I don't know, but
keep your wits about you. He's waited too long for this
by his lights."

Doyce allowed herself to be herded toward a cleared
area dotted with rough stone outbuildings near the base
of the path. Placids and others darted back and forth,
engaged in a variety of activities she didn't bother to
analyze, but she sensed they formed a tight, dense barrier
around the central area, so that no one but the chosen
could slip in and out with impunity.

At the far side of the circle, beyond the large, dancing
bonfire in its center, Vesey commanded all he surveyed.
Cloud rode on his good shoulder while Vesey gesticu-
lated at an Erakwan of less than medium height but with
a hard, muscled chest and shoulders and sturdy legs. The
Erakwan said little but kept shaking his head negatively
despite Vesey's angry expostulations. At times his hand
strayed to a red pouch dangling at his right hip and a
copper band glowed against one wrist, its flash giving
punctuation to his short, vehement rejoinders, body stiff
and formal as if not quite acceding to Vesey's authority.
Doyce recognized the face, the face she had seen watching as she had played her little game. He had the air of
the leader of the runners, those untiring guides who had
hemmed them on each side throughout their journey.
She wished she knew what thoughts were running through
his mind.

"I won't say it again!" Vesey's voice rose petulantly,
and he kicked at the dirt with his stubbed foot, pebbles
flying, spattering the Erakwan. "You'll all stay until I'm
finished with you, until I release you. Besides, I think
this might be salutary for you all to witness."

The Erakwan seemed to understand the tone if not the exact words. Again he shook his head in negation, braids swinging, and turned to leave. Then he stiffened, and as if every muscle in his body were fighting it, his hand tore free from the red leather pouch and he swung back reluctantly. With an effort that bulged his neck cords, he shook his head again, lips pulled back from his teeth in a snarl. Fingers splayed and rigid, he forced his hand back down to his pouch, fingers groping, but Vesey's face darkened with anger as the Erakwan fought to turn away again. He snapped back toward Vesey more quickly this time, yielding to some compulsive force he lacked the strength to gainsay.

Vesey reached out and tapped the pouch with his claw-like right hand. "You'll stay. You'll all stay and learn. Consider it another small tribute . . . unless you'd like to pay a larger one. Another mind or two, another life or two."

Without warning, the Erakwan struggled for balance, took a step back, then another, as if a support or a guy line had been severed. He corrected his misstep with a lithe move, then nodded grudgingly in Vesey's direction and left unopposed. With a guttural shout he gathered his followers in silent numbers from the fringes of the woods, their copper-colored skin adding a final metallic circlet or rim to the wheel of people around the roaring fire.

No longer absorbed by the altercation, Towbin continued to move Doyce deeper into the circle. A sense of relief almost beyond bearing shook her, left her heart singing as she realized she was being maneuvered to where Harrap and Mahafny and Jenret sat, unfettered but close-guarded, to the right of the fire.

"Doyce!" Jenret's yell soared high and boyish, relief cracking his voice into a higher register. He started to rise until Barbet, cudgel straddled between his hands, pressed it hard against the back of Jenret's neck and he subsided into a sitting position, rubbing the bruise, blue eyes drinking in the sight of her. Despite the dirt, the aches, the exhaustion, Doyce felt herself desired in a way she hadn't allowed herself to think about since Oriel's death. And to feel it here and now left her in awe of the resilience of the human spirit.

As she ducked under the arm of the standing placid, her knees buckled and landed her amongst them with ungraceful eagerness. Too many hands to clasp, too many shoulders to pat, and too many tears, at last, to dry. And nowhere to escape from the look in those blue eyes however much she strove for self-control. Harrap tucked her like a fledgling under one large arm, nestled her close, then reluctantly released her to Jenret who drew her to him hard, his lips fiercely grazing her forehead, leaving a brief, burning sensation. He rubbed his stubbled cheek against the top of her head, and the gesture seemed more intimate, more full of intimations than she could bear.

"Let the child breathe," Mahafny admonished as she reached for her turn, then stopped, face set, staring over her head. Evelien had breasted the outer fringe of the circle with her horse and was riding to greet Vesey, who met her with a long, low bow. She dismounted and Cloud pounced, an insolent strike at the flowing hem of her crimson cloak where it trailed the earth like a ribbon of blood. She laughed and bent to stroke his head, the ghatt quivering, rubbing up and down the length of her hand, marking her with his scent.

As if releasing its collective breath, the crowd sprang into action again, even the placids smiling, happy but unsure why. Vesey and Evelien stood in intimate converse, black-garbed figure and crimson-cloaked figure, her oval face tilted lovingly toward his, unflinching at the sight of scars and twisted, mutilated flesh.

With butterfly softness, Harrap brushed a strand of silver hair from Mahafny's set face. "Lady bless and keep those around Her," he comforted, broadening the sweep of his gaze and benediction to include Evelien as well.

Mahafny stirred, then looked unseeingly at her hands folded tightly in her lap. "I confess I fear that She may bless and keep those She shouldn't and forget those She should, Harrap."

"If you have done a procedure ten times over ten, then you have faith in the results, faith in the outcome. Grant the Lady that much faith, for She has more than ten times ten to Her credit than we can ever envision."

"Eumedicos make poor believers, but thank you, Harrap. I'll try."

Unexpected cups of strong, hot cha were thrust into
their hands, the squat mugs vaporish and cloyingly rich
with the scent of sweet amber honey and rum. As one
they lifted them to their faces and inhaled the headiness
of it. Motioning them to hold, Jenret sniffed and took a
small sip, swishing the liquid around in his mouth, then
swallowing with slow concentration. Doubtful, he sniffed
again. "Not drugged, I don't think. Mahafny, what's
your opinion?"

She, too, swirled the contents, looking for telltale hints
of undissolved crystals or powder, then inhaled the
aroma and tasted a minute amount.

Towbin spoke from behind her. "Safe, on whatever
honor you'll account me. The normal libation at the completion of a long and arduous journey. I made them
myself."

Jenret and Mahafny raised their mugs in ironic salute
and then drank as one. Doyce and Harrap followed suit,
but more circumspectly because of the heat.

"Honor doesn't require that you scald your tongue to
show your trust." Towbin pretended to cool his own
tongue by fanning a hand in front of his open mouth.
"At any rate, I figured you all deserved them for having
made it this far. Too bad we didn't meet in kinder days."
He sketched a minimal salute in Doyce's direction with
his own cup, then turned toward Vesey, ready to resume
his duties.

The hot rum coursed through her veins, she could map
its route by the blessed heat following in its wake. She
savored the light-headedness, the burning face, didn't
care in the least, gulped at the mug again. Ah, so good!
The faces around her looked almost expansive and
happy, as the others relaxed as well.

Then the voice slid into her mind, as seductively ap-
pealing as the rum's intoxicating warmth, but with an
after-chill that left her stone sober, heart racing to flee
or fight and with the wounding knowledge that she was
capable of neither.

"*Doyce,*" it insisted, "*come now, it's time. Don't make
me ask again.*"

She stumbled upright, the others adrift in their own
solitary enjoyment as she groped her way outside their

tight, private cluster. Her knee jostled Jenret, laughing at last and draining his mug, head thrown back and eyes closed, lashes long against his cheek. A part of her sensed that he made a belated, blind grab at her leg, but it came too late. She marched toward the central fire as Vesey had commanded.

"Well, well, you came after all. I was beginning to get very angry." He spoke aloud now, the words precisely articulated, each word distinct and with a carrying tone that encompassed the entire circle, binding it more tightly despite its will. "A little public humiliation now, rather than a strictly private one, don't you think?"

He paced back and forth in front of the fire but never too near it, the darting flames outlining his dark figure with a nimbus of orange-gold, an aura of cobalt blue. She noted now as she had before how he always kept a careful, more than respectful distance from any flame, near but not too near, simultaneously drawn to it and repelled by it.

He read her mind. "I was born of the fire. It fathered me more than your Varon, that putative father of mine, ever did. A hard birthing but a true one, for it made me Me. My mother would have approved of the fact that it wasn't an easy birth. Pain makes you learn quickly."

She stood there, feet apart, hands thrust deep in pockets to disguise her trembling. The medallion slid away from her questing fingers but still remained her captive.

"How did you escape?" she whispered. "Nothing could have lived through that fire. I tried to force my way through to find you, even after I knew in my heart that Varon and Briony were dead. I still kept trying to find you. Others tried as well." The crackling of the fire snapped obscenely loud and laughing in her ears, overpowering, smothering her words.

"I know. You have a sense of honor and duty—for whatever that's worth." His tone gentled her, almost caressing. "And perhaps that's why I've waited this long to make you repay your other debts to me."

She tried again. "How did you survive?" It seemed important to understand the how, even if not the why.

"Neighbors came from all around, remember? Moths to the flame, singeing themselves to try to save you and

your poor, precious loved ones. But there were two, their
names aren't important now, and one still lives in the old
town, who were distantly related to my mother and me.
They had her powers as well, though only a touch of
them, but that power allowed them to focus on me and
find me." He stopped short, shoulders hunched in remembered pain, then whirled to face her again.

"Do you have *any* inkling of what it's like to lie there,
the very floor searing your face, your shoulder, your
side, a pain so fierce your flesh shudders and tries to
crawl away despite the fact your body can't move? And
the flames cackling and screaming and fighting amongst
themselves like wolves tearing at each other, leaving the
victor to rip the sweetest, tenderest morsel from the live,
quivering flesh of the downed animal. Each individual
hair on your head rises and dances before it dies, shrivel-
ing in the heat, the fire scything it closer and closer to
your head.

"Do you have *any* idea? I doubt it." He moved toward
her, closer and closer, then stopped short several lengths
away. A tiny torch glowed in each eye, and the image
perplexed her because Vesey stood with his back to the
fire, impossible for his eyes to reflect it.

"I was lucky, lucky." The fused, clawed hand shook
in front of her nose, emphasizing his words. "There was
the thinnest margin of time. For some reason the spot
where I writhed on the floor was a fraction cooler than
the rest of the inferno. Who know why? At any rate, it
gave my friends just enough time to trace my mindcries
and pull me out, though they, too, were burned. Anyone
who saw us probably thought I was some blackened,
smoldering blanket, some rescued but unusable relic
from another life.

"They spirited me to a Hospice two days' ride away.
I begged them to take me as far away as they could. The
ride was agony. They rigged a sling, a hammock, in the
back of the wagon-bed and there wasn't a patch of my
flesh that wasn't blistered and oozing, crusted with char.
Luckily my mouth was too swollen to cry out in pain."
The bad hand came back, stroking the scarred mouth
corner.

"I was a curiosity to the eumedicos there. They'd never

seen anyone that badly burned live. And when, in my delirium, they discovered I was a Gleaner, they realized they had an opportunity such as they'd never had before. A chance to experiment and discover just what it was that made mindspeech humanly possible—if they could control me long enough to keep me from snatching the very ideas out of their heads and destroying them."

"That's when they brought you here, then?" Doyce gestured up toward the distant bulk of the Hospice, now a pale gray scar against the charcoal bulk of the mountain and the looming night, the long-set sun done with the delicate tintings which had decorated the building before.

His "Yes" floated out in a long, exhaled breath. "It was a long journey and by then I had healed enough so that I could scream in pain at every jolt and jounce, and at every dreaded stopover when they picked and peeled and scraped away the dead flesh to find the new underneath."

"Debriding, it's called," she corrected without thinking. And despite herself, despite knowing what the boy had become, she empathized with the long-lost child who had endured pain beyond enduring.

"Thank you." He made a sardonic half-bow. "Actual experience yields to superior medical terminology." Then his face flashed to a passionate seriousness as his nubbed fingers indicated the distant gray walls. "But I found something very special there. Not just the healing of my flesh and the training of my mind, because still—to most of them—I was a curiosity, a golden chance to chart the unknown. And they thought that what they could chart they could control. They played with me and I played with them. They know better now, much, much better.

"But there was someone else there, someone else like me, whose mind reached out as groping and unsure as mine had been before the fire."

"Evelien." She supplied the name although no response was necessary.

"Do you know what it's like to share a mind? Do you have *any* idea?" He stopped short before the fire. "Of course you do, how silly of me. It's just that so few understand. But a Seeker, even with the imperfect mind-blending the ghatti allow, knows far more than the common folk ever will of this gift.

"That, of course, is why we've been so interested in Seekers and ghatti over the past few years. Your gifts parallel but aren't identical to ours. They offer us a new way to discover and experiment as to how this ability works, is transmitted, whether it can be replicated in just anyone or if you have to be born to it as we are. You're our little laboratory rats, now that we've experimented as much as we can on some of our own less 'worthy,' less tractable members, not to mention an array of 'normal' minds. The Erakwa proved fascinating but a dead end. Naturally, Evelien and I are far too valuable for the more, shall we say, radical experiments and dissections."
She could detect no irony in his words and his passionate seriousness left her terrified.

"Stealing Cloud before he was weaned was another step. And a superlative stroke of fate, because surely had he lived any longer he would have been destroyed because he carried the seeds of evil, as you so quaintly put it. The mother ghatta and her Bond tracked us for days until we put them out of their misery. She would have destroyed Cloud, so it was only fair."

"Have you learned much from all your experiments?" The words left a lingering distaste in her mouth.

He looked back at her earnestly, the tiny fires in each eye still flickering. "Oh, enough, very nearly enough. But, of course, we shall learn even more now that you're here. A shame about Khar'pern, that would have made it perfect. But at least now we have the Shepherd plus Parm and Barbet as well as Saam, and even after all this time there's much to learn from slide sections, cell comparisons. If only we'd had him earlier when both brains could have been fresh. . . ."

Oriel, he was speaking of Oriel! Oriel, whose brain Vesey and Evelien had literally snatched, spied on, dissected and labeled and analyzed, as if the dead tissues could reveal what they needed to know about who and what Oriel was—friend, lover, a Seeker who sought so true. The tears willed themselves to slide down her face of their own accord, the rest of her statue-still, marble-cold.

"Ah. How insensitive of me. To rekindle old memories like that. Rekindle, what an interesting term regarding fire."

She pulled a hand free from her pocket to wipe her eyes and realized she clutched the medallion in her fist— a hot coal that she wanted to throw as far away from her as she could.

"It's time now, Doyce, it's time," Vesey crooned, just as he had crooned to Briony. "I've been so patient and waited this long, told you my story, but now it's time." His voice boomed hard and commanding. "I want it now, Doyce, the medallion. Give it to me, it's mine and I need it as a focus for the ultimate control and transmittal of my powers. That's why Mother gave it to me, though she didn't know how she'd carried tradition down through so many years. To her it was precious but still a medallion. I can see more than that, I can feel its power crying out to me, felt it increasing each time I invaded your dreams. I've grown into my powers now and so has it. Give it to me, now!"

Despite her overwhelming desire only moments earlier to rid herself of it, she perversely clutched it tighter, holding her clenched fist against her chest and protecting it with her other hand. The dark shapes around the perimeter of the circle were frozen, faces showing white and shadowed, mutable in the firelight. She could see Mahafny's and Jenret's and Harrap's faces since they sat closer, but she couldn't read them, or somehow couldn't spare the effort to do so.

"No," she responded, and then, surprised by the tenderness in her voice, spoke again. "No, I will not."

"Doyce, Doyce. I've spent enough time over this. I've asked politely when I simply could have taken what is mine. Or I could have Cloud do it, or Evelien, if you prefer. There's always your poor, lost soul, your fallen angel, Barbet." The words mist-runed the cold night air, and she shivered, remembering the white ghatt's lascivious thoughts, a vision that held a deeper meaning of an obscene relationship between Vesey and her. He glided into her thoughts smoothly. "Evelien would love to have the opportunity—she's still jealous of you, a trait I'll have to wean her from. She may have to learn how to share."

Should she give it to him? It was his, after all. How long had she unwittingly carried this poisonous thing? Her hand started out from her chest and she stopped it with an act of will, even though her hand throbbed and smoldered as if the medallion would escape by burning through the palm of her hand and out the other side. She bit her inner cheek for a counteracting pain and realized now the force the Erakwan had battled in trying to disobey Vesey's instructions. But he had managed to maintain his dignity.

She roared her defiant answer. *"No!"* And knew that they no longer spoke aloud but conversed in mindspeech, a deadly dueling intimacy with no weapons in sight in front of an uncomprehending audience.

The first sensation sparkled like hundreds of tiny, colored paper lanterns bursting into flame, one by one, flickering throughout her neural system, brighter and crueler and even more colorful in their succeeding heat and nearness. (Violet pulsation) *"I* (indigo) *will* (blue) *have* (green) *it* (yellow) *now,* (orange) *Doyce,* (red) *now!"* Then a pinwheeling explosion of white heat melding all colors into one, followed by blessed blackness, the absolute absence of color and action.

"No," she droned persistently, drawing the blackness across her like a cloak. *"You will not have it."*

Every thought within her felt buffeted, tossed and hurled high into the air, picked through, examined and discarded, as if a tornado whirled inside her head. She fought back, clinging to one tiny thought, then painstakingly grabbing another to join it and share her weight, as if her face pressed tight against the side of a cliff, fingers and toes scrabbling for any minute crack or crevice to gain a hold. And as she found one, another rough grip met her desperately questing thought, then another, until she stabilized, her mind holding firm against the sucking force that threatened to toss her and her thoughts high into the air and let them fall to the ground, limp and broken.

"Yet again, Doyce, with this unpleasantness? Why struggle to retain something you have no claim to?"

"No claim," she agreed, *"but neither do you. Not for the use you'd make of it."*

"Fine, as you choose. Less subtlety then, less artistry, but more pain. As you will it, then."

The anticipation slammed worse than any pain Vesey could visit on her, she told herself, steeling herself for the next bout and clenching her fingers ever tighter around the medallion. How long could this go on? (Eternally, her mind answered back.) And what worth to it when she knew that he would be the ultimate victor? (Are you enjoying the pain? her mind asked.) Why balk him with this foolishness? (Because that is exactly what he wants me to think, to feel, to fear.) Could she bargain? (No, it's beyond that.) Too late. (Let him snatch every thought, every hope, every piece of sentience from me and leave the empty husk. That's the only way he'll win!)

"Exactly my thought, my stubborn one. Or exactly your thoughts, to be precise. After all, you've been supplying me with them for such a long time now. I've come to thirst for them."

Parched, parched, every drop of moisture flowing out of her body, striking the ground, sizzling and dancing water droplets on a cast iron griddle. Parched, a thirst that would know no surcease, would never end, while flesh blistered and cracked open, oozing precious droplets of moisture. Burning, burning, locked in burning, hair flying out, each strand alive and stretching free, floating in the inferno, riding the heat waves as a spider clutches its ever-lengthening anchor thread as it floats to a new location on an errant breeze. Eyeballs crystallized diamond-bright from the heat and the pressure of a thousand, thousand, thousand centuries of searing pain.

Parched, parched. And the empty husk, the empty shell of Doyce withers, crackling, and starts to burst into flame, edges searing, the flame quickening and catching deeper and deeper, ravaging toward the core of her being.

Her hands dropped nervelessly to her sides, fingers starting to unclench. Her body swayed back and forth as if pounded by a pelting storm. The medallion began its slide from her fingers.

Then movement, motion. Her eyes registered the disruption, movement counter to the pattern of the flames. Strange that she should bother to notice, let alone recognize. The young Erakwan boy, Nakum—that was his name?—running, but hampered by some sort of burden. And as he darted by with an earsplitting yelp of warning, he heaved the bundle as hard as he could in her direction.

She threw up her arms protectively, ready to ward off whatever was flying toward her. Her hand clenched again on the medallion; it hindered her, but she refused to let go. And then she heard it.

"Com-ing!"

Khar's body unfurled itself from the folds of blanket wrapping, and Doyce heard the loud, inchoate scream of joy tearing from her throat as she desperately tried to estimate the ghatta's trajectory and catch her. The ghatta slammed into her chest with a satisfying thud that expelled the air from her lungs and she wrapped her arms around her.

Ah, to never, ever let her go again! *"Oh, my mind-mate, my love,"* she sobbed, hugging Khar close, rubbing her face into her fur, more sensuous than silk or satin, but with a faint, smoky tang rising over the normal talc-like scent. *"Where have you been? Are you alive? It's not a dream?"*

"Love," the ghatta moaned, muzzle crimped in the hollow of Doyce's collarbone. But her tone veered immediately practical and intense. **"Down now! Put me down. Before it's too late. We have to fight!"** And with a twist and a slither she struggled to free herself from Doyce's embrace.

In mute obedience, she dropped the ghatta between her feet. Vesey and the others within the center of the circle—Evelien, Cloud, Jenret, Mahafny, Harrap—remained transfixed, faces ranging the spectrum of emotions.

Flurries of activity harried her vision at various points along the rim of the circle where the spectators sat and watched, outbreaks of roiling activity, punctuated by shouts of dismay and surprise. The Erakwa seemed to be the cause of the action, as if her reunion with Khar had served as a catalyst.

Vesey's arm stretched, finger stubs pointing in accusation. "You, Doyce! The medallion, now! Even better that the ghatta is here to witness this. I will have it now!"

She looked at the medallion as if seeing it for the first time, then shrugged and thrust it into her pocket. He spoke aloud again, intent on commanding not only her but everything and everyone around her.

"**Be strong,**" Khar directed her. "**I will be vigilant.**"

"*But what can you do to stop him?*"

"**Perhaps not stop, but thwart, deflect. Try to hold strong a bit longer. Believe in our Bond, our love, as you never dared before.**"

Deflect? It didn't make sense. What could Khar possibly do to keep Vesey's mind from hers? And already she could sense Vesey gathering his powers, the air around him crawling with phosphene waves of energy as he gathered his strength for his next assault. The air blurred, as did her vision. A vague humming sound emanated from Khar, growing in pitch and intensity, a steady monotone she felt creeping up her legs, around her chest, and over the top of her head, cocooning her.

Everything beyond an arm's length away trembled, moved in limpid slow motion, faintly distorted as if staring into the depths of a lake, magnified. Easy now to pinpoint the running Erakwa, weaving their way amongst the frightened spectators, dashing to the pile of discarded baggage and slashing at large wicker panniers, knives flashing as they sawed and struck at the stubborn withes. Panniers? The panniers that imprisoned the ghatti? A smile split her face and a laugh of pure joy rumbled deep in her chest, but then she had no time to think further because Vesey's mind howled and clawed at her, searching for a hold at the very center of her being.

"**Hurry!**" Khar begged, but the message wasn't directed to Doyce.

Intent on the opening gambit of this new confrontation, muscles and sinews and mind rigid with anticipation, braced for the onslaught, she was oblivious to this opening move, so subtle the visitation.

Her feet sank deep in a carpet of richly verdant grass, soft, cushiony, the fragrance of unbridled spring hurtling toward summer. She could feel the lush texture of each individual and exuberant emerald-hued blade pushing its way between her toes, shooting up around her ankles,

waving and stretching and unfolding in the sunlight as it
danced greenly around her knees.

"It's not real, think about it," Khar instructed.

Delicate green fingerlings of grass tickled at the backs
of her knees as she protested. "But it's so peaceful, so
refreshing. Smell it! How could it possibly be. . . ."

The ghatta's voice, flat and prosaic. "It's not real."

She reveled in unfettered, luxuriant growth, each
green slip free and unrestrained. Interesting. Each limber
shoot sprouted sensitive hairlike tendrils, each questing
finger of green grasping and clawing, pinching, clasping
her in sinuous celadon loopings of vines harsher than
bands of iron. A band, a vise around her chest, crushing
her lungs, mocking each attempt at breath.

Choking, hard to breathe . . . how did it grow so fast,
a whole spring and summer compressed in the blinking
of an eye? Tighter, harder . . . no, expand, no, inhale
. . . what made Khar insist that it wasn't real? And then
the answer struck her as incredibly obvious: all ghatti
could identify the truth in any given situation, even if the
truth were unpleasant to hear. Falsehood could not and
would not be transmitted by the ghatti; they were incapable of being misled by it. She managed a shallow breath.
That she could question the sensation, not just accept it,
meant that Khar was battling to deflect at least some of
the falsehood, the false images invading her mind.

Vesey's expression tightened, eyes torch-enflamed,
lips compressed white-edged and hard as the scarring on
his face. Poor little boy! The ghatti never . . . what? And
as the grasping fingers of green trellised higher, probing,
wrenching, slithering up into ears, gouging behind her
eyes, prying open her mouth, creeping up her nose, she
forgot, dropped the thread of rightness she had tethered
herself to . . . it was gone. Writhing terror immobilized
her more strongly than the vines as the living green ran
its tendrils over and around her brain and prepared to
seize it, drag it forth in victorious display.

"Now!" Khar howled, and a familiar, lower baritone
thrumming joined with the ghatta's, increasing the force
around Doyce, causing the tendrils to hesitate and recede. A deep, rumbling purr so intimately familiar yet

withheld from her so long. If only the tendrils would escape her ears, she might recognize it.

"**Next! And carefully!**" A tenor trill wound in so butter smooth that its melding with the other two spun together without dissonance. No hesitation, no misstep in the joining, as perfect as if they had rehearsed for eons. The vines receded farther, began to wither and shrink, some blackened and rotting as if from the aftermath of a killing frost.

Of course! The ultimate rightness and sense of it left her breathless with relief, even though bands of vine still crushed at her chest. The baritone—Saam! Restored at last, mindspeaking, weaving his mind with Khar's, adding the warp to the woof to loom and weave the fabric of protection more densely with his baritone, and Parm, the tenor, sliding in with a practiced grace that belied his clowning mask.

"**Enter!**" Finally the bass joined in, ragged and cautious of its own power, but gaining resonance and rhythm as it continued, its deep vibrato adding the final resilience to the cloak of love that sheltered her from falsehood and deceit. Rawn, clumsy at first, but with a vibrant richness that melded all the others righter and tighter together in harmony.

The vines and greenery withered, decayed, leaving her gasping but aware, deep, shuddering breaths of relief whistling in and out of her lungs as she panted, staring back at Vesey triumphantly.

"You're not the only one to have friends to give you strength!" he screamed, furiously beckoning Evelien to his side. They clasped hands in front of the fire, Cloud materializing from nowhere at their feet. "I'm tired of toying with you, Doyce. I could do this on my own, but I want you to feel *our* combined power. Yield me what's mine and perhaps I'll let the others go."

She hesitated. *"Khar?"*

A harsh sob of exhaustion shook the ghatta. "**No! No compromise.**"

"**And the white one is mine,**" Saam added matter-of-factly. "**No other's. Understood?**"

"**Agreed,**" Parm sneezed in mock alarm. "**I've other interests.**" But Rawn coughed a polite ghatti cough of contradiction, "**If you should decide you'd like to**

share. . . ." He delicately left the thought unfinished, but the image cut crystal sharp.

Vesey and Evelien faced each other, hands clasped together near their hearts for all the world like a couple plighting their troth, their mindmeld blinding them from seeing, knowing, caring of anyone else's existence. When they turned, hands still intertwined, tiny flames flickered in their eyes, and a wave of power washed over Doyce with such lapidary brilliance that it reached beyond the very boundary of her soul and swept her away, helpless.

♣

The night shivered and pulsated with wave after wave of sound above the threshold of human hearing, but it vibrated them to the core, teeth buzzing, skulls throbbing, metalwork on saddles, bridles, and armor tingling, tinging and setting off their own sympathetic janglings. They galloped, Guardians and Seekers alike, exhaustion tossed aside as the strange sensation propelled them forward, faster, ever faster.

Rolf gasped with agony as the cold, thin air stabbed through his lungs. It seemed as if they galloped so fast that he could barely draw breath. Sound that was not sound transfixed all four ghatti, their more acute senses swimming in it so deeply that they seemed unaware of their Bondmates and their private terrors.

Laboring to force words through clenched teeth, Rolf wrenched himself sideways to shout at Swan Maclough. "What is it? What's causing it? By the name of all we hold sacred, what is it?" Give it a name, make it a thing and he could cope with it, conquer his fears and fight it. Without it, he felt craven, frozen by his own private phantoms of fear.

Indigo cloak whipping behind her, Sergeant Balthazar riding protectively at her side, at first it appeared she hadn't heard him. Then he saw her mouth move, the words dashed away, lost in their headlong rush. He pushed his own straining mount closer, lashing him with his reins, digging his spurs in, and he heard her this time.

"Battle! The sounds of battle as we've never heard before!"

It was not what he imagined it would sound like. The awed expression on Balthazar's face gave credence to that.

The ghatti conversed agitatedly amongst themselves, feverishly testing and tasting each wave of sound as the mindnet stretched to its limits, beckoned them.

"**There! Now!**"

"**No hold! Wait!**" Koom snarled back at T'ss. "**Don't break in yet!**"

"**Too perfect, too seamless,**" Per'la wailed. "**If we meld wrongly, our bridge will shatter them, not strengthen them!**"

Slit pupils dilating wide, Chak concentrated, listened to the music of his own heart, then launched his mind-voice through space with eerie precision, humming pinned to the pitch needed to merge with but not shatter the fragile melody of protection they all heard.

With a deep, steadying breath Koom balanced against the security of Chak's song, joined in without slipping or sliding. Soon the others followed suit. Four near, four far distant as yet, the eight sang their heartsongs.

She could feel the ghatti's concentration stretching, straining to encompass and protect her, leaving her cast up against the welcoming shore of their minds, brief respite from the devouring current of Vesey's thoughts.

But the water imagery abruptly ceased, abandoned. Instead, a crack appeared in the earth in front of her feet, zigzagging between her and Khar. It grew deeper, ever deeper and wider, until she stood trembling, tottering on the brink of a chasm that separated her from Khar.

"**It is false. Step across. We are right here.**" Khar strove to bridge the gap with her mindspeech, but it grew fainter, more indistinct. "**It is . . . right here,**" was the last Doyce heard.

Right here, and so it was. Her boot tips sought out the edge of the chasm, her toes testing the edge, unsurprised at the granular separation and crumbling, minute shifts and rivulets of sandy soil set free that she could distinctly feel through the soles of her boots. So easy to slide over the edge . . . right here. . . .

And she was falling. Down, down, and down again into the void, the walls of the chasm invisible to her eyes. Faster, faster, falling toward the heart of the earth . . . and then, suddenly, wheeling upward, soaring faster, ever faster in the opposite direction to seek out the very eye of the universe.

Nothingness sucking her up, spinning her round and round in an ever-expanding whirlpool of emptiness. Stars spinning by until they created a continuous band of light, a nimbus of brilliance wheeling around her and lifting her farther and higher and farther away from her world.

A faint cry wafted from the emptiness so far beneath her, probably only her imagination.

"Doyce, I am here. Do not believe in his lies, please!" And a triad of companion voices, **"Here, here, here . . . do not believe."**

Easy for them to say. There was nothing else here, any fool could see that: even the diamond points of light, the whirling disk of illumination had faded behind her in the immeasurable distance.

And with the totality of emptiness a groveling fear resonated, nagged, and twitched at her brain from all directions. She screamed with all the power of her lungs and heard no sound, no echo. She cast a thought out to all the compass points and it evaporated, faded away without a trace. The only thing . . . in all this emptiness . . . a small mote, flailing and bobbing in a sea of nothingness was . . . Doyce?

"So . . . you are nothing," a voice said. *"Absolutely worthless. Worth nothing, for you are nothing."*

"But I am," she insisted, fighting back tears. *"I am, I know I am. I exist. I am a sentient being, aren't I?"*

The rich boom of laughter tickled her, spun her head over heels or heels over head, no sureness to top or bottom. The laughter pealed again and then tapered off into a series of mocking chuckles. *"You are, are you? What makes you so sure of that?*

"What makes you think you're not a figment, a shard of some colossal cosmic joke that cracked into a billion pieces, a richly ludicrous fragment of nothingness unable to realize and appreciate the enormity of its nonexistence? And once you've dissipated the last of your puny

'thoughts,' as you seem to call them, nothing else remains." The laughter bounced her higher into the ether, dropped her in a belly-swooping descent, then snapped her from side to side as a dog shakes a rat.

"Am I really nothing?" Doyce asked in wonder. "Nothing." It seemed to make sense. "I am nothing." And she began to unencumber her mind, casting errant thoughts loose, sending them spinning free on their way to oblivion, except that they were already there.

"If you are nothing, then ask the voice what it is! Doyce, you must ask it! How can it exist if everything is nothingness?"

How unpleasant to have to assimilate a new thought when she was so busy casting out everything she had pack-ratted into her brain for so many years. Such clutter! She shook out each thought and idea and cast it off, watching it float and dissolve. But the new thought kept battering at her from all directions. Well, she had better let it in. The sooner she did, the sooner she could cast it forth. Now what was she supposed to ask?

"What are you? Who are you?" There, that was it.

"I am . . . Nothing."

A curious answer. "But how can you speak to me if I don't exist?"

An uncertain pause, and then the voice strove for a haughty tone. "Cannot Nothing speak to nothing?"

She worried it back and forth in her mind. "No, I don't think so," she responded at last, catching at the thought, examining it and thrusting it back into her head for further use. "In fact," she gathered her courage, "I think it's absurd!"

"Good, Doyce! Now more, more! Do it now!" The protective voices grew louder, jubilant, eight-strong now, their melody purling around her.

"Do what now? Oh!" And with dawning comprehension evolving faster and faster, she plummeted back down or up through the layers of nothingness as she realized what she must do. The brightness in front of her eyes grew, a beacon, a signal, a beckoning.

Doyce dug deep into her pocket and with all her remaining strength pulled the medallion free, stared down at it, felt it staring back at her. It glowed, pulsated with

a rhythmic, throbbing cold heat that did not burn her
hand but illuminated the very bones and blood coursing
through it, translucent and fragile—but real. At last it
began to spin in her hand, swifter and swifter, or perhaps
she only imagined it, a spinning disk of fire and flame
so whitely incandescent that the sight was beyond bearing
in its purity. It spun, engulfing her very being in a fiery
wheel, no beginning and no ending, locking her within
it, a mote in the fiery eye of god. She held her hand
higher, higher, the pale white beams blinding as a search-
light, cauterizing in its purity. And then, with something
approaching regret, she flung it into the very heart, the
core of the blazing bonfire in the center of the circle,
like calling to like, and she could but obey.

A high, keening wail tore from Vesey's throat as he
spun around and thrust his mutilated arm deep into the
center of the fire, groping for the medallion. "No, no!
Oh, Mother, no!" he screamed. Evelien grabbed at his
good arm, struggling to pull him back, and the hair on
Cloud's back stood stiff as he spat and screamed in unison with his mindmate, enduring the pain that he endured. With a burst of superhuman strength, Vesey
broke free and threw himself into the maw of the fire,
the flames welcoming him, caressing and wreathing him
with a white-hot, lucent brilliance, a circlet of fire crown-
ing his brow.

With a percussive slap of sound, a fireball exploded
outward, cannoning square into Evelien's breast, flames
quenched in her heart, and she dropped with a tiny murmured cry of dismay, charred crimson cloak puddled
around her.

Bright as shooting stars but far more deadly, fire
rained from the sky. From the outer rim, Erakwan after
Erakwan nocked and set loose a frenzy of arrow torches,
setting an outer perimeter of fire around the bonfire.
One shaft, in passing, whispered by Cloud's hackles, setting him alight. He rolled in a frenzy, legs flailing, but
the flames fanned themselves to greater heat. With a
final undulating scream, he dove headfirst into the fire
after his mindmate.

Other fireballs, large and small, shot in random, erratic patterns of bursting, spidery light, like a cache of

fireworks exploding from a misplaced match. And as each burst into scintillations, chrysanthemum-petaled with sparklers of light, Doyce saw a face inside, staring at her, young and old, innocent and dangerous alike. Some grimaced in rage, others smiled serenely, and she knew, knew without a shadow of a doubt that they introduced themselves as Gleaners, Gleaners spread across the whole of Canderis and beyond, some confident in their powers and their ability to hide them, others completely unaware they had the gift.

"Khar! There are others, others all around! Warn Mahafny, tell the others to beware! They've lived amongst us all the time! I can't tell how many, but they're there. Can't you see them?" she pleaded, shielding her eyes from the brilliance of their staring faces, dazzled by their light, eerie ghost-images imprinted inside her lids when she closed her eyes. Gradually the lights began to wink out, fade one by one, until she could no longer remember the faces, the voices, their hopes and fears, their honorable and dishonorable intentions. It was too much to bear, and she would not, she had done her duty.

Doyce saw it all, but refused to see any more. Crumpled on the ground, she watched the trails of brilliance crisscrossing the night sky. Once she'd wished on shooting stars; now she thought on nothingness. Perhaps not so absurd. There was nothingness, that was not an impossibility, it had only been the other voice that had been impossible. After all, what was nothingness but the absence of so many things: pain, loss, anger, suffering. And the absence of love, of course. Nothingness meant never having to choose, to make a decision to love and to suffer the consequences. She grabbed at the thought with every shred of her being. So very tired . . . and nothingness meant the absence of tiredness as well. Safe from so many hurts.

She could feel the ghatta trying to mindspeak her, sense her despair, her need to share, but she didn't have the strength. *"Oh, Khar,"* she sighed, *"let me go, please let me be free. But wait for me, beloved."* She let her eyes drift half-shut, jerked them open guiltily, then let them slide closed again and fell unconscious. Safe.

♣

"I don't know. It's up to her," Mahafny spoke more brusquely than she'd intended as she finished taking Doyce's pulse and refolded her limp arm over her chest. "The psychic wounds were great before we even began this chase. This may prove more than her mind can handle."

Jenret scraped a dark lock of hair off his sooty, sweat-stained forehead and pleaded, "But you can do *something,* can't you? You have to, you're a eumedico."

"That's perfectly correct: a eumedico, not the Lady or one of Her lesser companion disciples, only an imperfect eumedico with a will to do right but not always with the knowledge to do it." She kept her back to where her daughter Evelien's body was laid out. The living always counted for more than the dead. If action might help, mourning would have to wait.

"Can't Khar reach her? Khar, please try!" He crouched by the ghatta, hand hovering above her striped flank, wondering if he dared reach beyond toward Doyce's hand, pale against the blanket, until Rawn nudged his hand away.

Eyes wide and dark with fear, the ghatta cowered against Doyce's side, her breathing matching the rapid, shallow breaths of her Bondmate.

His hands and arms singed and oozing with blisters from trying to rescue Vesey from the fire, Harrap tugged Jenret back from the grieving ghatta. "Khar can't reach her unless Doyce decides she wants to be reached, you know that. Khar won't invade her privacy. And Mahafny's doing all she possibly can, but there are others who need tending, too." His face appeared naked, his eyebrows and eyelashes charred away, as if an artist had forgotten the final strokes in a portrait.

At last, the younger man turned and laid both hands on the Shepherd's broad shoulders. "You, for one. I'm sorry. I know, but I can't let anything more happen to her, hasn't she suffered enough?"

"I know, and perhaps that's why she's withdrawn, like a wounded animal buried deep in the woods trying to escape its own pain or learn to live through it and heal.

Always before she made herself go on living, but she never knew why she did, never felt she had a choice, that she chose of her own volition. She survived each time, but at what price? She's never forgiven herself for so many things, right or wrong, you could see it in her eyes. Now look around you, there are others besides Doyce and me needing your help. The Erakwa are implacable and thorough against their enemies, and, thank the Lady, they decided we weren't their enemies. I wonder what finally made them disloyal to Vesey?"

Jenret scowled in concentration, tried to marshal his thoughts which ranged so far away and yet focused on someone so tantalizingly near. If he could only reach her, touch her, but if Khar dared not, how could he dare? He grasped at the thread of the Shepherd's conversation. "Were they ever loyal to him?" he said and forced himself to continue. "Or were they submissive because they feared his powers over their earth-bonds until Doyce came along? She showed them there were other ways to use mindspeech, that it was meant to seek truth, not to control or dominate what they hold sacred with the earth."

"The Erakwa know entirely different things from what we know or think we perceive about ourselves and the world around us. Isn't that Addawanna with Mahafny now?" Harrap asked.

The Erakwan woman was easy to recognize, and Jenret had no doubt that it was she, though he had no idea how she had arrived so swiftly. Or had she been traveling with the others all along, shadowing them through the forest? She possessed the earth-link as well, the earth-bond, though it seemed hard to believe that it still offered such incredible powers to someone so advanced in years. Did it never fade? Did they never fade? He felt a momentary wonder at the thought, but it was the other white-haired woman standing between Mahafny and Addawanna who gave him pause. Impossible, he was sure. He grabbed Harrap's singed arm, unaware of the other's wince and jerking motion. "That's Swan, Swan Maclough! How did she get here? And Rolf Cardamon, and the others?"

Harrap cocked a missing eyebrow at him in puzzlement, moving beyond Jenret's eager reach as he nursed his burned arm against his chest. "Who is Swan?"

"The Seeker General! The head of the Seekers Veritas. Your leader now as well."

"Second in command only to our Lady," Harrap reproved as he smiled and formed the sign of the eight-pointed star.

♣

"What do you think, cousin? Will she live?" Swan's close-cropped helm of white hair made the rest of her face indistinct by comparison, attracting attention away from the dark circles sunk around her eyes, the new lines carved down the sides of her mouth, between her brows. "Or more accurately, will she ever be more than a shell, far worse than one of those lackwits over there?"

The eumedico considered, assessing the still form, covered to her chin with a blanket. They needed to move her someplace warm and quiet, and soon. She was in deep shock and near ready to slip beyond that. The Hospice, she supposed, it would have to do. It loomed there, waiting for them. It had been conceived as a place of healing and hope rather than as the place of grandiose dreams and mad meddling it had become. They all needed rest and warmth, food and peace for a night, though she expected no peace for herself, not with Evelien dead. Tomorrow they could leave, or some of them at least. She knew without a doubt that she would remain—someone had to create order, sanity, take control in the wake of Evelien's and Vesey's deaths.

"I wish I could say." She missed her white eumedico coat, fought to hold her hands in place, yearned for the pockets, the pockets that would hide the traitorous palsy of her hands. "Vesey never actually Gleaned her mind, I don't believe, although he came very close until the ghatti intervened. She yielded it up . . ." she rubbed her hands, searching for the right word, ". . . stored it away, abandoned it. . . . How much stress can the human mind and body endure before something snaps? It varies from person to person as you know full well, cousin. Some recover, learn, grow from the experience. Others . . ."

She let the thought trail off unfinished. Blast the ghatta for staring at her with those prescient amber eyes, but she had never let herself be receptive to ghatti mind-speech, and she wasn't about to let her guard down now, no matter how the animal pleaded with her. Nor would she ask Swan what the ghatta wanted.

But Addawanna had no qualms about squatting to stroke the ghatta, talking to her with a liquid stream of rushing vowels and occasional hard consonants.

"I t'ink she heal. But wedder she be Doyce we knew before, I no sure. Wait an see, mebbe long time, mebbe not."

Doyce shifted, sighed imperceptibly; she could hear the voices all around her, cajoling, pleading, begging to be let in, but she didn't have to answer this time, not if she didn't want to do so. She felt a twinge of longing at the caress of Khar's mindvoice, but she forced it back, too life-entangling. The ghatta had Chosen, she hadn't, and while she harbored no desire to hurt the beast—oh, Lady Bright, not to hurt anyone as she'd been hurt, deserted so many times—the ghatta would just have to wait. When she was ready to find herself, to seek out the real Doyce, she would do so, that was her choice.

Wait and see, that was all any of them could do until Doyce made her decision. Wait, and hope it would come soon.

Slumped behind the big mahogany desk, dwarfed by its size, Mahafny wondered if Evelien had ever had the same feeling when she had sat here. Somehow she doubted it. She had been up all night, rallying and chiv-vying cowed eumedicos, forcing them to face reality and tend to their new patients—innocent lackwits or placids, wounded by the Erakwa fire-arrows or their own panicky stumbling and bumbling in the melee. Erakwa injured by those who had fought back—a few turncoat eumedicos and novice Gleaners striving to channel their mindpowers for violent ends.

Whom to trust, whom to dismiss? Who remained loyal to Vesey and Evelien? How many would crumble, docile, at the sudden vacuum of power and who would remain a danger, smoldering resentment flaring into unexpected, unstoppable resistance from perfectly normal-looking people who harbored untapped, unskilled power in their minds? The razor's edge was very sharp and treacherous, that she knew all too well. And it was up to her to command, to take up the responsibility that she had abdicated all too long ago.

She had told, no, ordered Swan to have the ghatti scan every living soul in the place, regardless of Seeker etiquette. No time for niceties now, and Swan had done it without a demur, knowing it was crucial to find out who might present a danger. At least they had been able to separate Gleaners from "normals," and had instructed the ghatti to inform the Gleaners that their very lives depended on their good behavior, and that their truthfulness would be assayed.

She slid from behind the desk, from its drawers crammed with file upon file of research and experiments, and walked to the window, throwing back the shutters, looking at the ground below. A small party was gathering around a litter lashed between two horses. Jenret, Rolf, and four of Balthazar's Guardians were to transport Doyce, still unconscious, south to Gaernett, taking her away from this place as swiftly as possible. That Jenret would not leave Doyce's side until he had delivered her into safekeeping was clear to her, but then she knew his stubbornness, his determination, and his fears.

Addawanna and her kinsmen were somewhere near, she was sure, the Erakwan woman had gestured to the woods, the mountainous slopes, saying "Be seein' there be strays or no," and had faded away. Harrap, the other Seekers and Bondmates, and the rest of Balthazar's force had pledged to remain until fresh teams of eumedicos and Seeker pairs could reach the Hospice and aid in the reorganization, the rehabilitation. That had been Swan's suggestion and she had agreed with alacrity. Swan had seemed amazingly subdued, as if she had stared into the chasm before her feet and stepped back just in time. And for the Seekers, it had been just in time, Mahafny knew that too well.

A knock at the door and she yelled, "Enter," as she

swung around. She didn't dare turn her back on any-one—and realized what an outmoded notion of safety that was. Still, safer to face danger even if it were un-seen. Towbin Biddlecomb, Vesey's second-in-command, took three paces into the room, stiff with discomfort. Hands grasped his shoulders from behind, clutched tightly in the fabric, knuckles white, and a peaked face peered over. A red-headed woman with milk-pale skin and eyes the color and size of copper coins stared, un-easy, ready to bolt at the first untoward gesture. To com-pound her surprise, the ghatt Saam followed them in, trotting to a spot where he could survey everything and everyone, and sat, head cocked in her direction.

"I'm sorry." Towbin's raised eyebrows indicated the ghatt. "I promised him you was safe as houses with us, but he still insisted on coming. Mayhap he has his own . . . business with you."

"I doubt that. I don't converse with ghatti."

Biddlecomb regarded her, rubbing his thumb over and over the side seam on his trousers. "Well, that's for you to work out between you-like. But I . . . we . . . we've come to beg a boon of you."

She folded her arms across her chest, tired to the bone of having to deal in favors, in personalities, in private needs when everything around her was so pressing, so fraught with potential danger. Didn't the man realize that the whole of Canderis would have to be scoured for Gleaners or potential Gleaners, and what were they sup-posed to do when they found them? What would the High Conciliators and the Monitor do—condemn them all to death? Expect the eumedicos to devise an instanta-neous "cure"? Discover how to integrate them into the very fabric of Canderis?

She rubbed at her brow in a vain attempt to erase the questions, but they still remained, unanswered, taunting her for solutions. The woman's face floating over his shoulder like a disciple moon, he stood patient as stone, only the one thumb rubbing its ceaseless course across the seam. She had an ungovernable urge to slap his hand aside, stop the gesture. But Saam, front legs stretched high on Towbin's thigh, pushed the hand aside with his head.

He looked surprised, then trapped his thumb with his fingers. "Sorry. Used to be worse. Bad habit I've always had since I was a little'un. Used to pick at the seam without knowing it 'til my wife threatened to make me wear a sock over my hand." He rubbed the ghatt's head. "Did ye note he seemed to ken what ye were thinking?"

She countered with an explosive "phah" sound. "Stop shilly-shallying! You said you had a boon to ask me? And I'd advise you to introduce the woman lurking behind you."

He jerked to attention again, as if old habits under Vesey died hard. Reaching for one of the hands on his shoulder, he swung the woman in front of him, nestled her protectively in his arms, whispering reassurances. "This is my wife, Yulyn. She's a Gleaner." Lips pressed in a white line of fear, the woman managed a terse nod, whether in acknowledgment of her name or of her description, Mahafny couldn't decide. The woman was struggling not to flee, despite the comforting arms around her.

"You've no reason to trust me overmuch, that I ken," Towbin continued, "and her even less, though you don't know her. But I want to stay on and help out, have you help my wife. She didn't . . . we didn't . . . never meant to get caught up in something like this. We wanted help, and when the whispered word came through, we thought we had the opportunity. We didn't know he'd try to twist and bend as bad as he was twisted and bent himself. If you trust me . . . trust us . . . we'll trust you, support you best we can. My pledge on it."

" 'Tis my pledge she needs, Towbin," the woman protested in a soft but determined voice, working herself free from her husband's embrace until at last she stood alone, unprotected. A tall woman, angular, and made more so by continual stress and worry, Mahafny thought, but the pale face was luminous with resolve. "I've never hurt anyone wittingly, despite what *he*, what Vesey made me try to do. My pledge on that for the past, and for the future . . . if we have one." She started to take a step forward, entreaty clear on her face, but halted at Mahafny's involuntary flinch. "I wouldn't . . . I can't. . . !"

she cried. "If there's no place for me, then please don't hurt him!"

Towbin's expression contorted as he tried to express in words a concept that ranged beyond his usual thoughts. "Don't you see?" he implored. "The Shepherd Harrap would see. We're *all* part of this, part of the same root, the same stock, just different branches. Don't prune us off! You should know—the cousin of the Seeker General, the mother of Evelien, and you a eumedico yourself. As the branches are bent, so they grow. We *all* be part of the Lady's scheme of things, I beg you!"

She jammed her fists into the pockets of the borrowed white lab coat, glad she had confiscated it from a coat rack at some point during the long night. It didn't give her her usual confidence but it helped, reminded her who and what she was, of what she believed in, had striven to do all her life. A decision needed to be made, and she was the only one there to make it. "We all have much to learn, ways to grow for the good of everyone. I don't know what it will take to do it, or if it can be done. But the unknown is our enemy now. There may have to be experiments, perhaps painful ones," she warned, and saw Yulyn's chin rise, resolute. "But I'm willing to have you both with us. If you'll have us."

He had pulled her hand from her pocket, was pumping it with an enthusiasm that left her trying to rescue her hand for safety's sake. When had he crossed the room? she wondered. Had she been that adrift in her thoughts? He stopped at last, returned her hand to her with a curiously genteel gesture and fled the room. She had already seen the tears forming in his eyes. "You won't be sorry," his wife promised before she followed after him.

Flexing her wrist, cradling it in her other hand, she realized that the steel-blue ghatt still remained, regarding her, his mouth fractionally open as if he planned to vocalize. "Well, you'd better speak out loud, if you're going to," she advised him, "because I won't have it any other way. And you know it."

His head drooped, his eyes sought the floor as he offered a small, protesting "Meow." At length he looked up, yellow eyes bright, beseeching, his expression akin to the one she had just viewed on Yulyn's face. It sad-

dened her, made her wonder what she was missing, what
it would be like. Compelled by the loneliness, the misery,
the wanting, she wavered, started to yield. "No, I can't
do it!" She ground out the words between her teeth,
wrestling for self-control. "Not everyone has their wishes
granted, including me. I am . . . sorry. But I can't do it.
I don't have . . . Harrap's faith to take another step into
the unknown. There's enough of that around me now
and I can't allow myself to be diverted onto other paths,
not if we're to find a solution. Perhaps you could help
with that, but I can't afford the chance of distraction,
not now, not when so many others are depending on me.
You do see . . . don't you?" Somehow it seemed very
important that he should understand her reasons.

Nakum pelted into the room, startling them both. He
pulled up short, abashed by his interruption. "Being
sorry," his hand made a fluttering, self-deprecating gesture away from his chest as if to dissipate the abruptness
of his entry. "Dey be ready goin' now. You wan' say
good-byes?" All through his speech Mahafny noted he
stared at the ghatt, little side-glances of curiosity, of tentative friendship.

She turned her back on Saam, stared out the window
again. "No, I don't think it's necessary. I'll wave them
farewell from up here. Give them my best. Give my best
to them all. My love." But she kept watch from the corner of her eye.

He was hunkered down now, hand held steady and
unthreateningly in the ghatt's direction, waiting to see if
Saam would bridge the gap of his own volition.

"Saam, maybe you should go with them. Khar needs
your support. Take Nakum with you for company as
well, if his grandmother will allow it." The words cost
her, far more than she had anticipated as the yellow eyes
swept back to hers, searched her through and through.
Part of her wanted the ghatt to stay, just for the comfort
of his physical presence, the knowledge that if she later
changed her mind he would be there, and the thought of
leaving such a bolt-hole shamed her. She had made her
decision.

The ghatt's head swiveled back in Nakum's direction,
d the gray nose stretched, seeking, inquisitive toward

the waiting hand. He gave a little sniff, a deeper one, then inserted his head under the arm, rubbed along it. As he came closer to Nakum's pouch with the earth-bond he pulled back, then approached it with wary regard.

Eyes bright with the prospect of a journey into the unknown, an unknown land and civilization, Nakum made a salute of respect and dashed from the room. Saam trotted after him, but not before turning and rubbing against Mahafny's shins in farewell.

❖

Patience, the ghatta counseled herself, she will not leave me, cannot leave me like this. I cannot follow where she now goes, but I can wait. Wait until the end of the world and beyond and join her in the next if that is what fate has willed me. **"Do you hear me, I will wait!"** She thought Doyce heard, sensed somehow that the message had been received.

The medicinal smell of the Hospice stung her nose, had made her head throb the whole night through. So tired of the bustlers, the millers-around, the turmoil that continued as they readied for their departure, orbiting around the still, silent center of her beloved. She stared hard at her white paws, flexed her claws as if she could send them scattering far and wide. She, too, craved peace, the peace of perfect harmony and sharing. And then she heard the voices, not from outside but within.

"Khar'pern, Khar'pern Bondmate, we rejoice in your victory and your growth. Well met, courageous ghatta. The Truth is a hard lesson to learn, but you have made it yours."

The ghatta picked over several scathing, rude words in her mind, discarded them with an effort of ghatti politesse that made her grind her teeth. Ah, a nip on the collective tail of the Elderdom would justly serve them! **"Thank you, Elders, for your words, for your honor. But my ghatti brethren deserve honor too for coming to my aid, empowering me in my time of need."**

A breeze sigh that ruffled nothing else touched her delicate whiskers. A faint voice sounding like Mr'rhah, speaking at last. **"Still so obdurate at times. But wisdom** gained from one source does not mean wise in all ways. You still have time to learn—and we to teach."

How dare these mindvoices jabber and pluck at her when she must concentrate to parallel each breath, each heartbeat of her beloved? "I thank you for your 'speaking, but I have other concerns here." Do not distract me! Go tell your tales to some other credulous younglings!

"Ah, she thinks we toy with her, have toyed with her all along. Excusable when one is so torn between our world and the burden of the Chosen. Ah, Khar'pern, think of us less harshly, do not lash out at us—your claws will not shred phantom fears."

And because it was inevitable, because it was the ghatti way, she bowed her head, acquiesced to the voices, let them sweep her up and beyond and away, though her heart-kernel remained behind, watching, guarding—as it always had, as it always would. Others would watch if she could not, but not with the same unstinting fervor. The voices gamboled and played about her, jostled and tumbled like littermates, and she let herself ascend the first spiral of knowledge, glide past the bend into the second, an escalating climb into the third, where she prepared to halt, knowing and respecting her limits. But then, without volition, without any effort on her part, the slipstream of wisdom swooped her ever higher, lofted her into the fourth spiral!

"Congratulations, Khar'pern Bondmate! You have earned your knowledge and your elevation. Use it wisely and well to scale the spirals and you will succeed."

And with abrupt surprise Khar found herself still on the blanket, crouched close to Doyce. "Ah, beloved, I have wisdom for both of us! Go where you must go, as you must, but I am here, waiting to share!"

NOTES

Despite the fact that the planet Methuen and the country of Canderis bear a serendipitous similarity to the old Earth origins of its first settlers, history is unclear as to the origins of the ghatti. Some argue for a genetic mutation of the common house cat—aided by the eumedicos and their early fascination with gene-splicing in the pre-Plumb years; others that the ghatti are unique to the planet and their similarity to house cats and wildcats a mere coincidence. Yet others argue for an interbreeding of Earth house cats from the shuttles with the wildcats of Methuen—not impossible or improbable given the lineage of domesticated cats on Earth.

What is known is this: Ghatti show the basic conformation of common house cats with a slight blunting or coarsening of features—an obvious point in both the arguments for an indigenous wild species and for cross-breeding. Ghatti generally weigh from 30 to 40 pounds and are approximately 36″ to 40″ long from nose to tail-tip. If well-cared for as part of a Seeker-Bondmate pair, their longevity greatly exceeds that of a pampered house cat on Earth.

No hypothesis or controlled experiment has adequately explained their ability to mindspeak, although besotted cat lovers on Earth have long believed this to be possible. Should this be true, it might well add credence to the ancient Earth stories of "witches" and their feline "familiars." The ghatti themselves remain stubbornly reticent as to their beginnings and special powers.

PRONUNCIATION

To pronounce ghatti names, simply listen to any cat vocalize. Most names should be given a slightly rising inflection at the end, as if in query.

For example:

M'wa is pronounced much like the French "moi' with a question mark at the end.

Saam is the equivalent of our word "psalm."